For Emma,
my children, my brother
and in loving memory of
Dora, Mabel, Barbara,
and Flight Sergeant Clifton Wedd

Acknowledgements

I am thankful beyond words to the following people for the help, advice, loving kindness, support and encouragement that they have given to me throughout the creation of The Walnut Tree.

Emma Titterton, a powerhouse of strength and support; Irena Beaumont for editing, proof reading, and invaluable wisdom; Tim Hodges for all of the above and more besides; my son Peter for the cover design, technical knowhow and common sense; Helen Cooper for believing in me; Victoria Prince for invaluable guidance, organisation and motivation; my daughters Charlotte and Jessica; my mother, Mary; my brother, Peter; Ian Hewitt; Gerald Michaluk; Sylvia, Simon, Mark, Matthew and Tracie at Hawksworths Graphics and Print Ltd; Yi Jone Li and his staff at Dove Computers, Ashbourne; Brenda Croft; Alicia Mountford; Helen Crowson; Debbie Andrew; Gar Nevin; Anne Hawkins; Susanne Smith and The Stubwood Singers - Mary Spencer, Viv Edwards, Shirley Wagstaff, Dylys Delf, Rose Cope, Ann Johnson, Pat Boot, Mandy Ellis, Pauline Jilbert, Glenda Lovatt, Liz Oakes, Carolyn Zeller, Audrey McGuiness, Sue Allerton, Wendy Forrester, Ireana Beaumont; Laurie Becket-Fountain; Helen Woollaston; Annie Treacy; Julie Whitehurst; Katie Greene; Charlotte Jordan; Lisa Burke; Mark Davies; Mark Capewell; John and Gillyann Prince; Colin and Enid Prince; Andrew Fryer; Charlie Allen; Jayne Anders; Helen Wordley; Faye Whitefield; Christine Coxon; Rebecca Dalton; John Sanderson; Alan and Cath Bloxham; Geoff Carrington; Ruth and Peter Reeves; Joan Abraham; Terry Davies; Kate Hawley; Karen Boot; Steve and Tina Boot; Celine Whyte; Caroline Morton; Brenda Rhule; Jacqueline Ingerson; Sarah Orton; Karen Blake; Jon Bickle; Ken Winfield; Stan Sillitoe; Keith Hunt; Ron and Janet Tomkinson; Peter and Carole Dobey; Pat and Chris Hall; Marcia Gifford and family; John Birch; Kevin Grime; Olivia Grime; Dianne Poyser; Pascal Arnoux; Paul Williamson; Paul Barnett; Lionel and Denise Lethbridge; Alan Lethbridge; David Ogden; Terry Davies; Caroline Vernon; Jane and Stuart Smith; Jo Goodwin; Claire, Anthony and Holly Salt; Sally Holding; Kathleen Gregory; Mary Myatt; John Wedd; Marika Latham; Anna Felthouse; Pam and Dave Adams; Anne Woods; Sue Ross; Mavis Lund; Anna Bennett; Linda Thomson; Shirley Swift; Emma Manby; Alison Boot; Duncan and Janet Haines; Ian and Cynthia Gustard; Keith and Christine Norris; Jim Ottowell; Rev'd Geraldine Pond; Amanda Shaw; Anne Hall; Linda Allen; Mark Berry; Ian Copestake; Joan and Colin Gregory; Ian Lomas; Margaret Pearson; Alan and Carolyn Hutchinson; Vicki, Holly and Maddy Harris; Rebecca and Jack Doyle; Celia Heede; Harry Hitchen; Sarah Dawson; Ruth Downing; Melanie and Natasha Bell; John Chapman; Louise Eardley.

Contents

Part One
Spring – 'Beginnings…'
2

Part Two
Summer – 'The Heat Is On…'
100

Part Three
Autumn – 'All Is Gathered In…'
183

Part Four
Winter – 'A Very Dark Time…'
325

Part Five
Spring Again – 'New Life…'
502

Epilogue
535

Sources
538

Journey To The End Of The Night
539

About Caroline Wedd
540

Part One

Spring – 'Beginnings…'

Wednesday 5th April 1978

'You bloody idiot!'

She wasn't sure if she shouted the words out loud or if they screamed inside her head. It all happened so fast. She'd been following the battered old Land Rover for a good two miles since the railway bridge. She'd nearly reached the old oak tree next to the bend in the road that was her next time check point on her rally drive home from work. At first she'd been pleasantly distracted from her mission by the black and white collie dog that was continuously running from side to side on the front seat of the Land Rover cab. Ears pricked with excitement, tongue panting, he was looking forwards to where he was going.

'Wonder what it feels like to be that excited about something.'

The wonder soon turned back to irritation as the left indicator flashed at her yet again. The driver had been indicating left since the railway bridge as well, but there was nowhere 'left' to go.

'Why am I surrounded by people who can't get moving?'

She knew she spent far too much time talking in her head instead of out loud, but it saved a lot of time that way. She was about to run through the list of people who hadn't moved fast enough for her today when the Land Rover started to slow down and pulled into the left hand side of the road.

'Now's our chance!' she said to her little red car.

The road ahead was straight and clear. For all her rally driving games morning and night, she wasn't really a chance taker, but this guy had really, *really,* annoyed her and ruined her best run of the week to date. Like the dog in front, with ears pricked and tongue panting, she put her foot down flat on the accelerator pedal and swung out past her tormentor. What happened next turned her panting to panic. He was turning right! Right into *her* and not left!

'You bloody idiot!'

Her only hope was to keep going. Foot still flat down on the accelerator pedal she smashed her way onto the grass verge and hoped for the best. It didn't quite work. He hit the back of her car as he turned into the field gateway. She slewed back onto the road and stopped neatly by her favourite oak tree. She sat very still. Her heart was trying to get out from inside her buttoned up raincoat. Apart from this unusual thumping sound inside her coat and her head, all was quiet. Lovely pink and white flowers swayed gently by the side of the road, the only witnesses to her failed daring do.

'Get out of the car!'

The voice in her head sounded a bit different, but she knew it was hers. She got out of the car. She walked round to the back of it to see her bumper hanging on, or was it off, by a thread. One wheel arch was also buckled. Also buckled was her raincoat belt. Confident that her thumping heart couldn't escape its tight grip she turned to look at the man with the happy dog and the dodgy vehicle.

He'd got out of his Land Rover and was standing, still as a statue, behind it. She couldn't find any words in her head to describe how angry she felt at that moment, but her black stiletto shoes came close to the right expression as she pointed them in his direction and marched down the road towards him.

'How dare he stand still!' she hissed.

How dare he do otherwise than put a piece of metal Land Rover between himself and the formidable looking young woman who was swishing towards him at great speed in a very organised raincoat; only the soft, bouncing movement of her long, golden, hair as she charged towards him gave him hope that this tightly buttoned creature was not entirely made of metal also.

'What the hell do you think you're playing at?'

Her voice didn't sound like her own. She had to work hard to pull it back down to something resembling a normal, low, controlled pitch, instead of the high shriek that had just squeaked out of her dry mouth.

'You've been indicating left for over two miles and then you go and turn right. Right into my car!'

'Are y..you all r..right?' he said.

'Of course I'm all right!' she snapped. 'But look at my car – what are you going to do about *that?*'

'You'll h..have to t..talk t..to me d..dad up at the f..farm,' he said.

This made her even madder than before. No apology, no acknowledgement of fault, and he can't even deal with it himself. Got to run to his dad – at his age! He didn't even have the guts to speak clearly. She pressed her hands onto the hot Land Rover, in mirror image of two big, brown, muscular hands. He was young, but probably older than her. He was very tall. He was unshaven, swarthy either in complexion or from dirt, she couldn't tell which. And he had the most amazing shock of long, unkempt, curly dark hair that she'd ever seen on a man.

'Where's the farm, then?'

'J..Just over there.'

He turned and pointed to the red brick farmhouse that stood back from the road just past where all the trouble began.

'What's your name? How do I know you're telling the truth?' she asked in as legal a voice as possible.

'Speak to me d..dad. Our name is W..Wilson.'

———————◆———————

Carrie was two faced. At the ripe old age of twenty two she ran straight home to her dad, too.

'Ah, but,' she reasoned to herself as she finished the last ten miles of her journey home a bit more sedately than the first ten, fearing the loss of parts of her car along the way, 'my dad is a garage man. I'm only doing what any customer would do when they needed help.'

This was true, but, nevertheless, she melted inside at the sight of her dad's ever round, smiling face, and was much comforted by the familiar smell of his oily overalls.

As a little girl she'd spent hours playing around the edges of her dad's workshop, collecting iron filings with a big magnet, running her fingers through any oil and grease that she could find – how she loved getting dirty back then. Walking onto the cool concrete floor of the workshop now, she felt a sudden stab of regret that her own life had become so far removed from what she considered to be a real life. There was no hot and cold, dirt, fumes, or anything to really grab a hold of in her life at the office - and even less at home.

'That's not a big job, love.'

Dad smiled.

'Thanks Bill,' said Carrie.

She always called him by his name at the garage; everyone else there called him Bill and she'd copied them for as long as she could remember. Carrie was so proud of her dad. He was kind to everyone, always. She didn't know how he managed to do his job sometimes as he'd lost all the fingers on his left hand in a motorbike accident. Even now she couldn't help staring at his hand whenever she saw him. The skin on his fingerless knuckles stretched soft and white around them. The flat, square, ends of his knuckles looked like they'd never had fingers at all. There were no seams or scars. The imperfect was perfect, just like their owner. Carrie had spent so much time in her head imagining what it must be like to have a hand like that. She spent so much time imagining in her head about everything.

'*It's why I'm not progressing very well at the office,*' she excused herself. '*I'm not interested in facts and figures.*'

Living in her head had always been a protection from her life at home dictated by mother, and now also, to make up for the lack of 'real' things in her life right now. Carrie felt such a longing in her soul that it made her feel sick with pain sometimes.

'Go and see the farmer tomorrow,' said Dad as he ran his half hand along the car bumper.

She remembered the happy dog.

'*I want to be a happy dog,*' she thought.

Her dad brought her back to the uncomfortable reality of sorting out her car and the insurance. She was also mindful of the fact that it was really her own sheer recklessness that had caused the prang, and she knew that her dad knew that, but was too kind to say so.

'But how can I trust him? You know what farmers are like!'

This was just something to say to cover her embarrassment. She didn't know what farmers were like, only the farmers' sons at school, and she didn't have anything to do with silly boys in those days. She still didn't.

'You must go and sort it out. Look him in the eye. You'll be alright.'

Thursday 6th April

It was a lovely, warm, sunny day. Carrie wore her tightly fitting, tailored, black pencil skirt, her favourite black stiletto shoes and tightly buckled raincoat again. She didn't actually need the raincoat, but she felt safe inside these mature female garments; the girl on the inside was kept well out of sight as she parked her car up on some rough gravel in front of a small industrial unit that was to the left of the main drive up to the farmhouse and buildings. She could hear men's voices and singing as she got out of her car.

'I'll try here first,' she decided, knowing full well that it was probably nothing to do with the farmer that she was after.

Stepping into the shed she relaxed immediately – it was a tractor repair workshop and spare parts wholesaler. Dark and oily, calendars of ladies of a certain type. She felt right at home.

'Hello, is Mr Wilson about?'

'What do you want with him?' asked one of the boiler suits behind the counter.

'I've come to see him about my car – his son crashed into it yesterday.'

The boiler suits behind the counter started laughing.

'What's so funny?' asked Carrie, still feeling relaxed in their company.

'He's nowt to do with us,' said boiler suit number one. 'You'll have to go up to the farm.'

More laughing. No, it was silly giggling!

'You'll do no good with him,' said boiler suit number two. 'You be careful, duck, nobody messes with Wilson –he's mad!'

They stopped giggling.

'No, seriously, mind how you go with him, love. If he doesn't like you, you'll have trouble.'

'Good luck!'

With kindly smiles the boiler suits disappeared back into the depths of their workshop.

'Oh great,' sighed Carrie, 'just my luck to crash into an oddball!'

Forewarned is forearmed. Carrie pulled her little body up as tall as it would go, took a deep breath, and marched up the dazzlingly white gravel drive to find the mad Mr Wilson. He found her first.

He appeared from nowhere. Carrie was having to walk carefully in her lovely black stilettos up the incline of the white gravel drive, that was spotted with large chalky stones and bits of rubble that had been hastily dumped to fill the odd pothole.

Her eyes were looking down towards this dusty white minefield, when her view was obscured by two enormously long legs that landed slap bang in front of her path, in what seemed to be two or three strides, when it seemed like she'd been tottering along the same distance for hours.

'Mr Wilson?'

Carrie's voice sounded small. Her eyes travelled up the length of the longest pair of dark blue skinny jeans that she'd ever seen. Her eyes and neck had to keep going up, up, up, past a long, slender, body until they reached the face of mad Mr Wilson. He was staring at her.

'He must be nearly seven feet tall!'

Carrie felt like a little mouse beneath the gaze of a prize falcon that was about to have his sport with her, before eating her.

'That's right.'

'Look him in the eye! Even the smallest prey can still be brave!'

But what eyes! Was he really mad or did he just look mad? Carrie looked him in the eyes. Or did he command her eyes to go to him? Mr Wilson had the palest, pale blue, eyes that she'd ever seen. They were almost ice white and yet his gaze burned into her like acetylene torch.

He had a skinny long face and a skinny long nose, to balance his skinny long legs. Long, silver and white grey, wavy hair flowed past his shoulders like a King Charles I Cavalier. It was so uniformly wavy that it looked like he plaited it every night before he went to bed. Carrie was good at staring; she'd had plenty of practice, so she stared back at Mr Wilson.

A tingle of adrenalin shot up and out of her guts, and formed the words in her mouth that she hadn't planned.

'Your son crashed into my car on my way home from work yesterday, and I need your insurance details please.'

'You shouldn't have been overtaking him; it's your own fault.'

Carrie remembered how tall she felt in her stilettos.

'Your Land Rover was clearly faulty. The indicators didn't work and there were no mirrors on it *at all*, inside or out!'

The Falcon remained motionless. His icy focus burnt into the soft brown eyes of the little mouse. It was getting hot in that raincoat on such a lovely day.

'Don't mention anything about the mirrors or the indicators and I'll see that everything is alright.'

'But how do I know that you'll do what you say you'll do?'

'Do as I tell you and it'll be alright. I give you my word.'

Carrie hadn't met anyone before who was as good at staring as she was. She was shocked to find that she was actually enjoying herself. She felt that she was somehow having a telepathic experience with this most strange and powerful man. She knew that she was the mouse, she knew that she was going to lose, yet she didn't feel completely helpless. She hadn't planned to say:

'Alright, I'll trust what you say; I want to get this sorted quickly.'

But she said it.

'I give you my word,' he stared.

It's no wonder people think he's mad,' thought Carrie.

She was disappointed to end her ordeal so soon. She felt odd, turned upside down and inside out; the raincoat hadn't helped today. The Falcon hadn't finished with his prey.

'Close your eyes and hold out your hand,' he said.

'What for?'

Why couldn't you just say 'no' you stupid girl,' hissed Carrie to herself.

'Close your eyes and hold out your hand!' repeated mad Mr Wilson.

Carrie imagined him putting something horrible in her hand, a big hairy spider or something, just to make a point. Still, she closed her eyes. She held out her hand. She felt something hard, round, and very light, rest on her upturned palm. She opened her eyes.

'It's a walnut!' she gasped in surprise. 'Where did you get it from?'

'I have a tree in my orchard.'

'Thank you,' she smiled, 'I didn't think they grew in this country. Well, goodbye, then.'

But the Falcon was gone. He didn't say goodbye.

———————◆———————

Carrie pulled onto the drive and stopped her car. As usual, the sight of her mother's sparkling white lace curtains in the corners of the kitchen windows made her heart sink. Even the tightest of clothes could never stop that deflated feeling in her body and her mind every time she arrived home. Carrie didn't dislike her home, or her mother. She felt guilty and ungrateful that the shiny cleanliness and perfection of the house left her feeling so out of place.

Some people would give anything to live in such a wonderland –

beautiful, organised gardens with neat rows of flowers in weed-free beds; colour co-ordinated wall paper and plush carpets in every room; even picture frames that matched the lamp shades; photographs of family milestones strategically placed around the house to remind everyone who saw them what a successful and marvellous family they all were. And on paper, they were.

Carrie had been a good 'all-rounder' all her life to date. She'd joined in with everything, everywhere. She'd filled every moment of her life with gainful employment. Ironic then, that she felt so empty inside these days. Her father had his shelves of trophies from years of racing vintage motorbikes. He suddenly stopped racing ten years ago.

'I just woke up one morning and decided I was fed up of falling off and getting hurt,' he'd laugh to anyone who asked him about them. 'I'm too old to get hurt any more.'

He'd kept all his bikes, though. Nowadays, he escaped into their garage at weekends to tinker around with them. Carrie couldn't understand why he didn't fancy a change from the smell of oil and grease at weekends after being in his garage all week at work. She suspected that, just like her, he had an aversion to sparkling white lace curtains.

Carrie wondered why on earth her parents had chosen each other. Did they get a choice in the matter, or was she a mistake that had sealed their fate forever? Bill and Jill; their names rhymed, but that seemed to be the only part of them that did so. Their wacky alliance was a source of constant mystery to their only daughter. It put Carrie off the thought of ever getting tied to anyone, although her best friend, Debs, had just got married and seemed to be very happy about it.

Carrie's mother was formidable looking woman. Tall, slim, fine boned; Carrie had a lot to thank her mother for as she, too, had these lucky, hard-wearing, genes. But Carrie's mother also had nerves as highly strung as her high, fine, cheekbones. There had been many a weekend throughout Carrie's life when her mother would just take to her bed for no apparent reason. If she had a headache the rest of the household had to tiptoe around in sackcloth and ashes. No television, the only stir being the fetching and carrying of drinks and things that her mother needed. Then, on Monday morning, the fussing over, everyone's weekend spoilt, mother would be back to her usual, efficient, self. Carrie's mother was a pillar of the community. She was on more committees than there were days in the week.

'She fills her whole life with stuff, just like me,' thought Carrie, as she entered

the kitchen to find her mother nattering away on the phone, papers and lists in front of her on the kitchen table.

Carrie knew that she was a disappointment to her mother. She was not showing a healthy interest in joining her as a second pillar of the community, but preferred to don dirty overalls and poke about in the garage at home with her dad, or down at the big garage itself.

'I don't want to end up like her, full of stuff but no substance. I want to be real!'

Carrie reminded herself of this every time she came home to find her mother in overdrive. She just hadn't worked out what being 'real' was yet. No time to worry about that now. She didn't wait around in the kitchen to tell her mother about her car, or her walnut; she wouldn't mention that bit of the story to anyone just yet. Somehow, it made her feel a bit uncomfortable and she couldn't work out why. She went straight up to her bedroom and put the walnut on her dressing table. She showered away the grime of her working day, the injury to her pride and to her little red car.

But the happy dog, the Land Rover, the farmers and the walnut, she could not clean from her mind. They made a carousel inside her head. Round and round they went; she was in the middle and couldn't step out of it. She put the walnut inside her bedside table drawer. It didn't make any difference.

'I could eat it, and be done with it,' she thought.

No, she couldn't do that.

'I need to see Debs.'

It was still quite early in the evening, so Carrie felt sure that Debs wouldn't mind her dropping in on her wedded bliss. Carrie and Debs had stuck together like glue all through school. They still had that unexpected, unexplainable, bond between them, even though their lives had taken completely different paths. On paper their friendship seemed impossible.

Debs had left school at sixteen, to work in the local contact lens factory, and had just got married to Joe, who also worked at the contact lens factory. Carrie, on the other hand, had had a university education. She was on the ladder of life, she hoped, to get to the top of it; to be somebody; to do something; to make a difference; to make a success of her life, whatever that was. Carrie almost envied Debs for how easy she seemed to make everything.

Debs was happy and content and had everything worked out. Carrie was unhappy and discontented most of the time and had nothing worked out. Why? Debs would probably laugh and tell her to make a Waldorf salad, then the carousel would go away, and she could get back to normal.

———————◆———————

Carrie lived on the outskirts of town; it was country life only a few seconds from the civilisation of a busy town. She usually drove to Debs' house, but it was a lovely evening, and she didn't want to completely lose her car bumper, so she decided to walk.

She could relax as soon as she stepped across the threshold of Debs' newly painted, blue, front door. No lace curtains here. It was all ultra-modern. Minimalist. Raspberry coloured blinds and sharp, bright, square furniture everywhere, except for one very big, soft, leather, sofa in the middle of the living room. Debs was always pleased to see her.

With an eternal smile and bubbly laugh, her optimism was never blunted by Carrie's regular, angst ridden, visits. Carrie was very well aware that Debs was a very special friend. Sometimes it troubled her that she didn't feel that she was giving back to Debs in any way, but Debs never seemed to have any problems, so she didn't know how she could do any more than she was doing.

Carrie collapsed into the big, soft, leather, sofa and waited for Debs to make her feel better. A few minutes of laughing and jokes about walnuts and she'd be sorted. But she was wrong. Carrie told her story, acting out every last enraged detail. She got a smile from Debs, but *no* laughter. No jokes about walnuts.

'You must go back!' said Debs in a dead pan voice.

'What do you mean?' squeaked Carrie.

'You must go back to that farm. You've got a thing about that farmer. You must go back and find out!' said Debs with a big, satisfied, smile on her face.

'But which one?'

The blood drained from Carrie's face. She hadn't said 'but which one' out loud but it had horrified her that her unconscious mind had replied in this way without her permission. One was a staring, wild, old man, and the other was a great stammering, dirty brown, idiot.

'What a load of rubbish! Of course I haven't got any such thing!'

Colour rushing back into her cheeks, she continued:

'Anyway, how could I? I've no reason to go back there for anything.'

'I'm sure you can think of something! You want to be a journalist, don't you? You must be good with words, then.'

Debs' eyes were still smiling at her. Her steady gaze made Carrie feel like a microbe wriggling around underneath a microscope.

'Where's Joe tonight?'

Change of subject tactic.

'It's darts night,' said Debs. 'He'll be back late so I can watch what I want on the telly.'

'Why can't you watch what you want on the telly anyway?' thought Carrie, but she didn't say so.

They watched a bit of telly. They had a laugh and a joke until it was time for Carrie to go home.

'Let me know how you get on!' shouted Debs as Carrie turned to wave goodbye from the road.

'What? Oh, give over!' Carrie barked back.

For once, Carrie couldn't wait to get away from Debs' house. She was being slowly strangled by a very uncomfortable, tight, feeling in her stomach. The carousel whirled faster in her head. Debs had not made it better. Debs was right. She had to go back.

Friday 7th April

'Enter!'

Carrie pressed down extra hard on the door handle. Her hands felt clammy and sweaty; she feared losing her grip on both the handle and herself as she obeyed Mr Pike, and entered his office. Carrie did not have to see the editor in chief, and esteemed owner of the newspaper, very often; she was not important enough to do so.

Mr Pike was sitting behind his large, old fashioned, mahogany wooden desk. His telephones and other gadgets looked like they'd just dropped onto it through a hole in time. Or was it Mr Pike and his mahogany desk that were misplaced?

Carrie tried hard not to stare at him. In truth, he looked more like a trout than a pike. She always tried to be kind in her thoughts, but the trout would not go away. It was sitting there now, in a pin-striped suit. Great, round, jowls hid its gills. An enormous mouth, with rubbery lips that hung permanently open, continually blowing bubbles and gasping for air; a sheen of oily skin and hair slicked back in the direction of its scales; webbed fingers resting on the desk.

'I bet he keeps his tail under the desk and that's why he needs a big, old, wooden one to hide it.'

Horrified at her own unkindness, she temporarily forgot her nerves and the purpose of her mission. She smiled bravely.

'Good morning, Mr Pike.'

'Good morning.'

The rubbery lips did not move very far, but released the deepest, most booming, voice that Carrie had ever heard. It was so deep and dark that it was off the scale of resonance.

'What can I do for you, Carrie?'

Carrie pulled out her enthusiastic, high pitched, bright voice, by way of reply.

'Mr Pike, I've had the most brilliant idea for the newspaper...'

Debs pressed down extra hard on the office door handle with her elbow; she didn't want to drop the tray of contact lenses that she balanced in her hands. It was a privilege to be allowed up to the main offices to make the final check on the finished lenses before they made their way out into the world, where all eyes would be, literally, upon them. There was no room for mistakes. There could be no air bubbles or imperfections of any sort.

It wasn't physically demanding work but it was tiring, all the same. Still, it was only her eyes that would get tired today. She could relax into the comfort of a soft, office chair. She could sit at a lovely, polished wood, table. One of the secretaries would probably even bring her a cup of tea. Free for a few hours from the monotony of working the machines on the factory floor, she could let her mind wander. Only her eyes belonged to the factory today.

Joe would be downstairs somewhere, working his shift. The rest of her belonged to him. She was so happy to have her own home with Joe.

'That's what Carrie needs. A man in her life. I wish she could get fixed up with someone, but she never quite manages it. It's that mother of hers, pumping her full of guilt all the time. 'You can't do this, you can't do that, you mustn't do this, you shouldn't do that. It's wrong, it's dirty, it's disgusting!' It would do her good to have someone to love, you can't beat it...Mind you, it can be a bit tiring,' giggled Debs to herself. *'Maybe you can have a bit too much loving sometimes. Joe gets a rest when he gets home while I'm doing all the cooking and the cleaning and the garden. His idea of loving is full on, all the time. Sometimes, I'd just love a cuddle. Still, it's early days, we haven't been married long. He'll get tired eventually, and things will settle down.'*

Debs stretched out her legs underneath the big, wooden table. So far, she'd found no air bubbles or imperfections of any sort.

'I wonder if Carrie's found a way to get back onto that farm, yet. She'll have to make sure there are no air bubbles or imperfections in her plan, if she's going to get past that mother of hers. Go, Carrie, go! It's about time you started to break free...'

———◆———

Mr Pike opened the door, and stood in the doorway.

'He's got legs after all!'

Carrie was quite disappointed.

Mr Pike was booming again.

'Well, girl, if you're prepared to do the work in your own time, we'll have a look at what you come up with. I'm not making promises, mind. I've got a business to run, you know.'

'Yes, I know.'

Carrie needed to get through the doorway, but Mr Pike was still filling it. She walked purposefully towards the door.

'Thank you for your time, Mr Pike.'

Mr Pike turned into profile position as Carrie reached the door. His immense swim bladder protruded into the space that Carrie needed to get through.

'Let me know how you get on.'

Mr Pike adjusted his gills to produce a smile at each corner of his mouth.

'He's not going to move,' realised Carrie.

She took a deep breath, which made her even slimmer, and seized her moment. Swift as a silver minnow, she slid past the protruding Mr Pike and kept swimming, deep into the office pond.

Phase two. Wanting to avoid another tricky walk up the long, white, gravelled drive in her favourite stilettos, Carrie drove all the way up this time and pulled into the perfectly square farmyard. There were no signs of life anywhere. The driveway had taken her up close to the large, red brick, farmhouse. A low, red brick, wall and lawned gardens separated it from the drive.

Carrie had tried to scan as many of the rectangular Georgian windows for the twitch of a curtain or a presence of some kind, but she had seen none. That the farmyard also seemed derelict and unoccupied was equally a relief as it gave her a moment to think through her outrageous proposition once more, and push her thumping heart back down her throat so that she would at least be able to speak when she found him again. It hadn't actually taken her long to work out a reason to come back to the farm. Such was her enthusiasm for her idea that she feared she may have been doing it even without Debs' prodding. This worried her. She was behaving totally out of character, out of control, and she was loving every minute of it. She hadn't even stopped to consider that her plan might fail – until now.

'What if he tells me to f… off?'

Carrie did another sweep of the outbuildings that edged the farmyard. Nothing. The wooden shed doors were either closed or dropping to bits and couldn't be closed. There was one entrance with no door at all which led into total darkness.

'Where's the happy dog?'

Time to move. Carrie got out of her car. It was a good feeling to move her legs. It calmed her nerves to feel her heels pressing into her stilettos; she was used to tottering about in them all day, it made her feel professional. And Carrie meant to do her business today.

Unfortunately, the farmyard didn't have laminate flooring. Her stilettos sank into a quagmire of mud and gravel. The ground was soft from the rain of the night before. The yard was a minefield of puddles, clumps of weeds, cow pats and larger pieces of bricks and rubble. Carrie picked her way across the yard, hoping, with each step, that she had made the right choice each time, and would land on firm ground. It was not a very elegant passage. She didn't know how long he'd been standing at the back door of the farmhouse, watching her undignified progress.

'Hello again, Mr Wilson.'

'Ah do!'

'Oh God, what a terrible start!'

Carrie cringed inside. Stilettos in mouth, she garbled her unusual request.

'I'm talking too fast, too fast,' she panicked.

But she'd started so she pressed on and finished.

'I knew you'd be back.'

'He's going to make me sweat for this,' said the pores of the skin on her flushed face.

'It would be a fantastic opportunity for the town dwelling community to see inside the way of life of the farming community that's so often misunderstood,' raced on the raw, undergraduate, voice. 'And you'll get a worker on the farm for free!' she trilled at speed.

Carrie smiled her best smile.

'There doesn't look like there's much work in you.'

Mr Wilson looked down at her sodden, mud stained, stilettos. He slowly let his eyes scan all the way up from her dainty ankles, through her tightly fastened raincoat and finally come to rest inside her eyes. Carrie felt dizzy and completely undone. It was not unpleasant. She stood her ground.

'Of course I can work as well as any man,' she fought back. 'I grew up in the oil and grease of a large garage and I've worked hard all my life.'

'What's in it for you, then, missy?'

'My name is Carrie,' hissed Carrie.

She really was feeling angry now. The voice continued:

'My editor is keen for me to provide a monthly column. (Lie). It will take our readers through the seasons of the year, educate, inform, and entertain them (lie, lie, lie!). It will be something a little bit different for our newspaper to offer and, frankly, it will give my career a good boost if it's successful (true, true).'

But it wasn't the whole truth, and Carrie and the old man leaning in the doorway knew it. His eyes spoke:

'You're here for yourself, for me, and for my son. I know it, you know it, and you know that I know it.'

A calf called out in the distance. A sudden gust of wind tugged at her hair, wrapping it around her face, releasing her from his gaze.

'It'll be alright. I give you my word.'

Touché. She smiled defiantly at mad Mr Wilson.

'Very well. You can have a try. But we have to stay anonymous. I don't want any health and safety nonsense turning up around here. And I can fire as well as hire!'

Mission accomplished. Carrie was pleased.

'When can I start then?'

'Straight away. Come on Saturday and we'll see how you get on.'

'Oh thank you, Mr Wilson.'

Carrie genuinely forgot, for a moment, what a scary individual this old man was. She turned to go.

'I'll bring my wellies!'

She thought she caught a smile on his face as he disappeared back into the farmhouse. Carrie put on her seatbelt and started her little red car.

'Oh my God, what have I just done?'

Tuesday 11th April

It was only Tuesday. How could she possibly wait until Saturday? Carrie packed her wellingtons and her dad's old overalls into the boot of her car.

'There, I'm ready!'

She slammed the boot shut. What to do now, though? She had four more days to work at the office. Four more days of making tea, running errands, typing up other people's copy, collating Births and Deaths. Does anybody ever read them anyway? Just like flights in a busy airport, life arrives, stays awhile, and then departs.

'*Most of us, most of the time, spend our lives milling around in the foyer,*' she thought, '*looking for something or other, and never stopping to appreciate the real drama of arrivals and departures that are happening around us all the time. No matter who or what we are,*' she mused, '*we all have to make that departure flight, so best make good use of our time on the ground.*'

So how could she make the best use of four more days of routine and diffuse the agony of all that waiting?

'*I'm not going to see Debs until I've actually been there and done it.*'

Carrie was a bit proud and didn't like to admit to Debs that she'd been so right about everything. It still shocked her that she'd so quickly devised a plan to get herself onto that farm. Carrie had been trained to think; she'd been educated. She often had an uncomfortable feeling that sometimes, too much thinking was a bad thing, and it got in the way of doing real things. Thinking was an excuse for living and it covered up a multitude of uncomfortable truths and emptiness. To fill her emptiness now, Carrie decided to swot up on farming.

'*It's research for my article, and at least I'll be able to talk to them about farming,*' she convinced herself.

The list of topics was endless. She hadn't even stopped to consider what type of farm it was going to be. She started to feel worried inside. She was a total fraud. How on earth was she going to be able to work on a farm? And how was she going to turn this ordeal into an exciting article that people would want to read? After all, she wasn't doing it because she was interested in farming, or writing articles…

Saturday 15th April

The radio sang:
'BBC Radio1...'
Carrie's day of reckoning had begun. She got up earlier than usual, in order to avoid her mother's icy glare. Obviously, mother did not approve of what Carrie was about to do. She didn't like the idea of her daughter volunteering to get her hands dirty for free; it was the wrong sort of volunteering.

'If my articles are a success, though, she'll be crowing about them to everybody and basking in the reflected glory of having such a talented daughter.'
Carrie shuddered and put the thought of said articles out of her mind. Dad had just smiled and said 'Go to it, love, just watch what you're doing.'

That was exactly what Carrie intended to do. She began by putting her overalls on before she set off.

'It'll show them I mean business when I get there.'

Her unconscious mind continued *'and it will contain your nerves. Button down that thumping heart!'*

And that's exactly what it did. The aroma of oil and grease that came from her dad's old overalls acted like gas and air on her senses. The warm sun shining through the windscreen of her car, accompanied by music from the car radio, ensured that she felt most unusually relaxed by the time she pulled into the farm driveway. It was as if she'd done it a million times before. She even smiled and waved at the tractor mechanics as she passed their workshop.

'What's up with me today?'
The yard was deserted yet again. Carrie's bravado quickly disappeared. She looked around the farmyard buildings and towards the back of the house. Nothing. She had the uneasy feeling that they were all watching her, like their animals, hidden away in the darkness of their sheds.

'Come on, you daft thing,' Carrie said to herself as she got out of her car. *'They're men, not monsters.'*
She was bending forwards by the side of her car, just tucking in the last bit of overall into the last welly, when two firm hands took hold of her hips from behind and she felt the heat of a body pressing into her.

'Very nice, darlin',' said the body in a very deep voice.

Carrie pulled away from the hands in her bent double position like a sprinter off an Olympic starting block. She staggered forward after that, the adrenalin surge changing to shock as she turned to see him already sauntering away across the yard, grinning like a Cheshire cat from beneath that head of long, unkempt, curly dark hair. The last time she'd seen those big, brown, muscular hands, they'd been resting on his battered old Land Rover.

To suddenly feel them like that upon her body, to have felt the heat of his body pressing into her – no, no, no, it wasn't meant to be like that!

The heat of the moment lingered on her backside. The shock turned to shakes and then plain fear. Carrie leant against the body of her little red car for comfort and protection. Her body screamed at her to quickly get back in the car and leave. It had never occurred to her that she might not be safe here. She'd assumed that the farmers would be just like the men at her dad's garage. Sure, they'd tease her, and have a laugh and a joke, but not like that. But Carrie didn't have time to get in her car. The old man was upon her.

'Ah do!'

'Hello, Mr Wilson.'

Carrie wondered if Mr Wilson senior had seen what had just happened. She decided to wait and see what happened. Nothing happened.

'Let's get you cracking then,' was all he said as he turned, clearly intending her to follow him.

Carrie was speechless. She wanted to scream and shout the humiliation of the assault on her person, her outrage and indignation at that 'thing's' behaviour. But she couldn't do it. And she didn't know why. She was quite capable of going into that 'I can stick up for myself' routine that she'd seen her mother perform so many times over the slightest little misdemeanour. And yet here she was, meekly following this wild looking old man, as if drawn on by an invisible tractor beam.

Without thinking, without hesitating, she followed Mr Wilson through the entrance that led into total darkness. It was a corridor with enough room on either side of it to house all kinds of funny looking machinery, barrows and buckets. The daylight beyond it led to an alleyway.

An assortment of sheds made colourful walls. There was one large wooden shed with a sliding door, but everything else was made from corrugated zinc sheets. It was difficult to call them sheds. They were more like the hovels that she'd seen on T.V. in third world countries. Bits of zinc sheeting were tacked over rusty red old ones; there were even odd shaped pieces of wood nailed on here and there. The alleyway took a sharp left and the darkness of a large barn loomed at the end.

Mr Wilson stopped at the corner. There was a small shed here with a tiny door that an average sized man would have to stoop to get through. There was a tiny window that was so caked up with cobwebs and dirt that it couldn't do its job at all. The old man pulled open the door to reveal a step of rotting straw bedding and cow muck that was deeper than the height of her wellies.

'This has got to be cleaned out before we start with the new calves. Here's a fork.'

He handed Carrie the fork that had been leaning against the shed wall. Its handle was shiny and smooth and worn.

'We'll get the wheelbarrow and I'll show you where the muck spreader is.'

He set off down the alleyway leading towards the darkness of the barn. Daylight never reached down here. It was muddy and wet on this path even though they'd had a bright, sunny, few days. Green, furry, mildew glowed fluorescent all the way along the backside of the wooden shed with the sliding door. It was so beautiful Carrie wanted to touch it, but the old man marched on and she had to almost run to keep up with his long strides. They came out into another yard area where a large, orange, muck spreader was parked. It stank. Old man Wilson pointed a long bony finger:

'Here's the wheelbarrow,' said the expressionless farmer's face.

Carrie knew that he was laughing at her behind that straight gaze. She also knew he would test her to begin with, but she hadn't expected anything like this. But she wasn't going to be beaten by either a bit of shovelling or a cocky farmer's son. Her secret romantic vision of her adventure on the farm had already been destroyed by that fateful bend to put on her wellies. Her pride and dignity were at stake now. Too many people knew what she was doing. Debs, her parents, Mr Pike and the other staff at the newspaper. She had to finish what she had so deliberately started.

So Carrie said nothing. She smiled cheerfully, nodded, grabbed the wheelbarrow handles and pushed off purposefully in the direction of the calf shed. She tried to look as relaxed and normal as possible as she disappeared into the dark alley and away from his gaze. She was actually having to use all her strength to push and control the heavy wheelbarrow through the mud. He let her go. There was no mention of a tea break. Carrie was fuming by the time she reached the calf shed.

She flung the door open and rammed the fork into the compressed bedding. It stuck fast. She pulled and pulled and tugged until the fork came free, but it had no load attached to it. She was sweating already. Her back ached from pushing the heavy wheelbarrow.

'I'll not be beaten, not be beaten,' Carrie spat into the mud. 'Violence achieves nothing. I just need a better technique,' she said to herself.

The layers of straw and mud looked just like layers of flaky pastry. Carrie tried slicing away the top layer of bedding with the fork as if she was eating one of her mother's fancy 'milles feuilles' cherry gateau on a Sunday lunchtime. It worked.

It was going to take her longer than if she could dig deep with the fork but at least she'd found a way to do what she'd been asked to do. The adrenalin and anger she felt inside fuelled her energy and she sliced away at thousands of cherry topped gateaux. Thinking about cakes took her mind off the dirt and terrible rancid smell as she got deeper and deeper into the shed. Being an intelligent girl, Carrie didn't overfill her wheelbarrow. She remembered how hard it had been to push it through the mud when it was empty.

'I'll just have to make more trips to the muck spreader.'

Her back ached.

'Bastard, bastard, bastard.'

The wheelbarrow wheel squeaked in rhythm to her swearing every time she made the return trip to the muck spreader. Carrie didn't like swearing, and tried not to do too much of it. Today, however, even the worst swear words she knew were too polite. She'd worked halfway into the shed when a dark shadow blocked the doorway.

'It's lunchtime,' was all he said.

Carrie didn't expect him to say 'well done' or 'good work,' but she'd hoped he might have asked her if she was O.K. He'd already left by the time she'd propped her fork up against the wall. Trickles of sweat ran down her back and made her feel suddenly cold after her exertions.

'Yet another undignified progress back to the farmhouse.'

She was also on edge as she walked, especially through the dark corridor that led back to the main farmyard. The funny looking machinery turned into scary monsters now that she was on her own, and she feared another attack from those big, brown, muscular hands. But there was none. The old man was waiting for her in the yard.

'There's the toilet.'

Old man Wilson pointed at an old door that had holes in the bottom of its panels and was standing slightly ajar.

'And you can eat in here.'

He moved slightly to show her the doorway next to the outside toilet. This door was propped open; it led into a small shed. There was an old fashioned, Victorian, porcelain sink at one end with taps set up high in the wall above it. A very large wooden bookcase was stacked with jars and cans of paint and bottles of goodness knows what. It looked quite pretty, though, with its blues and greens and purple and red contents all jumbled together. There were bags of powdered calf milk, bags of cement, buckets, a hosepipe; it was a complete mess. In the middle of the shed there was a small wooden table with a plastic, chequered red, tablecloth and a wooden chair.

'I'll see you in a bit.'

Two strides later he had disappeared into the farmhouse. Carrie stood in the doorway to the shed in disbelief. On automatic pilot she fetched her sandwiches from the car and sat down on the wooden chair. It was *so good* to sit down on a chair.

'He's playing with me, pushing me to the limit.'

Carrie had never met anyone like Mr Wilson before. She stared at the sunlight in the open doorway in stunned silence and ate her sandwiches. She was ravenously hungry. Winston Churchill popped into her head.

'Never give in, never give in, never give in,' he said.

It was probably a bit dramatic to compare her first day at work on the farm to winning World War Two but it made Carrie smile inside, and she relaxed a bit. She suddenly realised that someone was watching her in the doorway. Two dark brown eyes stared up at her from the step – it was the happy dog! He still looked happy. Carrie froze. A split second later, the happy dog's owner walked past. He didn't even turn his head to look at her. He must have known she was there. Carrie didn't know whether to feel relieved or outraged after his behaviour that morning.

'Jip!' called the deep voice.

Her day was not going to plan.

'The happy dog is called Jip.'

Carrie smiled; she was an eternal optimist.

———◆———

Carrie had finished mucking out the calf shed and had started the next one by the time he came to tell her to knock off for the day.

'Same time tomorrow then,' was all he said.

'Will I be doing the same thing tomorrow?' she asked, as casually as

25

possible.

'You have to finish what you start, don't you?'

The pale blue icy eyes burned into her.

'Yes, of course. But I hope I'll be able to see a variety of things while I'm here, or I'll struggle to write my articles.'

'Oh, you'll see plenty. I'll make sure of that.'

Carrie squirmed inside. This old man wanted her to feel uncomfortable and he was succeeding very nicely. Carrie had the beginnings of blisters on her hands from gripping that fork all day. Her hands throbbed now. She felt that she had to fight back somehow.

'By the way, your son was very rude to me today. I'd be grateful if you could ask him to keep his hands to himself in future.'

No reaction.

'You're working for me, not him.'

'What's his name, anyway?'

'Best keep away from him. Same time tomorrow then.'

Same time tomorrow indeed.

———————◆———————

It was lovely to soak in the bath. Carrie usually showered, she got bored sitting in the bath beyond two minutes. But tonight it was wonderful. She was in serious pain all over and she felt seriously dirty as well. And tomorrow, she would have to put those smelly overalls on and do all that shovelling again. Maybe mother was right, after all. She could not have curled up her nose further in disgust when Carrie had arrived home. Carrie discovered that she still smelt of cow muck even after she'd taken her overalls off.

'It's just like dad,' she thought. *'He always smells of oil, even when he's scrubbed up. It's the smell of real life. It makes us who we are.'*

She was actually quite pleased that she had a real life smell at long last, and that it was so strong that it had got a reaction from her mother, even if it was a negative one. Carrie wasn't sure if she particularly liked the smell.

'But it's only temporary. It's not going to be for the rest of my life, is it? I'll find my own smell eventually.'

She sank down further into the bubbles of her bath.

'I'm just glad I didn't volunteer to work at a fishmongers!'

That thought reminded her of Mr Pike and her article.

'Oh no!' she groaned. 'Well, I don't have to think about that after just one day.'

All of a sudden, she needed to see Debs.

———◆———

As it always had been, Carrie talked and Debs listened. Debs could do the most amazing things with her eyebrows. Most peoples' eyebrows go up or down together, but Debs' eyebrows had a whole range of different positions. She could make one go up and the other one down at the same time. Debs' eyebrows had a really good workout of ups and downs as they reacted to Carrie's story.

'It all sounds very strange,' said Debs. 'I wonder why he wouldn't tell you his son's name? Are you sure you want to keep going back?' she asked. 'No one would blame you if you didn't after everything that's happened to you today.'

'I know it doesn't make any sense, but I'm determined to see it through,' said Carrie. 'I don't want to be beaten by a staring old man or that hairy, good for nothing, son of his. And I know it's not at all how I imagined it would be, and I know I wasn't really bothered about the newspaper articles, but if I *can* stick it for a few weeks, maybe I *can* write something that'll help me.'

'Then you'll just have to make sure that you do keep away from the son. If he dared to do what he did to you today, you can't trust him at all,' said Debs. 'Not all men are nice to women, you know.'

Debs' eyebrows were still and matter of fact.

'And the old man is hiding something. It's as if he doesn't want you there, he's trying to frighten you away but, at the same time, he wants you. Needs you, even.'

'Maybe,' said Carrie.

She thought about those palest of pale blue eyes, and how they stared at her.

'Joe will be home soon.'

This was Carrie's cue to say 'Yes, I'd better make a move.'

Carrie was silently aware that Debs seemed to like her to be gone by the time Joe came home. Carrie couldn't understand why it was such a big deal to have your best friend round to visit. Carrie would never outstay her welcome, and she knew that Debs knew that.

'No doubt it's the passion of true love and wedded bliss that I know nothing about,' she sighed.

Carrie was long gone before the front door slammed and Joe returned home. Debs was ready to receive him.

Wednesday 19th April

'Well, Carrie,' Mr Pike bubbled and boomed, 'it's most unusual, most unusual. I expected your first Spring article to have some fluffy chicks and new born lambs in it somewhere. I'm not sure if our readers will like this.'

'Please, Mr Pike, can't you give it a go? Look at my hands!'

Carrie held out her open hands to Mr Pike; they perfectly matched the colour of his mahogany red wooden desk. They were permanently red and sore these days. There were patches of hard skin, the beginnings of calluses on her palms, after her weekend of solid graft with that fork and wheelbarrow. By showing her hands in this way it looked as if she was begging but, actually, she was bristling inside.

'It's the truth!' she continued. 'Isn't our newspaper all about seeking out the truth? We don't invent the news to suit ourselves here, do we?'

'We most certainly do not,' boomed Mr Pike. 'We may be small, but we're a newspaper of quality, integrity, and the backbone of our community.'

Mr Pike launched into his favourite morale boosting speech that he gave at the end of every staff meeting. Carrie knew how to trigger his ego.

'And you're the editor and driving force behind all of that, Mr Pike. So if I'm prepared to do the work for you, won't you just give the truth a chance?'

'What shall you call the column?'

'Twentieth Century Land Girl.'

'Very well then, we'll give it a try for a few weeks.'

'Thank you, Mr Pike.'

The fish had taken the bait.

Friday 21st April

Dear Reader,

During both the First and the Second World War, young women from towns and cities were drafted into the countryside in their thousands, to work the land and help provide for the nation in its hour of need. They were the 'Women's Land Army.' During the First World War, by 1918, three hundred thousand women were working the land, milking cows, and caring for livestock. The army was called upon once more at the onset of the Second World War, under the directorship of Lady Denman:

'The Land Army fights in the fields. It is in the fields of Britain that the most critical battle of the present war may well be fought and won.'

My task is not such a matter of life and death; I am not so brave as those young women all those years ago. But I am a town girl who wants to know what it's really like to work the land. The World War Two slogan that advertised for recruits to the Women's Land Army read:

'For a healthy, happy job, join the Women's Land Army!'

And that's just what I'm going to try to share with you today, and in the coming months, for I have volunteered myself to work on a farm. I'm going to get my hands dirty, and find out if working the land really is 'a healthy, happy, job!'

It's the beginning of Spring. The fresh bright green of new life is all around. Flowers turn their faces towards the sun. The birds are busy working, working, working to build their nests. All of nature has to work, work, work continually, just to survive. It's only us humans who sometimes think that the world owes us a living. How wrong we are!

So far, down on the farm, all I have seen is a fork, a wheelbarrow, a muck spreader and tons of straw speckled animal poo! I have seen spiders and beetles and all sorts of insects living inside every forkful of dung. Every creature in their own universe, quite unaware that they are not alone. All this preparation is to welcome the new calves.

All day long, hour after hour, relentless, non-stop shovelling. One short stop for lunch sitting in an outhouse on a hard wooden chair, my only company the farm dog who looked like he knew what I was thinking and said 'So?'

The blisters on my hands, the pain in my back, the sweat on my shirt – this baptism of fire brings me as close as I can ever get to the blackbird in my garden. Remember that the next time you are shovelling s***! I've even got to quite like the smell of cow muck – it's bitter sweet. It's

30

a more straight forward, healthy bad smell, than human waste. How often do we moan about the stench from slurry and muck spreading farmers?

From the bowels of the muck spreader comes the fresh green grass and new crops to feed the cattle who in turn, will feed us all. It's looking like the World War Two slogan might be right, working the land is 'a healthy, happy, job!'

And I haven't even touched a cow yet!

Saturday 22nd April

Her mother finished reading the paper.

'I'm really not happy about you spending your weekends in this manner, Carrie. A young lady like you should not be doing that kind of thing, and it's outrageous the way that farmer treated you! And I *definitely* don't like that ghastly smell in my kitchen!'

Carrie said nothing.

———◆———

'Congratulations, love, on getting your first article in the paper! I'm very proud of you! Don't let that farmer take advantage of you, though. He's given you a tough time so far. Just watch what you're doing,' said dad.

Carrie said nothing.

———◆———

'I can't believe you've actually done all that shovelling! Why didn't you write anything about that nutcase of a farmer? Or his son? I want to meet the farmers next time, or else!!' said Debs.

Carrie said nothing.

———◆———

Old man Wilson said nothing. Carrie wondered if he read the local newspaper. She'd never so much as set foot inside the farmhouse yet to find out anything about him at all. She was desperate to know what he thought about her article. Debs was right of course, she had to write about the farmers themselves at some point, but at this point in time, she really didn't want to.

Old man Wilson had worked her into the ground and treated her quite harshly. She should hate him by now, and that ghastly, hairy, son of his, but she didn't. She wanted to keep them to herself. She felt an unspoken loyalty, a strange kind of bondage growing inside her that she couldn't explain. It made her uncomfortable. She didn't know where she was going.

Friday 28th April

Never mind all that. Today she knew exactly where she was going and that also put her in a panic inside – she was going shopping with Debs. She fancied a trip out. Debs loved shopping. Carrie hated shopping. Debs loved pottering about just looking at things, trying on whacky stuff just for fun with no intention of buying it. She loved just to sit and have a coffee. Debs loved having fun and was good at it. Carrie wanted to have fun but didn't feel very expert at it.

'Come on, let's try in here!'

Carrie heard the words from Debs' mouth even before she'd said them as she grabbed her arm and pulled her in the direction of yet another weird looking boutique full of glittery, spangly, clothes that shone like stars against the black interior of the shop. It was like stepping into a planetarium.

'Highly impractical, but they're all very beautiful,' said Carrie.

'Oh, lighten up, you silly old mare!' said Debs. 'Let's try something on.'

She picked a bright, fuchsia pink, dress from a rail, and a black one, with a flash of silver across it, for Carrie. It was a cheap and cheerful shop with just one communal changing room. Carrie was slim and trim but she still hated taking her clothes off in front of other women.

It made her feel fourteen again and back in the school changing rooms where everyone would be sniggering at each other to cover up their own feelings of embarrassment. And there were mirrors everywhere in this changing room. Carrie went to the opposite side of the room from Debs and tried not to look across at her friend. Debs had a beautiful figure. She had more flesh, was more rounded, than Carrie, but she wasn't fat. Carrie assumed that was why Debs had always been more popular with boys all her life. And she was married already! Carrie felt a bit jealous of her, but not, at the same time. She loved Debs to bits.

As Carrie finished pulling her dress down over her head she glanced across to see how Debs was getting on.

'Oh my God, what have you done there?' she cried.

'What?' said Debs.

'You've got bruises on your hips!'

Carrie was staring again. Debs quickly pulled her dress on – *'Maybe too quick,'* she thought.

'Ooh this one's a squeeze to get on. I was doing some gardening the

33

other day and bumped into the corner of the kitchen sink as I was carrying stuff outside, and then I did the same thing when I came back in. Got myself twice in one day!' said Debs. 'Hey, you look good in that!' she continued.

Carrie turned back to look in the mirror. She felt pale inside. Her flashback took her back to her wellies on her first visit to the farm. Those big, brown, muscular hands grabbing her hips. Carrie wasn't sure if she was imagining it, but the marks on Debs' hips looked hand shaped to her. No! Debs wouldn't lie about something like that. Would she? Carrie tried to be enthusiastic.

'Yeah, it looks great!'

'You should have it. You never know when it'll come in handy. Mine's a bit too tight so I'll give it a miss.'

Carrie couldn't help doing her old staring trick as they got changed. Debs pulled her top back on before taking the entire dress off.

'Is she covering herself up now? Does she usually get changed like that?'

Carrie was bothered by what she'd seen, and suspicious. Maybe she'd end up a good journalist after all. She had to get to the bottom of this. Carrie thought about Joe. Really, she hardly knew him at all. He was always just going out when Carrie arrived or just coming in as she was leaving. Debs always arranged their visits like that. Carrie had never thought about it before. But she thought about it now. Now, she needed the sit down and cup of coffee.

'Oh, my feet ache,' moaned Carrie.

'I'd have thought you'd have more stamina than that after all that shovelling!' laughed Debs.

'That's not the same thing. Shopping is much more stressful than mucking out a cowshed! I haven't got *you* trying to make me buy outrageous clothes that I'll never wear, and I don't have to worry about what I look like!'

'You don't have to worry about that anyway,' smiled Debs. 'You're one of those annoying people that always look gorgeous, even when they're not trying. You just don't realise it!'

Coffee and cake arrived at their table.

'So why don't I have any success with men if that's the case?'

Debs had hit a raw nerve. Deep inside, Carrie was distraught that, despite her efforts to keep herself in good shape, and be cheerful and snappily dressed at all times, Prince Charming had never appeared on horseback or in a Ferrari.

'You're tight aren't you?' said Debs. 'You can't let go of yourself, can you?'

'If you mean I work hard at everything I do, then I do. It's just the way I am!' replied Carrie, a little indignantly.

'It's not just that,' said Debs. 'All this working hard stuff is just a cover-up because you don't really know who you are. You're searching for something and you're frightened that you might never find what you're looking for, and that makes you even more tight and wary when you do meet anyone new or different.'

'How can she be so bloody clever,' thought Carrie. *'Am I so transparent as that?'*

Clearly, to Debs, she was, because Debs was on a roll, and she continued:

'For example, you loved that sparkly dress, you knew you looked *fab* in it, yet if I hadn't made you buy it, you would have denied yourself the pleasure of it. Why? Because you don't seem to think you deserve to have pleasure – you can't accept yourself and you certainly can't love yourself. You've spent too much time trying to please that mother of yours. At least, now, you've broken the mould a bit by going to that farm.'

Carrie sipped her coffee. She could do with something stronger.

'Am I that obvious?' was all she could say.

'Only to me!' beamed Debs.

'Not only to you,' squirmed Carrie's guts.

She was back at the farm for the first time; the Falcon's eyes were staring at her. Old man Wilson was bloody clever as well.

'Look at how you clam up at my house when Joe's around,' said Debs.

'Got you!' thought Carrie, as the mention of Joe brought her straight back to the smell of coffee, cake, shopping and those bruises.

'He's not a monster, you know,' said Debs. 'And yet you freeze up when he comes into the room.'

'Well, he might be your husband, but I don't really know him at all,' said Carrie. 'And to be honest, he frightens me a bit, makes me feel uncomfortable, like he doesn't want me to be friends with you. He never says anything.'

'Oh, what rubbish!' said Debs. 'He's actually quite shy. But he likes to be man of the house, king of the castle – like all men.'

'Not like all men.'

Carrie thought about her lovely dad.

'Are you happy like that?'

She wanted to say something about those funny bruises but she didn't feel able to.

'Oh I'm alright,' shrugged Debs. 'Nothing is ever perfect, is it? Except,' she continued, 'for that fabulous dress you've bought today. When are you going to wear it? Have you got any office parties coming up?'

'That's the end of anything serious, then.'

Carrie realised it was time to shut up – for the time being.

Saturday 29th April

'Hello, darlin', why don't you come on the grass with me?'

The big, brown, muscular hand slipped around her waist and came to rest on her right jeans pocket near to her groin. He'd caught her off her guard. She hadn't seen anything of him the last weekend she'd been at the farm. She'd started to relax. She'd been getting into a good routine. She knew old man Wilson was going to work her hard and she'd started to really thrive on the physical and mental challenge of it all. Her hands were no longer sore, they were tough as leather, just like her insides.

She'd just finished cleaning out the cowsheds. Sunlight streamed in through the doorway onto the antique, concrete, floor. It wasn't modern, boring, grey concrete. It was ancient pale brown, with millions of tiny little stones and pebbles in it. The wet floor shone like a bed of precious jewels in the warm sunshine. The cowshed looked neat and clean; Carrie was leaning on the yard brush in the doorway, admiring her handiwork, when the hand had caught her unawares. Panic stricken, her only escape was into the cowshed which made her feel even more trapped. He was blocking both the doorway and the sunlight.

'No thank you!' was all the defence she could muster.

Carrie was in bits. Strange, but he didn't make her feel like that when she'd first met him on the day of the accident. She felt dangerously unsafe; she was annoyed to find that she quite liked the feeling. She gripped the broom handle ready to defend herself. He leant on the doorpost.

'Well, if you're sure, darlin'.'

He was grinning that big grin again.

'Quite sure, thank you. And you shouldn't go sneaking up on people like that.'

He held his hands up in fake surrender.

'I'm just being friendly! Just being friendly! I'll be here when you change your mind!'

Sunlight blinded her. He was gone before she'd had a chance to reply, even if she could have thought of something clever enough to say.

Later that morning he waved at her from his tractor cab. At lunchtime he completely ignored her yet again as she ate her sandwiches in the outhouse. But as she drove down the drive at the end of the day he ran behind her car blowing kisses and laughing at her.

'There's got to be something wrong with him,' thought Carrie. *'He's as crackers as his dad. What am I doing here with these people?'*

Tuesday 2nd May

Carrie sat on her office chair at her office desk. The seat was padded and covered in a soft, tweed, fabric. The desk top shone like glass, being a pine veneer so hard that it was impossible to scratch, even with the sharpest pencil. Paper, pens, paperclips, telephone; all neatly arranged. There was not a speck of dust or dirt anywhere. Carrie looked across the large office and out of the window beyond. Birds were swooping and playing in the air outside. It was a beautiful sunny day, but the sky looked grey because of the tinted office windows.

Carrie felt trapped. Just at that moment she had a sudden panic and felt she'd be more free locked up in a prison cell, than in that shiny grey office. She stood up so quickly that she made her colleagues spasm with a nervous jump as her chair scraped the floor violently.

'I need coffee,' was all she said in answer to their silent alarm.

This wasn't true. Carrie needed dirt and sweat. She needed to be outside and hot and cold. She needed to feel alive, not sterilised. But, this morning, coffee would have to do. So she clicked her way down the corridor in her favourite, black, stiletto heels, that didn't seem to sound the same to her these days. There was not so much pleasure in their sharpness any more. What did it mean?

At the coffee machine she felt him behind her and he wasn't even touching her, yet she felt much more violated than when those big, brown, hands had been so recently placed upon her hips.

'Good morning, Carrie,' boomed Mr Pike. 'How are you getting on with that research of yours?'

'Which research is that, Mr Pike?'

'Into those farmers of yours!'

Carrie didn't like the way he said 'into.' She knew what he meant. She ignored it.

'Oh, very well, thank you.'

'You know, our readers like a bit of human interest, Carrie. Your articles are beautifully written, but we are a newspaper, and we need a bit of salt and vinegar on our fish and chips every now and then to liven things up a bit.'

'Oh why did he have to mention 'fish'!'

She'd tried with all her might not to think about Mr Pike in terms of swim bladders, scales and slime, and now she had failed.

'Of course I'll write about the farmers at some point, but I wanted our readers to feel what it's like doing the work and living a different kind of life from other people. And I must protect their right to privacy.'

'Well, to a degree, to a degree,' boomed Mr Pike.

'You're new to the game, Carrie. You've got to get in there and give me a bit of dirt.'

He leaned towards her, his swim bladder pressing against her thigh.

'A bit of dirt that isn't on the end of your shovel, eh?!'

His elbow fin flapped into her arm as he gave a deep chuckle. Carrie stood her ground. She was determined not to let him knock her off her balance in any way. She smiled back.

'I'll do my best, Mr Pike, to keep you entertained.'

She turned, and walked away with the sexiest swagger she could muster. In times gone by, she would have scuttled away and died of embarrassment in some corner after an encounter like that with the Mr Pikes of this world.

'You mean bitch!'

This was perhaps a bit too strong a sentiment, but it felt good to walk away and feel strong, and not intimidated.

'That's why my shoes don't sound the same any more – I don't need them!'

Superficial strength was being replaced by real strength. The image was becoming reality.

'You bitch!' said Carrie.

And she smiled.

———◆———

'Just put the kettle on quietly and make me a cup of tea, I've had the most ghastly headache all day. I haven't been able to do a thing. And I've got the W.I. meeting tonight. I shan't be able to go down early to set up, now. Cynthia and Rosalind will have to do it, for a change.'

'For a change!'

Carrie nearly exploded but said nothing. Poor Cynthia and Rosalind did it every time. Carrie's mother posed in the kitchen doorway like a tragic Greek Goddess. She was still in her dressing gown and it was past six o'clock. Carrie switched on the kettle as quietly as possible. Even so, its slow hiss was matched by a sharp intake of breath from the kitchen doorway. Carrie knew that by seven o'clock her mother would appear transformed into a triumphant Greek Goddess, with not a hair out of place.

She stabbed at the teabag with a teaspoon as it brewed in her mother's favourite china mug.

'If I want bitch lessons, I don't have far to go,' she thought. *'But it's the wrong kind of bitch. It's false.'*

'And cook some dinner for your father – you're not going out, are you?'

'No, not tonight.'

No, Carrie was saving up her night out for tomorrow when her mother had her 'LLN' meeting – the 'Local Ladies Network' – an organisation at the centre of the universe, populated by the great and the good; successful business women and ladies of means, putting the world to rights. Every time it was 'Local Ladies Network' night Carrie would get the same lecture, the same pleas from her mother to 'just pop along with me. It would be so advantageous for a young woman at the start of her career, such as yourself. And a lot of members have sons who are very eligible young bachelors, you know…'

Carrie knew. Unfortunately, she was always busy and never free to 'pop along.'

Mother disappeared with her cup of tea, and disappeared more permanently at seven o'clock sharp, as predicted. She wouldn't be back until ten-ish.

Yippee! Carrie could have a night in with her lovely dad. They could eat pie and chips in the lounge; sit with their legs swinging over the chair arms; watch rubbish telly. And no talking. No talking about nothing. And yet more would be communicated than on any other evening of the week. Because, when Carrie and her dad were in that room it was a *living room*, not a lounge.

'Had a good day, love?' was all he would say.

'Yes thanks, dad,' was all Carrie would reply.

He never pried. Yet he knew she was lying.

'I was grey and trapped!' is what she should have said.

'Just stick with it, love. It'll all work out in the end.'

'You see, he knows!' chirped Carrie's mind.

Wednesday 3rd May

Debs was wearing a big, baggy, sweatshirt and a silk scarf round her neck even though it was a warm, May, evening. She poked her head round her newly painted, blue, front door.

'Oh, it's you!' she said. 'Joe's just gone out. I thought he'd forgotten something.'

'Well, I just thought I'd drop in on you and say 'hi' for a few minutes if that's O.K. It's 'Local Ladies Network' night!'

'Oh, you'd better come in, then. Do you want a coffee?'

Debs was walking away down the corridor to the kitchen already.

'Yes, thanks,' said Carrie, closing the door behind her. She followed Debs down to the kitchen.

'Are you alright? You don't look too good.'

Debs busied herself with the kettle, coffee and mugs.

'Oh, I'm fine. I've had a bit of a sore throat. I feel cold, probably a bit of a virus, so I thought I'd wrap up and sweat it out.'

'Oh, what a shame,' said Carrie. 'There's nothing worse than a summer cold. Can I do anything for you?'

'No ta,' said Debs. 'But best not be late going so I can have an early night.'

'No problem,' said Carrie.

They drank the coffee. Carrie rabbited on about the calves and everything else she hadn't put in her article but she couldn't get the slightest flicker of interest out of Debs, who usually couldn't wait to hear the inside farmer story that Carrie point blank refused to share with Mr Pike and his readers. Carrie gave up in the end.

'Are you sure you're alright, Debs? You don't look like your usual self.'

'Oh yes, I'm fine. Just a bit tired, that's all. Joe's had a couple of days off and so we've been busy doing some jobs around the house.'

Everything looked the same to Carrie. Just then, the front door opened. Debs jumped out of her chair and moved towards the living room door. Joe was already standing in the doorway. He looked at Carrie but was speaking to his wife.

'I'm going up,' was all he said.

His eyes were fixed on Carrie the whole time.

'Yes, Joe, I'm coming straight away,' said Debs.

Carrie felt *so* uncomfortable, and tried to make a cheerful exit. She

41

found herself making excuses as she moved towards the front door.

'Thanks for the coffee, hope you feel better soon…Sorry, I shouldn't have kept you talking so long…I didn't realise it was so late…See you again when you're feeling better…'

'Bye,' said Debs.

The newly painted, blue, front door closed on her. It wasn't late. For a moment Carrie stood frozen on the front door mat. She listened.

'Yes, Joe, I'm coming straight away…'

Instinct made Carrie want to knock the door down and go back inside. Common sense took over, though; she walked away down the drive as loudly as she could. When she reached the road she turned slightly and just caught a glimpse of the front bedroom curtains swish. He had watched her leave.

Saturday 6th May

Right! It was time for action. After all these weeks of shovelling shit Carrie realised that she didn't actually know a great deal about Mr Wilson or his son, except that the son's dog was called 'Jip.' There was the occasional close encounter with him when he was in mood one, his 'hello darlin',' as she decided to call it. When in mood two, he was silent and oh so distant. The distance was key. Old man Wilson seemed to go out of his way to keep Carrie at a distance from anything exciting that was happening on the farm.

She comforted herself that the old man must know what a dangerous, womanising, villain his son was, so he protected her by keeping them as far apart as possible. But this was all imagination. She needed to get up close enough to talk to them, father or son, it didn't matter which one. She hadn't even spent a few minutes with either farmer the whole time she'd been there to be able to write about them; perhaps that's what they wanted.

On this particular Saturday morning she saw her chance. As she arrived she caught a flash of black and white through the hedgerow next to the farm drive; it was Jip, the happy dog. Son of Wilson was repairing a fence by the roadside. He didn't look up as her little red car slowed down to have a look at him.

'Right! I'm going to find the old man and ask to help with the fencing today. With a bit of luck he'll be inside the farmhouse and, if so, I'm going to walk straight in!'

Too late. He must have seen her arrive for he was waiting for her in the yard.

'Ah do!' he said.

'Hello, Mr Wilson,' she started.

'I want you to move the fence for the cows, feed the calves, and then there's the sheds to muck out.'

Carrie was about to argue about 'sheds to muck out' but she'd heard the word 'fence' and thought that that was progress; she'd seen the son fencing just now, so she said:

'O.K.'

'I'll show you what to do. Bring that sledge hammer.'

He pointed to a big hammer with a long, wooden, handle that was leaning against the wall. Then he was striding away up the drive towards the fields beyond. Carrie had to almost run to keep up with his crane-like long legs. It was lovely to get out into the open fields which sloped up to the blue horizon. The grass was very bright green, and long, in the new part of the field that the cows were about to graze. They'd stripped bare the section of field from the previous day – that was now lime green and spotted with dark brown cowpats. The dark hawthorn hedgerows around the edge of the field made it look like the beginnings of a patchwork quilt.

They'd walked past the cows, who were mooching around in the yard like a hoard of teenagers waiting to be let into the rides at an amusement park. The new grass looked so fresh and juicy Carrie thought it looked good enough to eat herself. And then, who should appear from nowhere but Jip, the happy dog. Running round in circles, running from the old man and back to Carrie. Carrie wanted to run as well, but she was carrying the sledgehammer. The old man suddenly stopped at a slim metal pole that was squewered into the ground. It held a thin wire in a loop at the top of it.

'Run up the field and undo the wire,' commanded old man Wilson.

Carrie enthusiastically grabbed the wire.

'Agh!' she shrieked.

It was live! It stung her whole body.

'Ow, that really hurt!'

'It's meant to. It's an electric fence. Wait while I disconnect it.'

She knew he was laughing at her. Nevertheless, she set off up the field, undoing the wire from the loops, never sure whether he would switch the power back on again at any minute. So Carrie ran as fast as she could. The field had quite an uphill slope so she was out of breath by the time she reached the top. Jip ran with her. She couldn't resist having a look through the open gateway at the top of the field. She let out a gasp of delight. The patchwork quilt on the other side of the hill was more complete and stretched out into a beautiful valley. A clump of trees waved to her from a hill on the other side.

'Hey!'

She heard a distant shout. As fast as she'd worked her way up the hill, the old man had been behind her, uprooting the metal poles and re-planting them with the sledgehammer amongst a new section of fresh grass. He'd been up and down the field in the time it had taken her to run to the top. She wondered just how long she'd been looking through the gateway.

'Hey!'

He was at the bottom of the field holding his end of the electric fence

44

wire up high in the air. It was a signal for Carrie to do the same. The wire was very long and actually very heavy as it dragged through the grass but Carrie didn't let go. It was obvious what to do next. So she did it. Running down the hill she re-looped the wire into the metal poles. By the time she got to the bottom of the hill again she felt so alive that she forgot that she was in the company of that strange old bird of prey. She babbled excitedly:

'Oh, that was great! Thank you! Can I do that again tomorrow? The view from the top of your field is just fantastic. How far does your farm stretch across the valley?'

He strode on. Carrie realised that she was running alongside him just like Jip, the happy dog.

'I'm a happy dog!'

A strange shiver suddenly came over her. She remembered that wish had popped into her head when she'd first seen Jip in the Land Rover all those weeks ago. They'd reached the gate by now. Old man Wilson was letting the cows out into the field. The cows didn't exactly stampede, but with happy feet and noses to equal those of Carrie and Jip, they knew where they were going and moved as one body, towards their new, fresh green delight. Carrie could feel their enthusiasm and sheer joy as they started their new day. How many times had she driven past a field of cows and never given them a second thought? So much beauty and life going on all around her, and she'd never even noticed it.

They returned to the farmyard a different way, around the edge of the buildings instead of through the middle. Here, there was a dirt track dotted with rubble, wild daisies and the odd shot of bright pink rosebay willow herb. To the right of the track there was a rickety, moss- eaten fence. Two stone gate pillars stood alone and without gate in the middle of the fence. And beyond there was an orchard. At least Carrie thought it must be an orchard because it was peopled by trees of different sorts. There were two large ones in the middle, edged with smaller ones. Far away, in one corner, one tree stood alone; it looked quite derelict and sad. Not dead exactly, but not alive either. Yet it had the most incredibly beautiful shape and branches. Beneath it, there sat a simple stone bench. It looked so old that it could have been lifted from Stonehenge itself. Carrie was drawn towards it as if by a magnet. A carpet of overgrown grasses and yellow buttercups completed the scene.

'Oh how beautiful!'

Without a second thought Carrie ran through the stone pillars and into the neglected little orchard. She swung herself in and out of the trees. It was a fairy wonderland of pink and white blossom better than any display of Christmas lights she'd ever seen.

'Oh, this is amazing!' she cried. 'It's just *so* beautiful!'

She stopped suddenly before the sad tree in the corner with its stone bench beneath. There was a slight rise in the ground in front of it. All at once the hairs stood up on the back of her neck. She felt like an irreverent child who'd been running around a church and had suddenly fallen upon the altar. The sad tree seemed to hold its branches out to her in a gentle and pleading sort of way.

Then she remembered the Falcon. Hardly daring to move she turned slowly, to see him standing in the stone pillar gateway. He looked just like a third stone pillar. He was watching her. He'd been watching her all this time. She felt undone all over again. As before, Carrie put on her brave, grown up, face, and walk, and returned to him.

'Your orchard is very beautiful, Mr Wilson. Thank you for showing it to me.'

'Well, he hasn't actually shown it to me, or has he?'

'I bet Mrs Wilson likes coming here, to pick the fruit.'

'My wife died.'

His gaze remained constant. Carrie shrivelled inside.

'Oh I'm really sorry, I didn't know. I just assumed that the lady I'd seen in the farm house was Mrs Wilson.'

'That's Mavis, the cleaner.'

'Oh,' was all Carrie could say.

She wanted to ask him what had happened. She had a feeling that he wanted to tell her. She really wasn't frightened of him at all any more. But they were being watched by other pairs of eyes. Jip the happy dog was sniffing at their wellies. And son of old man Wilson, in silent mood two, his eyes firmly fixed to the ground, walked past them, into the bowels of the farm buildings. He whistled to Jip. Carrie didn't know how long he'd been there.

———◆———

Carrie couldn't go straight home. She just couldn't face lace curtains and the smell of beeswax furniture polish after the day she'd had; it would have killed her. She needed a gentle let down back into her own world, so she called in at her dad's garage instead. With a bit of luck he'd still be there, just clearing up and doing the end of the day books and chores. His car was the only one left on the forecourt when she arrived. Perfect. Carrie's dad didn't need security cameras. He instinctively knew every creak and squeak in the place; the way familiar folk opened the door to the garage at the back. Only familiar folk knew how to turn the handle just to the right angle so that it opened. Maybe he should have got it fixed, but it was a kind of natural, in-built, security that worked if a stranger was near. Carrie was no stranger. He knew her entrances off by heart.

'Oh hello love. What are you doing here?'

His voice smiled at her from the office at the back of the little shop area. Her dad would be swaying to and fro on his swivel chair, rhythmically moving from paper and pen to the calculator with his one good set of fingers – the most reluctant job of the day for him.

'Nothing, really. I just didn't want to go straight home. Can I do anything to help?' said Carrie.

'No love, I've just about finished here.'

He continued with his papers. Eyes down. That's what Carrie loved about her dad. Never any fuss. Never any intrusion. And yet she knew he knew that she was only there because she'd had a wonderful day. Carrie reckoned it was about as close as anyone could get to a telepathic relationship, and it was just great. In fact, now she came to think about it, Carrie knew somebody else with that same ability. She'd just spent the day with him. Was that why she liked it at the farm so much? Carrie wandered into the workshop area. Oily black iron filings were scattered across the work bench. She started to slide them around with her fingers. She loved the smell and the gritty texture. She loved getting her fingers oily and dirty.

'I moved the fence for the cows today!' she shouted. 'And Mr Wilson says I can go to market with him the next time he takes some cattle in!'

Dad appeared in the doorway and stretched his good hand.

'I'm all done in here,' he said. 'Shall we go home in convoy? There's strength in numbers, you know!'

Carrie smiled. She let go of the iron filings and followed after her dad. On Monday morning he found a beautiful picture on top of the workbench. It was made out of black, iron, filings. It was a tree. It was a rather sad looking tree. The branches looked like arms, reaching out to him in a gentle and pleading sort of way.

Sunday 7th May

Debs was all better. It was a hot Sunday afternoon. They were walking through the park eating ice cream. They were walking through the park as they'd done so many times before throughout their young adult lives. It had been their route home from school. The path they took ran along the edge of the town's river. They had to steel themselves to cross the high, metal, Japanese style, pedestrian bridge to get to their favourite sloping bank and weeping willow tree on the other side. Even now, they had to lock arms and cling together to walk across that bridge. It just curved up so high above the water in the middle, with only widely spaced metal railings at the side, that they felt giddy and likely to fall into the river at any moment. It was fun, though, once they'd reached the other side.

Held invisible inside the long weeping fingers of their favourite weeping willow tree they settled down to eat their ice creams and watch the world go by. In years gone by they'd had great fun poking fun at the world from their anonymous shelter. Today, they still had a giggle at the world as it walked, skipped, cycled, ran, by but they were a bit quieter about it.

'Maybe the old man fancies you himself, and *that's* why he's keeping you away from his drop dead gorgeous, wild haired, son!'

Debs had finished her ice cream and was in bulldozer mode.

'Oh give over!' cried Carrie. 'Not everything is about sex, you know!'

'Of course it is! All men are the same, aren't they? That's all they ever want to be 'friends' with you for!'

'That's just not true! It's quite possible to be friends with a man and not do that!'

Unfortunately, this had been true for Carrie more often than she'd like to admit. Sometimes, she even wondered if there was something wrong with her, she almost seemed to frighten men away. And yet she had all the same female bits in the same proportions as Debs.

'Well, you must know some funny men, then,' laughed Debs.

She was suddenly blinded by a flash of sunlight that rippled up at her from the river below.

'What about Mr Pike?!'

Carrie's last bit of ice cream cone crumpled in her fist. She grabbed Debs by the scruff of the neck and rammed the crumbs down her back. They fell back onto the grass laughing.

'You cow!' said Carrie.

They laughed some more.

'Oh no! I just can't say that any more. Cows are the most gentle and beautiful creatures I've ever met. That's not an insult at all!'

'Well then, I shall be insulted if you *don't* call me a silly cow in future!' said Debs.

They laughed some more. But it was time to go. Debs wanted to be home before Joe got back from the football.

———————◆———————

It was very late. Past midnight. The sky was a piece of indigo velvet studded with millions of tiny white diamonds, stretched across her open bedroom window. All was quiet except for the ticking clock in the hall downstairs. Carrie lay in state in her bed, her arms crossed upon her chest. She held a breast in each hand. She felt the breath in her chest. She tried to make it as still and small as possible. She wondered.

She let her mind wander around its echoing corridors and open and close as many doors as it pleased. In and out it went. And she watched it like an interested spectator. These thoughts did not belong to her.

'I am not here,' a little voice said.

She stared up at the dark velvet sky. She travelled to the farthest star she could see, turned, and looked down upon herself, lying in bed. She was slowly and rhythmically caressing her own breasts. She came back from the stars. Her mind opened the door labelled 'sex.' She went in. Carrie's motto 'I can do it myself' came into her mind. So she did. But every now and then, she just longed for a bit of help. She longed to be held. Just held. There was a door at the far end of her corridor that remained sealed and locked. She'd never been brave enough to turn the key. But tonight she wanted to try. And she didn't know why. The door was labelled 'love.'

Monday 8th May

Dear Reader,

I have something really important to tell you. Cows are beautiful. Inside and out. The 'silly cow' myth must end. Forever. There is nothing silly about even the most average cow. That is the domain of the human being. If you want to insult your neighbour then call him or her a 'silly human' – it's a much more accurate insult.

Cows are, by and large, friendly, inquisitive, gentle, loving, never greedy, accepting of each other in their hierarchy, at peace with themselves and the world. And they work hard every day of their lives. They give us milk and meat, even the coat off their backs to warm and protect us, the gelatine from their feet. At the end of their life of love and service they give up their old bodies for dog food to feed our pets.

They fertilize the ground and so help to grow their own food. They are, by and large, never ill. They waste nothing. They shed their hair to furnish the birds with warm nests.

Whatever their colour or breed – unlike our creeds – they mingle happily together and bring colour to our countryside. So don't ever call me a silly cow; but if you do, I will take it as a compliment.

———◆———

It was Monday morning. Everything was back to normal. Carrie was back to normal. Mr Pike slithered along the edge of Carrie's desk on the way back to his office.

'This is all very fine, Carrie, but you're not writing a novel! You will have to do this again. You can't spend all these weeks working on that farm and never, not once, write about the farmers! What's the matter with you, girl?'

'Nothing.'

Time for subservience.

'Well then, get on with it!' he boomed.

Hot cheeked, Carrie got on with it. She knew she had no choice. On this occasion, she gave Mr Pike what he wanted.

She re-wrote her lovely article about beautiful cows and added the farmer, with striding muscular legs out in the field, with long, unkempt, curly dark hair, rugged checked shirt, and big, brown, muscular hands made of leather, pulsing through their daily work. The quip about the novel had stung her. She didn't know she was going to feel like this. She didn't need to write a novel – she was living in one, every weekend. But for the rest of the week, reality was where she had to be. So be it.

'Don't come over this week.'

'Oh, alright then.'

Carrie was taken aback. Debs had never ever told her she couldn't call in. She was really shocked.

'Are you alright?' was all she could manage to say.

'Yes, it's just that we've got visitors staying – Joe's Aunt and Uncle from down south. And we'll be going out at night. You know how it is, got to keep folk entertained.'

'Well, have a good time. Are they nice people?'

'Oh they're fine. No trouble really.'

'See you next week then,' said Carrie as cheerfully as possible.

'Maybe. Bye.'

And Debs was gone. Now Carrie had two problems. Problem one was that she had no escape route on her mother's 'Local Ladies Network' night. Problem two was that Debs didn't sound like Debs, and she didn't believe a word of what the person impersonating Debs had just said to her on the phone.

Solution one – do anything, go anywhere, just get out of the house on 'LLN' night – not difficult. Solution two – spy on Debs. Both solutions complemented each other. This sounded like it might be fun. But there was a more serious, dark, side to it. Carrie might discover something she didn't want to discover. What then?

Saturday 13th May

'The farmer's in his den, the farmer's in his den, ee- i-the-a-d-i-o, the farmer's in his den...'

Carrie smiled as she realised what her head had been singing to her all the way to the farm on this sunny Saturday morning. The sun always seemed to shine on her farm days. And today she was feeling rebellious and disobedient. She was determined to put herself in harm's way. She was going to be the one in charge today. She was going to tackle that ghastly farmer's son once and for all. It wasn't difficult to find him.

'Hello darlin', why don't you come on the hay with me!'

Always the same greeting, 'why don't you come on the...' in some different location or other. And always she started walking backwards as he got near to her. But not today.

'Well, maybe I *will* come and find you when I've finished my jobs today.'

Carrie smiled at him. Today, he stood still.

'That's my girl. I knew you weren't as dry as you looked. I'll be here all day for you darlin'. You only have to ask.'

With great effort, Carrie grinned back at him and then sauntered off to the farmhouse door.

What a horrible, infuriating man! And yet he's so good at it. He's so charming and good looking, so moody and unpredictable. Ugh! He drives me mad!'

Carrie was disgusted with herself. But she still couldn't help wanting to get to know him. A warm, welcoming, smell of baking – fruit cake or something like it – pulled her towards the open farmhouse kitchen door.

'Mavis must be in full swing today.'

Carrie only got the occasional glimpse of this busy woman. She was like a ghost in a frilly apron; her frills flickered across the farmhouse doorway or window in the sunlight, and then she was gone. Carrie never saw her arrive or leave. Was she really just the cleaner?

As she approached the farmhouse, Carrie could see that the red and black tiled floor had just been mopped. It was still wet and shining.

'Just like my cowshed floor!'

Carrie shared a moment of quiet satisfaction with Mavis as she remembered the first time she'd achieved such a shining floor in her first cowshed. Jip the happy dog was enjoying the sunshine by the kitchen door. He looked up at Carrie and wagged a welcome.

For the first time ever, Carrie knelt down to talk to Jip. She gently stroked the top of his glossy head and ears. He lifted his warm brown eyes to hers and she could feel the warm rays of affection from them just like the warm rays of the sun that were stroking her back at that moment. Carrie felt tempted to lie down in the doorway next to him. Then she noticed Jip's chin. Now that his head was upturned towards her, she could see a large swelling underneath it. The wound was open at the tip and it was gooey with a little puss and fluid.

'Oh Jip! What have you done!' exclaimed Carrie.

Jip carried on smiling up at her.

'Oh you poor thing! That must be so painful and sore.'

The sunshine on Carrie's back was no longer warm and relaxed; it was hot with rage.

How could they leave him like this? Untreated and in pain! Bloody farmers!'

'Got kicked by a cow.'

The sun had gone in. Old man Wilson had taken it away. He was standing right behind her. In the space available Carrie stood up. She could have done with grabbing on to those long legs of his to get her balance, but, obviously, she couldn't do that, so she had to struggle to stand up without treading on Jip.

'Can't you do anything for him?'

'We've tried everything. He's had antibiotics. The vet says he's stuck with it. Every time he knocks it, it opens up again.'

'Oh poor Jip.'

'He's alright. He loves his work. He's a good dog.'

Old man Wilson patted Jip on the head.

'Now, wait for me by the Land Rover. We're taking a beast to the slaughterhouse.'

Carrie felt hot again. At long last, something different. Some action. As she turned to walk across the yard, Carrie felt, rather than heard, the footsteps behind her. It was that confusing, annoying, farmer's son. Silent as the grave, he didn't even look at her but peeled away and disappeared into the sheds.

Carrie just couldn't make it out.

'One of us is crazy!' she said to herself *'And I don't know which one. But I do talk to myself a lot, don't I?'*

Wednesday 17th May

Dear Reader,

The merry month of May was named after the Greek Goddess 'Maia'. It wasn't actually called 'May' until about 1430. Traditionally, it's a time for great celebrations; 'May Day' signals the end of the harsh, winter months and welcomes the beginning of summer. 'May Day' is a time for love and romance. The Romans celebrated the 'festival of Flora', the Goddess of fruit and flowers, who was also their patron of prostitutes. Have you ever danced around a maypole? Be careful if you do! This ancient dance dates back to Pagan times, when tree spirits were worshipped. The maypole is a phallic symbol, planted into the womb of mother earth.

Decorated with flowers and ribbons, young girls danced around it to encourage fertility. Traditionally red and white ribbons were used. To spare you the blushes from questions from younger readers, I will not tell you what the colours of the ribbons, in relation to fertility, represent; you'll have to work that one out for yourself! Maypole dancing used to be a very lively, rowdy, affair, until the Victorians toned it down a bit by introducing the polite little dances we have today. No doubt, they introduced different coloured ribbons, too, to make it look more pretty.

There is nothing polite about the last dance of a different kind that I have just witnessed down on the farm. So far, on my journey, I've seen many different colours and smells of life that all combine to produce our Sunday roast joint. The brown stench and sweat of cow muck; the soft baby pink and vanilla of a new calf's nose; the sweetness of fresh green grass; today, it's bright red rivers of blood and the smell of fresh death.

The slaughterhouse is one part of Sunday lunch that we never see, appreciate, or even want to think about. Yet it is a necessity; the days of ritual slaughter of the fatted calf in our own back gardens is, thankfully, long gone.

The beast, as the farmer called it, for this word describes a four legged, gentle, bovine creature as far as the farmer is concerned, and not some horrific monster (leave that to the imagination and creation of humankind), was unloaded from the cattle trailer into a holding pen with lots of other 'beasts.' Our beast quickly disappeared into the mêlée of black, white, and brown hides, all quietly awaiting their final curtain call.

Inside the abattoir, I stood with my back against a cold, bare, red brick wall to watch, as 'beast' after 'beast' made their final entrance through a cattle crush, a metal pen that held them firm and tight. The air was quiet. There was some clanking of machinery in the background; wisps of music from a radio floated through the air, one small aroma of life amongst the overpowering smell of death.

There was kindness in the room. The slaughterman waited for his chance to catch the beast's neck in a trap at the front of the cattle crush so that its head had to stay still. Then came the final blow as the humane killer, the bolt gun, did its job. Machinery kicked in and whisked the beast away to be processed and produced. It was quick; it was O.K. It was time to go.

Through another door I passed row upon row of carcasses hanging up, scrubbed shiny and bright. Men in white coats were cutting bits off for our Sunday roast. It was quick; it was O.K.

Endless rivers of water washed the red away leaving the pebble-dashed concrete floor as shiny and wet as the performers suspended above it. My feet got wet; it was O.K.

I was O.K. all the way through the building until I stepped outside into the fresh air. There was no smell of death here, but there were large vats of offal; I had to struggle with all my might not to be sick at the sight and smell of this.

I went back to the abattoir the following day to collect the beast. It returned to the farm in the back of the Land Rover in baskets. I felt sick again but didn't say so. The farmer gave me the horns as a keepsake.

I enjoy my Sunday roast. I enjoy eating meat. But I shall make sure to appreciate it all the more now; after all, a lowly beast has given its all for me.

Thursday 18th May

Carrie had arranged to meet Debs for a coffee. Arranged. It sounded like a business meeting yet that's how it had seemed to be, recently. Carrie's attempts at spying on Debs had failed miserably. No matter how many extra times she'd taken a detour past Debs' house, past Joe's favourite club, the football ground, through the town centre, Carrie had seen nothing at all. This was not at all reassuring. When she hadn't been trying to spy on Debs, Carrie was sure that she'd bump into her at least a couple of times a week. Now her mind was beginning to play tricks on her.

Had she really bumped into her friend as often as that, or was she imagining it? Perhaps it was her timing that was off? Perhaps Debs was out and about as usual, and Carrie had just missed her by seconds. Perhaps Debs and the rest of the world was still there, carrying on as normal, and it was just Carrie's routine that was at fault, her life that was being turned upside down and inside out.

The phrase 'can't see for looking' popped into her head.

'Guilty as charged!'

Carrie's mind put its hands up in mock surrender.

'Yes, it's me! It must just be me!'

Debs had a black eye. But she was smiling and chattering away ten to the dozen.

'Well, you know we did some jobs around the house a few weeks back, and Joe put some new kitchen cupboards up. Well, the doors swing open very fast and I caught the corner of one yesterday morning. Joe opened the cupboard and I turned round at the same time and 'wham!' It got me in the eye! It's not too bad, not sore, and I can still see O.K. Anyway, tell me about the farm. Your article nearly put me off meat for good, but at least you were honest about it. Have you had any complaints from vegetarians yet? How's Jip? Have you got any further with that schizophrenic son? Found out any secrets? Oh, and have you used that lovely new dress yet...'

Debs was in overdrive tonight. Carrie tried to answer the flood of questions that came her way. It was true they had quite a lot of catching up to do, they hadn't had their usual get together for a while, and it was good to have a good old fashioned natter. But tonight, it was Debs doing most of the nattering, almost without a pause for breath.

What had happened to the wise and thoughtful Debs? The one that

57

listened and cut to the root of Carrie's problems with the wisdom and precision of a surgeon's scalpel? The Debs that told her just how it was? The Debs who was always right?

The only precision that Debs showed tonight was the frequency with which she checked the kitchen clock. They were sitting in the new kitchen at the new kitchen table. The clock chimed ten o'clock. The front door slammed. Debs snatched a sharp intake of breath. Carrie said:

'I'll be off then.'

Before the clock had finished chiming ten Carrie had reached the kitchen doorway to the hall, Debs was standing behind the kitchen table, and Joe was also standing in the kitchen doorway. He had Carrie pinned against its frame, one enormous hand leaning against the wall on either side of her shoulders.

'Hello, Joe, you're home early,' smiled Debs. 'Carrie's just going; we haven't seen each other for a while.'

Debs was pleading. Joe was grinning. He grinned stale sweat and alcohol into Carrie's face.

'Well, I need a woman now. Want to stay?'

The grin was getting closer and closer. Carrie gave him her best smile and disappeared from his view. Carrie had learnt, at self defence classes, to relax if someone grabs you tightly. This allowed her to become smaller and slip like jelly from Joe's vice. She now stood next to him in the hallway, as alert as a gazelle and ready to run to the front door if she had to.

Joe was clearly not capable of doing anything at speed. He slowly turned his grin to look at her. Then he slowly turned it the other way towards Debs. His beer vat of a body followed, until he was standing behind Debs, leaning his head over her shoulder. His big hands, made up of thick, sausage, fingers gripped her around the waist. Debs was gripping the kitchen chair just as tightly; her knuckles shone white in the fluorescent kitchen lighting. Debs' eyes met Carrie's. They said:

'Go! Just go! Please go!'

Joe gave Debs a heavy shove from behind. He was leaning on her so hard she looked like she was being cut in two by the top of the kitchen chair.

'Do you want to stay?' he grinned at Carrie.

Joe leant back towards the kitchen cupboards. He took Debs with him which at least allowed her to breath. He rocked her from side to side like a baby and dug his chin further into the soft flesh of her neck. Debs hadn't been to self defence classes so she had to rock with him.

'Now, now, Joe, it's O.K. You've just had one too many....Let me make you a coffee...'

Friday 19th May

'You look rough. Did you have a late night?'

'I just couldn't sleep. I've got a lot on my mind right now.'

'Oh? I can't think why. Mr Pike seems to be very pleased with you. I saw him yesterday. He says you have the makings of a fine journalist. He says he'd be happy to give you some of his time to help you with your writing.'

'I bet he would,' thought Carrie.

'You must make connections, Carrie,' her mother continued, 'if you want to get on in the world.'

For a second Carrie imagined 'connecting' with Mr Pike, but immediately had to disconnect.

'There are other things that matter besides careers and making money, mother!'

'Not for you, at your age. I hope you're not developing one of those 'social consciences.' You haven't got time to be feeling sorry for other people, and you certainly haven't got time to be socialising with friends, especially not so called 'friends' who are filling your head with their own troubles.'

'They're not doing that!' exploded Carrie.

But it was pointless to argue back. Carrie knew that, but still, she always tried, before having no choice but to give up, shrink deep into herself, shut herself off, shut herself down, and try to minimise the hurt that rained down on her from her mother's prejudiced and bigoted words.

'Sticks and stones will break my bones but words can never hurt me.'

Carrie had never believed this to be true. So frequently during her young life Carrie had thought that it would have been better to be physically thrashed with an iron bar than to undergo the lashings of continual criticism and condemnation from her mother's tongue. Unseen bruises and injuries are the most painful and, most lethal, as far as she was concerned, and no doubt if she had a medical training, she could prove it. So instead, Carrie chose to work with words for a living. Her mission was always to use the right words at the right time; to heal not harm.

The crunch of footsteps on the gravel path outside the kitchen window returned Carrie from her deep retreat and back to reality. Her dad was passing by at speed. He was one step ahead of her today. It was time to catch him up, time for work, and she felt totally wrecked already. The lace Roman blind on the back of the kitchen door clink – swished her mother's words away, as she followed in her father's footsteps outside. Carrie crunched the gravel as heavily as her slight body would allow. Even then she could still hear her mother shouting after her. She called out after her dad:

'Bye dad, have a good day.'

Carrie was really too tired to mean what she said. She wasn't going to have a good day.

'You can't help her unless she wants to help herself, you know,' he said.

Carrie froze. Bill wasn't talking about her mother, although he could have been.

'Do you know something?' she asked.

'No love. Only that he likes a drink, and he's starting to be noticed for it.'

Carrie was blank. Bill pointed to the clink - swishing lace Roman blind on their kitchen door that had just been re-arranged. It was closed now.

'It's the old closed door thing. Just be a friend to her, like you are doing. One day, she may come to you so be ready for it. But you can't force anything, so don't try.'

Carrie looked at her dad. She had no words. There was a tight knot in her throat, partly from lack of sleep, partly from spent emotion, and partly from the matter of fact blow that her father's words were both wise and true.

Saturday 20th May

'Sweep the yard!'

'What!'

The word didn't actually sound in Carrie's mouth but her face said it for her. The Falcon replied:

'Sweep the yard! The local farmers are having a do here next weekend. There'll be a marquee in the field round the back. I want this place spotless.'

'But that's not real farming work! It's just slave labour! I've had enough of being a lackey!'

But she didn't say it, did she? In truth, part of her did feel like that. In truth, another part of her reasoned that a morning of serious graft, sweeping the yard with the hot sun stroking her back as she worked, was the kind of workout her body relished after another long week sitting still at her stale and smell-less office desk.

Sweeping was a lovely switch off for her mind. She didn't have to think about anything. The rhythm of the brush could sweep away all her worries, fears, doubts – everything, for a few hours. Sun, sweat, brush, yard, dirt, was all she needed in the world at that moment.

So Carrie began to sweep. It was quite hard going at first. She had to think a bit as the rubble and potholes, cow pats, and occasional patches of weeds interfered with her rhythm. She planned the yard out in her mind into little squares, to make sure she didn't miss a bit. Each little section had its own little pile of gathered dirt. She decided to work a row of squares and then shovel up the piles of dirt into the wheelbarrow. Decisions, decisions. There are always choices to be made about everything.

Carrie was so happy at her work that she didn't hear the swallows chattering on the wire above her head. She didn't hear the tractor chugging up and down the drive, the calves bleating for their milk, Jip barking at the cows, the clanking of gates being opened and closed.

All she could hear was the rhythmic 'swish, swish, swish,' of the brush. All she could feel was the dust that caught in the back of her nose and throat as she swept, and the heat of the hot sun that massaged her back until it created rivers of sweat that soaked through her T-shirt and overalls.

So at first she really didn't notice the hand running freely up and down her back. His mistake was to start pressing on too hard or

62

otherwise she might not have noticed that he was there at all. But she did notice and she was furious to be disturbed from her love affair with the yard brush.

'Hello darlin', you're a busy little bee again today! Do you want to have a little dance around my maypole?'

'No I do not!'

Carrie turned around with such violence that she nearly broke his nose with the brush handle. For a moment, she'd felt complete panic, like being rudely awakened from a deep sleep by someone banging saucepans together in her ear. But she was awake now.

'And get your hands off me! Keep away from me! You've no business to go round touching people like that!'

'Well, I thought you liked it, darlin'. Look at you; you're all hot and bothered now and in a lather. And all because I've helped you with a little massage! I'd say you liked it very much, but don't want to admit it!'

'No I don't! How dare you!'

Carrie tried to look as ferocious and offended as possible. In truth, she was outraged to be disturbed. In truth, she knew that he was partly right also.

'Truth is a funny thing. Truth has as many sides as this yard.'

'You didn't come to find me, the other day, like you said you would,' he said.

'I was busy,' said Carrie. 'Now please, just go away and leave me alone. I want to get this yard finished by lunchtime. There's going to be a party here.'

'Oh yes, the party. Are you going to come and have a dance with me in the dark?'

'I haven't been invited.'

'Oh you will be, alright. He wants you here. Well darlin,' I must be off. You've got a good strong back, though, I'll give you that. I bet it can carry some weight.'

Carrie knew he wasn't thinking about carrying sacks of corn. He was outrageous, and some women would be impressed by a compliment like that, but Carrie fought with all her might not to let it creep into her head.

The brush seemed to lose its rhythm after he'd gone. The yard seemed as big as a continent. The work suddenly became hard. A real chore. Carrie's couldn't brush her anxiety away.

Who's he? Who wants me to be invited to the party? It can only be his father. Maybe Debs was right. Maybe the old man is some kind of weirdo. Maybe he does fancy me? Maybe he's just an older version of that overcharged son of his? Oh no!

Maybe I've been really gullible all along! Maybe I've read the old man wrong! Maybe I'm in love with a weird old man! Maybe that's why I keep coming here! Maybe my motives are all wrong! Maybe, I just don't know! Oh what shall I do? I wish Debs was here! Debs, where are you?'

◆

'Hi, you've reached Joe and Debs. Please leave a message after the tone…' said Debs' cheery voice at the other end of the phone. Carrie chose not to leave a message. She just couldn't have matched the cheeriness of the answer phone tone.

But Carrie was desperate. She wouldn't normally turn up unannounced; she'd been well brought up by mother. Good manners and etiquette are a hard habit to break, but right now she couldn't think of anything else but her need to see her friend.

It was only when she was knocking on the newly painted, blue, front door at Debs' house that she remembered Joe's behaviour on her last visit. Too late. She had already knocked. She thought she heard muffled voices deep inside the house but no one came to the door. The bedroom curtains were drawn upstairs.

'Perhaps Joe is making up with Debs after making such an arse of himself the other night. I bet he's sorry about it.'

The heat of her panic passed and she was left staring at the unopened, newly painted, blue, front door, feeling the bristles of a new 'welcome' mat poking at her conscience through the soles of her shoes.

'What are you here for?' it said. *'What's actually happened to you, that makes you stand on me and knock on my newly painted, blue, front door?'*

'Nothing really. I'm sorry,' said Carrie to the doormat. *'I'm sorry to disturb you. I'm going now.'*

Carrie went, her head hung low with shame and embarrassment. So when she reached the road she didn't notice the bedroom curtains swish. He had watched her leave.

◆

Carrie had also forgotten that her mother was having friends round for drinks and nibbles. She used the term 'friends' loosely, because she didn't know what else to call them. But they weren't friends like Debs. Her

64

mother's friends seemed to talk without actually saying anything. Nobody would ever give anything away or give ground on any topic, so their conversations never went anywhere, but they sounded impressive to the onlooker.

Normally, the prospect of one of these evenings would totally freak her out, but tonight, she felt so subdued, so physically and mentally exhausted, that she welcomed the distraction. So tonight, she meekly put on the dress that her mother had already chosen for her. It was laid out on her bed when she got home. Colours and styles had to be co-ordinated and complimentary; the guests must have a perfect experience from start to finish.

Carrie's dad did his bit as well. He wore a shirt and tie. He smiled at his guests as best as anyone could whilst wearing the equivalent of what was to him a hangman's noose around his neck. He was endlessly walking to and fro, to and fro, serving drinks to the honourable company (he couldn't carry a tray successfully with only one good hand, mother couldn't risk him dropping it, and it would only draw attention to his imperfection anyway).

Just like Carrie, he was a fish out of water on these social occasions. Carrie and her dad had developed a little system of smiles, eyebrows, and little hand signs, that allowed them to be disrespectful, to have fun at their guests' expense, without anyone noticing. It might not be a perfect system but it got them through the evening.

The other fish out of water this evening arrived in a very ornate, embroidered, waistcoat in the Jacobean style, except that the glittery threads on some of its flowers made its origins questionable, even though it looked very expensive.

'Good evening, Carrie,' boomed Mr Pike.

(Eyebrows at six o'clock and twelve to dad).

'Hello, Mr Pike. How are you? Let me get you a drink.'

'Thank you, my dear. And then you can come and sit next to me and tell me about what you've been up to on the farm today.'

'Of course I will,' smiled Carrie. 'But maybe a little later. It would be very selfish of me to sit next to you all evening when I see you all week at work. There are many other ladies here tonight who would be very pleased to enjoy your company as well, you know.'

'Oh well, yes, my dear, you may be right.'

'Why don't you say hello to my mother – she's just in the next room with Rosalind Greenacre. You know she lost her husband six months ago and has been having a difficult time. You might be able to cheer her up!'

Mr Pike breathed into Carrie's ear.

'Well, Carrie, you may be right. But I expect a little 'tête á tête' with my favourite employee before I leave.'

'I will never eat fish again,' vowed Carrie.

(Eyebrows at nine rotated to three to dad).

Thanks to their little system, Carrie and her dad had quite a pleasant evening. Always moving from room to room, always busy serving the needs of their guests, Carrie never had to speak to anyone beyond the first two or three pleasantries of a conversation. And her dad just smiled, and everyone just smiled back at him. Nobody was trying to impress him, so he was safe. For one thing, they all knew he didn't do 'being impressed', and secondly, he ran a garage anyway.

Mr Pike tried so hard to cheer up Rosalind Greenacre he nearly split his precious waistcoat laughing at his own jokes, and quite forgot his 'tête á tête' with his favourite employee until it was time to go, and then it was too late, as he was caught in the net of goodbyes from the other guests and hauled away into the darkness beyond the front door. The whole evening went so very smoothly. Carrie's mother was delighted.

'I'm so pleased to see that you finally realise what real life is all about, Carrie. You spoke very nicely to my guests this evening. Word will get round now, and we'll soon have you sorted out with a nice young man.'

'I'll just go and finish the washing up,' said Carrie.

'Well, I'm totally exhausted, so I'm off to bed, or I may end up with a migraine. Just make sure everything's put away before you go.'

'Yes mother.'

(Eyebrows at twelve o'clock to dad).

Thursday 25th May

The sky was grey. Sunday had been grey. Monday, Tuesday, Wednesday, Thursday – grey, grey, grey, grey and raining. The air smelt of grey. Grey can be a really beautiful, subtle, colour. It suits a lot of people. But it didn't suit Carrie. It wasn't a colour that she wanted in her life right now.

'Well tough!'

Carrie had heard nothing from Debs. The office windows were a darker shade of grey than usual because of the grey outside. She had impressed her mother at the drinks party so much that now said mother was in overdrive planning Carrie's next 'moves'. Grey, grey, grey.

She had received no invitation to the farmer's party. Black. Carrie took out from her wardrobe the slinky black dress with the flash of silver across it's waistline that she'd bought without reason, all those weeks ago with Debs, before her head had really started to unravel. She ran her fingertips across the silver threads. They were as coarse as sandpaper, and yet it was this gritty quality that made them shine out so in the light. The phrase 'silver threads among the gold' came to mind. And she remembered an old Victorian poem that she'd once read in an old Victorian book that she'd once found in an old Victorian bookshop.

It was all about how our lives are made up of dark, silver, and gold, threads. And we don't know, until we live our lives, what kind of pattern of light and dark we'll end up with by the time reach the end of life's tapestry. Some folk get more dark than silver and gold, some more silver, some more gold. It's just how it goes. Carrie wondered what sort of pattern she was weaving for herself right now. The flash of silver on her dress gave her a sign of hope that she would, perhaps, eventually be able to weave some permanent colour into her grey reality. She remembered the patchwork quilt of the fields on the hillside at the farm.

'No doubt all those fields and hedgerows, and all their inhabitants, will thrive on a few days of grey. The cold and the rain will refresh them and their colours will be the brighter for it. If the grass can do it, if the birds can do it, then I can do it,' she decided. *'I didn't want to go to a stupid farmer's party, anyway. I don't want to be stared at by a weird old man and I don't want to be man-handled by a rude lout of a hairy young man. I'm through with parties anyway, after coping with my mother's little soirée.'*

'That's alright then,' said the Walnut in her dressing table drawer, as Carrie put her dress back into her wardrobe.

Saturday 27th May

'Oh ye of little faith,' scolded Carrie's heart.

It was Saturday. The sun came out. It was a bright and shiny day. It was always a sunny day on Carrie's farm Saturdays. Always. Why had she thought it would be otherwise? Today it was brighter than usual.

The farmyard was full of vans of assorted shapes, colours and sizes. There was a hog roast van, a florist's van, a caterer's van, a lorry unloading trestle tables, chairs and coconut floor matting. There were men and women of assorted shapes, colours and sizes, walking to and fro carrying boxes and flowers and furniture. Like an army of ants they moved together in an orderly fashion, each instinctively knowing what the others were doing without having to talk about it, even though they'd all come from different locations, bringing different trades. It had an almost hypnotic effect on Carrie. She sat in her little red car and watched the choreography unfold.

'So, the party's on, then. They won't want me here today.'

She thought wrong. The Falcon stood, a fearsome centrepiece, in the yard and directed the proceedings with an occasional turn of his head and point of his long, bony, fingers. There was no escape for Carrie. She was easily consumed as an extra, dropped into the chorus line with no rehearsal. It was easy work. Fetching and carrying and helping and a bit of standing around. It was going to be a big party.

Eventually, the bit of standing around became a lot of standing around. Carrie made herself look busy but walked away from the extravaganza and into the wings, to the quiet of the calf sheds. The calves were pleased to see her. She talked to the calves for a while. Then she wandered back to the marquee in the field at the back of the buildings to see if anyone had missed her. But no. Even her tormentor, that hairy son, was too busy to notice her. There were plenty of other women there today who were happy to go along with his so called 'sense of humour.'

Somehow, Carrie didn't want to go home just yet, so she faded herself away further up the drive and escaped into that beautiful, if slightly neglected, orchard once more. There was life and movement here of a different sort. Here, in the orchard, Carrie became part of a graceful ballet instead of the brash, Broadway, showstopper that she had just exited herself from.

A gentle breeze pulsed through the long grass and the branches of the trees. Everything danced together. As Carrie walked towards the stone bench in the corner beneath that most strange of sad trees, the breeze wrapped itself around her legs. She felt that she was wearing an ancient medieval robe. The folds of its heavy material slowed her progress through the long grass.

It made her feel very beautiful all of a sudden. She became part of that beautiful place as much as the trees and the grass. She imagined herself to be a medieval maiden, pining for her knight in shining armour to appear. Fortunately, nobody showed up to spoil her little play.

She sat down on the cool stone bench, tipped her head back towards the sky, and closed her eyes. The stone bench was somehow very soft and comfortable to sit on. It was as if somebody had been sitting on it for such a long time that there was a ready-made, Carrie sized, dip for her to sink into.

Except that there was no visible dip. It just felt right. Carrie could feel herself falling into a deep sleep. The branches of the sad tree gently massaged her shoulders and stroked her long, golden, hair. They seemed to hold the weight of her head; she let them do so. It was beautiful. She felt beautiful.

'You'll come tonight.'

The Falcon was standing over her. All of a sudden, Carrie had to fight off the branches. Now they were grabbing her and pulling her head back so that she had no choice but to look up at old man Wilson as he towered above her.

She was in a total panic. It was a horrible way to have to leave her dreams of beautiful medieval maidens. She'd been fast asleep, for how long she didn't know. She had that terrible feeling that she'd been asleep with her mouth open; there was a trickle of saliva on her chin like her grandmother used to have when she'd fallen asleep in her chair without wearing her false teeth.

'I never want to be like that,' she'd thought at the time.

And here she was, doing a grandma at the ripe old age of twenty two. She shivered inside. She suddenly felt very cold indeed. She had a very strong sense of 'déjà-vu.' The last time she'd said 'yes' to this strange bird of prey, he'd given her a walnut. And look where that had landed her. And here she was, a meek little mouse once more.

Old man Wilson was already walking away. He'd turned to go before she'd had chance to reply. He knew the answer. The branches of the sad tree released her from their grip. Carrie stood up. The gentle breeze made one large, final, swish across her body. The branches of the sad tree wrapped themselves around her and held her very tight for a moment.

'It will be alright. We give you our word,' they said.

Then they let her go.

———————◆———————

'Oh for God's sake! Just wear the bloody dress!!' shouted Debs down the phone. 'And some red lippy!' she continued.

'I'm scared!' whined Carrie.

'What a pathetic and terrible thing to admit to at my age.'

But it was true. In fact, it was true of every social occasion that Carrie had ever been to. She'd never ever admitted it to a living soul before; tonight she was terrified to distraction and not just her usual scared. Like a swan swimming gracefully on the water, no one ever saw how hard she was having to paddle her feet just to stay afloat and look normal. She didn't know why she always felt like this. No one had ever hurt or embarrassed her in public; she just didn't feel real when she was dressed up and she was scared that someone would see who she really was. She didn't want anyone to know. And tonight, at the farmers' party, there would be at least one person there who would see straight through her straight away.

Dressed in that slinky black dress she would have no defence at all. But she wanted to feel that feeling at the same time. That was the rub. *That* was terrifying.

Debs was still talking away at her:

'...you might find yourself a rich farmer or landowner – and wouldn't that keep your mum happy!' she laughed.

'Alright, alright! I'll do it!' said Carrie. 'Now I'll have to finish getting ready or I'll be late.'

'Good luck, then! Let me know how you get on. It'll be fun! Go strut your stuff, girl! You never know, you might enjoy this one, it'll be different! Remember, it's only a party, you won't know anyone apart from those two Wilson's, and you can come straight home if you don't like it.'

'O.K. I'll do my best. I'll give you a call tomorrow!'

Carrie looked in the mirror. She looked beautiful, she knew that. But she didn't feel beautiful like she had done earlier that day in the orchard. She put on her favourite stilettos for a bit of confidence and support.

She hoped that somebody would notice her when she walked in to that marquee. She hoped somebody nice would come along and chat her up.

She hoped nobody would notice her as well. She hoped she could stop feeling like this.

She took two deep breaths and picked up her little black bag and car keys. It took a lot of effort to do that. Carrie comforted herself that tonight really didn't matter. It was research – she was just doing her job.

———————◆———————

Carrie parked her car about two thirds of the way up the sloping field at the back of the farm buildings. The ground was fairly hard and dry so she managed to totter down the hill without losing too much dignity. The large marquee at the bottom of the field looked like a giant pink marshmallow casually plonked on to the green field.

She followed a couple of groups of assorted guests who were also tottering as hard as her. All sorts of different shapes, sizes, textures and colours of ball gowns.

'*Liquorice Allsorts!*' thought Carrie. '*And I'm the liquorice stick tonight!*'

This thought nearly made her laugh out loud in the middle of the field. She relaxed. Her dress was figure hugging but very stretchy so that she could move freely. By the time she reached the entrance of the marquee she was still smiling at the happy childhood memories of bending her liquorice stick into all kinds of funny shapes before settling down to eat it. Right now she wanted to stop and feel the flower petals of the roses that decorated the entrance to the marquee – they looked too perfect to be real. Carrie knew they were real, she'd seen them delivered. But she stopped her childish urge and followed the other 'sweets' into the mouth of the marquee.

The soft, swishing, sound of a brush on cymbals, giving a gentle accompaniment to some big band tune or other that hissed through speakers at the far end of the marquee was disturbed by occasional outbursts of laughter, giggles, and guffaws from groups of 'sweets' that were dotted around the edge of the pink marshmallow marquee.

Carrie suddenly felt unsteady on her feet; she could taste liquorice in her mouth. Even though she was standing still in the entrance, she suddenly became a Liquorice Allsort being tossed and shaken in a tin whilst its unsuspecting owner searched for their favourite delight.

Around the edge of the tin, on every side, food was piled high on plates and in dishes. Carrie had never seen so much food before. And there was a hog roast tent outside as well. Carrie had never been so pleased to see the Falcon. He smiled a welcome to her with his eyes.

Old Mr Wilson looked amazing. Dressed in black tie, he towered over the proceedings. His long, silver grey, hair was brushed sleek and shiny and fell below his shoulders. Carrie knew his hair was long, but not that long. He looked like a very famous, aged, rock star.

'Good evening, Mr Wilson.'

'Ah do!'

Carrie had secretly hoped that the old man might have said something different from his usual 'ah do.' He might have said 'Welcome, Carrie, you look lovely in that dress.' But he didn't. Before she had chance to think or say anything else, a familiar voice touched her on the shoulder:

'Hello, darlin'! You scrub up pretty well! Are you going to come and have a dance with me?'

Carrie turned round to see son of Wilson grinning at her with all his annoyingly beautiful white teeth. Two 'sweets', a pink coconut and a blue one covered with tiny aniseed balls, were stuck to his arms, one lodged under each armpit. They also smiled at her with beautiful white teeth.

'*Look what we've got,*' the teeth said. '*Hands off, he's ours,*' they said.

'*You're welcome,*' smiled back Carrie's teeth.

But she felt rattled all the same.

'Maybe later, then, darlin', when it's a bit darker!'

More laughter, and poking of his ribs by the 'sweets,' and they rolled away towards the bar at the far side of the marquee. Exasperated, Carrie turned back to give the old man what for about his son, only to discover that he'd gone to the entrance and was in deep conversation with a man who wasn't dressed for the party. Carrie recognised him as Bob, one of the tractor mechanics, from the workshop down the drive. She'd seen him pottering about earlier that day. From what she could gather he'd been set on to look after the farm while the party was on. Carrie moved a bit closer to try to work out what they were saying. The old man turned and waved deep into the marquee.

Sure enough, a moment later, Carrie felt a large, casual, slap on her behind as son of old man Wilson sauntered past her and on towards his father. A moment after that he raised those big hands of his in exclamation. The hands were not pleased with what they heard. The thorns from the roses in the marquee entrance dug into the soft fabric of Carrie's dress and needled her to edge forward to within earshot of the two men.

A moment after that, there were three men. Carrie sat down, in total shock, so hard on the red rose in its ornate metal stand that only seconds ago had been supporting her and prickling her curiosity, that both she and it landed in a prickly heap on the floor. The three men turned together to look at her.

The Falcon stared at her with his palest of pale, pale blue eyes. The son grinned at her with all his beautiful white teeth and put his big hands away in his pockets. The third man looked down at the floor. None of them moved to help her. Carrie picked herself up. She was in a daze. She looked and felt like she'd had one too many to drink.

At that moment, the two 'sweets', the pink coconut and the blue one covered with tiny aniseed balls, giggled past her and, arms linked together, stuck themselves in the entrance, in between Carrie and the three men. They directed their beautiful white teeth in the direction of old man Wilson's son, and waited.

'Look!' he said, pointing at the two 'sweets,' 'I'm needed here! It's party night! Get 'J' to do it – you know how he loves his ladies!'

Without further ado, he walked away from them and re-attached himself to the 'sweets.' As he walked past Carrie, giving her his biggest smile yet, he said:

'Are you alright, darlin'? You look like a little lost teddy bear! Do you want to come and have a cuddle with me?'

He laughed out really loud. The 'sweets' laughed as well, a reflex laugh. To the tune of 'The Teddy Bear's Picnic,' he sang into Carrie's pale face, something about getting a big surprise. Thankfully then, he was gone. Devoured by the 'sweets', he disappeared into the depths of the pink marshmallow marquee.

He was right. Carrie did feel like a little lost teddy bear. And she had just had a big surprise. It wasn't the prickles from the roses, or the fall into the roses, that had bruised her, and frankly, knocked the stuffing out of her. It was the third man.

———— ◆ ————

Debs was having a quiet night in. Joe had gone down to the club. She was lying on her lovely, soft, leather, sofa, wrapped up in a soft, fluffy, blanket that covered her all the way up to her chin. She looked like a little lost teddy bear that had had the stuffing knocked out of it. The television was on. Debs was looking at the screen but she wasn't watching anything. Occasionally she slowly turned her head to look at the clock above the mantelpiece. She thought about Carrie. She hoped she was having a good time. She thought about going to parties like she used to do, not so long ago. She thought she was thirsty, but she couldn't be bothered to get up to make a drink. She wondered if Carrie had had a drink.

'Probably not, knowing her; she's driving.'

There was somebody dancing on the television now. It was Carrie, dressed in her slinky black dress with the flash of silver on it. She looked beautiful. Men were queuing up to dance with her, one after another. Carrie was laughing and smiling. Carrie looked happy. She was having a great time. The dancing ended and someone gave her some roses. Red roses. It was the end of the show.

Carrie left the stage arm in arm with a kind and lovely, handsome, Prince. Carrie was going to be alright now. Debs smiled. She felt relieved for her friend. It was late. The clock was ticking. Debs picked herself up from the sofa. She was in a daze. She looked and felt like she'd had one too many to drink. She was tired. Too tired for parties and dancing and roses. She needed to get to bed now. Joe would be home soon.

———◆———

Debs was right; Carrie hadn't had a drink, and she did look beautiful. But that was all she was right about. Carrie was not laughing, she was not smiling, she was not happy, she was not dancing and she was definitely not having a great time. Her brief encounter with red roses had done nothing but draw blood from her ankles when she had fallen onto their deadly thorns. Bright red crushed rose petals stuck to her dress. The petals added a random splash of colour to accompany the flash of silver that scratched at her trembling waistline:

'You wanted colour,' the silver scratch said, *'well, now you've got it!'*

Her eyes turned silver white with rage. They screamed at old man Wilson:

'Why didn't you tell me?!'

The third man was walking away in haste towards the farm buildings.

'You cruel bastard!' she hissed out loud as she stilettoed past the silver haired Falcon, sounding like a burst of machine gun fire.

He watched her progress until she disappeared round the corner of the farm buildings. He looked up at the sky. It was a beautiful night. A flash of silver stretched across the sky above his head. A million silver stars scratched at his eyes. He watched them for a while before returning to the party. From inside the marquee another pair of eyes had also been watching. It was dark inside the marquee; the 'sweets' didn't notice that their prize had temporarily lost his teethy grin. But not for long.

'Come on darlin', why don't you come on the grass with me, and we'll make some hay....'

———◆———

'I do hope Carrie won't be late home. I do *not* approve at all of her getting involved with those farmers,' said Jill to Bill.

Carrie's mother and father were having their usual Saturday night home alone routine. Dinner at seven, table cleared by seven thirty, retire to the lounge where Jill would sew and Bill would read, or pretend to read, so that he could watch the television.

The television was always on in the background for added company. Every time Jill left the room to make a drink or fetch more thread or whatever she needed to do, Bill would change the television channel to something that he wanted to watch. He waited then, when she came back, to see how long it would take her to notice the change; then watched as she changed it back again.

Bill wondered how she could sew and embroider and watch the television at the same time. He suspected very well that she couldn't, but best not go there, it wasn't worth an argument. Bill and Jill were both creatures of habit. For her, it was the habit of escape. She had become so good at it that she often forgot what she was escaping from in the first place. For him it was the habit of survival; he'd become so good at it because he loved his wife and knew that she needed him. They needed each other. Deep down, it was all still there.

'She's a sensible girl, she'll be alright,' said Bill.

'I just can't bear the thought of her getting involved with a rough, penniless, ruthless lout of a man,' said Jill, her voice getting louder and higher.

'Not all farmers are bad, you know. There are plenty of rough and ruthless louts around in all walks of life – just look at the husbands of some of your unfortunate friends.'

'Yes, yes, yes,' Jill hammered on impatiently, 'but you know very well why I don't like the idea of Carrie getting mixed up with people like that. I thought you'd back me up when it comes to bringing up our daughter.'

'You know I do,' stressed Bill. 'I'd do anything for Carrie. But you've got to let her find her own way. You like her articles in the paper, don't you? She's not forced to be like you, is she?' continued Bill.

Whoops. Bill didn't normally disagree or argue with Jill about anything, but her dig about not doing his bit for Carrie caused him to clench an invisible fist with the missing fingers of his left hand. Bill adored Carrie. He'd always tried to let her grow up to be herself, to have the freedom that he and Jill had never had because of how things were way back when.

Jill quietly gathered up her sewing materials and left the room without saying a further word. Bill had spoken a word or two too many already. He knew it immediately and he was sorry. He wasn't a cruel man. He turned the television back to his preferred programme and watched awhile, but the novelty soon wore off.

He thought about Carrie and how dangerously attractive she'd looked in that black and silver dress. He hoped that she was having a good, and safe, time, at the party. The girl really didn't go out much, she often got dragged into their 'Saturday night in' routine just because she was too polite and well brought up to stick two fingers up at her mother and do otherwise. So he hoped she was enjoying herself tonight. She deserved to be happy. She deserved to be free.

He switched everything off and made his way up to bed. All was quiet and dark in the bedroom. Jill was lying in her bed, her body turned towards the wall. Bill got ready for bed. He walked over to Jill and gently stroked the back of her hair with his good hand.

'Goodnight, love,' he whispered gently. 'I'm sorry.'

The hair pulled away from him and went further under the covers. Bill sighed and made for his bed on the other side of the room. He had a dream about a place where everyone was happy and everyone was free; his fingers were still missing though, and he couldn't find Jill.

———◆———

Carrie's stilettos ran out of bullets by the time they reached the farm buildings. This was good because there was no coconut matting in the farm yard and her ankles had already had enough of a bashing for one night without twisting them in a pothole or on a chunk of rubble. She slowed to a stop.

She suddenly realised how dark it was out here. After the lights and sounds of the pink marshmallow marquee, the thumping of the blood pulsing in her head and the throbbing pain in her torn ankles, all was quiet and still here. The red brick cow sheds, so warm and welcoming during the daytime, full of earthy smells and life, loomed cold. Like terrifying giants from a child's nightmare, their open doors gaped black; a host of open mouths, waiting to consume her if she got too close.

'What am I doing here? How did I get here? Why am I here?' asked Carrie's head.

'I don't know, it just happened,' answered Carrie's heart.

Across the yard, from one cowshed doorway, one single light battled the darkness.

'It's time to find out!' chorused her head and her heart.

Obediently, and oh so very elegantly, Carrie walked towards the light.

———◆———

He was there. Carrie met Bob, the tractor mechanic, as he walked across the yard carrying a bucket of steaming hot water and a bar of old fashioned, green, soap. A chequered towel, slung over his shoulder, and the swirls of steam that rose up around him as he moved, at once turned him into a mysterious Arabian knight. He waved a hand at Carrie as he disappeared into the cowshed. Carrie followed him.

She stood in the lit cowshed doorway. The light seemed bright, even though it wasn't, after her dark journey across the yard. The first thing she saw was a young cow, chained by the neck, standing in the cow stall opposite the doorway; her back was hunched up so that she looked more like a camel than a cow.

He was there. Rolling up his white shirt sleeves, he stood with his back to Carrie. His black tie dinner jacket and bow tie were cast aside, hanging over the concrete partition that separated the cow stalls. When he'd finished rolling up his sleeves he went up to the young cow's head and gently stroked behind her ears. He straightened up and ran a hand along the length of her back.

Those big, brown, muscular hands moved very slowly and gently. A pair of little hooves and a trickle of yellow jelly were sticking out of the young cow's rear end. His long, curly dark hair brushed against her flank as his hands continued onwards, and downwards, into the bucket of steaming hot water. He scrubbed his hands and forearms up to his elbows with the green soap. His eyes had moved straight from the cow to the bucket as well, so that Carrie wasn't sure if he knew she was there.

Just then she felt something warm lean against her leg – it was Jip the happy dog. Just like his master, he didn't raise his eyes to Carrie. He didn't need to speak in order to say 'hello, it's alright to be here.' And then Bob spoke for the dog, the cow, and the man with the rolled up shirt sleeves:

'This is a young heifer; it's her first time of calving. She's going to need a bit of help.'

The heifer groaned a long, low, groan. Carrie nodded to all of them; it wasn't the time or place for words of any sort. She stood, frozen on the spot, leaning into Jip the happy dog as much as he was leaning into her. She knew that she was about to take part in something very special.

The man with the rolled up shirt sleeves continued with his task. He moved from the bucket of hot water to stand behind the young heifer; he still hadn't looked at Carrie as far as she could tell. Gently, he slipped his fingers into the heifer's birth canal and slid them around the protruding feet. Then he repeated the action with the bar of soap. Then, without warning, he slipped one hand right inside her. He seemed to feel around with his hand as if searching for a lucky dip prize in a bran tub. The young heifer let out another long groan, arched her back even further, and turned her head round as far as she could to stare at her intruder; her eyes were bulging and scared.

'It's alright g..girl, it'll b..be al..r..right.'

Words of a sort, at last, from the man with the rolled up shirt sleeves.

'I c..can f..feel the h..head. B..Bob, g..get the r..ropes.'

Bob picked up a coil of old rope that was lying in the cowshed doorway. The rope was caked in some dark brown stuff that made it look very stiff and rigid rather than loose and rope-like. There were two small loops tied at each end of this worn out piece of rope. The young heifer suddenly strained as if she was trying to go to the toilet; a bit of wee splashed onto the floor.

As she did so, the man with the rolled up shirt sleeves took hold of one of the protruding hooves and attached one of the rope loops around it, pulling it quite tight. After a bit more fiddling about, he managed to do the same with the other loop to the other little hoof. He gently pulled on the rope until it was taut. The young heifer groaned and strained again. And again. And again.

The man with the rolled up shirt sleeves stepped away from the young heifer, still keeping a firm grip on the ropes, but not pulling on them. Without looking he stretched out one arm behind him and held out the rope. Without thinking, without hesitating, Carrie stepped forward and took hold of the rope. She knew it was meant for her. She stretched out her bare arms and took a firm grip on the ropes. She stood behind the man with the rolled up shirt sleeves. Behind her, Bob, the tractor mechanic took hold of the end of the rope. Jip the happy dog sat in the doorway; he was the anchorman.

'W..work with her,' said the man with the rolled up shirt sleeves.

And so they did. Moving as one, they pulled on the rope every time the young heifer strained; they relaxed when she relaxed. All was quiet, all was still.

The distant beat of the music from the party became a forgotten echo. All Carrie could hear was the rhythmic heavy breathing of dog, man, and beast, as they bore down together. They were creating something very beautiful together, and it was very painful.

The young heifer was really beginning to suffer now. The nose and part of the head appeared. Such was the pressure on her rear end from the straining and the rope that Carrie was frightened that her legs would snap in two. The young heifer staggered and nearly fell but managed to keep her balance. Part of Carrie wanted to run away from this terrible pain that she was witnessing, and part of her wanted to pull with all her might; to finish it, to end it. She got her wish. The end came quickly.

'N..Now!' commanded the man with the rolled up shirt sleeves.

The young heifer let out an almighty bellow as she strained again, much stronger than before. Carrie pulled on the rope with all her might. The man with the rolled up shirt sleeves elbowed her in the face as he caught the wet new life and lowered it to the floor. All was quiet, all was still. The new calf lying on the floor was still.

The man with the rolled up shirt sleeves was kneeling over it, doing something to its head. He lifted the calf's lifeless head and poked some straw up its nose. He grabbed a handful of straw and held it out to Carrie:

'R..rub the b..body.'

Without thinking, without hesitating, Carrie did as she was told. She knelt down on the cowshed floor and began rhythmically rubbing the calf's wet and slimy body. She wasn't sure how many seconds or minutes this went on for but, all of a sudden, the new calf sneezed itself into life. It raised its own head in a drunken stupor and shook its floppy ears.

Carrie and Jip the happy dog were the first to see this happen. The man with the rolled up shirt sleeves was quietly talking to the young heifer, stroking her ears once more. She stood still now, drooping and exhausted.

Bob appeared in the doorway with a fresh bucket of cold water. He passed the bucket to the man with the rolled up shirt sleeves, who offered it to the young heifer. She drank the whole lot without stopping. Jip the happy dog was walking to and fro excitedly in the doorway, wagging his tail. He knew a happy ending when he saw one.

The new life now breathing beneath Carrie's hands was squirming around, kicking at her with its legs, trying to stand up.

'He's alive!' squeaked Carrie in a voice she didn't recognise as her own.

It was helium filled with emotion, excitement, and pure joy. The man with the rolled up shirt sleeves was kneeling down alongside her now. He pulled apart the new calf's legs and dipped the remains of the its umbilical cord in a little pot of liquid that had a strong disinfectant smell.

'Sh..she's a..l..live!' he said.

'Oh a little girl!'

Carrie unashamedly babbled on. She completely forgot where she was and who she was with. She completely forgot how full of anger and rage she'd been; when and why that had been; where she'd been earlier that evening and why she was dressed in a slinky black evening dress. She was in ecstasy for the first time in her life and she was going to make sure she enjoyed every second of it, while it lasted.

'What will you call her?' she asked.

'Th.. the s..same as h..her m..mother,' said the man with the rolled up shirt sleeves.

'How about calling this one Carrie?' said Bob, as he stood in the doorway, re-coiling the rigid rope.

The man with the rolled up shirt sleeves picked up the struggling calf in his arms.

'C.. Carrie it is, then.'

And for the first time, he looked at Carrie.

———◆———

Jill was cold. She was tucked up and cosy in her bed, but sometimes she just couldn't get warm, no matter what she did. A flash of silver stretched across the sky. It scratched at her bed covers through a chink in the bedroom curtains. All the curtains and bedcovers in the world could not shut out this beautiful night, or any of the others that lived in her head. Jill lay now, drooping and exhausted. She drank a whole glass of water without stopping and cosied down under the covers; sleep would come eventually. It was a beautiful night.

———◆———

Carrie was cold. The young heifer, now a new mother, was tucked up on a bed of fresh straw with her newborn calf, little Carrie. They looked very cosy and happy together. Mother was licking dry the slimy black and white body of little Carrie. Big Carrie, standing in the doorway of the cowshed, suddenly let out a big shiver as she realised that she was also covered in the wet slime of new life.

Without thinking, without hesitating, the man with the rolled up shirt sleeves grabbed a handful of straw bedding and began to wipe away some of the slime that was clinging to the front of her once beautiful, slinky black dress. It didn't seem an odd thing to happen at all. She just stood still and let him do it.

'L..let's g..get c..cleaned up,' he said, simply, as he closed the shed door.

He turned, and set off in the direction of the farmhouse.

'What's your name?' she called out.

'J..Jon,' he replied.

He reached the kitchen door and went inside. Carrie followed him.

———◆———

Debs was cold. She let out a big shiver as she stood in the shower, waiting for the water to warm up and wash away the wet slime of married bliss. She stood still now, drooping and exhausted. Through the open bathroom door Debs could see Joe, tucked up and fast asleep in bed. He looked very cosy. It was a beautiful night.

———◆———

The wave of heat from the kitchen hit Carrie as if she was stepping into a furnace as she followed Jon, the man with the rolled up shirt sleeves, over the threshold of the kitchen door that had for so long fascinated and intrigued her. Even though it was a warm night, a fire burned bright orange inside the Rayburn cooker; a large, old fashioned, kettle gave out a low hiss of welcome from its steadily boiling spout.

The kitchen was large, square, sparsely furnished but very clean.

Shiningly clean. Carrie was shocked. She didn't know what she had expected to see. Standing on the red and black brick floor tiles just inside the doorway, she had a strong sense that she was stepping back in time. It was like stepping into one of those rooms created in a museum.

'See how we lived in the...*1940's*,' – Carrie's head completed the sentence.

Jon was leaning over the kitchen sink. He turned on the hot water tap. His hands were covered in the blood and slime of the young heifer's afterbirth. Bits of straw clung to the hairs on the skin of his bare, dark, arms. The kitchen sink was full of pots; cups and saucers, plates, an old, enamel, tin milk jug. He washed his hands and arms over the sink. He dried his hands on an old towel that was hanging from a hook at the end of the sink unit, and turned to offer the soap to Carrie.

'He's washed his slimy, bloody, hands over the household pots!'

A rush of colour blushed her face; he answered it:

'It's c..clean,' he said. 'It's c.. come from inside the c..cow. There's n..nothing wrong with th..that.'

As fast as she could, Carrie tried to regain her composure by smiling and nodding. A vision of her mother popped into her head as she washed her hands over the kitchen pots.

'Go away, mother,' she hissed alongside the kettle, which was now being poured to make tea by Jon, the man with the rolled up shirt sleeves.

'S..sugar?'

'Yes please.'

Thank goodness, he used two mugs from the draining board. He put the tea on the kitchen table that stood in the middle of the kitchen. They stood now, sipping their tea, on opposite sides of the table. It reminded Carrie of the first time they'd met, standing on opposite sides of that battered old Land Rover. Carrie wondered now, just how many times had she, in fact, been in contact with Jon, and how many times had it been the impostor – his brother. His twin brother?

A great many questions crowded her head. They all started with 'why?' A very plain looking clock was quietly ticking away above the large, white tiled, mantelpiece that jutted out into the room, a deep alcove that housed the Rayburn cooker. The hot tea and the ticking clock above the fire reminded Carrie how very wet and sticky and cold she still felt. She couldn't think of what to ask first of her many questions, so she decided to break the ice with Jon another way. She walked round to his side of the table and stood next to him in front of the little orange fire.

She slipped off her favourite stilettos. They were quiet now, completely run out of bullets and totally ruined. It was lovely to feel the soft tufts of the multi-coloured rag rug that made a hearth place of sorts in front of the cooker's little fire. She must have let out some sort of sound from her mouth, maybe an *'Ooh! that feels good,'* sound, or an *'Agh! relief at last,'* sound, because Jon said:

'A..are y..you al-r..right?'

Such was the comfort of the warm rag rug that Carrie had almost forgotten that she was standing next to the third man. He shared no such comfort. It was all for her. He stood still, frozen, and barely breathing. Frozen, his big hands locked themselves around his steaming mug of tea. Carrie had completely forgotten her manners.

'Fancy taking off my shoes and stretching out in front of somebody else's fire, completely uninvited!'

But she had been invited. Thump thump thud! The distant thunder of dance party music suddenly came back into focus.

'Oh no! The party! I haven't seen any of it yet! I can't go back now, my dress is ruined!'

'Oh no! Why did you just say that, you stupid girl!' said a sudden wave of heat from the fire. *'You've seen something far better! You don't care about the party, or your dress, so why say that you do?'*

Carrie felt totally ashamed of herself; it wasn't the real Carrie saying those words. That was the ambitious Carrie who needed her story for the paper; the Carrie who needed to please her mother; the Carrie who needed to fit in with the world. It wasn't the Carrie she wanted to be any more. She wanted to be warm Carrie. Here. Now.

'W..we h..have c..clothes. You c..can ch..change.'

'Yes, I can change...'

'Thank you, but I can't go to the party in a pair of old overalls!'

'Agh, why did you just say that, you stupid girl!'

Frozen, still Jon's eyes were studying his steaming mug of tea.

'Old bad habits are hard to break...'

'There is a d..dress. It will b..be al..r..right.'

'Like father, like son!'

The phrase 'it will be alright' was becoming a doorway to adventure in this place. So without thinking, without hesitating, she turned and, for the second time that night, obediently followed Jon, the man with the rolled up shirt sleeves, through a door from the kitchen that led into a long, dark, corridor. He suddenly turned left, climbing a flight of polished wood, steep, stairs that had a narrow piece of dark red carpet in their middle that was held in place by triangular wooden stair rods. The stairs would have been impossible to climb without the carpet. The wood at the edges was shining and slippy. Mavis popped into Carrie's head.

'She certainly does a good job here.'

She smiled as she climbed.

'I wonder if he's going to give me one of her dresses?'

Jon filled up the space in front of her as they climbed. He was a big man.

'Where am I going? What am I doing?' said her heart.

'I certainly wouldn't be doing this with his brother,' said her head.

'It will be alright,' replied her heart, as they reached a bedroom door at the end of the long, thin, upstairs landing.

The room was derelict. Literally. Standing in between bare, dusty, wooden floorboards and a white plaster ceiling that had holes in it so big that Carrie could see up into the rafters in the roof, a big, old fashioned, wardrobe with a large, tainted, oval mirror, stared at them in surprise as Jon switched on the single, yellow, electric light bulb that was hanging from a cable in the centre of the ceiling; somehow, it was still miraculously intact.

There was a tapestry covered chaise longue sofa, backed up against the wall, opposite the wardrobe, and an old wooden chest beneath the window. A million particles of dust filled the air as Jon lifted the lid of the old wooden chest.

He reached down into it, then raised his hands up high into the air, making swirls of silver white dust all around him. In his hands he held a very long black dress. He caught hold of the dress at its waistline as if it already contained the body of a woman inside it, and turned, as if with a ghostly dancing partner, and held out the dress towards Carrie.

'Oh!' Carrie gasped.

She was being offered the most beautiful dress that she'd ever seen. It was long, black, velvet. Velvet! How velvet used to be before the synthetic stuff was invented.

'Oh, it's so beautiful!' gasped Carrie again.

She couldn't help letting out another 'Ooh!' as she touched the soft fabric. It was as thrilling as stroking the fur of little Carrie for the first time.

'T..try it. It'll f..fit.'

He let the full weight of the dress fall into her arms – and it was very heavy – and then quickly disappeared, closing the bedroom door behind him.

Carrie was scared standing in the room on her own. The weight of the material was so heavy that it felt like there really was somebody already wearing the dress. There were no curtains across the window; the black night stared in at her as she removed her own dress. She had the feeling that ghosts in the rafters, and great big spiders (she didn't like big spiders) were watching her through the holes in the ceiling, waiting to pounce on her, so she got changed very quickly. But the oval wardrobe mirror was friendly.

'Oh!'

Carrie was speechless. She stared at the vision in front of her. Folds of long black velvet caressed her body. And the dress had a train. All of a sudden, Carrie was that beautiful medieval maiden in the orchard again; she was a Hollywood femme fatale!

She just couldn't stop her hands from touching her body inside that beautiful, beautiful, dress. She was seriously turned on. She didn't know how long she'd been standing there, admiring herself, until she noticed that the top of the V-necked bodice was gaping on her a little. She was a bit smaller chested than the previous owner.

'He said it would fit me! How did he know it would fit me?'

Carrie blushed as she remembered what Jon had said, and what that meant.

'Well, go on then!' said the oval mirror. *'You can't stay here all night. You have a party to go to!'*

Carrie went. For the second time that night, she walked, very slowly, and oh so elegantly, towards the light that was shining up the stairs from the kitchen down below. She hooked the little velvet loop, that was designed to carry the dress's train whilst walking, over her middle finger when she reached the top of the stairs.

'It will be alright,' swished the dress as she descended the shiny, polished, wooden stairs.

Jon, the third man, was standing by the fire, holding her favourite stilettos in his hands.

'It's al..r..right,' he said. 'They're d..dry.'

———◆———

Debs stood in front of the bathroom mirror. She was wearing her favourite soft, brushed cotton pyjamas, even though it was a warm night. The folds of soft cotton comforted her. Debs held herself tight with her hands as she looked in the mirror. She thought she looked pretty; the pattern of tiny pink roses gathered together with a blue bow caressed her body. Except for where the edge of the bathroom mirror tiles cracked and slightly distorted her reflection.

They couldn't afford a big mirror so Joe had stuck mirror tiles on to the wall. Some of the tiles were not stuck down very flat; there was a mirror crack at the height of Debs' mouth which meant she couldn't smile in the bathroom. It was a bit of a pain when she came to do her make-up; but she always tried to smile in that mirror nevertheless.

Standing in the warm leftover mist from her shower, she wondered what Carrie was doing. Had she found romance at long last at the party? Had she been swept off her feet by the farmer? And if so, which one? Debs remembered her first dates with Joe. He'd been *so* enthusiastic about her - wouldn't take no for an answer from early on. He was a big, strong man and Debs had enjoyed feeling wanted so strongly. It made her feel tired, but she was managing to get a break now and then. Joe liked his football and his trips down to the club. It wasn't the romance from a film or book; it was a real life romance with a chance for her to have a home of her own that she didn't have to share with umpteen brothers and sisters. Joe had taken notice of her, wanted to be with her all the time; he'd taken a firm hold of her and she had taken the chance.

At the very least, she hoped that someone had taken notice of her friend; she knew just how much this meant to Carrie, even though they'd never spoken about it out loud. Debs smiled. Carrie's adventure on that farm was like having a novel read aloud to her without having to make the effort to turn the pages - and she couldn't wait to find out what was going to happen next!

———————◆———————

Cursing and swearing with every breath, Carrie stumbled, hobbled and staggered across the dark expanse of the farmyard in her favourite stilettos that had been so shrivelled into a crisp by the heat from the fire after being previously so totally soaked, that she could hardly get them on her feet. Somehow, her feet had to carry the weight of this erotic, long, black velvet dress and the respect that she felt for its beauty. There was no room for mistakes; she couldn't fall into a pot hole or, worse still, a cow pat. But Jon was striding away from her in the dark, leaving her to cope alone with the dress, *and* all her questions *and* all her fury at how he, his father and his brother, had been playing her all these weeks.

Suddenly there weren't enough swear words to cover the distance back to the marquee and the party that she had to travel. Jon must have heard her muttering because, all of a sudden, he stopped and, without turning around, held out an elbow. In the dark his silhouette looked like a big tree with a funny shaped branch on one side. Carrie grabbed hold of the branch and dug her nails into its bark as hard and mean as she could; oh boy was she was going to make this tree bleed!

'Why didn't you tell me there were two of you!' she spat in between gasps of rage.

'It w..were n..nowt to d..do with m..me.'

'Well, whose idea was it then? And what was the point?'

Carrie didn't wait for an answer. She was in Mother mode.

'After all these weeks of working here, how dare you treat me like that...'

On and on she went. Apart from walking on, Jon was silent as he let Carrie rave at him. Carrie remembered his silence the first time she'd met him, when they'd stood on opposite sides of that Land Rover after the accident. He had no piece of metal to protect him from the long golden hair that was thrashing about alongside him now, and no escape from the long nails that bit into his elbow bone.

So Carrie raved some more. But it didn't do any good. Jon stayed as dark and silent as the trees in the orchard that they were just passing by. Without warning, he suddenly pulled away from her. Carrie was standing alone, a tall dark tree herself, suddenly dazzled by the lights and the sounds from the entrance to the marquee. Jon had disappeared into the hog roast tent nearby.

'Well that's not very chivalrous of him!'

Carrie felt hurt, until she remembered how she'd just been behaving. How could she so suddenly forget those unforgettable moments with little Carrie, and his kindness towards her with the dress and her shoes?

It was too late to escape. People had already started to notice her; look at her, whisper, or titter, and walk on by. She stood, frozen to the coconut matting. She didn't want to go into the marquee, but she didn't want to leave either. Standing in the moonlight her face looked ghostly pale contrasted against the depth of the rich black folds of the dress. She was a vision of loveliness yet it was causing her pain.

Inside the marquee Carrie could see a stone pillar standing tall and still amidst the whirling, twirling, tittering folk who waltzed and boogied round and around him. Old man Wilson was staring at Carrie with an intensity that she'd never experienced before. Now Carrie knew all about staring but this was something else. Her feet started to move. Like a tractor beam his furious eyes pulled her towards him. The whirlers and twirlers made way for her. They were all watching her but pretending not to.

Carrie stopped within breathing distance of old man Wilson. She looked up, up, up to meet his eyes. Palest, pale, ice blue yet they were on fire. How long did they stare? She didn't know. Her words sounded very feeble when they finally came:

'Your son Jon has lent me this dress from the house. My own dress got ruined - I helped to calve the heifer!'

'You can't have it.'

'Oh I know.'

'It's just to get home in; I'll bring it straight back.'

'No! It stays here. Take it off.'

Carrie stared. Old man Wilson stared back. Nobody moved.

Why is he so furious with me?' she trembled.

She wasn't used to being told 'no.' Her head dropped. Freed from his gaze she turned and began to walk away. She was just retreating nicely into herself when a familiar big hand slid around her waist and pulled her off balance. The brother of Jon hugged Carrie close to his hip.

'Hello darlin', you look good enough to eat. Did you enjoy getting down and dirty with 'J'? He's a real ladies man, you know. Loves his girls, doesn't he!'

Carrie tried to push away from him with both her hands against his arm. He wouldn't let her go; he held her even tighter.

'Ho Ho! What have we got here then?'

The brother of Jon poked a finger down the front of her dress which was now gaping forwards due to her pushing away from him so hard. He looked down into her dress and slid his finger from side to side.

'Jed!' commanded a voice.

Head first, 'Jed', the brother of Jon, disappeared from her view. Carrie was free. Old man Wilson held a few strands of long dark hair in his hand.

'All right, all right!' said impostor Jed, the brother of Jon. 'It was only a joke!'

He smiled and waved at Carrie as he walked away.

'I'll be seeing you later, darlin'!'

Five seconds later he was hooked up with the pink and blue 'sweets' from earlier that evening. Carrie had had enough. She looked around but she couldn't see Jon anywhere. She desperately wanted to see him. She wanted to say sorry. The music and the lights were thumping harder than ever, the smell of warm food and warm beer filled the air. The party was in full swing, but it was all over for Carrie.

On her return to the farmhouse she heard multiple giggling coming from the barn, and a deep, familiar, voice in the darkness. She wanted to look in on little Carrie before she left, but the deep voice, now labelled Jed, put her off. She didn't want to risk bumping in to that mouthy impostor again.

Carrie left the black velvet dress in its derelict bedroom. She didn't have the heart to fold it back into the chest. She carefully laid it out on the dusty, tapestry covered chaise long. In the moment between turning off the little yellow electric light bulb and turning to close the door, the reclining dress looked like there really was somebody lying inside it. Carrie felt a tingle down her spine. The dress seemed to hold its arms out towards her in a gentle and pleading sort of way.

Carrie drove home in her old overalls. She was too upset to notice the little yellow light across the yard in the cowshed. Jon was checking on little Carrie. He switched the light off when he saw her car leave. As she drove down the drive she didn't notice the third stone pillar, standing alone in the orchard, looking up at the flash of silver that stretched across the dark night sky. It was a beautiful night.

Sunday 28th May

Carrie's mother was having a migraine Sunday morning. For once, Carrie was relieved and pleased about it. She needed a quiet day too. Carrie had never before taken a 'sicky' - had a deceitful day off work - but she just couldn't face going to the farm this morning.

'No shovelling s***t today, no more s***t of any kind from them.'

As she lay in her bed she could feel two long, velvet, jackass ears sprout from her head. No matter how hard she pulled the covers over her head they kept poking out to laugh at her. She got up and tied her hair back with a scarf; she even put grips in at the sides, but still the ears grew and grew. The walnut in her dressing table drawer taunted her.

'Break me! Eat me!'

After checking on her mother, who had had no sleep because of the moonlight shining in through the curtains, Carrie went outside to sit in the garden. But the garden was full of red roses. So she went into the garage and sat on one of her dad's old bikes. He was down at the far end of the garage, working away at something that flashed silver as he turned it over and over.

'Not at the farm today, love?'

'No. I'm not needed today; they're clearing up after the party.'

Carrie's nose started to grow to match her ears. It was the first time in her life that she'd needed to lie to Bill, her own dad.

'Well they'll miss you, you've been a good help to them these last few weeks. I'd miss you! They'll look forward to seeing you more than you realise, Carrie. You have that effect on people. I'm looking forward to reading about the farmer's party!'

'Well, I'd better get on with it, then,' said Carrie, as she slid off the back of the bike; nowhere was comfortable today.

In the kitchen, the phone rang:

'Well, how did it go then?' chirped Debs. 'Did you knock 'em dead?'

'Sort of,' said Carrie, relieved to be truthful at last.

'Come over,' said Debs. 'Joe's down at the club tonight.'

Carrie was about to say 'No, I need to work,' but truth got the better of her and so she just said 'O.K.'

Carrie was not a church-goer; but it was Sunday, and she needed to confess.

'You bloody idiot!'

'I know,' said Carrie.

Her ears drooped low as she laid her head back on Debs' soft, leather, sofa. Debs was clapping her hands together with excitement.

'Why didn't we think of it before? *Two* brothers, like chalk and cheese!'

Debs laughed out loud. Carrie was glad that she said '*we* didn't think'; it made her feel slightly less stupid.

'Well, you can't leave it there! You'll just have to go back! You've got to find out if you want chalk or cheese for supper!'

'Give over!' said Carrie. 'I can't go back! Ever! I'm finished! I'll just have to tell Mr Pike that they don't want me any more, make up something for a last article about the farmer's party and leave it at that.'

'That doesn't sound like the Carrie I know,' said Debs. 'Don't you want to find out the truth? I thought that was why you wanted to be a journalist. Wasn't it something about using words for the good, or something?' Debs paused. 'Or did something else happen to you that you haven't told me about? Is that the real truth?'

'No!' said Carrie.

She felt her nose growing longer again. Carrie had told Debs everything *except* for her experience with the long, black, velvet dress. Why had she done that? It was a big part of her story; a great erotic moment in her life and a great humiliation also. That dress had swept down the corridors of her soul and knocked on those doors that she'd never tried to open before. Carrie was scared, so she'd lied. Very scared; she'd lied twice in one day.

'Well, it's a shame, then,' said Debs. 'I wanted to know about little Carrie.'

Carrie wanted to know about little Carrie. All of a sudden she was leaning back onto a sofa of soft, yellow, straw. Her clothes were sticking to her, wet with slime. She wanted to be back there more than anything, but found herself saying to Debs:

'How about you? Any more accidents recently? Whenever I see you these days, you always seem to have had a fight with the kitchen cupboards!'

'Oh no, I was just getting used to the new kitchen!'

Debs laughed out loud again, and pulled her sweatshirt sleeves down long over her hands as she spoke. Carrie saw Debs' nose grow in front of her eyes; she'd already seen the red marks on her wrists. She felt sick.

The truth will out, churned her stomach.

For both of them.
'Maybe, but not today,' swallowed her throat.

———◆———

Evening swallows swooped and dived around Carrie's little red car as it drove down country lanes, so familiar by now, that she really was certain that her car would find the way if she closed her eyes. When Debs had told her to go back, she probably hadn't meant immediately, now, straight away, this evening, but that's just what she was doing. Going back. It was late evening but not dark. Carrie needed to see little Carrie the new calf and that's all there was to it. She wasn't thinking about anybody else; at least that's what she kept telling herself with every press on the accelerator pedal.

She wasn't disappointed, then, to find the farmyard deserted and the farmhouse in darkness. Everywhere looked empty and derelict like it had done on her first fatal visit. It hadn't been empty then, and it wouldn't be empty now, either. It was a place full of lies and deceit. How could they do that to her? Carrie all of a sudden felt that mad with them all that she was spitting feathers as she crossed the yard in the direction of little Carrie's shed. The adrenalin lump in her throat told her that she was trespassing, that she shouldn't be there. But instead of tiptoeing in like a burglar as she'd planned, she marched across the yard like a soldier trooping the colour, head held high, feathers ruffled up into a grand display. But there was nobody watching. Carrie felt empty and derelict.

Quietly, she opened the door to little Carrie's shed. The single, yellow light bulb shone gold onto the straw bedding; it felt as soft as silk beneath big Carrie's feet. Mother and little Carrie the new calf were lying side by side in the far corner of the shed. They looked up at big Carrie. Nobody moved. Mother and daughter were together. Peaceful. Loving. Breathing together. Carrie joined in with them; it calmed her ruffled feathers. She thought about her own mother. Without warning tears welled up in her eyes. They came now, silently rolling down her cheeks and wouldn't stop.

'Ah do,' said a familiar voice.

Carrie kept her face turned away from old man Wilson. She couldn't speak anyway so just nodded her head by way of reply.

'He's up at the top field, looking the cattle.'

Carrie shrugged her shoulders and concentrated on her breathing.

How dare he assume that she was upset about Jon.

'Come on, I'll show you.'

There really was no need, she knew where he meant. But he was already striding away. Carrie let out a big sigh and then followed him. He didn't wait for her but kept on walking ahead.

'He's actually being kind to me; he knows I don't want him to see me like this.'

He stopped halfway up the field and pointed:

'Up there,' he said, as he doubled back and walked away from her without a pause in his long legged strides.

Carrie was recovering now; her breathlessness was due to the climb up the hill. The pink marshmallow marquee had disappeared. There was nothing to prove it had been there at all except for a few holes in the ground where poles and ropes had been tethered; a few stray pink ribbons floated along the ground in the evening breeze and a few crushed rose petals lay forgotten now amongst the flattened grass, their glory a distant memory. Party? What party?

He was standing just inside the gate at the top of the hill, with his hands inside his pockets. The cattle were standing in a semi-circle around him. They looked like they were in deep conversation together. Carrie felt embarrassed as she approached them. It was like walking into a crowded room where everybody turned to stare at you. No matter that she was in a big open space, that she was being stared at by a bunch of cows - the effect was just the same. Jon didn't stare. He was too busy looking up at the sky. He didn't speak. Carrie looked up too.

It was a very big sky tonight. Empty. There was nothing to see except sky. No sunset, no stars, no clouds. Just a cool, dark, evening, empty sky. Looking up into it made her feel giddy. It was like being sucked up into a vortex and it felt really good. Really peaceful.

A cow sniffed at her arm, then sneezed, and shook its head as if in disgust. Others followed. Sniffing at her body with their wet noses they touched her all over, they didn't seem to care where. Some pulled and licked at her clothing. The only sound she could hear was their heavy breathing and the odd burst of the birds' evening songs. She stood rigid and let them explore her. She closed her eyes and let the sky and the cows take her. She felt just as erotic as she had done the night before in that beautiful black velvet dress; it had nothing to do with the fact that she was standing next to Jon.

The world stopped turning at the top of that hill. Carrie was so glad that she'd come back. So glad.

'L..let's g..go n..now,' said Jon.

He turned and walked back to the gate.

'Oh but I want to stay here forever!'

She thought it but didn't dare say it out loud. It was starting to get dark and cold. As she turned to follow him the cows ran after her. Some of them leapt in the air and jumped about like rodeo horses, landing very close to her.

'K..keep w..walking, they're j..just p..playing, they w..won't h..hurt you.'

And they didn't. Jon closed the gate and they walked back down the hill to the farmyard in silence. The ground was black now and swallowed their feet. Every step was an act of faith. It was Sunday evening and therefore, quite fitting. She had been to confession with Debs, she had shared evensong with Jon and the cows. Carrie had seen the light.

Tuesday 30th May

Unfortunately, Mr Pike had not seen the light. Sales of his newspaper were down, and he'd just lost Brenda, his longest serving secretary for quite some time, to his arch rival at 'The Advertiser.' Everyone, except Mr Pike, was amazed that she'd lasted so long. Everyone, including Mr Pike, was sorry to see her go.

Being a lady of mature years, with looks to match, she had a knack of always being in the right place at the right time, making sure with an iron glare over the tops of her iron rimmed spectacles (they were very old looking glasses) that Mr Pike swam in a straight line, especially when dealing with the younger, female members of staff. She couldn't be there all the time, as Carrie had found to her cost on more than one occasion and now that she had gone for good, they were all easy prey for the big fish.

On this fine Tuesday morning Mr Pike was thrashing about like a fish out of water. He couldn't settle at his desk, couldn't find anything without Brenda, and flopped himself all over everybody else's desk in the main office, gasping for air and sucking up the slightest hint of sympathy that he could catch from anyone. It was a dangerous time. Nobody wanted to offend the boss; equally, nobody wanted to be promoted to become Brenda number one hundred and one. Especially not Carrie. There was a time when she might have risked it, just to get on, but not any more.

'Good morning, Carrie,' bubbled the boss. 'I'm looking for a little help in my office now that Brenda has been poached away from me.'

'I wish someone would poach, sauté and fry you out of the way!' thought Carrie as she tried to look politely back at Mr Pike.

He continued:

'You could take over some of her duties if we let Dennis cover the births and deaths columns for a while. Just think what sort of reference I could give you if I got to know you better!' he boomed.

Carrie was aware of a sudden flurry of papers and busy-ness on the rest of the office floor as everyone pretended not to be listening, relieved that he'd homed in on Carrie and not themselves, and intrigued as to how she would get out of this sticky situation.

'That's very kind of you, Mr Pike, but unfortunately, I have no secretarial skills at all. I'm never free at weekends and out of hours, and I'm very taken up with writing the 'Land Girl' articles that you wanted.

You deserve someone who can be totally devoted to you, Mr Pike. You pretty much run this paper single-handed, so why don't you advertise for a specialist secretary to help you?'

It certainly needed someone special to cope with Mr Pike, and he did run the paper single-handed, which was why they weren't doing so well. Still feeling full of light from the weekend, Carrie suddenly had a brilliant idea:

'Mr Pike, we all know how hard you work to produce the paper, but why don't you give yourself some thinking time? Find that new secretary, perhaps someone younger than Brenda - interview lots of them - you never know who you might find! And the editing team can take over the day to day running of the paper, in the spirit of your ideals, of course.'

The ego hook worked every time; Mr Pike was easy to catch with it.

'Well, yes, I have been working hard and I do need a permanent assistant. I'll look into it. Keep up the good work, Carrie, and bring me your hard copy first so that we can look it over together - I'm always happy to help you, you know.'

Carrie smiled with relief as Mr Pike slid away to his office, composing out loud the text for his secretarial ad as he went. The flurry of papers and busy-ness from the rest of the office floor continued but sounded less anxious for the rest of the day. Everybody smiled at Carrie and she smiled back at them. The sun actually shone through the grey office windows for the whole day. Carrie had given them hope.

———————◆———————

'Oh that's wonderful, Carrie. Wonderful news!'

After wanting it for so long, Carrie didn't know how to cope with her mother actually being pleased with her. It felt very strange; a bit of a let-down, really. Perhaps she didn't need love and affection from her mother as much as she thought she did; it was the wrong kind of love. Seeing little Carrie with *her* mother had prodded big Carrie into trying to build a bridge to connect with her own mother, something she'd never been able to do because her mother was like a shifting continent, her geographical plates were disturbed by perpetual earthquakes, landslides, hurricanes and tidal waves.

The country of 'Jill' that was Carrie's mother, was a hostile and unforgiving landscape. Completely enclosed behind a fortress of charm and sophistication, even Bill, her own husband, had to tiptoe in and out through the tradesman's entrance. And Carrie, her own daughter, her own flesh and blood was, by and large, enemy number one. Nothing - *nothing* that Carrie could ever do or say was ever quite enough for her mother. Yet to the rest of the world said mother praised her daughter to the heavens and beyond.

'*She's like the Wizard of Oz! A tiny person hiding behind a curtain and speaking out loud through a megaphone.*'

This was how Carrie had always pictured her mother. Why she was quite so tiny and hiding was a mystery to her. And was Carrie really to blame for this? Some questions could never be answered, and this was probably one of them. Still, she never gave up hope completely. Carrie had asked her mother if she could go along to the 'Local Ladies Network' night and this was the reason for her mother's unbridled joy. It was a sign to Jill that Carrie had seen the light and was finally realising what real life was all about.

Carrie hadn't been the same since she'd come back, oh so late, from the farmer's party at the weekend. Jill felt relieved that her daughter had no doubt seen what that rabble were really like. There would be no more cow muck in her washing machine at weekends, she was sure of it.

'Now just stick with me, Carrie, I'll introduce you to everyone,' said her mother as they pulled up in the hotel car park.

The town only had the one hotel; it was three star. The 'Local Ladies Network' hired a room there rather than meet in the village hall. At least, then, they had stripy carpet and china tea cups for their tea. A circle of gold chairs, covered in dark blue velour, met Carrie as she followed her mother through the door. Her mother immediately forgot her promise and sauntered away to greet her associates:

'Oh hello, Rosalind, how good of you to set up the room, I've had such a dreadful rush this evening...'

The purple and blue stripy carpet made Carrie feel dizzy. The room was spinning with women of all shapes and sizes, and all ages, not just the older end of the spectrum, which surprised her. Without warning they all sat down on the chairs - it was a bit like 'musical chairs' - and Carrie was left the odd one out. There was one spare chair at the far side of the circle. They all watched her in silence as she had to walk across the middle of the circle to take the seat. Her mother sat motionless, a queen before her courtiers, waiting for her to sit down.

What happened next was all a bit of a blur. Her mother was speaking to the group. There were words of welcome but Carrie couldn't take her eyes off the stripy carpet which was rolling to and fro like waves on a choppy sea; Carrie's chair was rolling too. By the time she was on her feet, introducing herself to the group, telling them about her journalistic hopes and dreams, she was far away. She was drowning in the sea, struggling for air. All she could see were blue and purple stripes in front of her eyes.

Then there was polite applause and she was sitting back down on her golden chair. She hadn't drowned after all because someone gave her a cup of tea. She rattled the saucer as she lifted her cup to drink. She felt dizzy and sick, and was very glad of the hot, sweet tea.

'Well done, Carrie,' said her mother as they got back in the car to go home. 'You gave a wonderful talk. Everyone was so impressed with you! You won't be able to speak every time, I can't be seen to favour you above anyone else, but I'll do my best!'

Carrie almost fell out of the car when they got home. She really thought that she was going to be sick. She concentrated on her breathing.

'Oh no, what have I done,' she groaned. 'There won't be a next time, and I'll hurt her! I don't want to hurt her.'

In the darkness of her bed, Carrie prayed:

'I just wanted to do the right thing. I tried. I just wanted to be loved.'

'You are loved more than you know,' said the Walnut in her bedside table drawer.

But Carrie didn't hear. She was drowning in a stripy sea, struggling for air, and there was nobody to help her.

———◆———

Debs was wide awake, but still drowning, struggling for air. She'd spent the evening with silence. Staring at the clock, staring at the fluffy carpet in the living room; its tufts, like frothy bubbles at the end of a wave on a sandy beach, were never still. Their movement made her feel dizzy and sick. Carrie had gone to 'LLN' night with her mum. Would she ever see her friend again? Was this the end?

Joe had been down to the club. But he was here with her now. Her husband. He broke her silence with his heavy breathing. He was struggling for air. He pulled her down, down, down; down with every beer stained breath, but somehow Debs held on. Everything was a bit of a blur.

Debs made a cup of tea; her hand shook as she lifted the mug to drink the sweet, hot tea. She really thought that she was going to be sick. She concentrated on her breathing.

'Oh no, what have I done?' whispered Debs to the silence. 'I just wanted to do the right thing. I tried. I just wanted to be loved.'

Debs listened a long time for an answer but none came. She didn't have a walnut in her bedside table drawer. There was no one to help her.

Part Two

Summer –
'The Heat Is On...'

Friday 2nd June

Dear Reader,

The merry month of May has turned into jolly June. It was time for the farmers to have a party. They can party as hard as anyone else! They can drink the same beer, eat the same food, dress up in fine clothes and dance the night away. The only difference between their parties and ours is that they have to bring their work along to the dance floor with them. Not just talking about work, but real work. They have to be back in time for milking the cows, feeding the animals.

During our party a young cow gave birth for the first time. She needed help and the farmer gave it. Party clothes were ruined. A few dances were missed. But it didn't matter. A new life was successfully brought into the world; a new investment as well. Work and fun, love and money, all rolled into one big party sausage roll! On and on it rolled until it was impossible to tell what was work, what was fun, what was love. And everything is money. Life on the farm is one continuous party; money is always at the top of the guest list.

Some of us don't love what we do for a living, some of us don't have fun when making a living, and some of us don't have to work hard to make a living. Farmers have to do all three all the time or they could not survive.

The month of June, named after the Roman Goddess Juno, continues the theme of love and romance begun by the merry month of May. Juno is the Goddess of marriage. June's flower is the red rose. Midsummer's day, which comes after the longest day on June 21st, is associated with magic, fairies and dancing. And there is magic and mystery in the soil beneath our feet, if we choose to look for it.

After several back breaking, hard days tilling the soil with a hoe, weeding crops of mangles and turnips which will feed the animals later in the year, the fine June weather brings with it the chance to make hay. My fingers are cut and sore, red from lifting the sharp twine of heavy bales. My back aches from dawn to dusk as I have followed the baler, raked hay at every corner, fetched and carried bales of hay, greased and oiled machinery, made flasks of tea, bottles of lemonade, sandwiches and cake. I am dirty and itchy with chaff. I am brown and sweaty from the heat of the sun on my back.

Dry grass prickles me if I try to sit down to rest in the field for a moment. There is no rest! I go back to the farm exhausted, but I still have to milk the cows, feed the animals, finish unloading bales of hay in case it rains...

There is no rest but I love every minute of my day. I feel like I've really done something that matters. I feel alive and I've worked to keep other things alive too. Work and fun, love and money. The greatest of these is love. Or is it money?

All things come from the soil. The rhythm of life. The romance of life. The magic of life. We must all till our own soil. It's hard work. It's a struggle. The weeds keep growing back. It's nature's way. But there is also great comfort and beauty in nature's way. Work hard, work together, work with what you've got and you will harvest a bumper crop from the field of your life! Start today! Find some soil, get down, get dirty - and get digging!

Saturday 3rd June

'Hello, darlin'! Do you want to come and make some hay with me?'

'I am doing, aren't I?' replied Carrie as Jed slid his hand around her waist.

Carrie was walking across the field to begin stacking, into towers of eight, the new crop of bales that had just been dropped by old man Wilson's tractor and baler. Jed was supposed to be taking over on the tractor but took a detour via Carrie's waist. Carrie just kept walking. The heat from Jed's big, heavy hand eased her aching muscles as she walked. It would have been so easy to just turn round and give in to him. With the hot sun dazzling her in the face it was impossible to tell whether he was Jed or his twin brother, Jon. So Carrie imagined. She imagined heat and hands. Not faces. Strangely, since the night of the party, she'd been feeling altogether more at ease on the farm. She knew that the Falcon was watching Jed's every move, so she felt relaxed and safe enough to freely give as good as she got now, like she'd always done in her dad's garage workshop with the men there.

Today they were working in the fields; Carrie felt part of the team in one big open workshop - a ceiling of blue sky, the rhythmic 'clunking' machinery sound of the tractor and baler as it chugged around the field, plenty of physical work to do, the deep smell of male sweat on the shirts of the men, much darker than her own little sweaty smell. Carrie was in heaven.

But Carrie didn't want to be in heaven on her own. Yet he stayed so far away from her. Was it deliberate? She just didn't know. All she knew was that she'd shared three of *the* most erotic moments of her life with a man who had barely touched her, barely spoken to her; a man who had not tried to connect with her in any way.

So why did she look for him all the time? She hoped that nobody would notice. Only Jip the happy dog understood. He made a bee-line for her at every opportunity. Carrie fussed him and held him and talked to his soft brown eyes.

'I need the toilet, Jip,' said Carrie. 'What shall I do?'

Jip wagged his tail. They were working in two fields that were far away from the farm. There were no bushes or hiding places of any sort, the whole space was taken up by field edged with hedge. The hay making was nearly done here and the field was as empty as a pale brown desert in the heat of the day. Carrie's only hope was a derelict, zinc tin shed in the corner by the gateway. It was dropping to bits. There was no door and the sides of the shed had rusty red holes in it around the bottom.

'It'll have to do, Jip,' said Carrie. 'I'll try to nip in when they're not looking.'

Carrie walked back to the gateway in the direction of the bottles of lemonade that were hidden in the hedge bottom, but veered off course at the last minute. Jip followed Carrie into the shed.

'No, Jip. Go!'

Jip ran out but came back again. He probably thought it was a game. He was running in and out of the shed door as if to say 'come on, then, chase me!' Carrie just couldn't wait a second longer.

'I'll just have to risk it.'

Carrie dropped her body, her jeans and her pants, all in one go in the far corner of the shed. She'd never had to wee outside before in her life. She felt ridiculous, squatting there, trying to hold her clothes out of the way of the splashing yellow wee that bounced back up at her as it hit the hardened cake of cow muck on the ground. She almost fell over trying not to laugh. Jip had gone.

Carrie rushed back outside. She was blinded by the heat and light of the sun after the darkness of the fusty shed. She almost trod on Jip the happy dog who was sitting obediently next to his master on the ground outside. Jon sat with his arm around Jip.

'Oh no!' panicked Carrie. 'Did he see me; did he hear what I was doing?'

That seemed worse than being seen having a pee at that moment. Carrie had been trying to speak to Jon all day and this was not how she wanted it to be, at all. Man and dog stood up. Jip stood still wagging his tail. Jon looked down at Jip.

'A..are you a..al..r..right?' he said.

'Yes, thanks,' said Carrie. 'I just needed a pee!'

Her face felt hot.

'It's O.K, w..we k..kept g..guard,' said Jon.

He turned to go without looking at her. He was immediately some distance away from her.

'Wait!' shouted Carrie.

She had to run to catch up with the strides from his long legs.

'Thank you,' she said. 'Can I help you with the cows later?'

'Y..yes,' he said, and carried on walking.

———— ♦ ————

Later came soon. The prickly heat of the day turned into a soft, warm evening of sticky cow muck and bad grass breath. Carrie and Jip were bringing in the cows for milking. Jip was zig-zagging from side to side, keeping the cows in line. Carrie just walked behind in the wake of their warm hides. The cows walked daintily despite the great udders clanging along in between their legs. Milking time was a bit late tonight because of the hay making and some of them were dribbling milk as they walked.

'*That could be me, one day,*' mused Carrie. '*Making milk for a baby! Ugh! It's horrible being a girl sometimes!*'

She suddenly felt sorry for the cows.

'*Their whole lives spent making babies and milk! And no choice in the matter! They deserve to be well treated and looked after.*'

Jed had said that Jon 'loves his ladies' and it was true. Gentle words, kind hands - this was all Jon's cows knew of life. And they did seem to be *his* cows. Brother Jed preferred tractors and machinery to the living parts of the farm. Carrie had noticed how Jip always gave Jed a wide berth; he knew. And Carrie knew too. There was no more confusion. Jon and Jed might wear the same clothes; the same boots. They might have the same bodies; the same hair; the same hands; the same eyes; even the same walk.

But that was all. Carrie could tell them apart now with ease, even from a great distance away. They really were 'chalk and cheese'. Jed, always in her face. Jon, always far away, looking down at the ground. And their Falcon father, old man Wilson, watching, staring. All the time.

Carrie had bounced half way across the yard before she noticed another, unknown, pair of eyes staring at her. These eyes were pale and misty with old age. The old man, dressed in a thick, black wool suit and matching waistcoat stood leaning against the silver handle bars of his old, black framed, bicycle. His scrawny trousers were clipped at the ankles with metal bicycle clips. His body, twisted with the arthritis of very old age, looked like an extension of the black bicycle frame. Just like a street statue performer, with a ghostly white painted face, the only sign that he was real and alive came from his staring eyes.

'I've come for me eggs,' he said eventually, after staring at Carrie, open mouthed for several seconds as she walked across the yard towards him.

'Oh, well I'll ask at the house for you,' she smiled.

She knew how to speak to old people, no matter how strange they looked or behaved. As usual, Carrie didn't get as far as the house before old man Wilson came out carrying a carton of eggs.

'Ah do, Ab,' he said.

'Ah do!' replied the old man.

Carrie stood to one side, unsure what to do next - go, stay, say something? She didn't want to be impolite so she just stood still. Both the old men ignored her and began a weird sort of conversation involving a lot of 'ooh this' and 'ah that'. It almost sounded like a foreign language so Carrie decided to slip away unnoticed. She hadn't got very far when old Ab, the egg man, said:

'Tat-tah, missy. By heck, you remind me of someone I used to know. I thought I'd seen a ghost!'

'Bye!' said Carrie.

She felt very uncomfortable as she walked away across the yard. Both men watched her go as if they were in a trance. She was never so relieved to get round the corner of the shed, out of sight. She popped her head back around the corner to see if they'd gone, but they were standing, heads close together, in deep conversation. It was the most talking to anyone that she'd seen old man Wilson do.

'I bet they're talking about me!' said Carrie. 'Having a laugh about me working here! Well, I don't care!'

'Don't care about what, darlin'?'

Carrie had backed away from the shed corner straight into the hot groin of Jed. He had her now, pinned up against the red hot brick wall, those big hands of his pressing on her shoulders, making her chest push out towards his body. Carrie looked Jed in the eye, relaxed her shoulders and started to drop *her* body away from his grasp.

But quick as a flash, he rammed a knee in between her falling legs so that she was left hanging. She had to grab onto his shoulders to keep upright. Her lovely self defence move had failed. She lost her balance, her cool, and her presence of mind. Jed was laughing at her. He let her squirm. He lifted his knee higher and took her away from the ground.

'Put me down, you big hairy oaf!'

More laughter.

'Let go of me!'

Carrie pushed against him with all her might. She forgot all her precious training. All she needed to do was pinch the skin underneath his upper arm, his thigh, or anywhere that she could reach, and she might have had a chance to get free of him. But she panicked. Easily done.

'Now that's not very nice!' laughed Jed. 'I only wanted to show you that *I* care!'

Jed's leg was like a padded steel girder. Fixed and unmovable.

'Hey!' a voice shouted.

The fixed and unmovable girder suddenly disappeared. Carrie was back on the ground. Jon was striding down the drive, at speed, towards them. Jed grinned his big grin at Carrie. Like members of a relay team, as Jon got near to Carrie, Jed continued the stride, away from them both, never looking back, like a good athlete. He wanted to win the race; Carrie had an uncomfortable feeling that she was the prize.

'T..time to f..feed the c..calves,' said Jon.

'Yes,' replied Carrie.

Carrie fed the calves. She fussed little Carrie. She stood in the yard with the cows. She watched Jon finish the milking. She talked to Jip. She opened and closed gates. She drove home in her little red car. She went to bed.

'Hey!'

The voice shouted at her over and over again. Louder and louder. It wouldn't go away. It didn't stammer. 'Jon loves his ladies,' Jed had said. Carrie had a funny dream. She was down on all fours eating grass. It was hard to chew. Her breasts were full and aching. But a pair of big, gentle hands was massaging them, so it was O.K. It was lovely. Carrie felt hot. She woke to find that she was holding her own breasts which had returned to normal.

'Remember you're a lady,' said the Walnut in her bedside table drawer.

Carrie smiled and went back to sleep.

Sunday 4th June

Carrie's mother, Jill, was down on all fours in the lounge. She had forgotten that she was a lady. She was busy reaching underneath the sofa for an escaped cotton reel that didn't want to be caught tonight. Jill's hands were full of rage; the more the reel rolled, the more her hands shook. She'd only dropped it because of Bill.

He sat now, silent and motionless, watching the shrieking banshee on the carpet in front of him. He knew the end was near. Jill was shaking uncontrollably and would soon need a cup of tea and tablets in bed. As usual, it was all his fault. His fault that Carrie was still going back to that farm. His fault that the kitchen still smelt of cow muck at weekends. His fault that Carrie was suddenly too busy again to go back to 'Local Ladies Network' night. His fault because he wouldn't do anything about anything! His fault! His fault!

Bill knew that his silence right now was making Jill's torment worse. But he also knew that it was the best and quickest way to end her suffering; she would burn up her rage far more quickly upon his silence. Arguing back would just fuel her fire.

Jill knew what Bill was doing and, deep down, she was grateful. He was her salvation. The Saviour was with her now. Alongside her on the floor, he rescued the cotton reel and gently put it into her shaking hands. The needle wedged in its end stabbed Jill's palm. Like a little hedgehog, she curled up into a little ball of self defence. She sobbed quietly. The Saviour took her in his arms and just held her for a moment; he ignored the prickles from the little hedgehog's body. He took her pain, and then he took her to bed and gave her a cup of tea and her tablets.

———◆———

Carrie nearly trod on the little hedgehog. It looked just like another brown cowpat. These days she didn't bother so much about not treading in or through one, especially if its top had slightly hardened off in the heat of the day. Then it would make a gorgeous squelching sensation as its skin hissed open beneath the weight of her foot. Jip alerted her to the little creature which just managed to reach the safety of the hedge bottom, closely escorted by Jip's interested pink nose.

A click of the fingers from his master, and Jip was back, walking alongside his rather unlikely looking band of companions. Carrie couldn't help thinking that she was in an episode of 'The Famous Five'; stories that she had loved as a girl, so many times imagined and now she was really living them at long last. Old man Wilson, Jed, Jon, Carrie and Jip. They were walking up the hill together, side by side, in one long line to look the cattle. The bull was with them; he was on loan from a neighbouring farm. Quite why Jed was there tonight Carrie didn't know. She did know that there was safety in numbers and Jed had reduced his greeting, by and large, to 'hello darlin'' without adding the 'why don't you come...' somewhere or other.

Perhaps he was harmless after all. And they'd done a good day's work together without any problems. The old man had kept his promise and was starting to let her have a go at lots more things on the farm; she was never short of stuff to write about these days.

Carrie had to go home soon, but she loved this last job of the day, looking the cattle. Usually it was just a silent trip with Jon; it was still a silent trip now. She didn't mind the extra company, as long as it wasn't going to be every night.

The bull was standing tall, the King with a golden ring in his nose and a glorious thick neck of white curls. His ladies in waiting, all dressed in co-ordinated black and white outfits, waited patiently in a circle around him.

He, dressed in royal red hide, surveyed his court with pale blue, slightly staring eyes. Carrie wondered how far he could actually see. Anyway, he seemed to be more interested in what he could smell rather than what he could see.

The famous five stood at the gate at the top of the hill and waited. Carrie waited too, but she wasn't sure what she was waiting for. She was getting a bit bored. The King and his ladies in waiting were milling around like race horses before a big race; everyone secretly looking to position themselves to the best advantage.

The King was busy sniffing the behinds of each and every one of his ladies. All of a sudden, he pulled a funny face and sneezed. He made a funny snorting sound, and something long, red raw, and slimy, dropped out from underneath the middle of his belly.

'Oh my God, what's that!' cried Carrie in alarm.

Too late she realised what it was because the bull was using it now on his chosen lady in waiting. The lady staggered forward a few steps, reaching for the ground with her feet for support. She reeled and shook as the King laid his full, immense, weight upon her. His lady was shaking uncontrollably as his end grew near.

'It's his pith!' said Jed. 'Haven't you seen one before?'

He grinned at Carrie.

So that's why he came tonight,' she squirmed.

'No, I haven't,' she replied as matter of factly as she could.

The King climbed down from his lady, and, with a snort and a shake of his head, had a sniff at another behind.

'He'll do,' said old man Wilson.

Jon said nothing and looked up at the sky. Jip said nothing and sat gently panting. Jed was still grinning at Carrie. Carrie said nothing. She felt a bit sick. She remembered:

'He's actually quite shy. But he likes to be man of the house. King of the castle - like all men.'

'Not like all men,' Carrie had said.

Now she was not quite so sure.

They were sitting on the new patio. The patterned concrete slabs shone white in the evening sun; the pots of bright red geraniums turned the little patio into an ancient, Mediterranean temple. The two Goddesses, Carrie and Debs, sat back in their stripy old deckchairs sipping gin and tonic. Flip flops swinging on the end of their feet in the breeze, they surveyed the pretty little empire in front of them; Debs with pride in her garden and Carrie with relief just to be there at long last.

'Well I can't see any weeds in your garden!' said Carrie.

'Oh, they're there alright!' said Debs. 'You just can't always see them.'

'I know,' replied Carrie.

Carrie looked across at her friend who was chilling beneath big purple sunglasses. Debs was looking better again these days. She was wearing more 'normal' for her clothes - a T-shirt and shorts tonight instead of covering herself up.

'Sometimes you need a bit of help to get rid of the weeds,' continued Carrie.

'You know, you're becoming very weird these days,' said Debs after a pause.

'What does the lovely Mr Pike have to say about your farm articles which aren't very much to do with farming? I'm not sure what to make of them! I like them, don't get me wrong. I kind of don't understand them, yet I do at the same time. They make me feel nice inside, the words make me feel nice. I don't know why, but they make me feel better. I just worry that a lot of folk won't get it.'

'Mr Pike is far too busy still fishing around for a new secretary and buying *the most amazing* waistcoats that you've ever seen, presumably to catch himself a minnow, to be interested in my work any more!' laughed Carrie. 'We're all having a great time just getting on with things. The paper is doing better and Dennis, the editor, doesn't seem to mind what I write. In fact, we've had a few 'comments letters' back agreeing with me! One, from Rosalind Greenacre, about 'the value of getting back to the basics in life' - and you can guess who put her up to that!' she smiled.

Debs smiled a little smile.

'You cow!' said Debs. 'Oops! Sorry! Not allowed to say that, am I?'

The old Debs was back.

'Come on then, how's it really going with the chalk and cheese?

Made your mind up yet? Or are you going to have both?'

'Certainly not!' said Carrie, indignantly.

'Well, you've got a bit of catching up to do!' said Debs. 'It's about time you took some of your own advice and got down and dirty in the soil yourself!'

Carrie wished the deckchair would snap and swallow her up so she didn't have to think of a clever answer - the old Debs was really back and there was no escape.

'Maybe, but I just can't, for all sorts of reasons you wouldn't understand.'

Carrie decided that honesty was the best reply tonight.

'I understand that you want what every girl and woman wants when they get to a certain age. I understand that you're scared of trying it because of what that mother of yours has drummed into you all these years. I understand that you want to fall in love and be rescued by your knight in shining armour. You might get some or all of that eventually, but you'll get nothing if you keep running away. Stand still. Stop running.'

'*I am standing still, very still!*' shouted Carrie in her head. '*I'm still and quiet, I love his dog, I watch him, I work with him, I smile at him, but he doesn't notice me! The wrong one notices me! What else can I do?*'

'I think *you* should be writing articles for the paper instead of working in that flipping factory,' said Carrie, out loud.

Still feeling honest, she admitted:

'You're right, though. I will try harder.'

'You don't need to try,' said Debs. 'Just look at yourself. You just don't realise how other people see you – you're *so* lovely!'

Carrie didn't know what to say so gave a nervous little laugh instead. The old Debs was really, really back.

'How's Joe?'

Change of subject.

'He's on nights at the minute, so I'm not seeing so much of him at the moment. I get back from work in time to get his tea ready, so it works quite well.'

'*Why can't he get his own bloody tea,*' thought Carrie. '*I wonder if the old Debs is back because he's on nights? Stupid thing to wonder about...*'

'How long for?' she asked.

'Don't know,' said Debs.

They left it there. It was getting cold and dark so the Goddesses left the temple. They went back to the kitchen and had a quick hot chocolate before one of them had to go home to her own temple. Back to her own thoughts. Back to the walnut in her bedside table drawer that she looked at every night before sleep.

'*Stand still. Stop running,*' it said.

Saturday 10th June

'Ah-do!' said old man Wilson.

Always the same greeting, even after all this time. And Carrie never knew what was coming next. She stood still and waited for a clue.

'Clamp the grains with 'J',' was all he said.

Carrie looked blankly at him. He pointed at her with his long, bony, finger just like he did to his sons. He pointed across the yard and up the drive.

'We've just had a delivery, it needs seeing to,' he continued.

'O.K.' said Carrie.

She knew better than to start asking complicated questions. She knew that she was expected to work it out for herself, and she usually did. Not only to work out which 'J' it was, Jon or Jed, but also, what it was she was supposed to be doing. Today, she hadn't got a clue what 'clamping grains' meant. Today she was going to stand still for as long as possible. She waited.

The bony finger and the ice blue stare were very slow to turn away from her. Old man Wilson still stared at her the same as the day she'd first met him. She still stared back. They were still Falcon and mouse. There was something behind that icy gaze that stopped the Falcon from killing the mouse.

'He still lets me come here, yet I think sometimes he really hates me and I want to know why. This little mouse is not so little any more.'

Carrie's little grey whiskers and nose twitched towards the funny smell that was coming from the direction of the drive. She turned and followed her nose. The smell got stronger and stronger and more rancid. 'J' for Jon was standing on the top of an enormous mountain of bright orange, stinky stuff which had been dumped in an enclosure made from old railway sleepers and slabs of old concrete, held together by rusty brown wire. The enclosure was round like the mountain of stuff that now sat in the once empty space.

'I've been sent to help,' she called up to him.

Her face screwed up tight like a crumpled ball of paper; the sun on the horizon behind Jon's head dazzled her. His shock of long, curly, dark hair was lit up around the edges by the same sun. He was a golden Saviour. He even looked like he was floating on thin air because Carrie couldn't see his feet. She was very aware that she, on the other hand, took the part of the lowly, ugly peasant girl. Blinded by white light, her face refused to

114

straighten itself out as she clawed her way up the ladder that was leaning against the orange mountain of stinky stuff.

Drawing level with the horizon at the top of the ladder Carrie's face might as well have been covered with lines drawn on in felt pen. The feeling of multiple creases wouldn't go away, yet she hadn't been having a big smiling session. Nevertheless, the Saviour held out a big brown hand to the ugly peasant girl.

Carrie stood still and let the big brown hand take hold of her little white hand. It fairly catapulted her into the sky and she landed with a soft bump on her bum on top of the orange mountain.

'Phew! What is this stuff?' she asked as she rolled round onto her knees and tried to stand up.

To stand still. It was a good job that she'd got wellies on. Her feet sank down into the orange mush, half a wellie deep. It was like standing on the top of a beautifully soft, Victoria sponge cake with the gravity of the moon. No gravity. She eventually managed to balance herself. Apart from the funny smell, it actually felt great now that she was up there. The big brown hand had moved across to the other side of the mountain.

'It's g..grains for the c..cattle to f..feed on in the w..winter.'

'Oh,' said Carrie, none the wiser. 'What's it made of then?'

'M..malted g..grain. It's the w..waste p..product from m..making b..beer. The c..cows l..love it.'

His words are bad today,' thought Carrie. *'I think I make him nervous. Stand still, stand still,'* she repeated to herself over and over again.

But Jon wasn't standing still. He was shuffling around the edge of the mountain of grains as if he was doing a little dance. Step - together - step - together went his feet, squashing down the orange stinky stuff and leaving a trail of foot marks as he went.

'So this is clamping grains! And today he's looking at his feet for a good reason!'

All of a sudden Carrie was no longer an ugly peasant. She set off with her feet, starting her own row of squishy footprints, following Jon's. She smiled:

'I've worked it out for myself. I'm still not sure why it needs doing, though, but it doesn't matter.'

What did matter to Carrie was that she wanted to catch up with Jon. To get a bit closer to him today. Carrie worked her feet and legs extra hard. The grains were soft and squishy; it was a lovely feeling. They could have just as easily been treading grapes in the south of France. The perfume rising from the stinky grains was just as intoxicating right now as the finest vintage. Except that it wasn't really all that pleasant. For some reason, the stink reminded Carrie of Joe. Jon had mentioned beer. Quickly, Carrie had to imagine grapes and Mediterranean sunshine again. She was catching Jon up a bit by now.

They were working in silence. Their circles were getting smaller and smaller and closer and closer as they worked into the centre of the mountain. Carrie found herself smiling at the thought that they were like two birds of paradise, shuffling around each other in a ritual dance of courtship. Closer and closer. There wasn't room now to look down at their feet.

'W..what?' said Jon.

He had no choice but to look into Carrie's upturned, smiling face.

'I was just thinking that this is one of the funniest things I've ever done! It's a bit like doing the cha-cha-cha on the moon!' she beamed. 'And we never did get to dance at the party the other week - well I didn't!'

'I c..can't d..dance.'

They stood still together in the middle of their beautiful Victoria sponge cake which was covered now with a crotchet of the most intricate footwork.

'Yes, you can!' said Carrie.

She was forgetting who she was with, again.

'Just look at what we've done here! It's just like dancing!'

Carrie leaned back towards the sunshine.

'Take me in your arms now, and dance with me some more!'

She longed to say it! How she longed to do it! She was feeling that erotic feeling again. Jon held out his arms to escort her down the ladder instead. His cheek bones were so brown with a tan that Carrie couldn't tell if he was blushing or not. She certainly was. He made her forget who she was, where she was, what she was. She was in bits. She was still dancing on the moon. She was free.

Jip was waiting for them at the bottom of the ladder, wagging his tail. He ran off immediately they touched the ground. Carrie could hear her own nervous little voice, chattering away nineteen to the dozen, as she walked alongside the silent Jon, following after Jip's happy tail. She was so busy feeling free that she wasn't sure what she was saying until Jip took a detour through the orchard. She ran after Jip and swung herself in and out of the trees until she reached the stone bench beneath the sad tree in the far corner. She sat down heavily, out of breath now, and realised that she was alone.

116

Jon was standing in the gateway to the orchard. He whistled to Jip who ran straightaway to his master. The branches of the sad tree poked her in the back and pushed her off the bench.

'Ouch! That hurt!'

Carrie almost turned to reprimand the tree for spoiling her fun, spoiling her moment. But it was just a tree. Her wellies were full of stinky orange grains. Stinky and embarrassed, she squelched across the orchard like a disobedient child, back to Jon and Jip, who were waiting for her. She didn't feel erotic any more.

'Are you cross with me?' she asked.

'C..cross with y..you? W..why?' he asked back.

'I just don't know if you like me being here.'

Jon fussed Jip's ears and talked to Jip by way of an answer:

'W..we d..don't m..mind, d..do we, J..Jip?'

Jip wagged his tail and his eyes smiled up at Jon. Carrie smiled too. She would have wagged her tail except she didn't have one. And for the first time, Jon's eyes looked up from the ground and smiled at her. They stood still; two trees standing together, growing together, in the orchard.

———◆———

'Hello, love! I'm beginning to think that you live here these days!'

'I could say the same to you!'

Bill smiled at the sound of his daughter's voice and the clink of her car keys as she threw them at his useful tin, the one he kept on the shelf at the back of the shop counter for useful things - she missed every time. He heard her swear slightly as she picked them up from the floor.

'One day! I'll get you one day!' she laughed as she appeared in the workshop doorway.

'Working late again?' she said.

'Just finishing off,' he said.

'You seem to be having a lot of finishing off to do these days,' said Carrie.

'It can't be helped, love. It won't be forever.'

'It feels like forever.'

She was getting fed up of evening meals alone with her mother. She wanted her dad back. She wanted a bit of 'normal' back at home. She was a grown up and it shouldn't matter to her what her parents did or didn't do. But it did matter, somehow.

'Are you cross with me?' she asked.

'Cross with you? Why?' he asked back.

'I don't know,' said Carrie. 'I just don't know if it's all my fault. You know, with mum, and everything.'

Carrie heard the clink of a spanner as he dropped his tool and appeared, quick as a flash on his trolley, from underneath the jacked up car that he'd been working on. He fell off his trolley as he tried to roll off it and pull himself upright.

'It's alright, Dad,' Carrie wanted to say. *'I love you. It's me and mum that are off our trolley, not you.'*

But she couldn't say it. Bill walked over to his daughter and stroked the top of her long, golden, hair with his good hand.

'I'm not cross with you. We're not cross with you. You've done nothing wrong. Just look at you! You're so lovely! No father could have a finer daughter than you. Your mother and I...Your mother carries a great burden in her heart, but that's nothing to do with you! She loves you, despite what you think. She puts a lot of pressure on herself sometimes and the only way to release it is for me to step away. We know this has to happen and we know that it will pass. Know that I'm not stepping away from you, or your mother, and I never will do.'

Tears welled up in Carrie's eyes. She smiled through them at her dad. She was in bits for the second time that day.

'Oh, dad, I've got so much to tell you! I've been clamping grains with Jon today! I've been dancing on the moon! I've been a happy dog! I've been a tree in the orchard!'

But, by way of an answer she just said:

'Can we go home together?'

They stood still. Father and daughter together. Holding each other. They were both in bits.

Saturday 1st July

'We're taking a beast to market.'

Carrie didn't know if the 'we' included her or not so she just said 'Oh.'

'Do you need to take anything with you?' said old man Wilson.

'I'll just get my bag, then,' replied Carrie, still not sure how many would be in the party of 'we.'

Just then Jon appeared. Carrie got her smile ready. Jon was totally preoccupied in escorting a lovely, mostly black, young cow into the back of the cattle trailer. Jon had his arm draped across her back. Quite a long time seemed to pass before he came out of it, so that Carrie began to wonder if he was going to travel with the cow.

When he finally emerged he was concentrating so hard on looking at the ground, that she could barely see his face at all. He lifted his side of the ramp and closed the catch on the trailer door, also without looking. And without looking, or even one word to his father, to Carrie, or to Jip, he walked away up the yard. Jip zigzagged behind him.

'I'm invisible! I got it wrong!'

Carrie tried to make herself feel better:

'Well, he must be wrong in the head!'

The Land Rover front passenger seat was muddied with hundreds of miles' worth of Jip's paw prints and upholstered with a thick layer of dog hairs and dust. In the foot well there was an assortment of dirty old rags, an old duffle coat and a can of antiseptic animal spray. There was hardly any room for feet at all.

'I expect that Jip is the only passenger in here most of the time.'

Carrie imagined how excited Jip would be if he was in her seat right now, wagging his tail with delight at the prospect of a journey to who knows where.

'I'm not a happy dog today. I don't really want to go to the cattle market any more.'

Carrie sat back in her seat and loosened the usual tight grip on her body. She gave up. She let the Land Rover shake, rattle and roll her in random directions. There was an occasional tug from the trailer behind. It was all the fun of a gentle fairground ride without having to pay. Carrie felt so loose that her teeth began to rattle together.

'Was your son alright this morning, Mr.Wilson? He seemed very quiet.'

'Ah, he'll be right. Didn't want to let this heifer go. She's just had her first calf.'

'Why are you selling her, then?'

'Got to. We can't run any more cows. Shame. She's a good 'un. She'll be a good milker for someone.'

'Oh.'

Carrie couldn't say anything else. Her mind was busy suddenly understanding a lot of things.

Monday 3rd July

'Mad Bull Attacks Girl at Cattle Market!'
There were dramatic scenes at the town's cattle market on Saturday morning when a raging bull escaped from its pen and nearly killed a young woman. Not just any young woman - but our very own reporter, 'Twentieth Century Land Girl' Carice Langford! Her life was saved by the great bravery and quick thinking of an elderly farmer.

Local girl, Carice, aged 22, was visiting the cattle market for the first time to carry out research for her 'Land Girl' articles for our readers.

'I was standing in a corridor in between the rows of cattle pens when, all of a sudden, I heard a lot of shouting and commotion coming from the other end of the shed. And then, I suddenly found myself in the wrong place at the wrong time, as a very large, red bull came charging down the corridor towards me!' said Carice. 'I froze! I've never been so terrified in my life! The bull's eyes flashed bright green as he charged towards me!'

The mature bull, described by his owner as 'gentle as a lamb,' had had an uncomfortable journey to market. His ring had been ripped from his nose by an accident inside the cattle lorry, so he was upset by the time he arrived at market. He was even more upset to be locked in a pen away from the cows that he could hear, see, and smell close by. When it was his turn to be sold he went berserk as the men arrived at his pen. He charged blindly through the gate and down the corridor towards our reporter. She faced a certain mauling to death.

But a knight in shining armour appeared on this dramatic day! A local farmer jumped over the rails of the nearby pens and, just in time, was able to pull a gate at the end of the corridor across his body and that of our young 'Land Girl'.

Showing great bravery and superhuman strength he held the gate fast, as the bull attacked them by pushing his immense weight against the gate. The cattle market vet was then able to shoot the animal humanely.

Our local hero is a sixty five year old farmer who wishes to remain anonymous. Our 'Twentieth Century Land Girl' said:

'This man has saved my life. I can't thank him enough. Apart from a few bruises from being squashed up against the railings, I'm fine. I'm more than fine, I'm lucky to be alive today!'

A review of Health and Safety procedures is being carried out at the cattle market. No charges related to this incident are expected. All the staff at the newspaper give their sincere thanks to the farmer who risked his own life for the sake of our 'Land Girl'. We shall look forward all the more in future to the next instalment of 'Twentieth Century Land Girl'!

Carrie froze. They were staring. Everywhere she went bright green eyes were mad and staring:

'That's it! You stupid girl! That's enough! Absolutely no more going to that farm any more!'

A very large mother, red with rage, charged blindly through the kitchen and onwards, up to bed for the day, even though it was a weekday.

'Oh Carrie!' stared dad. 'Please thank him for me.'

'Bloody hell!!' stared Debs.

'Well done, well done Carrie!' stared Mr Pike. The rest of the office staff stared and applauded and cheered and stared. Sales had gone up this week.

Carrie stared. The only light came from her eyes as they flashed bright green in the darkness. She froze. Her little grey body was suddenly smothered. The Falcon fell on her from the sky. He appeared from nowhere. She felt the warmth of his body, the ridges of every feather pressing down on her, as his wings outstretched in front of her.

She couldn't breathe. She surrendered her little grey life and let it live or die beneath the Falcon's wings. He wasn't there to kill her, but to protect her; she belonged to him. She had known it from the start; she just didn't know how it would end - in life or death.

She was breathing now. The Falcon had gone. Her little grey body stretched out its arms and legs. The heavy duvet that had been smothering her face fell away from her dream and woke her up.

Saturday 8th July

'Ah do!'

He'd been avoiding her all day, or so it seemed. Old man Wilson was sitting on the stone bench in the orchard, beneath that most strange of sad trees. It was the first time that she'd ever seen him *in* the orchard, even though she knew it was his special place - everyone kept telling her so - Mavis, old Ab, the egg man. Jed made mock of the 'precious' orchard. Jon said nothing. Carrie loved the orchard. She always felt that she was trespassing whenever she entered, but she still visited whenever she got the chance, even if it was just a quick swing through the trees and a swish through the long grass. She walked off the guilt afterwards and hoped that no one had seen her there.

She hesitated at the sight of the old man sitting on *her* stone bench. She really felt quite put out at the sight of him sitting there, even though she knew that she had no right to feel so; it was *his* stone bench, after all. Carrie had to speak to him. She really had to speak to him. She'd got a lot of things to say. He sat very still as she walked towards him.

'Ah do,' he said again.

Carrie sat down on the stone bench next to him. It took all her courage; it was like meeting the old man again for the very first time. Her favourite stilettos and tightly buttoned raincoat hadn't helped her then, and nothing at all could help her now as she sat next to the pale ice blue eyes that fixed upon her, freezing her into her place on the stone bench. The leaves from the fruit trees rustled around a bit in the breeze, as much as they dared. Carrie noticed for the first time that there wasn't much grass and no lovely yellow buttercups growing near to where they were sitting. It was as if the sad old tree had chased them away.

'Why put this lovely stone bench in a dead corner?'

The leaves from the fruit trees rustled round a bit more:

'We don't know,' they said.

The leaves from the fruit trees rustled round and around a bit more, and then a bit more, in the breeze, as much as they dared.

'Thank you,' said Carrie.

The leaves from the fruit trees rustled round:

'We know,' they said.

'My dad says thank you.'

The leaves from the fruit trees rustled round a bit more:

'We know,' they said.

'Are you cross with me?' she asked.

'Cross with you? Why?' he asked back.

'I don't know,' said Carrie. 'I just don't know if you like me being here.'

The pale ice blue eyes came closer. Two big, bony, hands were holding her face. They held her very still. They held her very tight. They held her very gently.

'You are *very* precious,' said the old man.

The leaves from the fruit trees rustled round and around a bit more, and then a bit more:

'We know,' they said.

He let her go. He made her forget who she was, where she was, what she was. She was in bits.

Tuesday 11th July

Carrie heard a voice. The gate at the side of the house was open.

'She must be gardening. Maybe she's heard me walking up the drive. Maybe she's cursing a weed that she's found in her beautiful garden...I'll sneak up on her!'

Carrie was twelve years old again and getting ready to jump out at Debs from the bushes at the bus stop. There was no finer start to the day in those days than giving her best friend a heart attack. 'Aagh!' Debs used to shout. It worked every time.

'It's a good job that Debs has a good, strong heart or she'd be dead by now!' thought Carrie as she crept, silent as a cat, along the edge of the house wall. The heart attack was always healed afterwards by lots of laughter and a hug; it kept them both alive.

'Aagh!' shouted Debs.

'Hang on a minute - I'm not there yet!' meowed Carrie, who was still creeping along the wall. Instinct told her to stay a cat.

When she reached the corner of the house her big jump was ready to go, but she had a quick peep first, just to get her bearings. But it was Carrie who had the heart attack. The quick peep became a peep show. Debs was standing at the kitchen sink. She was leaning forwards, hands in the sink. Joe was with her. At a first glance they looked like a loving couple - she, washing the pots, he, giving her a loving hug.

'Aagh!'

'Aagh!' Carrie shouted silently.

She was back at the gate at the top of the hill, watching with the famous five. Too late she realised what Joe was doing. He had dropped his trousers. Two big, sausage fingered, hands were holding Debs' head. They held her very still. They held her very tight. The sausage fingers wrapped themselves in a tourniquet around her long hair and forced her head forward, in between the taps on the sink. All of a sudden, Joe pulled a funny face. He made a funny snorting sound. Debs reeled and shook as he laid his full, immense weight upon her. She was shaking uncontrollably as his end grew near.

'That'll do,' said Joe.

Joe climbed down from Debs and, with a snort, gave her head a shake as he let her go. The cat pressed every sinew of its shaking body against the hard edges of the house wall.

'He's actually quite shy. But he likes to be man of the house. King of the castle - like all men.'

Some moments passed. It was time for the cat to be as brave as the Famous Five.

'Hello! Anybody home?' shouted the extra loud voice of an extra loud footed Carrie as she appeared from the path at the side of the house.

Carrie waved an extra big wave at Debs who was standing at the kitchen sink.

'Hello!' smiled Carrie with an extra wide smile. 'The side gate was open, I thought you were in the garden,' she said.

Joe was leaning against the kitchen door frame. He grinned at her. She squirmed inside. He stared at her. She looked back at him as matter of factly as she could.

'I'm just about to go in the garden,' said Debs in an extra cheerful voice. 'We've just finished tea and Joe's going to work.'

Joe unleaned himself from the kitchen door frame. He gave Debs an extra large slap on the backside and an extra large flick of the hair on the back of her head. All of a sudden he pulled a funny face and sneezed. He made a funny snorting sound. He turned towards the kitchen door and, leaning forward, pawed the floor with one foot.

Two big, sausage, fingers made horns at each side of his head. He charged, like a mad bull, through the door towards Carrie making an extra large snorting, bellowing sound.

His eyes flashed bright green as he charged towards her. Carrie froze. Until the last minute, when she took one little step to the side and the mad bull crashed into the bushes on the far side of the path.

'Aagh!' shouted the mad bull, amongst other things.

But he was a big, strong bull. He gave Carrie and Debs an extra large laugh and then he left for work with an extra large grin on his face.

The heart attack was over for today. The two good, strong hearts had a cup of tea together and a hug. It kept them alive.

Saturday 15th July

The cattle lorry pulled up in the farmyard. It was an unexpected visitor on a Saturday afternoon. Carrie was just having a lovely talk with the other visitor to the farmyard. Old Ab had come to collect his eggs. She was getting quite good, now, at 'ooh' and 'aah' language. She looked forwards to a chat with Old Ab. After nigh on seventy years of working the land, Old Ab was a living relic from the past; he always had a lovely story to tell about the old days. Jip loved him. He always had a friendly pat in his worn, kind, old hands for the happy dog and a warm shake of the hand for Carrie. He never stayed very long, but just long enough.

'Aah, I'll be off, then,' he would say.

Then he would put his carton of eggs in the wicker basket that was wired to the front of his arthritic old bicycle. And then he would turn to Carrie and take hold of both her hands in his and hold them for a moment. Carrie could feel the life flowing from them into her own hands. His blood, pulsing through exaggerated veins; his skin, so very, *very,* soft like a pebble worn smooth with a lifetime of work and weather. Kind hands. A kind man. And then, nimble as a lad from one of his farming tales, he pushed himself off with one leg and mounted his bicycle as it set off without him down the drive.

But today he watched with Carrie as the driver from the cattle lorry got out of his cab and started to undo the tailgate. Old man Wilson was there. He looked black with thunder. The lovely, mostly black, young cow who had made that fateful journey to the cattle market only a week ago, re-appeared. Down the ramp and into her old farmyard home she came as best she could.

Carrie had never seen a cow walk on three legs before. She'd seen plenty of dogs in the park with only three legs; with one leg amputated and a loving owner they always seemed to be quite happy, running around and having fun.

The lovely, mostly black, young cow still had her back leg attached to her body but she carried it like a weekend bag on her hip. It was hanging loose; the hoof was curled up tight into a ball. She could not or would not put it on the ground. At the bottom of the ramp, now, she stood still at the feet of old man Wilson. Her ears hung low to the ground. He reached down and stroked the top of her head. The lovely, mostly black, young cow was dribbling saliva from her mouth. She looked like she was crying.

Old man Wilson was whispering in her ear. He put one hand

underneath her chin and raised her head slightly. Then he stood up and, resting his arm across the top of her body, she hobbled alongside him as he led her to the nearest cowshed.

'Aah, it's a bad business, a bad business,' said Old Ab shaking his head sadly. 'Ta-ta Missy, bless you.'

Kind hands. A kind man. The second Old Ab pushed off down the drive Carrie pushed herself across the yard to the cowshed.

'You *poor* lady. You poor, *poor* lady,' said old man Wilson.

Over and over again he said it as he looked over the lovely, mostly black, young cow. The lovely, mostly black, young cow could not put her back foot on the ground because there was a deep cut in it where her hoof joined her ankle. One of the teats on her udder was ripped and part of it was hanging off. She stood hunched up like a camel, her ears hung so very low to the ground.

'They've thrashed the living daylights out of her!' said the old man. 'Her ribs must be black and blue. There was no need, no need.'

Carrie wasn't sure if he was talking to her, to the cow, or to himself.

'They said she wasn't a good milker, they said she wouldn't do as she was told, they want their money back...You poor lady. I'm so sorry...you poor, poor lady...there was no need, no need...'

Then Jon was standing in the doorway, with Jip. He said nothing.

'She'll never be the same again,' said the old man. 'She'll never get over this...She'll never do any good now.'

'Are you going to report this?' asked Carrie.

'Can't,' said old man Wilson. 'There's no telling what they'd do. But I'll make sure they know about this at the cattle market. They won't sell *them* any more cattle.'

Jon had disappeared as silently as he'd arrived. Jip stayed with Carrie. She wanted to weep but her eyes wouldn't let her. She wanted to be sick but her stomach wouldn't let her. So she just stood still in the doorway.

Jon returned with armfuls of stuff. Then father and son set to work on the poor lady. Kind hands. They covered her battered body with blankets; with local anaesthetic, needle and thread they repaired her; they sprayed her wounds with antiseptic; they injected her with penicillin to help her to fight infection; they set up a halogen light to keep her warm; they gave her a drink of water; offered fresh hay to eat. Kind hands.

She would not eat. She would not drink. Throughout all their attentions she stood as still as a statue. She never looked up. She never made a sound. Carrie hoped that she hadn't given up, but it looked that way.

Old man Wilson took the armfuls of stuff away. Jon stood with his lady. He gently stroked the back of her ears and neck. He never looked up. He never made a sound. He hadn't given up on her.

The other lady, that had been standing still all this time in the shed doorway, walked towards him. Without thinking, without hesitating, she wrapped her arms around his waist and pressed her body deep into his back. She held him tight. It didn't seem an odd thing to happen at all. He just stood still and let her do it.

'Come on,' she said.

She took hold of his big, kind, hand and led him to the door. His ears hung low to the ground. Carrie closed the shed door.

'Don't give up on him,' it creaked.

Friday 21st July

Dear Reader,

Sometimes life does not go according to plan; never more so than down on the farm where life and death is the bread and butter of the farmer's daily diet. Sandwiched in between we have to choose the type of filling that we want to eat - what kind of life do we want to live? And after we have chosen we have to make up the sandwich with our own hands. Someone once said that 'the eyes are the window of the soul'. Well I say 'the hands are the *expression* of the soul!'

Hands can be big or small; skin rough or smooth; they can have bits missing; they can be twisted with age or disease. Some folk have no hands at all and have to depend upon the choices made by the hands of others. Babies, tiny children, and animals – *all* completely innocent and dependent upon the hands of others. Your hands! My hands! What kind of hands have you got?

Kind hands? Cruel hands? The choice is yours. The farmer's choice is a matter of life and death every day. A cow will give more milk to the farmer with kind hands than it will to cruel hands. Cruel hands do not make a profit. Cruel hands that cause pain and suffering will reach the end of their sandwich much more quickly.

Down on the farm I have seen the terrible consequences of cruel hands. A lovely young cow was returned to our farm after being previously sold. She had been brutally beaten and abused. Cruel hands.

But down on our farm she was returned to the *kind* hands of our farmer who worked to heal her wounds and care for her. Kind hands. This young cow was lucky. She will stay amongst kind hands now, even though she may never fully recover from her injuries.

What kind of hands do you live with? Kind hands? Cruel Hands? You can choose. You do not have to *have* cruel hands. You do not have to *live* with cruel hands. You can choose. And if you see cruel hands at work on any living thing you can do something about it, can't you?

You can choose! I can choose! Kind hands. Cruel hands. Express yourself! *Choose!*

Saturday 22nd July

Carrie chose. She chose to go back to the farm when sunny Saturday morning arrived.

'I'll go to Debs tonight,' she repeated to herself over and over again as she drove along in her little red car.

'Tonight...I'll do it tonight.'

'Tonight!' sang the beautiful voice on the radio.

That beautiful song from 'West Side Story'. Romeo and Juliet. A beautiful story. Carrie was busy writing her own beautiful story in her head. How it would be on the farm today? A day with Jon?

'He won't sing to me, though!' she smiled.

The thought eased her pain. That terrible, tight, pain in her stomach that just would not go away. It was the pain of terrible emptiness. Terrible longing. An emptiness in her body and mind that longed to be filled. It needed to be filled by Jon. Thinking about it made the pain worse. And she longed to make the pain worse somehow, she just couldn't help it. So she thought about it some more.

And then there was that other terrible, tight, pain in her stomach that would not let her go. It allowed her to breath, it allowed her to watch her own torture. Just as she had watched Debs' torture. And then she had walked away. Walked straight into the arms of guilt. It was very slowly strangling her now. Guilt was a pain that Carrie was used to dealing with; but this guilt was different. This guilt was about someone else and it *was* killing her. So Carrie chose. She organised her pain.

'I don't do giving up about anything and I'm not going to start now.'

Carrie remembered her first aid training.

'When attending to a casualty, you must always attend to your own safety first.'

'D..do you w..want to t..try driving the t..tractor with me?'

Carrie felt safe. Jon had been waiting for her in the farmyard when she arrived.

'What about Jed? Doesn't he do all the tractor work?'

'H..he's g..gone to a f..farm sale with the old m..man,' replied Jon.

'Oh,' said Carrie, trying hard to hide her delight at the prospect of a day on her own with Jon.

Maybe she was going to get her own beautiful story today after all.

'Maybe he will talk to me a bit more if that ghastly brother of his isn't around.'

This certainly seemed to be the case. Jon still found it very difficult to look at Carrie. His eyes were glued to the ground as they walked over to the little grey Massey Ferguson tractor, but he seemed more willing to answer her questions in more detail than was usually the case. He was obviously still very nervous of her because his stammer was no better today.

'Where's Jip?' she asked, suddenly realising that they were completely alone.

'L..left him inside,' said Jon. 'H..he r..runs at the t..tractor wheels - it's d..dangerous'.

'Poor Jip,' thought Carrie. *'He won't like being shut in, but better safe than sorry. I am going to be driving the tractor after all!'*

'What a cute little tractor!' she exclaimed.

She immediately felt her face colour - how could she say something so silly to a hard edged farmer. But it really *was* the most pretty little grey thing. Small enough that a child could drive it, with big, round headlamps that looked like friendly eyes - only the eye lashes were missing. Jon swung himself into the seat and held out a hand for Carrie to join him.

She had to stand on the footplate at his side and sit back on the wheel arch of the little grey tractor. It was a very tight squeeze. Jon's enormous legs filled most of the space.

'Brrrm...brrrm...'

The little grey tractor even made a cute little noise as they chugged away to the fields at the back of the farm. Her knees kept bumping into his legs. She had to grab a hold of his shoulders now and then to balance. She felt very hot and maybe it wasn't entirely due to the sun in the sky.

'W..we're g..goin' to m..mow thistles,' said Jon as they arrived in a field that was dotted all over, in between the cow pats, with clumps of the dark green prickles.

He jumped off the tractor and it was obvious to Carrie that she should sit in the tractor seat. So she did. It was very warm. Jon released a lever at the side of the tractor which lowered the mower that they were towing to the ground. He jumped back on and rested his weight on the wheel arch, as she'd done moments before.

'I'm glad he's not leaving me on my own.'

Carrie was feeling hot *and* nervous now. She didn't want to make a fool of herself. She'd never driven anything bigger than her little red car before.

'I..it's j..just like a car,' said Jon. 'D..drive s..slow and s..straight.'

Jon reached down to the gear stick that sat on a raised platform in between her legs, and put the tractor in gear. The tractor jerked as she released the clutch pedal and they were off. Driving in a straight line had never been so difficult. Carrie could feel the mower behind her swishing, slashing, and tugging, as she sped along; she wasn't actually going very fast at all, but her heart was racing. They were going fast enough for the wind to lash through her long, golden hair. She deliberately threw her head back a bit to feel a bit more wind and sun on her face. She longed to close her eyes and feel the warmth of another face lean over her, but she had to look where she was going, and he was unlikely to do that anyway. But she was wrong.

Jon still didn't look at her, but he leant over her to keep her in a straight line. He reached across and put his hands over hers on the wheel. He whispered the odd word in her ear:

'T..there... l..like that...'

Carrie just smiled and nodded and carried on. Jon sat straddled alongside her. She had no choice but to rest her arm on his legs, especially when they had to turn at the end of the field. Her elbow almost brushed against his groin at every turn. She tried not to stare, not to look, but she failed miserably. Beads of sweat ran down her back. She hoped that she didn't look like the winner of a wet T-shirt contest, but she was so hot by now that she feared the worst. And she had a stomach ache deep down in her groin.

Jon said nothing. Eventually though, she got the hang of driving in a straight line. Jon started to annoy her as he continued to reach over her to correct her movements. She wanted to slap away his hands.

'*I can do it myself!*' she wanted to snap.

When they'd run out of thistles to mow Jon let her drive all the way back to the farm. When they reached the farm buildings he switched off the ignition and jumped down from the tractor first. And, for the first time that day, he lifted his eyes to hers. They were brown and smiling. He even had a little smile on his lips. Carrie smiled back. She was beside herself with excitement. It *was* a dream come true. As she stepped down from the cute little grey tractor Jon took a firm hold of her waist with both hands and lifted her down gently, as if she was made of porcelain. She relaxed and let him do it.

Her dream was coming true and she wanted to enjoy every moment of it. She felt free as a bird as she floated to the ground, safe in Jon's big hands. Jon's big hands didn't let her go. He held her still, his arms wrapped around her waist, and smiled deep into her eyes. Carrie smiled back, as hard as she could. The big hands were holding her head now, fingers wrapped in her hair. Jon leant forward and kissed her gently on the lips. Carrie just stood still and let him do it. It seemed the right thing to do. Then he did it again, and Carrie joined in. And again. And again. It made the pain in Carrie's groin a million times worse. It was lovely. And it lasted for a very long time, until:

'L..let's g..get Jip,' smiled Jon.

Carrie smiled back, as hard as she could. They walked back to the farmyard. She brazenly took hold of his hand as they swung along. Jon said nothing. Back in the farmyard, they walked over to the outhouse where she had spent so much time eating her sandwiches sitting on that hard wooden chair at the little table with the red and white plastic, chequered tablecloth. The door scraped along the ground as Jon pulled it open.

There was no Jip. Cold, wet, and pale, Carrie stood still in the doorway. It was the only thing she could do. Two big hands, closely followed by a big sweaty body, pressed her into the door frame. Two big hands held her head. The fingers wrapped themselves in a tourniquet around her long, golden, hair and held her tight. Jed was grinning deep into her eyes.

'I got you first!' he said.

He laughed into Carrie's pale face. He kissed her roughly on the lips. Then he let her go. He made her forget who she was, where she was, what she was. She was in bits.

———————◆———————

'You bloody idiot!' shouted Debs.

'I know,' whispered Carrie.

'*I know, I know, I know!*' shrieked her head, over and over again.

It was a beautiful sunny evening but Carrie had insisted on staying inside. The sight and feel of the sun on her face made her dissolve into a mush of embarrassment, just like the poor slug that had dared to trespass on Debs' garden path was dissolving in the salt that Debs had just poured out on him.

'I need a bloody big bag of salt to dissolve the pest trespassing in my life.'

For the moment, at least, she could hide in the folds of Debs' soft, leather, sofa, and try to forget the cute little grey tractor, the sunshine and everything that had happened to her today beneath its hot sunny stare.

'Could you *really* not tell that he wasn't Jon?' asked Debs with a gob-smacked look on her face. 'Not even when Jip wasn't there?'

'No!' said Carrie. 'I couldn't! Well, I didn't! I didn't pick up on the clues that were there,' she continued. 'He didn't look at me, and he stammered, but he *did* talk to me more than usual, and he had no problem being close to me, touching my hands on the tractor. And what he said about keeping Jip safe made sense to me,' justified Carrie.

From the comfort of Debs' soft, leather, sofa Carrie could easily logic the whole day away. Unfortunately, there was more to it than that, but Carrie just couldn't speak that truth out loud:

'I didn't read the signs because I was desperate! I was so full of longing and wanting and aching and dreaming. I was full of that song on the radio. I had a terrible pain in my groin. I was hot. I was writing a beautiful story and I was in it. I so wanted it to happen that I couldn't see anything else. And so he got me. He got me really good. Jed knows my truth now and I can't do a single thing about it...'

The truth in Carrie's head gave the pain in her gut a sharp twist.

'Write your story another day, you silly girl! You've come to no harm. Look at the real life sitting next to you!'

Debs was sipping her coffee. She always sat so that she could see the clock on the mantelpiece. Carrie straightened herself up. She sat bolt upright on the edge of the sofa; there could be no more comfort for her.

'Never mind all that. I made a fool of myself and that's all there is to it,' she started.

'It's easy to get caught out, you know,' said Debs, with a slight sigh.

'That sounds like the voice of experience,' said Carrie.

Debs smiled a little smile and looked past Carrie, through the window into the garden. It was now or never:

'I worry about you and Joe sometimes,' said Carrie.

'What do you mean?' asked Debs, squeezing her coffee mug with both hands.

'What kind of hands has he got?' she pressed on.

'You what?!' said Debs, sounding a touch defensive.

'You know I've got a thing about hands...good hands, bad hands, kind hands, cruel hands....Remember what I wrote in the paper last time?'

'So? What's that got to do with Joe - or me?' said a very prickly Debs.

'This is not going well, but I'll have to keep going now.'

Carrie's heart was thumping hard and fast.

'Nothing. Nothing at all. It's just that sometimes I get the feeling that Joe isn't always very kind to you. To be honest, Debs, your husband frightens me sometimes, and I've heard and seen things sometimes that make me worry about you.'

Debs said nothing.

'Sometimes, sometimes, sometimes - it's all the time! I'm glad she hasn't asked me what I've sometimes seen.'

'I'm sorry if I've got it wrong. I care about you that's all. I'm sorry if I've upset you.'

The clock on the mantelpiece ticked along in time to Carrie's fast beating heart. Every second of silence it filled seemed like a minute. And it seemed like hours before Debs spoke:

'He never *really* hurts me,' said Debs to her coffee cup. 'Joe likes a bit of rough. It was just a bit of fun at first...you know...But now he wants it all the time (*Carrie was out in the field watching the bull.*) He says I won't do as I'm told...I try my best...(*Carrie was in the yard watching the lovely young black cow walk down the ramp as best she could.*) Sometimes he frightens me a bit...but if I just let him have what he wants then he leaves me alone (*Carrie heard old man Wilson's voice 'You poor lady, you poor, poor lady.*) I'm alright, really...He's good with his hands round the house (*Carrie saw cruel hands wrapping their big fat sausage fingers in a tourniquet of long hair, tears blurred her vision and she couldn't tell whose hair it was.*) We haven't been married long, I'm sure he'll settle down...I just need to try a bit harder.'

Debs looked up from her coffee cup. She left her words sitting in the bottom of the mug with the coffee dregs. She turned to Carrie who was still sitting on the edge of the soft, leather, sofa and smiled a reassuring smile. Carrie couldn't see it because her vision was still blurred very badly. Debs' hands were holding her face. They held her very still. They held her very tight. They held her very gently.

'Don't worry,' said Debs. 'It'll be alright. You'll be alright and I'll be alright. Right?'

Debs let Carrie go. She made her forget who she was, where she was, what she was. She was in bits.

Sunday 23rd July

'What are you doing dressed like that?'

'I'm not going to the farm today, so I thought I'd have a pyjama day,' replied the pink dressing gown that stood with its back to its mother, making a cup of coffee.

'You most certainly are *not!*' replied the mother.

Carrie twisted her body round inside the pale pink dressing gown in disbelief.

'I thought you'd be pleased! You're always telling me to stop going to the farm! I thought you'd be happy that I've decided you're right, I'm not going back any more - it's too much hassle,' said Carrie, trying to hide a lot of emotions and failing miserably.

'Are you pregnant? Is that it?' asked her very matter of fact mother.

'Certainly not!' exploded Carrie.

'Of course I'd like to have the bit that comes before getting pregnant - but how can you possibly know that?'

Carrie was shaking all over with guilt of all sorts which she tried to pass off as outrage at her mother's comments. She wasn't sure how successful she sounded.

'How could you say such a thing!' she continued, as indignantly as possible.

'I'm not as stupid as you think,' snarled her mother. 'There's something going on with that farmer's son, without a shadow of a doubt.'

Carrie tried to calm herself:

'I haven't even told her there's two of them. How do I start to do that now?'

'It's not what you think at all,' said Carrie. 'They just mess me about all the time. I never know where I am with any of them. I get non-stop grotty jobs to do, and I just don't want to do it any more.'

'Well, if that's really the truth, then I don't know what you're getting so upset about. No daughter of mine is going to give in to anyone. Carice, get yourself upstairs, get into those disgusting overalls, and get back to that farm and finish the job. You're not going to be intimidated by those brutish farmers! Stop dithering and get back in there!'

Her mother's sharp words acted like a starting pistol on Carrie's body. She was in her overalls and getting in her car before she had time to think about what she was doing. What was she going to do when she got to the farm? What was she going to do about her mother? Her mother was weird. What was she going to do about Debs? What was she going to do full stop?

Dad waved to her as she pulled out of the drive.

'See, I told you she loved you!' he smiled.

'He must have heard us, maybe we were shouting!'

The gravel on the drive spat beneath her car tyres as she sped away. Carrie turned on the radio at full blast. A singer sang 'Love Hurts...'

Carrie quickly turned it off and drove the rest of the way in silence.

———◆———

Jip the happy dog was waiting for her in the yard.

'Oh Jip! I'm so pleased to see you!' said Carrie as she fussed Jip around the ears.

'Hello, darlin', do you want to come on the tractor with me? You're late today, aren't you? He thought you weren't coming!'

Jed hugged Carrie from behind. He put his arms around her waist and pressed himself into her back as if he'd been doing it all his life. She pushed away from him and turned round to glare at him. He made her feel oh so hot and bothered and she hated him and herself in equal measure for it. She didn't want to feel like that with him. The trouble was he looked and smelt and felt like that other body, the one that held the key to the locked door of her soul.

There was a sharp whistle from across the yard and Jip ran away in its direction. Carrie ran too. But not before Jed grabbed the back of her hair and whispered in her ear:

'You know you want it! Just remember, I got you first!'

He licked her ear as she freed herself from his grasp. Carrie didn't even look back to swear at him. She knew he would be laughing at her, watching her body move across the yard. She knew what he would be thinking, and there wasn't a single thing she could do about it except get out of the way.

'What am I going to do?'

She was so busy chasing after Jip that she almost missed the glare that Jon flashed across the yard in the direction of his brother. But it was there alright.

'D..did he h..hurt y..you?' he said.

'No, it's alright,' replied Carrie.

She decided to keep quiet. She didn't know if he was asking about just now in the yard, or about what had happened yesterday with the tractor and the thistle mowing. She didn't know how much he knew. Maybe Jed had been bragging, maybe he was just guessing; either way Carrie melted at the thought that he cared about her. It was a start.

They started together now, up the drive and on towards the cows that were waiting to be let out into the fields for the day. The trees in the orchard waved at Carrie as they walked past. She started to feel better; to feel safe. In fact, she found herself running around the back of the herd of cows just like Jip.

'I'm a happy dog again!' she smiled to herself. *'Is this how it feels to belong to him? If only I had soft pointy ears, a warm wet nose and a swishy tail, maybe he'd notice me more, love me more.'*

For the rest of the day Carrie decided to be a happy dog. Where Jip went, Carrie went. There could be no mistakes then. And so, one man and two happy dogs went out in the fields for a day of fixing fences and looking the cattle. The two happy dogs helped the best they could. One kept guard sitting on the back of the trailer or looking in the hedge bottoms.

The other happily fetched and carried tools and bravely held the wooden stake posts as Jon hammered them into the ground with a sledge hammer. The birds were singing in the hedgerows, the cows were mooching around and mooing; that was the only talk that was needed apart from the occasional command from the man to his two happy dogs. The happy crew returned to the farmyard, all pleased in their own way with the day's work.

'I'll p..park up the t..tractor,' said Jon.

Carrie and Jip jumped off the back of the trailer and walked down the drive together. As they rounded the corner to the yard they bumped straight into Jed, who was carrying a long plank of wood. Carrie braced herself for the impact. Jed swung his plank of wood forwards and low to the ground as if he'd lost his grip on it.

Jip yelped out in pain and staggered to one side. He stood with his head tilted; his laughing jaw was hanging loose. It looked dislocated.

'Whoops! Sorry!' grinned Jed. 'Must have caught him by accident under his bad chin. Never mind, eh?'

Jed gathered up his plank of wood and grinned away, blowing a kiss to Carrie as he went. Carrie sank to her knees in front of Jip.

'Oh Jip, Jip. What has he done to you? I'm so sorry, it's all my fault.'

Jip's jaw was showing no signs of straightening up.

'Oh Jip, I'm so sorry,' she sobbed over and over again.

Several days' worth of tears flowed now and would not stop. Carrie held Jip's head in her hands. She held him very still. She held him very gently. Her vision was very badly blurred so she couldn't see the love in Jip's eyes as he smiled up at her through his pain. He eventually managed to correct his jaw and straighten his head. He licked Carrie on the nose, a message from one happy dog to another.

And then, two big brown hands were underneath her armpits, picking her up off the ground. Carrie felt her feet touch the ground and turned round, straight into two big brown arms that held her very still, very tight, very gently. Without thinking, without hesitating, he pressed his body into hers. She stood still and let him hold her. It seemed the right thing to do. She cried until her tears soaked the front of his cotton checked shirt, and she had to move her face to a fresh piece of shirt.

'It'll b..be al..r..right,' said Jon.

Jip wagged his tail against her leg. They made her forget who she was, where she was, what she was. She was in bits; and she wanted to stay that way forever.

———◆———

Red, sore, swollen. Jip didn't mind what Carrie's face looked like, nor did he know that her whole body, inside and out, felt just the same. It didn't matter. It didn't matter to Carrie, either. Carrie and Jip took a detour through the orchard on their way back from seeing the cows out into the fields after milking. Jon was finishing off the end of the day jobs in the milking parlour; he was close by. And Carrie felt safe in the orchard with Jip. He was her four-legged knight in shining armour.

'*Well done,*' whispered the wind through the branches and the buttercups. '*You've reached the next level...love hurts...admit your pain...listen to your pain...speak it out loud...he will hear you call him...do it now...*'

'Ah do,' said an old, familiar, voice.

'Oh, Mr Wilson, you made me jump,' said Carrie.

She was expecting, hoping, for someone else to hear her thoughts. He sat down on the stone bench next to her. They listened to the wind together. But it was silent now; it had nothing more to say. All of a sudden, Carrie had plenty to say:

'Why didn't you tell me you had two sons? Do you know what's going on underneath your nose? Do you know what Jed has been doing to me?'

'I can see what Jon's been doing,' replied the old man.

In the cool air of the orchard Carrie had forgotten her tears and her red, swollen, face. Her old friend guilt stepped in to help her with a cover up:

'He's done nothing to me at all!' she cried, trying not to sound disappointed. 'In fact, he hardly ever speaks to me; it's like being in the company of a stone statue all day! And *why* is he so shy? And *why* does he stammer so? What have you done to make him like that? Why does he do most of the work around here?' spat Carrie. 'And why do you let Jed carry on like he does? It's not fair and it's not right!'

'Well, Mother, for better or worse, I'm doing it. I've stopped dithering. I'm finishing the job with these brutish farmers and I feel better for it.'

The branches and the buttercups waited with her for an answer.

'It's nature's way,' replied the old man eventually. 'There is great beauty *and* cruelty, darkness and light in nature. You can't have one without the other. It's in all of us, whether we like it or not. You must find the balance and then you can live. I'm not responsible for my sons. They've got to choose their own way, whether I like it or not.'

The old man's pale ice blue eyes stared deep into the orchard. Carrie had the feeling that he wasn't seeing trees and buttercups, though.

'But don't you feel guilty?' asked Carrie. 'If you know about something bad and you do nothing about it?'

'Guilt is man-made. It's not nature's way. It destroys. It doesn't want you to live...and you must live, Carrie...You must live as much as you can, every single day, even if it kills you. You must be prepared to step into the darkness, if you want to live in the light.'

Carrie stared at the trees and the buttercups, but she couldn't see them, either. She saw everything else - Debs, her mother, her father, herself, Jon, Jed, Jip, even Mr Pike.

'But what about that poor cow that came back in the cattle lorry?' she started.

'I said live. I didn't say do nothing. You must choose, Carrie...There is always a way...'

And then, old man Wilson chose a way; he walked away from her, through the trees.

'Well done,' whispered the wind through the branches and the buttercups. *'You've reached the next level...he talked to you...called you Carrie for the first time ever...twice...'*

'I want to live as much as I can, even if it kills me,' she replied. *'I choose*

to step into the darkness.'

'There is always a way,' she repeated to herself as she walked away, with Jip, from the stone bench and the sad tree in the orchard, back to the life that was waiting to say goodbye to her in the yard.

Jon chose to look down at the ground as she walked towards him.

'He knows about the darkness...'

She smiled up at him as she said goodbye. Jon still looked at the ground.

'But he has to; he's much taller than me! Choosing works...There is always a way...'

Through the kitchen window Jed watched Carrie choosing in the yard. As she drove away in her little red car, he opened the kitchen door and kicked his leg round the edge of the doorframe. Jip had heard him coming and chose to get out of the way.

'There is always a way,' grinned Jed.

Friday 4th August

Dear Reader,

It's holiday time! It's August! Time for the big school holidays. Buckets and spades at the seaside. A week in the sun. Sitting by the pool. Splashing. Relaxing. Days out. Getting away from it all. Here, in our office, we take turns at getting away from it all. There is always someone to take care of everything whilst someone else takes time out. We work in our office all year round. We expect to get a holiday; we need to take a holiday; we have to have a holiday or we get very cross and upset.

The farmer works the land all the year round. Yet he neither expects, needs or has a holiday - hardly ever. He doesn't get very cross and upset about it, although some folk may say he looks very cross and upset all the time anyway!

I expected to have not very much to write about for you, Reader. The month of August is a fairly quiet month down on the farm. But instead of a bucket and spade, a large brush is put into my hand and I spend hour after hour whitewashing the cowshed walls, preparing for another winter of housing the cows. The only waves I see are white. I still see them in my sleep! Washing up and down the walls, and stirring around the bucket. Occasionally splashing, the sound is quite relaxing. And then there are the visitors; the swallows, swooping in and out. These precious jewels flash blue, emerald, red and white. In all my life of holidays I have never seen a more beautiful sight!

Do you want more colours? More smells? The farmer is out on the tractor trimming the hedgerows. Waves of dark green prickles fall to the ground; be careful of your car tyres as you travel around on your days out. Then there's the yellow prickles of straw bales, which have to be baled up and collected. I lose more purifying sweat here than a week away in the sun.

My nails are manicured by lifting, catching and stacking the yellow bales of straw; into the barn with the hay they go. Priceless winter bedding must be stored.

And still there are the cows to be milked, cattle to be fed, fields to be tended, fences to be mended. Buying, selling, things living and dying all the time.

It's holiday time! We expect to get a holiday; we need to take a holiday; we have to have a holiday, or we get very cross and upset. Time to get away from it all. The farmer neither expects, needs, or has a holiday

- hardly ever. He doesn't have time to get away from it all.

But then, he's got it all, all the time, hasn't he? He has colours, smells, open air, sweat. He has the beauty of living things all around him and something different to do every day. He might have to milk the cows at each end of the day, but he loves his cows and he can have a sleep in between times if he wants. A week in the sun. Sitting by the pool. Splashing. Relaxing. Days out. These are our feeble attempts to create that same 'time out feeling'. Down on the farm, 'time out' is built in to every day by Mother Nature herself. In daily life for us ordinary folk, 'time out' is pushed out, only built in to the occasional holiday here and there. And we are crumbling because of it.

Maybe in this quiet month of August, we can find some 'holiday' in every day. Maybe find some 'time out' - in!

Monday 7th August

It was very quiet in the office. Carrie was taking care of almost everything, or so it seemed. Since she'd been writing her 'Land Girl' articles, she'd had more and more requests from the editing team. 'Carrie, can you just finish this', 'Carrie can you just check that' and so forth. But she was still the office junior making the tea and Mr Pike made no mention of a pay rise. It was very quiet outside the office as well; there was not much news around; the newspaper was getting thinner and thinner and thinner.

The only new news that Carrie could find was the fact that Mr Pike had finally found a secretary. Booming and shining in a silver waistcoat, he oiled the office floor with a new enthusiasm.

'Can't put that in the paper, though,' she sighed.

'Spy Infiltrates Newspaper!

In a surprise move, Mr Charles Pike, owner, and editor-in-chief, of this renowned newspaper, has appointed Mrs Rosalind Greenacre, leading light of the 'Local Ladies Network' and friend and associate of Mrs Jill Langford, as his personal secretary. Carice Langford, our star reporter, and daughter of Mrs Langford, is in shock.

'When I suggested to Mr Pike that he should take some time to appoint a secretary who would understand his needs, I didn't expect him to betray me in this most underhand fashion and appoint my mother's chief stooge! It's difficult enough having to come to work here all week. Being caged in this grey, faceless office with only the smell of coffee, the sound of shuffling feet and shuffling paper to listen to, is cruel enough. And I have to deal with Mr Pike fishing alongside me down the corridor, at my desk and into my private life.

But to be spied on every day by my mother's chief henchwoman is a mental cruelty beyond description! Whatever happened to privacy and human rights? I'll tell you what's happened to mine - they've been bloody eroded! Obliterated! Gone!'

Strong words spoken by our star reporter Carice. These dramatic events have literally just taken place in our office. Mr Pike gave a rousing speech to his staff; he was back at the helm. With Rosalind at his side, the newspaper would now go from strength to strength. Carice is considering her position, but she knows full well she hasn't got anywhere to go. At least she has weekends at the farm to look forward to. She is glad that Dennis, the much put upon editor and brains behind any success that the newspaper has had in recent weeks, is on holiday and didn't get 'roused' by Mr Pike.

Watch this space, readers. What kind of a fish will Rosalind Greenacre turn out to be - a shark, a minnow or an old trout? And what is going to become of our newspaper now - will it sink or swim? And what about our star reporter? Will she ever be free?'

'I'd love to put that in the paper,' chuckled Carrie.

It was the first time she'd laughed to herself in a while.

'Hello, Carrie, dear. It's lovely to see you so happy and enjoying your job,' said Rosalind. 'Your mother will be so proud of you when I tell her.'

Carrie smiled a friendly smile. As soon as she'd gone, Carrie looked in the small ads section:

'I think I need a drama teacher fast if I'm going to survive her being here all the time!' she chuckled to herself again.

'There's always a way...there's always a way...' she repeated.

Carrie went back to living in her head; after all, it would soon be the weekend again.

———◆———

'I don't know why you're looking so happy, love,' said dad.

Carrie had just finished telling him the fishy tale of Mr Pike and Rosalind Greenacre.

'That's bad luck,' he said.

'I know,' said Carrie. 'My mother and the 'Local Ladies Network' are like a bloody mafia! Still, it *might* work to my advantage. With Rosalind reporting back my every move at work, I might not get interrogated quite so much when I get home...hope so, anyway.'

Her dad shrugged his shoulders like a true Italian gangster and smiled. All he needed was the pin stripe suit and Tommy gun instead of oily overalls and a big spanner and he'd be there, in his own gangster movie. But he was too busy dismantling his latest purchase, a vintage Norton motorbike; a 1948. He was as happy as a pig in muck.

'I've been looking for one of these for ages,' he said.

'It's a dream come true! What about you, Carrie? You seem to be a bit happier these days...any dreams coming true for you?'

He knew better than to stare; he carried on working. Carrie tinkered with the tools on his workbench while she composed her reply:

'I don't really know what I'm doing, but I've decided to get on and do it anyway...I'm happier about some things...and I'm scared and worried sick about others.'

'That sounds fairly normal to me,' said her dad. 'You've got a fine set of guts, Carrie, and plenty of them, too. Trust them, fine tune them. Like the valves on this old engine, if you set them up right, they'll never let you down, and you'll run forever!'

'Thanks, dad. I love you.'

Carrie's dad stopped tweaking his engine for a moment. It was the first time that his daughter had ever said those words to him.

'I love you, too, sweetheart.' He tweaked some more. 'And remember, Carrie, if you just try to do the right thing, at the right time, for the right reasons, you can do no more. Things usually turn out for the best, you know, even if you can't see it at the time.'

'I know,' replied Carrie.

After a pause, she said:

'I'm just going round to see Debs.'

'O.K.' said her dad, without looking up.

He tweaked harder at his engine valves. He'd forgotten to tell Carrie about pure bad luck, and how some people get more of it than others.

———◆———

Joe answered the door.

'Hi, Joe, is Debs at home?'

Carrie hoped her panic didn't sound in her voice. Joe was never usually home at this time of night and he certainly never answered the door to anyone. Debs always did it.

'She's home, but you can't see her,' said Joe.

'Oh,' said Carrie as cheerfully as she could. 'Is she alright?'

'She's in bed. Fell down the stairs. She don't want any visitors.'

'Oh my God!' said Carrie, forgetting who she was speaking to for a moment. 'Can I see her for a minute? She won't mind a visit from me - I'm her best friend! Has she seen a doctor?'

'No, and no,' said Joe. 'She's having a rest. I'm seeing to her.'

Joe had about three days' worth of stubble all over his blotchy face. It stuck out from his skin even more as he leered at Carrie.

'You can come in for a bit and talk to me if you want,' he said.

'No, I'll not disturb you if that's how things are.'

Carrie took a step backwards.

'Please give Debs my love, and tell her I'll give her a ring in a day or two.'

'Oh ay, I'll give her plenty,' said Joe, as he closed his newly painted, blue, front door.

Carrie tried to fine tune her guts as she walked away, down the drive, from the newly painted, blue, front door. By the time she'd reached the road, all she'd managed to do was tie them up in some very tight knots. She could barely place her feet flat on the pavement due to the pain of them. Her feet wanted to do the right thing, at the right time, for the right reasons. Now they were walking plain wrong; this wasn't their chosen direction.

Carrie turned slightly as she hobbled past Debs' front garden border that was full of cheerful, bright, pink and white dahlias. She caught a glimpse of the front bedroom curtains swish.

'She's seen me leave...there's always a way...'

Saturday 12th August

For the first time in her life Carrie asked for help. She asked her dad to find out from his mates down at the club what shifts Joe was working this week. She asked her mother to pull a few strings at the factory and see to it that Joe got put back on nights. Her mother was delighted to have something underhand and powerful to do. Her dad didn't need to be told anything; he knew without knowing. Carrie could breathe and eat and sleep and go to the farm on this lovely Saturday morning knowing that on Sunday night Joe would be at work and she could check up on Debs. Not long to wait.

Even less long to wait before she saw Jon again. And she couldn't even wait that long. She'd had to put her feelings on hold for an entire week. Now they all came at once. Wave upon wave of beautiful, excited, happy feelings. As her little red car neared the farm drive bigger, darker, waves started to crash over the top of her warm, gentle ones.

Fear, humiliation, anxiety, dread; they were all there in the physical form of Jed. How was she going to deal with him? Carrie was scared. Would she, could she, ever be one hundred percent sure that she could tell the two brothers apart from a distance? How could she freely give of herself when she wasn't sure what she would get in return? And what about the old man, who told her to live every day, yet didn't seem to want to himself? Those piercing, pale ice blue eyes were always so far away...for some reason his talons had been clipped long ago and he was turning out to be a useless bird of prey.

They were all waiting for her in the yard, with wagons ready to roll. They were going to spend the day carting straw bales. Jon was sitting on the back of a large, flatbed trailer. Jed was sitting astride the tractor, revving the engine impatiently. Either the sun was in his eyes or he was scowling at Carrie as she climbed up on to the trailer to sit with Jip and Jon. The old man sat still and staring in command of a smaller, second tractor and trailer. Carrie looked across the top of Jip's ears at Jon.

'I wish I had you all to myself.'

Jon was looking straight ahead. Carrie put her arm round Jip and hugged him. It was some consolation. Her hand bumped into Jon's arm as she did so. He turned to look at her. For the first time ever, he really looked at her. She smiled back at the face that was so often hidden from view by that shock of wild, long, dark hair. The face nearly smiled back, but turned away just in time to stop itself.

A sudden jolt from the tractor hit Carrie like a tidal wave and nearly gave her whip-lash. She banged the back of her head on the trailer. They'd arrived at their destination; it was a very, very large, empty field of yellow stubble, dotted with what looked like thousands of small, yellow straw bales. Carrie jumped down from the trailer and landed on the stiff yellow stubble. It crunched hard underneath her boots as she landed and scratched her ankles above her sock line.

'Ouch!' she said.

For some reason she saw Joe's face as she bent down to rub her wounds.

'It's only a scratch!' said Jed as he charged past her and nearly knocked her over.

His boots made the stubble crack like the lashing of a whip. It was a hard, unforgiving sound. For the first time ever, Jed seemed to be in a bad mood. Much as she hated it, Carrie preferred the Jed that grinned and said 'Hello darlin', why don't you come with me, wherever...'

'I don't know how to cope with a bad tempered Jed at all. I wonder if the old man has said something to him...or maybe Jon...'

She was glad that she wasn't alone today. For some reason she saw Debs' face.

'Let's get cracking,' shouted the old man. 'Carrie, get on the trailer and stack.'

'But I don't know how to!' said Carrie.

'Show her, Jon,' said the old man.

Jip and Jon jumped back on to the trailer. Jed was already throwing straw bales at them. One after another they came, tossed from the end of a pitch fork.

'S..steady on,' said Jon.

'Y..you h..heard w..what h..he s..s...said,' mocked Jed. 'Got to g..get c..c...cracking!'

'You bastard, Jed Wilson!' mouthed Carrie.

Jed cracked and Jon stacked. Jon stacked the bales in a particular pattern. Carrie watched a bit and then tried to copy, starting down at the other end of the trailer. As soon as they'd finished one layer of bales they started again, overlapping the pattern of bales from the previous layer, like bricks in a wall. The two brothers moved as one, worked as one, breathed as one. It looked like perfect teamwork, although Carrie had the feeling that it was anything but. Every now and then Jed jumped back on the tractor and moved to a new spot for fresh bales.

'We'll never shift all these bales in a day,' said Carrie to Jip as they watched the three men work. 'And they'll never be able to keep this pace up, either.'

Jip was panting. It was a very hot August day already and there was no shade in this field. Every ounce of its soil had been devoted to growing corn. There was no space for lovely trees or hedgerows. Carrie and Jip were in a prickly desert with some pretty prickly companions; it was going to be a long day, and not the day that she'd so longed for.

Still, all was not lost. Once both trailers were full of bales they had to go back to the farm to unload and that involved a tractor ride. Carrie was suddenly getting ready to play netball; innocently manoeuvring her body into the best position as much as she could to make sure she got noticed and picked by the best team - Jon's tractor team. But the old Falcon was having none of it:

'You come back with me,' he pointed at Carrie.

'What about Jip?' said Carrie.

'He'll be right, he'll stay here this time,' said the old man Wilson.

The thrill of the tractor ride, high up off the ground, with the wind in her face and lashing through her hair, her clothes blown back tight against her underwear as if she wasn't wearing anything at all, made her feel as free as a bird. She was loving every minute of it, even though the driver was an icy eyed old man. Carrie shamelessly indulged herself as they sped along. She chose not to look at him but knew full well that he was smiling to himself; he wasn't a fool. He knew what she was thinking, and she didn't care. She carried on living.

'Carice Langford, what's happening to you?'

Nothing was happening, that was the problem. Old man Wilson didn't help her down from the tractor when they got back to the farm. She was pleased about that. She didn't want to be touched by him after what she'd just been thinking about.

The trailers were parked up alongside the barn. An elevator made quick work of unloading the straw bales and then they were back on the road again.

Carrie was expected to stack a trailer on her own this time round. The old man worked with her, passing her the bales. He worked her hard but allowed her to keep up. Jon and Jed still worked at each other like maniacs. They didn't seem to notice her at all; there was something altogether funny going on, and it made her feel as prickly inside, as she did on her shins above her stinky, sweaty, socks. She wanted to be noticed.

She wanted them to see that she was sweaty and working like them, that she could work like them, *and* be a desirable woman at the same time. Even a grin from a bad tempered Jed would have been something. But there was nothing.

It was tractor ride time again. This time, old man Wilson jumped on the tractor with Jed. Carrie completely lost her nerve. She was all fingers and thumbs as she climbed up to perch next to Jon on the tractor footplate. She'd got what she wanted but instead of feeling erotic her body went as stiff as a board. It was a very jolting, uncomfortable ride. For some reason, she suddenly felt very annoyed with Jon.

'You don't talk very much, do you?' she shouted at him over the sound of the revving engine.

'S..Some f..folk t..talk t..too much and still s..say n..nothing,' Jon shouted back.

'Well, I'd better shut up, then. No doubt you prefer the company of your precious cows to anyone else - just like your brother said!'

Jon said nothing. He carried on driving. Carrie was fuming. Any reaction was better than no reaction at all. She wanted him to fight back. Carrie suddenly found a strength and an energy she never knew she had. Back at the farm she was on the trailer with Jon, unloading the straw bales. Time after time, she threw bale after bale at his legs. She was aiming for the side of his knees; she wanted to knock him over. She had a pretty good aim, too. By and large she was unable to get even the slightest buckle from those big, strong legs. You can't fell an oak tree by kicking a football at it, but it didn't stop her trying. Occasionally he looked across at her as if to say 's..s...steady on' but he didn't actually say it.

Carrie felt more hot and prickly by now than an entire field full of yellow stubble. Even Jip just sat and looked at her when they returned instead of giving her the usual warm wag of his tail. Carrie moved as one now with the maniac brothers as they all worked together loading the trailers at a furious pace; she hated them both in equal measure.

She chose Jed's tractor for the next return journey. Once they were out on the road, Jed casually leaned one arm on her thigh and started stroking the side of her leg.

'Get your hands off me, you great big oaf!' spat Carrie as she pushed his arm off her leg. 'And take that stupid grin off your face!' she shouted in his ear for good measure.

'Every dog has his day - and I'll have mine!' Jed laughed back at her.

'In your dreams!' sneered Carrie.

'No, in the barn!' grinned Jed, as he slid his hand up the inside of her thigh.

Carrie slapped away his hand and then slapped the back of his head for good measure. His long, wavy hair was soft to touch and looked just like Jon's. She wished she hadn't touched it.

'What am I doing on a tractor with him?'

They still had one more load of bales to collect.

'This surely must be the last load,' she hoped. *'I've just about had enough of today. What have I been doing all week? Too much hope can be a bad thing.'*

Jon slammed the last bale into place at her feet, finishing the last layer of bales on the trailer.

'Oh no, he's cross with me now,' sighed Carrie.

They were high up on the trailer, standing on six layers of bales. Jon was already disappearing, climbing down the metals rails at the back of the trailer. Carrie followed after him; she knelt down and very confidently swung her leg over the side of the trailer to feel for the first rung of the metal railing. One thing that she wasn't afraid of was heights.

'All done!' shouted old man Wilson from somewhere on the ground at the side of the trailer.

The tractor revved and the trailer jolted as Jed put the tractor in gear. Carrie had barely got her first foothold on the railings. In a total panic she grabbed at the straw bales above her head in an attempt to hold on, but the force of the jolt as the tractor pulled away sent her backwards, flying into the air like a thrown stone.

Like a stone, she fell. Like a stone, she waited to land hard upon the ground. But in a perfect catch, two arms caught her, held her just long enough for the stone to turn into a feather, and then gently lowered her to the ground. Jon kept hold of Carrie. He gripped her elbows with those great big hands of his. Her bare arms rested on top of the hairs on the tops of his arms. Their sweat stuck them together like superglue.

'Y..you're v..very p..precious,' said Jon.

The tractor and trailer had pulled away from them, making its way towards the field gateway. It left them standing together, stuck together, in the middle of the enormous empty field of yellow, prickly, stubble. For a moment Jon seemed uncertain what to do as he looked down into Carrie's face. Then he let go of her arms and turned towards the tractor.

'T..time to g..go,' he said.

Like Adam and Eve suddenly ashamed of their nakedness, they climbed onto the tractor under the watchful eyes of Jip and the sun. They had nearly tasted the forbidden fruit of each other's lips, but Adam had resisted temptation; Eve was sticky, hot and furious.

———◆———

'Don't do that, he could break your arm!' shouted old man Wilson.

At the sharpness of his voice Carrie quickly snatched her outstretched hand and arm back from the space where she'd been dangling it, in between the feeding trough and the hayrack that made a wall along one side of the bull's shed. The Falcon had caught her up and was standing next to her.

'Why?' she said. 'He's a gentle soul. I've stood next to him lots of times out in the field.'

'Not now,' he answered. 'Bulls turn nasty in the month of August; that's why he's shut in here on his own. It's not safe to have him outside in the fields. He's very bad tempered. We won't go in to the shed with him until the 'August bull' is passed.'

'How odd,' said Carrie. 'He looks harmless enough.'

'Things are never as they seem, are they? Be vigilant, Carrie. Always look carefully; be careful you don't get caught out.'

Carrie turned to quiz the old man but he'd already gone. She caught a glimpse of his boot as it disappeared round the corner of the shed. He'd swooped in on her as he had done so many times before, only to fly before she could catch hold of him.

'Be vigilant? What does he see? What does he see in me that seems to fascinate him so? And what has he seen? Does he know about Jed? And Jon? Is he trying to tell me something, or am I seeing things that aren't there…Maybe I am, but I'm definitely feeling them, and so is he.'

She hugged her own elbows. She could feel the warm imprint left by Jon's hands, the look in his eyes as his face had blocked out the sun above her in that empty, yellow, field less than two hours ago. It made her shiver; goose bumps covered her arms but not the warm blood pulsing around her body.

'Too much hope might be a bad thing, but if this is what waiting for my hopes and dreams feels like, then I can stomach it for a bit longer.'

Carrie walked back to the farmyard with her hopes and dreams written all over her face and she didn't care who read it. Just then she saw Jed stride across the yard like a bad tempered bull, in front of her.

He didn't even bother to look at her, let alone read her face. He didn't need to. Quick as a flash he picked up a stone and skimmed it across the yard in Jip's direction. He missed - just. Jed turned back to grin at Carrie. He walked backwards, waving at her, before giving a mock bow and continuing on his way. Jed was pleased; his stone had missed Jip but it had got Carrie straight between the eyes. He'd seen the anger and the fear in her face; he'd shattered her hopes and dreams. It was just a matter of time.

Sunday 13th August

The waiting was over.

'Oh my God!' gasped Carrie and then wished she hadn't.

She stared and then wished she could stop this bad habit. It looked like Debs had applied mostly green, with a bit of purple, eye shadow very badly all around both eyes. It was the shiny, glittery stuff that they wore to discos when they were young and tasteless. The colours still complimented her lovely green eyes but the effect was particularly tasteless tonight; it was like a cuddly panda gone wrong.

'Well I did fall down the stairs, you know,' smiled Debs. 'I'm bound to have a few bruises. They're much better now.'

'It's very bad luck to bruise both eyes the same like that. I'd have thought you'd bruise more on your body than your face.'

'The bruises on my elbows weren't so bad,' said Debs. 'As you say, it was just bad luck...Coffee?'

Coffee was made and drunk, and made and drunk. Carrie put sugar in hers; she needed it. The disco make- up wouldn't go away.

'Do you remember when we used to do makeovers on each other?' asked Carrie.

'Yes!' said Debs. 'Weren't we outrageous!' she laughed. 'What hours and hours of fun we had putting on a face! We should do that again sometime!'

'We're doing it now, aren't we?' said Carrie, starting to feel a bit bad tempered, without quite knowing why. 'Here we are, sipping coffee, both of us putting a brave face on, and not a stick of eye liner in sight. How sad is that!'

'I told you, it was just an accident! You must believe me! Promise!' said Debs, starting to feel a bit bad tempered herself, without quite knowing why.

'That's guilt talking,' thought Carrie. *'Why have I got to promise?'*

'Things are never as they seem,' said Carrie.

'That's guilt talking,' thought Debs. *'What's she hiding?'*

'How odd,' said Debs. 'Maybe I'm seeing things, but I'm definitely feeling them, and you feel very bad tempered tonight, Carrie.'

'Is Joe on nights again?' demanded Carrie.

'Yes, and it's making *him* very bad-tempered and difficult to deal with,' sighed Debs. 'Never mind, I'll have to stomach it for a bit longer - three more weeks, in fact.'

Carrie suddenly wished that she'd carried on waving her arm at the bull and that he'd broken it after all. Then she'd be in 'A and E' by now and not having to listen to the harm she'd caused by getting her mother to meddle in Joe's shift pattern. Guilt was talking, and Carrie heard it. It wasn't easy listening:

'*I've not been vigilant! I've interfered, and now I've been caught out!*'

'I'm sorry,' said Carrie (*'sorry for more than you can ever know'.*) 'I think we must all have a touch of August bull.'

'You what?' said Debs.

'We're all like bad tempered bulls tonight. We're probably not safe in the same room together!'

Carrie tried to sound funny but she really meant it, unfortunately.

'Well you'd better sod off, then.'

Debs tried to sound funny but she really meant it, unfortunately.

'I am tired, actually,' said Carrie.

'Me, too,' said Debs.

'I'll perhaps catch up with you properly next week,' said Carrie.

'Great!' said Debs.

The makeovers had lasted just long enough; their faces were still intact. Carrie walked backwards, waving at Debs, before disappearing into the darkness at the end of her drive. Debs was pleased; she didn't watch her leave. She wanted to be alone. Carrie was pleased; she needed to be alone.

————◆————

It was dark. How could it be so dark and yet she could still see?

'*Where am I?*'

'*You are here, inside me. I'm your Walnut,*' answered the Walnut.

She reached out to feel the smooth, curved walls that held her in the terrible darkness.

'*But you're black velvet on the inside! How can this be?*' she asked. '*Let me out!*' she cried.

'*But you belong to me!*' said the Walnut. '*Time for a tractor ride - hold tight!*'

'*No! Let me out!*' she cried.

Too late, the tractor was already jolting her along in the velvet darkness. She gripped the steering wheel and tried to steer as best she could by the light of her own tight, white, knuckles.

'*Stop! Let me out!*' she shouted.

'*But you belong to me!*' said the Walnut. '*You must go and sort it out. Look him in*' *the eye...look him in the eye...'*

The wind lashed through her hair and made her nipples tingle.

'I knew you'd be back.'

Faster and faster went the tractor. Straight towards the sad looking tree. The branches looked like arms, reaching out to her in a gentle and pleading sort of way.

'Stop! Please stop!' she cried.

The branches of the sad tree held her tight. They scratched her face and tore at her clothing. Big hands came. They made a tourniquet with their fingers in her hair. More big hands ripped at her body, pulling her down to the ground:

'Hello darlin', why don't you come...Why don't you come...come...come...'

She fought the jerk of every word.

'Remember you're a lady,' reprimanded the Walnut.

Eyes were staring at her; bright green eyes flashed in the darkness and charged towards her; green panda eyes smiled; brown eyes grinned into her face:

'I got you first...got you first...'

'Help me!' she pleaded.

'Break me, eat me then,' replied the Walnut.

But she couldn't. The tree and the hands and the eyes held her fast. Her mother was screeching at her:

'You're never setting foot on that farm again...dangerous places...dirty things...it's outrageous...get rid of that ghastly smell...'

"'J' loves his ladies.'

'Oh my God!' she shouted. 'What's that?'

The Walnut pulled a funny face and sneezed. Something long, red raw, and slimy, came towards her:

'Haven't you seen one before?' said the Walnut.

'You know you want it! I got you first...it's only a matter of time...'

She looked up into the darkness. A flash of silver stretched across the sky. The Falcon was there, with the ridges of every feather outstretched above her.

'Help me!' she cried.

The Falcon stared down on her with pale ice blue eyes:

'You're very precious...you're very precious...'

Two big, brown, strong arms were pulling her away. Pulling her away from the tractor and the tree. Her bare, scratched and bleeding arms rested on the top of the hairs on the top of his arms. Jip's happy tail brushed her face. She grabbed hold of it as she was pulled away.

'T..Time to g..go.'

The arms held a very long, black, velvet dress...he caught hold of the waistline as if it already contained the body of a woman inside it. It did. Her body. He kept hold of her. He held her very still, very tight, very gently. He gripped her elbows with his hands. Without thinking, without hesitating, he pressed his body into hers.

'Ah do! I thought I'd seen a ghost.'

'No, it's only me,' said the Walnut. 'You belong to me!'

'No! I belong to him.'

'No, you belong to me!' said the sad looking tree as it caught hold of her hair and pulled her back towards its branches.

'No, you belong to me! Every dog has his day!'

'No, you belong to me!'

The Falcon swooped down on her:

'You can't have it...I have a tree in my orchard...'

The tractor was revving again. Coming straight towards her. Eyes and hands, grabbing, were coming, straight towards her. Quick as a flash she jumped - just in time. She was falling. Down and down. Over and over. The stairs were hard. There was no one to help her. Her ears hung low.

'You poor lady. You poor, poor, lady...'

Two big brown hands were underneath her armpits picking her up off the ground. Two big brown hands were wrestling with the tree branches. Grinning eyes and gripping hands ripped them away from her. The tractor was revving. Louder and louder, faster and faster. She couldn't see, but she could feel the black velvet smothering her.

'Help him!' she pleaded. 'They're killing him!'

Jip was howling. She reached for his face, but his jaw came away in her hand.

'Oh Jip! What have they done to you?'

'Love hurts,' said the Walnut. 'Are you hurting enough yet?'

'Yes! Yes! Please stop.'

'Close your eyes and hold out your hand,' said the Walnut.

She held out her hand. A big brown hand took hold of her little white one. A light behind his head dazzled her. His head was lit up around the edges. He was a golden Saviour. The big hand moved slowly and gently, stroking her hair.

'Help me!' she cried.

'Of course I'll help you, Carrie. It's alright, I'm here,' said her dad.

Carrie grabbed hold of her dad's one good hand and held it tight. Very tight. It was real. She stared up at her dad's face. It was real.

'You've just had a bad dream,' said Dad. 'Remember bad dreams aren't real - they can't hurt you.'

Carrie smiled in fake agreement. Dad smiled. He took the light away with him as he closed her bedroom door. The darkness returned. Carrie turned over and bumped into her bedside table. The Walnut rattled inside it.

'He's wrong,' she said to the Walnut. 'Bad dreams can and do hurt. They took him away from me.'

She took the Walnut out of the bedside table drawer, closed her fist around it and squeezed it hard.

'Let's see how you like being in the dark,' she hissed.

Carrie squeezed a bit harder; the shell started to crack. She slept no more. She could still see the sad looking tree reaching out to her in a gentle and pleading sort of way. Jon was in bits; his body was spread out amongst its blood red branches.

'Help him!' it said.

'It's alright,' said the Walnut. *'It's just a matter of time.'*

Saturday 19th August

Mavis was in charge. She was standing, in her ever frilly white apron, in the middle of the yard talking to Jon when Carrie pulled up in her little red car. She'd nearly crashed into the red brick wall that edged that corner of the yard. Jon was smiling down at Mavis. Carrie could see all his lovely white teeth. He had the same beautiful smile as his brother Jed. She knew it *wasn't* Jed because Jip made up the threesome who were smiling and laughing together. Jon had step ladders, one in each hand. Carrie's joy at seeing him, and seeing *him* lit up with such a lovely smile on his face quickly turned to all out jealousy.

'Why can't he smile like that at me!' she stewed. *'What's so special about plain old Mavis?'*

And Mavis was plain. Carrie felt bad for thinking such nasty thoughts. She was one of 'life's unfortunates' as her mother would so often say. Mavis wore very thick, large, plastic rimmed spectacles that magnified her pale blue eyes quite horrifically. She had a few teeth missing in her smile which she hadn't bothered to replace; she had a slightly hooked nose like a typical nasty witch nose, and a set of long, very fine, white whiskers that would be the pride and joy of any self-respecting cat. But her frilly apron and continually cheerful flowery dress turned her from nasty witch into ancient fairy godmother.

'Hello!' said Carrie.

Jon looked over at Carrie. She was able to share in the lovely smile that had been all for Mavis a moment ago.

'Hello, Carrie. You're going to pick plums for me jam today.'

Mavis might be an ancient fairy godmother but she definitely sounded nasty witch. Her voice was as hard and gritty as sandpaper; the only softness came from the content of her gentle words.

'Just me?' asked Carrie, as innocently as possible, glancing across at Jon.

'Jon'll show you what to do. Been picking plums for me all his life, he has, since he could barely reach the ladder. He's a good lad, isn't he, Jip?'

Jip looked up adoringly at Mavis and wagged his tail. His chin looked very swollen this morning and was leaking a little pus. Carrie looked down adoringly at Jip, with an adoration that was clearly intended for Jon, but she didn't want Mavis to catch hold of it.

An assortment of wicker baskets and plastic buckets were waiting for them at the entrance to the orchard. It was a chilly early morning start. The grass was still wet with dew. It fact, everything in the orchard was wet and glistening in the cold, morning sun. The bottom of Carrie's jeans got soaked as she walked alongside Jon, through the long grass, towards the plum trees in the far corner of the orchard. The rest of her jeans felt equally wet with excitement at the prospect of spending a whole day up a step ladder next to him in her most favourite place of all, this beautiful, peaceful, cathedral of an orchard.

There was quite a breeze in the air this morning; the odd leaf detached itself now and then from the trees and fell soft as confetti on them as they walked together. Jon walked tall and awkwardly with his step ladders. Carrie walked slowly, pulling along baskets and buckets as if weighed down by a long train on a wonderful, if slightly over the top, dress. The trees cheered and waved and bowed before them as they made their procession to the far end of the orchard.

Over in the other corner, the sad looking tree, sitting behind the stone bench, looked on. It held its branches out towards Carrie in a gentle and pleading sort of way. Carrie shivered. All of a sudden she remembered her terrible dream. The sad looking tree was not dripping with blood this morning but it still made her feel very anxious.

'Maybe my dream was a warning about today; maybe Jon is going to fall off a ladder and break his neck! What shall I do?'

There was no need to be anxious. The plum trees were so small that most of the time Jon didn't need step ladders at all. It looked like there was a good crop of plums; the shiny purple fruit almost matched the green leaves in number. Carrie set to with great enthusiasm pulling at the purple juice bombs. Sometimes they exploded in her hands.

'T..twist g..gently,' said Jon. 'It s..saves the t..tree and the p..plum.'

'O.K.' said Carrie.

She didn't like being told what to do, especially when it was something as simple as picking a plum off a tree. And she didn't like the fact that Jon was right. By twisting gently the plums came away easily in her hand and the tree branch didn't slap her in the face afterwards as if to say 'get off me!'

Up and down the ladder Carrie raced with her bucket, emptying it out into one of the large wicker baskets waiting in the long grass to be filled. She hadn't intended to race but, now they'd started, she wanted to pick more plums than Jon; the old Carrie who saw a competition in everything took over. For a time she even forgot to peep through the tree branches to study Jon's upturned face until he said:

'S ..slow is best. L..leave the d..damaged ones a..l..lone, and w..watch out for w..wasps. I'll b..be b..back in a b..bit to see how you're d..doing.'

'O.K.' said Carrie, just beginning to realise what a lot of time she'd wasted with all her racing and rushing.

He was gone now and she couldn't play peep-boh at him any more through the branches. By trying to win she'd lost out on the one thing she really wanted. The orchard was still just as beautiful as moments before but Carrie didn't feel beautiful now that she was picking plums on her own.

In fact, it was quite creepy being there on her own. Jip had gone. Even the breeze had left the trees. Carrie felt cold and goose bumpy despite all her hard work to-ing and fro-ing up and down the ladder. She felt watched.

'You're doing a good job there, missy!' replied a mind reading voice from far away.

It took Carrie a moment to register the familiar voice.

'Hello, Ab!' she shouted from the middle of her plum tree. 'Just a minute!'

Carrie jumped down from her ladder in relief at the sound of the friendly old voice. She ran across the orchard.

'How are you, Ab?' smiled Carrie. 'Would you like a plum?'

'Ay, I wouldn't dare take one, without Mavis' say so!' laughed Ab.

'Oh,' said Carrie, wondering if Mavis would be able to tell how many plums she'd been helping herself to in between picking them.

'By heck, missy, keep thinking as I've seen a ghost every time as I come here.'

Old Ab looked past Carrie far into the leaves on the trees from another time. He shook his head sadly.

'Ah, it were a bad business, a bad business!' he wailed.

'What bad business?' asked Carrie, trying to look at the same leaves on the same trees as old Ab.

Old Ab's eyes came back from the leaves on the trees from another time, and rested once more on her anxious face. He reached out with a long, bony, forefinger and wiped away a trickle of plum juice from the side of her mouth.

'Ah, I'm sorry, missy. Didn't mean to scare ya.'

'Nor me, you!' replied Carrie, just realising that her chin was stained with tell-tale trickles of blood red plum juice and her hair was a bird's nest of wisps and twigs, designed by the unforgiving branches of the plum trees.

'I must look like a ghostly vampire. Please don't tell Mavis that I've been eating her precious plums!' she pleaded.

'Best let sleeping ghosts lie,' said old Ab, looking around at the leaves on the trees once more.

Carrie was used to hearing old Ab's old fashioned little rhymes and sayings, but such was the sadness that darkened his face as he spoke these words, that he made her shiver. Old Ab seemed to really mean what he said about ghosts.

'Ah, it were a bad business...a bad business...'

The bright yellow buzz of a wasp interfered with the question that had formed on her lips. Old Ab batted it, and the wasp, away with one swipe of his withered old hand and returned to being sweet old Ab again.

'Ah well, I'd better be off, then, and get me eggs! Ta- ta, missy, bless ya. And don't fret, I shan't tell Mavis 'owt! Be seeing ya.'

Carrie watched him hobble away. The breeze returned to the trees. The orchard was still just as beautiful as moments before, but Carrie still didn't feel beautiful. In fact, it was quite creepy being there, feeling that she wasn't alone. Carrie felt cold and goose bumpy; watched.

Carrie chose not to listen. She chose not to look. All she saw was plums. If she had looked, she would have seen the daylight changing. If she had looked, she would have seen the tips of the sad looking tree dripping with the blood red light of the sun, reaching out to her in a gentle and pleading sort of way. If she had looked, she would have seen him, the third stone pillar, standing at the gateway to the orchard. If she had looked, she would have seen the fire in his pale, ice blue, stare. Carrie chose not to look. She knew he was there.

———◆———

Debs was in her most favourite place of all; her beautiful, peaceful garden. There was quite a breeze in the air this morning; the odd leaf detached itself now and then from the trees and fell soft as confetti on the path in front of her as she walked slowly, pushing her wheel barrow. The trees cheered and waved and bowed before her as she made her way to the far end of the garden. Behind her the garden gate down the path at the side of the house suddenly clanged shut in the breeze. It made her feel very anxious.

'It's early yet,' she said to herself. *'I should have plenty of time.'*

There was no need to be anxious. Debs set to with great enthusiasm, pulling at the weeds which were quite small and came away easily in her hands. In her garden Debs was in charge. It was the one place in her life where no one told her what to do. Up and down the path she raced with her wheelbarrow, emptying it out into the dustbin by the back door, and then returning for yet more weeds.

'Let's get on with it,' she whispered to the wheelbarrow. 'We need to make sure we finish in time. Then maybe he'll be pleased with me.'

Debs looked far past the weeds into the garden border from another time; she felt cold and goose bumpy.

I never used to like gardening.'

The weeds seemed to be bigger and more difficult to pull now. Debs forgot to listen. She forgot to look. If she had looked, she would have seen the daylight changing. If she had listened, she would have heard the garden gate slowly swing open. If she had listened, she would have heard footsteps upon the path.

But Debs forgot to listen. She forgot to look. Until it was too late.

———◆———

It was late. And Carrie forgot to look. Wasps had been floating around all day, and she'd been pretty good at avoiding them. Until now. Her arms were getting tired and she was snatching at the last few plums on the last plum tree when the wasp crept down the side of her face. She brushed it away feeling that it was just another branch tickling her with its leaves. There was nothing ticklish about the sting that drilled into her temple next to her right eye. Plums flew out of her bucket in every direction as Carrie fell off the step ladder clutching her face in shock and agony. Carrie staggered about, squashing plums and wasps as she went:

'Agh! I can't see! I can't see!' she cried. 'I hope I got you, you little bastard!'

Both her eyes were running and she felt her face changing underneath her hands - she was swelling up! She backed away from the scene of the crime, feeling behind her for the trunk of the big pear tree that she knew was close by. Relieved to find it she relaxed, still holding her tortured face in both hands. She was surprised to find that the trunk of the big pear tree had big arms and big hands that were turning her around and pulling her hands away from her face.

'W..who's a b..bastard?' it asked.

'You are!' she snapped back. 'You've left me alone here all day, picking

166

plums on my own and now a wasp has stung me!'

The big hands pulled at hers again. She resisted.

'It's al..r..right.'

The hands pulled and she was dragged, blind and aching, until she was pushed down. She landed on something cold and hard. It was the stone bench. Carrie was burning up. She lashed out with all her arms and legs at the hands that were holding her down.

'Get off me!' she shrieked.

The hands held her firmly by the wrists. Her wrists were returned to her arms. Her hands had no choice but to follow as they were placed on her lap. She felt the breeze lick her wet face. She felt a warm tongue lick her hands. The big hands took hold of her face for her. Warm breath dried her tears. Like a captured pirate, Carrie opened her one good eye to assess her situation.

Jip was leaning against her legs. Jon was holding her face, wiping away her tears as best he could with his great big dirty thumbs. He smiled down at her with a smile that was closer to her than it needed to be. Carrie was well and truly caught. It was a hopeless situation. So she surrendered.

'The s..swelling will go d..down by to..m..morrow,' he said.

Carrie put her hands on her captor's and tried to smile.

'I must look like the bride of Frankenstein. I feel like it, anyway.'

'Hey!' shouted an unwelcome voice. 'Steady on there, darlin', Jon was only going to kiss it better. Do you want me to do it, instead?'

Jed was upon them in a few strides. He grinned at them both.

'What a shiner! Jon, I'm surprised at you! You should take more care with your ladies. A bit of rough is one thing, but don't leave a mark afterwards!' laughed Jed.

Jon stood up. He towered over Jed who was standing at the bottom of the slope in front of the stone bench. He glared down at his brother. Carrie was burning up again. She took hold of Jon firmly by the wrist and pulled hard. He had no choice but to do as he was told.

'*It's alright!*' pulled her hand.

'M..M Mavis wants the p..plums. W..Wants to make a start on the j..j..jam,' said Jed.

He picked up the two nearest baskets of plums and, with one last grin, turned and walked away from them.

'Bastard!' hissed Carrie.

Like a captured pirate, Jon looked down at Carrie to assess his situation. Carrie still held him firmly by the wrist.

'It's alright,' she said. 'Forget about him, he's not worth it. I'm alright now. I'll pick up these last plums and bring them over. I'm not going to be beaten by a wasp or any other bastard - big or small!'

She let go of Jon's wrist. It was a hopeless situation. He was free.

'Come on, we can't keep Mavis waiting!' she said.

'O.K..K,' said Jon, ever so slightly annoyed she was telling him what to do. But he did it anyway, and walked away from her taking Jip and two plum baskets with him.

The breeze had returned to the trees. The orchard was still just as beautiful as moments before, when Carrie had been able to see it clearly with both eyes. Carrie clearly wasn't beautiful now, but she felt it. She rescued the last plums from the little bastards and sat back down on the stone bench. It was cold and hard. She was all burnt out. The sad looking tree massaged her aching shoulders.

'I can't see you, but I can feel you,' whispered Carrie.

'I can see you and I can feel you,' scratched the branches of the sad looking tree.

Carrie stared, with her one good eye, at the Falcon as he swooped past the gateway to the orchard. It was alight with the same fire that burned in the depths of his troubled, ice blue vision of the world. Old man Wilson chose not to look. He knew she was there.

Monday 21st August

Carrie needed some time alone. It was lucky, then, that it was Monday morning again, and she was back in the busy office. It was still holiday time so it was all hands on deck to make sure that everything got covered. It was easy for Carrie to sit at her desk and look like she was part of the team. She was, she prided herself in being a good worker. She didn't sit around with a coffee when she'd finished one job; she always asked 'what next?' It was easy to do her 'paper work' and let her mind wander free at the same time.

'Once upon a time, there was only 'paper' work. Being professional. Becoming a journalist. Keeping hands clean. Business lunches. Stilettos and pencil skirts. Intelligent conversation with equals. Being seen to be real...feeling real has upset the apple cart...upturned the plum bucket...stung me on the face...'

'My goodness, Carrie dear, what have those farmers been doing to you?' boomed Mr Pike. 'You look like you've done a few rounds in the ring!'

Mr Pike slithered into view. He leaned right across Carrie's desk to have a closer look at her still puffy, slightly distorted face. Carrie could smell the oils that oozed from the pores on his face and the Brylcreem that slinked back his thinning hair; he had more hair on one side than the other, so it slinked sideways - more than a bit off-putting close up.

'Poor Rosalind,' thought Carrie. *'But then, she doesn't seem to mind.'*

Rosalind Greenacre appeared in Mr Pike's wake.

'Oh, Carice,' she said. 'I know all about your face. My goodness, your mother was right, you have made a mess of yourself. I hope it's not going to leave a permanent mark.'

'It's only a wasp sting,' replied a tight lipped Carrie. 'I was picking plums. It was just bad luck.'

Carrie leaned back in her chair to try to put some distance between her face and Mr Pike's. He followed her like an optician examining an unusual eye.

'Well we look forward to some juicy stories from you this week then, Carrie. Eh?'

'Charles, we have an appointment at the bank at eleven thirty,' shrilled Rosalind.

Mr Pike lost his flow and nearly toppled off the desk.

'Goodbye Carrie, keep up the good work,' he boomed as Rosalind swept him away.

Carrie kept up the good work, editing a piece called 'Down Nature's

Way - Insights into Natural Habitats.'
'Poor Rosalind? Poor Mr.Pike! Looks like he's let a piranha into his river bed. It's always dangerous to introduce a predator into your natural habitat. It will take over and destroy...'

Tuesday 22nd August

'Jump in!' said Carrie. 'It's about time we had a trip out. We haven't been anywhere for ages.'

'Where are we going then?' asked Debs. 'I don't want to be late back.'

'Don't worry, we won't be. We'll just go for a drive in the countryside and then maybe stop for a drink somewhere on the way back.'

'O.K.' said Debs, settling herself in the front seat of Carrie's little red car.

Carrie put the radio on low and off they went. Things had been a bit awkward between them recently. Carrie thought it might be easier to relax if they were away from Debs' house; they'd got a bit of bridge building and a lot of catching up to do.

'Isn't this your route to work?' asked Debs.

'Yes, but I'm not taking you to the office,' smiled Carrie.

'Are we going to the farm?' asked Debs, suddenly all excited little child on the front seat.

'Not to it, but past it,' said Carrie.

'I hope we see something or somebody - maybe his body,' she prayed, but she didn't say anything to Debs.

Debs was bouncing up and down in excitement. The trip out was proving successful already; the old Debs was back.

'I'll slow down as we get near so you can have a good look at the farmhouse,' said Carrie. 'We probably won't see anybody, though.'

'Oh, can't you take me for a visit?' pleaded Debs. 'I'd love to see everything; I'd love to see all these strange men in your life - and little Carrie, too!'

'I can't do that, I don't think the old man would like it,' said Carrie. 'And little Carrie's not so little now, she's almost lost her 'cute' factor!'

'Just like you, then!' laughed Debs.

'Don't think I was ever cute in the first place!' said Carrie. 'Not like you!'

Carrie started to sing that well known Christmas carol:

'Ding dong merrily on high, with Debra in the graveyard...Wha...o...!'

Debs belted Carrie on the arm, and Carrie shouted:

'Steady on, you'll have us off the road!'

Debs sang back:

'The farmer wants a wife, the farmer wants a wife, ee- i-the a-d-i-o, the farmer wants a Carrie!'

'Give over! We're nearly there.'

They'd reached the oak tree next to the side of the road where Carrie had 'accidentally' met Jon for the first time. She gave Debs a blow by blow account of where everything had happened.

'It happened such a long time ago,' said Carrie, almost to herself.

'And you still haven't had your wicked way with him, yet!' laughed Debs. 'What are you waiting for?'

'He nearly kissed me,' she wanted to say, but it sounded a bit pathetic so she changed the subject.

'There's the farmhouse. You can look back into the yard as we go past and the orchard is up the drive on the left.'

Carrie slowed down so that Debs could take in all the sights that had become so much a part of her life. Driving past so slowly, it didn't look like anything much at all. It looked small and run down.

'Oh yeah,' said Debs. *'It looks small and run down, don't know what all the fuss is about,'* thought Debs, but she was too polite to say so.

She didn't want to start falling out with Carrie again, when they were doing so well at falling in.

'Can't see any hunky farmers,' said Debs. 'Perhaps they're all down the pub.'

'No chance,' said Carrie. 'They'll be just finishing the milking.'

'Shame,' said Debs. 'I'd love to meet one in the flesh. Can't trust what you say about them - you're a bloody journalist!'

'Let's find that drink,' said Carrie.

The suitably named 'Black Cow' was the first place they came to. All cream and white on the outside, with tubs of pink geraniums dotted about in between wooden trestle tables and benches, the 'Black Cow' looked a friendly enough place. The 'black cow' herself looked down on them from the pub sign as they got out of Carrie's little red car; she was badly painted and had unusually large, staring, eyes.

'Looks like she's had a few already,' said Debs, pointing up at the sign.

'Perhaps they should call it 'The Mad Cow,' and then you'd feel right at home,' said Carrie.

'I'd rather be a mad cow than a stupid cow!' laughed Debs. 'Anyway, whatever happened to all that love and respect for your four legged friends?'

'Nothing, I just want a night off from it all. I want to drink and swear and listen to your terrible jokes that I never get,' replied Carrie.

'One drink,' said Debs. 'You're driving, remember?'

'And,' said Carrie, with great feeling in her voice, 'NO mention of men of any sort! Promise?'

'Dib dib dib,' said Debs, giving a mock salute.

The sky was plain grey, but it was still just about warm enough to sit outside, so they did. Debs sipped her gin and tonic and Carrie had half a Guinness.

'That'll put hairs on your chest!' said Debs.

They had a laugh about all the people they knew with hairy chests; mostly, but not entirely, male. They imagined what sort of hair they'd have on their own chests.

'I'd have a fairly short cut, flat lawn, on mine,' said Carrie, 'and you'd be more rugged mountain, with tufts growing in between!'

Debs pulled at her T-shirt and bared a little more chest.

'Can you see anything growing yet?'

The old Debs was back. They collapsed in laughter over their trestle table; they didn't care who was watching. Well, Carrie didn't care because she didn't know anybody there, and Debs just didn't care.

'Good evening, ladies. You look like you're enjoying yourselves. Do you want to come and have a drink with me?'

The sound of his voice, the feel of his lips as he brushed the side of Carrie's hair next to her ear turned her instantly into stone. She froze. She stopped breathing. The world stopped turning. Debs was smiling and holding up her glass towards Jed as if to say 'cheers!' Debs was looking at him. Debs was in charge.

'No thanks, mate, we're fine. Got to go in a minute anyway,' she said.

Carrie found some breath and some voice.

'Yes, we've got to go. Debs, this is Jed from the farm. Jed, this is my friend, Debs.'

'Darlin', you can come on the farm anytime with me. I'll show you everything!'

Jed was standing behind Carrie. He had both his hands on her shoulders; he was massaging them as he spoke. He held her so firmly that Carrie couldn't escape his grip without making a scene, so she just sat there, paralysed. She knew he would be grinning his best grin, with all his lovely white teeth, at Debs. She knew he was shaking with laughter at her.

'Isn't that right, Carrie?'

Carrie pushed hard with her legs and stood up, forcing Jed to finally let go of her.

'Sorry, but we need to get back,' said Carrie.

'Well, it's been lovely to see you and meet your gorgeous friend. You'll have to come again one night.'

'Thanks, we will!' said Debs.

Debs was in charge. She waved a cheeky little wave at Jed as she walked away from the trestle table. Carrie took her cue and followed Debs. She didn't wave at Jed. She didn't even look at him. She still felt so frozen that she could hardly move her legs. She walked in a daze back to the car and fumbled about in her bag for the car keys. She was in bits.

'Are you alright?' asked Debs. 'You look very pale.'

'Yes, I'm fine,' snapped Carrie. 'I just wanted to have some down time with you, without a man interfering - and not that ghastly man, for sure!'

'Ghastly? How can you honestly say that?' spluttered Debs. 'He's one of *the most* drop dead gorgeous blokes I've ever seen! Why haven't you taken him up on all his offers? I bet he's a really good kisser with a smile like that!'

Carrie put the fan on maximum in her little car; it was getting hot in there despite driving through the grey, still, night.

'And his brother, Jon, looks just like him?'

'Yes, exactly like him. They're identical twins.'

'Bloody hell!' said Debs. 'You lucky bitch!'

'Don't say that,' groaned Carrie. 'There's nothing lucky about it at all.'

'Well, I wouldn't say that,' continued Debs. 'Looks a bit like a case of 'have your cake and eat it' if you've got the appetite!'

Debs made a lip smacking sound with her mouth and smiled at Carrie. The old Debs was back. Carrie jammed the brakes on full and hard on her little red car. The little red car squealed in disbelief; it wasn't used to such harsh treatment. Debs catapulted forwards in her seat; the seatbelt cut into her neck. The little red car slid to an abrupt halt at the side of the road.

'What's up? Have you hit something?' said a jolted Debs.

'No, but I'll hit you if you don't shut up,' bristled Carrie.

Debs started to say 'sorry, what have I said...' but she didn't get that far before Carrie exploded:

'You've got no idea at all what it's like. It's torture...every time I go there! I'm so so desperate to be with him, to see him...to touch him...I so so want him to see me, to be with me...to touch me...and there's that brother of his...always there...always spoiling things...and then when I see him I can't always be sure whether it's him or his brother...and then, I feel so so guilty, I still can't help feeling hot for the wrong one...when he touches me, like tonight, there's a fire in *his* hands that drives me wild...and yet, at the same time, his fire is like a faded candle compared to the furnace I step into when I'm near his brother...it drives me mad...the waiting...the waiting is killing me...and then I feel like a pathetic and useless girl...I'm all in bits and I like it but I don't like it...I don't want to be a girl...I want to be a strong woman...and I don't know how to be...and it's driving me nuts...and then there's all this weird stuff...the old man keeps staring at me...and it's creepy in the orchard...but I love the orchard...and it's weird...they're tearing me to bits and I like it...it makes me feel real...I can't leave it alone but it's killing me...I just don't know what to do...the pain is unbearable...'

Carrie sank her head onto her hands that gripped the steering wheel. The car horn hooted once in dismay. She was relieved it was all out in the open; she was too exhausted to care any more. The grey, still, night sat silent upon the roof of the little red car. Debs sat silent inside the little red car. Eventually she reached out a hand and rubbed Carrie in the small of the back.

'I'm so sorry,' said Debs. 'I didn't know it was like that, and I'm sorry if I've upset you.'

Carrie didn't stir. Debs battled on:

'One thing's for sure, Carice Langford, it's that you *are* a strong woman - a very strong woman. There's nothing wrong with you, so stop all this feeling guilty nonsense. You're in love and you're not used to it...You don't like it because you can't control it. You're letting all these other people and things get in the way of it. You're fighting it and using them as an excuse...You know what's real...You know the truth...It's killing you, yes...because love hurts, Carrie, it really hurts...but it hurts worse if you try to run away from it...It will haunt you forever...like the old man in the orchard...You don't want to end up like him, do you?'

Still Carrie didn't stir; her head wouldn't let go of the steering wheel.

'You know,' said Debs, after a pause, 'do you know what the French word is for orgasm?'

Carrie involuntarily picked up her head and said:

'What?'

'Petit-mort! It means little death. I think that about sums it all up, don't you?' said Debs. 'And you're not going to feel better until you've died, so start saying your prayers and getting ready, Carrie. It's only a matter of time...Now, are you feeling better yet, because I can't drive your car and I need to get home, or I'll really be dead by morning!'

Friday 25th August

Dear Reader,

'Waste not, want not!'

This is the life of the pig. Some cute, pink little piglets have just arrived on the farm. Really cute, really pink and, yes, they really stink! Despite the very unpleasant 'pig' smell they looked so lovable and cuddly when they were first put into their shed. But they quickly started to snout around and eat the cow muck in the straw bedding and the man who delivered them said that if you fell down in a pig shed and couldn't get up the pigs would eat you alive. So I won't be cuddling a pig any time soon!

The pig is an ancient and totally useful animal. It has been a life saver for farmers and ordinary folk throughout history. A pig will eat anything. Anything! It will hoover up vegetable waste, bones, dead rabbits – uncooked - anything. And from anything eventually comes everything.

Every part of the pig can be used - there's meat, joints, sausages, bacon; pork scratchings made from the skin; you can even make a football out of the bladder by blowing it up and tying a knot in it if you really wanted to!

But our cute, pink, useful little piglets quite often get a bad press. And it's not just their smell or their odd, unfortunate appearance as their bodies grow enormous while their floppy ears and little piggy eyes stay small. Their meat and presence is taboo in some cultures; perhaps they are considered unclean because they don't live 'clean'; they will eat each other if they got hungry enough - but would we do that?

How many pig jokes and insults do you know?

'Fat pig' is the obvious one, and there may be some truth in that. But did you know that pigs are very intelligent? They love to play, to explore, to sunbathe, to play football if given a chance! They enjoy music and each other's' company. They are inquisitive and can be trained to perform tricks. They are actually clean animals and won't soil where they sleep. They can't sweat so have to bathe in mud or water to keep cool; they always prefer clean water. They have an excellent sense of smell. *And*, they sleep nose to nose. They sleep nose to nose!

During the Second World War many folk kept a pig in their back garden; a pig can be kept in a very small space quite successfully. They were the family pet that eventually joined the family at the dinner table in person. And much appreciated and welcome they were too. So, how many pig jokes and insults will you use today? It's not really fair, is it? But then, life's not always fair, is it? The life of the average pig is proof of that. Perhaps there is more 'pig' in all of us than we would like to think, and that's not necessarily a bad thing.

'Waste not, want not' is the life of the pig. The pig makes the most of everything it's given, whatever it's given, and turns itself into something really useful. How about you? What kind of an animal are you?

Saturday 26th August

Old man Wilson paused. He'd just let the cows out to their morning grass. He and Carrie watched them go, like proud parents releasing their excited children into a new playground. Carrie had just asked her question. He rested one of his very long legs on the middle rung of the gate. Still as a praying mantis he waited. Carrie stood straight against the gate, a stick insect wondering if the mantis was going to suddenly turn round and bite her head off.

'She died,' was all he said, with a shake of his head.

Carrie realised that her head was still intact so she pressed on a bit further:

'I'm sorry,' was all she said.

'Ah,' was all he said.

'What happened?'

The praying mantis lowered his leg from the gate and became simply a man praying, clasping his aged hands together over the worn edge of the wooden gate; a worn man:

'I watched her die...they called me back from the fields...It was a beautiful day...We'd just had a beautiful night together, the most beautiful night we'd ever had...The lads...they found her collapsed...They were only little, not at school...She'd had a brain haemorrhage. The hospital said there was nothing they could do. They laid her on a bed...laid her out naked on a bed...took away her dignity...By the time I got there...she was shaking...she couldn't stop shaking...I knew she was already gone...I watched her go...'

The stick insect broke in two and became simply a woman grieving, clasping her hands together over the worn edge of the gate; a broken woman:

'Oh, I'm so sorry...so sorry,' she sobbed into the worn edge of the gate.

'Ah,' was all he said.

Still Carrie didn't stir; her head wouldn't let go of the worn edge of the gate.

'You know,' he said, after a pause, 'do you know that she's pleased you're here.'

Carrie involuntarily picked up her head and said:

'What?'

'I feel it. You've come to us for a reason, Carrie. And you're not going to feel better until you've worked out what it is. It's only a matter of time...Now, are you feeling better yet, because I need to get on. A farmer's work is never done - waste not, want not, remember?'

———◆———

Carrie needed to get on. She needed to work. No feeling. No thinking. Plain, honest, simple work. With old man Wilson's blessing, she went back to doing one of her most favourite jobs - mucking out. With every shovel of shit and every bead of sweat she felt better and better and stronger and stronger and freer and freer. She barely noticed Jed sauntering past, except that he had to spoil things by giving her his usual greeting:

'Hello darlin'! Do you want to come hunting with me?'

Carrie looked up from her shovel, not quite taking in what he'd said, so he said, waving his shotgun at her:

'Do you fancy a bit of sport up in the woods?'

Carrie looked at Jed in complete disgust:

'Don't you ever do any work around here?'

'Course I do!' grinned Jed.

Quick as a flash he pointed his double barrelled shotgun up at the sky. There was a deafening bang followed by a dull thudding sound as a crow fell out of the sky and landed near his feet.

'Ah! What did you have to go and do that for!' shouted Carrie.

'Cos I can!' grinned Jed.

'You shouldn't have done that,' said Carrie. 'This bird probably had a mate and young ones to look after. Why don't you think for once before shooting off that big mouth or that big gun of yours? Crows mate for life, you know.'

'Are you a crow then, Carrie? If your mate got accidentally shot to bits, (Jed poked at the dead crow with the end of his boot) would you go to bits and grieve yourself to death, or would you get fed up after a while and look for a bit of something else, even if it was a rook or a magpie, to tide you over?'

Carrie shivered. She stooped down in front of Jed and snatched the dead crow away from him. She wanted to protect it, even in death, from Jed.

'You're a callous bastard, aren't you?'

Jed laughed out long and loud.

'Carrie, you sound like you're starting to care about me!'

Jed stroked the barrel of his shotgun.

179

'I'm a good shot, Carrie! Straight up!'

Carrie stood her ground as he walked towards her. Jed made to push the barrel of the gun in between her legs but she saw it coming and moved out of the way.

'You're nuts!' said Carrie.

'All the compliments on one day!' said Jed. 'I'm a lucky man!'

He walked towards her again but Carrie held out the crow in front of her, its blood dripping from her hands, as if it was some sort of talisman. The crow, even in death, was protecting her from Jed. It did the trick because Jed froze as if he'd seen the ghost of the crow in front of his eyes:

'Well darlin', I'm just off up the fields to shoot some rabbits for dinner. As I said, you're welcome to come along. I'm a good shot and I always get what I want. Why don't you stay for some rabbit stew afterwards - Mavis is a good cook, you know!'

Jed gave Carrie his best smile and waved at her with his gun in farewell. Carrie gave him her best sneer and backed away from him.

'I'm so sorry,' she said to the crow. 'I've been the cause of your death.'

Carrie mourned the life of the crow before placing him in her wheelbarrow of shovelled cow muck like a true unsentimental twentieth century land girl. She returned to her shovel, to her beloved work. She didn't see the other bird that had been hovering, watching, protecting. The Falcon had seen and heard everything and then he flew away.

————◆————

There was beautiful singing. Yodelling. It was very loud and very good. It filled the milking parlour and the surrounding cowsheds.

'Jon's got the radio on loud tonight,' Carrie said to the calves that she'd just finished feeding.

She was in the corner shed and stood, rubbing her backside. Little Carrie was sharing this shed with three other calves. Little Carrie had just turned round and kicked big Carrie on the backside with both back hooves.

'Fine payment that is for feeding you, you ungrateful child!' rubbed Carrie.

Maybe it was just her imagination, but the calves appeared to pause with her to marvel at the sound of singing that broke the silent antics in their shed. Carrie went to her little spy hole. There was a gap in between the planks of wood that made up the shed wall that was shared by the milking parlour at one end. At every opportunity she spied on Jon through this little hole in the wall at milking time. It was a guilty pleasure that she'd been enjoying for quite some time.

Quite often there wasn't much to see. Quite often the cows got in the way. But quite often she got a close up look at his lovely long hair as he bent down to feed or fuss one of his ladies. Sometimes she even got a close up look at his butt. Very often she wished that she was one of Jon's ladies, wished that he would bend over her and lean his lovely long hair against her flank, wished that he would see to her needs. Very often also a large spider would appear above her head and chase her away. And then the calves would jump around her again, wanting to play, and that would be the end of her imaginary playtime with Jon.

Tonight was different. Tonight he was singing. Carrie could see his beautiful teeth inside his beautiful mouth. She could see his beautiful tongue and the beautiful smile on his lips as he moved from cow to cow. His beautiful mouth was wide open, letting out a flow of sounds at full volume. Not words, but sounds. Syllables. It didn't matter that they had no meaning. They meant everything to Carrie.

'He looks happy!' she whispered to the calves. 'I wonder what he's thinking about? Do you think he's thinking about me?'

Carrie desperately wanted to stay and listen some more but she still had the baby calves to feed in the next door shed. It was a real struggle to carry six buckets, each half filled with milk, from the outhouse near the farmhouse door to the calf shed without spilling any of it, but she just about managed it every time. Tonight was different.

Jip appeared from nowhere, and so did Jon. He took hold of three of her buckets from her left hand and walked along with her to the calf shed. Carrie smiled her thanks to him. She knew better these days than to try to start a conversation with him, especially when there was no need. They fed the calves together.

When Carrie had finished feeding her three little charges, she waited for Jon to do the same. He got the awkward one at the end of the shed, who wouldn't drink. He got his trousers soaked with milk, trying to make it take the milk from the bucket with his finger. He swore softly underneath his breath. Carrie leaned on the straw bale wall of her calf's compartment and watched him struggle. She smiled to herself, like a true, unsentimental Land Girl, that she could do a better job than him with this awkward little calf. She enjoyed watching him struggle. When he'd finished and climbed out of the calf's little compartment, she was still smiling at him.

'W..What?' he said.

'I heard you singing tonight,' she said.

'Oh,' he said.

'You're very good,' she said.

Jon changed colour in the glow of the golden halogen calf lamp that heated the calf's living space.

'The c..cows like m..music. They g..give m..more m..milk if they're relaxed.'

'It made me feel relaxed, too,' said Carrie, digging her elbows deep into the top of the straw bale wall.

They both stared at the golden light from the calf lamp. It was lovely and warm. They stood together, bathed in the tiny pool of light. The rest of the calf shed disappeared into darkness; it could have been an eternity deep. After an eternity, she said:

'Do you want to kiss me?'

After an eternity he replied. It lasted for an eternity. Except that he didn't really know how to do it. But it didn't matter. She reached her arms up and held his hair gently in her hands. She pressed her whole body into his. She got her trousers wet with milk from leaning against his trousers. He pressed his lips gently onto hers and had no choice but to put his arms around her because she was standing so close to him. Except that he didn't really know how to do it. But it didn't matter. It lasted for an eternity. That was all that mattered.

They both shared the golden light from the calf lamp. It was lovely and warm. They were lovely and warm. They stood together, bathed in the tiny pool of light. The rest of the calf shed disappeared into darkness; it could have been an eternity deep. After an eternity Jip growled. A shadow passed across the windows of the calf shed.

'You go f..first,' said Jon.

'O.K.' said Carrie.

Quiet as a mouse Carrie slid open the shed door and looked outside. But there was nobody there. She picked up her buckets and bolted.

Jed was in the yard. He swung a dead rabbit in front of her face as she returned the calf buckets to the outhouse. Jon walked past on his way to the milking parlour; he was singing. Carrie didn't see the rabbit. Jon didn't see Jed. Jed didn't see Jip, sniffing at his rabbit. And all the while the falcon hovered. He'd seen everything that he needed to see and then he flew away. Into eternity.

Part Three

Autumn –
'All Is Gathered In…'

Saturday 2nd September

Something was wrong. Jip was sitting in the middle of the yard. He had a length of baler twine tied to his collar. He looked down at the ground just like his master. Except the master holding the other end of the baler twine this morning was Jed. Carrie exploded out of her little red car.

'What are you doing to Jip? Let him go!'

'No chance. Jip's with me today. I'm in charge, and he's going to learn some manners,' said Jed, as he gave Jip's makeshift lead a hefty tug.

'You can't do that! He's Jon's dog, not yours!'

'And he's not yours either,' said Jed. 'I think it's about time you learned some manners as well. I'm the boss today and you'll have to do as you're told, Miss Tight Lipped, Tight Legged, Land Girl.'

'You'll never be the boss of me,' snapped Carrie, 'and you'll never be the boss here either, not while Jon and your father are around!'

Jed laughed.

'Well, they're not here today. They're busy being good neighbours, helping a farmer whose herd's got to be put down 'cos they've got TB. They'll be gone *all* day!'

Carrie suddenly found she'd lost all feeling in her legs. After going home from the farm last weekend, after a whole week of sleeping in her bed, getting up every morning, having a shower, eating breakfast and going to work at the office, her legs had stayed wet with milk from when she'd pressed herself against Jon's trousers in the calf shed. Her legs had taken it for granted that they'd be doing a bit more pressing today; that she'd be getting wet again today.

'Here!' grinned Jed.

He rooted around in one of his pockets and then threw something at her. Her reflexes caught it. It was a length of baler twine.

'Now, are you going to do as you're told, or do I have to tie you up by the neck as well?'

Carrie suddenly found that she'd lost all control of her legs. She was moving now, like a big cat that had just had its kill taken away from her. With a silent shriek and claws extended she lashed out at the predator who had just taken away her means of survival. Jed saw her coming and moved out of the way; he had to move several times because the big cat was a viciously angry cat by now.

'Whoa there!' he half laughed, half shouted. 'You'll frighten Jip!'

Jip! Jip!

The name trickled down Carrie's miaowing nerve endings and reached her legs. She slowed to a stop. She had to protect Jip.

'Jed!' screeched a voice from the farmhouse door. 'Stop mucking about! Those cows need seeing to, and the pigs still need feeding. And Carrie, love, you're going to pick damsons for me jam today.'

It was Mavis. Mavis was in charge.

'She can do the mucking out first!' Jed shouted back at Mavis.

'You heard me the first time, Jed Wilson! He says *you're* to do the mucking out and Carrie's to have the day in the orchard; it's damson time and he knows it.'

'Well he's not here today, I am!' replied Jed, less than politely to the fairy hagmother who brandished her duster at him as if she was about to blow him away with one flick of her wrist.

'And so am I, so you'd better get on. It's about time you learned some manners, young Jed. He'll have to do as he's told, won't he, Miss Carrie?'

Carrie nodded agreement with Mavis and smiled her best smile at Jed. 'Here!'

She held out her hand and offered the length of baler twine to Jed.

'Now, Jed, are you going to do as you're told, or does Mavis have to tie you up by the neck?'

Jed glared at Carrie and, with an almighty yank on Jip's baler twine, started off across the yard towards the cow sheds dragging Jip behind him.

'And let go of that dog!' shouted Mavis. 'He's to stay with Carrie in the orchard - Jon says so!'

Carrie thought Jed was about to argue with Mavis again, but obviously he thought better of it because he let go of his end of the baler twine. Jip ran straight to Carrie. He didn't need words to tell her how relieved he was to be free. Carrie undid the baler twine from his collar and he licked her hands in gratitude. Carrie suddenly found all the feeling back in her legs as she knelt at Jip's side; she pressed herself against his warm body. She was wet with milk again.

Carrie stood up and looked up at the sky. It was a funny colour this morning, neither white nor grey nor blue, but all of them at the same time.

'Come on, Jip, let's make a start. I think there's a storm coming.'

Jip wagged his tail. His chin looked good today. The lead sky pressed down heavily on them as they made their way to the orchard. The trees of the orchard propped up one little corner of sky, like a bed frame holding up a heavy blanket over injured legs, to let Carrie and Jip pass under it.

It was dark underneath the orchard blanket. The air was thick with an oppressive heat, but Carrie and Jip were happy together beneath the little damson trees. They felt safe. Occasionally, far off in the distance, they heard a gate clanking and Jed swearing. It was merely an echo from another time and another place. It had no meaning to Carrie and Jip; they were far away in their own beautiful world, and nothing and nobody could take that away from them.

The damsons were small, dark and sweet. They matched the colour of the air this morning. They were easier to pick than plums because there were thousands of them in one place so Carrie didn't have to move her step ladder so often in order to fill her bucket. There was beautiful singing. Yodelling. The sound cut through the heavy air and filled the orchard.

'It's me!' marvelled Carrie.

Not words, but sounds. Syllables. It didn't matter that they had no meaning. They meant everything to her. Carrie was about to burst into song again when she heard Jip growling. A shadow passed over them.

'What's up, Jip?'

Jip hugged the bottom of the step ladder and whined up at her. Carrie climbed down the ladder and stroked the top of his head. Jip wagged his tail but his ears stayed flat.

'It's alright, Jip, it's alright.'

Just then the ground rumbled beneath their feet. Jip trembled and pressed his body against hers. Carrie looked around. Bathed in the warm light of her own beautiful thoughts and feelings, she hadn't noticed the darkness creeping towards them. Carrie and Jip could not escape the storm which was bearing down on their beautiful world. The trees of the orchard were struggling to keep the sky from falling in on them.

Thunder rumbled through them once more. Even the leaves on the damson trees sat still, holding their breath. The sad looking tree in the corner of the orchard looked straight at Carrie. Black and menacing, it seemed to be using its branches to climb over the stone bench. It was coming straight for Carrie and Jip.

Just then there was an enormous clap of thunder. Jip yelped. Carrie ducked down in panic. Was it Jed with his shotgun, fooling around? By way of answer, a flash of purple lightning lit up the orchard, proving that there was no Jed. There was just a beautiful orchard, a girl and a terrified dog, caught together, in a terrible storm.

'Come on Jip, we need to get away from these trees,' whispered Carrie.

She didn't want the storm to know that they planned an escape. She was too late. Jip bolted out of her arms and ran at top speed towards the farm buildings. Carrie ran after him as fast as she could but she couldn't catch him; he'd disappeared. Out on the farm drive, free from the clutches of the dark and menacing sad looking tree, Carrie looked up at the sky. Even as the leaves on the damson trees, she stood still and held her breath. She bathed still, in the strange, golden light, yet the sky above her was pitch black. In the black light, clouds bubbled across the sky in diagonal patterns of the most intricate, frilly lace. Delicate and oh so breathtakingly beautiful; violent and oh so deadly.

Then came the rain. Arranged into large sheets as hard as steel, it fell into the ground and made an impenetrable wall around her. Carrie was trapped. She could barely see the farm buildings in front of her. Craters appeared in the dry dust of the drive. Instinct took over and, just like Jip moments before, she bolted in the vague direction of the red brick buildings. The rain stabbed her in the back like knives, falling from a box held up at great height. She didn't stop running until she reached the safety of the newborn calf shed. The calves were quiet; surprised, but still pleased to see her.

'I didn't see this coming,' she said to the calves as she shook the wet off her body. 'I hope Jip's alright.'

Carrie stared at the golden light from the calf lamp. Last Saturday she was wet with milk in here. She dug her elbows into the top of the straw bale wall like a true, unsentimental, twentieth century land girl. She remembered. Then she remembered Jip.

'Poor Jip, he must be terrified. I must find him.'

A shadow passed across the windows closely followed by a blinding white light.

'Looks like it's over,' she said to the calves.

Quiet as a mouse she slid open the shed door and looked outside. There was nobody there. And no Jip.

Jed was in the yard.

'Have you seen Jip?' she asked him.

'He wouldn't come with me to fetch the cows in, so I've given him a good thrashing,' replied Jed sounding very satisfied with his day's work.

'You bastard!' shouted Carrie. 'He was terrified of the thunder. He wouldn't have gone out in it, even with Jon. Where is he?' she demanded.

Jed paused to enjoy a grin at Carrie.

'He's up the yard. You haven't done a very good job of keeping an eye on his precious dog, have you? What's he going to say about that?'

Jed laughed at Carrie but she was already gone. She ran at top speed up the drive. Jip was tied to the gate that let the cows in from the field with a length of baler twine. He was stuck to the gate, so tightly was he tied by the twine. He looked down at the ground just like his master. He was soaking wet. His chin was bleeding. He held his mouth open, with his jaw to one side, as if he was laughing his head off. Carrie wasn't laughing.

'Jip! Jip!' she called softly as she reached the gate.

Jip kept his eyes firmly fixed to the ground. He trembled as Carrie worked to untie the baler twine from the gate; the knot was pulled so tight it was impossible. In the end, Carrie undid Jip's collar instead. Jip just stood still and let her do it.

Without thinking, without hesitating, Carrie picked him up and carried him to the calf shed. It seemed the right thing to do. She lifted him over the straw bale wall of the nearest cubicle and placed him gently underneath the calf's halogen heated lamp. The calf backed itself into a corner at the sight of the dog. Carrie sat down on the muck soaked straw and cuddled Jip dry as if he was a childhood long lost teddy bear. She held Jip long after he dried, long after he stopped trembling, long after his jaw had stopped laughing and returned to normal.

'Oh I'm so sorry, so sorry,' she sobbed into the warm, aching fur that was breathing life into her hands.

'It's alright,' licked Jip.

The girl, the dog and the calf shared the golden light from the calf lamp. It was lovely and warm. They sat together, bathed in this tiny pool of light. The rest of the calf shed disappeared into darkness; it could have been an eternity deep. They felt safe.

After an eternity the door to the calf shed slid open. Jip looked up to greet his master. He held Jip's empty collar in his hand. Now it was Carrie's turn to look down at the ground. Jon climbed over the straw bale wall, banging his head on the calf's halogen lamp. The tiny pool of light spun out of control and lit up the darkness that surrounded them.

There was no more dark. He knelt down on the muck soaked straw and put his arms around Carrie and Jip. He held Carrie long after she'd stopped trembling, long after Jip had finished licking his hands. He lifted her tear drained face and kissed her gently on the forehead.

'Oh I'm so sorry, so sorry,' she sobbed into the big, warm, hand that was holding her face.

He kissed her again. He really knew how to do it this time. So did she. He pressed his whole body into hers. He got his shirt wet from the rain on her back. Jip panted in the heat. It lasted for an eternity. The girl, the man, the dog and the calf shared the golden light from the calf lamp. It was tropical. They sat together, bathed in wonderful, golden light. They felt safe. They were far away in their own beautiful world, and nothing and nobody could take that away from them.

————◆————

'It's a 1933 Brough-Superior!' said Bill, shining with pride as brilliant as the silver exhaust pipe that he'd just finished polishing.

'Is that good?' asked Carrie, not really interested in getting an answer.

'Good! It's amazing! I've always wanted one, all my life!' shone her excited father.

Carrie smiled at her dad. To the rest of the world, even to her mother, he might look like a gentle, middle of the road type of guy, but Carrie could see and feel his youthful passion right now as he caressed his beloved vintage motorbike.

'*That's why we get on so well,*' thought Carrie. '*He knows passion, lives it, understands it. He would understand if I told him...*'

Passion continued:

'They were known as the 'Rolls Royce' of motorcycles. Did you know that Lawrence of Arabia was killed riding one of these at ninety miles an hour?'

'Oh,' said Carrie, thinking that Lawrence of Arabia was better known for riding camels in the desert, fighting and having a famous film made about him, than motorbikes.

'How much did this cost you, then?'

'Best not go there,' smiled her dad. 'But safe to say I shan't be buying any more bikes after this one. Did you know that the neurosurgeon Hugh Cairns was so upset that he couldn't save Lawrence of Arabia after his accident that he went on to invent the crash helmet?'

'No, I didn't know that,' said Carrie, wondering how or if she could somehow use these useful facts for her next 'Land Girl' article, and save herself a bit of time and trouble.

'It just goes to show,' said Bill as he paused to find a fresh chamois leather, 'that something good always comes from something bad, one way or another, even if we can't see it at the time.'

'Maybe,' said Carrie. 'But sometimes, aren't there just some people who are just plain bad, through and through, and nothing good will ever come from them?'

Jed, for example...'

'There's always a reason for it somewhere, Carrie. Always choices to be made. There's good and bad in all of us. Nobody can be good all the time, not even your mother!'

Carrie laughed. It was a relief.

'I don't know what's most funny - the thought of mother being bad, or being good!'

'And exactly what do you mean by 'bad' and 'good, anyway?' said her dad.

Carrie squirmed.

'He knows about the calf shed. Does that make me bad or good?'

'It's just best not to judge folk in the first place; then life's a lot better!' he continued. *'And,* don't be too hard on yourself, either.'

Bill was polishing hard, he was on to the fuel tank now.

'He knows about Jip. How can he know?'

'How's things down on the farm, these days? You don't seem to want to talk about it so much when you get home.'

'I suppose I'm just too worn out from the physical work,' said Carrie, starting to edge towards the garage door. 'I've been picking damsons all day today, I got soaking wet in a terrible storm, and I ache all over *(in heart, mind, body and soul).'*

'I suppose you are, then. Just be careful they don't start to take advantage of you, that's all. You know what men can be like.'

Bill wasn't looking at her, but Carrie knew he could see her, nevertheless.

'He knows. How can he know?'

She opened the garage door and put one foot outside.

'Yes, Dad, I know. I'm fine. I shall have muscles as big as yours by the time I've finished.'

'I'm not so sure that's such a good idea,' said Bill, flexing his one good hand at her.

'Anyway, I've got a pot of plum jam in the car that Mavis gave me. I'd better get it inside before it starts to melt.'

Bill waved his chamois leather at Carrie in farewell but she'd already gone. He looked at the door as it closed shut. For the first time, Carrie had closed the door on her life to him. Bill hoped that she'd closed it for the right reasons. He hoped that it would only be temporary. He only had one good hand and it took all his strength to keep his wife's door ajar. He reached for his oil can. It was empty.

'Better get some more!'

He had a feeling that he'd be needing to pour oil on more than his beloved Brough-Superior motorbike before the year was out.

———◆———

'Mavis has sent you some plum jam.'

'Oh, that was very kind of her.'

Carrie's mother took hold of the glass jar that was being held out to her with one finger and one thumb. She carried it at arm's length across the kitchen and put it on the worktop. She backed away from the dark purple contents as if Carrie had just given her a jar of the most deadly poison.

'Mavis says it'll make a good Bakewell tart.'

'Well I'm sure we can use it for something.'

'Yeah, like poisoning next door's cat!'

Carrie longed to say it, but sarcasm was pointless with her mother. It would have just started a row about how she didn't really have anything against next door's cat, even though it did use her lawn as a toilet far too often. Still, she couldn't help feeling a stab of pain at her mother's obvious loathing and rejection of Mavis' gift. It was her achievement too; she'd picked the plums that had made the jam. A lot of love had gone into that jam in more ways than one.

'But she wouldn't understand anything about that. She doesn't want to know. I'm on my own.'

So instead, Carrie took the path of least resistance:

'Dad and I can use it on our toast in the mornings.'

'Well, I'm not sure about that,' said her mother. 'I never buy homemade produce from anywhere. You just don't know what's in it, or how clean people are.'

'Mavis is perfectly clean!' said Carrie.

'I'm sure she is, but it still might be best to pass it on at the next bazaar.'

'Bazaar! You're bizarre!'

Carrie said nothing. She was used to knock backs great and small; it hurt the same, whatever the size. She shut down. She sat frozen in her seat, waiting for her mother to leave the room, waiting to be free again. She achieved some warmth in her soul by thinking about Mavis.

'I've never ever seen Mavis wash her hands, even after she's just fed the pigs or let the hens out. The pigs and the hens share the same apron with the cooker and the tea

towel!'

When her mother had left the kitchen Carrie made a piece of toast and opened Mavis' jam. She spread a thick layer onto her toast. She ate without a plate. She let the crumbs and droplets of jam fall onto the polished, wooden kitchen table. It was delicious. Carrie felt delicious. She smiled to herself:

'I'm unclean, and I love it!'

Carrie hid the jar of plum jam at the back of the kitchen cupboard.

'I'm going to keep you all to myself,' she said to the jar.

She wasn't ready to share her love with anyone. She cleaned the polished, wooden table before she left the kitchen. She needed to keep her secret safe.

———◆———

'Bloody hell! It sounds like you've died and gone to heaven!' spluttered Debs.

'Well, not quite,' replied Carrie, 'but I'm on the way, aren't I?'

'Bloody hell!' said Debs again. 'This is getting more exciting than anything that's on the telly. It's making me go hot and cold just thinking about it!'

Carrie squirmed and squeaked, deep into Debs' lovely, soft, leather, sofa - there wasn't anything comfy like this to sit on at home, let alone slouch into. Carrie slouched now. She relaxed into her embarrassment with pride; she'd floated her friend's boat just by telling her what happened in the calf shed, and that wasn't really all that much. She smiled at Debs who was squirming around, tucking her legs underneath her body and smoothing down her disturbed T-shirt.

'Ooh!' she moaned, 'tell me again, quick. And don't miss out any details - I want to know every last little thing!'

'Give over!' groaned Carrie, 'I've told you twice already! It's not that exciting compared to what you've got up to in your time!'

Carrie immediately wished she hadn't said that; they'd been having such a lovely time together. She didn't want to hurt Debs; remind her of things that she might be trying to forget. Carrie held her breath.

'I tell you straight, Carrie, what's happening to you is a *million* times more exciting and erotic and passionate than anything that's happened to me! You can't compare it to a quick fumble in the bushes, even if I have done it a lot more times than you. So, come on, tell me again!'

So Carrie told her again. Debs' lovely, soft, leather, sofa squeaked and squirmed and tossed and turned in all directions.

'Do you know,' said Debs, when Carrie had finished her tale for the third time, 'we should write all this down and send it off to the BBC. It would make the most fantastic drama series!'

Carrie squirmed and squeaked.

'Just imagine it!' said Debs.

'I don't need to imagine it, but clearly you are!'

'Ooh! Hot, hot, hot! Actually, we'd better not send it to the BBC, I think it's going to end up more porn than Saturday night drama. We might have more luck sending it to a film company, one that specialises in Certificate 18! Do you fancy playing yourself, Carrie, or can I be your stuntwoman for the love scenes!'

Carrie threw a fluffy cushion at Debs' and pounced on her. Debs wrestled her off. Debs was laughing. Carrie was laughing too, but her laugh sounded a bit hollow next to Debs'. Carrie hadn't imagined like Debs. The trouble was, Debs' imagination contained alarm bells of truth.

'Debs dreams it all and it's just a film on T.V. I'm living it all. I am a dreamer by day. It's dangerous and real. I'm dangerously real.'

Friday 8th September

Dear Reader,

September came in, dark as a damson. Beware! The world will erupt! There will be fire and earthquakes, volcanoes and hurricanes! This is what the Romans believed about the month of September. September was ruled for them by the God Vulcan, the God of fire and forge. And Michaelmas Day, St.Michael's Day, is the 29th September. St.Michael was the angel who hurled Lucifer (the Devil) out of heaven for his treachery.

Michaelmas Day marks the end of the harvest season and heralds the beginning of nature's move towards winter, as the nights start to draw in. 'All change!' shouts this little month of only thirty days, as the year moves from the glory of summer and harvest to the sadness and grief of the return to winter. Everything is getting ready to die to the old life, and there is no guarantee of a return. No wonder then, that the Romans feared fire and earthquakes, volcanoes and hurricanes!

The Anglo-Saxons, on the other hand, decided to go out with a bang! September to them was called the 'Barley Month' or 'Harvest Month'. This was the time that they made their favourite drink - 'The Barley Brew!' If they had to go into the darkness and uncertainty of winter, they were going to live life to the full while they had it and party, party, party!

Down on the farm, I could take the Roman or the Anglo-Saxon point of view. Having just picked a crop of damsons, I was a Roman caught up in the violence of a terrible and terrifying thunderstorm. The God Vulcan, the God of fire and forge, rained down his wrath upon me and the innocent and helpless animals around me. Was I being punished by all of nature for taking the damsons? If I was a Roman, I should surely think it so.

The Anglo-Saxon in me turned my damsons into jam and I had the best of feasts! I got my knuckles rapped playing the ancient game of conkers. I will eat a goose on Michaelmas Day and then not want for money all the year through! I will give thanks for the harvest, 'all is safely gathered in', and celebrate by sharing what I have with those less fortunate than myself.

In the month of summer's ghost, my glass can be half full or half empty. I shall have the glory and the grief of September. I shall be Anglo-Saxon, and go out of September with a bang! After all, something good always comes from something bad, one way or another, even if we can't see it at the time.'

Monday 11th September

'Mr Pike wants to see you now,' clicked Rosalind Greenacre. Carrie watched her stilettos disappear down the corridor.

'Sounds like she's wearing my old shoes.'

Except that Rosalind Greenacre had to force her feet into her sharp toed footwear. Her ankles flopped over the sides and wobbled slightly as she slapped and flapped her way back to her office. Rosalind's office adjoined Mr Pike's. Anyone needing to see him had to get past her before reaching the depths of his lair. It wasn't an easy thing to do. Few members of staff managed to escape a mauling by 'Rosalind the Rottweiler,' as she was affectionately known.

Carrie still saw a piranha as she followed Rosalind, but 'Rosalind the Piranha' didn't have the same ring as 'Rosalind the Rottweiler', and quite possibly her colleagues wouldn't see the fishy side of what was going on between her and Mr Pike. Carrie had never been able to share her marine imagination with anyone at the office, not even Dennis the editor, for fear of being caught in a net of betrayal.

So she kept her eyes firmly fixed to the floor now as she edged along the walls of Rosalind's office, hoping to reach Mr Pike's door unseen and unscathed. She failed.

'Mr Pike has some exciting news for you, Carrie dear. I hope you're going to be suitably grateful.'

Carrie could find no suitable words to reply to Rosalind. Alarm bells and klaxon horns were sounding in her head as she neared Mr Pike's door. She just managed a nervous smile at Rosalind, who continued:

'Let me get the door for you, Carrie.'

Rosalind pushed past her and opened Mr Pike's office door - without knocking.

'Here's Carrie to see you, Charles.'

'Ah, thank you, Rosalind, thank you. Come in, Carrie dear. Take a seat.'

'Thank you,' said Carrie, wondering what on earth all the fuss was about.

Rosalind stood firmly behind Carrie's chair.

'Thank you, Rosalind,' boomed Mr Pike.

'Oh!' replied Rosalind.

She very grudgingly retreated through the doorway.

'Please close the door behind you, Rosalind. We don't want to be disturbed for a few minutes, do we, Carrie dear?'

Carrie smiled a nervous smile. Rosalind flashed a gnash of sharp white teeth at Mr Pike as she reluctantly closed the door. It seemed to take forever to finally click shut. Carrie was all alone and unprotected from the big fish, but she couldn't help liking him for a moment; he had just boomed Rosalind away. Mr Pike was not completely dead in the water.

'I wanted to congratulate you, Carrie, on the quality of your 'Twentieth Century Landgirl' articles.'

'Thank you,' said Carrie, still trying to figure out where he was going.

'We've had a great many compliments and positive comments coming in from our readers, so we've decided it's time to make better use of your talents....'

It's time to start panicking! Who's 'we' for starters?' panicked Carrie, but still she said nothing.

Mr Pike had just finished his usual rousing of the staff speech, and was continuing. Carrie heard her name mentioned as he said:

'...so we're going to move you from the Births and Deaths columns and start to send you out and about more as one of our reporters at local events. We can use your poetic skills to good effect to bring news of what's happening in the town to our readers. The 'Local Ladies Network Harvest Bazaar' is coming up next weekend, for example. Your mother would be so proud to have it reported by her very own daughter...'

'No, no, no, No!' exploded Carrie.

The force of her word made the office door rattle behind her. Or was there someone pressed up against the other side of it, suddenly knocked off their balance by the aftershock? Mr Pike looked fit to boom but Carrie got in first.

'I'm sorry, Mr Pike, I'd love to help you, but I do my research at the farm at weekends for the 'Land Girl' articles, and they still have some time to run.'

'Only if I say so,' he boomed quietly.

Carrie stared at Mr Pike.

'But you've just said how much your readers like my articles!'

'For all this time you spend down on the farm, Carrie, there's never much mention of these farmers in your articles. It makes me wonder exactly what kind of research you're doing!'

'The farming content and historical facts of my articles are correct and so is my respect for the privacy of my farming sources. You taught me that, Mr Pike. And I'm sure you wouldn't want me to let either yourself or the paper down by not completing the year's worth of 'Land Girl' reports; they're so very popular, as you say. They just wouldn't be the same without the hands on experience that I'm getting and, by the time I've finished there, I'll be so much more able to report on anything, do anything for you!'

(Smile, smile, smile).

'Maybe, maybe,' boomed Mr Pike, quietly, again. 'We just thought you might like a bit more variety in your weekend work.'

'I love working here for you, Mr Pike, and I thank you for offering me this new opportunity, but I have to finish what I started for the good of the paper. I'm still young and have a lot to learn from you. You always make the right decisions, so please let me stay as I am!'

(Smile, flutter, flutter, eyelids).

Mr Pike boomed joyfully:

'Yes, you're right about me, Carrie! Very well, we will continue. Rosalind will be disappointed, I'm sure, but I shall probably go with her idea to restrict travel claims to beyond a twenty mile radius, so that will keep the peace, there.'

Carrie stared at Mr Pike and smiled for all she was worth. She knew what was coming next.

'Very good, Carrie, dear. Keep up the good work.'

The office door was open now and Mr Pike was standing in it, his swim bladder pulsing with anticipation. Carrie didn't disappoint.

'Thank you very much, Mr Pike. I'd like to personally show you my next hard copy when it's ready.'

Carrie pretended to get stuck in the doorway with Mr.Pike. She pressed herself hard into his swim bladder as she spoke the words 'hard copy.'

Mr Pike leaked silver with oil and sweat.

'Yes, of course,' he boomed.

There was a little more pulsing and pushing. It was a small price to pay for her freedom. As she left, she heard him saying 'What a lovely young woman...' to 'Rosalind the Rottweiler.' Rosalind growled agreement as Mr Pike relived his doorway 'hard copy' drama as he returned to his office. Rosalind flashed a gnash of her teeth in Carrie's wake and kicked out her sharp footwear underneath her desk; she banged her floppy ankle on the waste paper basket. It hurt. She'd been unable to trap and devour the young minnow; how was she going to explain that to her victim's mother?

Saturday 16th September

'Do you need a hand?'

Jon was in the cowshed when she arrived. It looked like a cow was calving. He had his back to her. With one hand he held up the cow's tail while he examined her behind. He was stripped to the waist.

'He must be expecting trouble.'

She turned hot and cold and hot and cold at the sight of all that bare, beautiful skin, that covered a perfect arrangement of well-defined muscles. As he leaned into the cow Carrie realised that Michelangelo's marble statue of 'The Dying Slave' hadn't died after all. He was real, standing in front of her now. She'd always had a thing about wanting to touch ancient relics in museums and churches; she secretly felt that if she sneaked a quick touch it would bring her good luck or give her secret powers of some sort. It turned her on to think about all the other human beings who had touched that very same relic who were no longer living. It was some kind of morbid fascination that was a bit weird.

There was nothing weird or morbid about wanting to touch the living, breathing statue that had its back to her right now. It was just a case of being plain 'turned on'. Carrie wanted to press her whole self against the naked back that invited her towards it, but she faltered at the last minute, and just stretched out a hand towards his shoulder instead.

'He's busy with the cow, he might not like it.'

She had no need to worry.

'A h..hand is g..good,' he said.

Smiling out of sight, Carrie decided to continue with the back press. Jon reached out and took hold of her hand with his slimy one. He pulled it down in front of his body until it rested over his groin. Carrie pulled back in alarm but he had a firm grip on her wrist by now. He forced her hand, rubbing it up and down against the front of his groin. Jed tossed his hair in Carrie's direction and kissed the side of her head. He held her very tight.

'A hand is always good, darlin'!'

'Let go of me, you vile creature!' spat Carrie.

She wrestled with Jed. Her head was level with the cow's struggling birth canal. She had a very close up view of two little feet pushing their way into the world. The cow suddenly strained. A splash of wee hit Carrie in the face. Jed laughed. He let her go. Carrie staggered back and wiped her face on her shirt sleeve. She felt horrible. Horrible!

He'd caught her out yet again. Blinded by her passion for Jon she'd missed all the signs that shook their head in disgust at her now. She'd seen a cow calving so assumed it would be Jon. But Jon would never have taken his shirt off; he didn't mind getting wet and dirty. And there was no Jip. And Jon would never have lifted up the cow's tail like that, as if it was something disgusting.

What a fool! What a fool I am!' she shivered.

The cow groaned low and deep.

'Jon! Yes, I've been a fool. Yes, I'm blind. Love is blind! But Jon would put the cow first. I can feel sorry for myself later. This cow needs help. I must find Jon. I don't fancy this cow's chances with Jed as the midwife.'

'You leave that cow alone,' demanded Carrie. 'I'm going to find Jon and your dad.'

'You'll have a long walk, then,' laughed Jed. 'They've gone to market; there's a special dairy sale.'

'Well I'll fetch Bob, then, from the tractor workshop. He'll know what to do.'

'They're closed. Short time working.'

Carrie had run out of options.

'Besides, any fool can calve a cow. I've done it hundreds of times. Pass me those ropes,' said Jed.

The two little feet were protruding quite nicely now from their mother's birth canal. Carrie saw the familiar ropes curled up on the floor. The sight of them filled her with warm memories and reassured her. She remembered every last detail of the miracle that she'd shared with little Carrie, little Carrie's mother, Jon, Jip, and Bob. It was going to happen again right now. It needed to happen. Maybe Jed did know what he was doing; maybe he had done it hundreds of times before. Carrie passed him the ropes and got ready to pull.

'Work with her,' Jon had said.

Jed put the little loops on the end of the ropes around the two new little feet. The cow heaved and groaned once more. Carrie got ready. But Jed picked up what looked like a wide plank of wood and threaded the ropes through holes in the middle of the plank. Attached to the plank was a metal wheel, around which he threaded the ropes. It was a pulley. He gave his usual grin at Carrie as he pushed her out of the cowshed, followed himself, and wedged the plank across the doorway.

'Now you'll see what real life's all about,' said Jed.

He didn't take hold of the ropes. He took hold of a handle on the pulley and started to turn it.

'What are you doing?' said Carrie.

'Calving the cow,' replied Jed.

Jed turned and turned the pulley handle. He didn't stop. The cow was battling to stand still as the ropes pulled her body towards the door. Her neck was chained. Eventually she ran out of neck and the chain started to choke her. She was frothing at the mouth. She was very quiet, except for the fast and heavy breathing coming from her nostrils. The two little feet stubbornly would not budge. The cow's backside started to bulge out like a football.

'Stop it!' shouted Carrie. 'You're hurting her! You're supposed to work with her contractions!'

'And just how many times have you calved a cow?' said Jed, turning, turning, turning his cruel handle.

'Please, please stop, Jed!'

'What's the matter? Can't you take a bit of real life? Life hurts, Carrie.'

Somehow the cow managed to make some noise. It was a scream that hissed out of her trapped windpipe.

'Just remember, this might be you, one day! Do you want to do this for a man?'

It was getting harder and harder to turn the pulley handle. Jed was having to strain like the poor cow that he was tormenting.

'Come on, you bugger!' he groaned.

Carrie's windpipe was trapped. She couldn't breathe for the lump of pain that she felt at the back of her throat and the scream that welled up in her belly. Jed turned and turned and turned.

They all exploded at once. The cow exploded her calf. Her birth canal ripped open and catapulted the two new little feet to the ground. The two new little feet landed with a bang on the hard concrete floor. They lay still and quiet. The cow stood still and quiet. Her neck returned to its usual length. Jed dropped the pulley on the floor and stretched himself out; his muscles ached after all that pulling. Carrie let out a small hiss as her windpipe ripped open to allow air back into it. With the return of breath came movement and senses. The two new little feet appeared to have neither.

'Quick!' said Carrie. 'The calf's not breathing!'

Jed bent down and lifted one of the little feet into the air.

'Agh! He said in disgust. 'It's a bull calf, anyway. They're not worth anything.' He stood up. 'Leave it, it's not worth bothering about.'

Jed left it. He picked up his shirt and slung it over the shoulder that Carrie had so lovingly reached out for, not so many minutes ago. She hadn't expected her helping hand to end like this. He picked up his ropes and pulley and plank of wood and walked away.

Carrie felt cold. But she made herself move. She got down on the floor next to the new little feet and rubbed his little body with all her might. She poked straw into his nostrils. She lifted his head. She shook him. She rubbed him again. She tried and tried. She didn't tell him to 'come on' like she had done to little Carrie; she knew he wasn't going to.

The cow stood still and quiet. Carrie and the new little feet sat still and quiet on the floor. The only movement came from the swallows that swooped in and out of the shed to feed their young. They were very quiet. An occasional drip of blood landed on Carrie and the new little feet. It was a gift from his mother. It was all she had to give him. She couldn't give him a warm lick or a drop of milk.

His mother was hurting. Carrie didn't really know what to do but she did it anyway. She fetched his mother a bucket of water to drink. She stroked her neck that had returned to its usual length. She fetched some ice from Mavis at the farmhouse and made a compress with it from an old towel in the outhouse; she held it against the ripped open birth canal. The cow stood still and quiet. She held it until the bleeding stopped. The tear had almost doubled the size of the mother's birth canal. The cow's bottom smiled at her with two enormous, red, swollen lips. It looked like a botox treatment that had gone wrong instead of a cow's bottom.

Carrie shuddered. She thought about little Carrie. She thought about a lot of things. And all the while the new little feet lay still and quiet, as they had done throughout their brief visit to the world.

———◆———

Debs lay still and quiet. Joe was lying next to her, fast asleep. They were having a lie-in. He had his back to her. She turned hot and cold and hot and cold at the sight of all that bare flesh, rising and falling. She tried to get up quietly out of bed, but Joe stirred. Joe reached behind him and took hold of her hand as she tried to move. He pulled it down in front of his body until it rested over his groin. He forced her hand, rubbing it up and down; Joe was awake again.

'A hand is always good,' he said.

'I need to get up now, Joe. Let me make you a cup of tea.'

Debs pulled away from him but he had a firm grip on her wrist. Joe kissed the side of her head as he rolled over towards her. She had a very close up view of two slightly yellow, slightly bloodshot eyes as he rolled. She had no choice but to roll with him. He'd caught her out again. Debs had run out of options. She got ready. Joe groaned low and deep.

'Joe, what are you doing?'

'Now you'll see what real life's all about,' said Joe.

'Please, please stop, Joe! You're hurting me!'

'What's the matter? Can't you take a bit of real life?' Joe was having to strain now. 'Come on, you bugger!' he groaned.

Debs' windpipe was trapped. She couldn't breathe for the lump of pain that she felt at the back of her throat, and the scream that welled up in her belly. She swelled up like a football. Joe pushed and pushed and pushed. They all exploded at once. Debs let out the scream that escaped from her trapped windpipe as she tore. Joe rolled off her and stretched out on the bed; his muscles ached after all that pushing.

Debs lay still and quiet on the bed, her face buried in her pillow. She cried softly.

'Agh!' said Joe in disgust, as he rolled off the bed and left for the bathroom.

Debs had not expected her lie-in to end like this. She felt cold. But she made herself move. An occasional drip of blood landed on the bedroom carpet as she walked towards the door. It was a gift from Joe. She fetched some ice from the kitchen and made a compress from it with an old towel. She sat down on it on a kitchen chair until the bleeding stopped. Debs was hurting. She shuddered. She thought that she would never be able to go to the toilet again.

She thought about a lot of things. And all the while she could hear Joe's feet pacing about upstairs. It was his weekend off; there would be another lie-in tomorrow.

———————◆———————

Carrie was sitting on the stone bench in the orchard; her body melted and fused with the stone of the bench. She marvelled at herself with a morbid fascination; but since she was made of stone she couldn't touch herself for good luck; she didn't expect to find any, anyway. Shadows and light were the only visitors to the statue that was awkwardly propped back against the sad looking tree. Its eyes followed the stripes of light and dark flickering across the orchard trees made by swift moving clouds above.

Was the light chasing the shadows, or the shadows chasing the light? Either way, it filled the statue with wonder at the sheer speed of the change from light to dark. How quickly the world turns. Suddenly, above the tree line, four white doves exploded across the sky. Shining brilliant white, like four guardian angels, they brought movement and senses back to the stone statue. Or was it his voice that did that?

'Carrie.'

'Ah do,' said Carrie.

The weight of the old man suddenly sitting down on the bench next to her broke her away from her stone bench base, and blood flooded back into her veins. Old man Wilson sat still and quiet. Carrie sat still and quiet. The sad looking tree stood still and quiet. They watched the shadows and light play with the trees. The white doves had gone. After a while, the old man said:

'He's a dirty rotten scoundrel.'

Carrie said:

'Why don't you cut this tree down? It's virtually dead. It bears no fruit, and nothing will grow near it. Maybe it brings you bad luck.'

The old man slowly turned his head, tilting it to one side as he did so. He stared at Carrie.

'*You be careful, duck! Nobody messes with Wilson — he's mad!*'

She had forgotten the tractor mechanic's warning.

'*This is it! I've made him mad!*'

Once again Carrie felt like a little mouse beneath the gaze of a prize falcon that was about to have his sport with her, before eating her.

'*Look him in the eye! Even the smallest prey can still be brave!*'

But what eyes! Was he really mad or did he just look mad? Carrie looked him in the eyes. Or did he command her eyes to go to him? The old man had the palest, pale blue eyes that she had ever seen.

'Your eyes are the colour of pain.'

'It's my walnut tree.'

'I can't tell them apart sometimes.'

'Look them in the eye, then you'll see.'

The Falcon was rubbing his hands together, one over the other. His knuckles were red and sore on his right hand. She knew that she was the mouse, she knew she was going to lose, yet she didn't feel completely helpless.

'My dad told me to do that, the first time I came here.'

'Then he was right then, wasn't he? Jon's patching her up, now. Go to him, Carrie. He wants to thank you.'

Carrie felt odd; turned upside down and inside out. The Falcon hadn't finished with his prey. He took hold of her hand. He was warm.

'It'll be alright. I give you my word.'

Why couldn't you just say 'no!' you stupid girl… 'I have a tree in my orchard."

The Falcon watched her go; he didn't say goodbye.

On her way back to the cowshed Carrie saw the Land Rover parked up in the yard. Its back door was open. Two new little feet were sticking out of it. Jip was sniffing at them. But he followed Carrie over to the cowshed door; life was more interesting than death.

Carrie's eyes were drawn straight to the cow's bottom. A neat row of blanket stitches covered her gaping wound and returned her smiling botox bottom to a recognizable cow's bottom. Jon was there. Carrie stood still and quiet. She looked him in the eye. He held out a hand to her. She took it.

He pulled her into the shadows of the cowshed. Shadows and light. Was the light chasing the shadows, or the shadows chasing the light? Either way, it filled them with wonder at the sheer speed of the change from dark to light. How quickly the world turns. Jip stood on guard at the cowshed door. Suddenly, he barked.

The Land Rover engine revved up in the yard. Jed was driving away with the two new little feet. His face looked red and swollen on one side, his eye swelled up like a football; it looked like the cow's bottom.

'What bad luck, two new little feet, to have Jed as your undertaker.'

But today was for living and breathing.

'Look him in the eye. You'll be alright.'

So she did. And she was. How quickly the world turns. And Jip stood on guard at the cowshed door.

Saturday 23rd September

Bill stood on guard at the Town Hall door. For one Saturday every year he sacrificed a day's work at the garage to help his wife with the annual 'Local Ladies Network Harvest Bazaar.' Standing in the doorway now, at the top of a flight of grand stone steps which led up to the entrance and which were sheltered by two large, stone pillars that supported a grand porch in grand Victorian style, Bill prostituted himself to everybody who came along. Brandishing a large floor plan instead of a set of jangling car keys, his task was to ush everybody, upon their arrival, into the exactly correct place at exactly the correct time.

Deep inside, at the far end of the hall, his esteemed wife, Jill, stood in state with her own clipboard overseeing the proceedings. By the time anybody had reached the stage so that they were close enough to look up at the underneath of her esteemed clipboard, everything was done and dusted. Everybody knew where they were and what they were doing and when they were doing it, thanks to Bill, and the horde of 'LLN' ladies who were sandwiched in between himself and his all-seeing, all-knowing, all-smiling, majestic, clipboard swinging pimp.

Carrie hid amongst the trestle tables and tablecloths as best she could. Everybody admired her parents' successful partnership and frequently said so:

'Carrie, we're so lucky to have both of your parents here to help today, they work so well together,' said Rosalind Greenacre.

Carrie smiled and carried on putting out chairs around the edge of the room.

'Nobody can see for looking. And is it my imagination, or is Rosalind developing a 'boom' in her voice? Is there no escape from Mr Pike?'

Apparently not, since the esteemed Mr Pike had been invited to open this year's Harvest Bazaar.

'So that's why he made such a fuss about wanting it reported.'

Being such an important event in the life of the town, Dennis had got the honour of describing it for the world, much to Carrie's relief. However, she'd been unable to achieve the complete relief of not being there at all. Her mother had insisted that she give the farm a miss this day. She *'absolutely'* could not manage without her. It was one day a year that Carrie had 'absolutely' attended without fail since she was in nappies, although quite what her contribution had been back in those days she couldn't imagine; probably about the same as today - smile at everybody, and do as she was told, and then smile at everybody again, and keep quiet.

This was her mother's finest hour. It was quite irrelevant that her mother took all the credit for the day and yet elegantly managed to do none of the work; that was a given lovingly accepted by one and all. The 'LLN' always had their big fundraiser at Harvest time; everybody else did Christmas and summer; in their town they had to be different, and always the best.

The Town Hall was only part of this mega event. Stalls, attractions and entertainment spread out onto the streets around and into the town's three star hotel which was coerced every year to provide refreshments – the 'LLN' ladies would be far too busy to serve tea to their minions. This was a shame really because at least then, Carrie would have had something definite to do by the way of washing up, instead of having to hang around like a lost soul. But at least she could hang around instead of being hung up on display like her dad; in the doorway all day for all and sundry to trample past and have a quick stare at his one faulty hand, as he stamped one of their good ones with an entrance marker.

The 'LLN' knew how to make money; Carrie couldn't think of any other such events where you had to pay to get in - *'I'd pay to get out if I could!'*

Debs had promised to come down to keep her company. So with great joy she swung round ready to greet her friend when a hand tapped her on the back of the shoulder, as she grabbed the last velvet chair from the store cupboard.

'Ah do,' said a voice from another world.

Carrie would have dropped down on the chair in shock if she could, but the room was getting so tightly packed with folk that there was hardly room to stand up straight. And then a 'boom booming' sound came into focus. Mr Pike was delivering his rousing welcome speech. It was exactly the same as his favourite, rousing staff meeting speech so the words bubbled easily out of his mouth; as easily as the soapy bubbles being blown by the small child standing in front of her. Mr Pike's words created the same feeling of awe and wonder in his audience as the child's soapy bubbles:

'Cor, look at that one!' exclaimed the child with delight, only to be sharply 'hushed' by his mother because 'Mr Pike was still speaking.'

A moment later, however, Mr Pike's voice ran out of froth and the sea of people in the room began to wind their way around it like a set of well-oiled teeth in an enormous clock mechanism. Everybody ticked around the edge of the room patiently in time together; everybody taking turns to get to where they wanted to be. Old man Wilson stood still in the crowd, sticking up into the room like an enormous spanner in the works; he wasn't going anywhere for anybody. With all her might Carrie pushed back the fingers on the hands of time as she worked her way towards him through the clockwise folk.

'What are you doing here?' she shouted up at him.

She felt overjoyed to see the old man.

'It's my turn to rescue you like you rescued me at the cattle market.'

'The 'Local Ladies Network' asked the Farmer's Union for some straw bales for their 'Anglo Saxon Corner' - wonder where they got that idea from?'

The old man kept a straight face; Carrie felt her face blushing red hot.

'So he does read my articles!'

'So we were asked to bring some down,' he finished.

'We!'

Carrie was gone. She forgot to rescue old man Wilson and made straight for the door. She didn't even stop to ask which 'we' he meant. Bill was still stamping hands but he was less busy now. So he had chance to look up and see Carrie standing opposite him in the doorway, scouring the chaotic scene on the street.

Chaos can be a beautiful thing. The straight lines of the road and pavement were obscured by the colours, sounds and smells of human beings having fun. Children with painted faces eating candyfloss; balloons, flags, ice cream sellers, cake stalls, cheese stalls; the buskers and the troop of Morris Men getting ready to strut their stuff; the whole town doing their own thing which became a whole thing.

Yes indeed, chaos is a formula of great beauty, although it may not always be a welcome guest in the minds of those who are not open to receive it. Right now Carrie's mind was focused on finding the other half of 'we' - or third - she hadn't considered that possibility. Of course he would be here, he would come to see her, wouldn't he?

'She's over there!' said Bill.

The sound of her dad's voice slowed Carrie's focus and helped her to see more clearly. Now she suddenly saw a crowd of people in front of her instead of an impossible sea of vibrating colours. She looked across blankly at her dad, as if to say 'who is she?'

'If you're looking for Debs she's over there!' he pointed. 'She's in the Anglo Saxon Corner having a barley brew!'

Carrie looked.

'It's good to see her out and about; she looks like she's enjoying herself with her friend.'

Carrie stared.

'I've not seen him around here before, though. Maybe he's from the factory.'

Carrie stared.

'Do you know him, love?' Carrie stared.

'What? Oh, no,' she replied.

Carrie stood frozen to the steps; she couldn't move. The clockwise crowds were streaming by but time stood still for her. Debs was sitting on a straw bale in the Anglo Saxon Corner sipping some 'barley brew' from a large plastic cup. Jed was sitting next to her, also with a large plastic cup in one hand. His other hand and arm leant around the back of Debs. Carrie knew from how he was sitting just exactly what he would be looking at, and it wasn't Debs' face or colourful personality.

'He couldn't come,' said a voice from high up behind her. 'We've got a young heifer calving.'

'Oh,' said Carrie.

His words melted her a little. And now, this is how it was:

Carrie's dad was staring at Carrie and the old man, a tall stranger who had just leant forward and whispered into his daughter's ear; Jed was staring at Debs' cleavage; Debs was staring into her barley brew and giggling like a silly schoolgirl; Carrie's mum was staring at Bill because he wasn't doing very much; two slightly yellow, bloodshot eyes that bulged out from the doorway of the barley brew tent alongside his barley brew gut, stared at Debs and Jed; Carrie just stared. And the Falcon hovered over them all.

———————◆———————

'I'm just thrilled beyond words!' thrilled Jill as Carrie and her dad struggled through the kitchen door behind her carrying an assortment of leftovers from the Harvest Bazaar.

The second the doors closed on the Harvest Bazaar signalled the end of 'Local Ladies Network' and the beginning of dog eat dog as every lady grabbed, very politely of course, as many leftovers and treats that they could carry home; as many as Carrie and her dad could carry in Jill's case. Carrie dumped her box of stuff on the kitchen table and looked at her mother's face to see what she was so thrilled about - the success of the day or her illicit swag.

'It was a brilliant idea of mine to have the Anglo Saxon Corner! Selling that 'barley brew' will have doubled our usual profits, I'm sure of it.'

'It was plain old fashioned beer, of course the whole town's going to turn out for that!' snapped Carrie. 'You've probably given the whole town a hangover and nothing will work tomorrow.'

Carrie was thinking about Debs - and Joe.

'Well!' spluttered Jill, 'that's not very grateful! I was about to thank you for giving me the idea from your 'Land Girl' article, but I don't think I'll bother now. I'm exhausted, I'm going up to bed. Bill, can you put these things away? At least that would make up for all the time you spent standing around doing nothing this afternoon.'

And then she was gone. Bill shrugged his shoulders by way of a little stretch and smiled kindly at Carrie.

'That wasn't very subtle, love. Are you alright?'

'Yes, of course I am,' snapped Carrie again.

Then she felt sorry, and softened a little:

'Sorry, Dad, it's not your fault. I just get fed up with her sometimes - always criticising. And all that cheap 'barley brew' *will* cause trouble for some folk in the town tonight.'

'Don't fret yourself; she wasn't doing any harm.'

Her dad walked round the kitchen table and took hold of Carrie by the shoulders. She felt the warm, heavy grip of his fingers on the top of one shoulder, and an invisible grip on the other one.

Just because I can't feel it doesn't mean it's not there.'

Carrie felt the warmth of both his hands in equal measure.

'She's a grown up, she can look after herself, you know.'

'It was Jed.'

'Who?'

Carrie sat down heavily on a kitchen chair and rested her arms on a box of her mother's swag for support. She started talking. She talked and talked and couldn't stop. His hands on her shoulders had set her free. She told him everything. Bill kept making cups of tea but Carrie didn't notice. She just kept talking. She was barely aware at times that he was there at all, and she didn't even care if he was listening or not. Of course he was listening. To every word. He saw everything. He saw the shadows and light flicker across her face as she watched the clouds play with the trees in the orchard. He saw swallows swooping. And he saw the Falcon hovering over them all.

———◆———

The Falcon flew home from the Harvest Bazaar very fast in his Land Rover. Falcons have tapered wings which allow them to move very swiftly. Jed had had a few too many to drink and burped out of the Land Rover window as it sped along.

'Steady on!' he groaned.

Falcons are highly intelligent birds of prey with exceptional powers of vision - more than two and a half times that of a normal human being. The Falcon used his powers of vision now to absorb what he'd seen. Time stood still for him today when he wasn't rescued by Carrie from the cogs of the human clock that ticked away the seconds of his understanding. He'd seen why Carrie hadn't rescued him.

He'd also seen the tall, striking woman with the vicious looking clipboard standing on the stage; she had same golden hair and graceful bones as Carrie. He'd seen the kind, humble man standing in the doorway with the disfigured hand which worked with great elegance; he had the same warm smile as Carrie. He'd seen his son Jed in the Anglo Saxon Corner. He'd seen it all.

Being a solitary bird, he had a walk up in the fields to check on the cows, and called in on the orchard on his way back; he was glad he lived in the country. He didn't like towns. The falcon is a ruthless, dominant, predator. One day, he will swoop down from the skies; and no one will see him coming.

———◆———

The curtains were closed early at Debs' house; they were having an early night. The clock ticked to itself on the mantelpiece. Joe had had a few too many – that 'barley brew' was strong stuff and he had a headache. He was asleep in bed. Debs had a headache too. She also had backache, front ache, inbetween ache, leg ache, arm ache, and neck ache. Debs couldn't sleep; how could one glass of 'barley brew' have had such a big impact on her day? It was truly strong stuff. But not strong enough to keep the peace that she now enjoyed; Joe would be awake in a few hours' time. A small chink of moonlight sneaked into the bedroom through the edges of the closed curtains. She couldn't see the moon.

'Just because I can't see it doesn't mean it's not there.'

Debs felt the silver light her face.

'One day I'll fly up high into the sky. One day I will fly free.'

Joe was asleep; he didn't hear her silver prayer.

Wednesday 27th September

Dear Reader,

Christmas comes early down on the farm! It's still only September yet a cardboard box containing the gift of a hundred one day old chicks has arrived. The beginnings of Christmas Dinner. Tiny, helpless, bright yellow balls of breathing fluff; tiny, pale pink matchstick legs and beaks. A hundred pairs of big, soulful eyes stare as they are unloaded from their box by big, sandpaper hands. They may feel the rough skin of the farmer's hands but no rough treatment; they are precious. They will pay for the farmer's Christmas with their lives!

Clean and warm in a small enclosure made by straw bales, lit and heated by a halogen lamp and resting on a carpet of soft wood shavings, the bright yellow balls of breathing fluff huddle together to make one big, cuddly toy in one corner; they are frightened. Who is this giant that picks them up and puts them down at random, squeezes their fluff and talks to them in a loud voice? Why it's me, of course!

Who could resist the temptation to hold a real live warm ball of yellow fluff in their hand, to stroke its tiny, delicate head and say 'Aaah!'? Why the farmer, of course!

It's the same warm ball of yellow fluff; it's just a different point of view. But having a point of view can be a dangerous thing. Such is my enthusiasm for fluff and cuddles I volunteer to look after the warm balls of yellow fluff at every opportunity. But life's not all about fluff and cuddles, as anyone with a tiny baby of any sort will tell you; stuff comes out of the other end too!

And I soon discover that there is no worse smell or texture in the world than sawdust soaked with chicken 'poo'. None at all! Even tiny warm balls of yellow fluff make quite a lot of poo!

And after a few short weeks the warm balls of yellow fluff start to grow gangly white feathers. They get dirty very quickly; they fight and peck at each other and at my hands. They need more space and make more poo. No more cuddles for me; now the hard work begins. I volunteered according to my point of view; now they are getting harder to love but I'm stuck with the job, I've got to see it through.

But at least I have a cut off point - I'll be done by Christmas Day. No such luck for human parents. When the warm balls of yellow fluff first 'cheeped' at me I imagined they were saying 'Help me! Save me from Christmas Day!' and I felt so sorry for them. Now I cheep back 'Happy

Christmas to you!'

I wonder if my parents want to sing the same to me?

Yes indeed, having a point of view can be a dangerous thing. We all need them. They can be dangerous if they don't change, and equally dangerous if they do. We have no choice but to make all our choices based upon them. The best we can hope for is to do the right thing at the right time for the right reasons, be careful what we wish for, and enjoy as much fluff and cuddles as we can fit in along the way.

Happy Christmas!

Friday 29th September

Carrie knew just as soon as the door opened that she had made a wrong choice. Debs' face said 'it's not a good time' but, before she could speak, Joe had shouted from the kitchen:

'Who is it?'

'It's Carrie!' replied Debs.

'Well let her in then, don't keep her waiting!' he shouted back.

'Yes, Joe,' replied Debs.

Carrie was starting to back away with the 'sorry if I've called at a bad time routine' but Joe was upon them:

'Come in, come in! Any friend of Debs is a friend of mine! Not that she's got many friends, mind, so you must come in and have a cuppa.'

Carrie came in. Debs pushed her after Joe into the kitchen, where she sat down on a chair at the kitchen table, opposite Joe. Carrie smiled politely because she didn't know what else to do; she wasn't expecting to see Joe at home. He leaned back in his chair and slapped Debs on the leg as she walked past him to the kettle.

'She's making the tea,' said Joe. 'We've just had some fluff and cuddles. Read in the paper you wrote that we'd got to get it when we can - isn't that right?'

Joe leaned the opposite way in his chair, sliding his elbows across the table in Carrie's direction. Carrie was determined not to panic, and to help her friend if she could.

'After all, what can he do to me?' Well, quite a lot, except I don't think he'd dare.'

Still, she found her mind and body on red alert.

'Well, it depends on your point of view and we're all entitled to one of those.'

'Not necessarily,' proclaimed Joe, looking pointedly over at Debs. 'Are you making that tea yet? Carrie's thirsty!'

Carrie doubted that Joe was thirsty; he smelt like he'd had a few already.

'Yes, Joe, it's coming now.'

'Good job something is.'

Joe smiled across his elbows at Carrie. His teeth were as yellow as his eyes.

'Is there a football match tomorrow?' asked Carrie, trying to sound genuine.

'Yeah, there is, but I can't go, can I?'

'I don't know,' said Carrie.

Debs was still working on the tea; she had her back to them both.

'No, I *can't*, and I'll tell you why!'

Joe raised a handful of podgy, pork sausage, fingers and pointed one menacingly at Carrie. Carrie didn't flinch, but she wanted to.

'Because of her! You women are all the same. Give them a bit of slack, and they get slack! Slack! They start going out, drinking and cavorting!'

Debs brought over two mugs of tea and put them on the kitchen table. She kept her eyes on the table cloth. Joe suddenly grabbed the end of her neck scarf and gave it an almighty tug, pulling her face level with his, bending her body forwards over the table top. Carrie reached for her mug of tea with the intention of accidentally spilling it over the pork sausage fingers in front of her, but Joe released Debs as quickly as he'd caught her. He gave her another friendly slap on the back of the leg as she retreated to stand next to the work top.

'I've known Debs all my life and I can promise you that she never has and never would go 'cavorting', as you put it.'

'It might not be much, but I've got to try something.'

Joe grinned and waited for what Carrie was going to say next:

'And, Debs is the most kind, big hearted person you will ever meet. You're a very lucky man to be married to her!'

'I don't know about a big heart, but she's certainly got plenty of arse to go at!'

More yellow teeth.

'Joe, please!' pleaded Debs.

'Oh yeah, sorry, I forgot there's a lady present.'

'Ladies!' stressed Carrie.

She tried to smile reassuringly at Debs, and Debs tried to do the same back.

'Joe's got a funny sense of humour,' said Debs.

'Did I tell you to speak?' snapped Joe.

'No, Joe. Sorry.'

The sorry was meant for Carrie too. Carrie stared into Joe's yellow eyes. She had never met a man like this before; she could barely describe him as 'man'. She hoped the daggers in her stare would either blind him, silence him, or shame him – but she achieved absolutely nothing, for he continued:

'You see, Carrie, *my* point of view is that a slack arse is no good for anything. Yours looks tight enough, though. She'll have to watch out she doesn't start having sprogs!'

Joe stood up, if a little unsteadily.

'*And*' he continued, pointing a pork sausage finger in her direction, 'my other point of view is that it's about time you fucked off and left my missus alone. She doesn't need any more fancy ideas from you. Carrie says this and Carrie says that. You and that mother of yours got my missus slack at that Bazaar and I'm a laughing stock, *a laughing stock!* I say she'll do as she's told in my house, so fuck off and put that in your paper!'

Carrie and Debs shared a staring moment; Joe was holding open the back door. It was no time to argue about leaving by the same door that you came in by.

'*I was right - a point of view is a very dangerous thing. What the bloody hell am I going to do now? Be very careful what you wish for!*' sobbed Carrie, all the way home. '*Debs! Oh Debs!*'

Saturday 30th September

They were all in the garden at the side of the house when Carrie arrived. They had all made a slight lift and turn of their heads as her little red car crunched against the pot holes and rubble of the farm drive. But only for a moment. There was no big 'show' of greeting as Carrie walked around the side of the house to say hello, but she felt very welcome, all the same. They were still leaning, heads together deep in conversation, each with one foot on the fence at the entrance to the pigs' enclosure. Was it Shakespeare or the bible that wrote about the seven ages of man? Three of them were standing with their backs to her now; the very old Ab; the old man Wilson; the young man Jon.

'Hello,' said Carrie.

The trio turned together as if they'd been practicing this move ready for her arrival. Heads up, feet down, let go of the fence and turn around. Old Ab's height didn't alter much whether he was standing up or leaning. Old man Wilson unfolded into a tower of steel, the centrepiece of the trio. Jon stood, not quite as tall as his father, but broader, curved with softer edges of flesh that life had not yet worn away. Only time would tell if he was built of the same steel as his father.

The trio smiled greeting and affection to her in their own unique way. Old Ab rearranged the wrinkles on his face to make space for an open mouth to show a gummy grin; old man Wilson's face, unchanged, said 'ah do', but his eyes glistened more than that in the sunshine. And Jon? Jon could talk with his eyes, just like his father. Carrie could barely hold herself together, but it was a different kind of shaking feeling than the one she'd experienced last night in Debs' kitchen.

Last night, Debs' kitchen had shattered her into a thousand sharp and tiny pieces, just like the time, when she was a little girl, that she'd broken one of her mother's prize porcelain dolls. It was so pretty she'd just wanted to hold it. But it had fallen from the shelf and her mother had never forgiven her. Carrie came unstuck then, just like she was now; here was her punishment at long last. She had become that broken porcelain doll; that is how she had arrived at the farm. That is how she had expected to stay all day - unstuck.

But she was wrong; she had had punishment enough. The three ages of man stuck her back together. The look in Jon's eyes burned across the wet morning lawn like a gunpowder fuse; Carrie felt the thousand sharp and tiny pieces that made up her body melt and fuse back together. And

Mavis sealed the final cracks by bringing out a tray of mugs of steaming hot tea and scones, with her lovely, dark plum jam - it wasn't afternoon tea time, but nobody cared.

'Sit ya down, Carrie love,' said Mavis, pointing to a set of old, wicker garden chairs that used to be painted white.

'Thank you,' said Carrie.

'Come and get your tea lads, afore it gets cold!' called Mavis.

This made Carrie smile. The three 'lads' came over for their tea. There were only three chairs so Jon and his father remained standing. They stood opposite Carrie; old Ab sat on one side of her, Mavis on the other and Jip at her feet.

'Ah do, missy!' said old Ab as he crunched down into his chair, patting Carrie on the hand as he sat down.

And there they all sat and stood and sipped their steaming hot tea and ate scones with lovely, dark plum jam. The sun shone. The grass was wet and quite long. The pigs grunted occasionally. The hens clucked about at a safe distance from the assembled party. Jip watched them, ears pricked. Carrie could sense that he was having to use all his will power to stay put when he clearly longed to give the chickens a good chase round. Poor Jip! Carrie stroked his ears and he smiled up at her, but he went straight back to coveting chickens when she let go of him.

All was quiet for a time. Once all the scones had been eaten, mostly scoffed by the 'lads', the lads had a spot of 'ooh aah' talk. Mavis chipped in occasionally. It was mostly talk about when to 'do' the pig. Carrie sat still and looked and listened. She felt so welcome and accepted that not only was her broken porcelain body fully repaired, it became fully clothed in its fine Edwardian muslin.

'I wonder if this is what 'normal' families are like? At home I never feel like I belong like this - I like this!'

Carrie liked it some more. She looked across at Jon. Her eye line was level with his groin. She couldn't stop herself looking. Thinking.

'Oh help! I hope no one notices!'

But if they did they didn't let on. A date for 'doing' the pig had been decided. Carrie decided to join in with the conversation:

'Where's Jed today?'

'Why did I just say that? He's the last person I want to see or hear or think about! So why did I say it? Because you'd been thinking about groins!' came the uncomfortable reply.

Carrie started to come unstuck at the edges again. There was an uncomfortable silence from the assembled party; looks were exchanged between the 'lads'.

'He's in the house,' said old man Wilson.

'He's not well,' said Mavis.

'Oh,' said Carrie.

Jon looked at the ground.

'Well, best be getting on,' said old man Wilson.

And as usual, he was gone in the blink of an eye. This signalled the end of the party; old Ab followed Mavis and her empty tray back to the kitchen. Even Jon turned to walk away from Carrie without looking at her. Carrie was in a total panic. She chased after Jon.

'Wait!' she called after him.

He waited.

'Have I said something wrong?'

'N..no,' he replied.

Jon started walking again. He had big strides, just like his father, and she had to run to keep up with him.

'Well, what shall I do today? Your father didn't say. And where is Jed? And why did everybody just walk away like that?'

They had reached the farm buildings by now.

'They d..don't w..want anyone to k..know,' said Jon.

'Know what?' asked Carrie.

Jon looked down at the ground; the colour in his face changed.

'He's g..got the p..p..pox,' he said simply.

Carrie looked at him blankly.

'You kn..know!' he said, raising his face to meet hers.

'The? Oh,' said Carrie, thoughts of groins giving her the answer.

Now Carrie looked down at the ground; the colour in her face changed to a shade near to Jon's. They'd reached the newborn calf shed by now. They stood outside the shed door like a pair of embarrassed teenagers standing alone and exposed together at a bus stop for all the world to see. But there was no one there to see; the shed door was closed so even the calves couldn't see. Jon looked down at Carrie. He answered her look:

'It was after the H...Harvest B...B...Bazaar. (Carrie started to feel faint) He'd h..had a f..few and (Carrie felt her legs starting to go...) w..went on d..down to 'The B..Black Cow.' There were some g..girls there f..from t..town (Carrie's legs were coming back).That's what d..did him.'

This was the biggest sentence that Jon had ever spoken to her. She was so pleased with both the length of the sentence *and* its content that she wanted to grab him and shout and leap for joy. Somehow she managed to control this urge given the content of the story. It didn't stop her mind having a quick carnival to celebrate. The only sign of what was going on in her head at that moment was the lovely smile that she gave him.

'He thinks I'm pleased that Jed's got the pox. Well, I suppose I am. There is karma. I hope he has a good dose of it. But I'm most pleased for Debs, and the length of his speech!'

'Shall I work with you, today?'

Jon didn't reply but opened the door to the calf shed and went inside. Carrie and Jip followed him. He closed the door quietly. After what they'd just been talking about the calves might not approve. But they just looked on in wonder.

'Never, *never* stop kissing me!' said Carrie.

And he didn't.

———◆———

'Bloody hell!' said Debs. 'Just take it slow. Sounds like he's never kissed a girl before.'

'I don't know,' said Carrie.

'He just needs some practice!' smiled Debs down the phone.

'Well, we're getting lots of that. When we're alone, it's all the time. He just holds me. It's amazing!' Carrie blushed down the phone.

'Sounds like you're both as green as the grass you'll eventually lie in. How exciting is that!'

Carrie blushed some more. She wanted to share her secret happiness with Debs, but at the same time she didn't and she didn't quite know why. Yes she did, it was the thought of Joe. So she quickly changed the subject and told Debs what had happened to Jed.

'Bloody hell!' said Debs. 'That must be humiliating for the poor bloke!'

'Serves him right!' spat Carrie. 'How can you be so kind hearted towards him? Look at all the trouble he's caused you!'

'It wasn't his fault, it was mine,' said Debs, simply.

'No, it wasn't!' spat Carrie once again.

'I'm married now. I can't go putting myself about like I used to. It's all my fault.'

'No it's not!' shouted Carrie down the phone. 'Putting yourself about? They don't sound like your words, Debs. There's nothing wrong with going out and having a laugh and a joke every now and then. You did *nothing* wrong. It's Joe's fault! He's jealous and controlling and I don't like the way he treats you!'

'Well that's none of your business, is it? He's my husband, not yours. I was wrong to go flirting with Jed and I've hurt Joe's feelings.'

'Has he got any feelings, except for himself?'

'He's a very proud man with very old fashioned values. I love him and he loves me!'

Carrie was starting to say 'sorry' but Debs didn't give her chance:

'If it's anybody's fault it's probably yours! You got yourself mixed up with these farmers. They probably wouldn't have brought those bales to the bazaar if it wasn't for you! Joe's right, I don't need to listen to all your romantic rubbish all the time. 'Ooh he kissed me in the calf shed and it lasted forever!' So bloody what? It's just a little game you play at weekends and then make out that it's life and death the rest of the week. Sounds just like that mother of yours if you ask me, and look where that got her! Some of us have to work and live real life every day, and it's not always beautiful and full of meaning, it's just surviving the daily shit - you should try it sometime! Joe's right – fuck off and put that in your paper! Don't you come calling on me again! I don't want to see you *ever* again!'

Monday 2nd October

Carrie was trying the daily shit and surviving - just - by the skin of her teeth. It was Monday morning. It wasn't beautiful and meaningful. It was work and real life. It was necessary. It was polystyrene coffee, too hot to handle. It was sugar spilt on the shiny tiled floor that ground into the sharp toed shoes that didn't notice it was there. Carrie heard every gruelling crunch. It was plastic lighting that cancelled out the sun that banged on grey glass windows begging to be let in. Carrie heard it call to her, but she didn't have the strength, or the authority, to open the window.

It was words, spoken out loud by human bodies, and dead ones, written on paper. Carrie heard them, saw them, but their worth was filtered away by the continuous hum of normal, happy office life that surrounded her; the scrape of chairs, the telephone bells, the sudden outbursts of laughter at lewd jokes, the white noise of the building itself. It was Monday morning, and it had to be survived.

Monday morning became Monday afternoon, and it had to be survived. Carrie went swimming with Mr Pike. Nine times out of ten, she was elected to run errands to and from him. It was an added bonus that 'Rosalind the Rottweiler' was a pal of her mother's and therefore less likely to challenge Carrie if the news was bad. And Mr Pike always sent for Carrie if he had tidings ill or glad for his staff.

Of course he was genuinely fond of Carrie and wanted to help her journalistic ambitions; he knew talent when he saw it. This fact provided 'Rosalind the Rottweiler' with a big enough bone to chew on throughout the day, without her needing to pick on anybody else.

The system worked swimmingly for everyone - except Carrie. But today she didn't mind. At least it was a kind of daily shit that had some fondness, affection, and respect at its heart from the various parties that pushed, pulled, gnashed, and boomed her around. She might be the smallest pawn on the office chessboard, but she was wanted and needed, and nobody told her to 'f... off'. She had survived Monday by the skin of her teeth. Tomorrow is Tuesday. Tuesday must be survived as well.

But first she needed some honest dirt. She couldn't face another day of daily shit without a change of texture. It was 'LLN' night. Bill would be working late at the garage because of that, and she would normally be at a friend's house...

———◆———

'Need a hand, Dad?' said Carrie, as her car keys clinked straight into the bottom of his useful tin - the one he kept on the shelf at the back of the shop counter for useful things - funny, usually she always missed.

Not tonight. He heard her swear slightly at her success.

'No thanks, love, I'm happy with the one I've got!' laughed Bill, from deep inside the garage workshop.

'Well, you're getting two more whether you like it or not!' Carrie shouted back.

She rummaged around in the cupboard underneath the counter for a spare pair of overalls.

'I thought you'd be at Debs' tonight,' he shouted.

'No! Something *really* terrible's happened, and I don't know what to do about it,' started Carrie as she pushed herself into the arms and legs of an oversized pair of oily overalls.

She rolled up the sleeves as best she could and waddled into the garage workshop. She hadn't bothered to take off her pencil skirt but rolled it up to the top of her legs. She didn't care that her dad might look up and see her pants and the ugly dark top bit of her tights. She stood in the doorway wrestling with the poppers on the overalls.

'I need to talk to you about Debs,' started Carrie.

'Ah do,' said a familiar voice.

Carrie's dad lifted his head out from underneath the bonnet of the battered old Land Rover. Carrie stared. The Falcon sat perched on the old swivel chair that her dad used to make life easier when he worked at the bench at the far end of the workshop. She shuddered at the thought that he must have seen and heard everything, as she fastened the last popper at the top of her overalls. Her embarrassment was replaced by a sudden surge of anger:

'What are *you* doing here?'

How dare you swoop into my territory! Invade my privacy! Get back where you belong!

'Getting my motor fixed,' said the Falcon.

You enter my territory every weekend! You shatter my privacy, and yet I welcome you!

Carrie glared at old man Wilson; her dad was talking:

'...met Mr.Wilson on the steps at the Harvest Bazaar...(*'that bloody Harvest Bazaar!'*)...fix up his motor - after all, he did save your life, Carrie. I've been hearing about what a good worker you are on the farm! I think Mr Wilson would hire you if you weren't so keen on the journalism.'

'What have you told him?' stared Carrie's eyes.

'Nothing,' replied the old man's face.

'Pass me that small spanner, Carrie,' said her dad.

Carrie did as she was told. She doubted that her day could get any worse. But it did.

'Hello darlin'! Fancy meeting you here!'

'I thought you were ill!' snapped Carrie, trying to hide her disgust of Jed from her dad.

'Antibiotics work wonders! I'll soon be up and at it before long!'

Jed walked into the workshop waving a paper chemist's bag at her. He wore a bandage around his forehead. Small sticking plasters were dotted randomly around his face. He was sweating. He looked like he'd just won a gruelling tennis match; no doubt the bandage was for the benefit of the nurse he had no doubt just been to see. Carrie felt sick at the sight of him but she had to pretend to be normal in front of her dad and old man Wilson. All she could see was Debs shouting at her to 'f… off'.

'Get in!' said the old man to his son, pointing to the Land Rover.

He knew. Very meekly, Jed did as he was told without another word. Carrie stared a 'thank you' to the old man; she saw the pain in his eyes.

'All done!' said her dad.

The battered old Land Rover had brand new wing mirrors. Well, new to it. They weren't the right colour or style; they were some that had been kicking about the workshop for some time.

'I knew they'd come in handy for something one day,' smiled her dad as he shook hands with Mr Wilson; they said their goodbyes.

Carrie didn't say goodbye; she just managed a wave and a stare as the Land Rover reversed out of the workshop and sped away into the orange dusk of evening. Her two worlds had collided; opened a dialogue, touched flesh, breathed the same air. Contaminated each other. Nothing would ever be the same again.

Now Jed knew about the garage. Her dad was pals with old man Wilson. He had seen Jed. What would he be thinking? She'd never told him the whole truth about Jed. Maybe he thought he was Jon. What would they tell Jon? And Debs. Debs! What was she going to do about Debs? And what had Debs said about her mother? She had needed to talk to her dad tonight, but it was too late now. They had taken it all away. Carrie felt ill.

'I'll just finish up, love, and then we can go. Are you alright, Carrie?

You look very pale.'

'Yeah, I'll wait for you outside.'

Carrie went outside. She was sick in the gorse bush that was behind the air and water spray pumps. She wiped the spatter off her shoes onto the wet grass; the overalls protected her work clothes. She rolled up the overalls and put them in the boot of her little red car. She could wash them with the farm ones; wash away the evidence of her day. She had survived Monday by the skin of her teeth. Tomorrow is Tuesday. Tuesday must be survived as well.

Friday 6th October

It happened in the supermarket. Carrie was in desperate need of junk food. Comfort food. Cosy food. Fat food. She was wandering aimlessly, up and down the aisles of the town's tiny supermarket, throwing in everything that she knew was bad for her, and she intended to spend this Friday night feeling miserable, scoffing the lot, and enjoying every abusive mouthful. It was whilst reaching up to the top shelf for another bar of chocolate that she saw the top of his head, standing like a sentry at the end of the next shopping aisle.

Carrie quickly unreached her hand, the chocolate came with it, and ducked down in the hope that he hadn't seen her. Joe was standing, hands in pockets, shuffling from side to side at the end of the aisle as busy shoppers pushed past him with their trolleys. Carrie could almost hear their 'tut-tut' as they passed him by.

He was one more obstacle in the way of their weekly shop when they just wanted to get on with it and get home. He would have attracted less scorn if he'd been an obstacle with a trolley. He would have been even more of an actual obstacle, but at least he would have been shopping too, enduring that weekly, stressful, ritual, instead of standing around and waiting while he put his wife through it on her own.

'Tut-tut.'

The shoppers were too busy to notice that Joe was actually working very hard at that moment. Carrie noticed. His hands might be in his pockets but his yellow eyes focussed like neon on an object in the distance. Every now and then he changed aisles and lent his yellow glow to a different set of products for sale. Carrie set off at great pace to the opposite end of her aisle; her timing would be crucial if she wanted to see Debs. She would have to catch her on a corner so that Joe couldn't see her. She parked her trolley up at the end of her aisle with the precision of a grand-prix racing driver, and waited.

She studied intensely a packet of fish fingers, whilst watching for the starter flag to drop - racing drivers didn't have to cope with pretending to buy fish fingers. Adrenalin pierced little holes in the fish finger box where Carrie had been gripping it. She quietly put it back, hiding it underneath another box, just in time, for Debs was suddenly walking straight towards her.

'Wait...Wait!'

As Debs reached the corner of Carrie's aisle, Carrie pushed her trolley out, colliding with hers. Bright white reversing lights lit up Debs' eyes as she reversed her trolley. For a fraction of a second (Carrie wasn't very good at maths so she couldn't say how short the time was) the white lights disappeared from Debs' eyes as they connected with hers.

For a fraction of a second the light of a lifetime of love and friendship spontaneously ignited in her eyes. Carrie felt it, saw it, was deeply moved by it. But Debs very quickly changed gear. She smashed past Carrie's trolley leaving a trace from the red lights of her staring eyes like an over exposed photograph.

'Red light spells danger...' sang the song over the supermarket tannoy.

How very true,' thought Carrie. *'Red light also spells fear. Debs, I can hold out for you as long as it takes.'*

Carrie couldn't hold out, however, as she walked down the chocolate aisle once more on her way to the checkout.

Saturday 7th October

'We're doing the pig today, so you might want to go home,' said old man Wilson.

'But I've only just got here!' exclaimed Carrie. 'Are you trying to get rid of me?'

'No, but I don't want any of this reporting in the paper. Our pigs don't have a licence.'

His eyes continued:

'They're illegal - you understand?'

'I'm not stupid!' replied Carrie's glare.

Did he seriously doubt her loyalty? But then, what had her dad said to him about her being 'keen' on journalism? Was there a coldness about the Falcon this morning? Or was he just on edge about the impending execution?

His two henchman, Jon and Jed, were in the cowshed putting the finishing touches to their preparations. They were normal. Jon looked at the ground; he barely acknowledged her when in any company. Carrie was used to this by now, and it suited her just fine. She didn't want anyone to know about her secret love. It was just like the walnut in her dressing table drawer. Something special, given just for her. And both had come from this rather odd, decrepit old farm - old farmer.

Jed looked pock marked on his face where the blisters were healing up around his mouth; he was walking a bit funny too (he'd no doubt had blisters in places other than his face) but he still managed his customary 'Hello darlin'.' Despite Carrie's general loathing of Jed, she couldn't help but we warmed by his greeting this morning - it was the only one she'd got from anybody. Even Jip sat at a distance in the yard. He was not a happy dog this morning. Carrie had to go over to him; there was no warm wag of the tail for her today.

'Hello, Jip!' stroked Carrie.

But Jip just flattened his ears and laid his body down flat on the ground. Carrie turned round just in time to see why Jip was trying so hard to disappear. Jon and Jed were escorting the big pig, who was sandwiched in between two corrugated zinc sheets like the pork sausage that he was to become. He had bright blue piggy eyes that looked almost cross-eyed with confusion. The pig was so big that it made the eyes in his face look small and close together. But it didn't mean that he couldn't see where he was going or feel that something was up.

'Poor big pig!' whispered Carrie to Jip.

The big pig grunted as he entered the shining, freshly washed, cowshed. It was a lovely sunny day. What happened next looked comical and funny in a way. Except it wasn't.

The tractor was parked up alongside the shed door, blocking it slightly. Old man Wilson turned up the tractor onto full revs so that it made a very loud noise. Carrie was standing right next to it and had to put her hands over her ears. Old man Wilson pushed the yard brush at her and shouted something about the drain next to the doorway, before disappearing into the cowshed.

'There's a lot to think about when you're planning a murder. You have to be quite clever to think about everything to make sure you don't get caught out afterwards. I'm glad I'm not one of the henchmen today!'

Jon and Jed held the big pig tight in his zinc sheet sandwich. With all their might they were having to lean against him. The big pig was getting a bit upset at being hugged so close. Old man Wilson picked up a large, black hand gun; it was a humane killer.

'Funny name for such an instrument of death. It's a pity I can't write about this in the paper.'

Carrie started to write the story in her head. But she didn't get very far. Nobody likes to have their ears pulled, even if it's just for fun. This is exactly what Jon and Jed were doing right now to the big pig. He didn't like this game at all. He went berserk!

The pig had a very fine coat of tiny hairs all over his body that made him very soft and silky to touch. He'd worked up a bit of a sweat by now with all the hugging and heaving, so that the henchmen were finding it almost impossible to get a good grip on his ears. Each time they tried to pull on an ear their hands either slid off or were shaken off by the violent struggles of the big pig who didn't want to play any more. They needed his head to stay still long enough to be shot through with the bolt from the humane killer.

Old man Wilson was shouting and swearing at his henchmen to hold the big pig still. It was the first time that Carrie had ever heard the old man swear. She didn't like it. She didn't like him like this. The tractor was revving its revs as loud as it could. The big pig was screaming and screeching at the top of his voice and his little piggy eyes were rolling around in circles as he tried to shake himself free.

The big pig's voice was louder than anything else. It was a terrifying sound. It was just like the scream of a young child in pain. Carrie stood in the doorway holding onto the yard brush for dear life. The noise seemed to go on forever. There was a small cracking sound and then there was just the sound of the tractor revving.

Forever had probably only been a few seconds or a minute or so. There was more shouting and struggling as the big pig was rolled on his side onto a low bench next to where he'd been standing on his last piggy legs only a moment ago. Quick as a flash, old man Wilson dug a sharp knife into the big pig's throat and made a deep cut upwards towards his chin. A big red hole opened up and rivers of blood started to flow towards Carrie's wellies. It took her by surprise.

'Get sweeping!' old man Wilson shouted at her.

It was the first time he'd ever shouted at her. She didn't like it. Bright red washed around her wellies. So Carrie started to sweep. Big waves of red rolled into the drain. Carrie felt sick but didn't say so. It was quiet now.

Very hot water from a large copper was poured onto the big pig's body. The henchmen were scratching and scraping to remove the bristles from his skin. The big pig's body was still twitching; it looked like they were giving him a massage. The ordeal was over for them all. Jon and his father hung the big pig on a meat hook hanging down from the cowshed beam.

The old man started the job of butchering the big pig. He split his body open with an axe and started to empty the entrails into an old dustbin. Carrie had seen enough. She couldn't write about it anyway. Anyway, she'd had enough of feeling sick recently. She was determined that she wasn't going to do it again today.

With all the dignity she could muster, she quietly propped her red yard brush against the cowshed wall and walked away up the drive towards the fresh green air of the fields above the farm buildings. The trees from the orchard grabbed her by the scruff of the neck as she passed them by and she found herself sitting on the stone bench, breathing in deeply the smell of fresh, dead wood from the sad looking tree whose branches remorselessly tapped at her, like a blind man seeking the comfort of company of either the living or the dead.

Right now, Carrie would have settled for either, as well. She coughed up the dead wood smell like she had done the first time she'd inhaled a cigarette at the bus stop with Debs. Debs had laughed as she'd coughed up her guts and told her to stick to puffing on cigars in future.

'Oh Debs!'

This had turned out to be good advice; Carrie enjoyed the bitterness of cigar smoke. She kept a small tin of cigars and very occasionally indulged her secret passion for dead wood smells.

'What's wrong with me? Why do I have to keep everything that matters to me a secret?'

'We don't know,' tapped the tips of the branches of the sad looking tree onto Carrie's long, golden hair by way of reply, as she leaned back, closed her eyes and lifted her face to the sky.

The light from the sky blinded her closed eyes. Blotches of purple and blue, flashes of gold.

'I wonder if this is what the blind see.'

Suddenly, the pretty blotches went away; shadow covered her uplifted face. Fearing real blindness, she opened her eyes just to check that they were still working properly. They were. Jon was standing over her. She quickly straightened herself up; she didn't want to appear vulnerable.

'A..are you al..r..r..right?'

'Yes thanks,' said Carrie, trying not to sound too indignant.

'You d..didn't h..have to s..stay,' said Jon.

'I suppose you're bothered about what I might write in the paper as well,' she snapped, and then immediately regretted her words.

She didn't mean them at all. Jon sat down next to her on the stone bench. The sad looking tree tapped impatiently, waiting for him to continue:

'I d..didn't w..want you to s..see it. I w..would n..n..never hurt you.'

The sad looking tree stopped tapping, waiting for her to answer:

'I know,' said Carrie. 'I'm sorry.'

The sad looking tree started tapping again.

'Go on!' it said.

So she went. She'd had enough of secrets. She reached across and took hold of Jon's hands; they were still warm and slightly damp, no doubt from washing them after 'doing' the big pig. The sad looking tree tapped louder.

'Go on!' it said.

So he did. He reached across and took hold of Carrie in his arms. He pulled her into his shirt that stank of big pig. He held her tight, as tight as the big pig. But Carrie didn't scream and struggle. She kissed him back with all her might. The sad looking tree tapped louder still.

'Go on!' it said.

So they did. But the daylight had betrayed them. Jip flattened his ears and laid his body down flat on the ground. They didn't turn round in time to see why Jip was trying so hard to disappear. Like the big pig an hour before, Jip had seen everything; everybody. He knew something was up. He was not a happy dog.

Sunday 8th October

'Come in!' said old man Wilson.

They were all there; Jon, Jed, Mavis and old Ab. Waiting for her. It wasn't a dream or a nightmare. It was real. It was Sunday lunch in the farmhouse. Carrie nervously stepped across the threshold onto the splendid red and black brick tiles of the farmhouse kitchen floor.

'Come and sit ye down, Carrie love, the dinner's just about ready,' cackled Mavis, as she briefly looked up from her Rayburn cooker.

Her glasses were so steamed up by the heat from this ancient cooking relic that Carrie marvelled at how she managed to see to do anything.

'She probably doesn't need to see, she's done it so many times before; Mavis is Queen of this kitchen.'

Carrie could smell roasting meat and something sweet - apple sauce. Of course, they were having roast pork today. That's why she'd been invited; old Ab too. They'd all shared an interest in the life and death of the big pig. Was this Sunday lunch a symbolic ritual rather than an act of simple hospitality? Carrie wasn't sure, but old Ab didn't seem to mind so why should she?

She had a lot more to mind about - she would have to be on her guard all the time she was in that farmhouse. She had to protect both herself and Jon. She wondered if he was feeling as awkward inside as her. If he was, he was very good at hiding it.

He sat in a chair by the big, square, kitchen table, deep in 'ooh aahs' with old Ab. His eyes were fixed downwards on the wizened old man who sat next to him at the table. Once upon a time old Ab would have been a young Ab, a throbbing young man just like Jon. Now, all the roast dinners in the world could not return the flesh to his bones. Now, this roast pork dinner would feed his heart and keep his soul upon the earth for one more day and his eyes shone with delight at the prospect of it.

That's the best way to be - enjoying life for one more day!'

Carrie sat down on a chair at the dinner table opposite Jon and waited, politely. She missed her overalls; she was used to wearing them all the time at the farm. She missed the layer of protection that they gave her, just like she used to depend on her favourite stilettos when she first worked at the paper. Today, she was wearing a white cotton shirt patterned with tiny blue flowers and jeans. She felt so exposed sitting at that table that she could just as well have been sitting in her underwear. Jed didn't help matters, either.

'Hello darlin', looks like you've chosen to sit next to me!' he said, as he brushed a hand along the back of her shoulders on the way to sitting in the chair next to her.

Carrie swayed to one side to try to avoid his touch. But Jed leaned into her as he sat down and whispered, in a low voice:

'And I know why.'

Carrie didn't reply. She didn't look at Jed. She didn't need to. She knew what he meant. Just at that moment, there was a scraping sound as old man Wilson got up from his old armchair next to the Rayburn cooker to take his place at the head of the table.

Mavis was just putting the finishing touches to an overwhelming array of beautiful food that she had placed in pretty, fine bone china dishes and plates in the middle of the large table. The pretty, fine bone china dishes had a chain of pink flowers around their edge; the table took Carrie right back to her childhood days when she would bury her head and as much of her body as she could manage, into the depths of her doll's house. Her doll had had a table of beautiful food, just like the one in front of her now and she'd always wanted to share that meal.

Better late than never; now she had her chance at long last. Of course her mother always laid out a beautiful table at mealtimes, even when they didn't have company, but it was all doilies and silver crockery. This table was all food; meat, vegetables, more vegetables. One battered silver cruet set was the only manmade decoration on the table, yet it was a table alive with all the colours of life.

Quite how a plate of food could create such an erotic feeling in Carrie's guts she didn't know. She looked across her roast pork at Jon and felt her legs quiver beneath the white cotton tablecloth. She pulled in her tummy muscles with all her might because she feared she was going to wet herself. It was only then that she noticed the back of Jed's hand sliding itself up and down the side of her leg underneath the tablecloth. Carrie gave a little cough and reached down to her jeans pocket for her handkerchief, pinching the skin on the back of Jed's hand as sharp and tight as she could on the way. He immediately let go of her leg.

She glared at him with the side of her eye like a mad bull. Jed grinned at her and carried on eating his dinner; he left her alone after that, though. Jon was totally focussed on eating his dinner. In fact, they all were. Old Ab slurped a bit; he was short of a few teeth. Sometimes he spat out a little gravy as he chewed; droplets pinged across the table, sometimes landing on his neighbour's plate.

'Ab is lovely but I'm glad I'm not sitting next to him!'
The roast pork really was delicious. Carrie couldn't cope with the silence so she tried to start a conversation:

'This meat is beautiful, Mavis.'

'Ah, he were a good 'un,' she replied.

The food focus continued.

'Thank you for inviting me for lunch today.'

Carrie addressed old man Wilson who had just finished his meal.

'Ah,' was all he said, and nodded in her direction.

He leaned back in his chair and rested the fingers of one hand inside the little pocket on the front of his wiry tweed waistcoat. A thick gold chain disappeared into this pocket. Carrie assumed he had a fob watch in there but she'd never seen him use it. He didn't use it now, either, but sat still on his perch, just watching. This bird of prey was satisfied with his dinner; he wasn't hunting today.

He didn't need to, for Mavis brought forth yet more food. Damson crumble and custard. Carrie was stuffed already, but it wouldn't be polite to refuse Mavis' efforts. Eroticism was replaced by stoicism as Carrie loyally dug into her damson crumble; she wouldn't be able to run away from Jed if he decided to chase her this afternoon. But she had no need to worry on that score.

'I'm off to the football,' said Jed, pushing back his chair and having one last brush of Carrie's shoulders as he took his dish to the kitchen sink.

'Don't be late back for milking,' said old man Wilson.

'Oh I'll be back in time. I'm not like Jon you know. I don't keep my ladies waiting when they need something!'

With an almighty grin at Carrie that froze her to her seat, he flourished out of the kitchen door, releasing a hearty burp out into the open air as he did so. A slight commotion of footsteps, closely followed by a growl and then a yelp, completed his exit. Jon leapt up and tore open the kitchen door; Jip ran to his legs, his laughing jaw hanging wide again and bleeding. Jon knelt down next to Jip and held him fast until his jaw recovered itself. Jed's Land Rover roared fast away down the drive.

Old Ab and old man Wilson shared a silent eye to eye moment before returning to the chairs that sat either side of the Rayburn cooker. Old man Wilson turned on the radio that sat perched above the mantelpiece.

The warm and smoochy sounds of Glenn Miller's band playing

'Moonlight Serenade' melted Carrie so that she was free to get up from her chair. She wanted to go over to Jon and Jip who were just outside the kitchen door, mostly obscured from view as Jon had pushed the door to, but it was a private moment for them, just as the two old men were enjoying their private moment sitting by the fire, each no doubt thinking what only Mavis said out loud:

'Ee Jed! He's a bad lad and no mistake - he'll come to no good! You'll have to do somat, Ezra.'

Who the hell's Ezra?

It took Carrie a moment to realise that she was talking to old man Wilson. Ezra Wilson fumbled his fingers about in his waistcoat pocket and said 'Ah.'

Tutting all the way Mavis disappeared down a dark corridor at the far end of the kitchen carrying a dish of leftovers. Carrie decided to follow Mavis, hoping she could 'share' a moment with her as no one else was available and she felt a bit out of place. At the end of the dark corridor Mavis walked into an even colder, darker room.

White washed walls were the only source of light in this damp and dingy place. Where the walls met the ground the white wash became blackwash, covered with damp patches and mould that looked a thousand years old. At the ceiling end of the walls the whitewash was decorated with the lace of a thousand silver grey cobwebs, so well established that they too looked a thousand years old. It was the pantry.

Fresh food, plates of cakes and boxes of apples sat upon a very large table pushed back against one wall. In the centre of the table sat the complete head of the big pig, wearing a tea towel as a neck scarf as if to keep himself warm. Carrie must have jumped at the sight as Mavis cackled:

'Ah, I'm going to make a brawn with him!'

'Oh,' said Carrie.

She had no idea what 'a brawn' was, but guessed it was something to do with mashed up pig's head.

Think I'll skip any offer to stay for tea.

On their return to the kitchen Glenn Miller had smooched off to be replaced by Vera Lynne singing 'We'll Meet Again…' accompanied by some low growling sounds that alarmed Carrie at first, it sounded like Jip again. But it was old Ab singing. Carrie wanted, needed, to be with Jon. She was desperately trying to think of an excuse to get outside when he poked his head around the door:

'I'm g..goin' to check the t..top field.'

Old man Wilson nodded without turning to look at his son who was blocking the light from the kitchen doorway. His nod instead was turned towards Carrie, but she had already bolted towards the kitchen door. She felt, rather than saw, the silent eye to eye moment shared by the old men as she brought light streaming back in through the kitchen doorway as Jon made way for her. Was that Vera Lynne or Mavis cackling? As Jon closed the kitchen door behind them, Carrie heard Mavis saying 'Ee Jon!...' but then they were away with Jip, up the yard and towards the top field, so that neither of them got to hear what Mavis had to say. No matter. It was their time now to share a private moment.

———◆———

Mr Pike had just shared a private moment over lunch with Rosalind Greenacre. It was the third time that she'd invited him to her house for lunch. Rosalind was a good cook and had filled his waistcoat to the brim with fine things to eat and drink. Today he was even offered a little port after his meal. He had sat in Rosalind's lounge and admired her collection of fine bone china and her deceased husband's collection of rare antique books. He was surprised therefore, upon his departure, to receive a slap around the gills when he put his hands upon her ample bosom instead of his customary hug of her arms.

'Well, well, well,' he blubbed all the way home, 'I just can't understand it! She invited me after all!'

Mr Pike worried for a moment that he may be in need of a secretary on Monday morning, but decided to put the thought out of his mind for the time being. He gave up trying to understand the female race and called in on his elderly mother who lived in the local nursing home instead. There would be plenty of cups of tea and sympathy from the nurses there; and anyway, he had plenty of other lady friends that he could visit at any time, who were always pleased to see him. Mr Pike congratulated himself with this thought.

'Yes indeed, I am a very kind and generous man!'

———◆———

Debs and Joe had not shared a private moment for some time. Joe was asleep on the soft, leather, sofa; Debs was working in the garden. The sky was blue and there was sunshine in the sky. She said a little thank you that she could still see it with her one good eye; she was just about used to wearing the eye patch that the doctor said she must wear to give her cornea a chance to heal properly.

She was just about used to folk staring at her; just about bored sick of all the eye patch, 'can't see for looking' jokes, at the contact lens factory. But her sense of humour was still intact.

'Well, I can see the funny side of it all, working where I do.'

It had been a nasty accident with the car door; she knew that she was lucky that a couple of paramedics had pulled into the supermarket car park just after it had happened. Their quick actions had probably saved her sight. As she knelt down upon the grass to do a spot of weeding she gave a little thank you for all the private moments that she shared with her lovely garden; it was much better company than all those wasted hours with Carrie Langford.

'Can you imagine the fuss she'd be making about it? I'm glad she's not here to stare at me!'

She gave a little thank you for the peace and quiet that her accident had brought her; that she could enjoy it, despite the likelihood that it wasn't going to last forever.

———◆———

The sky was blue and there was sunshine in the sky. Jip zigzagged a pathway through the buffeting wind in front of them as they walked up the long, slow hill towards the 'top field'. Carrie and Jon's hair followed Jip whilst their bodies continued in a straight line. Occasionally they flicked each other with their long hair as they bounced along; it wasn't the sting of the flick of a tea towel but the electric shock effect was the same on Carrie's senses.

For the first time she realised that Jon's hair was nearly as long as hers. How little she really knew about this silent, gentle giant that walked, fairly slowly, in measured out paces this afternoon, alongside her. He had big feet.

'Why does he have such big feet? He barely talks to me, hardly looks at me a lot of the time, so why do I want to hold his hand?'

Carrie's thoughts and voice babbled along quite separately as they reached the top field. Jip was first to slip through the gate before Jon had time to finish opening it.

'What are we going to 'check' up here? Do you never stop working? You're very different from your dad and brother. Why don't you stand up to them more? Is it those cattle that we're going to look at? You don't talk very much, do you?'

'You t..talk enough for b..both of us!'

Thoughts and voice babbled together; they didn't take the hint:

'Do you think so?'

Jon closed the gate behind her. Carrie breathed in the gust of wind that hit her body as she stepped into the 'top field.' She stretched out her arms as wide as they would go and gave her body up to the ravages of the wind that swooped across the open valley before her, and focussed itself in on her loose, white cotton shirt with the little blue flowers on it. Her white wings flapped in anticipation of a glorious flight, up, up, up into the empty blue sky. She made ready to let go her feet from the ground.

'Oh I love it out here! I want this to last forever!'

But Jon wouldn't let her fly. He weighed her down with those big hands of his, pressing hard on her shoulders. He turned her shoulders towards him, put a finger over his lips and then pointed up at the sky.

Above their heads, only a short distance away, a falcon hovered. Motionless, seemingly far away from them, yet so close that they could see every detail of its outstretched wings, Carrie and Jon froze. Was the predator's eye upon them? Carrie held her breath and waited. She felt safe standing beneath Jon's hands that held her, firm and still. It was not unpleasant.

The end came suddenly. In less than the blink of an eye the falcon swooped upon his prey. Three cow pats away, the soft, little brown field mouse had no big hands to protect him. There would be no return home to the hedgerow for him today, or any other day. Carrie winced. The falcon flew away with his prize.

'It's n..nature's way,' said Jon.

He let Carrie go free and began walking away down the rippling hill of the 'top field.' The ground rose and fell in ridges. Carrie stumbled after him.

'Beautiful, and yet so cruel,' she said, catching up with him and taking hold of his hand.

He closed his fingers around her soft little white hand. They were walking uphill again now, towards a small clump of trees that stood all alone at the top of this next hill. Like sentries on duty, they watched

Carrie and Jon approach; they waved their branches in noisy welcome, guiding them towards their outpost. The man, the woman and the dog, who sought their sanctuary, walked gratefully towards them.

The three faceless creatures pushed through the vortex of swirling hair and wind, pushed their knees into the sloping hill before them. On this day sanctuary was given. The trees made way for the three visitors. Space, stillness and the hospitality of an ancient chaise longue in the form of a fallen tree greeted them. Carrie dropped down on it in relief; her legs ached from trying to keep up with Jon's stride and still look elegant in all that wind. Jon stood, an extra sentry, looking out at the horizon. He kept his back to her.

The voice babbled and blundered on:

'What's your real name, then? What's Jon short for? And Jed, what's that short for? Don't you think it's a bit funny that both your names begin with 'J'?'

'Can't you just shut up for a minute and enjoy the view!'

The 'view' turned slowly round and sat down next to her on the wooden chaise longue.

'You r..really can't s..stop t..talking, c..can you?'

Carrie looked, felt, and sounded as dumb as the old tree trunk that she was sitting on. She squirmed inside and out, possessed by millions of tiny creatures, plant, animal, and insect, that swarmed and gnawed at her embarrassed trunk. She was powerless. In Jon's presence she couldn't control her body, her feelings, her thoughts and most especially the words that came out of her mouth. It really was like being eaten alive, from the inside out and she was loving every minute of the agony of it all.

'It's you,' she said simply. 'I can't think straight when I'm with you.'

'Why's t..that?' asked Jon.

Carrie didn't need to look to feel his eyes smiling down at her. He was enjoying her discomfort. All of a sudden it was Carrie who was short of words:

'Well, you know...' she tried. 'You affect me...I can't say...'

Carrie tried to look at him. Jon had a small smile on his face.

'It's J..Jonathan and J..Jed..ded..ded..diah. Our m..mother loved words. The s..sound of w..words. She r..read to us all the t..time when we were l..little. I r..re..m..member. K...kept her b..books. P..poetry. W..words that rhymed. J..Jon and Jed. J..Jed hates his n..name. He's n..not a coper. She left us. I h..had to l..look after him. H..he is my t..twin. I am him and he is m..me. We're in each other. He is angry and l..loud. I am quiet. I l..lost my w..words when she l..left. I f..find them b..better when I'm..w..with you.'

'I love words, too,' breathed Carrie.

'I know you d..do!' Jon laughed.

It was a lovely laugh. Deep and hearty. He let it ring out across the valley. It was the first time he'd really let himself go, really let himself be himself in her company. The trees whispered in the background:

'Bet he's going to kiss her...any minute now...'

Carrie and Jon didn't hear them. They were lost inside a vortex of their own making. Faceless creatures once more. Their hair wrapped around each other's faces and necks. It was a truly private moment. Jip stood on guard with the other sentries who kept watch for them, all the while trying not to look, not to giggle in the breeze. But they couldn't help it. The wind laughed with them and caressed their leaves.

Deep inside the vortex, the man and the woman were still and quiet. Her lips held his. His hands held hers, silent, on her lap. It was more than enough to send them flying together up, up, up into the empty blue sky. This time he didn't hold her down, but flew alongside her.

'I'm flying! I love it out here!'

'I k..know.'

'I want this to last forever!'

'I k..know...'

But no bird can fly forever. There was always work to be done. And flying was exhausting. The man, the woman and the dog walked back to the farm buildings in silence. It was all they needed. There were no words left for them today.

The Falcon was waiting for them in the yard. Motionless, seemingly far away from them, yet so close that they could see every detail of his weathered face.

'Go home, Carrie. You've done enough for today.'

Jon let Carrie go free and began walking away in the direction of the cowsheds. It was milking time. With no big hands to protect her Carrie could see that it was pointless to try to argue with the Falcon. She'd done enough for today. She winced. The Falcon flew away.

She stumbled across the yard to collect her rucksack from the outhouse.

'Been practising, have we?'

Jed was blocking the doorway. Carrie made to walk past him. But Jed wouldn't let her. He weighed her down with those big hands of his,

241

pressing hard on her shoulders. He pushed her back against the inside of the outhouse door, brushed a finger over her lips, and then held her, firm and still. It was very unpleasant.

'You know we're twins, don't you?'

'Let me go!'

Carrie pushed back at Jed with all her might.

'When we were little, we shared all our toys. 'J''s a good sharer, he always looked after me. So when are you going to kiss me like you do him?' laughed Jed.

'Let me go, you cruel bastard!'

Carrie fought back but, like the soft little brown mouse out in the 'top field', she was caught in the talons of Jed's words and hands.

'Well I just want my share...you know.'

Jed licked the side of Carrie's face. Carrie kicked back at the outhouse door and it made an enormous banging sound.

'That's the spirit, darling. There's nothing like a good bang at the end of the day, is there?'

'Jed! Jed! Where are you?'

'Coming!' leered Jed at Carrie.

In less than the blink of an eye, he was gone. So was Carrie.

Monday 9th October

'Go home, Rosalind. You've done enough for today. I'm very grateful to you.'

Mr Pike had been in his lair all day. Nobody had seen him come out of it, not even to the coffee machine, which was most unusual. The last time he'd made himself so scarce, the wonderful Brenda had given her notice, cleared her desk and was gone before lunchtime without saying a single goodbye to anybody.

It had all been very strange. Today, everyone had been getting on swimmingly in the office. The mechanics of the daily grind had run more smoothly than usual thanks to the absence of the big fish; too much oil in the works was just as bad as too little. Everyone gave a little thank you for 'Rosalind the Rottweiler'. She'd been looking more vicious than usual all day. She'd been so bad tempered, banging doors, barking orders down the telephone that the 'distemper' and 'rabies' jokes were starting to wear a bit thin.

'Had Mr Pike finally got to Rosalind? Had she bitten off more than she could chew? Or had she discovered a new way to take control of him? Was this Rosalind's mission all along? 'LLN' spy infiltrates local newspaper in a daring takeover bid...'

Nobody else, apart from Carrie, seemed to notice or care about the significance of Rosalind's behaviour. They were just pleased that fish was not on the menu today. So nobody else noticed or cared that Mr Pike emerged, at this late hour, oozing charm from every scale on his shiny face, to tell Rosalind to knock off for the day.

'He's lost his boom! We really are in trouble.'

'And you jolly well should be grateful,' snapped Rosalind. 'But I will speak with you, Charles, before I go home. I haven't quite done with you today. I have a very important matter to discuss with you.'

'Well, of course my dear, if you wish,' bubbled Mr Pike.

Rosalind bore down on him and closed the door behind her with a slam.

'All she needs is a sharp spear in her hand, some tribal headgear, and she'd be fishing for food in the Amazon,' thought Carrie. *'Mind you, she had daggers enough in her eyes. Poor Mr Pike,'* she sighed. *'I knew it wouldn't end well with her here.'*

But she was wrong. It was a very quiet affair. Rosalind was in Mr Pike's office for what seemed a very long time. Carrie hung around a bit, wandered up and down the corridor a few times, but she couldn't hear a word that was, or was not, being said. When the door finally opened,

'Rosalind the Rottweiler' appeared first.

'Goodbye, Rosalind, mind how you go,' he whispered.

Rosalind had already gone. The edge of her coat slapped Carrie on the legs as she overtook her, at great speed, in the corridor. It stopped Carrie in her tracks and she turned to watch Rosalind, who was now actually wearing Amazonian tribal headgear in the form of a burgundy felt hat adorned with feathers (*'no doubt trophies from her previous kills'*), disappear around the corner in the direction of the stairs. As she did so she glanced back at Carrie. Her eyes threw their last dagger of the day. She missed. Carrie turned to find Mr Pike standing behind her.

'She didn't miss then! She wasn't aiming for me!'

Carrie looked at Mr Pike. His nose was running. He took out a large, silk handkerchief and blew on it, loudly.

'Good night, Mr Pike,' said Carrie.

'Ah, good night, Carrie dear.'

'I've just finished my next 'Land Girl' article. Would you like me to leave it with you before I go?'

'Why yes, of course! What a good idea!'

A little 'boom' had returned to Mr Pike's voice. By the time Carrie came back to him with her article, he was 'booming' up to speed. Carrie was pleased. She might not like oily fish, she might not like Mr Pike's oily behaviour, but she liked cruel words and harsh behaviour even less. She knew what it felt like to be on the receiving end of them. She felt sorry for Mr Pike. She pitied him, even though she didn't quite know why.

'I'll read this straight away,' he boomed.

'Thank you,' said Carrie.

Mr Pike smiled after Carrie as she walked down the corridor. He congratulated himself with a happy thought:

'Yes indeed, I am a very kind and generous man!'

He chuckled to himself as he read Carrie's new article. Not because it was funny, or particularly his 'cup of tea', but because Carrie had reminded him of another young lady, a dear friend, who would be pleased to see him if he called in for a 'cup of tea' on his way home...

Friday 13th October

Dear Reader,

I've got backache! It aches so badly that I can hardly sit on a chair to write for you! I've been tricked. Duped. Conned. The farmer was in his den. He lured me into it with an invitation to a hearty Sunday lunch - roast pork with all the trimmings; damson crumble and custard. I had neither seen nor eaten so much food at one sitting in my entire life! Yes indeed, the farmer is all heart.

And with his big heart he let me wander free, in the afternoon, in the rolling green fields to walk off my roast pork and damson crumble. And afterwards, he even let me go home early; no more work for the Twentieth Century Land Girl. Yes indeed, what a big heart he's got - except it was a trick! He was fattening me up, my romantic notions too, only to thin me down again on my return visit.

For on my return I was faced with a rolling green field of a different kind. A darker green with splashes of red and cherry pink. There were no pretty cherries to pick at this time of year. Only mangles. Row upon row of mangles stubbornly growing in the ground. What a funny name for a vegetable! I don't think we would like to eat them. They look a bit tough, watery and tasteless, but the cows, apparently, love them.

Our days shorten; it's getting colder. The grass feels it as we do. Soon it will stop growing and the cows will need a different source of fodder; they will need the mangles.

Like over-sized, pinky-red turnips sprouting large, beetroot type leaves, endless rows of mangles stared at me like whisky red faced little old men, hiding beneath camouflaged green tin hats. Each one was a unique and scary faced old man with whiskers, wrinkles and warts all of their own.

Whether the ridges on their faces smile or frown at me I am ordered to pull them out of the ground, twist off their green camouflage and leave them lying in a row, heads bare, until they are collected by the tractor and trailer that follow behind me, ever pressing me to 'go faster.'

Can you remember sports day at school? Wanting to win against all the odds? Did you ever have to do the potato race? Bent double, as you run to be the first to fill your bucket with potatoes or bean bags and reach that finish line.

This is the cause of my achingingly bad back. Facing row upon row of mangles that had to be pulled out of the ground, I wanted to beat, or at least keep up with, the men working alongside me. With rows of vegetables the length of a thousand allotments there was no such thing as a finish line in sight.

With my eyes bent upon the ground, I used the backsides on either side of me as my marker. Sometimes I got level with them; mostly I was a bit behind. I was never going to reach that finishing line, and if I did, I wouldn't win first place. In a way this was a relief - I didn't want those farmers using my behind as a marker to their progress!

Saturday 14th October

Hello darlin', how's that aching back of yours? Do you want me to rub it better for you?'

'It's fine now, thank you,' replied a very formal Carrie.

She was a touch on the anxious side after the publication of her last article. She'd been so angry with Jed for spoiling her flight with Jon that she couldn't help releasing a drop of venom into her words. And now she regretted it; she hadn't been fair. She'd enjoyed her Sunday lunch at the farm. They'd made her a welcome, wanted guest. She'd even enjoyed her midweek afternoon of pulling mangles.

She'd just made herself look petty, cynical and ungrateful. She hated herself for she'd done the one thing that she loathed to do. She'd lashed out. She had tried to hurt the very people she held so very dear and close to her heart. Even Jed. He was just a sad, attention seeking, silly little boy inside a big man's body. Carrie knew she would have to learn to deal with Jed if she wanted to be with Jon.

Watching 'Rosalind the Rottweiler' had inspired her to try a different approach. All week, Rosalind had been very strict and firm with Mr Pike. She had been polite, formal, but had basically treated him like a naughty little boy. And he appeared to like it that way. He was booming with a new confidence. So, with her new, pretended confidence, Carrie started work on Jed:

'What are you doing today?'

'Well, if you don't want me to rub your back or keep my eyes on your behind, I've got to help Jon finish the cows and then I'm off to buy some corn.'

'You don't usually help with the cows. I thought you didn't like work?'

'I don't! You're right there, darlin" laughed Jed. 'But Jon got kicked by one of his precious cows yesterday. Slowed him down a bit.'

Jed watched Carrie run across the yard in the direction of the milking parlour. Just like his father, he hovered. He saw everything he needed to see. He shouted after Carrie:

'Funny that, isn't it?'

Jed smiled with all his beautiful white teeth. But there was no one there to see it, or to see what was inside it.

Inside the milking parlour, the backside letting the last cow out into the yard looked normal enough. It was a touch slower moving than normal for it was sitting on top of quite a severely limping leg. But Jon smiled with all his beautiful white teeth at the sound of Carrie's voice as she draped her arm over the other side of the cow and walked along with them both.

'Jed told me. How's the leg?'

'I'll l..live,' said Jon.

'I'm so sorry. Can I help you today? Where's your dad? I haven't seen him yet. I'm sorry about my article. Is he cross with me? It was Jed...after last week...out in the field...and your dad sent me away.'

Carrie ran out of steam. Jon was so lovely. He just let her talk and talk and talk, and he never seemed to mind.

'Ah do,' replied a familiar voice.

Old man Wilson appeared from nowhere. Carrie quickly let go of the cow and stepped out of the way as he closed the gate on Jon and the cow.

'Get your breakfast, Jon. I'll finish off here.'

Without a word Jon limped away to get his breakfast. He didn't look at Carrie.

This is it, then. The old man has had enough of me, he doesn't want me here any more, doesn't want me anywhere near Jon. Doesn't like my article...he's going to sack me...'

Just then, Jip appeared from nowhere. He was wearing a rather fetching Easter bonnet made out of a small, blue, plastic bucket. It covered his whole head. Like a blinkered racehorse he could only see straight in front of him; there wasn't even room for him to prick his ears in either welcome or warning. He looked sad, but still wagged his tail at Carrie. Carrie forgot all about getting the sack:

'Oh Jip, what have you done?'

'Hurt his side,' said old man Wilson. 'Must have caught it on a fence somewhere.'

Sure enough, a round, dark red wound gaped back at Carrie's open mouth. A square patch of Jip's fur had been shaved away from around the wound. It looked like a red button on the side of a toy dog.

'Press me and see me run!' it said.

Instead, Carrie pressed her hands gently on either side of Jip's blue Easter bonnet.

'It's to stop him licking the wound. The vet looked at it; he'll soon be right.'

'And what about your son? Will he soon be right? Why do you want to keep me

away from him?'

'Poor Jip, you're always in the wars, aren't you? You do look very cute in that bonnet, though. You could pass as a girl!' said Carrie, bending down to stroke Jip's soft, white, warm chest.

'The 'Land Girl' had better get on with some work now she's here, hadn't she, Jip?'

Carrie straightened herself up.

'Seems you prefer a spot of hard graft instead of hospitality, so you can start by cleaning out the cockerels, then feed the pigs for Mavis, then see to the calves.'

'Fine!' breezed Carrie, relieved not to be sacked but down hearted that, in effect, she'd hit snake number ninety-nine on the 'snakes and ladders' board, and slid all the way back down to square number one.

Her stupid article had destroyed her good relations with the old man. She was back to day one on the farm, being worked into the ground and not trusted.

'It's all Jed's fault!'

Carrie was spitting feathers as fast as she shovelled feathers in the cockerel shed. It was quite possibly the worst job on the farm. The sticky, ammonia filled, cockerel offerings were like shovelling acid. The smell burned the inside of her nose as she worked. And then, there were the pigs to look forward to.

'I get the message, I get it!' heaved Carrie as she worked.

She saw no one for the rest of the morning. As promised, Jed had gone out in the Land Rover to fetch some corn; as far as she could tell Jon was inside the house.

'Bet the old man's locked him in the house, so I can't see him.'

Carrie moved on to the pigs.

'Maybe he's resting his leg. You want him to get better, don't you?'

Carrie moved on to the calves. She took her time. The calves always made her feel better. The calf shed always made her feel better.

Jed was back in the yard now, unloading bags of corn from the Land Rover.

'Me dad says, can you fetch the cows up, then you can go.'

'O.K.' said Carrie, feeling even more down hearted that even Jed was not being Jed towards her any more.

Her clever plan had failed. Carrie fetched the cows. She stood with them, next to the gate in the yard. Little Carrie's mother was a favourite of hers. She talked to her now just as she had once talked to Debs; she was truly a very special friend. She was a good listener; oh how she missed Debs...

'You're just as much of a soppy animal lover as that brother of mine, aren't you?'

Jed appeared, swinging a big stick.

'There's nothing wrong with a bit of kindness, Jed. You should try it sometime.'

Little Carrie's mother backed away from the gate as Jed made to open it.

'I can see why they like you, though. You're quite the natural little farm girl, aren't you? Nothing he throws at you ever breaks you, does it?'

'I don't know what you mean,' said Carrie, as indignantly as possible. 'I'm here to do a job for my newspaper, that's all. And, at the moment, I don't think anyone around here likes me very much.'

'Never mind, darlin'. As I've said, many a time, you can always come on the grass with me! You know, I wouldn't leave you on your own all day - I'd never leave you alone! Shame about his dog, though, eh?'

Jed poked at Carrie with his big stick.

'Ouch! That really hurt!' snapped Carrie.

She rubbed the side of her thigh.

'Whoops, sorry!' said Jed. 'It's amazing how accidents can so easily happen. Anyway, I've got to get these cows in and don't worry darlin', they'll only get a poking if they don't do as they're told. Remember that, won't you?'

Carrie shuddered. She doubted that even the most vicious 'Rosalind the Rottweiler' could ever sort Jed out. Jed swung his stick in the direction of little Carrie's mother's behind; he prodded her with it. The young cow suddenly lost control of her senses and leapt into the air, kicking out as she did so.

'You bugger, I'll teach you to kick out at me!' snarled Jed.

Carrie cringed as his stick came down upon the young cow's back. She knew that this display was entirely for her benefit.

'You don't have to be like this, you know,' she said.

Jed laughed at her as she walked away.

'What's the matter, darlin', can't you take a bit of fun?'

Carrie was not going to keep quiet about Jed's idea of fun. She'd felt it, seen it, with her own eyes. She felt sick and afraid. She had to find Jon straight away.

Jip was sitting outside the outhouse door.

'Oh Jip, where's Jon?'

'H..here,' limped a voice from inside the outhouse.

'Oh Jon, do something, it's just terrible!'

'I k..know.'

Jon pushed her back against the inside of the outhouse door; his lips pressed onto hers. It was very terrible. He'd not seen her all day, and soon she had to go. She was quite right, he had to do something.

So he did it. And so did Carrie. She told him about Jed's big stick, the one with the nail stuck in the end of it. She told him about the side of her thigh, about little Carrie's mother. Jon looked down at his own leg. He looked down at Jip's blue Easter bonnet that made him look like a cute girl.

'G..Go home, C..Carrie. I've g..got to d..do s..s..something.'

'No, I'm not leaving you! He's dangerous!'

'You m..must. T..trust me. I g..give you my word. It'll be al..r..right.'

'Ah, go home, Carrie. You've done enough for today. We'll see to it.'

Quite how long old man Wilson had been standing there, Carrie didn't know. She stared back at the old man. Jon was still holding her, the ridges of worn wood on the old outhouse door pressed into her back. She couldn't breathe.

A fire was well and truly alight in the Falcon's pale, ice blue, eyes. His eyes showed her the way to a big ladder that took her back up to square ninety-nine on the 'snakes and ladders' board. Carrie turned back to Jon, thinking she could better argue with his dark eyes. Like father, like son, Carrie saw the same fire burning into her. Jon put a finger over her lips to make extra sure that she wasn't going to argue back. Jip looked up at her with reassuring eyes and waved a goodbye with his tail.

The two men watched the red glow from the lights on Carrie's little red car disappear down the drive. It was a good job that her little red car knew the way home, for Carrie's eyes were on fire. All the tears in the world could not put out their flames.

'You must trust me. I give you my word...'

'The word is love...'

'Ah, you'll be alright. I'll see to it,' said the Walnut in her bedside table drawer.

Sunday 15th October

Morning came, bringing with it a copper horizon and a sad song. Carrie had managed to get down to the kitchen without fully opening her eyelids. The sad song, which seemed to be lasting forever, floated across the kitchen from her mother's little radio. The kettle boiled in harmony with it, releasing its steam at the climax. Carrie opened her eyelids a little more and allowed the rays of light that were finding their way through the delicate lace of her mother's kitchen curtains to touch her.

'Wake up! The sun is shining!' they said.

'I am awake!' hissed Carrie.

She tried to return to her dreams by closing her eyelids once more but the sunshine burned into them like a red hot poker; so did her mother's voice:

'Well you certainly don't look very awake this morning. Is your back still giving you trouble? I'm absolutely appalled that you keep going back to that wretched farm. Surely you can see the madness of what you're doing?'

'Yes, I can see all too well! It's a good job you can't!'

'My back is fine now, Mother, but I'm not going to the farm today.'

'About time too,' triumphed her mother. 'We can have a proper Sunday lunch for a change, instead of waiting around for you all day.'

Carrie ignored her mother's little dig. In a way, it was comforting to have a bit of normality back in her weekend, after the pain of yesterday.

'Do you want me to help you with lunch, or anything else today?' asked Carrie.

Unfortunately, Carrie's mother was still in 'waiting around for her' mode; she'd forgotten that her daughter was going to be home all day:

'What are you trying to prove by going back to that farm *every* single weekend? It's not as though you're producing articles of great literature for that pathetic little newspaper. Rosalind Greenacre's been telling me a few things about that place that make my hair stand on end! It's not the right place for you to be furthering your career. From what I can see you're not going to do much good as a writer anyway. It's about time you gave up and looked for a proper job, suitable for a young woman of your standing...'

'Mother!'

'And don't 'Mother' me! You know I'm right. I'm always right. What *are* you trying to prove, anyway? That you can work like a man, or something? Why have you always got to be different, Carrie? We've always done our best for you, and yet you seem to be so ungrateful all the time.' 'Mother' was shaking her head. 'You're doing yourself great harm carrying on like this. You're lowering yourself to their level. No good will come of it, I'm telling you. Don't come crawling to me when you find out the truth.'

'Mother' departed the kitchen at speed and with great purpose. She had forgotten what a good, old fashioned Sunday at home with her daughter was like. It was a kind of relief of sorts that it was still there. 'Daughter' stayed in the kitchen for a while longer with the sunshine and yet another sad song on the little radio. Her dad would already be in the garage reading his secret newspaper.

It's Sunday. I've done my good deed for the day; she's given me a good kicking now so maybe dad will get a break. Think I'll go for a walk, then I'll spend a bit of time with dad; a bit of 'normal' might do me good. What am I trying to prove? That I'm right?'

———◆———

She wasn't sure if she could safely cross the bridge on her own. She'd never had to do it before - she'd always had a friend with her...but she had no need to worry. As she walked through the park towards the high, Japanese style bridge with the widely spaced metal railings she saw that there was already a woman standing on it, slap bang in the middle, staring down at the water. Given her mood as she made her long promised, afternoon walk, Carrie had another panic - she hoped that the woman was not planning to jump off it, right in front of her.

'Well if she can do it, so can I!' thought Carrie. *'Walk to the middle of it, not jump off it, you idiot!'*

Carrie's mind continued the conversation without her:

'Do you seriously think you're the first woman to suffer the pain of waiting? The pain of longing?'

'Haven't you heard about the 'cloud of unknowing'?'

'What's that, then?'

'It's a medieval poem all about waiting in the darkness for something. Just wait in the darkness for as long as you need to. Be patient, and eventually the light, or whatever it is you're waiting for, will come to you.'

'That's a lovely way of putting it...but I still can't stand the pain of not knowing.'

Well it's good job you're not a real Land Girl, then. How would you have coped in the war? Waiting for your man to come home. Not knowing, from one moment to the next, if he would ever come home at all, or if he did, whether he'd still own all his arms and legs? Not knowing if he'd ever be the same again...'

'I'm sorry,' said Carrie to the path in front of her.

She'd reached the high Japanese bridge by now and was determined to get across it on her own. The woman was still there in the middle of it anyway. So Carrie walked, keeping her ashamed eyes down on the path. She held on to the railing at one side with her arm held out at full stretch, so that she was as far away from the edge of the bridge as she could get. The woman at the top didn't offer to move as Carrie got closer to her.

She was staring very intently down into the water. She was wearing an eye patch and a wide brimmed hat, no doubt so that folk wouldn't stare at her face. So it was no surprise that she didn't react when Carrie quietly stopped next to her at the top of the bridge. She reminded Carrie of Jip. Blinkered like Jip, she could probably only see straight in front of her with her one good eye. Her hat covered her whole head.

'There's probably a pretty lady underneath all that cover. Poor Jip, you're always in the wars, aren't you?'

Carrie couldn't see any buttons to press on the woman's coat; she was all zipped up, but something about her made Carrie want to try, anyway.

'Can you see any fish?' asked Carrie.

'You should know, you work for one!' said the woman with the eye patch and the wide brimmed hat.

'Nah, they've gone to ground. It's too cold for them today. They know when winter is coming. They wait in the darkness. Living in their own little cloud of unknowing, they wait for the light to come back.'

'What if the light never comes back?' asked the woman with the eye patch and the wide brimmed hat.

'It always comes back,' said Carrie, gently. 'It has to. It's been scientifically proven. Light is stronger than dark. Even the tiniest flame from a candle can battle the blackest darkness. These fish know it.'

'Quite the budding poet, aren't you?'

'No I'm not...I just need a hug...'

The man on the bicycle rang his bell repeatedly and loudly. Violently. He was shouting some very rude words. Unpleasant words. Bad words. Two teenage boys were laughing. Pointing. One of them threw a stone. It hit the metal railing of the high, Japanese style bridge and crashed into the darkness of the river below. The fish knew it was just a stone. They knew that it wasn't time for them to come out of their darkness just yet. The light belonged to someone else today.

It belonged to the two women, who held on to each other now, in the middle of the high, Japanese style bridge with the widely spaced metal railings. They were not afraid of falling. They fell now, into each other. Heads, hands, arms, faces, hair. Each held on tight to the other. Their cloud of unknowing lifted, their bodies trembled like the darkness of the river below, in the wake of the stone's crash.

They held on long after the trembling subsided; long after the sound of the bicycle bell faded into the distance; long after the echo of unpleasant words and laughter had left the path running alongside the river, chased away by the strong light from the Autumn sunshine, that suddenly seemed so much brighter than a few moments ago.

'I've got to be back before....'

'You *are* back! I'm back! We're *both* back!' whispered Carrie, gently.

'You're back!' said Bill.

'Yes, I am!' announced Carrie.

'That's said with great feeling,' replied Bill. 'I thought you'd be heartbroken not to be at the farm today.'

'I was. I am!' said Carrie, sticking her nose inside the open petrol can on the top of her dad's workbench. 'Agh!' she sighed with pleasure at the smell of happy memories spent with him down at the garage.

'Hey, steady on with that! I don't want fuel spilling all over the floor!'

'Sorry,' she said, reluctantly putting the cap back onto the can. 'I can't begin to tell you everything that's happened, but I *can* tell you that I've just seen Debs in the park.'

'Oh, good,' said Bill. 'And how is she?'

Carrie pushed the pains in her chest and the lumps in her throat away with as many words as she could pack in to an answer for her dad:

'Well, she was standing on the Japanese bridge. I didn't realise it was her at first, but she knew me straight away. She was wearing an eye patch. She had a terrible accident a few weeks ago with the corner of the car door; she nearly lost her eye. It's pretty much better now, but she's going to carry on wearing the patch a bit longer, just to be on the safe side. Joe's been really upset about it. He's takes her everywhere, even helps with the shopping and everything. He's changed, she says. He's devoted to her now, never lets her out of his sight. He's wanting to look after her all the time.'

'I see,' said Bill, taking a wire brush to the spark plug that he'd just wedged into the vice at the end of his workbench. 'And she doesn't mind being looked after all the time?'

'She says not. She says it's what she dreamed married life to be. He trusts her now, and she understands that all he wanted all along was to look after her. She's sorry about falling out with me, and Joe says so, too.'

'What was she doing in the park on her own, then?'

'Sometimes Joe still goes to the football, so sometimes she can go out for a walk.'

'So are you two going to meet up again?'

'I don't know. She says she's busy most nights nowadays. They go out more. I might be able to meet her for a walk in the park, but I'm usually not around at weekends, am I?'

'No, you're not,' said Bill.

'She says she'll let me know. Oh, I can't tell you how good it was to see her again! I'm just so relieved she's alright. The old Debs is back. We just couldn't stop talking. She was more bothered about me, than herself.'

'And is she right to be bothered about you, Carrie?' asked Bill, rasping away a bit harder at the stubborn rust on his spark plug.

'Me? No, I'm alright,' said Carrie. 'I had been feeling a bit down that they didn't want me at the farm today, I miss the routine of it. I haven't missed Mother having a go at me like she did this morning, though.'

'A lot of 'missing' going on, then,' said Bill, 'just like these wretched spark plugs that won't fire up!'

'If only it was easier to keep in touch,' said Carrie.

'With the farm, or Debs?'

'Both,' said Carrie, suddenly feeling guilty again, as the thought of wartime telegrams popped into her head.

'Can't you 'wire brush' the rust off them with a simple telephone call?' suggested Bill.

'The trouble with that is, that it's never very private at the office or here, and you never know who's going to pick it up at the other end,' said Carrie. 'I wish we could have our own personal phones that we could carry round with us. Wouldn't that change lives?'

'Well, the men in white suits are working on that right now,' said Bill. 'It's only a matter of time.'

'It's only a matter of time...break me...eat me, then...'

Bill stopped rasping for a moment and looked at his beautiful daughter who had her nose in his petrol can again. He walked over to her and took it out of her hands. He knew what she was doing, but he didn't know why.

'We all have to have some pain in our lives, Carrie. It's how we deal with it that counts.'

'I know. Like the 'cloud of unknowing.' Anyway, I've got to go now, Dad.'

Carrie wire brushed his words out of her mind as she made towards the garage door. After she'd gone, Bill swept up the stubborn rust filings from his wretched spark plugs as best he could.

'I'm losing her. She doesn't want me to see...doesn't want to see for herself, either...'

Bill couldn't wire brush his own words out of his mind. He walked back to the house, content to wait patiently, beneath his own little cloud of unknowing, knowing full well that bigger storm clouds, full of thunder and lightning, would be waiting for him when he got there.

'It's how we deal with it that counts...'

Saturday 21st October

It looked as though Jed had been well and truly dealt with. He wasn't there. In fact, the entire farmyard looked derelict and unoccupied just like on her first visit all those months ago. The only difference between then and now was that there was a greater choice of 'him', and there was a cold wind blowing and a miserable rain falling on her, instead of lovely sunshine. Otherwise, this morning felt like a spot of 'déjà-vu.'

'Where's Jip?'

Time to move. All week she'd been living and re-living the dream of her return here this morning; fine tuning every last detail until she'd got it just right:

The sun is shining and Jip is the first to greet me when I pull up in the yard. His wound is better, so is his chin, and the blue Easter bonnet bucket is gone. Old man Wilson tells me to spend the day with Jon. Jon smiles, hugs me and kisses me, whilst everyone else looks on and smiles at us. Jed smiles too.

Jon and his dad have talked to him; he says he's sorry for all the bad things he's done, and he's changed for good. To prove it, he pats Jip gently on the head and Jip wags his tail with delight at his new friend. We all go inside the house for a cup of tea and cake with Mavis before we start the day's work. I trusted them and everything is alright.'

Just like her first visit, it had never occurred to Carrie, until now, that her dream might turn into a nightmare:

What if they've all killed each other, Mavis too, because she got in the way trying to stop them, and they're all lying dead, spread out all over the farm. It's too early for old Ab to call for his eggs so I'll be the first to find them…Oh no, what shall I do?'

'You want to be a journalist, don't you? So get on and be one! What a fantastic scoop of a story - 'Twentieth Century Land Girl finds murdered farmers…Butchered each other in a deadly family feud fuelled by love and jealousy. Land Girl admits guilt…Writes a best-seller and lives happily ever after…'

'Ah do!'

'Hello again, Mr Wilson.'

'Been waiting for you,' said the old man. 'Thought you'd come with me to cattle market, got to pick up some supplies.'

Carrie stared blankly at the old man, shocked that he was still alive. Then she looked down at her miserable, rain soaked jeans and watched the rain drops gently kick the life out of her legs. Her dreams, that had kept her alive all week, soaked away with the rain and disappeared into the mud of the farmyard.

'But I was going to spend the day with Jon! Where is he? Why do you want to keep me away from him?'

'You keep telling me you need to do research for that paper of yours,' finished the old man.

'Well, yes, but…'

'Jump in then,' he said, already making for the Land Rover.

'Bloody newspaper…' thought Carrie, knowing she was in for a jolting ride with the old man in more ways than one. It was time to put disappointment to one side and bravely face the day.

'Where's Jon today?' *('Didn't he want to see me? What have you done with him? Why do you want to keep me away from him?')*

'Out fencing. Sheep'll be coming, soon.'

'Oh.' *(But didn't he want to see me first? What have you done with him? Why do you want to keep me away from him?')*

'And what about Jed? What about all that trouble last weekend?' *(Do you remember last weekend? What did you see? What have you done with him?)*

'Trouble with Jed is, he doesn't really want farming…doesn't know what he wants.'

'Oh.'

'Sent him to the workshop down the drive. I own the site, they said they'd take him. Give him a try. He's always preferred machinery to 'owt else. He'll perhaps do better there. I haven't got enough work for him here and I can't trust him to work for anybody else.'

'Oh!' *(So you do remember last weekend!)*

'Can I trust you not to get into any trouble at the market, today?'

'Of course you can trust me. After the last time we came here, I'm not letting you out of my sight. It's a dangerous place!' *(You don't trust me! Is that why you want to keep me away from him?')*

'Ah, you'll be right. Shan't be long.'

Old man Wilson parked his battered old Land Rover next to one that looked even older, or at least, dirtier. Carrie could tell that his boredom was pretended as he spoke these words. Wet nosed in the rain, he could barely contain his excitement as he set off at great speed in the direction of the cattle market buildings.

The rain withered his long hair into dreadlocks that danced off beat to the march of his feet; 'step - bob - step - bob…' Equally wet nosed, a miserable Carrie tried to keep up with him. Her feet moved more like the 'Charge of the Light Brigade.' Even then she couldn't match the pace of the relaxed Bob Marley in front of her, who was syncopating his way

259

through the mud, puddles and folk who, increasingly now, blocked their path to the main attractions.

The rhythm of the scene unfolding in front of her, accompanied by the excellent backing group of relentless wind and rain, lifted Carrie out of her misery like the best of gigs. Caught up in the wake of the old man's excitement, her mind started to 'research for that paper of hers' against her will. Now she was there, she found she just wanted to enjoy being there.

There were burger vans, straw and sawdust carpeted tea rooms, stalls selling all sorts of useful stuff, weird looking stuff; healthy smells; sudden loud noises and voices caught in the air; all sorts of colourful people, birds, animals, machinery. If you had an interest in being there, it was like a day out at a lively seaside resort without the sea or the rides. There was cow muck and straw a-plenty to make up for the lack of soft brown sand; muddy puddles a plenty substituted as rock pools.

Carrie was splashed from all angles by fun loving boots and wellies which crashed through them without a second thought for their contents or the legs of the passers-by who might be strolling by, making effort to keep dry. There were four legged friends a-plenty, as fluffy and cute as any seaside donkey. There was even an ice cream van tucked away in one corner, braving the seasonal weather like the most bulldoggish of English seaside towns.

'Maybe the old man fancies you himself, and that's why he's keeping you away from his son!'

Debs had finished her ice cream and rammed a handful of crumbs down the back of Carrie's jumper.'

Carrie stared after old man Wilson as he suddenly ducked his head and disappeared through a dark green door. Determined not to get lost and in trouble like her last visit to the cattle market, she tried to ignore the crumbs of Debs' sense of seaside humour. She had no choice but to follow the old man. She too, ducked her head as she stepped through the dark green doorway, even though she wasn't nearly seven feet tall.

It turned out that there were no crumbs rammed down her back; only a trickle of wet rain from her coat collar. This fact didn't make her feel any better about being in the company of this strange old bird of prey.

'Oh give over, Debs!' cried Carrie. 'Not everything is about sex, you know!'

'Of course it is! All men are the same, aren't they? That's all they ever want to be 'friends' with you for!'

But 'better the devil you know', for Carrie was pressed on all sides now by predators; they were standing in the audience of the auction ring. A Shakespearean theatre in the round, the audience jostled each other, stood up, sat down, pushed each other out of the way, talked, guffawed and prodded each other, quite oblivious to the drama that was taking place in the auction ring.

'They're mangles!' smiled Carrie to herself. *'Whisky red faced, each one unique and scary faced, with whiskers, wrinkles and warts all of their own.'*

There was nothing vegetable about the behaviour of the red faced mangles; they all seemed to know what was happening in the ring and more besides, without seeming to pay any attention to it. The play today was the sale of dairy cows. The auctioneer sat in his high tower, judge, and sometimes executioner, as the fate of cow after cow was decided. Speaking a language all of his own that no one else shared yet all seemed to understand, Carrie's ears worked hard trying to work out the plot of these most strange mini dramas.

'Oh give over, Debs!' cried Carrie. *'Not everything is about sex, you know!'*

'Of course it is!'

'You know, Debs, you may be right…'

The most personal secrets of every cow that came into the ring were shared with the audience; breeding history, milk yield, good calver. It all came down to sex, sex, sex.

'No wonder they've all got such red faces,' chuckled Carrie to herself. *'Their livelihoods depend on successful sex…it's bound to affect the way they look at life!'*

Carrie looked around. She suddenly felt very uncomfortable. All eyes yet no eyes were upon her; she could feel it, see it.

'Keep still,' commanded old man Wilson. 'Don't want you buying a cow by mistake.'

Carrie wasn't aware that she'd been moving at all. Now she came to think about it, nobody else seemed to be, either. But on closer inspection, the mangles were twitching. Every now and then, eyes winked, or a thumb thumbed. A cow was bought and sold, literally, in the blink of an eye. It was a secret language belonging to a secret society which Carrie had not a chance of joining. She felt very vulnerable and alone all of a sudden.

'You do remember last weekend, don't you? Is that why you brought me here? To prove that I don't fit in? Are all men the same? Are you the same? Why do you want to keep me away from him? What are you so scared of?'

'Ah do.'

Old man Wilson was talking to one of the mangles.

'This is Carrie. She works for me at weekends. Writes for the local paper.'

'Ah, yes. Very good, very good.'

The mangle examined Carrie, using the same secret language that was being used on the cows in the auction ring. Eyes winking, thumbs thumbing.

'Ah well, we must be off,' said old man Wilson.

He turned, pushing Carrie in front of him, pointing her towards the dark green door.

There was still a cold wind blowing and a miserable rain falling outside. They walked back to the Land Rover to the same musical beat as when they arrived. But this time Carrie's misery was lifted. This time, the old man slowed his pace a little, and Carrie speeded up a little, so that they 'step-bobbed' together in perfect syncopation.

'The last time we came here you saved my life. You just did it again, didn't you?'

'Let's get home, see how Jon's getting on.'

'So you do remember last weekend.'

Carrie watched the miserable rain turn into tears of joy all the way back to the farm. She was soaked. Her eyes winked through the Land Rover window. The Falcon kept his eyes on the road.

'You are very precious.'

The priceless jewel sitting next to him in the Land Rover cab did not understand secret language. She had no idea just how valuable she was, even though everyone else today had seen her pedigree.

———————◆———————

Carrie couldn't understand it. Debs had promised her she'd get in touch.

'Doesn't she remember last weekend? The bridge? The fish? It's been a whole week!'

Despite the fact that her own life was becoming more 'real' and exciting with the passing of each week, Carrie couldn't completely stop her old bad habit of living inside her head. No longer needed as an escape from the disappointment of reality, or a time saving exercise to avoid taking part in reality, this most annoying of old bad habits was now causing her the very disappointment from which she had, once upon a time, needed to escape.

'The old Debs is back, and so am I, collapsing into her soft, leather, sofa, having a coffee and a natter…having a giggle…going shopping. Walking home through the park, crossing that ridiculous bridge. Maybe she's been trying to call me all week and

I've just missed her! Maybe she's sitting at home, just as disappointed as me, waiting for me now, the coffee mugs standing empty on the kitchen worktop. She said Joe was sorry about everything. She's bound to have talked to him by now, it's been a whole week. It wouldn't hurt to just drive by, see if they're at home. After all, Jon was there, waiting for me after my cattle market trip, my dream wasn't completely out of tune with reality then…no doubt Debs will be, too. It proves the power of positive thinking!'

Carrie pressed her little red car and her mind to travel at full power in the direction of Debs' house. The frequency of the vibrations coming from both the engine of her little red car and her mind united and strengthened as they neared their destination. Carrie could feel the high Japanese style bridge sway underneath her foot pedals as she had held on to Debs; she could hear the river giggling at them as they had tried to look for fish in its darkness.

'Without the darkness we might not have seen the light.'

Carrie had arrived. Debs' house was in darkness.

'It won't hurt to try the front door; they might be watching telly.'

The evening sky rained tears of joy on Carrie as she walked down the drive to Debs' newly painted, blue, front door.

'I can't wait to tell her about Jon!'

'What are you doing here?' asked a poker faced Joe, opening the newly painted, blue, front door, and standing squarely on his own 'Welcome' mat.

Her mind fully charged with the power of positive thinking, Carrie didn't hesitate in her cheerfully polite reply:

'Well, I was just passing and thought I'd drop by to see if Debs was in. I've a feeling I might have missed a call from her this week.'

'And why do ya think that?' said Joe, leaning against his own newly painted, blue, front door frame.

'Well, after I bumped into her in the park last weekend, she said she'd talk to you and let me know about meeting up for a coffee sometime.'

'Well if that's what she said, that's what she'll do.'

Joe turned his neck and called into the darkness of the house:

'Deb, can you come a minute. You've got company.'

Joe returned his neck towards Carrie's face. Carrie wanted to jump out of her skin. From out of the darkness, Debs' pale face, still wearing her eye patch, appeared behind Joe's shoulder, like the phantom of the opera. But Debs wasn't singing. Carrie could see tears of joy welling up in Debs' eyes and start to run down her face; even on the eye patch side too.

263

'Carrie here says she met you in the park last week. Thinks she's missed a call from you about coming round for a coffee. Is that right?' asked a very relaxed Joe.

'Wow, he must be drinking different beer these days. He really is a changed man.'

'Well, yes, we did bump into each other by accident in the park. I'm really sorry, Joe, I haven't had chance to tell you about it with work and everything but *no*, I haven't made any calls,' said a very quiet Debs.

'There you go. No calls. As I said, she'll call you if she wants to. She'll see you if she wants to, and not before.'

'I'm sorry if I've called at a bad time,' said a very flat, de-charged, Carrie.

'Don't worry about it,' said a very casual Joe. 'No harm done. But don't come round here again. She belongs to me. Not you, not anyone else. Got it?'

Carrie 'got it' but Joe didn't care. He was already closing the newly painted, blue, front door. Carrie caught one last glimpse of the phantom as she backed away into the darkness of her hallway.

'What if the light never comes back?' asked the woman with the eye patch and the wide brimmed hat.

'It always comes back,' said Carrie, gently, to the paint on the newly painted, blue, front door.

'It has to. It has to. It's been scientifically proven. Light is stronger than dark, isn't it?'

'Isn't it?' she called out to the evening sky.

Carrie quickly got into her little red car and slammed the door shut. It was still raining. A trickle of rain rolled down her back from her coat collar.

Debs was laughing. She had finished her ice cream and rammed a handful of crumbs down the back of Carrie's jumper.

A different sort of rain was falling here at Debs' house; it was plain, old fashioned, miserable rain. Carrie wept plain, old fashioned, tears all the way home. Crumbs of understanding, all that was left of her powers of positive thinking, stuck to the back of her miserable head. She was soaked.

'I need a hug.'

'Don't we all!' said the Walnut in her bedside table drawer.

Sunday 22nd October

'Tomorrow is another day!'

'How true,' thought Carrie. *'If Scarlett O'Hara had had a little red car like mine at the end of 'Gone with the Wind' she'd have jumped in it and pressed her accelerator pedal in the direction of the new day's blue horizon, wouldn't she?'*

As luck would have it, Scarlett had just spoken this well-known proverb last night when Carrie had got home from her disastrous visit to Debs' newly painted, blue, front door. She'd walked in on her parents just as the film was finishing. Whether the heroine's words had filled her mother with hope, optimism and comfort, Carrie couldn't tell because said mother made a very hasty exit up to bed; it just would not do to be seen to be moved by the 'goings on' in a film, or in real life, for that matter.

Her dad had smiled his usual, reassuring smile; he didn't need to watch a film in order to be filled with hope and optimism. Fortunately, he had a ready supply of his own. 'Comfort' was his middle name; Carrie had got her much needed hug before she went up to bed.

The 'big tune' from the end of this beautiful film had eventually brought her sleep and dreams that would have otherwise been impossible. This morning, as she drove to the farm, the melody wrapped itself around her, soothed her soul, protected her body, healed her mind, in a way that only music can.

'It speaks without speaking, and that's what I need to do.'

'Shut up, then. We're nearly there,' whirred the engine of her little red car.

Even after all this time there was still a doubt niggling at the back of Carrie's eyes when she arrived at the farm. Which 'J' would be the first one to greet her? The physical adrenalin rush in her body was the same every time; whether it would be a 'fight or a flight' after that was in the lap of the Gods. No, it was even beyond their control; it was entirely Jip's gift to give or take away, for he would not be parted from his beloved master. So Carrie's eyes scanned the yard for a flash of black and white, a wagging tail, or a friendly bark in the distance. From this information she could calculate what sort of a start to the day she would have, and she didn't have to waste time focussing on the wrong 'J.'

'Hello darlin', want to come for a ride with me?'

Carrie set off across the yard in search of Jon. Jed followed her:

'It's Sunday, you know. The day of rest! Take some time to lie back and take it easy!'

Jip came out of the door-less dark entrance that led to the calf sheds. He waited for Carrie to reach him, then stood squarely in front it. He spoke without speaking to Jed, who suddenly seemed to give up following Carrie. Jed laughed as he turned away:

'Are you sure you don't want to have some fun with me, darling? Don't think there'll be much of that around here today - Jon's got more work to do now I'm not farming any more - he's missing me already!'

Jip bristled slightly. Carrie stroked the top of his head.

'Enjoy your day off,' she said.

'Now, get lost, Jed,' thought Carrie, turning into the darkness trusting that a light, that shone just for her, was waiting inside.

Jip ran in front as Carrie walked; she could hear a machine chomping and grinding. The noise came from the darkness on the left of the passageway. In the gloom Carrie could see a large, 'V' shaped, machine standing up on high legs; the metal bars that formed the 'V' could have been the teeth of a ferocious monster. Not just a monster, but a cannibal too. For the teeth were piled high with the heads of whisky red faced little old men; the mangles were being eaten alive by the machine and spat out into little pieces onto the floor below.

Just then, another monster re-appeared. Jed's face leaned out of the darkness and came to rest on Carrie's shoulder. This phantom wrapped his arms around her, cloaking her in his dark presence as he sang his dreadful song into her ear:

'Farms can be such dangerous places, Carrie. You can be trapped, crushed, squeezed and pulped in the blink of an eye if you're not careful.'

Jed jerked Carrie from side to side as he acted out his little drama.

'Do you know there was once a farmer down the road from here who got his arm cut off by his baler? He slung his arm over his shoulder and carried it across the fields, all the way home, without blinking an eye. Got it sewed back on, and went back to work. All in the blink of an eye, so watch out darlin'! Are you sure you don't want to Sunday with me? We don't want you to lose that pretty little head of yours, do we?'

Carrie spoke to Jed without speaking. She wasn't even sure what she'd said to him but it was enough to make phantom Jed suddenly fade away again. She heard him whistling across the yard. The friendly whistle from a wheelbarrow wheel took his place; a wheelbarrow full of red faced mangles, Jip, and Jon had arrived.

Jed was right. Jon had more work to do, but that was all he was right about. The pulping machine was in full swing now. Carrie had a great deal of fun throwing the red faced mangle heads into the pulping machine as fast as Jon shovelled them out into the wheelbarrow ready to feed the cattle. Carrie, Jon, and Jip, had a fun packed Sunday full of jobs to do. Nobody missed Jed.

And in between the jobs in the cowsheds, the barn, the yard, the top field and the calf sheds, Carrie and Jon found plenty of time to speak without speaking. Jip joined in and wagged his tail too. The newly formed trio composed a new melody, all their own, that wrapped itself around them, soothed their souls, protected their bodies and healed their minds in a way that only music played from the heart can do.

When Jed parked up the Land Rover after his busy 'day of rest' down at 'The Black Cow' he was surprised to see Carrie's little red car still sitting in the yard.

It was late. Jon was still milking. In between the familiar tunes of farm life - the clanking and whirring of the milking machine, the animal voices - that he was, frankly, pleased to be rid of for the day, he heard alien notes that did not belong in his despised familiarity.

He heard voices talking, nineteen to the dozen - *his* as well as hers! He heard singing - *hers* as well as his! He heard laughter. He heard giggling. He heard silence. He heard everything that it said. Jip stood squarely at the cowshed doorway and barked loudly at Jed. Jip heard everything that Jed said as he disappeared into the darkness of the yard. He growled. Unfortunately, Jip could only speak without speaking.

Monday 23rd October

There had never been a more miserable Monday morning than the one in which Carrie was now sitting. Miserable chair, miserable desk, miserable work, miserable peace and quiet in which to work; even the miserable rain was back, a bad tempered toddler banging erratically on the grey window panes. Miserable office. The entrance of a cheerful Mr Pike heralded the prospect of a truly miserable week ahead for Carrie.

'Good morning, good morning,' he boomed through the office floor.

These days, he was kept on a tight leash by 'Rosalind the Rottweiler,' so that he never got quite far enough to oil the edge of Carrie's desk like he used to. If he strayed too far from Rosalind's office HQ she pressed the retraction button on his invisible leash:

'Charles, a moment if you please.'

Mr Charles Pike was then hauled, unceremoniously, all the way back into Rosalind's lair, to give her a moment. Rosalind had truly earned her nickname in a way that no other member of staff at the paper had ever achieved; her supremacy was total.

Carrie, the lowly office junior, was the only member of staff who did not fear and revere. She had a history with Rosalind that went way back before thoughts of working for the newspaper. Carrie had grown up in the company of the great pretender who currently ruled over them all. Carrie knew the truth. Perhaps that was why Rosalind was keeping Mr Pike away from her desk, everyone else too, as far as she could manage it.

Carrie was stuck doing increasingly boring jobs, all on her own. She was still, by and large, stuck in the 'Births and Deaths' columns. She occasionally got out into 'Jobs' or 'Adverts'; there was nothing in them for her, not even a bit of relief from the boredom. She was even starting to miss visits from the big fish.

Carrie tried to work on her article. She usually wrote them at home. On this miserable Monday morning she remembered why. It was just too painful. It was cruel to be reminded of dirt, sweat, smells, cold, back breaking, aching long hours of work, the company of fellow workers. How could she write about that sitting in this miserably clean office?

She wasn't stuck doing increasingly boring jobs; she'd been doing them all her life. She'd never realised it before. She realised it now. 'Rosalind the Rottweiler' had done her an enormous favour. Carrie went back to scanning the week's 'Jobs' and 'Adverts' page. She noticed that the local cinema was having a 'vintage night.'

'*Gone with the Wind' again. What a coincidence. Thanks, Scarlett!'*

'*Tomorrow is another day...there is always a way...It's only a matter of time...It's how we deal with it that counts...*'

'*I'm not the only person who's seen it, am I?*'

Carrie returned to the 'Jobs' and 'Adverts' page. It had stopped raining outside. She was glad of the peace and quiet at her end of the office; the privacy of her desk. She used it to book herself a couple of days' holiday for the following week; she hadn't taken any time off in ages. The week ahead was looking slightly less miserable, after all.

Saturday 28th October

'Hello, Carrie love. How are ya?'

'Pleased to be here, Mavis, after a week sitting at my desk,' said Carrie.

'By heck, can't think as you'd want mucking out and feeding the pigs, when you can be sitting clean at a desk, all clever like.'

'It's not that clever, and neither am I,' replied Carrie.

'Course you are. And our Jon says you're just lovely with the calves, and a good worker too. They all say that. I don't know what we'll do when you're done here.'

'Well, I'm not planning on going anywhere just yet,' smiled Carrie.

'Well I was hoping you'd fetch me eggs for me!'

Old Ab was laughing and braking and climbing off his bicycle all at once.

'Hello Ab, of course I will!' said Carrie. 'My, you look smart today!'

Old Ab was wearing his usual black wool suit, complete with waistcoat and gold fob watch chain. He wore a small posy of flowers on his lapel.

'Ah well, I'm spoken for, aren't I? The missus won't let me work for anyone else.'

This most ancient of old men had a twinkle in his eyes as he continued:

'How about you, Carrie. And you, Mavis. Are you spoken for?'

Carrie tried and failed to hide her blushes; Mavis cackled cheerfully.

'What are you still doing holding that there mop, Mavis? Hasn't he given you any flowers yet?'

Mavis cackled some more:

'He ain't never going to give me flowers, is he? 'Sides, he knows my mop's staying here. I don't need to look for more work than I've already got!'

As if to prove her point, Mavis propped her mop up against the wall by the kitchen door and busied herself with the kettle, making tea for old Ab in her battered, old, tin teapot with its squeaky handle, whilst removing scones from the oven and stoking the little cooker's orange fire with coal, all in one swift flurry of hands, teatowel, and frilly apron.

Carrie watched Mavis work. She was busy puzzling about the significance of Mavis' mop and who was going to give her flowers for it. Wily old Ab had a stop from laughing with Mavis to answer the question on her thoughtful face. His lovely stories always began with 'When I were a lad...' Today, he told her about the 'Mop Fair.' His stories always ended with 'Ah, life was hard back then. But we had good times, all the same.'

'Ah,' replied Carrie, by way of thanks and appreciation to the ancient old man.

And then it was back to a bit more laughing.

'Ah,' said Mavis, 'we still do have good times. Look at Miss Carrie here, writing in that paper! She'll be right famous one day; she's that clever at it, I'm sure.'

Carrie put her hands up and tried to disagree with Mavis.

'Ah, and right pretty she is too!' finished old Ab. 'You'll make some fine fella a very happy man, one day.'

Carrie blushed and retreated in the direction of the hen house, mumbling something about fetching his eggs. She'd seen the wink that he'd given Mavis. She'd heard Mavis' cackling reply. The two elderly troublemakers set about drinking their cups of tea.

Feeling a mixture of shame and embarrassment no doubt equal to that of the hens as she shoved her hand underneath their warm bottoms in search of soft, new, pink eggs, Carrie thought about what she'd just heard.

They must know about Jon and me (someone is shoving their hand under my bottom, is there no privacy or dignity these days?); they think I'm cleverer than them (they expect me to lay eggs); they think I like writing and working at the paper (they think I like being a hen). But they don't know what it's like being cooped up like that all day (but they don't know what it's like being cooped up all day). I don't want to be it any more (I didn't want to be a hen in the first place).'

Carrie found enough eggs and picked her way across the wet lawn back to the farmhouse door. The geraniums in the garden were still holding out against the cold.

'I bet Debs' garden is still full of flowers. What did he mean about 'him' giving Mavis flowers? Is Mavis more than chief cook and bottle washer here? I've suspected it for a long time...it's all a bit strange though. I'll ask Jon... Jon...Where's Jon?'

Carrie filled old Ab's egg cartons and put them back in his bicycle basket. The kitchen door opened and Jon came out. Carrie smiled at him. She couldn't help it. From inside the kitchen an ancient pair of eyes twinkled at her. From inside the top of her wet wellies Jon picked out a posy of bright red geraniums that had got caught there on her return trip from the hens. He put them in her hair at the side of her head; they were cold and wet. Carrie shivered. She looked back into the farmhouse. She smiled at old Ab.

'I'm spoken for!'

Mavis cackled some more.

Monday 30th October

Dear Reader,

Have you noticed how the nights are drawing in? It's getting colder. We close the curtains earlier. It feels good to shut out the dark. It feels good to be warm and cosy inside our homes. Down on the farm, the cattle feel it too. The cows and the other cattle are brought inside to live during the dark months. They are a very noisy community! They shout, they argue, they fight, they play, they spend a lot of time eating, they make a mess - just like us! It's noisy here in this office; it's noisy in the factory down the road; it's noisy at home in the hustle and bustle of daily life. But it's a manmade noise and it's a different sort of noise. It's relentless and unforgiving.

There is another noise that binds everything and everyone together; it's the stillness and peace of quiet time. Sometimes it's hard to find. Sometimes it's hard to keep. Some folk get more than they want; some folk never get enough. Packed together in one living room the cattle achieve the stillness and peace of a quiet time that is second to none. Working alongside the farmer as I feed, water and clean out these riotous animals I feel privileged to have seen it, felt it, shared in it. How do they do it?

There is the answer; they don't 'do' anything except be themselves. They respect themselves and each other. Now you may say that's all very well for the cattle; they don't have as many things to think about as we do. That's true. We have to 'do' and 'think' a lot of things. We are relentless and unforgiving. Now it's very hard work down on the farm, working alongside nature every day. But the farmer has taught me that a little discomfort is a good thing. At my office desk I am clean and warm and relentless in my duties. I am comfortable. On the farm I am often cold and dirty and aching through my duties. I am not relentless; I am uncomfortable.

And it's great! It's natural. All of nature knows the order of things. The cattle slow down in between doing the things they have to do. Why don't you try it? It works!

We can't all be farmers, but we can work in our gardens, walk in the park, look after a pet, or help out at an animal sanctuary. The next time you close your curtains and you breathe in that feeling of relief as you shut out the darkness, see how long you can make that feeling last. The next time you serve up a meal to your hungry family and you hear the contented silence as they begin to eat, see how long you can hear it.

Can you speak without speaking? Why don't you try it? It works! You'll be amazed at how much will be said. If you ever want to buy a cow at auction you'll need to do it! The secret language of bidding is a leftover from our ancestors who depended on signs and symbols for their very survival.

Years ago, the 'Mop Fair' took place around the 10th October. Folk looking for work, dressed in their best clothes, would go to town carrying a symbol of the type of work that they could do - a mop for a maid, wool for a shepherd and so forth. When you'd been hired you wore flowers and ribbons to prove it. Doesn't that sound like a lovely way of doing things? Shall you wear flowers and ribbons when that new job comes along?

Halloween is coming! It's the season of superstition sprinkled with a seasoning of religious beliefs. Throughout the ages the human race has been looking for a sign; it's what everyone longs for.

And in the stillness and peace of quiet time, wherever we may be and whatever we are doing, we can find that sign. You may have flower fairies in your garden. Remember, help and hope are always at hand when we need them; no front door ever built is strong enough to keep them out.

Halloween is coming! You may have skeletons in your cupboard, ghosts in your attic, witches in your wardrobe, but don't look back on your life for you can't change anything. But, just like the cattle, you can quieten down and see the signs.

You can begin a new life here, today. Everything that you've ever loved lives or dies in your heart; it speaks to you without speaking. So listen up!

Tuesday 31st October

'I don't want you to be too late going home, Carrie. You should be back afore it gets dark.'

'Oh it's alright,' replied Carrie cheerfully. 'I don't mind driving in the dark.'

'I do. Make sure you're home before sunset tonight.'

Old man Wilson stared at Carrie as if she had some kind of horrific disfigurement he'd never seen before. He'd been such a solitary bird of prey on her last visit to the farm that she was beginning to think he'd migrated south for the winter with the swallows. But he was here today.

'Maybe he's furious that I've turned up on a week day, without asking.'

She'd taken it as a positive that he'd been leaving her alone so that she could be with Jon; work with Jon. Not so today. He ran her ragged with a string of chores which kept her away from the farmhouse, away from Jon, away from everything that she'd come to take for granted on a Saturday - entertainment from comedy duo Mavis and old Ab and the ecstasy of working alongside Jon.

All she got today was the pain of watching his body from a distance, without ever being able to connect with it. The old man had her cleaning out buckets with a hosepipe. He even had her cleaning the battered old Land Rover; there was at least a decade's worth of mud to remove.

'This isn't real work; this has nothing to do with farming. Perhaps it was a mistake to come here today. He's turned on me again, and I don't know why.'

The Falcon hovered and swooped, swooped and hovered so that Carrie was feeling dizzy and on edge by lunchtime. Old man Wilson was clearly on the edge about something; after barking his ridiculous orders to her he would disappear, only to return a short time later to do some more barking and staring.

'Think he's taking the comment in my article about a little bit of discomfort being a good thing a bit far,' she growled.

'Lunchtime!'

Old man Wilson came upon her so sharply with this longed for order that she slipped and fell flat on her back in the cow muck as she crossed the yard. He overtook her and disappeared into the farmhouse. He must have heard her call out as she fell but he didn't turn round to help her.

'Agh!'

The muck and the wet quickly soaked through her overalls and into her jeans; the cuffs on her sleeves got caught as well as she tried to stand up as cleanly as possible. She always kept spare clothes in the boot of her car but prided herself that she'd never had to use them, until now.

'I was wrong. There's nothing pleasant or romantic about cow muck when you get this close to it.'

Carrie stood in the cold at the backdoor of the farmhouse and slid her overalls to the ground. But she couldn't take her jeans off outside. She thought about going to the outhouse but the door didn't shut properly. And it was freezing cold today anyway. Stinking and stuck Carrie decided to knock on the farmhouse door. A broomstick swept through the door before Carrie had a chance to get near to it.

'Carrie love, get thee inside, it's right cold day today,' said a frilly aproned Mavis.

Mavis clutching her broom reminded Carrie what day it was:

'It's Halloween! If I didn't know better, I should think Mavis wants to lure me inside with promises of unlimited food and drink, so that she can fatten me up and eat me like the witch in Hansel and Gretel! But where's Hansel?'

The witch was squinting at Carrie now through her fogged up plastic spectacles. Carrie turned to show her that there wasn't much fat on her behind:

'I can't come in Mavis, I'm covered in cow muck!'

The witch cackled herself silly; her frilly bosom bent forward beneath the weight of the sound of her own laughter, turning her body into a letter 'R' shape that filled the kitchen doorway completely.

'Come in you daft thing! We don't mind a bit of muck in here. Where there's muck there's brass, isn't that right, lads?' said Mavis.

'She can fatten me up all she wants if Hansel's already in there.'

But old Ab and old man Wilson were the only 'lads' sitting at the kitchen table. Carrie's heart sank. It was lunchtime, and she'd hoped to spend it with Jon.

Mavis had put down her broomstick and was pushing Carrie through the warm kitchen in the direction of the stairs; she was no longer a witch, just a friendly fairy hagmother once more.

'Getcha upstairs and change, and then come down for a bit of dinner,' she commanded.

Carrie obeyed. As she left the warmth of the crackling fire and cackling Mavis there was an immediate change of temperature as she climbed the heavily polished, wooden stairs, creaking into the cold of the upstairs corridor with every upward step. She knew where she was going; the door on the left at the end of the hallway.

The derelict room was waiting for her, door ajar. Carrie reached round the doorframe for the electric light switch; there was no way she was stepping in there without a little company from the single, yellow, electric light bulb. She remembered the last time she'd been in there. Her body started to tingle.

The big holes in the white plaster ceiling were still there. Carrie didn't look up at the rafters. It was Halloween and therefore they were likely to be definitely full of ghosts and big spiders. But the friendly oval wardrobe mirror was still there, too. Carrie made straight for it and stared deep into it, hoping to see and feel the erotic, beautiful, turned on Carrie that had looked into its rusty reflection the last time she was here.

'Yes, she's still here. I can see her!'

She could also see the tapestry covered chaise longue. The long, black, velvet dress sat reclined upon it, staring at her, as if she had some kind of horrific disfigurement. Carrie jumped out of her skin. The dress hadn't moved since she'd laid it out after the party all those months ago.

'Have you forgotten me?' said the beautiful, long, black velvet dress.

Carrie backed up against the comfort of the friendly oval mirror.

'Oh!'

Carrie was speechless. She stared at the vision in front of her. Folds of long black velvet called to her.

'You're so beautiful. Come to me!'

Carrie fumbled with her jeans. She ripped at the zip. She wrestled the stinking, soaking wet, material from her buttocks and nearly fell over in her rush to be rid of it. Her pants were cold and wet. She was cold and wet. She didn't care. She just had to feel the weight of that black velvet body pressing on her one more time.

'Ooh!'

She gently lifted the long black dress, caught hold of its waistline, and held it against her trembling body. She remembered Jon's hands.

'Oh!'

She was speechless. The folds of long black velvet caressed her body. She folded her arms around the weight of the dress and clung to it with all her might. She didn't waste any time looking in the mirror. Carrie closed her eyes. She was that beautiful medieval maiden in the orchard again; she was the Hollywood femme fatale. She just couldn't stop her hands from touching the beautiful, beautiful dress. She was seriously turned on again. She didn't know how long she'd been standing there but suddenly, a floorboard creaked in the hallway, and, even more suddenly, the door opened on her derelict passions.

He stood in the doorway and stared at her. Carrie stared back at him because she wasn't wearing much else. The long, black, velvet dress stared too.

'You're so beautiful. Come to me!'

Only the friendly oval wardrobe mirror heard who spoke without speaking first. It didn't really matter because they all came together in front of its rusty yellow reflection. The uneven creak of the bare and dusty floorboards from his still slightly limping leg chased the ghosts in the rafters away. He caught hold of the dress and the woman who was holding it at the waistline. He gently held them both in his hands. He let the full weight of the woman and the dress fall into him. He ignored the dress and kissed the woman. She couldn't help letting out an 'Ooh!' as he pressed the soft fabric deep into her body.

They didn't know how long they'd been standing there but suddenly, a cackle called out:

'Carrie, shall you have a bit of dinner?'

'Yes thank you, Mavis, I'm coming.'

Carrie felt a tingle down her spine, for she very nearly was. The uneven creak of the bare and dusty floorboards took Jon away as suddenly as he'd arrived. The bedroom door closed behind him.

'Well, go on then!' said the oval mirror. *'You can't stay here all day. You have dinner to eat.'*

Carrie quickly got changed into her fresh clothes. She laid the long, black, velvet dress back onto the tapestry covered chaise longue.

'Oh, you're so beautiful!'

'So are you,' replied the friendly oval mirror.

Carrie didn't hear for she was already creaking away down the cold corridor as fast as she could, back to the warmth of crackling fire and cackling Mavis in the kitchen. She didn't see the long, black, velvet dress hold its arms out to her in a gentle and pleading sort of way as she switched off the yellow, electric light bulb. It was Halloween. The ghosts could return from the rafters now that the breathing folk had gone away.

Jon was standing by the fire, staring at the steaming, boiling, kettle.

'He feels the cold like me.'

Carrie shivered. It had been so cold and spooky upstairs but she only started to feel it now that she was returned to the warm welcome of the farmhouse kitchen. Or was it the pair of pale ice blue eyes of old man

277

Wilson that followed her to the kitchen table that were responsible for her shakes? Or the guilt of creaking bare and dusty floorboards? Either way, Carrie was just as dizzy and on edge as she was before she'd fallen in the cowmuck.

She continued to fall, over and over again, throughout the eating of beef stew and mashed potatoes. Her stomach churned, her throat struggled to swallow, as black velvet and cow muck touched her mind, her stomach and her cold, wet, behind.

Jon went outside to 'get on'; Mavis got on with the pots; old Ab got out his pipe and flavoured her last mouthfuls of stew with a friendly smoky wood smell. Old man Wilson sat back in his big wooden chair like father bear from the 'Goldilocks' story, endlessly fumbling with his thumb and forefinger inside the fob watch pocket on his wiry old waistcoat. For all the time he spent fumbling he never pulled on the chain to look at his watch.

'Might as well get home early,' he said.

'I'm happy to do some more cleaning,' said Carrie.

'Not today,' replied the Falcon, abruptly.

'Well, I'll just finish off then.'

Carrie's heart sank yet again. She'd hoped to spend the afternoon with Jon and do a bit more 'finishing off.'

'Thanks for the dinner Mavis, it was lovely.'

'You're welcome, Carrie love, anytime, isn't she, Ezra?'

The Falcon scraped his big wooden chair back from the table, and suddenly flew away through the kitchen door without even so much as an 'Ah.'

'Perhaps he doesn't like his name, or her calling him it in front of me?'

'Take no notice of him,' said Mavis. 'He don't mean no harm.'

She took a small bowl of stew to the back door.

'Jip! Jip!' she called.

Jip came running for his stew. Carrie smiled nervously at old Ab and made to follow her through the door.

'Ah, you were right, missy. Everything lives or dies in here.'

Old Ab pointed to his withered chest with his pipe; a flake or two of ash fell onto the tablecloth as he tipped it up. He brushed it away with his marble hand. Carrie looked blankly at him.

'He feels it, Miss Carrie, he feels it.'

Carrie still looked blank.

'It's Halloween! If you've got ghosts in your life it means more to you, especially when you can't let them go.'

Old Ab shook his head sadly.

'I don't understand,' said Carrie.

'You've seen him. I've seen you watching him, working that chain in his pocket.'

'What is it?' asked Carrie.

'He keeps her ring in a little tin. He's never let her go. Drove him mad when he lost her. He lay in a ditch for two weeks, nearly lost everything. Folk rallied round. Mavis came and saw to the lads, they were right little. She was her cousin. Been here ever since. Neighbours came and kept the farm going. He got going again, but he were never the same.'

Carrie watched the smoke from old Ab's pipe curl and uncurl like the thoughts in her head. She shivered. It was Halloween. All of a sudden she needed to get home early before it got dark. Before sunset; she'd had her fill of ghosts today.

The dress! No wonder I struggled to eat my dinner.'

Carrie needed to do some breathing. The smoke from old Ab's pipe was choking her and making her eyes run. She gestured to old Ab and made for the door just as Mavis came back in with Jip's empty bowl. She pushed the fairy hagmother out of the way; she needed to shake with cold. The sound of creaking floorboards haunted her all the way across the yard; the soft fabric of the mud beneath her running feet pressed into their soles like the deepest black velvet.

'Everything that you've ever loved lives or dies in your heart; it speaks to you without speaking. So listen up!'

Carrie ran to the one place on the farm where she felt safe. She needed to be alone. She needed to listen. Jip ran with her. He loved this game with Carrie. They had run together through the trees in the orchard many times before....

———————◆———————

Debs was working in her garden, even though it was a freezing cold day. There wasn't much to do, really, at this time of year, but she could always find a bit of tidying up. It was Halloween. The ghosts from her past kept her company. Trick or treating. Dressing up. Badly fitting plastic vampire teeth, outrageous make up and fake blood - Debs was a master of disguise. Nobody could ever guess it was really her, not even Carrie sometimes. Debs smiled to herself.

'Dopey cow! She didn't even recognise me at first, on the bridge the other week - I've not lost my touch. I'm still the cover up Queen!'

As she grubbed around beneath the shadows of the bushes, gathering stray leaves and the odd weed that refused to die, a succession of ghosts, ghouls, witches and demons appeared, arms raised, woefully wailing in ridiculous high pitched voices, to trick or treat her memories. She could remember every last detail of the great lengths that she and Carrie went to, to turn themselves into the living dead. Even the smells.

They spent many happy hours trying to make the greatest stench possible by mixing the contents of her mother's kitchen cupboards with the oil and grease from her dad's garage. It always looked like the finest witches brew but never really achieved much of a smell, except in the year that they bought a piece of meat from the butcher and soaked it for a couple of weeks beforehand.

Their scariest year by far was the year of the vampire. Carrie found an old velvet curtain at home, so they cut it in half to make two cloaks. It didn't matter that it was dark red instead of the traditional black. They terrified themselves a treat beneath the weight of the folds of that mysteriously soft and wonderful material. It was such touchy feely stuff that it made them feel really special. They didn't feel quite so special when Carrie's mother couldn't find one of her best red velvet curtains that she'd taken down for dry cleaning. That was the end of playing with velvet.

Debs smiled to herself again. Not quite the end, for her hands smoothed out the velvet soil now. Soft and dark red, her top soil contained quite a lot of clay. She couldn't help letting out an 'Ooh!' as she pressed her hands deep into its soft fabric.

'Have you forgotten me?' said the pale blue flower fairy with silver wings that was lying on her side at the back of the bushes.

She'd been knocked off her stand and one of her silver wings was chipped.

'Oh!'

Debs was speechless. She stared at the vision in front of her.

'You're so beautiful. You can still fly,' she said, gently lifting the fairy up and placing her back onto her stand. She remembered Carrie's article.

'She said look for the signs. Well, I've got a fairy in my garden! What does that mean, then?'

Debs heard her front door bang. It was time to stop working in the garden; it was a freezing cold day anyway. She stood up. She said 'goodbye' to the pale blue flower fairy with the chipped silver wing.

'I won't forget you,' she whispered as she walked down the garden path back to the house.

'You're so beautiful. You can still fly,' replied the pale blue flower fairy.

Debs didn't hear her. She was inside the house, looking for signs. It was quite possible to be spooked and scared on any day of the year; the tricks played by ghosts, witches and demons on Halloween were a treat compared to the horrors of daily life.

———◆———

Jill looked out of her kitchen window. She 'tutted.' There were brown finger marks on her lace curtains; it was either oil or cow muck, she couldn't tell which.

'It's just hopeless. Hopeless! How on earth do they expect me to keep this house clean when they can't stop touching things with their dirty fingers!'

Jill was full of despair. And Bill had only got one hand anyway. Her kitchen curtains were dirty. The late afternoon sun was drowning in its own blood, congealing into the evening, and Carrie wasn't home yet. Jill had planned a cosy night in by the fire, with them all safe at home together. She had planned to close the curtains early tonight; to shut out the dark and hold on to the feeling for as long as possible.

It was Halloween. Not that Jill was superstitious; she was only religious when she had to be seen to be, so she was certainly not going to believe in all that ancient 'ghost' nonsense. No, she just wanted to keep all those ridiculous 'Trick or Treaters' away; tonight had nothing to do with shutting out the dark or the fact that it was Halloween.

'The only spirits I'm having here tonight will be at the bottom of my glass!' snapped Jill, checking the kitchen window and lace curtains again for the sight or sound of Carrie's little red car, and to count exactly how many black finger marks she would have to battle on Monday morning.

A light was on in the garage; Bill was home early as requested.

'He doesn't like 'Trick or Treaters' either. It's only Carrie who's silly about it.'

Jill shuddered. She suddenly remembered what Carrie did to one of her best dark red velvet curtains one Halloween not so very long ago.

'Silly little girl! And she's still being silly now. Only she could think it's funny to be deliberately late home in the dark, tonight of all nights. She's just doing this on purpose to spite me.'

She might be silly, and awkward, and disobedient, even a disappointment at times, but Carrie was still her one and only daughter. It didn't have to be Halloween for Jill to feel anxious until she returned safe and sound in her little red car; she felt it every second of every minute of every hour of every day and every night about something or other. Jill made her own 'comfort anxiety' like some people ate 'comfort food'. Halloween gave her the perfect opportunity for a secret 'binge'.

There's no telling who'll be about on the roads tonight. I just couldn't bear it if anything happened to her. What a terrible fate to have to bury your own child, your own love, and leave her all alone in the dark...I should weep forever...'

But in the meantime, Jill got on with preparing the dinner and setting the table. She glanced up at the kitchen window, looking for a sign. All she saw was the ghostly reflection of her own face staring back at her. It had some kind of horrific disfigurement that she'd never seen before:

'Have you forgotten me?' said the face.

'Oh!'

Jill was speechless. She stared at the vision in front of her.

'You're so beautiful. Why do you weep so?'

'Ooh!' shrieked Jill.

The vision suddenly grinned and waved at her.

'Trick or treat!' shouted Bill through the kitchen window.

Jill staggered backwards, clutching her chest in the terrible pain of real anxiety. She breathed heavily:

'You nearly gave me a heart attack, you ridiculous man!'

The ridiculous man was coming in through the kitchen door now; there would be no treats for him tonight, and he knew it. Jill was standing in the kitchen holding on tight to her fast beating heart.

'Everything that you've ever loved lives or dies in your heart; it speaks to you without speaking. So listen up...What does my daughter know about hearts?'

---◆---

'W..wait for m..me in the orchard.'

'Did Jon say 'Wait for me in the orchard,' or 'Wait for me in the orchard?' I'll wait for you forever. You don't need to command or request. Don't you know that?'

Carrie forgot all about Halloween; she forgot that she'd promised more than one person, as well as herself, that she'd be home before dark. She listened to her heart. In the orchard the stone bench beneath the sad looking tree was waiting for her. Pale and white, the bench was the only source of light in that darkening place. Carrie sat, cold, upon it and set about the task of waiting forever. She sat, all folded up, like a pale dove, sad and alone at sunset, singing a sad song, waiting for her mate to join her. She was surrounded by the soundless murmur of rustling leaves. It was the sad song of the trees as they were slowly eaten alive by the encroaching darkness.

Roots first, they disappeared into the black earth. Their branches wailed with pain in the night wind. Carrie's feet sat on the edge of the terrible darkness. There was no carpet of beautiful green grass left, only a black hole stretching all the way to the stone pillars at the gateway; the galaxy of lights from the farm buildings looked light years away.

'Jon might be an old man by the time he reaches me! Never mind, I'll still wait for him forever.'

Carrie waited. The sad looking tree waited with her. It was very quiet. Its branches, dressed in the soft black velvet of the night, caressed her face, they held her close, they creaked as they pressed into her body.

'You're so beautiful. Come to me!'

'Oh!'

Carrie was speechless. She remembered the beautiful medieval maiden in the orchard. She remembered the uneven creak of bare and dusty floorboards. She closed her eyes. Carrie felt a tingle down her spine; she very nearly was, again.

'Everything that you've ever loved lives or dies in your heart; it speaks to you without speaking. So listen up...'

Carrie listened. She heard breathing. The soft black velvet tree was breathing. Carrie listened again. The soft black velvet tree had a heart that was beating. It was alive. She could feel its life force pulsing, thumping, vibrating through her own body - or was it just her own heart, living, waiting...But she still heard breathing.

He gently held her face in his big, strong, hands. They were cold. Carrie tried to jump out of her skin but he was holding on to her face.

'Oh!'

Carrie was speechless. She stared at the vision in front of her.

'What are you doing here?' he said.

Carrie backed up against the comfort of the soft black velvet, sad looking tree. Its heart was still beating hard in to hers. She stared at old man Wilson as if he had some kind of horrific disfigurement. Pale ice blue eyes stared back at her; they burnt into her face, turning it to ash. Suddenly, dark with understanding, the eyes let her go. Carrie ran, shedding flakes of ash as she flew through the trees. She ran straight across the black hole towards the galaxy of lights from the farm buildings beyond.

'Carrie! Carrie! I'm sorry!'

But Carrie didn't hear his call; she was already light years away. It was Halloween; she'd promised more than one person, as well as herself, that she'd be home before sunset. But she hadn't done it. She had ignored the signs, and now she was well and truly spooked.

She ran straight into two familiar, big, strong arms. Without thinking, without hesitating, he put his arms around her and held her tight; he could tell she'd been spooked by something because she was shaking. It was Halloween, after all. She buried her head in his old jumper.

'Hold me! Please hold me tight!' she sobbed into it.

'Your dad scared me.'

'Shhh...' he said gently.

He held her tight. Carrie listened. She heard breathing. He was breathing with her. Carrie listened again. His heart was beating. She could feel his life force pulsing, thumping, vibrating through her body, with her body, in her body. She breathed with him. She stopped shaking. She breathed deeply. The ghost of childhood smells, oil and grease, calmed her haunted senses.

'Oh!'

Carrie was speechless. Too late, she stared at the vision in front of her. Jed smiled down at her and continued to hold her tight in his loving embrace; he was shaking with silent laughter.

'Jip!' called out a ghostly voice.

'Oh!'

Carrie was speechless. Jon was walking away across the yard. He switched the cowshed lights off one by one as he went. He kept his eyes fixed to the ground. The farmyard, and everything in it, was being slowly eaten alive by the encroaching darkness. Without thinking, without hesitating, he walked across its black hole to the farmhouse kitchen; another world was waiting for him there. It would be warm in the farmhouse kitchen; he really felt the cold these days.

———◆———

The immense night weighed heavily upon her. Carrie lay in her bed, waiting for sleep to take her. She was shaking with cold. The soft, black, velvet cloak of midnight spread like a shroud over her body and her bed. There was no warmth in it, even though it pressed deep into her.

Carrie touched her body. She touched it in the places that no one else had visited. She held herself tight in a loving embrace. She was cold and wet. Her skin was soft as velvet. Her body started to tingle.

'Oh!'

She was speechless.

'He hasn't actually touched me anywhere that I want him to, even when he had the chance! Why did he walk away?

It's Halloween, after all. 'Trick or treat?' asked the Walnut in her bedside table drawer.

The Walnut listened, but Carrie gave no answer. She had turned over to the other side of the bed; it would be warmer over there. She breathed her way into the soft, black, velvet folds of deep sleep. The Walnut listened to her breathing.

'You're so beautiful, I'll wait for you forever...Everything you've ever loved lives or dies in my heart...Don't you know that?'

Wednesday 1st November

Mr Pike heard giggling coming from conference room number one. Even though this room doubled as a staffroom, he felt duty bound to investigate the sound. It wasn't the usual sound of happy office staff; there was far too much laughter. And it wasn't coffee time, either. It was going home time, and Mr Pike wanted to go, but first he wanted to get to the bottom of the happy sound that had no right to be there. His thick, rubbery lips bubbled with anticipation as his cold, clammy, hand quietly pressed down the door handle.

He was ready to boom outrage and indignation at the person or persons who were on the other side of the door, who were no doubt engaging in illicit behaviour of some sort or other; he had no idea what he was about to see and he was looking forwards to catching them at it, whatever 'it' might be.

He hadn't caught anyone 'at it' in his office empire for quite some time; either the young folk of today were different from in his day, or, they were a lot better at hiding it, or, they didn't dare do it on his watch; he congratulated himself that this last reason was most certainly the true one. Someone behind conference room number one, however, didn't know the truth...

'Carrie!' boomed Mr Pike, 'What are you doing in here?'

Mr Pike's boom of outrage and anticipation quickly faded to a bubble of disappointment. Carrie was sitting on the conference room table clutching nothing more than a cup of coffee. Her feet were resting on a chair. At the sound of Mr Pike's 'boom' she quickly dropped her legs to the floor and stood up, pulling her pencil skirt down over her knees as fast as possible, hoping that he didn't see her feet resting on the chair. Mr Pike saw everything. Carrie blushed.

'This is my friend, Debbie Harrington, Mr Pike.'

Debbie Harrington dutifully stood up from the chair that she'd been sitting in; her cup of coffee was on the table.

'Debbie's come in with an item for our 'Deaths' column. It's difficult for her to get here earlier in the day because of work, and we were just having a chat because we haven't seen each other in a while. I hope you don't mind; we were just going now, actually.'

'Mind? Of course I don't mind! Any lady friend of yours, Carrie, is a friend of mine. Condolences to you, dear lady.'

Mr Pike boomed generously in Debs' direction.

'So you wouldn't mind if she occasionally called in now and then on her way home from work?'

Carrie smiled her best, reassuring, smile at the big fish. He waved a friendly fin in Carrie's direction, and talked to her knees, one of which was still showing slightly after her failed attempt to cover up the fact that she'd been sitting with her feet on one of his best conference room chairs.

'Of course not, of course not, just so long as it doesn't eat into your working day. Just make sure you switch the light off before you leave.'

'Oh thank you Mr Pike, you're very kind,' said a relieved Carrie.

Mr Pike heard the relief in her voice. He spoke quietly as he closed the door behind him.

'I understand the need for privacy, now and then.'

Carrie and Debs waited until the last ripple left by Mr Pike's wake had completely disappeared.

'Come on, let's get out of here,' said Carrie.

Debs giggled quietly.

'You lying toad! What are you going to put in the 'Deaths' column now? You'll have to invent somebody! Did you see the look on his face when he walked in? I bet he could see right up your skirt!'

'Don't remind me,' groaned Carrie.

'Remember to switch the light off, though,' reprimanded Debs.

'Don't mock! He's going to let you call in here, which means we can keep in touch better from now on,' said Carrie. 'I must say, I'm a bit puzzled by what he said, though.'

'It doesn't matter,' said Debs. 'He likes you. Just keep sitting on the edge of the desk and show him your knees every now and then, and he'll be happy,' she laughed.

'Give over!'

Carrie pushed Debs through the door, and they tiptoed away, down the corridor, onto the stairs and out into reality once more.

Mr Pike was sitting in his office. The happy sound disappeared down the stairwell and into the busy street. For some reason, he didn't want to go home any more. Disappointment and a touch of sadness swelled his swim bladder so that he couldn't move. He sank to the bottom of his chair and stayed there.

'*So that's why she never writes about the farmers,*' he blubbed.

'*Oh well, each to his own, each to his own,*' he sighed. '*She's still a lovely girl.*'

The thought of lovely girls raised Mr Pike from his chair. His swim bladder returned to normal; he wanted to go home now. He congratulated himself:

'Everybody's entitled to a little bit of privacy now and then. Yes, indeed, I am a very kind and generous man.'

Mr Pike forgot to switch the lights off as he left his office. He was in need of a little privacy, and he needed it now.

———◆———

'You're late!'

'Sorry! I met up with Debs for a coffee on the way home. We don't get chance to meet up as often as we used to.'

'Well whose fault is that?' spat her mother. 'You're never here at weekends, and you're always late home. Late, late, late. You promised me you'd be home before dark on Halloween! I was beside myself with worry; I thought something terrible had happened to you.'

'It did.'

'I've said I was sorry about that.'

'Can you remember what a state you were in? You frightened your father and me to death!'

'I remember.'

Carrie wanted to go now, but her mother hadn't finished.

'I heard you moaning and groaning in your sleep. I didn't get a single wink of sleep all night for worrying about you, and here you are, late again, and the dinner's ruined! Why don't you ever let me know what's going on? Am I so unimportant or unreasonable that you can't just let me know if you're running late?'

'I'm sorry, Mother, I just forgot. It was a spur of the moment thing; it wasn't planned.'

'Well don't you think it's about time you did some planning for a change? Where are you going, Carrie? What are you doing with your life?'

'I don't know. I don't know!'

'I know very well that you earn peanuts at that newspaper! You're stuck in the 'Births' and 'Deaths' columns. What sort of a career is that?''

'Actually, they're probably the two most important events in our lives...'

'And, to finish off, you spend every weekend working for nothing at that disgusting, dirty farm. You let those farmers take advantage of you, goodness knows what they have you doing, you almost always come back in a terrible state, and I don't just mean stinking of cow muck, but that as well. Where's your self-respect, Carrie? Why can't you be a respectable, responsible, young woman like your friend, Deborah?'

'I am respectable and responsible!' cried an angry Carrie

'And I don't need reminding about terrible states right now!'

Carrie could cry at the top of her voice but her mother wasn't going to listen.

'She's the same age as you, yet she works full time, she's happily married, she runs her own home, supports her husband and no doubt she'll be planning children before too long. That's respectable and responsible! What do you do? Pretend to be a journalist, play down on the farm at weekends like a love struck teenager, chasing some romantic notion of country life, being at one with nature. If that's how you're going to waste your life you might as well give up now. If all you want to be is a nothing, you might as well get married and have a family, like Deborah. At least we'd have some grandchildren to be proud of, then.'

'She must be finished now, surely. I'm finished. How can all of that come out of me being a bit late for dinner?'

'I'll go and waste my life upstairs out of your way, then,' said Carrie.

'Don't be ridiculous! The dinner's ready. Go and tell your dad, he's in the garage.'

Carrie told her dad. She also told him that she wasn't feeling hungry right now; perhaps he could leave her some dinner on a plate that she could eat later. Then she went straight upstairs, out of the way. Her mother was outraged. She told Bill all about it over dinner:

'She's always late. She never tells me anything. I try to help her, give her good advice, but she never listens to anything I say. I spend all my time worrying about her and she doesn't care. I only want the best for her, but she doesn't seem to want it for herself. I don't know where we've gone wrong with her, I really don't. What have we done to deserve all this trouble all the time? She's all I've got. Doesn't she know that?'

Bill reassured Carrie's mother that her daughter knew that.

'Look at the state you're in. You frighten me to death!'

After dinner, Bill went back to the garage, out of the way. Carrie's mother left a place laid and a plate of dinner for her daughter. She moved the jug of fresh flowers from the kitchen window and put them on the table. She knew that Carrie liked flowers and she wanted to make the table pretty for her whilst she ate her dinner. The flowers were still on the table the following morning. So was the dinner.

Friday 3rd November

She was waiting in the middle of the high Japanese bridge. Even though it was made of metal, the bridge swayed to and fro with every gust of wind. It seemed like she'd been waiting forever; she held onto the railing with her arms fully outstretched so as to keep herself away from the edge. Her feet were cold. She tried a little cha- cha-cha, a little heel - toe tap dance, finishing with a low level can-can, to fight the cold and the edge, but the high Japanese bridge wasn't in the mood for dancing.

It was such a bitter November day that the park was deserted even though it was a Friday lunchtime. She relaxed into the comfort of the emptiness around her. Maybe it would be a good meeting place after all. She suddenly felt brave enough to peer over the edge and have a look at the darkness of the water below. There were still no fish.

'The fish might be far away, but so is the darkness.'

She didn't know how long she'd been standing there, staring down very intently into the water, when she felt footsteps dancing along the bridge towards her. The bridge shook violently again as if trying to shake off the intruder; it failed. She turned to smile at her friend.

'What are you doing here?' said the familiar voice.

A man on his bicycle rang his bell repeatedly and loudly. He smiled and waved at the happy couple as he passed by. Two teenage boys were laughing. Pointing. They carried on walking along the path; they were too embarrassed to walk past the happy couple who were locked together in a passionate embrace at the top of the high Japanese bridge.

Beneath the shadows cast by her favourite weeping willow tree Carrie kept out of the way. They were supposed to meet up at two o'clock, but it was nearly quarter past now; Carrie had been running late. It had been her idea. She had listened to her mother. She had planned her Friday lunchtime; the plan had gone wrong.

'Never listen to your mother! What are you doing, Carrie? Where are you going, Carrie? I don't know. Everything I do goes wrong! Everybody I touch gets hurt!'

Carrie stood still and quiet beneath the shadows and watched her plan, the plot that failed, fail. She backed up against the weeping willow tree for support; its damp silver bark wept onto her back.

The happy couple were still standing together in the middle of the high Japanese style bridge with the widely spaced metal railings. Carrie was afraid that Debs was going to fall. Joe fell into her. Head, hands, arms, face, hair. He held onto her very tight. Her body trembled in the cold

November wind day. She trembled long after the sound of the friendly bicycle bell faded into the distance; long after he'd finished whispering in her ear, long after he locked his fingers in hers and started to walk her away down the path alongside the river.

'Oh!'

Carrie was speechless. She stared at the vision in front of her. Joe's face looked like he had some kind of horrific disfigurement.

'Oh!'

Debs was speechless. She stared at Carrie standing beneath the shadows of the weeping willow tree. Carrie stood still. She knew that it wasn't time for her to come out of the shadows; it was a cold November wind day. Debs' face had turned to ash; she shed a few flakes as she walked along the path with her husband. Carrie stared back at the happy, respectable, responsible, couple.

'Debs! Debs! I'm so sorry!'

Debs' eyes, dark with understanding, let her go. Carrie walked away through the park.

'I've got to be back before...two thirty.'

Her cloud of unknowing lifted.

'Hold me! Please hold me tight!' she sobbed into the cold November wind day.

She kept her eyes fixed to the ground. She remembered Jon's hands. She was being slowly eaten alive by the light of understanding. She needed to get back to the office; another world would be waiting for her there. It would be warm in the office; she really felt the cold today.

———◆———

Dear Reader,

Few people find the month of November to be a pleasant one. The Anglo-Saxons called it 'wind monath', the month when the cold winds begin to blow. In Finland it's called 'marraskuu', meaning 'month of the dead.' Our ancestors associated death with fertility; celebrations took place at the beginning of November which marked the end of harvest and the beginning of winter. Folk believed that to honour their dead at this dark time would increase the prosperity and fertility of the living.

Down on the farm there is no finer example of fertility flourishing than a flock of sheep, toughing out the 'wind monath' in their thick wool coats. The expectant mothers are quite happy to live out in the fields, in the wet or the frost, as long as they are fed. A diet of grass and hay is all they need to sustain their heavily pregnant little bodies. They might look like nothing more than overfilled beanbags tottering about on matchstick legs, but this curious, opportunist, gregarious flock of fluffy ladies could give any 'Local Ladies Network' a run for their money in many a social situation!

Sheep have a reputation for being rather silly, woolly headed individuals, who don't have very much going on in their lives. If you take a look underneath their fluffy exteriors you will discover that this is not the case at all. Sheep do like to be in a group and they like to follow a leader. The leader does not have to necessarily be a born leader, but is often just the first individual to move in a certain direction. Sheep don't like being separated from each other and, just like us, they have 'best friends.'

The similarities do not end there. Just like us, they have their own, unique, bleat (a 'baa' to us town folk), a voice which they use to 'network' in their community. Walk into any meeting of four or more people and you will hear the same bleats, grunts, rumbles and snorts as if you were standing in the middle of a flock of sheep. Unlike us, they stay silent when in pain. Just like us, sheep are food orientated, although some folk may be outraged at such a comparison.

Sheep have some truly amazing abilities. They have good hearing and are sensitive to noise; they have an excellent sense of smell; they have excellent peripheral vision so that they can see behind themselves without turning their heads! They have good memories and can recognise up to fifty faces, both sheep and human and remember them for years. They can work out how you're feeling from the expression on your face, and they can show their own feelings through the position of their ears. All skills that would be the envy of many a 'Local Ladies Network' member.

But being a sheep does have its drawbacks. Sheep have no depth of vision; they don't like shadows and dips in the ground and will always move uphill and into the light wherever they can. Their only means of defence is to run away from danger. If they are attacked and survive they are likely to die of panic afterwards. Even more unfortunately, they can't right themselves if they fall down in certain positions and will die within an hour or so if not given help.

Sheep can do problem solving but are not as bright as pigs. Nevertheless, they were sacred animals to the Egyptians and, as one of the twelve animals in the Chinese Zodiac, they represent righteousness, sincerity, gentleness and compassion. So if someone calls you a 'black sheep' it's not necessarily a bad thing. Instead of counting sheep, why not try counting the talents of sheep? Why not try counting your own talents? If you look underneath your fluffy exterior, you will be surprised at how many you might find, and you'll get to sleep faster!

Saturday 4th November

Jed wasn't working at the tractor workshop. Carrie had a bad feeling about the day ahead. It was going to be difficult enough to talk to Jon about what happened last weekend without him hanging around, making the damage even worse.

'Hello, darlin'! Do you want to come and help me oil my machinery?'

Carrie ignored Jed and set off across the yard in search of just about anybody else she could find who wasn't Jed. She knew that he hadn't finished with her yet. He walked alongside her keeping so close to her ankles that he'd win the top prize at Crufts for walking to heel if he were a dog. Jip, the dog that she wanted to find, was nowhere to be seen.

'How about it, then? Why don't you come down to the workshop with me instead of slaving away in the dirt here?'

'Go away, Jed, you're starting to sound like my mother! Agh! Go away, thoughts of mother!'

Carrie walked on. She caught the sound of a familiar whistle on the wind. She quickened her pace; Jed obediently did the same. He was moving so closely with her that they might as well have had their legs tied together at the ankle. This was a three legged race that Jed intended to win. Carrie was furious with him. She didn't like how he was making her feel right now. She concentrated as hard as she could on looking where she was going, but even then, she couldn't help but see and feel the edges of Jed. Her primitive body saw and felt Jon. He even smelt the same as his brother and there was the added distraction of that oily garage perfume on his shirt that had always sent her on a trip to paradise. And he was still rattling on about garages:

'Don't you fancy a day in the right sort of dirt with me? Think about all that oil and grease, Carrie! You know your way round an engine, don't you? Wouldn't you like to fiddle about with me and undo some nuts? Then we could screw them back up together!'

Carrie fought her senses and the adrenalin rush that swelled up in her belly. She was plain angry with him, now. She stopped walking. Jed nearly lost his balance and grabbed onto her shoulder for support just as Jon came whistling round the corner with Jip.

'No! Enough!' she shouted at Jed. 'I do *not* want to spend the day in a garage with you, or spend the day, any day, with you, full stop. I'm here to learn about farming, and that's all, so leave me alone!'

Jon and Jip slowed to a stop. They made up a foursome with Carrie and Jed as if they were getting ready for a square dance. But there was no music. This was a good thing because Carrie didn't feel like dancing, Jon had already said that he couldn't dance, Jip wouldn't do anything without his master; only Jed had all the moves worked out. He moved now:

'Alright, alright!' he smiled, letting go of her shoulder.

'I was only being friendly! You were friendly with my jumper, last week, weren't you? Just thought you might like a bit more of the same. We don't want you to be bored while you're here, do we, Jon?'

Jon said nothing. Jip sat down. Carrie looked at Jip.

'That was a mistake, it was dark and I let Halloween get to me, I'm sorry.'

'I'm all for mistakes, I've made plenty in my time!'

Jon said nothing. He looked down at Jip and stroked the top of his head.

'Looks like you've made a mistake as well, brother. The lady's only interested in learning farming. And when she's done it, she'll be back in her shiny office until she decides to learn something else. Isn't that right, Carrie? You mark my words; she's using us just as much as the old man is using her. Still, I'm sure there'll be plenty you can teach her in the meantime. Just like me is our Jon, he's good with his hands…Aren't you, J..Jon?'

'B..better g..get on, then.'

'Thought I'd stick around and give you a hand,' said Jed. 'The workshop's closed today.'

'N..no n..need,' said Jon, turning to walk away.

'Oh b..but I w..want to,' mocked Jed. 'That'll free you up to teach Carrie some more f..f..f..farming.'

'D..do what you w..want.'

Carrie glared at Jed with every atom of hatred that she could muster. Jon and Jip were fast disappearing around the red brick wall corner of the nearest cowshed. Carrie ran after them having no idea what she was going to say or do when she caught up with them. Jed smiled to himself with all his beautiful white teeth. He knew exactly what he was going to do today.

———◆———

Bill wasn't working at the garage. He had a bad feeling about the day ahead.

'It was a lover and his lass, with a hey and a ho and a hey nonny no, and a hey, nonny nonny no...' he sang.

'No! Enough!' snapped Jill. 'I do *not* want to spend my day listening to your infernal singing. I've got enough jobs to get through today, without coping with that as well.'

'But it's a classic! Shakespeare!' replied Bill.

Jill ignored Bill and set off across the car park in the direction of the shopping centre. She knew that he hadn't finished singing yet. The tune was, however, reduced to a small hum underneath his teeth as they rattled along. He walked alongside her so close to her ankles that he'd win the top prize at 'Crufts' for walking to heel if he were a dog. But today, he was a dog nuisance, embarrassing her with his cheerful song. Still, she needed his help today; he'd got a lot of heavy shopping to carry for her. It was November already and time to start planning Christmas.

Jill walked on. She quickened her pace; Bill obediently did the same. He was moving so closely with her that they might as well have had their legs tied together at the ankle. Jill was furious with him. She didn't like how he was making her feel right now. She concentrated as hard as she could on looking where she was going, but even then, she could not help but see and feel the stub of his fingerless hand as it brushed against her coat. He was suffocating her with helpfulness. And he was still singing under his breath.

'Can you please keep a respectable distance, you're crushing me! And stop making that noise! You're embarrassing me!'

Bill smothered his senses. He stopped walking. Jill nearly lost her balance as she angrily turned round to see why he'd stopped. Bill stopped singing.

'Alright! Alright!' he smiled. 'I was just trying to be helpful and keep cheerful. Just thought we could enjoy our day out together, that's all.'

Jill looked at Bill.

'Well, that's a mistake, then. I'm far too busy to be enjoying a day out.'

Bill said nothing.

'And when we're done shopping there'll be plenty more jobs to do at home.'

'Better get on, then.'

'It's about time you gave me a hand at weekends,' said Jill.

Bill held out his one good hand to Jill. She glared at him. Why did he always have to make such a joke, such a show of his disability in public? She turned, and walked into the nearest department store entrance. Bill ran after her having no idea what he was going to say or do when he caught her up. He knew that he was an embarrassment to his wife in public. He hummed along to the cheerful music that was playing over the tannoy. He knew exactly what he was going to be doing today.

———————◆———————

Carrie caught up with Jon and Jip in the dark passageway that led on to the calf sheds. Jon was busy loading buckets onto the feeding trolley. From out of the darkness the menacing face of the pulper machine grinned at her with its ferocious, metal barred teeth. It was silent today. Just like Jon and Jip.

'What shall I do today?' asked Carrie as cheerfully as she could.

'D..do what you w..want.'

'I want to be with you!'

Jon was walking away down the alleyway, pushing the trolley in front of him.

'Please, wait for me!' pleaded Carrie. 'I need to talk to you, tell you what happened. You don't really believe all that rubbish that Jed came out with, do you?'

Jon picked up a bucket of calf pellets and opened the calf shed door. Jip, the conscientious security guard, ran in first to check out the premises before his master entered. Ears pricked, on full alert, he darted into every corner to check for mice, rats, or anybody else who shouldn't be there.

'Talk to me!' cried Carrie.

'I c..can't t..talk. You k..know that.'

'Yes, you can,' said Carrie gently. 'You don't need words to talk to me, especially not in here.'

Jon watched as the bucket of calf pellets was pulled away from his hand. It was replaced by something soft, white and warm. He closed his fingers around it as he had done so many times before in recent weeks. He knew he had the power to crush it in an instant. He chose not to. It felt good to hold. He wanted to hold it, to protect it, just like the rest of her. He was never sure if he was doing it right. He was relieved to find her other hand freely giving itself to his other free hand. Not only her hand. He gave back to her as freely as he received, taking care not to crush her.

'Crush me! Crush me to a pulp!' begged Carrie's body.

'I can't get close enough!' cried her mind.

Jip growled; Jon suddenly let her go. They listened with Jip as the whistling got louder and louder in the alleyway.

'Need a hand in here?' asked a smiling Jed.

He jokingly held out his hands through the part open sliding door. Jon shook his head at Jed. Jip bristled. So did Carrie.

'I've just finished the cowsheds,' said Jed. 'I'll get on with the feeding under the barn, then.'

Jed closed the calf shed door and whistled away.

'Why don't you stand up to him more?' asked Carrie.

Jon shrugged his heavy shoulders.

'N..no point,' he said. 'W..wouldn't change anything, and I d..don't w..want to h..hurt him.'

'Well he wants to hurt you, I'm sure of it,' said Carrie.

Jon shrugged his shoulders again.

'He's always looking for a chance to hurt Jip, surely you can see that?'

'J..Jip can look after himself and s..s..so c..can I,' said Jon. 'J..Jed's just plain d..daft.'

'Your dad can see it. Why don't you ask him?'

'He sees a l..lot of things that aren't th..there,' said Jon.

Carrie felt a tingle down her spine; she hadn't seen old man Wilson since Halloween night when he'd well and truly spooked her in the orchard. She had a feeling he was avoiding her today.

'Well I think he's made a mistake sending him to the tractor workshop. It'll just make him worse, even more jealous of you.'

Jon laughed out loud. The shock of the noise prompted the calves to join in with the joke. They were all laughing at her.

'J..Jed? J..jealous of me? You m..must be j..j..joking!' said Jon, looking down at himself dressed in his mucky overalls and ragged overcoat.

Jip wagged his tail in agreement. Jon walked over to Carrie and put his arms round her. His smile held her tight.

'Have you heard the saying 'keep your friends close but your enemy closer?' said Carrie.

'Are y..you my enemy then?'

His words were improving.

'That's for you to decide!' smiled Carrie, reaching up to run her fingers through his glorious long, dark, hair.

'W..working with the t..tractors keeps J..J..Jed out of mischief,' said Jon.

'He's not there today, is he? I don't trust him one little bit,' said Carrie.

'D..don't b..bother about him. The only m..mischief he's likely to do will be down at 'The B..Black Cow' later.'

'I could play with your hair all day,' said Carrie, happily playing.

'Got to get on,' said Jon.

'I know,' sighed Carrie.

They walked back to the farmyard together. Mavis was standing in the yard, hands on hips, getting on at Jed:

'...and don't you go getting into any mischief, Jed Wilson, or you'll answer to me!'

Her frilly apron, caught in a blast of bitter November wind, shooed Jed away to the Land Rover; he was laughing at Mavis as he went. Mavis turned to squint across the yard to Carrie and Jon. Her big, plastic, spectacles burned into them with the reflection of the late afternoon sun.

'Sent him to fetch me shopping, so's you'll have a bit of peace,' said Mavis. 'Do ya want a cup of tea, Carrie, love?'

'No thanks, Mavis. I'll just help Jon get ready for milking.'

'Right you are,' said Mavis. 'He reckoned as much.'

'He reckoned right, then.'

Carrie shivered at the thought of old man Wilson, Jed, Mavis, or old Ab putting two and two together about her and Jon; it was getting harder to hide the truth every time she came to the farm. At least they'd have a bit of peace for a while now, thanks to wonderful Mavis.

Carrie couldn't milk the cows but she'd learnt enough of the routine to help to get ready for milking. One of her most favourite jobs was to switch on all the lights in the cowsheds. There was something truly magical about the moment, the first sliver of the second, when the warm yellow lights lit up the darkness. Carrie longed to have faith in the dark, just like the cows.

The cows have each other, maybe that's their secret. Maybe one day, I'll live and breathe in the dark like them; maybe one day I'll have company...I must have faith...'

The cows had faith in the light, too; it brought them food and a release from the tension of udders swollen with milk. She wondered if having their udders milked by a machine made them feel sexy. Debs always used to joke about her liking for a hand up her jumper in the days when Carrie found all that sort of thing disgusting; she wasn't so disgusted

299

these days, and was quite keen to find out for herself.

So the flick of the switch that brought the warm yellow light to the cowshed was a signal to the cows to wake up; mostly they would already be standing up, chained by the neck, in their standing places. The bull was tethered in the same way in the stall at the far end of the cowshed; being in the company of the cows kept him happy and easy to manage.

Carrie flicked the switch, looking forward to sharing the magical moment. She flinched. There was no magic here; there was sorcery of the darkest kind. The bull, who had been standing, quietly chewing, let out an enormous bellow and dropped his body to the ground as if he'd been shot between the eyes.

His legs splayed out underneath him; his mad, staring, eyes were more mad than usual. He looked like he was wearing a pair of joke glasses where the eyes stick out on stalks and roll around on springs. He upset the cows who were all up on their feet by now, bellowing back in answer to the bull's distress call. The noise was deafening. Carrie was scared. She didn't know what to do so she quickly turned the light off in the hope that the return of darkness would calm the madness. She ran to fetch Jon.

By the time a puzzled Jon arrived at the cowshed door the bull was back on his feet, the cows were chewing and gently 'mooing' as normal. Jon turned his puzzled look on Carrie; Carrie shrugged her shoulders in embarrassment. Surely she wasn't going mad? Jon flicked the flicked the light switch; the madness returned. The bull bellowed and dropped; the cows bellowed in alarm. Jip started barking.

'Jip!' said Jon sharply.

Jip stopped barking. It was the only thing that stopped. The bull looked like he was having a fit. He was writhing around on the floor doing a very bad job of acting out a death scene. It was quite possible that he wasn't acting; the chain around his neck was getting tighter and tighter.

'I'll have to g..get the b..bolt cutters,' said Jon.

He switched off the light in the hope of achieving some calmness and ran across the yard shouting in the direction of the farmhouse. Carrie and Jip stood in the doorway and watched the sorcery fade away once more.

'It's stopped again!' she shouted across the yard.

Jon came running with bolt cutters; old man Wilson turned up, too. He didn't look at Carrie.

'He's alright in the dark,' said Carrie. 'Maybe there's something wrong with his eyes?'

The two farmers said nothing; a mad bull was a very dangerous thing, whatever the cause. Old man Wilson was holding a shotgun in his hand. Jon switched the light on again and they watched the madness take hold of the bull once more.

'He's ch..choking,' shouted Jon, 'I'll have to cut the ch..chain!'

'Can't!' shouted old man Wilson. 'He'd kill you. I'll have to shoot him!'

The two men walked over to the bull's stall. The enormous, unhappy, creature was writhing around in agony on the floor.

'On my count, switch the light off, Carrie. I'll do it in the dark, so as not to upset the cows.'

Carrie nodded. The old man lined the end of his gun up with the centre of the bull's head.

'Now!' he shouted at Carrie.

Carrie flicked the switch.

'Wait!' shouted Jon. 'Hang on a m..minute.'

He pushed the barrel of his father's gun away from the bull's head. As soon as the lights went out the bull stopped writhing. He was breathing heavily but that was all; even his eyes popped back inside his furry, white, head. He sat on the floor, looking like nothing more dangerous than an old, overstuffed, soft and fluffy, teddy bear. The bolt cutters and the shotgun waited, unsure which one, if any, would be needed. Their owners were hesitating.

'Carrie, switch the light on again,' said old man Wilson.

She flicked and the bull flipped yet again. The bolt cutters took hold of the bull's chain, the shot gun stood ready.

'Agh!' shouted Jon. 'C..cut the l..lights!'

Carrie cut the lights.

'He's b..being electroc..c..cuted by his ch..chain! It's live!' said Jon.

'Well I'll be damned!' said old man Wilson. 'I was going to shoot him! You poor devil!' he said, rubbing the top of the old bull's head.

The bull was too exhausted to care whether anybody shot him or stroked the top of his head. Jon quickly dressed the bull in his rope halter that was usually used to lead him and tied him to the railings at the front of the stall. Then he cut the metal chain from around the bull's neck. Carrie switched the lights back on; faith in the light had been restored.

Jon found a 'live' wire, running from the bull's chain, through a hole in the wall and connected to the wiring on the other side of the shed wall. He looked across the shed at Carrie; Carrie looked back.

For the second time that day, he didn't need words to tell her what he was thinking; neither did she. She felt sad that her eyes said *'told you so';* she didn't like to give anybody bad news, least of all, him.

'It'll be that Jed, you mark my words,' said Mavis, who had just joined the party standing in the cowshed doorway. 'He's been hanging around here all day, getting under me feet, making out as he was going to help out today. I told him more than once to keep out of mischief. It's probably my fault,' sighed Mavis.

Carrie looked at Mavis as if to say 'why?' for she continued:

'Mischief Night! I was talking to Ab about it today, he must have heard and decided to do a bit of mischief himself. He's a few days late, it's really the night before Halloween. But not like this! Years ago it were all about playing tricks on folk, moving things round a bit, moving the neighbours cows from one field to another, hiding stuff and having a bit of fun. Ab used to do it when he were a lad.'

'I've never heard of 'Mischief Night' before,' said Carrie.

'Ah, 'trick or treating' on bonfire night comes from it,' finished old man Wilson. 'Where's Jed?' he asked, sharply.

'He's not back with me shopping yet. Bet he's stopped off at 'The Black Cow,' said Mavis.

'I'll give him a treat when he gets back,' said old man Wilson, quietly.

'I wish I'd known about 'Mischief Night,' thought Carrie, *'I could have used that in my last article.'*

She shuddered at her thought: *'Oh, please stop, head. I don't want to be a user; I don't want to use these people. I love them. I love him. It's doing my head in, and, if something like this can happen on Jed's 'Mischief Night', what on earth's going to happen tomorrow, when it's 'Bonfire Night?' There's going to be fireworks...'*

Sunday 5th November

'Have you read this?'

Jill threw the local paper across the table at Bill; it landed on his hot buttered toast. Bill didn't need to look at the paper to know at which page it would be open; he'd already seen it.

'Yes,' he replied, as neutrally as possible.

The silence at the kitchen table was so loud that Bill could hear it.

'This is going to be bad.'

He bit down hard into his hot buttered toast like a man biting on a piece of wood who was about to have his leg amputated without anaesthetic. He allowed himself a smile as he realised what he was doing.

'I can't afford to lose any more limbs, can I? I'll have to try to stay in one piece or she'll completely disown me!'

'What are you smirking at?'

Jill broke the silence.

'Nothing,' replied Bill, knowing full well that he'd just made things a million times worse by enjoying his own thought.

'She thinks I'm laughing at her! What a shame.'

Bill quietly picked up the newspaper and folded it up.

'I just hope Carrie's not wearing her overalls already; that's the spark that'll well and truly light the fuse on her pyrotechnics.'

'Morning!' chirped the cheerfully polite, hated, figure who came into the kitchen already dressed in her overalls, and cheerfully began to make herself a coffee. Bill sat well back in his chair and waited for the show to begin.

'Oh, Carrie! What have you done! It's 'Bonfire Night'! 'Remember, remember the fifth of November, gunpowder, treason and plot!' And you've committed treason against the most unforgiving ruler that ever lived!'

Carrie looked out of the kitchen window at the sharp, hard, November sun. It was a very cold, clean, morning.

'Looks like it'll be a great night for fireworks with a sky like this,' said Carrie.

'Never play with fireworks, Carrie.'

'Shall we go down to the bonfire in town tonight?' she continued.

'Hold fireworks at arm's length, Carrie.'

'It's very quiet in here this morning. Are you alright?'

Carrie turned away from the sunny kitchen window to look at the kitchen table; she was blinded by the darkness of the kitchen as she turned.

'Never go near a lit firework, Carrie!'

'Baa..baa..baa!' bleated Jill.

Bill watched his daughter's face ignite with understanding.

'People get hurt when they play with fireworks.'

'It was meant to be a compliment!' said Carrie quietly.

'Throwing a firework in a public place is an offence, Carrie. The fine is five thousand pounds!'

Bang! The show had begun. Rocket after rocket exploded at point blank range in his daughter's face. Bill watched his daughter burning in the flames of her mother's highly organised fireworks display. Sparks of many different colours melted Jill's fluffy exterior as she banged, bleated, crackled, grunted, whistled, rumbled and snorted at her daughter's treason. Bill sat on his kitchen chair, roasting to a crisp, like a chestnut placed at the edge of a large bonfire. The noise, light, smell and smoke coming from Jill's seemingly endless supply of gunpowder was beginning to make his eyes run.

'Guy Fawkes jumped from the scaffold at his execution and broke his neck, so as to avoid the pain of mutilation; you're not so lucky, Carrie, you've got nowhere to jump to in this kitchen.'

Bill watched as his daughter was finally hung, drawn and quartered. Her executioner, who had doubled as judge, jury and master of fireworks had put on a fantastic show. Her talent for organising displays for great occasions was envied and admired by her loyal followers at the 'Local Ladies Network'; that's why she was always put in charge. She wasn't about to let her standards slip just because she was in the privacy of her own kitchen; besides, she was protecting the reputation of her flock.

When her last sparkler was spent, Jill dropped it into her bucket of cold satisfaction, and walked away to get on with the rest of her day.

Bill spent the first part of his day emptying the bucket, putting the matches away and trying to deal with the damage left behind in the wake of his wife's premature November 5th celebrations that had got so horribly out of hand.

'Half of all accidents on Bonfire Night involve children.'

Bill looked at his child now. Apart from being welded to the kitchen sink by the sheer force of the blasting that she'd just received, he could see no fire damage to his daughter's face; any burn marks would be internal. More painful, more difficult to treat, taking longer to heal than an open wound, the only medicine he had to hand was a hug and a few kind words. He tried to think of as many as he could; he was not a poet but he knew a few catchy rhymes and songs. He sang in her ear now:

'Remember, remember the fifth of November,

Gunpowder, treason and plot.

We see no reason why gunpowder treason

Should ever be forgot...but she will forget, Carrie, love, she will...and so must you!'

Carrie was spent; she looked at him blankly. He smiled at her and continued:

'Come on, now, Carrie. Don't let her spoil your day and don't go doing anything stupid!'

'Don't you start on me as well,' said Carrie. 'What do you think I'm going to do? Run away and leave home?'

'*Yes!*'

'Of course not!' cried Bill. 'You get off to that farm of yours! They'll be no fireworks there; animals don't like them, you know. He makes you happy doesn't he?'

Carrie tried to stay blank.

'It's alright! You're allowed to be happy, Carrie. And if he makes you happy, then I like him already.'

Tears welled up in his daughter's eyes; unwittingly he'd thrown a firecracker of his own. The spark of truth it contained was more lethal than all her mother's sound and fury put together.

'It's not my f..f..farm,' she stuttered in-between gentle sobs, 'and he m..makes me m..miserable most of the time, you wouldn't unders..s..stand.'

'Perhaps not. But I see how miserable you are all week and I see you come alive on Saturday and Sunday mornings. I understand that much.'

Bill raised Carrie's face with his one, good, kind, hand. It was hot and sweaty but it didn't burn her.

'And I say live, Carrie. Don't mind me or your mother. 'Seize the day!' We've never quite managed it but you can! Start making a few fireworks of your own. Real ones that are going to light up the night sky of your life and stay lit forever.'

For the second time that morning, Bill watched his daughter's face ignite with understanding.

'Now, get in your car and go!'

'I c..can't t..talk,' stumbled Carrie.

'I know. You don't need words to talk to me,' said Bill. 'Go! I'll deal with your mother.'

Carrie kissed her dad on the cheek before walking away to seize her little red car and her day. When she'd gone, he opened up the newspaper and read her article again. He allowed himself a smile as he realised how much he was enjoying the thoughts inside his head.

'So, sheep don't like being separated from each other, they have no depth of vision, their only defence is to run. If attacked, they die of panic…can't right themselves without help…'

Jill was all alone, cornered upstairs. She heard him coming up the stairs. She didn't need to turn her head to know that he was standing in the bedroom doorway, or to see the expression on his face. She didn't want to see it. Bill was not singing this morning, there was not even a small hum from underneath his teeth. His silence was so loud that Jill couldn't bear to listen to it. Panic set in. She thought she was going to die. Bill turned and walked away to get on with the rest of his day.

'She'll need my help to right herself before the day is out, but she can wait an hour or two….Three sparklers burning together make the same heat as a blow torch, and I'm a dab hand with one of them…'

———◆———

Debs was sitting at the kitchen table reading Joe's newspaper; he hadn't come down for his breakfast yet. She always got up first at weekends and made him a cup of tea before nipping down to the shop to fetch his paper. The silence at the kitchen table kept her company as she read, making sure not to crease the pages. She quietly folded the newspaper and put it in Joe's place at the table when she heard him clumping down the stairs.

'Have you been reading my paper?'

Joe threw a suspicious look at Debs as he sat down heavily in his chair.

'No, of course not,' replied Debs as neutrally as possible.

'I'll have toast.'

'Yes, Joe.'

Joe bit down hard into his hot buttered toast and started to read his paper. Debs looked out of the kitchen window at the sharp, hard, November sun that was slowly cleaning the frost away from her garden.

'It's bonfire night! I love fireworks. They're really pretty, like flowers in the sky. And it's fun!'

Debs allowed herself a smile at the thought of sparklers, toffee apples and standing out in the cold watching other people's fireworks because they never had any of their own when she was little.

'What are you smirking at?' crunched Joe, enjoying his own thought as he dropped crumbs all over the page three girl.

'Nothing,' replied cheerfully polite Debs. 'It's bonfire night and it looks like it'll be a great night for fireworks. Shall we go down to the bonfire in town?'

'Have you been reading my paper, then?'

'No! I just saw a poster about it at the shop.'

Joe quietly picked up the newspaper and folded it up.

'Suppose you plan to meet up with that Carrie bitch,' said Joe.

This is going to be bad.'

'No! I just thought that we could go together, have a night out.'

Remember, remember the fifth of November, gunpowder, treason and plot! He thinks I'm plotting.'

'I'd pay to see that nosey parker friend of yours go up in smoke,' said Joe.

'He wants me to light his fuse.'

'She's not my friend any more.'

'I'll never play with fireworks again.'

'So you don't go sneaking off to meet her in the park or anywhere?' asked Joe.

'I'll hold fireworks at arm's length in future.'

'No! I'm finished with her!'

'I'll never go near a lit firework again.'

'Blah blah blah,' sang Joe. 'I've seen ya!'

Joe pointed a sausage shaped finger at Debs. Her face lit up with understanding.

'People get hurt when they play with fireworks.'

'It was only once,' said Debs quietly. 'It won't happen again, I promise.'

'Throwing a firework in a public place is an offence. There's a heavy price to pay…'

Debs leaned against the kitchen worktop and got ready to pay up.

'If you want fireworks, then I'll give you fireworks!' snapped Joe.

Bang! Joe gave Debs a rocket. Then another one. And another. She burned in the flames of Joe's very personal fireworks display. Sparks of many different colours lit up the white kitchen cupboards as Debs was banged, cracked and rumbled. Joe whistled, grunted and snorted at her plotting. The noise, light, smell and smoke coming from Joe's seemingly endless supply of gunpowder, made her eyes run.

'Guy Fawkes jumped from the scaffold at his execution and broke his neck, so as to avoid the pain of mutilation; I've got nowhere to jump to in this kitchen.'

Debs was finally hung, drawn and quartered. Joe had put on a fantastic show. She'd had her fill of fireworks; she wouldn't need to go to the bonfire in town tonight, after all. Joe could go out for a drink instead.

When his last sparkler was spent, Joe dropped his newspaper in the bin, he'd finished with it, and got down on the sofa for a nap. Debs dropped down on a kitchen chair and tried to deal with the damage left behind in the wake of Joe's premature November 5th celebrations that had got so horribly out of hand.

'Remember, remember the fifth of November,
Gunpowder, treason and plot.
I see no reason why gunpowder treason
Should ever be forgot…He will never forget…Oh Carrie…'

Debs went up to the bathroom. She looked at herself in the mirror tiles on the wall. After the force of the blasting that she'd just received, she was pleased that there was very little damage to her face; the burn marks were only on her knees. Debs gave herself a hug and tried to think of as many happy times as she could. She looked blankly at the mirror tiles.

'Come on now, Debs. Don't let it spoil your day! I can't run away so I may as well get on with some gardening. Gardening makes me happy.'

Tears welled up in her eyes; unwittingly, she'd thrown a firecracker at herself. The spark of truth it contained was more lethal than all of Joe's sound and fury put together.

'He makes me miserable most of the time, but I've got to live. I don't understand him.'

Debs sobbed gently. She heard sounds coming from the T.V. downstairs. She stopped crying. Debs saw her own face light up with understanding despite the unfortunate crack in the bathroom mirror tiles.

'I've got to seize the day. Start making a few fireworks of my own!'

Debs went downstairs. She was relieved to see that Joe was fast asleep on the soft, leather, sofa. She quietly picked the newspaper out of the kitchen bin and had a good look at it again.

'He'll be asleep for an hour or two; there'll be plenty of time for me to get back.'

Debs put on her coat and made for the newly painted, blue, front door.

'Are you there?' shouted Joe.

'Yes, Joe. I'm coming,' said Debs, slipping her coat off and hanging it up by the front door.

Panic set in. She thought she was going to die. But he only wanted another cup of tea.

She put the football on the telly. Joe turned over and went back to sleep. He was snoring, very loudly. Holding the newspaper in one hand, Debs picked up the telephone with her other, free, hand.

'I c..can't t..talk here…' she stumbled.

———◆———

'By heck, you're a clever lass, and no mistake,' cackled Mavis.

Carrie wanted to hug and kiss Mavis. She didn't care about her long white whiskers, her fogged up spectacles, her missing front teeth, her frilly apron speckled with something brown that didn't come from the kitchen, her funny 'old lady' smell. She wanted to so badly but she couldn't. For a start, she wasn't sure if her arms would reach around Mavis' ample bosom; second, Mavis didn't make a big show of her affections.

'She'd think I was weird if I tried to hug her!'

In fact, none of them made a big show about anything; Jed's behaviour didn't really count. By and large, Carrie was lucky to get an 'ah do' by way of welcome these days. By and large, they never welcomed anyone anyway. That didn't mean that Carrie didn't feel welcome; quite the opposite.

'Dad's right, it is my farm!'

Mavis would never say 'hello, how are you?' She always got straight to the point with her sandpaper sentences, but there was more warmth in her harsh tones, kindness in her lack of words and welcome in her magnified eyes, than the grandest state welcome that the Queen could ever receive. Carrie received now.

'Thank you, Mavis.'

'By heck, who'd have thought sheep were that clever. I should like to have a memory like a sheep, I can tell you!' chuckled Mavis.

'Where are the lads?'

'Putting the cows out to the kale and feeding the sheep!'

Then, as if committing deadly treason, she whispered through her whiskers:

'By heck, Carrie, there weren't half some fireworks after you'd gone last night! He went mad at Jed. Mad! Surprised you didn't hear him raving at home!'

'About the bull,' said Carrie.

'Ah! He gave him a rocket and no mistake. He was going to give him a right good hiding too but Jon stepped in. He's a grand lad, isn't he?'

Carrie smiled at Mavis and tried to stay blank.

'She's not a sheep so she can't read my face.'

'And Jed, well, I don't know what's up with him. One thing's for sure, we've had enough fireworks round here to last a lifetime! We don't want any more tonight, do we?'

'She is a sheep after all.'

Carrie smiled at Mavis and tried to stay blank.

'But I've got to seize the day! Start making a few fireworks of my own!'

'Any road, best get on,' said Mavis.

'Ah,' replied Carrie.

Mavis had lit the fuse that fired Carrie up the drive in the direction of the kale field. She had to find the 'grand lad.' She crunched across the empty farmyard and up the sharp, hard, drive in the direction of the fields. The November sun had not yet cleaned the frost from the rubble on the drive; it was like going for a walk on the dark side of the moon. She passed the orchard; it was still asleep. The sad looking tree in the far corner stood sombre and alone in its own shadow.

'I hope I'm not the cause of your sorrow. He frightened me and I can't trust you any more. I don't think I'll ever visit you again.'

The silence of the orchard was so loud that Carrie could hear it; there was not even the slightest rustle from a single leaf.

'Ah do.'

Carrie nodded a silent 'ah do' in return to old man Wilson; she didn't make a big show of her affections.

'Will you walk with me, Carrie?'

'Look him in the eye! Even the smallest prey can still be brave!'

'Please!'

The Falcon remained motionless. His icy focus burned into her. Carrie had had her fill of being set on fire for one day so she started walking.

'I'm not sure it's such a good idea you working here. How long were you planning on staying?'

'Forever! It's my farm!'

'I want to do a year's worth of articles, that's what I promised to do.'

'I said I could fire as well as hire.'

'I know you did. But I'm a good worker, aren't I? You told my dad so.'

'You're upsetting the lads.'

Bang! It was a fairly small firecracker coming from a man with such a reputation for violence. Nevertheless, it made an impact that echoed in the corridors of her memory.

"Maybe the old man fancies you himself" chirped Debs...'

'I'm sure they can look after themselves, they've always had to, haven't they?'

Bang! Carrie's rocket got him straight between the eyes. Old man Wilson stayed blank.

'And so can I for that matter,' she finished.

'I can see that.'

'It's time to seize the day! Start making a few fireworks of my own!'

'You once told me, right here in this orchard, to live. To live every single day as much as I can, even if it kills me.'

'I did.'

'Well, I'm doing it. I'm living here today. Right now. I'm fed up of people telling me what I can and can't do, can and can't think, can and can't be. I'm fed up of people wanting me to be what they want me to be because they want me for themselves. I want to be free to be me, and I'm going to be it. Don't you dare try to take that away from me when I'm just starting to be it.'

The Falcon stared at his prey; he wasn't used to it fighting back.

'I can see that.'

Carrie looked him in the eyes.

'I c..can't t..talk,' stumbled Carrie.

'I know. You don't need words to talk to me.'

Jip had arrived; he jumped up at Carrie. He was pleased to see her. He didn't need words, either.

'Go!' he said.

Carrie smiled defiantly at him before walking away to seize her day with Jon and Jip.

Old man Wilson watched her go. She was very precious; he wasn't sure that he could protect her. He was spent; the impact of her smile echoed in the corridors of his memory. He allowed himself a smile as he realised how much he was enjoying the thoughts inside his head. Then he walked away to get on with the rest of his day. The sad looking tree in the orchard reached out to him in a gentle and pleading sort of way. He paused for a moment to look at it. The cold November sun kindled sparkles of many different colours in between its branches.

'It'll be alright. I give you my word,' said the tree.

'I know,' he mouthed, as he walked away.

───────◆───────

It was a big bonfire. Most of the town turned out to see Guy Fawkes burn. The hated figure had been made by children from the local junior school. They'd been doing a project about him in history. They'd done a good job. They had tortured Guy into shape with straw and old corn sacks that were usually reserved for the sports day torture of the sack race. The children were pleased to see the sacks go up in smoke; they didn't know that their teacher was secretly plotting to get some new ones for the next sports day. If they had known, they'd have made Guy look like their teacher and taken pleasure in seeing her burn, keeping alive the true spirit of bonfire night, like conscientious students of history.

But they didn't know. A great cheer went up from the crowd as Guy's straw entrails caught fire and he started to burn; he quickly disappeared into the flames of his own making. Bang! The show had begun. It was a fantastic fireworks display. Rocket after rocket exploded in the cold, clean, November sky. Sparks of many different colours melted the darkness away; they looked like flowers in the sky. They were really pretty. The folk nearest to the bonfire were roasting to a crisp like the chestnuts that were being passed from hand to hand in the crowd.

The noise, light, smell and smoke coming from the seemingly endless supply of gunpowder was making everybody's eyes run; still, it was fun. When the last sparkler was spent and the last toffee apple eaten, everybody walked away, home to bed. Nobody threw a firework; nobody got hurt. Even though the children sang all the way home, everybody forgot what they'd been celebrating; still, it had been fun.

'Remember, remember the fifth of November,
Gunpowder, treason and plot.
We see no reason, why gunpowder treason
Should ever be forgot.'

───────◆───────

Bill had lit a big fire in the lounge; it was a cold November night, and Jill was cold. They were having a quiet night in. Jill didn't want to go to the big bonfire in the town. Bill didn't want to see Guy Fawkes burn.

Carrie wasn't home yet. Bang! The show had begun. Jill was worried about the fireworks; she was frightened that a rocket might explode on Carrie's little red car. Fireworks can get so horribly out of hand in the wrong hands. She folded and unfolded her hands as she listened in between the bangs and whistles of the celebrations, for the sound car tyres crackling on the gravel of the drive; that would be celebration enough for her tonight.

'She's not back yet! What shall we do?'

'It'll be alright. I give you my word. She'll be back.'

Bill sat with Jill next to the big fire in the lounge. He nearly burned to a crisp but Jill was still cold. The heat and light coming from the fire made their eyes run.

'I hope she's not hurt somewhere. I couldn't bear her to be burnt...disfigured for life...' thought Jill as she wiped her eyes.

'I hope she's lighting up her life with some fireworks of her own!' thought Bill, wiping his eyes.

When the last sparks from the big fire died down Jill and Bill went up to bed. Carrie wasn't home yet. Bill remembered that she wasn't a child; Jill could never forget her child. Bill watched the fireworks light up the night sky from the bedroom window; he wondered what Carrie was doing.

———◆———

The farm was quiet. It was a cold November night. Mavis had stoked up the little fire in the Rayburn cooker in the kitchen. She sat next to it, opposite old man Wilson in his favourite 'father bear' big, wooden, chair. They were burnt to a crisp like the chestnuts that Mavis was toasting in the flames; they were a little treat, their own little celebration of bonfire night. They were listening to the radio; there was always good music on Sunday nights; it was peaceful. They liked music. Bang! Jed had just gone out, banging the kitchen door behind him.

'He spends a lot of time at that 'Black Cow' for saying as he doesn't like cows!' tutted Mavis.

She got no reply from old man Wilson. She didn't expect one. He'd had enough fireworks for one day. He kept his eyes fixed on the flames that burned into the chestnuts and his ears fixed on the beautiful love song of 'Samson and Delilah.' It was from the opera by Saint- Saens; he liked opera, liked a good tune. He gently moved his hand in shape to the music as Delilah exploded:

'My heart opens at your voice...Samson, Samson, I love you!'

In the distance of the night sky the occasional bang, crackle and whistle, interfered with his ecstasy. So did Mavis.

'Jip won't like all this noise,' said Mavis.

Mavis didn't particularly like the noise coming from the radio, but she was too kind to say so. She couldn't share Delilah's ecstasy; she'd never had a Samson of her own. If she had, she'd have told him to get his hair cut without all this fuss, anyway.

'He'll be right with Jon. He'll keep him inside,' said old man Wilson.

He didn't particularly feel like talking, but was too kind to say so.

'Ah,' said Mavis, keeping quiet because she knew he wanted to listen to the end of the music; Delilah's shouting was really loud now.

The noise from the radio and the heat from the fire made his eyes run. Mavis fished the chestnuts out of the fire and put them in a bowl. She was used to the heat of the fire; her eyes didn't run. They shared the chestnuts.

Remember, remember the fifth of November,
Gunpowder, treason and plot.
We see no reason, why gunpowder treason
Should ever be forgot...Samson, Samson, I love you.'

———————◆———————

Bang! Poor Jip was terrified of the bangs, crackles and whistles that fell on him from the night sky all around the farm. He lay low in his basket in the outhouse shivering and shaking with cold terror; no words of comfort from either Carrie or Jon could ease his pain. Jon closed the outhouse door; he was too kind to make Jip come outside with him to check the cattle tonight. It was the one night of the year when roles reversed and Jon protected Jip. He cursed the hated figure Guy Fawkes who was the cause of all the noise, light, smell and smoke that was upsetting Jip and the cattle.

Bang! Carrie's plan to share a few fireworks with Jon fizzled out like the last spent sparkler, dropped into a bucket of cold disappointment. As they crossed the yard another noise filled the night sky; it was a woman singing. She sounded as if she was in terrible pain but glad to be suffering at the same time.

'I know just how you feel,' thought Carrie as she tried to keep up with a quite bad tempered Jon marching towards the cowsheds.

'What's that beautiful singing?' she asked, not expecting an answer.

'S..Samson and D..Delilah,' came the reply.

Jon switched off a cowshed light and marched on to the next one.

'Old m..man likes m..music. Opera.'

'Well it sounds gorgeous,' said Carrie. 'I don't know what she's saying; it sounds French.'

'She's t..telling him she l..loves him, just b..before she t..tricks him and c..cuts off his h..hair.'

Crack! Another cowshed light burnt to a crisp.

'I promise I'll never cut your hair off!' said Carrie.

She wanted to reach out and touch his beautiful hair.

'You know about a lot of stuff, don't you?'

The beautiful hair didn't reply. The darkness of the farm buildings and the night sky exploded in her face as the last spark from the last cowshed light floated away in the cold November air. Carrie held her hands out in front of her to see if she still existed; she wasn't sure, she could barely see her own hands.

Suddenly, the darkness was pulling her up the drive; it had warm hands. She followed, trusting that it wasn't playing tricks on her. It wasn't. Its beautiful hair was so dark that it became one with the night sky; she wanted to reach out and touch it. She felt grass underneath her feet; they were walking uphill. It was a very long way to the top of the top field. The gate stopped them from falling over the edge into the abyss on the other side. They stopped. It was completely dark and completely quiet.

Jon pulled Carrie towards him and folded her body inside his coat. She could feel his beautiful hair become still as it rested itself against hers. Bang! The show had begun. It was a fantastic fireworks display. Across the valley, rocket after rocket exploded in the cold, clean, November sky. Sparks of many different colours melted the darkness away; they looked like flowers in the sky. Carrie was roasting to a crisp inside Jon's coat. She got her real fireworks after all. Their celebrations were very quiet; there was no singing. They burned in the flames of their own making; they burned long after the last sparkles had faded from the night sky. It made Carrie's eyes run.

They walked back down the hill, guided by the darkness of the night sky and the farm buildings; they felt their way together. They breathed together. As they reached the drive they heard another noise. It was a familiar voice; it sounded in terrible pain. It was whining and yelping. It was coming from the orchard. They ran:

'J..J..Jip!' called Jon. 'J..Jip!'

Jip called back.

'*I don't know what he's saying, but it doesn't sound good,*' shivered Carrie.

They found Jip tied to a tree in the orchard. His chin was bleeding.

'I'll k..k..kill him!' exploded Jon.

'*Never play with fireworks, Jed!*

'*Remember, remember the fifth of November,*

Gunpowder, treason and plot.

We see no reason, why gunpowder treason

Should ever be forgot...He will never forget tonight, Jed...and neither will I. My heart opens at your voice...Jon, Jon, I love you...oh Jip!'

Monday 6th November

'Mr Pike wants to see you immediately,' gnashed 'Rosalind the Rottweiler.'

She slammed a pile of papers down on Carrie's desk so hard that she would have chopped her hands off at the wrists if Carrie hadn't anticipated the guillotine strike and quickly moved them out of the way.

'I know what this is about,' winced Carrie as she clicked across the shiny office floor to be seen to immediately by Mr Pike.

She didn't need to turn her head to see her colleagues silently laughing at her from underneath their own piles of paperwork; they knew what it was about as well.

'Have you found your sheep, yet, Bo Peep?' and 'Where's your lamb, Mary?' were still hilariously funny questions that greeted Carrie wherever she went in the building. In fact, she'd found an anonymous note taped to her desk this very morning which read:

'Mary had a little lamb, she tied it to a pylon, ten thousand volts went up its arse and turned its fur to nylon!'

Dennis had warned her about the consequences of her last article. Dennis was a bushy moustached Irishman who hadn't got to be editor-in-chief without taking a risk or two in his long career, so he had cheerfully turned a blind eye it. He was secretly pleased that she'd had the guts to shake up the paper and shake up the town with a touch of poetic licence. Now she would have to pay for it, of course. He'd already denied knowledge of the offence due to sick leave. Somehow Carrie's article had slipped through the editorial net, leaving her entirely responsible for everything.

Even though Carrie had been pretty fed up at work recently, she hadn't actually planned to get herself the sack quite so soon or quite like this. She would have preferred to leave in a blaze of glory even if she couldn't stand the job than leave in a blaze.

As she knocked on Mr Pike's door she prepared to have her fur turned to nylon. She was already starting to melt around the edges; the heat from Rosalind's laser stare was burning holes in the small of her back and the back of her head. 'Rosalind the Rottweiler' was filling the holes with pure hatred with every scratch and stab of her pencil on her jotter.

'Enter!' boomed Mr Pike.

Carrie was pleased to enter.

'Close the door, close the door, Carrie. We both like a little privacy now and then, don't we?' he boomed, more quietly.

'*Where's this going?*' puzzled Carrie as she closed the door on 'Hatred.'

'Sit down, Carrie, dear. Will you take tea?' asked Mr Pike, suddenly sounding like a sweet old lady speaking to an even older sweet old lady.

'*What's he up to? I hope he's not going to suggest that I go for a swim with him, or else get the sack for bringing the paper into disrepute! Mind you, he does have an elderly mother so he probably talks 'tea' as a matter of course.*'

'No thank you, Mr Pike.'

Mr Pike was sitting behind his large, old fashioned, mahogany wooden desk. He still looked more like a trout than a pike. His cold, watery eyes were set deep inside his great, round jowls. He was staring at Carrie.

'*He's put on a lot of weight recently,*' thought Carrie, and then wished she hadn't; she'd got to get out through the door at the end of this booming.

His webbed fingers were drumming on his desk; his tail was flapping underneath it. Heel, toe, heel, toe, went his shoes against the hard mahogany.

'*What on earth is he going to do to me?*'

Mr Pike's enormous rubbery lips took a break from blowing bubbles and gasping for air. They were slowing changing shape to form words.

'I've received a letter of complaint, a very harsh, letter of complaint, about your last 'Land Girl' article,' he boomed dramatically.

'*This is it, then.*'

Carrie said nothing. She suddenly remembered that sheep stayed silent when in pain. Perhaps Mr Pike saw straight through the sheep's behaviour as it stared silently back at him, for he suddenly let go of his boom and became a sweet old tea lady once more.

'*He's gone falsetto again so that Rosalind can't hear him!*'

'This letter is from the President of the 'Local Ladies Network,' he shrilled.

The sheep stayed silent; she was busy trying to read the expression on Mr Pike's face. She made sure to keep her own ears covered by her long, golden, hair; she was giving nothing away of herself that she didn't have to. He was quoting from the esteemed letter:

'...We are extremely outraged and offended...flock of fluffy ladies...rather silly, woolly headed individuals...like to follow a leader...bleats, grunts, rumbles and snorts...a highly irregular and insulting publication...demand an apology and immediate removal of the

'Twentieth Century Land Girl' articles from your newspaper...focus on the charitable work of the 'Local Ladies Network'...a powerhouse of the community...influential members... consequences...'

Mr Pike finished reading. His cold, watery eyes looked across the depth of his big, mahogany desk at the silent sheep sitting bolt upright on the edge of her chair. He could just make out the tops of her knees sticking out from underneath her tightly fitting pencil skirt. He tried to read the expression on her face. Her ears were hidden underneath her beautiful, long, golden hair; she had well and truly pulled the wool over his eyes for he could see nothing. Eventually she spoke:

'So you're going to sack me, then?'

'Please don't sack me just yet! I want to finish what I started! I know you're weird, and you look like a fish, but I think I'd miss you, and your booming!'

Mr Pike swallowed an air bubble, flapped his tail underneath the desk, and came back to life.

'Sack you? Of course I'm not going to sack you, dear girl!' he boomed. 'You'll have to put an apology in the paper, but that's all. I'm not going to sack one of my best members of staff or change the content of my newspaper on the say so of the President of the 'Local Ladies Network' or anyone else, for that matter.'

Mr Pike threw a glance in the direction of his office door, before continuing in a quieter boom:

'You're like me, Carrie.'

Mr Pike leaned forward across his desk as far as his swim bladder would allow.

'How am I like you? Oh no, he does want something from me after all!'

'You're greatly misunderstood. You're a creative like me! A fellow sufferer! It's not easy having to live a double life, being surrounded by people who don't understand you. Bearing your affliction, living with the guilt.'

'What on earth is he talking about?'

'You may feel weak, Carrie, but I tell you, you're strong! Each to his own, I say! Now you must chase after your dream, Carrie, and don't stop till you've caught it. You'll always be surrounded by folk who don't understand; don't mind them, you just keep going. Your secret is safe with me,' he sweet old ladied.

'How can he know about Jon?'

Carrie didn't know what to say so she tried to smile politely to Mr Pike as if she knew what he was talking about. Mr Pike was on his feet.

He slid round to Carrie's side of the desk.

'Here comes the swim bladder.'

Carrie got ready to receive Mr Pike. But he just reached forwards and took hold of her hands in his webbing. His skin was very white and cold. His eyes closed in on her face. Carrie was shocked, for she saw great kindness and a touch of sadness in them.

'Now, you're going to write for me the best article that you've ever written. Leave the sheep to safely graze in their own fields of self-righteousness and get on with your life how you want to get on with it.'

Mr Pike was flapping Carrie's hands up and down inside his own with excitement. He was booming again for all to hear:

'It's November, Remembrance is coming up, we've just had Bonfire Night, so let's have some fireworks from you now, Carrie. Set this paper on fire! I want to be swamped with letters of congratulations from our readers about our 'Twentieth Century Land Girl!' Now, go to it!'

'Thank you, Mr Pike, I'll do my best.'

Carrie smiled a smile of genuine affection to Mr Pike. For a moment of an unknown length, she willingly and joyfully connected with him. She looked into his eyes, she shook his hand back and shared in an unspoken understanding of something, she didn't quite know what, but it seemed to do them both good. Until the office door opened and Rosalind bleated:

'The editing team's waiting for you in conference room one.'

'Thank you, Rosalind.'

Mr Pike turned his back on Carrie and swam away through the open office door to his meeting; he didn't wait for Carrie. Neither did Rosalind. She let the door close in her face as she got near it. Carrie didn't mind. She gave Rosalind a smile as wide as any gnash of a Rottweiler's teeth and clicked swiftly back to her desk. The occasional sheep bleated at her as she walked across the office floor but she ignored them. They'd already been fed this morning; they were getting nothing else out of her today. Carrie put pen to paper; it was time to start a fire.

Friday 17th November

'Have you read this?' asked Bill.

He pushed the paper across the table towards Jill's coffee cup. She glanced at him from over the top of her reading glasses.

'No,' she replied.

She fluttered her larger, national, newspaper at him.

'I'm reading a real newspaper, in case you haven't noticed. I'm not wasting my time with that local 'rag' rubbish any more.'

'That's a shame. Your daughter's written something in here for you, and I don't just mean the disclaimer about her 'sheep' article.'

'What disclaimer?' asked Jill, sharply.

'Apparently there'd been some complaints,' said Bill.

Jill carried on reading; she felt intellectual when she was wearing her reading glasses.

'Apparently so,' she said, in as disinterested a voice as she could manage.

She carried on reading. But Bill didn't take the hint that their conversation was over:

'Well, I'll leave it with you. Apparently some folk liked it; Carrie's got herself a full page spread on page three this week, and not for taking her clothes off either!'

Jill was about to give him a disgusted look but the telephone rang and saved her the bother.

'I'll get that,' she said.

'Oh hello!'

Bill could hear Jill's over the top reply; she was still wearing her reading glasses.

'Oh thank you. Yes, she's always wanted a career in journalism...'

Bill sighed. It was one of Jill's 'network' pals; he could tell what it was about. As promised, he left the local 'rag' rubbish open at page three and went out to read his own paper in the garage. Jill found the page three spread waiting for her on the kitchen table. She quickly folded it up and put it on the side. She'd have a quick look at it later, if she'd got time.

She didn't get time. Jill's morning was spoilt by endless phone calls from the great and the good, all wanting to congratulate her on her daughter's wonderful, most moving, 'Land Girl' article on the 'Remembrance' page three special. She congratulated herself on her success;

'I knew I was right to complain. She needed telling. Look where she is now! And it's all thanks to me. She's going to be a success after all...'

———————◆———————

Dear Reader,

So far down on the farm I have written about cows, calves, sheep (to my cost, please note the disclaimer on page twenty two), pigs, chicks, the toil and sweat of tilling the soil, crops both wild and farmed, fruit and vegetables of all shapes and sizes. There can be nothing more, I hear you say. I have thought so myself at times; maybe this is getting boring for my readers. Just more of the same. But you are wrong. Very wrong, and so was I. For I need to tell you about sacks of corn.

A flat bed lorry is standing in the middle of the farm yard. It delivers sacks of corn to feed the cattle over the coming winter months. The lorry is in a hurry; lots of deliveries to make before the end of the day. The farmer's sons run to unload their sacks of corn. Each sack is as big and heavy as a full grown man. Time after time their knees take the strain as their backs carry their precious burden into the corn store. They have neither time nor energy for talking, apart from the occasional grunt as the weight of the corn sack connects with their backbone.

They compete silently with both the lorry and each other to see who can unload the most corn sacks, as if their lives depended upon it. Human beings like to win, don't they? No doubt the children who stuffed the corn sack that became Guy Fawkes on bonfire night battled to see who could stuff the most straw into his belly. Call it a challenge or a battle; we humans like to win, either way.

A very old man stood alongside me in the farmyard, watching the battle of the corn sacks. He stood to attention as best as his ancient, twisted body would allow. I saw tears form in his eyes as he watched the corn sacks fly from lorry to man. The November sun was not in his eyes so I asked him why. It was the eleventh day of the eleventh month; Remembrance Day. The very old man had been a young man once, a soldier, a Private during World War One.

The tears in his eyes that would not flow turned his eye sockets into reservoirs. His eyelids held them fast as I asked him why; they held fast while he told me. He was a strong man. He was dammed up. He was damned to remember. I will tell you now, just as he told me, in his own words, as well as I can remember, about the sacks of corn.

'I were just a lad when I got called up. Nineteen years old. I was from the town, an ordinary town lad; never been to the country, never seen a gun before in me life! I got sent to Northern Ireland first. It turned out that I were a good shot! The best in my regiment! Any road, I ended up in the Somme. I was made adjutant to my Captain, his servant, like. He were a grand chap. He were well to do, but he was brave and he looked after his men as best he could. He led us over the top and he didn't get killed, he was one of the few to survive.

Any road, one night we had a really bad night. The Germans opened up an offensive to take our position. They blitzed us! They fired all night - all night - onto our trenches. Me and another bloke had been sent out on a job, reconnoitring, like. We were out on the top, trying to get back to our trenches.

Oh the shells! The shells! The noise! It were terrible! We were stuck on top, and we couldn't get back! We were surrounded by dead bodies. So we piled them up! We stacked up dead bodies like they was sacks of corn and we stayed under them all night. And in the morning, when it were quiet, we went back to our trenches.

Well! Everybody was dead! Walking down the trenches I saw all the lads I went to school with, even my wife's first husband. All dead. Only four of us had survived.'

The very old man watched the last sack of corn disappear into the corn store.

'I've got no words to say about it,' he said, simply.

Neither had I. The farm dog sniffed a welcome at the old man's black wool trousers. He patted the warm welcome on his warm head.

'And in the middle of the war, when we were in the middle of the trenches, one day a column of horses towing guns turned up and pulled into a small field at the side of us. My Captain went mad!

'What are they doing?' he shouted. 'They'll get blasted!' And they did. An enemy aeroplane flew overhead and gave the German guns the position of the field of horses. Well! What a sight! You've never seen such a sight in your life! We could do nothing but watch. All the horses and men were killed. The noise were terrible. Terrible! I'll never forget it. The worst thing was the noise. The noise was dreadful.

After the war I did a farming course, run by the Government. Thought I should like to work with horses. I won a bit of money; it were enough to start farming. So I did. I had a little dairy and I made butter. Worked the land the rest of my life.'

The very old man chuckled to himself:

'When I started farming I weren't much good at it! I got in all sorts of scrapes! One time I'd reared a bull and had to take it to market. You walked them to market in those days. Well there I was, walking this here bull down through the town to market. He was quiet, like, no trouble. But I forgot he'd got long horns! We walked past a sweet shop and his horns smashed the shop window! Well, I had to pay for the damage, didn't I!'

The very old man turned to towards me and smiled; the November sun was in his eyes, but still his tears would not flow; only mine could do that. You and I were born free because his tears would not flow. He is a strong man. He doesn't make a fuss. He has no words to say about it; neither have I. He is damned to remember. We are damned if we forget:

'They shall not grow old, as we that are left grow old:
Age shall not weary them, nor the years condemn.
At the going down of the sun and in the morning
We will remember them.....we will remember them.' [†]

Part Four

Winter –
'A Very Dark Time…'

Friday 1st December

'It's a bit early for Christmas shopping, isn't it?'

'Nah, Christmas or not, it's never too early for a bit of shopping!' laughed Debs.

'Come on, let's try in here!'

It was Debs' idea to go Christmas shopping; her idea that Carrie should take a half day's holiday so that they didn't have to go on a Saturday when it would be really crowded. And she wouldn't take 'no' for an answer.

Carrie was taken aback at first by the new, assertive, Debs that had so suddenly and mysteriously appeared inside the clothes of the old Debs. The 'new' old Debs was happily dragging her into every corner of every store pottering, looking, trying on and buying up everything in sight. Carrie struggled to keep up with her; she walked three paces behind most of the time, weighed down by armfuls of Debs' shopping that she loyally volunteered to carry around every shop so that Debs could be 'hands free' to potter, look, try and buy. It was just like old times and more besides.

'It's great to see her looking so happy, so why do I feel a bit uncomfortable about this 'new' old Debs?'

'Are you sure you can afford all this?' asked Carrie, as Debs handed her yet another carrier bag of stuff.

'Oh, lighten up, you silly old mare!' said Debs. 'Of course I can! You only live once and anyway, it's Christmas! Joe's working back to back double shifts at the moment to make some extra money for the holidays, so I've got to get him some decent presents, haven't I?'

'If you say so...so that's why she wanted to come shopping today, she knows he'll be at work till late...Still, she's behaving a bit weird...'

'Oh look here! It's your favourite shop!'

Debs' happy smile and determined pull catapulted Carrie into the weird looking boutique full of glittery, spangly clothes that shone like stars against the black interior of the shop. It was the planetarium shop where she'd bought her little black dress with the flash of silver across it so many, many, months ago. Carrie was glad it was so dark in the shop; she felt certain that she was blushing as bright as the Scarlett dress that Debs holding against her bagged figure. She was damned to remember and it felt good. Very, very, good:

The pink marshmallow...the third man...little Carrie...black velvet. The orchard, the sad looking tree...wet with milk...creaking floorboards...fireworks...How do I begin to tell her...'

Debs was giggling:

'You must have the office Christmas party coming up. Mr Pike will be wanting to give you his Christmas box in person!'

'Oh just shut up!' groaned Carrie.

'I bet he's got some mistletoe!'

'Leave the big fish alone!'

'He's actually not a bad old trout, you know,' said Carrie, quietly. 'I think he might just be very lonely; I don't think he means any harm.'

Debs was too busy giggling to hear:

'And they'll definitely have mistletoe on the farm! Who are you going to kiss first?'

'Jip the dog! Are you sure you're alright, Debs? Have you been drinking?'

This made Debs laugh even louder. The spotty, spindly youth who looked down at the floor, embarrassed to find that he was the only shop assistant on duty this afternoon, eyed them suspiciously as best he could with the tops of his eyes from behind the safety of his till. He was new to the job; he wasn't sure how to deal with the loud woman who was touching all the dresses in the shop. She may have been drinking, or worse. He didn't want to make a mistake and lose his job. The other woman looked sensible enough, though. He just hoped they'd hurry up and go away.

'Certainly not! I'm allowed to have a bit of fun, aren't I?'

Carrie smiled back nervously at Debs as if to agree with her.

'What on earth has got into her?'

'Let's try something on! Please!' pleaded Debs.

'O.K. but I'm not a scarlet woman,' said Carrie, pushing Debs' outstretched hand containing the little, very little, Scarlett number away from her.

'Ah, I bet you will be before you're done! You haven't mentioned the farm or those hunky farmer's sons once all afternoon. You're hiding something from me, I can feel it!'

'So are you!'

'Let's be honest, you've hardly let me get a word in edgeways all afternoon to tell you anything. You've been in overdrive today - what's up with you?'

'I need black velvet...'

'I don't know, really,' said Debs, picking out white chiffon with a gold trim. 'Oh yes, this is definitely me - Lady D comes to tea! Oh no, can't you think of any other colour than black?'

'Feel it, it's beautiful. Velvet!'

'If you say so. It's a bit stuffy for a party, isn't it? At least try the green one and then you'll be camouflaged when you're lying in the long green grass with farmer chalk and or farmer cheese!'

'Don't you ever give up?'

'Nah, it's too much fun watching you squirm!' laughed Debs

I wish I could say the same about you.

'Just to make you happy I'll take the one with the floaty chiffon sleeves,' said Carrie. 'Now, can we please stop shopping and have a coffee!'

The spotty, spindly youth who served them was pleased that the loud woman agreed to have coffee with the sensible one. He was glad to see them go, although he wouldn't have minded hearing a few more details about the hunky farmers. But they were already far away, sitting down at a café table in the middle of the shopping centre foyer. Heads bent, close together, the loud woman and the sensible one, were oblivious to the noise, the crowds and the spotty spindly youth who stared after them. They'd left him behind, struggling with his imagination, in between serving customers for the rest of his relentless day and, quite possibly, beyond it.

'We've had a fair few ups and downs since we last sat here,' said Carrie.

'Your last article was brilliant!' replied Debs. 'You'll be leaving us for the big lights before too long!'

'Thanks, but I don't think so,' said Carrie.

She tried again:

'How's things with Joe now?'

'What? Oh fine. Hasn't this been a great trip out? We must do it again, hit the January sales. Now, about the chalk and cheese. Spill!'

'It's complicated,' began Carrie.

'Rubbish!' said Debs. 'Come on, out with it! What's going on?'

'What's going on with you?'

All of a sudden Carrie was glad she was training to be a journalist.

'Bloody hell!' said Debs every now and then.

The old Debs was back in bulldozer mode. Carrie had to use all her editorial skill to tell her the whole truth without telling her the whole truth. The old Debs was back; oh how she loved her friend.

'You're right, this has been great,' said Carrie. 'Just like old times. I thought I'd lost you for a while.'

'No chance!' said Debs. 'Just because I'm married doesn't mean I can't

328

see my best friend, does it?'

'No. Are you sure Joe won't mind you shopping like this?'

'What are you doing over Christmas?'

'Don't know. The usual, I suppose.'

'Listen, Carrie. I need to tell you something.'

'What?'

'I mean, I'm going to do something.'

'I think you've done enough for a while now,' laughed Carrie. 'Just look at all this shopping, and most of it's yours! What are you going to do?'

'Oh nothing, never mind,' said Debs. 'We'd better get a move on. I'll have to put all this away before Joe gets home. Can you give me a lift?'

'You never need to ask,' smiled Carrie. 'Come on!'

Carrie gave Debs what she asked for.

'Thanks!' said Debs as Carrie helped her bags of shopping and her empty purse to her newly painted, blue, front door.

'Ooh you daft thing, I need a hug!' said Carrie.

They had a hug.

'I must get on now,' said Debs, quietly.

The 'new' old Debs was folded into her handbag as the old Debs reached into it to pull out her house key. She smiled and waved at Carrie until the newly painted, blue, front door closed upon her day out.

Carrie smiled to herself all the way home. At every junction she had a little stroke of her new black velvet dress with chiffon sleeves. In the dark it looked like Jip the happy dog curled up on the front passenger seat. She smiled at the thought of 'new' old Debs, who would be frantically hiding away all that shopping before Joe got home by now.

It's only a little house; she might have to bury some of it in the garden. Oh my God, what am I thinking? What have I missed? I was too busy enjoying myself to hear! She was trying to tell me something! Oh Debs, I'm so sorry, I've just spent the afternoon with an impostor! Oh Debs, what are you going to do?'

———◆———

'It's a bit early for Christmas shopping, isn't it?'

'Of course it's not, you silly man! Have you any idea how busy I am in the run up to Christmas? It's an extremely stressful time of year!'

Jill tapped her fingernails rhythmically on the car window sill as Bill chugged along in the queue to get into the town's main car park.

'It's only stressful if you make it so,' he replied.

'Well you never do anything to help me, do you? And Carrie's even worse! Most daughters love to go Christmas shopping with their mothers, help to make Christmas special. If it was left up to the two of you, we'd have no presents and bread and water for Christmas dinner!'

'That's a bit harsh,' said Bill.

He had to look out of the window to hide his smile from his wife's view. He couldn't help imagining a Christmas organized by himself and Carrie; Jill's assessment of such a possibility was not far short of the mark.

'I just mean that you take on a lot of extra responsibility every year that you don't have to.'

Bill pulled into a parking space.

'Such as what?'

Bill replied carefully:

'Well, you do a lot of great work for the community with the 'Local Ladies Network'. All the charity stuff, the carol singing in care homes, and all the entertaining over Christmas and New Year. Why not give yourself a year off? We could have a quiet Christmas with just the three of us and a Christmas tree for company. Then you wouldn't have the stress of all this shopping and preparation.'

Jill got out of the car and slammed to door.

'As I've just said, you really have no idea about anything!'

Bill struggled to keep up with Jill; he walked three paces behind most of the time, weighed down by an armful of Jill's shopping that he loyally volunteered to carry around every shop so that she could be 'hands free' to purchase as much Christmas stress as possible. When his arm was completely stressed, he walked back to the car to unburden himself.

He knew he was an especial nuisance at this time of year; he only had one good hand so he couldn't cope with as much stress as a normal person when out Christmas shopping. He wasted Jill's precious time with his repeated trips to the car; she got more and more annoyed with him upon his every return.

'What about this? What about that? Can we afford this? Can we afford that? You're never here when I need to decide anything!'

It was just like old times and more besides. Bill really enjoyed his trips to the car; he walked to it as if his life depended upon it. But once stress free, he could take his time and enjoy the town's pretty Christmas lights and the joy of the happy shoppers all around him. A group of young children were gathered around a shop window that was covered in fake snow apart from little peep holes dotted around it at different heights. A row of parents were standing behind them, leaning across to the higher holes. Hundreds of tiny white lights lit up their 'oohs and 'aahs' as they spied through the peepholes. Bill pretended to be a parent and had a look himself through a peephole at the end of the top row.

'Ooh!'

Bill was lit up. 'Snow White and the Seven Dwarfs' were having a visit from Father Christmas who had just plopped down their chimney. He was busy giving presents to everyone. Snow White was surrounded by all the birds and animals from the forest. They were all nodding and smiling to each other. Snow White was being kind to all the animals. Everybody loved her. Everybody was happy.

'Aah!'

Bill 'aahed' with the children and the real parents. A mirror on the wall containing the face of Snow White's wicked step mother, the evil Queen, broke in two; a door opened, and a handsome Prince appeared in the doorway on a white horse.

'Lucky old Snow White!' chuckled Bill to himself. *'I bet she didn't expect to find a handsome Prince in her sack on Christmas morning!'*

The young children laughed too. Bill watched Snow White get her Christmas surprise a few more times until his peep hole fogged up with the heat from his breath.

'I'd best give Snow White a bit of privacy! I'd better find my evil Queen before she cuts my heart out for being late again.'

The fog hadn't cleared from his peephole as he turned to walk away.

'I'd forgotten how cold it is; bet we're going to get some snow, Snow White. I wonder what Carrie's doing? I bet she's being kind to all the animals. Is he loving her? Is she happy? Is he her handsome Prince? Or is he just trying to get her in the sack? It will break her mother in two. What sort of surprise am I due? Oh Carrie! What are you going to do?'

'Where on earth have you been?' cried evil Queen Jill.

'I bumped into 'Snow White and the Seven Dwarves!' said Bill.

'Well, Mr Dopey, it's time for work now!' snapped Jill.

'I've had to buy all your presents for me on my own, and I do like you to look at them with me! We need to get home quick sharp now so that I can get them wrapped up, and then you can hide them. I can forget about them then, and at least have a bit of a surprise on Christmas morning. Agh! I'm fed up with Christmas already. It's the same every year; I end up having to do all the work...'

Bill was too busy to hear. He whistled as he worked his way back to the car; the sound of his hot breath fogged up the cold air around him. Through the peep holes in his mind he could still Snow White; she was singing:

'Some day my Prince will come...'

The sound of her singing was drowned out by a loud noise; the handsome Prince had turned up on a tractor instead of a white horse, and Snow White was dressed in mucky old overalls...He'd never worked on tractor engines, it could be quite interesting and profitable. Jill was revving the car engine as he finished loading her Christmas presents into the boot of the car.

'What are you looking so happy about?' said Jill.

'I've enjoyed Christmas shopping,' replied Bill, bashfully.

'Huh!' said grumpy Jill.

'Heigh-Ho!'

'No more singing! I'm sleepy. I'll need a rest when we get home.'

It was time to stop digging; Bill stopped singing. He'd got a lot of presents to hide when he got home.

'You're not seriously going out in this weather are you?'

'Of course I am! The roads will be fine and I've got winter tyres. Isn't it pretty?'

The snow light dazzled Carrie's eyes; she had to cover her forehead with her hand to look outside at the radiant, cold heaven that had fallen silently to earth during the night. A host of crystal angels had settled on the hedge around the edge of the garden. With their arms raised in welcome they called to Carrie to 'come out and play' just like they had done when she was a little girl.

And just like she had done when she was a little girl she hesitated. Sure, she wanted to go outside and play with the angels, she wanted to gather as many diamonds as she could that glistened in the white air, she wanted to join in with the silent snow carol; she wanted to go to Heaven.

But she also knew that she wasn't perfect. She knew that if she took even one step into heaven the beauty and stillness of its white perfection would be lost forever. Taking that first step was so hard. The guilt was terrible. Still, the angels called to her. Once she was there, standing in the middle of the dazzling whiteness, she was fine. It was fun. But she had only ever played in the back garden of heaven, never in front of the house. Her mother didn't want her to go to Heaven; especially not at the front of the house where everyone could see that she wasn't perfect.

'It's madness! Look at the sky! There's definitely more snow on the way. What will you do if you can't get back?' said her mother, also having to shield her eyes from the ghastly snow light.

'I'm sure they'd give me a bed for the night,' said Carrie.

'I'm sure they would. But whose bed? And who'd be in it with you?'

'Mother! They're not like that!' *('Well, one of them is!')*

'Of course they are, you naive girl! All men are, haven't you learnt that yet?'

('Maybe the old man fancies you himself, and that's why he's keeping you away from his son!' Debs had finished her ice cream and was in bulldozer mode.

'Oh give over!' cried Carrie. 'Not everything is about sex, you know!'

'Of course it is! All men are the same, aren't they? That's all they ever want to be 'friends' with you for!' Go away Debs...Oh Debs, come back!)

'Well what about you, then. I bet you tried out a few fellas before you settled on Dad!'

'How *dare* you cast aspersions at me!' exploded her mother.

'I'm not!' replied Carrie. 'It's just life, isn't it? It's not such a big deal, surely!'

'It is when you're suggesting that you're own mother's nothing more than a common tart!' shouted Jill.

'I'm not suggesting any such thing!'

The kitchen was suddenly getting very warm in the white hot winter sunshine. The host of crystal angels outside must have heard the commotion in the kitchen because Carrie could see them suddenly packing up and flying away over the hedge. With every gust of winter wind a few more of them departed, no doubt in search of a more peaceful garden in which to sing their silent winter song. Carrie wanted to fly with them but her mother was reminding her once more that she wasn't perfect. She sang to Carrie at the top of her voice:

'...I thought we'd brought you up to have a better moral code than that. You make sure you keep away from that farmer's son!'

'I intend to!' tried Carrie. *('One of them, anyway.')*

'I'm all cold now. And Christmas is coming up. Here I am, slaving away trying to make Christmas perfect for you and what do you do?'

'What have I done?' tried Carrie again.

'I just don't know how you could be so cruel. How could you do this to me, how could you!'

'I'm sorry,' tried Carrie. 'I don't understand.'

'Understand this, then!'

Jill threw open the kitchen door, grabbed both of Carrie's mud caked wellies and wanged them, one after the other, as far as she could out onto the drive. Heaven's radiant morning broke with a thud, thud. But only for a moment. The silent snow carol muffled Jill's despair as it buried Carrie's mud caked imperfections in the pretty snow. The silence stung Jill's face; the bitter winter wind made her eyes run.

'Oh, I'm so cold!'

Carrie tried again; her mother very kindly threw her coat and car keys at her.

'If you want dirty farmers, go and live with dirty farmers and see how you like it, then!'

'Maybe I will!' shouted Carrie.

Jill didn't hear; she wanged herself back through the kitchen door and on up to bed. The silent snow carol was so loud that it stifled every other sound. It was so cold.

'Oh, I'm so cold,' shivered Jill.

'Maybe I will stay the night!' Carrie skidded defiantly down the drive. *'I'll stay the night in Jon's bed!'*

Carrie thought about staying in Jon's bed all the way to the farm; the pretty snow melted away beneath the heat of her winter car tyres. The snow light dazzled her eyes. She knew she wasn't perfect, but she still wanted to go to Heaven.

———————◆———————

Somewhere, there has to be a borderline between Heaven and Hell. Carrie had clearly crossed the line with her mother this morning, and she still didn't quite understand why. Her disappointment was complete by the time she parked up in her usual spot in the corner of the farmyard. She had clearly crossed the line once more; there was no radiant cold Heaven and no crystal angels in the farmyard. There was no snow here at all, only freezing cold. The bitter winter wind rushed everybody about the yard and farm buildings. Nobody had time for her, there was clearly going to be no offer of a bed for the night. It was looking like she'd arrived in the Farmyard from Hell.

'Get those sheds done!' shouted old man Wilson, striding across the yard as sharp and pointed as a gigantic icicle that had just been ripped from its comfortable roots by a gust of wind.

He'd just appeared from the warmth of the farm house. He wore an old, felt, trilby hat pulled down tight over his eyes. His nose stuck out from underneath it blowing steam in time to his marching feet. Carrie couldn't see his eyes this morning which made him seem more fire breathing dragon or out of control steam train than an all-seeing, all knowing, Falcon.

'I'm doing it!' shouted a familiar voice from across the farmyard.

A shovel full of cow muck flew through the cowshed door and landed in the muck spreader that was parked alongside it. It was followed by the body of a reluctant Jed.

'Hello darling! Are you going to give me a hand?'

Jed looked genuinely pleased to see Carrie. Old man Wilson turned his frozen trilby in her direction. For less than a fraction of a second, he stabbed Carrie with an ice white glare from the corner of one eye. Carrie's long, golden hair nodded back to him as she pulled her own woolly hat down over her ears. She walked across the yard to 'give Jed a hand' as she'd just been ordered to do. Jed held the yard brush out towards her.

'Never mind, darling! Put your back into it and we'll soon get you warmed up!' he grinned.

'What are you doing here, today? And why's your dad in such a bad mood?'

'Me? I just thought I'd help out a bit. Got to keep my muscles in good working order with all those Christmas parties coming up!'

Jed took a break from shovelling to show Carrie his best Mr Universe pose.

'*Where's Jon?*'

'And him? Well, that's your fault! You were late this morning, maybe he thought you weren't going to show. He's like a bear with a sore head without you,' laughed Jed.

It was a horrible, really dirty, laugh. Jed was right; he'd soon got her warmed up.

'What do you mean?'

'*I should not have taken the bait! Stupid!*'

Jed took another break from shovelling. He grinned straight into her eyes with all the beauty of his twin brother's soft brown ones; Carrie was in bits.

'*It's not Jon, it's not Jon...It's not real...*'

'For some reason, I reckon he's soft on you! Has been since the day you first came here.'

Jed laughed again:

'Can't think why! Don't know why you're wearing that hat today; you're the original ice maiden. But don't fret, darling, it's probably just because you're a bargain! Slave labour for free and you keep us all entertained! You've even livened up that brother of mine, and I thought he'd never get past 'go.''

'*I should not have taken the bait!*'

'Mind you, we don't know whether he has or not, do we?'

'*The eyes, the hair, the teeth, the tongue, the lips...Go away, Jed!*'

The original ice maiden tried to freeze Jed away, but failed completely.

'I'd choose him over you any day!' she hit back.

'*I should not have taken the bait!*'

'Ooh!' shivered Jed. 'Blow, blow thou winter wind, thy sting is not so sharp as Carrie's tongue! Ooh, Carrie, give me some more tongue!'

Carrie brandished her yard brush as if to say 'on guard' to fight Jed to the death. She was really mad now; mad with him and mad with herself for letting him get to her. Jed grabbed the end of the brush, muck and all and pulled her in towards him. It didn't occur to Carrie to let go of the brush; she was too busy being mad and defending Jon.

'Don't quote Shakespeare at me!' she shouted with every tug of the yard brush.

'Well I can't exactly compare you to a summer's day wearing a hat like that, can I?' he laughed.

Jed wasn't mad; he had the presence of mind to let go of the brush. He caught hold of Carrie as she staggered backwards. His hands were wet and mucky.

'You know, darling, I don't think you're such an original ice maiden after all. He has got past 'go' hasn't he?'

'Let go of me!' struggled Carrie.

"Love is a spirit all compact of fire.' [†] Are you on fire, Carrie?'

Jed had her backed up against a freezing cold concrete cow stall; she knew what was coming next and she couldn't do a single thing about it. Jed was just too powerful and too big. The padded steel girder of his leg fixed her into position so that she couldn't move. Carrie decided not to take the bait any more; she figured that he wouldn't really dare to do anything to her so she made herself stop struggling at him. She bit her lips together. Jed pulled Carrie's woolly hat from her head. Her hair fell over his mucky hands. Trying first ice and then fire, she glared at Jed.

'Now that's better. I can see you now. 'The prize of all too precious you.' [‡] That's who you are, isn't it, darlin'?'

Jed breathed into Carrie's face.

"So sweet was never so fatal.' [Δ] That's what Othello said to Desdemona just before he murdered her. He thought she'd been a naughty girl. What do you think Jon would do if he knew you'd been thinking about being a naughty girl? I know you think about it. I can see it on your face. Saw it this morning. You know you want me, you can't help it, can you? I make you feel like he does and you hate me for it. You can't deny it, can you?'

'Yes..I..can!' shouted Carrie, pushing against Jed with all her might and getting precisely nowhere.

'I should not have taken the bait!'

'You'll not deny me, in the end,' finished Jed. 'Some day your Prince will come, right inside you, and it'll be me not him, just you wait and see...'

Suddenly, the sound of Jip barking exploded around the echoing cowshed like a volley of machine gun fire. Jip was standing in the cowshed doorway; he was more bristled than the world's biggest yard brush. The padded steel girder disappeared from in between Carrie's legs. Jed threw her hat back at her, picked up the yard brush and swung it at a snarling Jip as he walked towards the door. Jip stood his ground until the very last minute.

'Ah! 'Parting is such sweet sorrow!" [†] laughed Jed. 'Catch you later, darlin'.'

'Jip! Good boy, Jip! Come here!'

The tractor revved Jed away to empty the muck spreader. Carrie hugged Jip close and tight.

'He's crackers, Jip, totally crackers. Never mind the muck spreader; he needs to empty the filth from his own mind first.'

Jip listened carefully to Carrie but could offer no advice beyond a friendly wag of his tail. It was enough to make her feel better. She stood up. She didn't put her woolly hat back on, though. She shoved it into her coat pocket instead. Jed's Shakespearean outburst had stung her in more ways than one. She felt guilty for taking the bait in the first place, and guilty for tasting the bait in the second; Jed had clearly inherited his father's predatory vision. It was also clear that he didn't intend to use it for the good. For a moment Carrie felt genuinely scared. Jed had crossed a line and dragged her with him.

'Maybe the old man fancies you himself, and that's why he's keeping you away from his son!'

'For some reason, I reckon he's soft on you! Has been since the day you first came here.'

Carrie shivered. It was time to get back to heaven, even if there was no snow light to show her the way.

'Come on, Jip. Let's find Jon.'

Jip didn't need a light of any sort to find his master. He raced ahead of Carrie in the direction of the barn. Jon was standing in the middle of the large cattle shed. He looked like he was throwing pale yellow cushions amongst the feet of the cattle. He was; it was their straw bedding. At the sound of Carrie's voice he looked up; he wanged the last few chunks of straw bale into the far corner of the shed. They landed with a muffled thud, thud. Jon looked fed up.

'If you want dirty farmers, go and live with dirty farmers and see how you like it, then!'

Carrie watched the dirty farmer walk across the shed in her direction. His silence stung her face. Less than two hours ago she was defiantly planning to stay the night in his bed. She had wanted to go to heaven, and all she'd managed so far today was a hellish diversion in the company of dirty farmer Jed, with his wet and mucky hands, and wet and mucky mind. Carrie tried:

'Oh I'm so cold,' she said, thinking they could soon get warmed up in the calf shed.

She reached up to put her arms around his neck; just a touch of his warm hair in her fingers would be enough. Jon pulled her hands away and gave them back to her.

'C..can't s..stop. G..got to g..get r..ready to d..do the c..c..cockerels.'

'Oh. O.K.'

Carrie understood very well what they were going to 'do' to the cockerels.

'S..sorry.'

Just like his father, he was walking, no, striding away at speed.

'You're not as sorry as me! I thought he'd never get past 'go'...Someday your Prince will come...and it'll be me not him...See how you like it...My mother doesn't want me to see how I like it...Still, I want to, need to see it...Heaven or Hell...There has to be a borderline somewhere...'

The bitter winter wind chased after Carrie who chased after Jon down the alleyway in the direction of the farmyard. In the newly cleaned cowshed, the first cockerels were arriving at the borderline. They didn't know if they were about to see Heaven or Hell; neither did Carrie.

———◆———

'Your mother's in bed. Migraine. She's overdone Christmas already. It's strange. It's happened earlier than usual.'

'Oh.'

Carrie hoped her dad didn't hear the guilt in her 'oh.' He was busy in the kitchen dishing up two plates of overcooked pie, chips, and mushy peas. Everything was decorated with slightly curled, brown edges, even the mushy peas, which had stuck to the bottom of the saucepan because he'd forgotten to give them a stir. It didn't matter. It was warm, friendly, food and it tasted of love and comfort.

Outside, the veil of snow had almost totally melted away. Inside, the stillness of the white day lingered into their evening, stifling every movement and spoken word, even the solemn air that they were forced to breath. They ate quietly in the kitchen; they dared not take food into the

339

lounge whilst Jill was in the house. It had been a joyless, brown edged, winter day. But Bill couldn't help being Bill.

By the time he'd analysed a thousand and one options as to what to do with the burnt bottom of the mushy pea saucepan, including burying it in the last snow drift or using it as a crash helmet, before finally deciding that it would mysteriously disappear because he wanted more than anything to surprise Jill with a new set of saucepans for Christmas, Carrie was feeling a little less brown edged, even if she did wish that she could also mysteriously disappear and be replaced by a shiny new Carrie.

Instead, she disappeared into the lounge to watch a bit of telly with her dad. It seemed like an age since they'd had any comfy time with just the two of them together. Carrie tried, as she'd done all day, but it just wouldn't work; she couldn't feel comfy or cosy. After a while, Bill said:

'What's up, Carrie? You don't look very happy!'

After a while, a very long while, Carrie replied:

'I've been cold, wet, mucky, abused and ignored all day!'

'All day? Are you sure? You're starting to sound just like your mother!'

'Ugh! And I think it's my fault she's got a migraine!'

'Why?'

Carrie told him why. After a while, Bill said:

'You know she's a very sensitive soul. It doesn't make her a bad person. We can never see behind another person's closed door. If your mother's not ready to open up and share with you, then you'll just have to accept that there'll always be things about her that you don't understand. Try to remember that she loves you, though. Just imagine how it must feel to feel like you do tonight, every moment of your life.'

Carrie imagined.

'So there is something, then? Why can't you tell me?'

'Would you like me to tell her about Jon and Jed?'

'No! But I'm not like her! You can trust me!'

'It's not about trust, it's about respect. When we can't respect ourselves or each other, that's when all the trouble starts in the first place. Look at Debs. If she told you something you'd respect her, wouldn't you?'

Carrie's face melted like the snow on the windowsill outside. The salt from her tears stung her skin and she melted faster and faster in the heat of comfy time with her dad. Bill put his arm with the good hand around his daughter's shoulders and tried to stop her melting.

'Hey! What's up, love?'

'She was trying to tell me something the last time we went shopping, and I didn't listen. She was acting funny, spending lots of money. I think she needed me and I didn't listen! I haven't heard from her since. I can't go and see her, I think something's wrong behind her closed door, and I didn't listen...'

'Sometimes too much imagining can be a bad thing,' tried Bill. 'Debs enjoyed Christmas shopping with you, didn't she? Maybe it was good news she wanted to tell you and she was a bit embarrassed. Maybe she's pregnant and couldn't find the right words to tell you, that would explain the shopping, the 'nesting' instinct, wouldn't it? You've been lifelong friends and she knows you're there for her. You made up after that last little fallout didn't you? And the run up to Christmas can be a very stressful time for lots of people for lots of reasons, so don't be too hard on yourself, about your mother, neither.'

'Oh Debs, you're not are you?'

'I just seem to get everything wrong, all the time! I just upset everybody, all the time!'

'Well you don't upset me! And you don't upset your mother, despite what you think. She upsets herself and you're not responsible for that. And I bet you don't upset Jon; well, maybe you do, but in a good way!' tried Bill, again.

'I'm not getting any time with him to upset him or otherwise. He just works, all the time. All I get is hassle from that brother of his! I wish I'd never set foot in the place...'

'Oh help! I am starting to sound just like my mother!'

Bill couldn't help being Bill. He waited for Carrie to stop sounding like her mother, before he spoke:

'Lots of folk have to work hard, long, hours. Just look at your mother!'

Carrie heard the twinkle in his eyes, and managed a little smile.

'Jon is a farmer. It's the life that he has, that's his choice. The life that you have is yours to choose also.'

Carrie chose.

The Falcon had not finished with his prey.

'Close your eyes and hold out your hand,' he said.

'I have a tree in my orchard...'

'And I saw Snow White in the shopping centre yesterday,' continued Bill. 'Now she had a fair bit of trouble before she finally connected with Prince Charming, didn't she?'

Carrie nodded.

'Some day your Prince will come, right inside you, and it'll be me not him, just

you wait and see...'

'So come on, my beautiful Princess! Why don't you get up to bed? You must be exhausted after what you've done with all those cockerels today. Take the positives, and sleep on them. Everything will look better in the morning. You never know, we might have so much snow in the night that you can't get in to the office on Monday!'

Bill had walked his daughter to the foot of the stairs. He whispered:

'Christmas is coming! Let's you and me work together to make sure it's a really boring, peaceful and uneventful one!'

Carrie smiled and nodded. She kissed her dad on the cheek; she still couldn't speak.

'Night night, love. Sleep tight.'

Carrie did as she was told and slept very tight.

The Falcon fell on her from the sky. He appeared from nowhere. She felt the warmth of his body, the ridges of every feather pressing down on her, as his wings outstretched in front of her. She couldn't breathe. She surrendered her little grey life and let it live or die beneath the Falcon's wings. But he was not there to kill her, but to protect her; she belonged to him. She had known it from the start; she just didn't know how it would end - in l..life or d..death....s..sorry...'

Friday 22nd December

Dear Reader,

Christmas comes early down on the farm. It has to so that the rest of us can enjoy our Christmas dinner. December marks the beginning of winter. The days are short; there is wind, rain, snow, dark and cold. It's miserable! No wonder the ancient Anglo Saxons lit a yule log at the start of 'Yule Monath', their name for the tenth Roman month of December, to cheer themselves up. We do the same with pretty lights, carols, cards, Christmas shopping, brightly coloured wrapping paper and ribbons for our presents, and decorating our houses.

Down on the farm, the winter jobs take all day. There is a continuous cold, dark, slog of feeding animals, bedding animals and mucking out, over and over again. And there is still the extra work of preparing for Christmas; instead of Christmas shopping there's plucking turkeys or cockerels; instead of wrapping presents there's dressing (and I don't mean in party clothes) turkeys or cockerels; instead of ribbons for our presents there's string to tie together the naked, goose bumpy legs of turkeys or cockerels; instead of pretty lights there's just one old, dust covered, light bulb to shine in every turkey or cockerel's eye as it's turned upside down and sent to heaven by the hands of the farmer. I'd never seen it done before; I didn't realise how difficult it is to break a neck, even one as small as a cockerel neck.

The farmer has to be strong, and quick, and kind. I had to be strong, not because I was upset at the sight of death, although at times it was grim if the farmer got it wrong and pulled the bird's head off by mistake, or worse, if the bird wouldn't die no matter how far he stretched its neck. No, I had to be strong to hold the bird upside down by the legs while it flapped its way up to heaven. I have heard stories of the nervous reflex action of birds being so strong that headless, they could still run around. After what I've seen, I believe the old 'headless chicken' joke could easily be true. Read on, you still want your Christmas dinner, don't you?

Our snow has just melted, for the time being, but there are white feathers a plenty to create the perfect 'Farmyard at Christmas' picture postcard scene. I didn't realise how difficult it was to pluck the feathers from a bird. Dunking them in scalding hot water for however many seconds so that the skin doesn't burn didn't seem to help me much, either. Wet or dry, the feathers are greasy, often caked in poo, and well and truly stuck beneath the skin of their owner; they weren't designed to fall out easily for our convenience. My fingers are still bright red, raw and sore from endless dunks in the boiling water and stabs from pulling on dandruff ridden, stinking, feathers.

There was no point trying to sweep them up; the darned things got everywhere. They looked pretty and charming from a distance, blowing around the farmyard beneath the crystal glow of moonlight, stars and yard lamp. But close up, they were a mush of pale brown chicken poo, chicken dandruff, and the still warm, feathery smell, of fresh death.

The smell of raw death was everywhere. There were dead cockerels on the table in the farmhouse pantry; dead cockerels hanging up in the outhouse next to the farmhouse kitchen back door; dead cockerels hanging up in some of the cowsheds. The cows had to wander and weave underneath them to get to their stalls at milking time; it was a festive decoration of sorts for the cows which could never be surpassed by the beauty and intricacy of the spiders' cobwebs and decades of dust that turned the cowsheds into a Christmas snowy wonderland all year round. Decorating the farmhouse with tinsel and baubles will have to wait until much later. Read on, you still want your Christmas dinner, don't you?

Dressing up for Christmas parties would also have to wait; the cockerels needed dressing first. You may well agree with me, reader, that dressing up for a Christmas party can be difficult. What shall we wear? Have we got enough make up on? Shall we put our hair up or down? I have to tell you that dressing a cockerel is far more difficult! We may find that some of the company or some of the food at our Christmas party makes us feel sick, but I promise you that it is nothing compared to the smell and texture of putting your hand inside a cockerel's bum and pulling its insides outside and watching them plop into a bucket at your feet. Why this act is called 'dressing' I cannot understand. The smell made me heave until I was just about sick! Read on, you still want your Christmas dinner, don't you?

Don't fret, your Christmas dinner is almost ready. The cockerel's legs are tied together with string. It's not much of a party game, but there's quite a skill to getting it just right so that the legs look even and the breast is plumped up in all the right places, a bit like choosing the correct underwear for your Christmas party outfit. And after all of that, there's entertaining to be done, as customers call to collect their Christmas dinners; the farmer sees his profits disappear in endless cups of tea and glasses of sherry. It's Christmas, after all!

A lot of ancient December customs have been swallowed up by Christmas. 'The Lord of Misrule', 17th December, in ancient Roman times, was the beginning of the festival of 'Saturnalia', in honour of the God of agriculture. This was a week-long orgy of feasting and merrymaking. It was a holiday time for all slaves who were waited on by their masters. Presents were exchanged, informal clothes were worn and gambling games were allowed. It sounds just like Christmas, doesn't it, although perhaps parents, especially mothers, might disagree about it being a holiday time for slaves!

A 'master of the revels' was appointed to organise the goings on. This character was called the 'Lord of Misrule' - every family has at least one of these, every Christmas. Is it going to be you?

December marks the beginning of winter. The days are short; there is wind, rain, snow, dark and cold. It's miserable! So why not have lights, warmth and parties?

Whether it's a single light in a cowshed where your Christmas dinner begins, a single star above a stable where a baby boy was born to be a light in the world, or the light and warmth of a simple Anglo Saxon Yule log, we can all celebrate light in the midst of darkness. There is an old saying:

'Good luck will come to the home where a fire is kept burning throughout the Christmas season.'

So good luck to you and yours! And there is another old saying that I long to be true:

'On Christmas Eve, all animals can speak. However, it's bad luck to test this.'

Please don't test it, just in case. I wonder what the cockerel in the cowshed, or the donkey in the stable, would have to say about Christmas?

———◆———

'Hey! Watch out, Carrie, your string's showing!'

'Well you just be careful I don't decide to use it to tie your legs together and put an orange where you don't want it!'

Dad would be proud of me, mother would be horrified with me, if she heard me talking like that. She's permanently horrified anyway, so what the hell...It's the office Christmas party and I don't care what any of them think about me any more, anyway...'

This wasn't entirely true. Carrie had stopped joining in with Mr Pike jokes since her 'moment' with him in his office a few weeks ago; she still hadn't worked out why she no longer found him funny. Mr Pike was the only person at work, apart from Dennis the editor, of course, that she really cared about; they were the only people whom she really cared what they thought about her, too.

In previous years, the office Christmas party had been a stingy affair. A few cheap bottles of mulled wine and packets of mince pies from the local supermarket, barely enough for one each, drinks as well as mince pies, and all taking place in the drab, undecorated, plastic conference room one which doubled as the staff room. Mr Pike got a lot of stick a lot of the time, and he'd probably deserved a lot of it, especially at Christmas time. But this year was different.

This year he'd hired a room at the local three star hotel. There was a buffet with real food. There was a bar selling real drinks. There was even a man playing a baby grand piano in the corner. There was a complimentary drink of sherry on arrival, courtesy of Mr Pike. All you had to do to get one, was to shake his hand on arrival and say 'Happy Christmas' and you were boomed onto the sherry table with 'a Merry Christmas to you too!' After that, the evening was yours to spend as you wished without a single thought for the big fish, who had provided all the facilities, sitting alone on the gold and dark blue velour three star hotel chair in the corner. Yes indeed, Mr Pike was a very kind and generous man, but nobody noticed. It was Christmas, after all. Carrie noticed.

'This is a lovely party, Mr Pike. Thank you for organising it.'

'Not at all, not at all, Carrie dear. You look very fine in that dress. Have you brought your friend along with you?'

'No, I haven't got a friend to bring,' said Carrie, feeling a little confused. 'I assumed it would be staff only anyway.'

'Friends are always welcome, especially when you don't get to see them very often, eh?' sneaked Mr Pike, nudging Carrie with his elbow.

'I might have been able to bring someone, I suppose,' said Carrie, almost thinking out loud to herself more than in answer to him. 'But they have a lot of work on at this time of year and wouldn't be able to get away.'

'I wonder what it would be like to go to a party with Jon. To walk into the room on his arm; to dance with him all night; to feel so proud of him; to protect him from all the other women who would try to get their hands on him - the jealousy would kill me, I'd be exhausted! To go home with him afterwards...Suppose I've already been to one party with him, when little Carrie was born...but I'd love to do it again, properly...'

'I know just what you mean,' boomed Mr Pike. 'They worry that they

346

won't fit in, and so you have to always come to occasions on your own. It shouldn't be like that, but it is. The world can be a cruel place, Carrie. It's my belief that ignorance is the greatest evil and the cause of a great deal of misery and unhappiness in the world. The spirit of Christmas never lasts long into each New Year does it?'

'No, I don't suppose it does.'

Carrie wasn't really prepared for a philosophy lecture, so she tried:

'Shall I get you another glass of sherry?'

'Yes, Carrie, that would be grand. And go and get yourself something to eat while you're at it. I shall sit here and listen to the music.'

Carrie left Mr Pike blowing bubbles. The piano man had reached the opening chords of 'I'm Dreaming of a White Christmas' by the time she reached the food queue. Sandwiched in between sweaty, beery bodies she was manhandled along towards the paper plates and sausage rolls.

'Hey up, Carrie, are you feeling sick yet?'

The 'String' idiot was pushing into her behind.

'No, but I will be if I have to listen to your verbal diarrhoea much longer!'

'Well, that's not very Christmassy!'

Carrie picked up a paper plate and a sausage roll.

'String' tried again:

'Hey! Watch out, Carrie, you've lost your place. Rosalind the Rottweiler's got Mr P backed into a corner. Just look at the state of her. Looks like she's not picked the right underwear for her Christmas party outfit. She's plumped up alright, but in none of the right places! And look at the state of those legs! You haven't plucked them for her, have you, Carrie, 'cos they look goose bumpy enough. Bet she's after his sausage roll. Go and tell her there's plenty over here, just the same size as his!'

Carrie suddenly lost her balance. Without warning, she took a step backwards. Unfortunately, the heel of her razor sharp stiletto pierced straight through the top of 'String's' cheap, leather shoes.

'Ow! You idiot! You've broken me foot!' hopped 'String.'

Everybody turned to laugh at 'String' who was doing a very silly dance in the middle of the room.

'Excuse me,' said Carrie.

She pushed past the entertainment that was twirling faster and faster in the middle of the room:

'I feel sick.'

Unfortunately, she was in such a hurry that she spilt her glass of sherry down its back; everybody laughed even louder. Everybody agreed; it was a good party. Good old Mr Pike. He's a very kind and generous man.

'Three cheers for Mr Pike!' called out Dennis the editor.

Everyone stopped laughing for a moment to give three cheers for Mr Pike, in an Irish accent, of course. Why pass up an opportunity to mock an Irishman if you got the chance? Dennis laughed and said he'd tell his 'mudder'. Everybody started laughing again. Everybody liked Dennis; he was a good sort.

'String' was right. It did look like 'Rosalind the Rottweiler' was after Mr Pike's sausage roll. She did have him backed into a corner. It was difficult to tell whether he was being chatted up or interrogated by the Gestapo.

'Knowing Rosalind, it'll be one and the same. Don't worry Mr Pike, I'll rescue you!'

'....you could come round for a meal in the holidays. I'll be on my own, otherwise...'

'Here's your sherry, Mr Pike. Sorry for the delay. I'm afraid I had a little accident and spilt it, had to go back for some more. Have you had anything to eat yet, Rosalind? There's a big queue, I wouldn't leave it too long or there'll be no sausage rolls left.'

Carrie held up her plate to show Rosalind her sausage roll.

'Yes, indeed, Rosalind, don't miss out on your party food.'

'I'll look after your bag for you,' said Carrie, pulling the silver clutch bag from underneath Rosalind's ample chicken wings. Rosalind gnashed her teeth at Carrie and flapped reluctantly away to the food table. Mr Pike was sweating a little oil on his forehead so he sat back down on his gold and dark blue velour three star hotel chair as soon as Rosalind departed. Carrie put Rosalind's silver clutch bag on a table a few feet away. She sat down next to Mr Pike.

'I wouldn't be at all surprised if she had a machine gun tucked away in that bag of hers, it weighed a tonne!'

Mr Pike turned his head slightly to look at the bag on the table; his thick, rubbery, lips bubbled slightly.

'I think he's smiling.'

Carrie looked across the room at the other silver bag who was standing next to the food table, filling her plate with sausage rolls and every other kind of roll on offer.

'Was Rosalind bothering you, Mr Pike?'

'Bothering me? Why of course not! I don't fraternise with my staff outside of work. That sort of thing always ends in disaster. I've had problems with all my secretaries over the years, Carrie. All of them. I don't understand it. They make a fuss of me, I try to be kind back to them, a lot of them are lonely, you know, and then they turn on me! What do you make of that?'

Carrie smiled and shrugged her shoulders. She didn't know what to make of that. She did know that Rosalind was throwing daggers and every knife and sharp fork she could muster at her as she chugged helplessly along the food queue.

'She's jealous! Jealous of me sitting here with Mr Pike! Well I never! Her hatred of me has nothing to do with being my mother's henchwoman after all!'

Carrie smiled and waved across the room at Rosalind. She decided to give Mr Pike an early Christmas present:

'You're a kind and well-meaning person, Mr Pike. I hope you don't mind me saying so, but it's just bad luck that you get misunderstood sometimes. You have unusual features which can't be easy for you. You've perhaps missed out on something when you were younger and it's affected you, but that's not your fault. It makes you vulnerable to ladies who might seek to take advantage of you. I think you're right to keep away from women like that; you could end up getting hurt. Sorry if I've spoken out of turn.'

Carrie kissed Mr Pike on the cheek; she didn't care who saw her do it, either. Mr Pike stopped bubbling.

'You're an incredible, most lovely young woman, Carrie. Don't ever forget it. Nobody has ever spoken so kindly to me. And you're right. Nothing good ever comes from living a secret life. But times change. I hope you won't have to live your life in the shadows, Carrie. What was your friend's name again?'

'My friend? Oh, you mean Debs. Oh! *(Oh! Mr Pike, how could you think...)* She's my best friend from school. She's married, Mr Pike. She *is* just my best friend.'

Mr Pike boomed so loudly that Carrie thought he was going to fall off his chair. Everybody turned to look as he reached out to give Carrie a Christmas box she'd never forget. He put his arm round her and pulled her into his gold velvet, embroidered with silver holly leaves, waistcoat. Carrie could feel his swim bladder sloshing around underneath it like a very loose pin cushion. His gills homed in on her face; his thick rubbery lips bubbled open. Wider and wider they went. Nearer and nearer they came.

'*He's going to swallow me whole!*'

A cold clammy hand grabbed her around the rib cage. It ever so slightly brushed against her left breast before it came to rest around her back. Carrie's body was sweating enough water to swim in, but she drowned instead. Mr Pike connected with Carrie - on the lips.

'Chestnuts roasting on an open fire...' sang the piano man. There was cheering in the background. Everybody agreed; it was a great party. Good old Mr Pike! He's a very kind and generous man.

Carrie didn't know where to put her hands. She wished the piano man would stop singing about chestnuts. She settled on standing up at speed in the hope of loosening Mr Pike's grip with as much dignity as possible. There was a great risk that he might accidentally touch her breasts again but she had no better options. He did.

'Please, Mr Pike!'

Mr Pike didn't hear the emotion in her voice. He was in full boom by now.

'Oh, Carrie, I'm so delighted, so delighted! It would have been such a terrible waste...How wonderful! Just a friend you say....That's made my Christmas, it was worth paying for all this after all...'

'I'm sorry, I have to go now,' said Carrie.

She backed away from Mr Pike. She felt genuinely sick.

'So soon? Well, I don't understand!' blubbed Mr Pike.

'We were getting on fine, like I always knew we would...'

'I feel sick!' said Carrie.

Carrie left the Christmas party at the three star hotel a good deal faster than she'd arrived. She didn't hear 'String' laughing, she didn't see Rosalind's smug gnash of satisfaction as she walked across the room to pick up Mr Pike who was standing alone, drowning like a fish out of water in the corner of the room. He might not be much of a catch, but he was better than nothing, and she was going to be all alone at Christmas otherwise. She'd be alright if she had a few sherries.

But Dennis, being a bushy moustached Irishman who'd had a few sherries already, caught the big fish first. He hadn't got to be editor-in-chief without taking a risk or two in his long career. He'd cheerfully turn a blind eye to a fair few things, but not everything, and certainly not where a lady was concerned. He was going to give Mr Pike a Christmas box he'd never forget; he should have done it years ago, he could see that now.

Carrie didn't see anything. All she could feel was her heart going 'thud' against the inside of her new velvet dress with the chiffon sleeves in time to her every step. It was like being hit by a small hammer, over and over again. She hastily, shakily, walked down the stairs to the lobby of the three star hotel.

Outside, it was really, really December dark. She breathed in bitter black ice air. She breathed out iced whited air that was her only source of light as she made her way to her faithful, little red car. The crystal car park cracked open beneath her feet; she wished it would swallow her up. But it didn't, and here was her little red car, anyway.

'I want a word with you!'

Carrie dropped her keys; the car park was happy to swallow them up. She couldn't see a thing. She could barely make out the outline of the creature that seemed to rise up from underneath the cracked car park tarmac.

The large, black, silhouette was pressing down on her now, bending her backwards over the bonnet of her little red car; not far enough to break her back, but far enough to render her completely helpless. The small hammer beating on her velvet dress turned into a big one. She'd just dropped her car keys so she couldn't even gouge out the creature's eyes; it was so dark she couldn't see its eyes, anyway. The sherry and the after effects of Mr Pike's Christmas box were still clouding her judgement. She almost laughed at it; what further humiliation could it do to her, that hadn't already been done tonight?

Carrie felt sick enough already, so she tried to make herself sick over the creature, but she was being held backwards at too sharp an angle to make it work. The creature was alive because she could feel and smell its breath. Beer.

'Happy Christmas! I've got no money,' said Carrie.

'I don't want your filthy money. I said I want a word with you!'

The penny dropped. The outline of the creature suddenly changed shape. It had a round head and a large belly; it had pork sausage fingers and slightly yellow eyes. It was a man of sorts. It was Joe. Carrie said nothing.

'I told you to keep away from my missus! I told you, didn't I?'

Carrie said nothing.

'Answer me, you bitch!'

Joe shoved Carrie a bit harder down onto the bonnet of her little red car.

'You're hurting my back!' said Carrie.

'I'll hurt more than your back before I've finished with you, if you don't leave my missus alone!'

Carrie said nothing. The after effects of Mr Pike's Christmas box were a distant memory all of a sudden. All of a sudden, Carrie realised that she might be in a tight spot here; she started to madly race through her options and found that she hadn't got many.

'Let me go, Joe, and then I can talk to you. You don't want to get into trouble just before Christmas, do you? Think about Debs?'

'I think about her all the time!'

Joe pulled Carrie from the bonnet of her little red car and rammed her up against the driver's side window. The poor little car shook violently; its coating of ice frosting stuck to her back.

'I think about you taking her shopping, spending all my money, sneaking around behind my back, taking her for fancy coffees...'

With every thought, Joe slammed Carrie backwards; the ridge of her little red car's roof cut into her back like the lash of a whip. She kicked out at Joe's shin with her stiletto.

'Ow! Bitch!'

Joe pulled Carrie again. This time she landed face down over the top of her little red car's bonnet. Joe laid his immense weight on her and shoved into her with his every word. Carrie wanted to be sick more than she'd ever wanted to be sick in her whole life, but it wouldn't come.

'Keep..a..way..from..my..mis..sus!!'

'Help!' shouted Carrie.

The trouble was, she didn't sound very loud because her face was being pressed into her little red car bonnet. Carrie felt all of Joe's body parts as he gave her one final, enormous, shove.

'Chestnuts roasting on an open fire...'

Joe was speaking fast and low now:

'Keep away from my missus, bitch, or next time, I'll teach you a lesson you'll never forget!'

'Ow! Agh! Get off!'

Something was whistling through the air. It landed with a dull, thudding, sound. Again and again. Joe got off Carrie.

'Unhand that lady, you monster!'

Joe unhanded. He had to use his pork sausage fingers to protect himself from the blows that were raining down on him. With every word, Mr Pike's ornate, silver topped, walking stick whistled and thudded onto the monster.

'You...vile...sick...creat..ure! Leave...her...a...lone!'

Joe had already left. He half ran, half staggered, one set of sausage fingers covering his head, the other clutching his belly as it followed behind his stumbling legs. Joe had no trouble being sick. He'd had a few too many tonight and so he sicked himself away, all down his clothes, and all over the crystal car park. A crack opened beneath Joe's feet and he slipped silently into it, sealing his despair, hurting his hip. He crawled away on all fours out into the street. If Carrie wanted to press charges the police would have no trouble tracing his sick trail all the way home.

'Oh Carrie, Carrie! Are you alright?'

'Yes, I'm alright. Thank you.'

Mr Pike was blubbing and bubbling:

'Oh, Carrie, I'm so sorry, so sorry. It's all my fault, what shall I do, I'm so sorry...'

'I'm alright, Mr Pike. It's not your fault. Thank you for rescuing me.'

'Oh, but it *is* my fault!' he wailed. 'I frightened you and chased you away and now that ghastly creature has further assaulted you. Carrie, I'm so sorry. Are you hurt?'

Carrie was kneeling down on the ground, her hands spread out over the crystal diamonds that still managed to shine in the darkness, in the few places where they hadn't been crushed by Joe's monster feet.

'No, I'm looking for my car keys...Here they are!' replied a suddenly very happy Carrie.

'Well I must say, you seem remarkably calm,' said Mr Pike.

Carrie stood up, shrugged her shoulders and looked blankly, very blankly, at Mr Pike.

'Yes, I suppose I am,' she said. 'Actually, I don't feel anything.'

'You poor girl, you must be in shock. I'll send for an ambulance, send for the police. Oh, what have I done, what have I done!'

'You helped me, rescued me from Joe. Thank you,' said Carrie, simply.

'Why am I not feeling anything?'

'Do you mean to tell me, that you know that man? He's not your secret friend is he?'

Carrie even managed a smile in the darkness:

'No! He's my friend Debs' husband.'

'Oh...oh dear,' murmured Mr Pike.

His penny dropped. It started him off again:

'Oh, what have I done! To think what I thought! To do what I've done! Oh Carrie, please forgive me.'

Mr Pike stood hunched over his silver topped walking stick; he looked like he'd skewered himself into place.

'It's alright, really. There's no harm done. I'll be alright. I'll go home now.'

Why am I not feeling anything?'

Carrie unlocked and opened her little red car door. The gentle yellow light from inside the car lit up Mr Pike's presence. He glowed silver all over, from the top of his silver walking stick, through his gold velvet, embroidered with silver holly leaves, waistcoat and on up to his face, which was coated in a silver sheen of oil and sweat. He was gasping for breath; he was drowning in a sea of tears which were rolling down his face.

'Are you alright, Mr Pike. You don't look very well. Shall I take you back inside the hotel?'

'No, Carrie dear, no. I came out here to find you and I'm jolly glad I did. Dennis...Dennis put me straight...I didn't mean any harm...I never mean any harm...'

'I know,' said Carrie.

'Please, Carrie, please just listen to me. I'm sorry for my behaviour in the hotel, sorry from the bottom of my heart. I would never ever hurt you. I am just so very, very fond of you. You have always been so very, very kind to me. You have no idea how much your kindness has meant to me, what you've done for me. I just wanted to express my affection for you and I have overstepped the mark. I didn't realise what I was doing, I got carried away. Please accept my most humble apology. You can rest assured that it will never happen again. Never. I value your friendship and hope I haven't spoilt it. Please forgive me.'

'I forgive you, Mr Pike. Don't let it spoil your Christmas. I want to go home now,' said Carrie.

Why am I still not feeling anything?'

'Will you shake my hand?' asked Mr Pike.

Carrie took a step back.

'I don't want to.'

Mr. Pike seemed to slip even lower down his silver topped walking stick skewer.

'I have to go now,' said Carrie, blankly.

'Yes, of course. Very well dear. Thankyou.'

Carrie climbed into her little red car and made to pull the door to; Mr

Pike put his tail in the way and stopped her.

'Good bye, Carrie dear. Your friend, the one that you don't see very often…'

Carrie looked away from Mr Pike, and busied herself with putting her car keys in the ignition. He still looked more like a trout than a pike.

'I'm going now.'

'He's a very lucky man. My advice to you, Carrie dear, is to enjoy the pleasure of being alive. Don't hide from it. Promise me that, Carrie…'

'Goodbye.'

Carrie's little red car was reversing before she'd finished shutting her car door.

'Happy Christmas!' boomed Mr Pike.

He smiled and waved cheerfully at the little red car. A few other folk were leaving the three star hotel. Mr Pike stood alone in the freezing cold, crystal car park. The moon came out from behind a cloud. Mr Pike was suddenly surrounded on all sides by a carpet of diamonds, riches beyond his wildest dreams. He stood alone for a moment longer and enjoyed the riches and his wildest dreams. But the party was over. It was time for Mr Pike to pay.

'Yes, indeed, it was a great party. I'm a very kind and generous man. It's Christmas, after all.'

Inside the three star hotel, the piano man was still playing; he was a very kind and generous man, given what they were paying him for tonight. Mr Pike listened from the privacy of an armchair in the foyer; it was one of his mother's favourite songs. He knew it well:

'Have yourself a merry little Christmas…' he boomed, quietly.

Sunday 24th December
Christmas Eve

'Come in, Carrie love, and take the weight off your feet!'

'Thanks Mavis!'

'I didn't expect to see you today. It's Christmas Eve!'

'I wanted to come. I wanted to see you all and wish you a Happy Christmas!' said Carrie.

'Ah, suppose you did,' cackled Mavis.

Mavis never ever seemed to run out of cackle whatever the time of day or night.

'Come and sit ye down and have a spot of tea with me. We don't get much time to talk when the lads are hanging round all the time.'

Carrie made to sit down at a wooden chair at the kitchen table but Mavis blocked her path.

'Get you down here by the fire!'

She was pointing to old man Wilson's 'father bear' chair next to the square little fire of the Rayburn cooker. Carrie started to say that she couldn't sit in Mr Wilson's chair, but found herself sitting in it before she'd had time to finish her sentence. Mavis stood, now, next to an enthroned Carrie, making the tea with boiling water from the friendly farmhouse kettle; it worked as hard as anyone else on the farm, endlessly making cups of tea for 'the lads.'

Carrie watched Mavis make the tea. She soon forgot her discomfort at the thought of sitting in the Falcon's chair. Like Goldilocks, it was far too big for her, but she could see why he liked it so much. Its wood was worn with a natural warmth. An old, hand knitted, blanket hanging over the back gave just enough padding that could be adjusted to taste.

From this spot by the fire, Carrie could see everything in the kitchen, she could see through one window out into the garden and the main road beyond; through the other one, and the kitchen door, she could see out into the farmyard and the buildings beyond it. Sitting here, she could see everything. It was the perfect roost for the old bird of prey.

Somebody had slapped up a few Christmas decorations around the kitchen. There was a tiny Christmas tree on the windowsill. Hanging from the meat hooks and clothes pulley, garlands made of crepe paper zigzagged all over the kitchen ceiling. The colours were faded with the memories of a thousand Christmases. Carrie wondered who had made them. Maybe the little hands of Jon and Jed with their mother. She wondered what that did to Jon and Jed every Christmas now that they had big hands. A big silver star hung down from the meat hook above the kitchen table; it looked quite new.

'Your decorations look lovely, Mavis.'

'Ah, he don't like Christmas, but I always put a few up for the lads. Look at me star! Jon bought it me this time. 'Put this up for us, Mavis' he said. 'It's a light in the darkness.' And look at me angel! He bought me that as well!'

Mavis dropped the friendly farmhouse kettle and rushed over to the kitchen table.

'She's an angel called 'Hope'. Here, see?'

Mavis walked very slowly and carefully back towards Carrie. She held her hands out in front of her, cupped, as if she was carrying a little lost baby bird inside them.

'Look at her. Isn't she beautiful?' whispered Mavis.

Mavis bent forward into her familiar letter 'R' shape and opened her hands so slowly and carefully that Carrie really expected a little lost baby bird to fly out at her. Angel 'Hope' lay cushioned in between the large, soft, knuckles and hard, round, calluses of Mavis' hands. All of a sudden, Carrie thought she was going to be sick. Mavis' hands were scrubbed, cold, and white as the dusting of snow that lay outside on the farmyard, but they still reeked of chicken giblets and cockerel feathers. Or was it her clothes? The wool tights or the frilly apron? Or was it Angel Hope's long, golden, hair?

'Oh yes, she's lovely!'

Carrie didn't want to offend Mavis. The tiny, porcelain, angel dressed in a long white gown, smiled back at her as she returned her to Mavis for safe keeping.

'Well look at that, she smiles just like you, Carrie, love! You'll be sitting in the middle of the table with us and no mistake on Christmas day!'

Carrie smiled back politely and put some more sugar in her tea; she needed it. She'd already worked out where she'd be sitting on Christmas day, and who wanted her there. 'Hope' was a little angel with a big message; Carrie heard her loud and clear, even if Mavis didn't. She was in bits.

'Here, Mavis, I've brought you a little present.'

'Ah, they're lovely! You shouldn't have bothered. I'll put them on the table with 'Hope'.'

Mavis put the flower arrangement, based on a Yule log, on the kitchen table next to the little angel.

'There you are, some company for you, little lady.'

Carrie smiled. On her Yule log, there was a Father Christmas, a reindeer, and a snowman. Angel 'Hope' towered above them like the 'Statue of Liberty' but Mavis didn't seem to mind. Company's company and that's that.

'And I've brought a few little things for Mr Wilson and 'the lads', and Ab, of course. Can you hide them for me until tomorrow?'

'Ah, Carrie, love, you're an angel. They never bother about presents. That'll give them a shock! Here, come with me. I know where to put them.'

Mavis rustled away down the corridor, past the stairs with the shiny wooden edges and the strip of carpet in the middle, that had led her to two of the most erotic moments of her life to date, and on to a closed door at the end. Mavis opened the door; it sounded letter 'R' shaped at the hinges.

'This is me best room!' said Mavis, proudly.

Stepping from the warmth of the kitchen into this arctic, best room, was really like stepping into another world, and not just because of the dramatic change in temperature. Carrie had entered a fairy wonderland of row upon row of beautiful dolls and knitted toys which sat the entire length of a very long, bench type, padded sofa. All sorts of beautiful, polished, wooden furniture and chairs were adorned with embroidered table cloths, crocheted mats, and hundreds of knick-knack ornaments; little birds and painted vases.

'Angel 'Hope' and her friends will end up in here after Christmas!'

'Aah!' said Carrie, and not just because of the sudden cold. 'This is amazing, Mavis! It's so beautiful! Have you made all of these?'

'I feel the need to bow my head. I want to bow my head to this amazing lady!'

'Ah! I just like making things. Don't use a pattern or nowt like that. Just me eyes!'

The eyes were squinting at Carrie now, smiling their smile, and cackling again:

'Take one, Carrie, love. Take one for Christmas!'

'Oh no, I couldn't take your beautiful things!'

'Yes, you shall have one. You choose. Anything you like! There's a Santa here, is he any good?'

'She wants to give me something, I mustn't offend her.'

With as much reverence as she could muster, Carrie gently walked across the room to the very long sofa. She walked up and down looking at all the beautiful toys as if she was the Queen inspecting a royal guard of honour. She wanted to honour Mavis.

She took her time. It was hard to choose. She was drawn to the animals that sat together at one end of the bench. Little lambs, a donkey, a giraffe, several cows...'

'This looks like someone I know! Can I have this one?'

'I knew it. I knew you'd take that one!'

Mavis was almost jumping up and down with delight.

'He's been made for you, hasn't he?'

'Yes, he has!'

Carrie couldn't let go of the smile on her face to reply to Mavis straight away. She held the black and white collie dog in her hands, cupped, as if she was carrying a little lost baby bird.

'I'll treasure this, always. Thank you Mavis. I'll call him Jip!'

'Ah,' said Mavis, turning to go back to the kitchen.

There was another closed door at the far end of the room.

'What's in there, Mavis?'

'It's me room.'

'Do you live here, then?'

'That I do.'

'I didn't know that.'

Carrie did know that Mavis' replies were getting shorter and shorter. It was time to shut up.

'He's been good to me.'

Carrie's 'ah' was lost in the echo of their feet on the hard tiles of the corridor; the heat of the kitchen brought Mavis back to normal.

'Well I never, it looks like we'll have a white Christmas after all.'

Carrie nodded.

'You'll stay and have a bit of tea with us, afore you go, won't you, Carrie, love?'

'Well, I shouldn't be late back...'

'You can just have another cup of tea. They'd like to see you. It'd do the old man good!'

'Alright, I'll have another cup of tea...'

———◆———

'Well, I'm expected at home, I can't stay any longer,' said Carrie, trying to keep her heartache from breaking her voice into uncontrollable syllables of disappointment.

'Silent night, holy night,' sang the radio on the mantelpiece. It had been so quiet and calm at the tea table that despite the radio's relay of endless Christmas carols, Carrie had heard every tick tock of the mantelpiece clock, ticking away the tocks until she had to leave, and still Jon wasn't back from delivering last minute cockerels.

Neither was Jed, so there was at least a little something to feel cheerful about. If she couldn't see Jon, then Jed was the last person she wanted to see last before she had to go home. Old man Wilson had settled down to roost in his favourite chair. He'd hardly said a word all through tea time, just an 'ah' and a nod when Mavis told him about 'the fancy biscuits' that Carrie had bought them for Christmas. The fancy biscuits couldn't compete with Mavis' juicy mince pies; the open tin sat next to Angel 'Hope' on the table looking hopeless despite the glamour of their colourful tin and swirls of chocolate.

They look like I felt at the Christmas party; over dressed and out of place, attracting all the wrong sort of attention. I bet Jed will come in and scoff the lot!'

Old man Wilson sat with eyes closed, his long, silver, hair resting against his old, hand knitted, blanket, while Mavis cackled, chuckled and quizzed Carrie about her Christmas day. Mavis was mostly about food:

'You shall take a bit of me ham for Boxing Day! Can't beat a bit of ham on Boxing Day, can you, Ezra?'

'Ah,' hummed old man Wilson.

Carrie had the uncomfortable feeling that he was staring at her in-between pretending to be asleep or listening to his Christmas music, but she couldn't catch him at it. She was having to concentrate hard on Mavis, who was clearly enjoying having someone to talk to, who wasn't made of porcelain, this Christmas Eve teatime.

'I'm sorry, I really do have to go now.'

'Ah, shame the lads won't see you.'

Carrie wasn't the only one who was heartbroken at 'the lads' missing teatime; she heard it in Mavis' voice. The cackle had gone. Mavis was quiet. But not for long.

'Who won't we see?'

Jed burst in through the kitchen door bringing a flurry of white Christmas Eve with him. He shook his overcoat like a shaggy dog; tiny white flakes of snow fell to the floor making tiny puddles of ice all around him.

'Shut the door, you're letting all the cold in,' said old man Wilson.

'If you say so,' said Jed, kicking back a leg like a dog stretching itself out after a long walk.

The kitchen door slammed shut. Old man Wilson shut his eyes. White Christmas Eve, and everything that came with it, was not wanted in the warm, farmhouse kitchen; Carrie could see that as plain as the puddles that Jed was leaving on the floor as he chased Mavis around the far side of the kitchen table.

'Here you are, Mavis!'

Jed grabbed hold of Mavis and hugged her with one arm:

'Mm...'posh' biscuits!' he said, helping himself to a chocolate swirl with his other one.

'Hands off, Jed Wilson, they're a present from our Carrie!'

Jed grinned at Carrie and grabbed another biscuit.

'And here's a present for you from me, Mavis! Come here, gorgeous!'

Jed reached inside his overcoat. He pulled out a large sprig of mistletoe and gave Mavis a loud kiss on the cheek:

'Mmmm....!'

'Give over, you daft beggar!' cackled Mavis.

'Who's next, then?' laughed Jed.

Carrie started edging towards the kitchen door; this wasn't the kind of Christmas Eve that she wanted at all.

'Thanks for the tea, Mavis, I'd best make a move now.'

'You certainly had!' said Jed. 'We can't let you go without a Christmas kiss under the mistletoe now, can we?'

Jed was coming at Carrie at speed. Mavis was cackling. Old man Wilson was sleeping. The radio was singing 'On the first day of Christmas my true love gave to me...'

Jed had reached Carrie. His arm was reaching out to grab her. Mistletoe above her head, his lips were about to touch hers; she could smell the whisky on them. How many cockerels had he delivered? Christmas drinks collected? A fair few by the smell of things. Jed's lips had barely made contact with Carrie's cheek before they were gone. Taken away.

The Falcon stood, all seven feet of him, or thereabouts, in between Carrie and Jed. Jed suddenly looked like a shy little boy peering around the back of his father's legs, at the visitor to their farmhouse kitchen. The Falcon turned his back on his son, and turned to face Carrie. She knew that she was the mouse, all over again. He reached down and took both of her hands in his.

'Look him in the eye! Even the smallest prey can still be brave! But what eyes! Is he really mad or does he just look mad?'

Carrie looked up into old man Wilson's palest of pale, pale blue, eyes. They were as ice white as the Christmas Eve on the other side of the farmhouse door. Yet they were on fire. They burned her still, just the same as the very first day they'd met. She still felt odd, turned upside down and inside out; nothing ever helped that feeling. The Falcon hadn't finished with his prey.

'Happy Christmas, Carrie, and all the best to you and yours.'

The Falcon had still not finished with his prey. His long, silver, hair fell down over her head, touched her upturned face. Gentle as the tip of a feather, old man Wilson kissed Carrie on her forehead.

'How silently, how silently, the wondrous gift is given,' [†] sang the radio.

Whiskers grown on soft pink porcelain and the strange perfume of rosewater mixed with chicken giblets and a little wee were kissing her now.

'Take care, Carrie love. I hope Santa comes to you!'

'Thanks. You too, Mavis!'

Carrie reached for the farmhouse kitchen door, but it opened by itself. Jon and Jip were standing on the other side of it.

'Hey, Jon!' said Jed, pushing forwards, grabbing the sprig of mistletoe out of Mavis' hands.

He waved it in Jon's face:

'You're not too late! We've all had a go with her! Now it's your turn!'

Jon stood stock still in the doorway. He looked cold enough to be frozen to the spot. Just like Jip, he was covered in a dusting of white sugar frosting, except there was nothing sweet about the white Christmas Eve blowing in through the open farmhouse door, or the look on Jon's face as he stared at his all smiling twin brother.

'I'll w..walk you to your c..car,' he said, turning, returning to the coldness and bitterness of the icy farmyard as if they were preferred, comfortable, old friends.

Carrie smiled a final good bye to Mavis and followed after Jon. Jed leaned against the open kitchen doorway and followed Carrie with his eyes; it was too cold to go back out side.

'Never mind 'to be, or not to be', the question is 'will he or won't he?' smirked Jed. 'Wait for it, wait for it...He's saying something to her now. Oo...Oo...Oo...Oh bloody hell! He's shaking her hand, for God's sake!'

'Jed, I've told you to close the door, you're letting all the cold in.'

Jed went back to the 'fancy' biscuit tin; he scoffed the lot. From his perfect roost by the fire, the Falcon saw everything, even after the door closed. He went back to sleep.

'What can I give him, poor as I am? If I were a shepherd, I would bring a lamb. Yet what I can I give him, give my heart...give, my heart,' [†] sang the radio.

———◆———

The little red car stood alone, dark, and silent, parked up in the freezing cold gateway. The moon came out from behind a cloud. Through the bars of the five barred gate, a field full of diamonds glistened in the white, night, air as far as the eye could see. Carrie looked through the fogged up windows of her little red car. Sure, she wanted to join in with the silent snow carol; she wanted to go to Heaven. She wanted to go outside and play. But he wasn't here yet. She had to wait a bit longer. The guilt was terrible; she was already very late going home. Her mother would be furious with her. It wouldn't be a good start to Christmas.

He's a very lucky man. My advice to you, Carrie dear, is to enjoy the pleasure of being alive. Don't hide from it. Promise me that...'

Heaven arrived, without warning. A dull thud from a large fist broke the silence of the snow carol, as the moon had broken its darkness. Carrie didn't hesitate. She didn't hide. She got out of the car and raised her arms in welcome; she wanted to go to heaven. It wasn't hard. He caught her. They stood together in the middle of the dazzling whiteness.

'I c..can't when he's w..watching.'

'I know,' said Carrie.

She opened a hand. Sitting in her palm was a small piece of mistletoe that she'd 'borrowed' from Jed.

'It's evergreen. It'll keep!'

'No, it won't k..keep,' he said.

And it didn't. The guilt was terrible; Carrie couldn't stay in heaven for ever. She knew that she had to break the beauty and stillness of their perfection.

'I've got to go,' she whispered.

'C..close your eyes and h..hold out your h..hand,' he said.

'What for?'

'C..close your eyes!'

363

A shiver ran down Carrie's spine, and not because of the cold.

'I have a tree in my orchard...'

Carrie remembered. But only for a moment. She closed her eyes. She held out her hand. She thought he was going to kiss her again. She smiled as she felt something hard, and very light, rest on her upturned palm. It was wrapped up in a paper bag.

'H..happy C..C..Christmas,' said Jon.

'Thank you,' said Carrie. 'I've got nothing to give you, except for the socks that I've left for you, with Mavis!'

Jon smiled down at Carrie. He almost spoke.

'G..go!' he said, simply.

'What do you do on Christmas Day?'

'W..work as usual.'

'Me, too,' sighed Carrie. 'Except I'll be working my mother's guests; I'd rather be mucking out here, with you!'

'H..have a g..good one!' he said.

A dull thud from his fist closed the door of her little red car. The moon disappeared behind a cloud. Jon watched as the little red car flew away. He stood alone in the freezing cold, dark, silent gateway. He couldn't see a thing. He stood alone a moment longer. The little red car had taken all the light away, and the moon sat stubbornly behind its cloud. No matter; he knew his way back to the farmhouse off by heart. His heart raced back faster than his feet.

He kept his fist tightly closed as he walked from memory.

'It's evergreen. It'll keep.'

And it did. Safe in the palm of his hand.

———————◆———————

Her dad had done a good job.

'Ah, there you are, Carrie. You've missed dinner, I'm afraid. Come and have a sherry and a mince pie.'

Carrie's mother sat on the new sofa in the lounge, her high cheekbones as bright red as the Yule log burning happily away in the grate. Her dad winked at her when she came into the room and held up two fingers with his good hand. He wasn't swearing at her for being late; on the contrary, he was telling her how many sherries her mother had already had. Carrie was in the clear. She didn't even need to apologise for being late.

'Mavis has sent us some of her ham for Boxing Day.'

'Mince pie!' commanded Jill.

'I've put it in the fridge,' said Carrie, smiling across at her dad.

'A card came for you today. It was dropped off by hand, but I didn't see who it was from,' he said.

'Oh thanks,' said Carrie.

'Never mind that!' said Jill, loudly. 'You can look at that later. We need to run through the arrangements for tomorrow and Boxing Day and the day after. I don't want *any* problems this year!'

'Have another sherry, then,' said Bill.

'That's just the sort of interruption we don't need!' said Jill, sharply. 'Just pay attention for a few minutes. I will have another sherry, though, now you mention it.'

Carrie smiled.

'Christmas is a very difficult time of year for a lot of people,' said Bill.

'That's why *we* need to be organized! There's a copy of my schedule in the kitchen, and I expect both of you to look at it by the end of tomorrow morning, but I'll talk you through the main parts now....'

Jill talked; Bill and Carrie ate the perfectly bought mince pies.

'They're not as good as yours, Mavis! Oh Mavis!'

Nobody listened.

'Now Carrie, are you going up to bed, please. Your father and I have a lot of work to do.'

Even now, Carrie still had to go up to bed first before her mother would put the presents under the tree. Thank goodness she'd stopped putting out a glass of sherry, a mince pie and a carrot, for Father Christmas and Rudolf the red nosed reindeer, although it was embarrassing to remember just how recently she'd stopped doing that. Tonight, she was very pleased to go up to bed so early. She had something of her own to hide; the pain in her chest might very well be indigestion from eating too many mince pies, but she doubted it, somehow...

'Good night, love,' said dad.

He made to kiss her on the forehead. Carrie backed away from her dad as best she could.

'I don't need mistletoe to kiss my own daughter now, do I?'

'No, of course not, but I smell of the farm,' she smiled, uneasily.

'Or the farmer,' whispered her dad, planting his Christmas kiss gently on her forehead.

There was no point trying to hide. Her mother was helping herself to 'one last sherry.' Bill was smiling at his daughter. She almost spoke.

'Go!' he said simply. She hugged him.

'Don't forget your card!'

'No, it's here! I haven't forgotten it.'

Bill watched Carrie go through the lounge door.

'No, she won't forget a lot of things this Christmas. Christmas is a difficult time for a lot of people.'

His difficult time had just fallen asleep on the sofa.

'Come on Sleepy! Why don't you get up to bed? I'll put the presents under the tree.'

Bill didn't have enough fingers to show Jill how many sherries she'd had; he'd have to pay for it tomorrow, but at least it had got Carrie through Christmas Eve in one piece. Bill hadn't forgotten Snow White in the shopping centre.

'It's nearly Christmas, let the pantomime begin...'

———————◆———————

The moonlight was her chosen landscape. Carrie curled, wrapped up in her fluffy, pale pink, dressing gown, on the little bench beneath her bedroom window. Her curtains were open wide; her window was open, a little less than wide. Outside, the wintry sky was so soft and so sad and so sleepy that she needed to feel it on her skin. Its touch had the same gentle, deep, feeling that had made her feel so happy and so sad at the same time, standing beneath Jon's kisses in the field gateway less than two hours ago. She held Jon's paper bag present in her hands. She couldn't wait until Christmas Day.

She hesitated. She couldn't open it. She was hiding again. She decided to open her hand delivered Christmas card first. An angel, with long, golden, hair, dressed in a long white gown, smiled up at her. She was covered in glitter. She was beautiful.

'Oh, Mavis!'

'Happy Christmas, Carrie. Don't contact me over Christmas, or anytime. It was a mistake to get in touch again. I can't do it any more. Leave me be, D.'

'Christmas is a difficult time for a lot of people. Oh, Debs! What do you mean? I got it wrong before, I don't want to get it wrong again. Where are you, Angel 'Hope'?'

Outside, the wintry sky looked troubled, all of a sudden. A gust of wind disturbed Carrie's long, golden, hair. It cut her face.

'I'm not made of porcelain or glitter, Debs. I'll not make the same mistake twice! I wasn't made of porcelain two hours ago, either...'

Carrie stopped hiding. She opened her paper bag present. A familiar face looked up at her. Its black and white features weren't perfect. It was a pencil drawing. It was the style of the artist; strong; straightforward; raw. It was Jon. It wasn't so much the portrait of little Carrie that so disabled big Carrie's eyes so that she could barely see beyond the black and white blur in her moonlit hands. It was the charcoal thumb prints and pencil scratchings around its edges.

There was no glass in the simple, wooden, frame. In fact, it was so rough at the edges, it was quite likely handmade by the artist himself. Carrie laid her thumbs over the charcoal ghosts of the artist. She saw what he saw. She felt what he felt. She felt the weight of his thumbs as they pressed into the soft paper, deep in concentration and creation. The paper yielded to her now as she had yielded to him less than two hours ago.

'It's evergreen. It'll keep!'

'No, it won't k..keep,' he'd said.

'Yes it will, yes it will, I hold it now...I hold you now...'

Carrie dreamed that she was beautiful. Dressed in a long, white, gown; her long, golden, hair was covered in glitter.

'Oh Mavis!'

'Look at you! You're beautiful!' whispered Mavis. 'I'll sit you in the middle of the table with the fancy biscuits!'

'Mm...'posh' biscuits!' said Jed, helping himself to a chocolate swirl. 'Hey Jon! You've had a go with her, now it's my turn!'

His arm was reaching out to grab her. Mistletoe above her head, his lips were about to touch hers. He'd had a fair few by the smell of things. He grinned. He knocked her over as he grabbed another chocolate swirl. She broke into a thousand pieces.

'Christmas is a difficult time for a lot of people. Oh, Debs! I got it wrong. I am made of porcelain! Help me!'

'I c..can't when he's w..watching. You'll k..keep in the p..paper b..bag.'

'No, I won't! Let me out. I want to enjoy the pleasure of being alive. I promised. Where are you, Angel Hope? I don't want to make the same mistake twice!'

'Mince pie!'

'Oh Mavis!'

'He's been good to me!'

'I have a tree in my orchard.'

'I smell farmer.'
'It's evergreen. It'll keep.'

Carrie stopped dreaming. She climbed out of her paper bag. She opened her hand. Sitting in her palm was a small knitted Jip. He smelt of rosewater and chicken giblets, mixed with a little wee.

'Oh Mavis!'

She sat on the edge of her bed. She stopped hiding. Two familiar, black and white, faces looked up at her in the black and white moonlight. Both in the style of their artists; strong; straightforward; raw. Little Carrie and knitted Jip.

She held them. She saw them. She felt them. She wasn't made of porcelain after all. She held herself. She saw herself. She felt herself. She yielded to herself as she had yielded to him less than two hours ago. Her thumbs became his thumbs as she pressed, deep in concentration and creation, into her flesh. She wasn't made of porcelain; she wasn't going to break.

'It's evergreen. It'll keep.'
'No, it won't.'

And it didn't.

'Have a good one.'

And she did.

'Happy Christmas...'

Monday 25th December
Christmas Day

The short arm of the winter sun stretched through Carrie's bedroom window, erasing the charcoal night sky. A few smudges of darkness remained, here and there. This Christmas morning sky had been painted by a five year old who was short of paint. With only one shade of grey, their heavy streaks left random gaps with no colour at all. If a grown-up had produced such a scene, it would have been praised as having 'a profoundly mysterious and solitary quality.' In fact, it was just a joyless winter day. No breath. No sound. This Christmas morning sky was the same sky no matter who looked up at it. Flat. Cold. Hard.

'Agh!' sighed Carrie, looking out of the window on her way to the stairs, 'Act One, Scene One, let the ritual of Christmas begin.'

Carrie knew the routine off by heart; it had been the same aged three as at nearly twenty three.

'How can all this stuff come from a little baby being born in a lowly stable?'

Being the child of the family, Carrie led the Christmas party into the lounge, and dutifully expressed excitement at the presents waiting for everyone underneath the tree.

'There's nothing lowly about our Christmas! And no evidence of a baby anywhere, either.'

It wasn't difficult to say 'aah!' when the lounge door was opened onto her mother's vision of the perfect Christmas morning; it all looked very beautiful indeed. Colour co-ordinated decorations and wrapping paper, presents arranged according to shape, size, and importance; aged three or nearly twenty three, Carrie stuck to the schedule, without question.

'She needs a perfect Christmas. I don't think baby Jesus would have got very far if she'd been his mother.'

Her dad sat on the sofa, ever round, ever smiling, enjoying everything.

'But dad makes the perfect Joseph. What a brick! What does that leave for me? The donkey?'

The thought of donkeys and stables brought Carrie back to the farmyard. The sight of her mother's fine decorations, there was never any tinsel because the bits made a mess, brought her back to the farmhouse kitchen; there were no garlands spread across their kitchen ceiling. Carrie kept one eye on the Christmas morning sky. Flat. Cold. Hard.

'This is all so perfect, like it is every year, yet I feel more empty than usual. I wonder what he's doing now. Wonder what he's thinking...'

'Your eyes look dark this morning, didn't you sleep?' Carrie didn't get chance to answer her mother.

'Well, I didn't sleep at all well. You shouldn't have let me drink all that sherry, last night, Bill. You know how busy I am today and tomorrow.'

'I know, love. But Carrie and I will help you, and you could have a rest this afternoon.'

'I'm not missing half of my Christmas day! We should be spending it together.'

Bill kept one eye on the Christmas morning sky. Flat. Cold. Hard.

'Christmas is a difficult time of year for a lot of people.'

With his other eye he watched Carrie looking out of the window.

'Her eyes are dark with love, not lack of sleep...'

'Well, why don't we spend it together now. I'll give you a hand in the kitchen while Carrie clears up in here. You're right, she does look tired. A few minutes peace and quiet will liven her up before lunch, won't it?'

Jill looked at Carrie looking out of the window.

'What is she looking at? There is no Christmas morning sky. It's empty. Flat. Cold. Hard.'

Jill shuddered and looked away.

'Yes, alright, then. There doesn't look like there's going to be much in the way of help coming from her this morning, she's miles away, no doubt looking for angels in the sky...'

Bill encouraged Jill through the lounge door and closed it with one of his ever round, smiles.

'Thanks, Dad. You're a brick! The thought of angels in the sky brought her hope. Angel 'Hope'. Oh Mavis!'

———◆———

Old man Wilson walked across the farmyard; he was going inside for his breakfast. The short arm of the winter sun didn't reach as far as here. The yard was a perfect reflection of the Christmas morning sky. Flat. Cold. Hard. With only one shade of grey, it was just another joyless winter day. No breath. No sound. He knew the routine off by heart; it had been the same Christmas day every year since he'd stopped remembering them, whatever the colour of the farmyard. Flat. Cold. Hard.

Inside the farmhouse kitchen, the warmth of bacon and eggs and sounds from the Christmas morning radio would be waiting for him.

Mavis would be busy cooking the Christmas dinner. Old Ab would be dropped in for a cup of coffee, sitting in the chair by the fire, smoking his pipe.

Jed would be baiting Mavis, getting under her feet, laughing at her flicks of the tea towel, before finally giving up and moping by the window. Jon would be following in his footsteps shortly, a mysterious and solitary figure, who made no sound. With dark eyes he would sit at the kitchen table and eat his bacon and eggs. Flat. Cold. Hard.

'Ah do,' he said, stepping into the ritual of Christmas morning.

'Where is the little baby being born in a lowly stable?'

Jip was sitting curled up by the fire; old Ab sat gently stroking the top of his head with the veins on the back of his hand. Jon was already sitting at the table, eating his bacon and eggs; somehow he'd beaten him to it this morning.

'Sit you down, Ezra, and I'll get your breakfast.'

He sat down at the kitchen table opposite Jon. He stared at his son, who, in turn, stared at the tiny porcelain angel who sat in between them, in the middle of the table. She had long, golden, hair, and was dressed in a long white gown. She had a lovely smile. 'Angel Hope' said a little plaque at her feet.

'There you are!' said Mavis.

He looked up as Mavis placed his plate of bacon and eggs in front of him; a big silver star hung above his head.

'Jon bought it. It's me light in the darkness,' said Mavis, on her way back to the kettle to make his tea.

Old man Wilson ate his bacon and eggs. He kept one eye on the flat, cold, hard, Christmas morning sky, and one eye on the tiny porcelain angel in the middle of the kitchen table.

'It's me 'Angel Hope,' he bought me that as well. Isn't she beautiful?' said Mavis, dropping his mug of tea onto the table.

All of a sudden, he thought he was going to be sick. Was it too much bacon, or Angel Hope's long, golden, hair, and familiar smile? Through the window, random gaps appeared in the Christmas morning sky; it was no longer one shade of grey.

'She's here...'

Old man Wilson looked around the kitchen. Garlands made of crepe paper zigzagged all over the ceiling; their colours were faded. It was warm in the kitchen.

'I wonder if it was warm in the first Christmas stable?'

Mavis was cackling with old Ab.

'She'd have been a good mother Mary; that baby would have been alright with her. And old Ab, he's a good shepherd. What does that leave me? A Wise Man? I don't think so...'

'Hark, the herald angels sing,' sang the radio. Mavis was cackling again:

'Come and open your presents, lads. Carrie left them for you!'

The winter sun reached in through the kitchen window, lighting up the big silver star hanging above the kitchen table. He kept one eye on the Christmas morning sky while everybody opened Carrie's presents. It was a perfect Christmas morning. It was the Christmas day that he'd stopped remembering. No longer flat. No longer cold. No longer hard. The tiny, porcelain, angel, dressed in the long white gown, smiled back at him as he opened his present. Socks. Jed was laughing. But the tiny, porcelain, angel was not smiling at him, or at Jed. Her eyes were fixed on the dark ones, that had not let go of her all morning. He knew that they would never let her go.

"A light in the darkness,' Mavis said. An angel called 'Hope.' Oh Carrie...'

———◆———

Debs scrubbed at her face in the cracked bathroom mirror tiles. A few smudges of darkness remained, here and there, leftover charcoal eye shadow and mascara from the night before that she'd been too tired to wash off properly. The short arm of the winter sun reached through the open bathroom window. Its reflection on the cracked bathroom mirror tiles temporarily blinded her.

'Agh!' she said softly, remembering the colour of blindness.

Her old eye patch was still on the bathroom shelf, staring at her. Debs applied just one shade of grey eye shadow this morning; a thin layer so as to avoid heavy streaks. She needed to look good all day. She was entertaining, cooking Christmas lunch for Joe's family. She needed a perfect Christmas day. At the top of the landing there was no breath, no sound. Everyone else was still fast asleep.

Downstairs, the kitchen was grey except for the streaks of fluorescent white light shining around the edge of the kitchen cupboards. Flat. Cold. Hard. Debs took her cup of coffee out into the garden. She looked up at the Christmas morning sky. She looked for angels in the sky, but it was just a joyless, winter, day. Flat. Cold. Hard.

'Ah, there you are!' sighed Debs, in relief. Her pale blue flower fairy with the chipped silver wing smiled up at her from the flat, cold, hard, garden border.

'It's Christmas day! Baby Jesus had angels above his stable, and I've got you!'

Inside the kitchen, Joe was shouting for his bacon and eggs.

'Yes, Joe, I'm coming!'

'Be near me, Lord Jesus, I ask you to stay close by me forever, and love me I pray,' [†] sang the radio.

'Turn that bloody rubbish off; we don't want to hear that first thing in a morning!'

'I thought your mother might like the Christmas carols.'

'Well, you thought wrong.'

'Yes, Joe.'

'I'll do the thinking, you do the cooking,' said Joe, pointing a pork sausage shaped finger at her. 'And then,' Joe paused in the kitchen doorway to think for a moment, 'and then, if you do a good job of the cooking, I'll give you a good something that rhymes with 'cooking' later.' Joe grinned. 'Make sure you cook enough food this year!'

'How can all this come from a little baby being born in a lowly stable?'

Debs knew the Christmas routine off by heart. Eyes down, she concentrated on cooking the bacon; she was going to be busy today and tomorrow.

'I wonder if there's room for me in that stable?'

There was no point looking outside at the Christmas morning sky. There wasn't one. It was empty. Flat. Cold. Hard. All of a sudden, Debs thought she was going to be sick. Was it the smell of the cooking bacon, or the lack of angels in the sky?

'I used to have an angel, but I sent her away. Oh Carrie...'

Tuesday 26th December
Boxing Day

'Welcome, everybody! Happy Christmas!' gushed Jill.

'Carrie will take your coats. Come on through, and get a drink.'

Jill ushed the early arrivals through to the dining room. She glanced over her shoulder at Carrie as she left the hallway. She didn't need to tell her daughter what to do next; Carrie knew the Boxing Day routine off by heart.

'Agh!' she sighed. *'Act Two, Scene One. Let the Boxing Day Bonanza begin!'*

Carrie stood in the hallway and gushed and ushed and ushed and gushed until the house was so heaving with people that it was difficult to move beyond the little bit of space that each person had for their feet, backside, wine glass and plate of nibbles. The lucky few early arrivals got the chairs; they weren't so lucky when it came to getting up to go to the toilet, though. They were quite likely to wet themselves waiting for a clear space in which to pull out into the passing traffic of people ruthlessly socialising around the room; and, of course, they would lose their seat forever once they did finally manage to escape to the toilet queue.

'How can all this stuff come from a little baby being born in a stable? She never invites anyone with babies or children, and if she did, they'd never dare to bring them over our threshold. I was embarrassment enough when I was little. No, our Christmas is a sophisticated, very grown up affair, for the great and the good! A chance for them to show each other how perfectly happy they are and how kind-hearted they can be towards each other, once a year!'

Technically, Boxing Day was a Bank Holiday, but it was, without a doubt, the hardest day's work Carrie had to do in an entire year. Somehow, she had to stay kind-hearted and perfectly happy all day whilst servicing the needs of the great and the good, until the second they departed their Boxing Day experience.

Somehow, she had to manoeuvre herself through the traffic delivering life-saving supplies of nibbles and drinks, reassuring smiles, witty conversation; with very little hard shoulder around the edge of each room, she was frequently trodden on or touched up as she loyally carried out her duties.

So there was no 'bank holiday' for Carrie, or her dad. Entertaining was the name of the game. She'd have to go back to work at the office if she wanted to have a 'relaxing day' after the strain of the Christmas holidays. This year, however, she planned to have a few days off so that she could go back to the farm; she was finding it increasingly difficult to get through a whole week without seeing Jon. To make the time pass more quickly today, she threw herself into the job at hand. Someone had dropped their plate of nibbles on the carpet behind the lounge door.

'The pigs at the farm have more sophisticated manners than some of our guests; they wouldn't waste their food, or trample it into the ground!'

Carrie knelt down to pick up the pieces.

'And there's not a ham sandwich in sight! Oh Mavis!'

Thoughts of ham gave Carrie a sudden lump in her throat.

'They won't be eating this rubbish today, they'll be tucking into Mavis' ham! I bet my mother's already thrown ours out!'

Thoughts of picking up the pieces suddenly made her feel close to Jon.

'Just like me, he'll be working today. Just like me, he'll be mucking out, feeding the animals, clearing up after them, making sure they've got a drink. Just like me, he'll talk to them and won't get a response, except for the occasional stare. Just like me, he might get trodden on while he's carrying out his duties. Just like me, he won't get a day off, it'll be work, work, work, like any other day. At least on the farm, it's honest dirt, and not the sort that's coming out of all these false mouths full of false food and false good wishes.'

A familiar pair of floppy ankles were blocking Carrie's return from behind the lounge door. They were talking now to Carrie's mother. Carrie decided to play dead; she sat, slumped in the corner behind the door and listened.

'Charles Pike sends his profound apologies that he can't come today. His mother's very ill, you know…of course I've done what I could for him…a very difficult person to deal with…He's set to inherit a fortune, you know, an absolute fortune. Tell Carrie her holiday leave next week is cancelled, I need her in at work…'

'…good job, too, she's better occupied at work than messing about with those ghastly farmers…'

Carrie waited until they'd gone before she rose from the dead; unfortunately, now, she really felt completely dead, and there was a lot more Boxing Day to get through. Now, she had to play at being alive.

'Oh Mavis! What on earth am I going to do?'

Thursday 28th December

Carrie did what she had to do; go back to work at the office. It was December 28th, Holy Innocents day. In the Christmas story, it was the day that King Herod had all the baby boys in Bethlehem murdered. Regarded by many as the most unlucky day of the year, it was a fitting finale to end the ritual of her Christmas. Only three days long yet it had felt like three thousand years long. Spectator or performer, the end of any event brings with it a quiet time of reflection. Daily life is either elated or deflated by the experience.

'Dad was right, Christmas is a difficult time of year for a lot of people.'

There might be very little news around at this time of year, but the merry-go-round of life continued without a care for Christmas. The Births and Deaths columns were still as busy as ever. Mr Pike wasn't in the office. 'Rosalind the Rottweiler' was enjoying every second of being in charge in his absence. Only a skeleton staff had been called in this week and Carrie appeared to be the backbone, getting the brunt of the daily chores. She wondered how Mr Pike's mother was doing, but she couldn't bear to look at Rosalind let alone speak to her to find out. This was easy to achieve for Rosalind herself ignored Carrie completely; she had left written instructions on her desk this morning. If she ventured out of her lair to have a gnash at anyone else, she walked sideways like a crab, keeping her back to Carrie's desk.

'She's not forgiven me for coming between her and Mr Pike at the office Christmas party. That's why she's cancelled my holiday, given me all the rubbish jobs. She'll trip over her own flabby ankles walking like that on this shiny floor. She's about due for a fall...and I won't pick her up when she does...'

Thoughts of the many different ways in which Rosalind could meet a sticky end on the shiny office floor got Carrie through her unlucky day. Once or twice, it even looked like the power of her wicked thoughts might work; the flabby ankles nearly gave way, but never in the right place to be impaled by the scissors or sharp pencils that someone had carelessly left hanging over the edge of the table near the coffee machine. Carrie needed to pick herself up before she went home, where she was likely to be impaled by her mother; she never missed her target, either.

'I wonder what sort of Christmas Debs had? But she doesn't want to see me.'

Even so, Carrie couldn't resist driving home past Debs' house. The front bedroom curtains were closed. The only sign of life came from a fat, jolly, snowman, who was hanging on the newly painted, blue, front door. On the windowsill of the lounge window, Carrie could just make out some flowers.

'Hope she liked the present, it's the same as the one I got for Mavis. It's in the window, anyway.'

There was nothing in the front window at home, except her mother's face, watching as she pulled into the driveway.

'She looks like the ghost of Christmas past.'

Despite the perfection of their Christmas, her mother was still running on empty. It was the same every year. All their guests, all their hard work; nothing was ever enough.

'I'll never understand her but, at least, this year, I know how she feels. Nothing real ever happens in our house. It catches up with you, after a while. The strain of pretending is just too great. With her, it's headaches. What's it going to be for me?'

It was her dad. He got to her before she reached the back door to the house.

'Hello, love. Survived the day?' he said, cheerfully.

'Just about. Why?' asked Carrie, suspiciously. 'What are you doing home so early?'

'Shut up shop early; no customers this afternoon. Some post came for you, today, to the garage. Hand delivered.'

He held out a blank, sealed, envelope in her direction.

'What is he so excited about?'

'Who's it from?'

'See for yourself!' beamed her dad.

Carrie didn't need to open the envelope to see who it was from. The thumb print on the back of it said more than any words it could contain. Carrie tried to stay looking normal in front of her dad.

'It's an invitation to a dinner and dance on New Year's Eve,' she said, flatly.

'I know!' said her dad. 'My Princess is going to get to dance with her Prince after all!'

Carrie stared at the gold edged invitation.

'What's the matter? I thought you'd be pleased!' said her dad, looking concerned.

'It must be a trick! It's that brother of his!' shouted Carrie. 'Jon says he can't dance! He'd never dress up and go to something like this!'

'Calm down, Carrie! Old man Wilson delivered this himself, this morning. It's to say thank you for all the hard work you've done for them this year. There's one ticket for you, and one ticket for Jon. He says you both missed out at the last party because you were calving a cow. It's not a trick, it's real! Best not say anything to your mother about this, though. Not until the last minute. You know she doesn't like New Year celebrations.'

Carrie smiled at her dad. Reality was sinking in.

'Now, you'd better start thinking about a dress to wear. You're not Cinderella, you know. You can't depend on a last minute fairy godmother, although I'm sure Debs would love to give you a hand. It's more than I can do!' laughed her dad.

'Oh please stop, dad! I know you mean well, but I can't cope with any more...'

'Now, how about a nice cup of tea?'

'Great!' said Carrie.

'I could do with something stronger...Oh Debs, where are you?'

Sunday 31st December
New Year's Eve

'I've had funny phone calls all day, today,' complained Jill. 'That was another one. No sound at all. Not even heavy breathing.'

Carrie's mother was slamming cupboard doors in the kitchen.

'That's the thanks you get for being public spirited and working for your community. I put myself out there, make myself available and what do I get? Some prankster with nothing better to do on New Year's Eve than try to spoil the peace and quiet of my last day of the year!'

The sharpness in her mother's tone of voice made the nylon fluff of Carrie's pale pink dressing gown stand on end; it was a mistake to come downstairs to make that cup of tea, after all. She tried to duck down into its ample collar and make good her escape. She crackled noisily, a pale pink pylon full of static, across the kitchen. She had almost reached the safety of the hallway but it was impossible not to be seen and heard, most especially when her mother was in overdrive about some outrage or other. When this happened it was a particularly dangerous time. When this happened, she seemed to develop a sixth, seventh and eighth sense.

'Where are you going?'

'To my room.'

'Why are you dressed like that?'

'It's New Year's Eve. I'm going out. Remember? With my friends from the office.'

'I didn't think you had any friends at the office.'

'Well, you don't know everything about me, do you?'

'Rosalind never mentioned anything about a party.'

'We young folk wouldn't want to go out on New Year's Eve with her, would we?'

'I suppose not,' said her mother, suspiciously. 'It seems a bit early for you to be getting ready to go out, you don't normally go to so much trouble. A quick five minutes is all you usually take when you go anywhere.'

'Well, I want to make an effort tonight. It's New Year's Eve. Time to turn over a new leaf. You're always so immaculately dressed when you go out, I thought I'd try to do the same for a change,' urged Carrie.

Her mother paused for a moment. Digested.

'Where did you say you were going?'

'Oh, it's just a dinner and dance at a hotel in the country. Dad's got all the details. He offered to take me, but I'm happy to drive myself. I don't want to drink.'

'Quite right, too,' agreed her mother. 'I can't stand all the fuss people make about New Year. It's just another day, when all is said and done. One year is much the same as another.'

'Not when you're young and looking forwards,' suggested Carrie.

'Sometimes. But not always.'

Her mother paused again. Digested. Carrie paused too. She looked at her mother. Now it was her turn to develop a sixth, seventh and eighth sense. It was time to change the subject.

'Well, I must finish getting ready. You'll have some peace and quiet without me.'

Her mother didn't reply. She stood still in the middle of the kitchen, surrounded by the peace and quiet that had been left in the wake of the static from her daughter's nylon pale pink fluffy dressing gown. As Carrie crackled away up the stairs to her bedroom, she heard her mother call out after her:

'If the phone rings again, can you answer it? I don't want to hear that silent nonsense again. It's given me a headache...'

———◆———

Things were hotting up. Outside, there wasn't even a night frost on the ground. The sudden thaw made the world look darker and colder than before; the world was wrong. Inside, standing in front of her bedroom mirror, wearing her slinky black dress with the flash of silver across its front, Carrie was burning up. Dressed in the memory of her first meeting with Jon, at the birth of little Carrie, big Carrie's reflection re-lived every second of the last time she wore this fateful dress. She'd had it dry cleaned but she could still smell every smell of that night, she could still feel the traces of the wet slime of new life on her body and trace with her hand where Jon had rubbed her down with straw afterwards.

Debs was shouting at her now:

'Oh for God's sake! Just wear the bloody dress! And some red lippy!'

'Yes, you're right, Debs. I need red lippy.'

Carrie struggled to apply it; her hand couldn't stop shaking.

'Oh, Debs, where are you? I miss you shouting down the phone at me. I miss you full stop.'

Her reflection didn't reply, except to show her that she was ready to go. She tried a smile with the red lippy. It worked.

'I don't need to be scared. A bit nervous, yes, but not scared. It'll be different this time. It'll be a proper date. After all this time, our first date! And I'll finally get to dance with him all night. Oh no! I can smell grains! I wish that farmyard would go away for once...'

'Carrie! Carrie! Get the phone! I'm not doing it again!' shouted her mother.

Carrie had been so lost in farmyard sounds and smells that she'd completely missed the ringing sound that was shaking the whole house.

'Alright!' shouted Carrie. 'I'm on my way!'

'It's time to go, anyway...'

'Hello?'

There was no sound at all. Not even heavy breathing.

'Is it another funny phone call?' shouted her mother.

'Hello?'

In the background, behind the sound of the silent nonsense, Carrie could hear football on the telly. Carrie was burning up. She struggled to hold the phone; her hand couldn't stop shaking.

'Oh for God's sake! Just wear the bloody dress! And some red lippy!'

'I'm on my way,' whispered Carrie, gently.

'Tell them we'll report them to the police if they do this again!' shouted her mother.

'It was a mistake,' said Carrie. 'It's time for me to go now.'

'I've made a mistake; a big mistake...'

'Well wear a coat, for goodness sake, you're shaking with cold,' said her mother, holding out her coat for her.

'I'm not cold,' said Carrie.

'Well, you look very cold. You should have put a bit more make up on. I don't hold with all this pale English rose complexion nonsense. A bit of colour in your face is much more attractive. There's no harm in letting a man know you're made of flesh and blood, you know.'

Carrie stared at her mother.

'Well, good manners tell me to tell you to have a good time and watch what you're doing. Choose your friends, especially your gentleman friends, wisely, Carrie. Happy New Year!' said her mother.

Carrie stared at her mother.

'Yes, Happy New Year...I must go now....'

The world wasn't wrong after all. It was cold and dark this New Year's Eve for more than one good reason. It was fit for purpose; it allowed Carrie to park her little red car on the road just down from Debs' house, unseen; it shielded her as she tiptoed up the drive towards Debs' house; it perfectly suited her mood. She quickly realised that she couldn't tiptoe very quietly or fast in her stilettos, so she nipped back to her car and slipped on her wellies that she kept on the floor behind the driver's seat. The slap-flap sound of a tiptoe from a welly boot covered in a long, tightly fitting, evening dress, seemed a much softer, less obvious, kind of tiptoe than the clickety-clack-clack that she had tried first.

All the curtains at the front of Debs' house were closed. The fat, jolly snowman, hanging on the newly painted, blue, front door no longer showed any signs of life; in the darkness he was simply left hanging. Carrie couldn't see his smiling face or any other face, as she stretched her eyes and ears to find sight or sound of Debs.

'I'm so dark in this darkness that she might not see me!'

Carrie opened her coat to release the flash of silver on her dress.

'I just hope she'll see the sign. I'll try round the back.'

The flash of silver gave Carrie some small sense of light as she edged down the side of the house into total blackness. Her hands scraped along the rough brick wall until she reached the corner. The kitchen window and back of the house was as dark and lifeless as the front. Carrie was starting to feel very panicked.

'My mother was right for a change without knowing it. Maybe I should have just called the police. Oh Debs, where are you?'

Carrie stared at the gaping black hole where Debs' beloved garden used to be. Carrie knew this garden, off by heart. She'd spent so many happy hours here. She knew where the wheelbarrow was propped up against the wall of the garden shed; she knew the water butt; the compost heap; the flower tubs; the dustbin; the two stripy folding deckchairs on the patio where they used to sit and drink coffee. She saw them all. They were all still there, staring back at her in the darkness. She didn't remember there being a pile of rocks in the middle of the lawn, though.

'Funny place to build a rockery...'

The rocks were moving, ever so slightly. Carrie felt a shaking sensation rising up from her feet, through her legs and on to her body and head. It wasn't an earthquake shaking her feet or the rocks in the middle of the lawn. The rocks weren't rocks; they were Debs.

She was curled up tight like a little hedgehog. She opened up a little at the sight of the flash of silver which appeared above her head; it was talking to her in a gentle voice. In her hands she held the body of her pale blue flower fairy, the one with the chipped wing. The flash of silver was pulling at her, ever so gently, trying to pick her up. It was talking again:

'It's alright, Debs. It's me, Carrie. Can you get up? You need to get up! We need to get out of here!'

Debs was holding onto the body of her flower fairy with all her might; she wouldn't let go.

'See, silver prayers do work,' she whispered.

'What?' said Carrie.

Carrie realised that Debs wasn't going to let go of the broken little body anytime soon. Feeling relieved she'd changed into her wellies, Carrie stood firm, bent her knees, took hold of Debs underneath her armpits, and pulled both friend and fairy out of the gaping black hole that used to be Debs' garden.

'No!' cried Debs, hoarsely.

Carrie had to fight to hold on to her as she pulled back towards the ground.

'It's alright, I've got you. Let go!' whispered Carrie. 'Shhh, we need to be quiet!'

Debs was mumbling, quite loudly now, '...won't leave her, I won't leave her...'

'Alright, we won't leave her!' said Carrie, frantically trying to work out what Debs was looking for.

Then she saw it. The pale blue flower fairy with the chipped wing had been kicked in the face. Her head had been knocked off and was lying in the bushes a few feet away from them.

'I've got her,' whispered Carrie.

She somehow managed to reach down and rescue the flower fairy's head whilst holding onto Debs' body. The body relaxed as soon as the fairy's head was reunited with the hands that were clutching its body. For one terrible moment Carrie remembered old Ab and his sacks of corn as she felt the full weight of Debs slumped over her shoulder.

'My sack of corn is still very much alive, thank God!'

It was also cold and soaking wet all over, but at least it had feet and legs that would move with a bit of encouragement.

'Quietly now,' whispered Carrie. 'My car's on the road.'

There was no sound at all. Not even heavy breathing. Carrie had to turn slightly just to check that she hadn't been tricked into carrying a sack of corn down the path in the darkness, instead of rescuing her friend. Debs was still there, hanging on; the pale blue flower fairy was digging into Carrie's shoulder blade. Slap-flap-slap-drag. Carrie had no idea how long or how noisy they were as they made their way across the last few feet of the drive. She kept one eye on the fat, jolly snowman hanging on the newly painted, blue, front door. As long as he stayed dead there was a good chance they'd get away without being hung, drawn and quartered by Joe.

'*Wonder where he is? Bastard.*'

Carrie didn't have time to wonder beyond half a second. They'd got back to her little red car unseen and that was all that mattered. Debs didn't make a sound as Carrie collapsed her into the passenger seat.

'I don't know how long you've been out there, but you're soaking wet. Let's get out of here, you'll catch pneumonia!'

The pale blue flower fairy on Debs' lap glowed slightly blue by the light of the car dashboard; it was the only proof Carrie had that Debs hadn't turned into a sack of corn. She was barely breathing. Carrie switched on the car engine and pulled away without putting her headlights on until they were well away from Debs' house.

'It's alright,' said Carrie. 'You're safe now.'

'Déjà-vu, déjà-vu,' revved the car engine.

Carrie shivered and turned the car heater onto full. She was too busy just getting away from Debs' house to listen carefully to what her car engine was actually telling her:

'Check the rear view, check the rear view,' it revved. But she didn't. She missed the glimpse of the front bedroom curtains swish. He had watched them leave.

———◆———

'Help!' shouted Carrie. 'I need help!'

'Bang!' went the kitchen door; it wasn't used to such rough treatment. The shock of the noise shook the whole house. Carrie, Debs and the pale blue flower fairy arrived through its doorframe in one big push. The flower fairy's wing tip scratched the paintwork. Jill arrived in the kitchen at the same moment, claws extended, ready to pounce on the intruder who'd disturbed her New Year's Eve peace and quiet.

Carrie and the pale blue flower fairy immediately stood to attention in the middle of the kitchen as best they could. Between them they tried to support the weight of the wounded soldier who slumped unashamedly on Carrie's shoulder. It took Jill less than a moment to put her claws away, assess the situation, and take charge like a true commander in chief. Carrie stared at her mother.

'Don't just stand there! Get her sat down on this chair!'

Her mother was already moving, moving Debs onto a kitchen chair. Carrie stared at Debs.

'It's Debs!' said Carrie, feeling the need to convince herself as well as tell her mother who was sitting on their kitchen chair for, in truth, the person she'd just dragged into their home looked nothing like Debs; it wasn't even human.

'Of course I know who this is!'

Carrie's mother kept her eyes firmly fixed on Debs' face. She smiled at her and spoke in the most gentle, most soft, voice that Carrie had ever heard. She stared at her mother; this woman looked and behaved nothing like her mother. She was human.

'Oh Debs, you *have* been in the wars, but don't worry, everything's going to be just fine now.'

Her mother was pressing down on the top of Debs' head with the kitchen tea towel.

'I found her in the garden.'

Carrie stared at Debs. She wasn't cold and wet from lying on the night dew of the lawn and it wasn't too much make up that had put the colour in her face. There was too much colour. The colour of blood and roses. There was no doubt that she was made of flesh and blood; it was written all over her face for everyone to see. Joe had proved that to her just like he'd done to her pale blue flower fairy. Carrie, on the other hand, was carrying the pale English rose complexion to the extreme. There was no blood in her face; she was feeling dizzy by now, starting to see spots in front of her eyes. She was cold and wet and wanted to lie down on the floor.

'Carrie!'

Her mother's voice returned to normal to speak her name.

'I need ice from the freezer, more towels, the soft blanket off my bed and the first aid kit from the bathroom cupboard. Move, girl! Do it now!'

Somehow Carrie moved. She managed to get upstairs to the bathroom before doing it; she was violently sick in the toilet. She found the towels, the blanket and the first aid kit, and then found her way back down the stairs to the kitchen, where she started to see spots all over again so she ducked her head down as low as she could in the bottom of the freezer; the bags of ice cubes burnt into her shaking hands. The sudden stab of real pain soothed her heaving stomach; at least she wasn't sick in the bottom of the freezer.

Debs wasn't shaking; she sat as still as a statue on her kitchen chair. Carrie's mother looked like she was playing the 'mummies' game with her that she and Debs had enjoyed playing at parties when they were little. The aim of the game was to wrap your partner up in toilet roll from head to toe to make them look like an Egyptian mummy. You had to leave eye, nose and mouth holes, of course.

'We'll get you tidied up, then get you to hospital and call the police,' said Jill.

'No!' groaned the mummy, suddenly coming back to life. Debs pulled at the bandages.

'No hospital! No police! He'll f..find m..me.'

Now it was Jill's turn to stare. She stared at the blood on her hands. She looked down at the bandages that were fast unravelling beneath her hands, and then she looked up at Carrie; there were tears in her eyes.

'Of course, dear,' she said, in her gentle voice. 'Don't get upset. You can stay here with us.'

Carrie's sixth, seventh and eighth sense told her that her mother was lying.

'Where's dad?' asked Carrie.

'Out on a call. Emergency breakdown.'

'Like us, then.'

Bang! Bang! Bang!

Debs stared at the sound coming from the hallway.

'It's alright Deborah.'

Jill took hold of her trembling hands firmly enough to stop her shaking.

'Go and see who that is, Carrie, and get rid of them. We can't be doing with visitors tonight.'

Bang! Bang! Bang!

Carrie didn't need to go and see to know who it was, but she pretended to go just to keep her mother happy. She edged herself around the doorway as thinly as possible to have a look at the front door.

Bang!

'Open up, bitch! I know you're in there! What have you done with my missus?'

There were two hand prints and part of a face print where Joe had pressed himself up against the stained glass panels on the front door.

Bang! Bang!

Joe was repeatedly throwing himself at the front door. Carrie wondered how long the old stained glass could stand such a beating. Debs had stood it. And so must they all, if need be. The police would never get here in time even if she called them now. She swallowed her fear and slid back round the corner to the kitchen.

'It's Joe,' she said, as simply and calmly as she could.

Debs started shaking again as Jill let go of her hands and straightened herself up.

'Right!' snapped Jill, returning to her commander in chief voice. 'This is what we're going to do. I will distract the creature at the front door, Carrie, whilst you take Deborah through the back door; get her in your car, and away from here.'

'We can't do that, Mum, he's far too dangerous. He could really hurt you, and what if he sees us?'

'And what if we do nothing? They'll always be an 'if', Carrie, but this one hasn't happened yet and we're not going to let it. It's not me he wants, it's you two. I shall call the police now and they can pick up the pieces after I've finished with him.'

Bang! Bang! Bang!

'But...'

'Absolutely no 'buts', Carrie. Look at Deborah, she's shaking like a leaf. You told me you were turning over a new leaf this New Year's Eve, well, this is it, for me too. This is real...I've been such a fool, Carrie...'

Carrie stared at her mother as she picked up the sweeping brush in the corner of the kitchen and twirled it in one hand like a cheerleader's baton.

'Mum. I've just called you Mum for the first time ever.'

'No more pretending. Look at her!' cried her mum. 'All these years! I'm through with pretending. I've had enough!'

Carrie saw her mum for the first time ever.

'Open this door, bitch, or I'll kick it down!'

Bang! Bang! Bang! Bang!

'Coming!' shouted her mum in a high pitched, cheerful, voice.

'I'll take her to the farm.'

'Good idea, now go!'

Carrie stared at her mum.

'Go!' she hissed.

Mum went, sweeping brush in hand, to answer the front door. Carrie, Debs, and the pale blue flower fairy with the chipped wing, pushed through the back door of the kitchen in one big push; it was even harder this time because Debs was wrapped up in a blanket and Carrie wanted to be wrapped up in a blanket. But that would have to wait.

'I'm coming, just give me a moment,' chirped Jill.

The banging on the door stopped. Carrie heard her mother rattling the security chain, slowly pulling back the bolts at the top and bottom of the door, finally releasing the latch. That was her cue to move Debs to her car. She could hear her mother's voice, how it always used to be, in full flow. The creature at the door couldn't even get started on her. There was an almighty crashing sound followed by a series of grunts and snorts.

As her little red car slipped around the corner of the house and pulled away down the drive, Carrie saw her mum. Light from inside the house poured out onto the front garden where the New Year's Eve celebrations looked like they were in full swing. Her mum even had time to stop what she was doing and wave to Carrie's little red car as it disappeared down the drive and away into New Year's Eve. Joe, who had clearly had one too many, lay flat on his back, spread eagled on their rockery. He was wedged in between two large, stone, urns, one of which had fallen off its stand and now rested on one of his legs.

Every time Joe tried to move her mum cheered him on with her sweeping brush baton, whacking him in the groin with the brush end and finishing off with a stab in the belly with the stick end. It was the best New Year's Eve celebration she'd had in years.

———◆———

Bill returned home from his emergency breakdown call out to find two policemen drinking tea and eating cake in his front room. He heard all about his wife's bravery in tackling the drunken thug who had turned up out of the blue and trashed her garden; he'd been taken to hospital by ambulance with a broken leg and suspected broken ribs and they'd be catching up with him later. He wouldn't be walking, let alone running anywhere, after what they'd seen his wife doing to him with her sweeping brush. It was pure self defence, of course. He also heard that Carrie had taken a friend with her to the New Year's Eve party in the country and that she'd probably stay the night with her friends at the farm.

Bill smiled at the two policemen. He stared at his wife. Reality was sinking in.

'Now, how about a nice glass of sherry?' said Jill.

'Great!' said Bill.

'Make mine a large one...'

'Happy New Year!' said Jill.

'Yes, Happy New Year!' said Bill.

'Oh, Carrie, where are you?'

———————◆———————

'Help!' shouted Carrie. 'I need help!'

'Bang!' went the farmhouse kitchen door; the shock of the noise shook the whole house. Everybody stared at her. Jip had been asleep in his basket; he looked up at her, too surprised to bark. They'd been enjoying some New Year's Eve peace and quiet. Old man Wilson was sitting in his chair, listening to his music from the radio on the mantelpiece. Mavis was sitting in the chair opposite him, busy with her knitting, listening to the clickety-clack-clack of her knitting needles and looking forwards to seeing Carrie again. Jed was sitting at the kitchen table reading his newspaper; he was looking forwards to seeing Carrie again so that he could bait his brother. Jon was listening to the kitchen clock tick tock.

Jon was standing by the fire dressed in his black tie outfit just where he had been standing with Carrie the night little Carrie was born. His were the first eyes she met; everyone else was sitting or lying down. They were definitely his eyes, but he looked odd, somehow. In the time it took her to work out that it was because his shirt sleeves weren't rolled up and that he was wearing a black dinner jacket, he was already moving across the kitchen in her direction. Without uttering another word to anyone Carrie turned and ran back outside before anyone else had had time to stand up. Jed laughed:

'Look at him go! Following her like a little lap dog! Doesn't look like he'll be going to any party tonight!'

Jed folded up his newspaper and rushed off in the direction of the shiny polished stairs. Nobody noticed.

'Bang!' went the kitchen door once more. Carrie came in first, closely followed by Jon. He was carrying something that looked like a brightly coloured sack of corn.

'She's fainting!' said Carrie by way of explanation.

'She's lost a lot of blood.'

'Oh heck,' said Mavis, 'best get the kettle on.'

'Here!' commanded old man Wilson, 'put her down here,' he said, pointing to his own chair by the fire that he'd vacated the very second that Carrie had burst in on them the first time.

Carrie hadn't noticed; she'd only had eyes for Jon. Jon did as he was told. He very gently lowered Debs into his father's chair by the fire. Her head fell back against the old, hand knitted, blanket that hung over the back of it, then it lolled forward, then side to side, before coming to rest on the knitted blanket again.

Beneath the decoration of congealing blood and brightly coloured soft, fluffy blanket, Debs looked like a ghost. Her face was transparent, barely visible; her swollen, rearranged facial features were the only clue that she was real. Even her long hair, matted with blood and dirt from her beloved garden, looked like a wig that had been hastily stuck in place to give anyone looking at her confidence that she actually had a top of her head. Old man Wilson knelt down at her feet.

'You poor lady! You poor, poor, lady. It's alright now. It's alright.'

Debs started shaking. Old man Wilson, nearly all seven feet of him, wrapped himself around Debs and her brightly coloured, soft, fluffy blanket and held her. He held her. He bowed his head before her so that his long, silver hair fell upon her trembling hands. Debs took hold of his hair. She wrapped it around her fingers. She held it tight. The trembling moved from her hands to her eyes. Her tears fell upon his hair. Slow and silent they came. And came. And came.

'By heck, Carrie. The poor lass has had a right to do. What's happened?'

Mavis held out a steaming hot mug of tea towards Carrie. Carrie couldn't take her eyes off old man Wilson and Debs. Her own hands were trembling so much by now that she couldn't hold the mug even if she wanted to. Mavis grabbed hold of her, breaking the spell of the long, silver hair and forced the mug of tea into her hands, forced her to drink from it. It was very sweet.

"See, silver prayers do work.' That's what she said to me when I found her.'

'You what?' said Mavis.

Carrie reached down to feel the flash of silver on her dress. The sweetness of the tea and Mavis' familiar cackle brought her back from somewhere very far away. It was the high, Japanese style, bridge. There was a woman wearing an eye patch and a wide brimmed hat standing in the middle of it:

There's probably a pretty lady underneath all that cover. Poor Jip, you're always in the wars, aren't you?...'

She looked across at Jip. He was lying down, ears flat, in his basket. Jon was kneeling down next to him, stroking the top of his head, talking very gently to him.

'What if the light never comes back?' asked the woman with the eye patch and the wide brimmed hat.

'It always comes back...You are back! I'm back! We're both back!'

'Her husband happened. Joe.'

Mavis stared at Carrie. Jon stared at Jip. Carrie tried to take charge.

'She needs a doctor.'

'No! No doctors!'

Debs might have looked and sounded like the walking dead but she was still very much alive; strangely alert, all of a sudden.

'No doctors!' she mouthed again, trying to get up out of old man Wilson's chair and his hold on her.

But he wouldn't let her go. Old man Wilson kept his eyes firmly fixed on Debs' face and spoke to Carrie:

'No! No doctors. Do as I tell you and it'll be alright. I give you my word.'

'Bang!' went the door from the hallway.

'Ta da!' announced Jed.

Wearing a white tuxedo, matching blood red cummerbund and bow tie, a very gelled up, slicked down, Jed posed in the doorway to the kitchen. Everybody stared at Jed.

'Whoa!' said Jed, as if trying to calm a runaway horse.

With difficulty he pulled himself to a stop. He stared at Debs. For less than a moment he was speechless.

'I know who this is! Hello, Debs.'

Debs squinted at Carrie through the eye holes left by her bruises. Through the gap left for her mouth she mouthed to Carrie:

'Cheese!'

Carrie nodded. The old Debs was still there, even after all this. She had to turn away so as not to let Debs see her tears, so she glared at Jed instead. For a moment, Jed looked at the floor.

'Jon, fetch Alec!'

'He'll be at the party already,' offered Jed. 'And he's a...'

'He'll come for Jon!' cut in old man Wilson.

Jon stood up. He'd been kneeling down with Jip all this time. Debs squinted across at Carrie again.

'Prince!' she mouthed.

Carrie looked across at Jon. He still looked odd. He looked stunning. He was as immaculately dressed as his brother and more besides. She nodded to Debs. Jon studied the black and red floor tiles; a trail of blood on them led him to the kitchen door.

'You may as well give me a lift,' said Jed. 'There's no point in letting these tickets go to waste, or my talent. You won't be needing them now, will you?'

Jon said nothing; he was already walking away through the door. Jed paused in the doorway:

'Don't expect me back tonight, I'm sure I'll find someone who'll give me a bed for the night. Happy New Year!'

He threw Carrie a token smile.

'I'm sorry for your trouble, though, Debs.'

'And good riddance!' said Carrie, at once realising that she'd spoken these words out loud.

Nobody seemed to register them.

'Here you are, Debs, love. Have a cuddle with this hot water bottle. Come on Carrie, let's get this lady up to bed. Our Alec will set you right.'

Debs was getting ready to fight again when old man Wilson took charge once more.

'Alec is our friend. He's not a doctor. He's a vet, but he can help you. He will help you.'

Debs stared at old man Wilson.

'Let him help you. You have to do it.'

Old man Wilson stood up, a little awkwardly. He'd been kneeling down for quite some time now. Debs made no reply. Mavis tried a second time to give Debs the hot water bottle and succeeded.

'There, that's better. Look here, little Angel Hope is smiling at you!'

Mavis picked up Angel Hope from the kitchen table and took it over to show Debs.

'There!' she whispered. 'She'll be a friend to your little blue fairy.'

Mavis put Angel Hope in Debs' free hand. Now it was old man Wilson's turn to stare. He stared at the blood and tears on his hands.

He reached down and stoked the top of Debs' head and then he looked up at Carrie; there were tears in his eyes. Now he was whispering in Debs' ear. She let him do it. Like a tired little child, she let him pick her up. He carried her. Somehow, he carried her all the way up the shiny polished stairs with the strip of carpet in the middle.

Neither the pale blue flower fairy nor Angel Hope made the slightest scratch on the walls as they travelled up the steep, narrow, stairs. He laid her down in his own bed.

'I'll look out for Jon and Alec. It'll be alright, I give you my word,' he said.

He caught a glimpse of a flash of silver leaning over the bed as he closed the bedroom door.

'I have a tree in my orchard...'

And then he was gone.

———◆———

The clock was ticking. It would soon be midnight.

'Out with the old and in with the new.'

It was a difficult time. There was no time; only silence. Even the ticking clock on the mantelpiece could not make itself heard. Behind closed doors there was only waiting. There was blood, rose red, on the kitchen floor; remembering. There were no words then; there were none now. The shiny polished stairs creaked some comfort.

'I've done my best for the poor lass,' said Alec.

'Thank you, Alec. I'll make it right with you,' said old man Wilson.

'There's no need. No need,' replied the vet. 'She really should have seen a doctor. She needed stitches in more places than her face.'

He shook his head sadly.

'She was very brave and so was that young friend of hers, Carrie. 'She saved me, she saved me' was all she kept saying to me. Found her in her garden, in the dark. Do you know that slip of a girl picked her up off the ground and carried her, single handed! Just like she was a sack of corn. And she's a big girl, too. I don't know how she did it. I've given her a mild dose of penicillin just to be on the safe side, but she must get checked out properly in a day or too. And I'd call the police if it were up to me, but she'll have none of it. That monster wants stringing up after what he's done!'

Jon stared in the direction of the stairs.

'Thank you, Alec, Happy New Year!' said old man Wilson.

'And the same to you and yours. I'd better get back to the party. I'll just about get there before midnight! And don't worry, it was a difficult calving!'

As one door closed, another one opened. Mavis appeared. She looked so tired she became a capital letter 'R' with her head bent low.

'She's asleep now. Carrie's sitting with her.'

Jon was already climbing the shiny polished stairs.

'I've made up your bed for her, Jon, and shall you go down to the end room, just for tonight?'

Mavis got no reply.

His father's bedroom door was ajar when Jon reached the top of the stairs. A flash of silver was fast coming towards him.

'H..hope you weren't p..planning to g..go d..dancing in those,' he said, stepping gently on one of her feet.

Carrie looked down. She was still wearing her wellies. She looked around her. There was a trail of muddy boot prints all the way up the stairs and all over the bedroom carpet. Everywhere. Her slinky black evening dress with the flash of silver on it was covered in dirt and bloodstains. Her hair was dishevelled, half up, half down. Her face was black with tear stained mascara.

'I'm sorry,' she said. She looked up at Jon. 'You look beautiful.'

'And so do you.'

He picked up the half of her hair that was hanging over her face and smoothed it away with his hand. She tried her best to keep cheerful, it was New Year's Eve, after all.

'We'll never get to d..dance,' she whispered.

The tears and the trembling would not stop.

'We d..don't need m..music to d..dance.'

Jon stood with his lady. Without thinking, without hesitating, he wrapped his arms around her and pressed his beautifully dressed body into hers. He held her tight. She just stood still and let him do it. As if to order, strains of beautiful music floated up through the floorboards from the kitchen radio beneath. Without thinking, without hesitating, they swayed together with the rise and fall of every phrase. Through the slightly open bedroom door Debs saw and heard the beautiful music that was being played out on the muddy carpet in the hallway. Her face allowed her a small smile.

'See, silver prayers do work,' she whispered to her pale blue flower fairy and Angel Hope.

'Happy New Year, Carrie!'

The chimes of Big Ben were ringing in the New Year on the kitchen radio downstairs. Carrie and Jon didn't hear them. They didn't wish each other a Happy New Year. There was no time; they were already too busy living it.

———————◆———————

The best New Year's Eve she'd had in years was over. She was lying awake now, in the dark of a new year; it felt great. Jill couldn't sleep. She was used to not being able to sleep so she wasn't troubled by the feeling. It was all her other feelings that were giving her trouble. They wouldn't go away. Jill lay flat on her back in bed. Through the moonlit curtains of her bedroom window the shadows of the leaves on the trees in her garden played with both her cream coloured cotton curtains and her mind. Over and over, the leaves turned, turned, turned. She watched them until her head started to ache; it was the wrong sort of ache. Her body was aching too. Jill closed her eyes and waited a bit longer. It was no good; she knew she was in trouble. She couldn't wait any longer.

Jill jumped out of bed. She took her nightie off. She took her pants off. She took her socks off. The carpet felt tickly beneath her naked feet. The cool air of the night bedroom tingled against her skin as she walked across the room towards Bill's bed. It gave her goose bumps. She wanted to giggle. So she giggled. Clothed in a smile she slipped, lithe as a nymph, under Bill's bedcovers. She reached down into his pyjamas and took hold of him. He jerked awake.

'Hello, love.' He turned towards Jill. 'Are you alright?'

He spoke in alarm as much as anything else.

'Yes, I'm fine,' purred Jill. 'I just need to make sure that you are...'

'Oh,' he said.

There was nothing else he could say or do. He caught a brief glimpse of a flash of silver moonlight through the cream coloured cotton curtains of the bedroom window; it played with the shadows of the leaves on the trees from the garden until the shadow that was Jill's body underneath his bedcovers blocked his view.

'Happy New Year! Oh..Bloody hell!'

———————◆———————

Joe had just had a New Year's Eve that he would never forget. He was lying awake now, in the plastic light of the hospital ward; it felt terrible. Joe couldn't sleep. He wasn't used to not sleeping; he was sorely troubled. He was going to make sure she got a New Year she'd never forget as soon as he got out of here. Joe lay flat on his back in his hospital bed. Through the window looking into the nurses' office at the end of the ward, fluorescent strip lights dazzled him. Shadows, on the dark walls outside, haunted him. He watched the nurses chatting, laughing and drinking cups of coffee until his neck started to ache and he had to turn the other cheek. He was hurting. All over. He was in terrible pain. All over. Joe closed his eyes and waited a bit longer. It was no good; he knew he was in trouble. He couldn't wait any longer.

'Nurse! Nurse!' he slurred.

He pressed his red, emergency, button with his swollen, pork sausage finger. He couldn't tell if it was working or not. The nurses carried on drinking their coffee.

'Nurse! I need help!' shouted Joe.

The nurses carried on drinking their coffee. Joe had a vague feeling that he needed the toilet. He had a vague feeling that he was going to be sick again. He couldn't get out of bed because his leg was in plaster; he was in such terrible pain. All over. They said he was drunk. They'd pumped his stomach; he'd never had any problems before if he'd had one too many. They said he'd been violent. Breaking and entering! Well, that mad woman with the brush had been violent! She'd done the breaking and those bloody nurses had done the entering with that pipe. He was going to make a complaint when he got out of here.

'Nurse! Nurse!'

He couldn't wait any longer. Joe was sick all over himself and the bed; he did everything else all over himself and the bed as well. The shadows on the walls were getting bigger and darker; they were coming straight at him.

'Oh bloody hell! Happy New Year!' said the first shadow.

'Be quiet now, Joe, you're disturbing the other patients,' said the second shadow.

Joe could smell coffee. It was making him feel sick again.

'Oh the pain!' he groaned.

The first shadow lifted his bedcovers; the cool air of the hospital ward stung his bruises.

'What are you going to do to me?' alarmed Joe.

A flash of silver temporarily blinded Joe as the lights above his bed were switched on. The shadows disappeared, leaving two nurses standing on either side of his bed.

'We're going to get you cleaned, up, love,' said the first nurse. 'And then we're going to give you a catheter so you don't get into any more trouble like this!'

'I don't think he'll be causing any more trouble with this for a long time!' said the second nurse, reaching down and taking hold of him.

The nurses had a little giggle.

'Might as well give him an enema at the same time and then we won't have any more trouble with that for a couple of days, either.'

The nurses had another little giggle and then set about making sure that Joe was alright.

'Oh bloody hell!' cried Joe, as they flipped him over.

He cried like a baby. The tears and trembling would not stop. There was nothing else he could say or do.

———————◆———————

Carrie didn't want her New Year's Eve to end, but she knew that Jon had to get up for milking. He needed to sleep; she was heartbroken that it wasn't with her. She was lying awake now, in his bed; it felt amazing. She couldn't sleep. She could smell him all around her. He wouldn't go away. She hadn't wanted him to go away tonight. She lay flat on her back in his bed. She could feel the imprint of his body on the well-worn mattress underneath the fresh sheet.

Through the moonlit curtains of his bedroom window the shadows of the leaves on the trees outside played with both the stuff in his room and her mind. Over and over, the leaves turned, turned, turned. She had planned to turn over a new leaf this New Year's Eve; she never expected it to be such a big one as this. She watched the shadows come and go until her head started to ache. Her slinky, black, bloodstained dress with the flash of silver across the waistline lay draped over the back of the chair across the room. It lay on top of Jon's work clothes; she could just make out the checked pattern of the cotton sleeves in the darkness. Her head was hurting:

It should be me lying draped over him, not you!

In sympathy or reprimand the moonlight suddenly shifted. She was temporarily blinded by a second flash of silver reflected from her dress by the large oval mirror in the middle of Jon's wardrobe. It was exactly the same sort of wardrobe as the one in the derelict room where he had been volunteered to sleep. If Carrie lifted her hurting head slightly she could see herself, lying in his bed. The shadows of the leaves on the trees played with her reflection and echoed around the walls of his room. It was a very plain room. Apart from the wardrobe and his bed, there was only a small chest of drawers, a small desk and a chair. In the silver shadows they looked so small that Carrie wondered how he managed to get his legs under the desk to sit at it.

They looked small enough to be children's furniture; perhaps they were. Above the desk there was a small bookcase, screwed onto the wall. It was full of small books. Old books. Carrie screwed up her eyes to try to read their titles. Grey and fading in the darkness, and no doubt the same in the daylight, too, once upon a time these books would have been brightly coloured and brightly loved by little hands; they were all children's books. 'Ned the Lonely Donkey', 'Janet and John', 'Peter and Jane'.

'I can't see one called 'Jon and Carrie.' Well, I haven't finished writing that one, yet...They belong to the other woman in his life, his mother is here. He said she loved words and reading...It's all he's got left of her...'

On the wall around the edge of the bookcase several dark shapes spooked her. At first, they looked like real leaves that had been magicked in through the window by the moonlight and stuck to the wall. But it was just the style of the artist; strong, straightforward, raw. Jip was there, the cows were there; there were sketches of trees, leaves and flowers...and she was there. Dressed in a long, black dress, she was smiling. Her eyes, as black as her dress, looked steadily down on her; they were alive. They reached out to her in a gentle and pleading sort of way. Carrie shivered.

'Your eyes are the colour of pain...'

But it was just the style of the artist; strong, straightforward, raw. She pictured Jon now, curled up, fast asleep on the chaise longue in the derelict room. For less than a moment, she caught a glimpse of him in her own mirror; he had dark eyes, too. But the shadows on the walls were getting bigger and darker; they took him away. She could have put the bedroom light on, but she definitely wouldn't see him then, and she didn't want to disturb Debs in the room across the corridor. And then, she didn't want to see the life that he'd had, in that room, trying to tuck his lovely long legs under such a small desk. The moonlight had been light enough to see, to feel, everything.

Carrie pressed her body hard into his mattress; her body was aching all over, and she still had a headache. She closed her eyes and waited a bit longer. It was no good; she couldn't wait any longer.

Her skin tingled; she had goose bumps. She reached down under Jon's bedcovers and took hold of herself. She lifted her head slightly to look for his reflection in the oval wardrobe mirror; she could see his eyes again.

'Oh...bloody hell! Happy New Year...'

The tears and the trembling would not stop. There was nothing she could do. But dreams could do what neither sleep or Carrie could do for herself.

'Carrie! Carrie! Help me!'

Carrie jerked awake; she leapt out of bed; it was Debs. She grabbed Jon's cotton checked work shirt from the back of his chair and hastily threw it on. She rushed out into the hallway:

'I'm here!' she called out gently.

She pushed at old man Wilson's door. The bedside lamp was switched on; Debs was lying in bed, flat on her back. She was fast asleep. She looked peaceful. Carrie watched her breathing just to make sure.

'She must be dreaming.'

Filled with silver moonlight, the hallway looked peaceful. Empty. It touched Carrie, too, guiding her to Jon's bed. She climbed back into his bed, still wearing his shirt.

She wanted to giggle. So she giggled:

'If he needs his shirt in the morning, he'll have to come and get it, won't he?'

1979
Monday 1st January
New Year's Day

Jill got up early. It was New Year's Day; time to turn over a new leaf. She studied her face in the bathroom mirror. She thought she looked a bit different but she wasn't sure. She wasn't sure if she was turning over a brand new leaf by getting up so early this morning, or if it was still the same one from last night. The early morning light glowed through the stained glass on her front door. It was very old glass with an old fashioned pattern of red roses. Jill wasn't a church goer but she'd always found the presence of that stained glass comforting. It was her very own little piece of church at the entrance to her own home; it was protection; reverence; sanctuary.

And it had been broken. Violated. Abused. In the morning light Jill could see Joe's hand and face prints in-between the red roses on the stained glass of her front door. She backed away from them, holding on tight to her cream cotton dressing gown. She shivered. She felt broken. Violated. Abused. Her body felt funny, as if Joe's hands and face prints were imprinted on *her* body, instead of the stained glass. She almost ran down the last part of the hallway to the kitchen; she needed coffee.

Such was her desperation that she switched the kettle and the radio on, reached for the coffee, milk and a mug before finally switching on the kitchen lights; that felt funny too. The kettle was whistling at her; that sounded funny. The kitchen looked funny. Jill stood in the middle of the kitchen; she couldn't find anywhere safe. There was blood everywhere; in the sink, on the taps, on the kitchen table, on the door handles, on the floor. There were muddy footprints all over that, too.

The tears and the trembling would not stop. The radio would not stop. The echoes of sounds and smells would not stop. The memories would not stop. The kettle stopped eventually. When Bill came whistling down the stairs to make his coffee he stopped immediately when he saw the state of the kitchen and the state of Jill, in the middle of it all, shaking like a leaf.

'It's alright, love,' he said gently. 'Here, take my hand, and walk with me to the lounge.'

In the end, he had to take hers. He was relieved that, eventually, her feet agreed to move. He would have struggled to pick her up and carry her; she wouldn't have let him anyway. She'd have been more likely to stab him with a kitchen knife than let him touch her this morning. He led his broken lady through to the new sofa in the lounge and sat her down. He rushed back to the kitchen, made the coffee and rushed back to her even faster.

'Here, drink this, love,' he said.

Jill stared into her coffee cup; she didn't want to drink it. She wasn't sure if it was coffee or blood.

'I think I did things...'

Her voice wouldn't, couldn't, speak.

'It's alright, love. You're my wife. You're allowed to love me, and it was lovely for me to love you back.'

Bill wanted to love her back now and put his arm around her, but it was too soon.

'After all these years...'

'It's alright, love, there's nothing to be afraid about any more. Nothing to be guilty or ashamed about. Time doesn't matter. We're here now aren't we, nothing else matters.'

'Well, I'm having new glass in that door and I want it today!' cried Jill.

'Not today, love; it's New Year's Day. It's a holiday.'

'And you've just told me time doesn't matter! Of course it matters! Oh what have I done? All these years...I tried, I saw Carrie and I wanted to turn over a new leaf...and then Debs...Oh, you didn't see her...those cruel hands...all that blood...I had to do something for her...I lost it, Bill, I lost it...I can't remember what I did....What am I going to do?'

'You've done and did nothing wrong! In fact, you were very brave. I know you remember exactly what you did, Jill. You're good at remembering; too good. You're very upset and exhausted now, you've barely had any sleep last night and neither did I!'

Bill was too kind to look at Jill's face, but he heard the sharp intake of breath from her mouth. He was trying to say and do the right thing; he knew he was on the edge of her reason.

'Why don't you go back to bed this morning and rest? The police will be calling this afternoon to take your statement. I'll get in touch with Carrie before then and find out what's what at her end. We must respect Debs' wishes. Jill, are you listening to me? We must respect Debs' wishes.'

Jill nodded. The mention of word 'police' did more than any of Bill's words of reassurance to return her to her old, familiar, self. Suddenly, she wasn't feeling so funny any more.

'Now, you go and relax. I'll clear up in the kitchen.'

'Yes, you're right. I must be ready for the police.'
Jill paused in the doorway for a moment:
'She called me 'Mum'!'
'Well you are,' smiled Bill, 'and a great one at that.'
'Happy New Year! She's looking a bit less broken...'
The kitchen, however, looked as though all the children from the local primary school had passed through it, having lessons in gardening and modern art on the way. Bill sighed as he started to clear up.
'Oh bloody hell! Happy New Year!'
It was going to be a long first day of the year and, almost certainly, a long year...
'Oh Carrie! Where are you?'

———— ◆ ————

Carrie woke up in alarm; she'd been fast asleep and was disappointed to find that it was past nine o'clock already. She'd wanted to make an early start on New Year's Day; it was time to turn over that new leaf. She was also disappointed that Jon hadn't come in to get his shirt off her back or anything else for that matter, not even a good morning kiss. She jumped out of bed; Jon would have nearly finished half a day's work by now and she didn't want to be the last up.
'Debs will still be in bed, I bet she's still fast asleep.'
Still wearing nothing but Jon's work shirt, which she decided that she was never going to give up, not even for washing, she tiptoed across the hallway to check on Debs.
'Sleep well?' said Debs.
She was sitting up in bed sipping a mug of tea. She was wearing an enormous, white cotton, nightie. Her hair wasn't brushed, but it had been neatly arranged on the pillow behind her; she smelt of rosewater and antiseptic. She had clearly had a visit from a Fairy Hagmother who had worked her own, unique, magic on her friend. Debs was smiling, as best she could; she'd always had an eternal smile...
'Mavis!' said Carrie.
'Aren't I the great white whale? You'll have to start calling me 'Moby Dick!'
Carrie laughed and sat on the end of the bed.
'Why didn't you tell me you were awake?'
'Thought you'd need to catch up on your sleep after last night!' said

Debs.

'Not as much as you!' said Carrie.

Debs tried to smile a bit wider.

'I saw you last night, Carrie!'

Carrie blushed at her midnight memories of standing in the hall in her wellies.

'I saw you last night, sneaking along the hallway in that slinky black dress of yours. You went down to his room, didn't you?'

'No! I certainly did not! He had to get up for milking this morning. You must have been dreaming.'

'No, I wasn't. I couldn't sleep. I was hurting. Aching. I was wide awake. I definitely saw you go past!'

'Well, I heard you calling *me,* and when I came to you, you were fast asleep, so you must have been dreaming!'

'It's O.K. You don't need to lie to me. I wouldn't blame you!'

'Honestly Debs, I'm not lying. Much as I'd have loved to go to him, it wouldn't have been the right time, after everything that happened last night...'

Carrie's voice trailed off. She realised, too late, that she was returning Debs to that horror.

'I'm so sorry, about everything,' said Carrie. 'I've been such a fool. I've known all along, saw the signs, and I did nothing to help you, even when you tried to tell me...'

Carrie broke down; the tears and trembling would not stop. She hadn't been violated and abused; quite the opposite, in fact. That fact made her feel even worse. Instead of turning over a new leaf, she was shaking like a leaf.

'It's alright, Carrie,' said Debs gently, taking hold of her hand. 'You were there when it really mattered. You saved me, probably saved my life!'

She squeezed Carrie's hand.

'You know, I think he might have killed me this time. He wouldn't mean to, of course. He never means to. Look at me, Carrie! You've got nothing to be guilty or ashamed of - especially not your little trip down the corridor. I'd do the same if I was you, he's so lovely!'

Carrie looked up in protest but Debs was having none of it; the old Debs was still there, bursting out of her broken body.

'It's me that's been the fool! Me that's guilty! Me that's ashamed! Me!'

Carrie started groaning and shaking her head violently.

'I chose to marry him; I ignored the signs, until it was too late. I

403

thought it would go away. 'It's your own fault!' he said. All the time. And I believed him. I thought it must be me, it had to be me. So I tried. Harder and harder, but it was never enough. I was in and I couldn't get out. I was afraid and I just got more and more afraid. And by the time I finally tried to get away over Christmas...' Debs' purple bruises seemed to change colour, become paler, 'I was sure he was fast asleep, but he caught me at the front door with my suitcase, and that was it...for several days...until I managed to call you...'

Debs sank back into her neatly arranged pillow. Talking, feeling, had exhausted her.

'I need a hug!' sobbed Carrie.

Ever so gently, they had a hug.

'Now, are you going to get changed? That shirt stinks! You can't go home to your mother in that - she'd have a heart attack.'

'Perhaps not, after last night,' said Carrie.

'Yeah, she was great, wasn't she?'

Tears welled up in Carrie's eyes again.

'Yes, she was great.'

A sudden, loud, knock on the bedroom door made them both jump and pushed the bedroom door open; old man Wilson had to bend his head to get through it. He stood in the doorway like a roosting bird of prey. Shoulders hunched, his head sank down into them, yet his eyes remained alert; all-seeing, all knowing. Carrie wondered how long he'd been there, how much he'd heard; probably everything, knowing him. He'd caught her in a state of undress on more than one occasion, both of body and of mind. She tried to cover up her legs with Jon's work shirt, failed, and nearly fell off the bed; she couldn't do anything about her words so she sat still and resigned herself to that little brown mouse feeling that she so often experienced when he was hovering.

'Ah do,' he said.

Debs smiled at him.

'She's not embarrassed or afraid of him! How odd! So why does he do that to me?'

'Hello,' said Carrie, summoning the courage to turn slightly towards him.

Old man Wilson was looking out of the window.

'It's him that's embarrassed! How odd!'

Carrie suddenly felt a bit better; she relaxed a little and turned more fully towards him, showing herself and her knees.

'I've just spoken to Bill on the phone. Everything is sorted. You're going to stay with us.'

'Brilliant! More nights in his bed...'

'Our doctor will call in on you. The police are taking a statement from Carrie's mother this afternoon. He's in hospital with a broken leg and ribs, he's not going anywhere. Do you want to press charges?'

Debs shook her head; she started trembling again. He must have noticed:

'I thought not, I'll tell Bill. Don't worry. You're safe here, and you can stay as long as you like.'

'Thanks, I'd like to stay forever, please.'

'Carrie and her Dad will get your things from your house. It'll be safe, he's going to be in hospital for a while. Carrie will go home today, she's got work tomorrow. She can let the factory know that you're ill, so no worry there. Everything must carry on as normal while you decide what you want to do.'

'But I want to stay here with Debs!'

'If you can manage for a few days, Carrie will bring your things when she comes here at the weekend so as not to raise any suspicion that you're here.'

Old man Wilson stood awkwardly in the doorway, still hunched up inside his folded feathers. He looked very tired; very pale.

'Thank you for your kindness...'

Debs's voice trailed away, to be replaced by quiet tears.

'Ah,' said old man Wilson, retreating through the door.

'He's not been talking to me at all! Where did he sleep last night?'

Debs needed to sleep. She collapsed further into her pillows. Old man Wilson's face reappeared around the edge of the doorway:

'Get changed out of that stinking shirt, Carrie. I'm not letting you go home from here looking and smelling like that.'

Carrie wanted to argue, *'but I love this smell, it's his smell; it's the best smell in the world!'* but he was gone.

So was Debs, already the healing power of sleep was taking control of her weeping body. Carrie and Debs had experimented with many things together during their lives; kissing wasn't one of them. But Carrie suddenly wanted to do it now.

She leaned over a dopey Debs, risked disturbing her with the perfume from her stinking shirt and gently kissed her on the forehead. Debs opened her eyes for a moment, tried a little smile and then returned to the oblivion of sleep. In one hand she held the body of her pale blue flower fairy with the chipped wing; in the other she held her head. Tiny porcelain Angel 'Hope' sat smiling on the bedside table. Carrie picked her up and laid her on Debs's chest; it was a symbolic act as much for her own benefit as for Debs. It didn't make her feel any better but she hoped it would make Debs smile when she woke up.

'If she ever wakes up. I'd think twice about it if I was her. She looks so peaceful now...Oh Debs, I'm so, so sorry...'

As Carrie pulled the bedroom door to on Debs she nervously looked up and down the hallway.

'I saw you last night, sneaking along the hallway in that slinky black dress of yours. You went down to his room, didn't you? No! It couldn't be...What nonsense! There's no such thing as ghosts...'

Even so, she just had to have a look inside the derelict room at the end of the hallway where Jon had, no doubt, spent an uncomfortable night. There were blankets on the floor, he hadn't even tried to fit on the chaise longue. The long black velvet dress was hanging down the front of the wardrobe; Carrie could see the reflection of its back in the faded oval mirror. She walked in and held the sleeves in her hands.

'Have you been sleep walking? Why would you do that when you could have had him pressed up against you all night?'

Carrie stroked the soft black velvet sleeves.

'Ooh,' she moaned, 'it should have been me...'

'Carrie, love, are you there? Shall you come and have a bit of breakfast?' Mavis called up the stairs.

'Is there anybody there?' smiled Carrie to the black velvet dress.

By way of answer the door to the derelict bedroom creaked shut.

'Yes, I'm here!' called Carrie, reaching for the door handle in a blind panic.

'Yes, thanks, Mavis. I'll be right down!'

Carrie had no choice; instead of dressing for dinner, she had to dress for breakfast in her slinky black evening dress. It was less smelly than Jon's shirt, but just as dirty, if not more so.

Downstairs, Jon was already tucking into bacon and eggs at the kitchen table, Mavis was 'making tea' and old man Wilson was sitting, eyes closed, in his father bear chair by the fire; the hand knitted blankets were spread all over it.

'So that's where he slept last night...'

Fortunately, there was no Jed as yet. Mavis smiled as she presented her with an enormous plate of fried food and a mug of tea. Jon carried on eating without saying a word, although he did pass her the sugar bowl and brown sauce bottle by way of welcome to the kitchen table. Old man Wilson appeared to be fast asleep.

'She's asleep now,' said Carrie, just because she needed to say something for herself, to prove she'd been doing something all morning.

She looked across the table at Jon. This was not exactly a romantic, first dinner date but, as far as she was concerned, it couldn't get any better than this...

Wednesday 3rd January

Carrie was sitting on her padded tweed chair at her desk. She was back at work and, as far as she was concerned, it couldn't get any worse than this. It was still early January, but the camaraderie, community spirit and good will of the recent Christmas season was soon forgotten as the grindstone of the daily office routine started up once more. The deadlines, the lewd jokes, the smell of stale coffee, the sound of telephones endlessly ringing and office machinery clunking and clicking; it was all was made a million times worse by the short, dark, January days and the return of 'Boredom', a member of the office staff that seemed to enjoy sitting at Carrie's desk more than anyone else's.

A note, triumphantly pinned upon the staff notice board by Rosalind the Rottweiler suddenly created a new level of worseness. Mr Pike's mother had, very sadly, died over the Christmas holidays. He would not be returning to work until after the funeral; all editorial matters should be referred to Dennis whilst Rosalind would continue to see to the everyday running of the newspaper. Carrie returned to her desk after reading the notice board, to find that 'Boredom' had made a space on her desk for 'Despair' to join it. Rosalind was already out and about, doing the rounds on the office floor, issuing her orders and enjoying every moment of her extended time as the 'big fish.'

'Poor Mr Pike, I wonder how he's coping,' thought Carrie. *'I don't expect he'll be doing very well, despite his 'booming' bravado.'*

Carrie thought about her own mother:

'I don't really know her at all! I expected her to go to pieces when she saw Debs on New Year's Eve, and yet she was quite the opposite. She was brave and strong. Fearless! And now she's gone back to her usual self; she's worse than she's been for a long time. Something's got a hold on her and I'd love to know what it is. It's the old 'closed door' syndrome. We've all got some of those...even if you've got a key to unlock it, you've still got to want to put the key in the lock and turn it...'

Carrie felt inside her trouser pocket; Debs' house key sat at the bottom of it. She was meeting her dad after work and they were going to get her stuff. The edge of the key dug into her flesh every time she moved; Carrie pushed back at it through the material of her trouser pocket.

'Don't you dare dig into me! You're pointless! You're the most utterly pointless key I've ever had in my possession! Debs' door has been kicked open as wide as he kicked open her face, so don't you dare pretend to me that you're important, because you're not!'

'What's the matter, Carrie?'

'Rosalind the Rottweiler' was bearing down on Carrie's desk. She rested her hands on it, squashing 'Boredom' and 'Despair' beneath the weight of her floppy palms, just as her ankles flopped over her shiny new shoes.

'Nothing,' said Carrie.

'Why are you crying, then?'

'I'm not!'

Carrie tried to argue back, only just realising that she'd opened her own flood gates, quite by accident, in full view of everyone. Her face was wet and stinging.

'Well, you don't look very happy. I suppose you're pining for Mr Pike!'

You bitch!

'I'm very sorry for his loss. I suppose I was thinking about how it must feel to lose someone close to you like that. I've been typing up the Deaths column all morning, and I suppose it's got to me a bit.'

'Yes, well I know all about that. Your mother will be relieved to hear that you do have some family feeling after all; it's just a pity you can't show her some of it, sometimes. Go and wash your face, pull yourself together and get on with some work instead of day dreaming about nonsense. Mr Pike will be back soon enough; save your tears for him, because they don't impress me.'

Carrie left 'Boredom' on her desk, took 'Despair' with her, and went to the toilets. She washed her face and then sat on a toilet until two other women had been in and then out of the other cubicle next door to her. She didn't cry any more. Debs' house key fell out of her pocket when she pulled her trousers up. It made a pretty ringing sound as it hit the tiled floor; it sounded just like a front door bell.

I don't need reminding! I hope you break inside the lock! Oh Debs, I'm so sorry...

Carrie was about to leave the toilet cubicle when somebody else came in, so she waited until they were in full flow on their toilet before making her escape; she didn't want to have to speak to anybody; certainly not 'Rosalind the Rottweiler'. The shoes that had just come in sounded suspiciously pointed, as did the smell from the next door toilet cubicle. Either way, Carrie knew that she would be hounded for the rest of the week now that she had let Rosalind see that she was breakable.

Carrie deliberately dug Debs' key into her leg as she walked back to her desk; she felt every sharp ridge of its teeth.

She's not going to break me any more than I can break you! She's not the only one with sharp teeth...Oh Debs...'

———◆———

The fat jolly snowman, hanging on the newly painted, blue, front door watched them walk up the drive towards him. Bill was having none of it. He lifted the snowman off the door and propped him up against the wall around the side of the house.

'We don't want any witnesses to our breaking and entering do we, Carrie?'

Carrie stared at her dad.

'Hey, don't look at me like that, it's your Mother's 'look of disgust' face, and I was only trying to cheer you up,' said Bill.

'I know,' sighed Carrie. 'Sorry. Let's get this over with.'

Carrie rooted around inside her trouser pocket for the offending key; having needled at her all day, now it seemed to be stuck inside the folds of her pocket's material and didn't want to come out. As she fumbled about and finally succeeded in connecting the key with its front door lock, Bill interrupted her with another cheerful thought:

'I had to take him down. It's bad luck to keep Christmas decorations up after Twelfth Night.'

Carrie looked like her mother again.

'Sorry, I'll shut up now,' said Bill.

The newly painted, blue, front door was open. Carrie and her dad stood on the welcome mat and peered into the darkness of Debs' empty house. They didn't feel very welcome.

'She said her suitcase was in the hall by the door, but he could have moved it,' said Carrie.

'There's only one way to find out. Go on, love, you go get it for her.'

Carrie stepped into the darkness of the house. There was something very soft underneath her feet. She took another step and found the same sensation underneath that next step, too.

'There's something on the floor here. I'll have to put a light on.'

'That's O.K.' said her dad. 'I was only joking before about the breaking and entering, you know. She asked us to be here, so don't worry.'

'I'm not worried about that. I'm worried about what I'm going to see when I switch the lights on. Oh...'

Debs' suitcase was in the hall just as she'd described, but it was lying on the floor, wide open.

'I see her here, lying on the floor; wide open.'

Debs' clothes were scattered all over the hall and up the stairs. Some were ripped to pieces; the softness beneath Carrie's feet was Debs' favourite, pale pink, fluffy jumper.

'I hear her here, crying; he rips her.'

There was a funny smell in the hallway.

'Dad, I need some help,' called Carrie, quietly.

Now it was her dad's turn to stare with the 'look of disgust' face.

'He's ruined all her clothes!' cried Carrie. 'Look!' She held the pale pink fluffy jumper out towards him. 'He's even urinated on them!'

'Sick bastard,' said Bill.

Bill very, very, rarely swore, so when he did, he really meant it. Carrie could see the anger welling up inside her dad's body; the knuckles on his fingerless hand were shining white with fury. Carrie wondered what he was going to do next. He looked as though he was about the punch his fist through the wall. But Bill was as finely tuned as the engines on his beloved vintage motorbikes; he was in full control of his throttle. He quietly closed the newly painted, blue, front door.

'I'm going to clean up this mess here, see if there's anything that's alright, while you go upstairs and see if you can find some more clothes and personal stuff up there.'

'I don't want to go upstairs. I don't want to see her bedroom. I don't want to hear or see or smell or feel. I don't want to remember. I don't want to imagine...Oh Debs!'

Carrie climbed the stairs trying not to look or touch anything as she went. It was hopeless. There was blood on the bed sheets; blood in the bathroom; blood on the door handles; blood on the carpet. Instead of painting the town red, Joe had painted his wife instead. He'd got his choice of colour horribly wrong; Debs loved pink. Pale pink fluffy jumpers and pale blue flower fairies, pretty flowers and fairy lights.

Carrie was suddenly seeing fairy lights all around her; she crouched down and tried to put her head between her knees until the sick, fainting feeling had passed. Whilst she was down she remembered and imagined; she heard, saw, smelt and felt.

'How are you doing, Carrie?' called her dad.

'Nearly done!' she called back.

'Come on, you silly mare! That's what she'd say if she was here!'

Carrie stood up. If she listened very carefully, she could hear Debs laughing; the sound was coming from downstairs, from the soft, leather, sofa. Carrie found plenty of underwear and make up, an old sweat shirt and her gardening shoes.

'Come on, Carrie, that'll have to do. Let's go home. We can buy her some new stuff before the weekend. I doubt whether she'd want anything out of this house anyway.'

Carrie locked the newly painted, blue, front door in agreement.

'I hope I never have to come here again,' she said. 'I hope she never has to come here again.'

'She'd never get rid of the red. Pink is her favourite colour. She loves pink...'

———◆———

Joe was seeing red. He was waiting for a taxi, sitting in the lobby at the entrance of the hospital. He'd just been discharged. He didn't think it was right; he wasn't ready to go home yet. He needed looking after. He could hardly move with this heavy plaster cast on his leg and every breath he took was agony because of the bruising around his cracked ribs. And he'd just had a visit from the police. Why couldn't they have visited him whilst he was still on the ward, instead of humiliating him in front of everyone down here?

It wasn't right. He had rights, didn't he? He might have had a bit too much to drink, but he'd a right to some privacy, didn't he? He'd a right to some dignity! He'd learnt his lesson; he'd got a broken leg and ribs! And they weren't even going to press charges so long as he paid up for the damage to that crazy woman's garden. It should be her that's paying up for the damage she's done to him. He might never recover from this; he might be in pain for the rest of his life! He'd a good mind to make a formal complaint. His taxi arrived.

'You poor devil!' said the taxi driver, as he helped Joe into the back seat.

'I know,' said Joe.

He gave the taxi driver the address.

'Have you got anyone to help you at home?' asked the taxi driver as he pulled up in front of the newly painted, blue, front door.

'The missus is away, visiting family,' said Joe. 'But she'll be back afore too long. She'll have to come back.'

'You're right there mate! She'll have to. I can't see you managing on your own like this.'

'No, I shan't,' said Joe.

The taxi driver helped Joe out of his taxi, passed him his crutches and

412

watched him struggle to his front door.

'Got your key, mate?'

'Yes, ta.'

'I should get straight on the phone to that missus of yours. When she sees what a state you're in, she'll be all over you like a rash! She'll be full of tea and sympathy. I bet she'll fuss you to death.'

'Probably,' replied Joe, hesitating with his key in the lock, but not turning it. 'She gets things wrong a lot. She's very annoying, like women are, sometimes. You know...'

The taxi driver smiled and waved in agreement:

'Oh I know, alright! Still, I couldn't be without my old lady. She's lovely. Just lovely. I carry folk about all day in this taxi, and when I get home, she carries me about! I can live with a bit of nagging now and then. Love her to bits, I do! Just like you do, with your missus.'

Now it was Joe's turn to smile and wave agreement; he managed a grimace of sorts. He was hurting; the crutches were digging into the flesh beneath his armpits, as if he hadn't got enough bruises already.

'Well, good luck, mate. Be seeing ya.'

Joe watched the taxi and its driver disappear down the road before opening his front door.

'What a prat!' he hissed under his breath.

Talking too loud hurt him. Joe stood on his own welcome mat and peered into the darkness of his house. It wasn't much of a welcome home. Debs' suitcase was folded up, propped up against the wall just inside the front door. Joe had a feeling that it wasn't like that when he'd left the house, but he couldn't be sure. He couldn't really remember much about New Year's Eve, except that she'd upset him again, and now look what a state he was in.

'Bitch.'

Joe squeezed himself down the hallway and switched the lights on in the kitchen. The chairs were neatly arranged around the kitchen table. He had a feeling that they weren't like that when he'd left them on New Year's Eve, either. In fact, he'd broken one. It had been propped up against the wall by the back door.

'Bloody stupid chairs! I'd never put it there! Someone's been here! Breaking and entering! I've a good mind to call those bloody police!'

Joe looked around the kitchen; it looked tidier than usual.

'I don't think they've taken anything. It must be her! She's been back, tidied up and then left me again! Bitch! Just wait till she gets back...'

There was a funny smell everywhere. Joe remembered very clearly what the smell was and why it was there. He saw his reflection in the kitchen clock face.

'Agh! Disgusting!' he snarled.

The clock was unmoved by his 'look of disgust' face; it carried on ticking.

Why couldn't she have cleaned up properly? And I could do with a cup of tea! I need some help!'

Joe decided against trying to make tea; he couldn't carry it and walk on his crutches at the same time, anyway. He could, however, slip a can of lager in his pocket and make it to the soft, leather, sofa in the lounge. He switched the television on; at least that worked properly.

'I don't want to go upstairs. I don't need to go upstairs, anyway I can sleep down here just as well. I'll show her! I don't need her and her ridiculous fairies and flowers and fluffy stuff. There's going to be some changes around here when she gets back.'

'Ouch! Bloody coffee table!'

Joe collapsed down into the soft, leather, sofa.

He was suddenly feeling sick and faint after the strain of getting from the kitchen to the lounge. He lay still but the feeling wouldn't pass. He noticed that there was some blood on the corner of the coffee table; it couldn't have been from his leg because it was covered in plaster cast.

'She made me cross! She's always been accident prone, anyway. There's no point ringing up, she'll be back soon enough, crawling in on her knees...'

Joe leaned over the edge of the soft, leather, sofa and was sick on the carpet. He'd got his choice of T.V. channel horribly wrong; there was no football on this one. His knees felt too weak even to crawl across the floor to change channels. He was done for today. If he listened very carefully, he could hear Debs singing along with the radio in the kitchen:

'Yes, Joe! Coming, Joe!'

'She made me cross! But I'll buy her some new stuff when she gets back; maybe we'll have a new carpet in here...and some curtains...She likes pink, doesn't she?...'

———◆———

'No expense is to be spared for Deborah. You know what she likes, Carrie. You get her lots of new stuff and I'll pay for it.'

'You've never said that to me!' said Carrie.

Jill stared at her daughter with her 'look of disgust' face.

'Fortunately for you, you've never experienced real trauma in your life. We're going to help Deborah get over hers, and we do that by giving her as much kindness and caring as we can, whatever it takes. I'm not going to let her linger and suffer for the rest of her life like I...like I...' Jill's voice faltered to a stop.

She stared down at the kitchen table.

'Like you, what?' asked Carrie.

Jill closed her eyes and released a quiet reply when she was able to open them again.

'Like I've read about. Studies have shown that good care after any kind of trauma, physical or mental, speeds up healing and recovery.'

'That makes perfect sense to me,' said Carrie. 'Are you alright, Mum? You make this business with Debs all sound very personal, somehow. And you've not been the same since that night I brought her here.'

'Personal? Of course it's personal!' shouted Jill. 'I've known Deborah all your life! I just can't bear to think about what that poor girl has gone through. The pain, the humiliation, the degradation. It's unbearable! And all this time, nobody knew, she carried it inside of herself. She was all alone and nobody cared...'

'I knew! I knew! How do you think I feel?'

Jill was definitely not alright. She let her head fall down onto the kitchen table and sobbed into its hard, shiny, polished wood; her tears gathered in pools beneath her face. She was, literally, drowning in her own tears and she didn't appear to care who saw her doing it. She was definitely not alright. Given what they'd just been talking about, Carrie did her best:

'Mum! Mum! It's alright,' she soothed.

She tried to put her hand on her Mum's shoulder.

'And don't call me Mum!'

Jill leapt up from her kitchen chair and backed away from Carrie.

'But you are my mum, aren't you?' asked Carrie, suddenly looking and feeling scared. 'Or is there something you want to tell me? Is that what this is about? Did something happen to you? It's O.K. You can tell me. I'll still love you. You'll still be my Mum.'

Jill started shaking; she hugged herself in her arms.

'Of course I'm your Mother! But you've only just started calling me 'Mum'. You're always so formal and distant with me!'

'Me?' exploded Carrie.

'And all I ever wanted was a daughter to love me back, to call me 'Mum'. But I can't cope with it, somehow. I want it, but I just can't bear it! I don't know why...'

'You know,' said Carrie as kindly as she could, 'that's not my fault. I really try. Maybe you should talk to someone. There's probably something haunting you from your past. Maybe the shock of seeing Debs injured like that jogged your memory in some way. Did somebody hurt you?'

Her Mother's face achieved a new level of disgust before her jaw hardened into a familiar reply:

'Certainly not! How dare you suggest that I'm mentally unfit!'

'I wasn't...'

'There I was, trying to do the best for your friend, trying to accept your belated attempts at daughterly affection, and you manage to turn it round so that there's something wrong with me! Rosalind was quite wrong about you! Family feeling indeed! Agh, I need to lie down.'

'*So do I...*'

Saturday 6th January

Debs was glowing. Pinky red. She was sitting by the fire in old man Wilson's chair, watching the flames dance amongst the lumps of coal. She had one of his old, hand knitted, blankets over her knees. She had old Ab sitting opposite her for company. The reds and purples on her face from a week ago were being gradually replaced by gentler, pastel shades of pink, pale greens and yellows. But here was another visitor.

'Ah do, missy!' said old Ab, as Carrie knelt down at Debs' feet.

'Hello Ab!' said Carrie, feeling the warmth on her face from the fire and from the glowing Debs who was smiling down at her.

'Wow, you look great!'

'Don't tell lies, Carrie!'

Carrie laughed.

'Beauty's in the eye of the beholder!' said old Ab. 'Isn't that right, Mavis?'

Mavis bustled in carrying a plate of cakes from the pantry.

'Ah, reckon it is,' cackled Mavis. 'It's a good job too, for the likes of me! Let's have a cup of tea,' she cackled again.

Debs smiled at Mavis:

'I've had so much tea and sympathy. I'm being fussed to death!'

'And quite right, too,' said Carrie. 'I've brought you some things.'

'I'm not ready to go home yet,' said Debs, her voice and her body backing themselves deep into old man Wilson's chair.

Carrie could see the distress that even the thought of her home had brought her.

'Of course you're not. I should have said 'bought' you some things, because that's what we've done. I just hope you'll like them, you know what I'm like with shopping. I'm no good without you!'

Tears welled up in Debs' eyes.

'Oh no, I've just upset her even worse, reminding her about happy times.'

'You shouldn't have done that, I can't pay for them!'

Tears welled up in Carrie's eyes.

'Of course she should,' said Mavis. 'There's nowt wrong with accepting a gift now and then, especially one that's kindly meant, is there, Ab?'

'Not at all!' said old Ab. 'Look at all the eggs and ham and cakes I've had out of you, all these years, Mavis! By heck, ladies, I wouldn't be the fine figure of a man I am today, if it weren't for Mavis' cakes; she's kept me alive!'

Old Ab brandished his stick thin arms, then had a good old fashioned chuckle with Mavis. Carrie looked up at Debs who was looking exhausted again.

'You've kept me alive,' thought Carrie.

Debs reached out for Carrie's hand and squeezed it, gently.

'No, we've kept each other alive,' came the reply.

'I can see the garden from here,' said Debs. 'It's beautiful here, isn't it?'

'Yes, I told you!' said Carrie. 'I see you've got your flower fairy fixed!'

'Jon did it for me,' said Debs.

She smiled an all-seeing, all knowing, smile at Carrie.

'I'd better go and find him; I'm supposed to be here for work experience!'

Carrie stood up. Her face was burning hot from sitting in front of the fire all that time; she tried to let it cool down away from the all-seeing, all knowing, old Ab and Mavis.

'Have you met Jed, yet?' she asked as casually as possible.

'Only briefly,' said Debs. 'I think he's a bit squeamish, to be honest. He can't seem to bear looking at my bruises. I think I frighten him.'

'That'd be a first, then,' said Carrie.

'He's been very polite, though,' said Debs.

'He hasn't been any such thing!' interupted old Ab. 'He's been like a bear with a sore head at my house.'

'It'll do our Jed good to have to put himself out a bit, he's too fond of getting his own way,' joined in Mavis.

'Brilliant, no more Jed!'

'Don't you worry, Miss Debs, it won't hurt him to stay with old Ab for a while. He's only down the road.'

'Oh, I'm sorry,' said Debs. 'It's all my fault.'

Carrie could feel Debs slipping away to her old way of being; she suddenly felt full of anger.

'Of course it's not your fault. Nothing's your fault! You're as innocent as that fairy you hold in your hands. She's been fixed, and so will you be! Don't ever say that again, Debs. Never!'

Debs stared at Carrie.

'You sound just like your Mother! You look like her, too!'

'Oh, please don't say that!' cried Carrie, achieving a new level of disgust with her face.

'That's no bad thing,' said Debs, quietly. 'Just remember how brave and

418

strong she was on New Year's Eve! There's something very good inside her, it just needs a chance to come out, doesn't it?'

The old Debs is still there, alright! She's still too clever for her own good.'

Just then, the kitchen door banged open and the all-seeing, all knowing, who was also too clever for his own good, old man Wilson burst in through the door.

'Look what we've got here!' he said.

From the folds of his open coat he produced an old piece of blanket; he placed it on Debs's lap. Inside the blanket was the tiniest of tiny lambs.

'Aah!' said Debs.

'He's been born a bit too soon. He needs a bit of looking after,' said old man Wilson. 'I think you can do it,' he finished.

'Of course she can,' said Mavis. 'Now, you rub his back, Miss Debs, and get him going, and I'll find a box for him. He can sleep by the fire with our Jip.'

'Aah,' said Debs, stroking the half awake, half asleep, little beauty.

'Don't be afraid to rub him a bit harder, you won't hurt him,' said old Ab. 'He needs to wake up!'

Carrie was glowing. She glowed at old man Wilson, the all-seeing, all knowing, the definitely very clever man who was backing out of the kitchen door, his work done.

'Something for her to love. Thank you, you're wonderful...'

'Carrie, I think you've got work to do! The cold is back. We're struggling to get water to the cattle; there's pipes to be thawed out.'

'There's no cold here! I'm not cold. This is the warmest place on earth!'

'Yes, I'm on my way. I'll find Jon.'

'No need for that. I'm sure you can remember how to break the ice on your own. Some hot water is all the heat you'll need.'

Debs the all-seeing, all knowing, glowed at Carrie.

'Lighten up, you silly old mare! You're so transparent. Go and find him, Carrie! He's wonderful.'

———◆———

Jon might be wonderful, but Carrie couldn't find him anywhere. Old man Wilson gave her a hammer, a chisel and a big, old, tin jug full of boiling water.

'Start with the sheds under the barn and work your way back to the cowsheds.'

Carrie knew better than to ask what Jon was doing. She set off happily with her tools; it felt great to be trusted to get on with things. She was a real farmer now, even it if was just thawing out a few pipes and water troughs.

'How hard can it be? And I'll soon find him, anyway.'

Thawing out the pipes turned out to be a very hard and unpleasant job. It was a soaking wet, swearing, job. She'd reached the small calf shed before he found her.

'H..here, let m..me w..warm you up!' he said, pressing himself into her from behind.

He put his arms around her and rested his big warm hands on her tiny frozen ones. Carrie looked down at his hands.

'Back off Jed,' she snapped.

There was no Jip. She gripped the chisel tight in her hand. Jed must have either seen or felt her tense up with it because he let her go.

'Alright, darlin', I was only trying to help. Those hands of yours look really painful, but that's fine by me, it makes less work for me while you're playing 'busy bee.' You know, I'm surprised at you, Carrie. You could be having such a great life and yet you choose to put yourself through all this hard slog every weekend. Who are you trying to please? And why? You're just like that friend of yours - except your bruises are on the inside.'

'Deep down, you're just a coward, aren't you?' said Carrie, pointing her chisel at him and trying not to shake.

He'd stung her. Until he'd turned up she hadn't felt the cold. Her hands were so cold now that they could barely hold the chisel; at the same time they were on fire. She was determined not to let Jed get to her, not to let him see her pain.

'I'd rather be a coward than a doormat,' said Jed.

Carrie smiled her best smile at him:

'You're jealous, aren't you? You make out you don't want to work on the farm and yet you do, really. You don't like me being here at weekends, taking the work that you'd normally get to do, taking away your chance to complain about how you're so hard done to.'

Carrie must have been affected by Debs this morning, because she suddenly found herself in bulldozer mode, all-seeing and all knowing:

'And you're afraid! You're afraid that you're losing your stake in the farm, that Jon is taking over. That's what you're about, Jed Wilson -

money. Greed and selfishness, powered by a love of money above all else. That's why you've been at me all this time! You're jealous of Jon, and you don't want him to have anything you've not got. You might look just like him, sound like him, walk like him, but you're just a weak, cowardly bully inside! You're less than half the man he is and everybody knows it, including you!'

Jed grinned at Carrie with all his beautiful white teeth:

'Well, darlin', if that's the case, why don't I bully you up against this wall?'

Jed started to undo the buckle on his trouser belt; he was blocking the doorway.

'Let go your chisel, Carrie. You're delirious with cold; I'm going to have to warm you up, for your own good.'

Jed started walking towards her:

'And I'll warm you up if you take one step closer!' threatened Carrie, brandishing the tin jug of boiling water.

Jed couldn't see that there was actually very little water left in it, but there was an impressive amount of steam coming out of the top of it.

'Do you want more scars down there, than you've already got?'

'I wonder if Jon knows what a bitch he's got on his hands. Perhaps I should tell him about how you've begged me to warm you up this morning, tell him exactly where you wanted to put your hands!'

'You're sick,' said Carrie, making ready to swing her jug of boiling water at him.

'And you're not worth bothering about! You're a pale, skinny little stick insect. I'd split you open and be done with you in less than five minutes! Where's the pleasure or the fun in that? At least your friend's got something worth grabbing hold of. I bet she's a right little 'goer.' Pity she's gone a bit too far this time! She'll probably never be any good again.'

Jed fastened his belt buckle and turned to go:

'It's a shame,' he said as he stooped to go through the low, calf shed door, 'I'd give her a ride on my tractor any day!'

Carrie couldn't feel her hands but her arms were still working. She swung the arm holding the tin jug with as much speed as she could muster and threw the jug and its contents at Jed. She missed and hit the doorframe. Jed laughed and sauntered away. Carrie picked up the old tin jug and leaned against the doorframe; both she and the jug were empty and dented. She couldn't get Jed's cruel words out of her head:

'You're just like that friend of yours - except your bruises are on the inside.'

Her bruises were so deep inside her at that moment that she couldn't reach to rub them better herself; she needed someone to help soothe them.

———————◆———————

She found him in the milking parlour, just finishing off the last cows of the morning. She leant against the doorframe and watched him. He was down in the milking pit, busily cleaning the cows' udders. When he got to the end of the row he saw her legs. He smiled up at her, which was a new and instantly warming experience as he usually towered above her by quite some way, so that she got neck ache whenever she was near him. She got lots of other aches as well, and they all started up again now.

He held out a hand to her to invite her down into the pit.

'H..here, let m..me w..warm you up!' he said, closing his big, warm hands around her frozen ones.

Carrie let out an enormous shiver at his words that sounded exactly like Jed's terrifying impersonation of only minutes ago.

'You're so c..cold!' he said. 'Here!'

Jon took her hands and placed them on the nearest cow's udder; then he placed his own hands over hers and held them there. Carrie could feel the warm sack of milk throbbing and pulsing under her hands as the milking machine rhythmically sucked away at the milk, like a very hungry baby. A fine layer of hairs covered the cow's udder, making it as soft as silk. Jon stood behind her. Carrie kept her eyes focussed on his big, warm hands and let her body fall back against his. His arms wrapped around her and he breathed warm air into her ear.

Carrie said nothing; she glanced across at the empty, dented jug that she'd left in the doorway. She felt sorry for the jug for she was filled to the brim and overflowing now with warmth as intense as the hottest boiling water, and all her dents and bruises were melting away. She felt shooting pains in her breasts:

'I need you to put your hands on me, like this! Do you feel as erotic as this every time you milk a cow?'

Carrie twisted her neck and turned to look up at him; how she longed to ask him.

'W..what?' he said.

'Nothing,' said Carrie. 'Thanks for warming me up!'

Jon leaned forward and kissed her on the lips.

'I've g..got to see to the c..cows.'

Like a newly thawed out frozen pipe, Carrie's juices were flowing; she was on fire and didn't want her erotic moment to end:

'Can I have a go at milking?'

'Yes, if you w..want to.'

They were so busy with the 'milking lesson' that they didn't notice Jip edge himself into the parlour and sit just inside the door. He knew he wasn't allowed in here, but the footsteps approaching the door left him no other option.

'Hey 'J'!' called Jed, 'you'll never guess what your Carrie just asked me to do!'

Jed appeared in the doorway:

'Oh, I see she's already got you doing it as well! Glad to see your hands are nice and warmed up now, darlin'!'

Jed laughed a dirty laugh, trod on Jip's tail, and disappeared as fast as he'd arrived. Jip was in pain; he had no other option but to let out a yelp. His ears hung low. He knew he wasn't supposed to be in there in the first place, let alone upset the cows with a yelp like that. But all he got by way of punishment were two, very warm hands, holding him, stroking him, soothing his bruises.

'Come on, Jip, why don't you come and feed the calves with me!' said Carrie, picking up the empty tin jug that Jed had knocked over.

'G..good idea,' said Jon. 'Jip, g..go with Carrie!'

Jip wagged his tail at Carrie. Carrie set off happily with Jip; it felt great to be trusted with his dog. She'd just had a first go at milking a cow as well. She was a real farmer now. And Jed Wilson would just have to get used to it.

———◆———

'By heck, Carrie, I knew we'd make a farmer of you, the moment I set eyes on you! Come and have a cup of tea. I'm right proud of you!'

Carrie had just told Mavis what had happened in the milking parlour; but not everything.

'Thanks, Mavis. Where's Debs?'

'Gone for a lie down. He knocked her about good and proper, the swine. It'll take her a while to get over it, you know.'

Carrie nodded agreement.

'I'd wring his sorry neck if I got hold of him! Here's your tea, Carrie, love.'

'Do you think Mr Wilson minds her staying here this long? I know it's putting you all to a lot of trouble.'

'Mind? Of course he doesn't mind! None of us do!'

'Jed minds!'

'Carrie, love, you've brought nothing but good to this house and that includes Miss Debs. Can't you see? She's a light for his eyes! Something for him to love better. She's his little lamb!' said Mavis, pointing to Debs' little lamb that was fast asleep in his box by the fire.

'But he loves you, doesn't he?'

Carrie squirmed. Her mouth had blurted out her words before her mind had had time to think about what she was saying. Mavis didn't do feelings and emotions. Mavis sat very still and watched 'Boxer' the lamb sleeping peacefully with his little chin resting on the edge of his box. Debs had chosen his name because of his box.

'I'm sorry, Mavis, I didn't mean to pry. I just assumed you and he were...you know...Debs sleeps in his room...I'm sorry if I've upset you, Mavis.'

Mavis waved her hand at Carrie as if she was giving her a dust and polish with one of her magic dusters. The strong, magnifying effect of her large plastic glasses left Carrie nowhere to look but straight back at the extra large, all-seeing, all knowing pair of blue eyes that answered her.

'He's been good to me. Look at me, Carrie. Who'd have wanted me? I knew he belonged to her. She were my cousin, you know. When she died, I helped him with the lads. They were right little. Lost without their mother, they were. Yes, he belonged to her. Always would do. Always will do. As time went on...well...he's a passionate man, Carrie. He had needs....And I, well, you know how it is, Carrie, love...'

Mavis' face almost opened up to let out a cackle; the extra large eyes gave a smile:

'Underneath me whiskers and me frump, I'm still a woman the same as any other woman. Don't judge him, Carrie. Love him.'

'No I don't, I mean, yes I do, but not like that...'

Carrie shrivelled. The all-seeing, all knowing, large eyed Mavis hadn't finished:

'And you belong to Jon!'

Carrie squirmed. Mavis didn't do emotions and feelings; she was happy to blurt and pry.

'I've seen it. We all have - except him, of course. But give him time, Carrie. He'll come to it one of these days. He had a poor start in life, you know, losing his mother like that. It changed him. Now you're changing him back.'

Carrie had such a lump in her throat that she couldn't swallow her tea. It was her turn to sit very still and watch Boxer the lamb; he was starting to wake up.

'He's waking up, he'll need feeding,' said all-seeing, all knowing Carrie. 'I'll get Debs. She'll want to feed him herself.'

Carrie jumped up out of her chair and headed in the direction of the stairs to fetch Debs.

'Ah she will. I'll make up a bottle for him,' said Mavis.

I don't do emotions and feelings; I'm a Mavis, now.'

Monday 8th January

Once upon a time Carrie used to be conscientious. Maybe she still was, deep down inside, but she kept it very deep and down when it came to turning up on time for work these days. She had fine-tuned her routine so that she arrived for the start of her working day with only seconds to spare rather than the enthusiastic hour she used to give to the office every morning when she began with her journalistic ambitions.

This Monday morning she rushed in to her desk as usual, throwing off her coat onto the back of her dreaded, tweed padded, chair and then on to the coffee machine queue before she noticed that the office was quieter than usual. It was quieter because most of the staff were already gathering in conference room one. There was no queue at the coffee machine, either.

'Staff meeting, I bet the big fish is back.'

The 'String' idiot from the office Christmas party had just finished putting sugar in his coffee. He was wearing a new pair of cheap, leather, shoes.

'He must be an apprentice from the printing room.'

In fact, conference room one was filling with all sorts of people that Carrie had never seen before; it must be an important meeting.

'Hurry up, 'String' idiot, I need my coffee.'

'What's going on this morning?' Carrie asked him as he turned to walk past her.

'What planet do you live on!' said 'String'. 'Haven't you heard? The old Pike has been found dead at home. Committed suicide is the formal line, but that's only the half of it!' he grinned. 'This is going to be the story of the year! Typical of him, the great big show off! I don't expect he expected to show off quite as much of himself as he did, *and* give his precious paper the best story and boost of sales it's ever had, *and* all at his expense. Hurry up or you'll miss the meeting! Dennis is in charge now. It's bloody hilarious, isn't it?'

Carrie found the news so hilarious that she spilt her coffee that she'd been quietly pouring whilst 'String' had been talking all over his new, cheap, shoes.

'Ow! You idiot! You've burnt me foot!' he hopped.

He began, once more, to do a very silly dance in the middle of the corridor.

'Déjà vu.'

'Excuse me,' said Carrie, pushing past 'String' who was twirling faster and faster, trying to rip his shoes off his burning feet, 'I feel sick.'

Carrie was in such a hurry to get to the toilets that she spilt the rest of her coffee down his back.

'Ouch, you bloody idiot!' he shouted.

Nobody laughed at this party trick because they were all too busy waiting for Dennis in conference room one. He would be unlikely to start the meeting with 'Three cheers for Mr Pike!' Everybody liked Dennis; he was a good sort.

'Well he just might, knowing Dennis' sense of humour.'

Meeting or no, Carrie needed to be alone. She really thought she was going to be sick. She locked herself in her favourite toilet cubicle. She leant over the toilet but nothing would come so she sat down on the seat instead. She stared at the beige painted toilet door. She examined every brush stroke of paint; up and down and up and down went her eyes over every inch of the door as if she'd just painted it herself and was checking for any gaps that she'd missed.

'Come on, Carrie! Pull yourself together. The one thing you can't miss is this meeting. Get up! Now! You don't do emotions and feelings, remember? You're a journalist, that's what he was helping you to be, so get in there and be it. For him.'

Carrie left her favourite toilet cubicle, took plenty of time to wash and dry her hands, and walked, as slowly and elegantly as she could, especially as she passed 'Rosalind the Rottweiler' who was sitting on the front row by the door, clutching an embroidered handkerchief to her face, into conference room one. She even found a spare seat at the grey window side of the room. It was a brilliantly sunny winter morning. She let the plastic veneer on the desk top warm her hands. It wasn't quite the same as a cow's udder but it would have to do. She held a pencil in one hand and a notebook in the other; it stopped them shaking. She was a real journalist this morning; she would just have to get used to it.

Dennis the editor walked in to the breathing silence of conference room one. It was very comforting that his gentle, Irish drawl was the only sound that broke the roar that was on the other side of the silence in Carrie's head.

'Good morning to you all, and thanks for coming to the meeting,' began Dennis. 'It's my sad duty to inform you of the sudden death of Mr Charles Pike, our respected editor-in-chief, and owner of this newspaper. We all know that Mr Pike was a truly unique man...'

'In truth, he looked more like a trout than a pike...'

'...and because we remember his familiar words from the end of every speech that he ever made, 'we may be small, but we are a newspaper of quality, integrity, and the backbone of our community...'

'Boom, bubble, boom...'

'...I'm going to tell you all the truth about what's happened to Mr Pike...'

Mr Pike slithered into view.

'Isn't our newspaper all about seeking out the truth? We don't invent the news to suit ourselves here, do we, Mr Pike?'

'We most certainly do not...'

'You will remember that Mr Pike's elderly mother died at Christmas. This lady had been the one consistent thread in his life. Now Mr Pike was a very private man...'

'I understand the need for privacy now and then, Carrie.'

'...and nobody knew, beneath all the 'boom' and bravado, just how difficult and lonely his life had become.'

The big fish swam away.

Dennis, being a bushy moustached Irishman, and editor-in-chief, who knew a thing or two about how to tell a story, paused, breathed in the silence before continuing.

'I knew! Is he waiting for me to confess?'

'We all know that Mr Pike was a very kind and generous man...'

'Yes indeed, I am a very kind and generous man...'

'...and so the tragic seeds of circumstance were sown that have led to his unnatural and untimely death...'

The silence roared a little louder.

'The world can be a cruel place, Carrie...'

'...and so he was drawn into a secret, sad, world, taking comfort in the company of women of questionable morals...'

'It's not easy having to live a double life, being surrounded by people who don't understand you. Bearing your affliction, living with the guilt...'

'...dangerous practices...'

'Friends are always welcome, especially when you don't get to see them very often, eh?'

'....asphyxiation...'

'I don't understand it. They make a fuss of me, I try to be kind back to them - a lot of them are lonely, you know - and then they turn on me! What do you make of that?'

'...sex game gone wrong...'

'I didn't mean any harm...'

'...accidental death...'

'I would never ever hurt you. I am just so very very fond of you. You have always been so very very kind to me. You have no idea how much your kindness has meant to me, what you've done for me. I just wanted to express my affection for you and I have overstepped the mark. I didn't realise what I was doing, I got carried away...'

'...investigation by the police....they'll be coming into the office...'

'Please accept my most humble apology...I value your friendship and hope I haven't spoilt it. Please forgive me.'

'I forgive you, Mr Pike.'

'Will you shake my hand?'

'I don't want to.'

'...out of respect to him...this truth will remain forever, confidential, within these four walls. Any member of staff who discloses this information will be dismissed immediately. This paper is going to keep its integrity to the last. We are *not* going to report any of this in our paper. We are going to lie like we've never lied before. Anyone who can't agree to these terms can leave now.'

Dennis paused once more to check that the silence was still intact; it was. It was booming.

'He's a very lucky man. My advice to you, Carrie dear, is to enjoy the pleasure of being alive. Don't hide from it. Promise me that, Carrie...'

'Goodbye...'

'Please stand for a minute's silence in remembrance...'

He still looked more like a trout than a pike.

'Three cheers for Mr Pike!'

The silence finally broke as everyone gave three cheers for Mr Pike, in an Irish accent, of course. Why pass up an opportunity to mock an Irishman if you got the chance. Dennis smiled and told everyone:

'We may be small, but we are a newspaper of quality, integrity, and the backbone of our community', so go, and get on with it!'

Everybody liked Dennis; he was a good sort.

Carrie took a deep breath and seized her moment. Swift as a silver minnow, she slid past Dennis the editor and kept swimming, deep into the office pond. She hid there for the rest of the day. The big fish was gone forever. He'd finally been caught. Caught out.

'Now you must chase after your dream, Carrie, and don't stop till you've caught it. You'll always be surrounded by folk who don't understand; don't mind them, you just keep going...'

He'd been gutted, stuffed, seasoned and hung up to dry; after all that, still nobody wanted him. The tweed padding on her office chair dug into the backs of her legs, reminding her that she was a journalist; she didn't do emotions and feelings.

'Here comes the swim bladder:

'Now, you're going to write for me the best article that you've ever written. Set this paper on fire! I want to be swamped with letters of congratulations from our readers about our 'Twentieth Century Land Girl!' Now, go to it!'

'Thank you, Mr. Pike, I'll do my best...I'll always do my best.'

Carrie put pen to paper and the big fish swam away.

Friday 12th January

Dear Reader,

It's the beginning of the New Year; time to make those New Year resolutions! To plan; to look forward. January was established as the first month of the year by the Roman calendar. It was named after the God 'Janus' which is the Latin word for 'door.'

Janus has two faces which allow him to look both backwards into the old year and forwards into the new one at the same time. But he's not two faced; he's not a hypocrite. He hides neither face but, just like us, he can choose to look forwards or backwards.

Janus represented the 'spirit of opening.' How many times have you heard the phrase 'when one door closes another one opens' or 'if you push against enough doors, eventually one will open for you?'

We all know that an open door is much more healthy than a closed one. It allows a free flow of air around us that keeps us healthy and feeling well; it gives light. Keep your doors and windows closed and the air stagnates, damp and mould eventually set in, and dis-ease follows in the darkness that it brings.

So at the start of this New Year, which face will you choose to wear? Are you brave enough to wear both? Bad things are happening all the time. Truth can be a very difficult thing to face up to, but there can be no peace of mind without it. And you can never tell how soon it might be too late for you to do so. What about those New Year resolutions then, Reader?

What has all this got to do with a 'Twentieth Century Land Girl', I hear you cry! Here is your answer. The man who gave me the chance to write these articles for you, Mr Charles Pike, our beloved owner of this newspaper, is lost to us, suddenly taken away by a broken heart in the wake of his own mother's passing. He was brave. He was brave enough to have faith in me when I didn't really believe in myself. He was brave enough to face up to the sadness and difficulties of his own life.

How many of us are brave enough to do that? How many times do we hide behind our faces? Keep our doors closed? Locked, even.

Mr Pike was an encourager. He encouraged me to live life to the full. He believed in quality and integrity and encouraged us all, here at our paper, to do the best job that we could whatever we were doing; to support each other and serve our community. Put simply, he cared.

'Life is a quality rather than a quantity and can't be measured by time alone; our years, months, hours and minutes mean nothing on their own. Some moments may only last for seconds but the memory of them is so powerful that they live on in us forever. Over and over again, we can feel the joy of them.' [†]

Down on the farm I've just had my first try at milking a cow; my first touch of a silky, warm, cow's udder; that is one such moment for me. During the slog of daily life, whether it's thawing out frozen pipes so that the animals can get drinking water, sitting on the tweed of an office chair, or working at a machine, we can experience a new great moment or re-live an old one.

Another word for memory is remembrance, another word for remembrance is celebration, and another word for celebration is thanksgiving. So keep your doors open, Reader, your forward and backwards faces, too. Keep the 'spirit of opening' in your hearts. You just don't know who or what's going to come along your way next.

In Memoriam
Mr Charles Pike
(1918 - 1979)

Saturday 3rd February

Boxer the lamb was asleep by the fire. So was Debs. She was sitting, as usual, in old man Wilson's chair; Boxer was curled up, as usual, on her lap. He was lovely and warm. So was Debs. Even though she was, to all intents and purposes, fast asleep, her hand was awake enough to keep stroking the silken wool jacket of Boxer's rising and falling little ribcage. The clinking sound of tea cups on the kitchen table gave her a gentle 'wake up' call.

'The lads'll be in for tea in a minute,' said Mavis, now clunking plates of cakes onto the table.

Debs straightened herself up in her chair. She was looking forwards to a catch up with Carrie; she'd missed her first thing that morning. Carrie was now officially one of 'the lads' as Mavis called them. She'd got so used to Carrie being there at weekends, working out on the farm, coming in mucky and cold like the men, that she no longer needed to say 'Carrie, love' any more, except to her face. Of course, Carrie wasn't supposed to know that Mavis now rated her as a real man, but Debs, being Debs, couldn't keep a secret like that from her friend.

'Hello!' called Carrie as she burst in through the kitchen door bringing a blast of cold air with her.

She was closely followed by three pairs of heavy boots owned by Jon, Jed and their father. For some reason that no one could fathom, Jed had suddenly developed a healthy interest in farming after spending a lifetime complaining about it and trying to get away from it. And now Carrie was having to spend all her time trying to get away from Jed; it was difficult to get time alone with Jon and even when she did, she'd always got one eye on the nearest corner, expecting to see Jed's leering face and hear his leering voice. Jon loved his brother's new found affection for the farm; Carrie hated him for it; old man Wilson said nothing.

'He's t..turned a c..corner,' said Jon.

'You can't trust him,' said Carrie.

'I'm starving!' said Jed, rushing to the kitchen table.

Jed had spoken for them all. Much as Carrie would have loved to have stayed outside with Jon a bit longer, leaving Jed to come in and stuff his face with cakes, it was a bitterly cold day. There was snow and ice and a razor sharp wind outside; the ground was frozen solid. They all needed cake.

'How are ya?' said old man Wilson, gently touching Debs on the top of her head with his hand as he walked past her to the kitchen table.

'Fine!' glowed Debs.

She had never shied away from his hands the entire time she'd been staying at the farm.

'*Strange,*' thought Carrie, '*she wouldn't stand that from anyone else. There's something magic about that man.*'

There was nothing magic about Jed who watched his father and then smirked across the table at Carrie, reaching out, very obviously, to grab two coconut macaroons, one in each hand, as he licked his lips.

'*You disgusting bastard, I hope you choke on them.*'

There was a little silence as everyone tucked into their tea and cakes. Boxer stayed fast asleep with his little chin resting over the edge of Debs' knees. All of a sudden Debs cried out:

'No!'

Tears formed in her eyes.

'I think he's going to stay asleep now.'

Everybody stopped eating mid cake. Boxer's little silken jacket had stopped breathing.

'He's just been born too soon,' said old man Wilson. 'At least he's had a bit of life. He's tried his best.'

'Ah, don't fret, love. He's been loved and warm by the fire, hasn't he?' said Mavis, kindly.

Debs let her tears fall on him in answer.

'I'll nip him down to the muck spreader then,' volunteered Jed.

Everybody ignored Jed. Debs stroked Boxer one last time before lifting her hands away to let old man Wilson pick him up. Despite the fact that he'd had almost a month of life he was still so tiny that he almost totally fitted inside the bony outstretched fingers of the one farmer's hand. Old man Wilson made for the door.

'I'll take him,' said Carrie, without thinking about it. 'I'll bury him.'

'The ground's too hard!' laughed Jed, sliding back in his chair to show Carrie his open groin.

'I shall pour hot water on the ground first,' she said defiantly. 'That does the trick just fine, every time, doesn't it, Jed?' said Carrie, as icily as possible.

For a moment of unknown length everybody in the kitchen froze, caught and held by Carrie's tone of voice. Then Jon scraped his chair back.

'I'll g..give you a h..hand,' he said.

'I'm so sorry, Debs. I'll look after him for you, I promise,' whispered

Carrie, as she took Boxer from old man Wilson.

She cradled him in her arms like a baby. Boxer left the warmth of the kitchen just as he'd arrived, wrapped up inside his piece of old blanket, inside the folds of a coat. As Carrie walked through the door, followed by Jon, who was carrying his box, there was nothing to prove that he'd ever existed at all, except the still warm imprint that he'd left on the blanket on Debs's lap and her quiet tears, shed in his memory.

Jed got up as if to follow them but stopped in the doorway.

'What a pair!' he smirked. 'The ice maiden and her lap-dog. Since when did we all get sentimental about animals round here?'

'You hush your mouth Jed Wilson, or I'll wash it out with soap,' threatened Mavis. 'There's nowt sentimental about being kind to animals, and don't you forget it!' she finished. 'And shut that door, you're letting all the cold in!'

Jed shrugged and shut the kitchen door.

'If you say so, Mrs Mavis. Anyway, I'm off up for a sleep cos' I'm out tonight.'

'You'll finish feeding the livestock under the barn first,' said old man Wilson.

'What?!' said Jed, turning back from the passageway to the stairs. 'Jon can do that, he's not going anywhere.'

'All the more reason for you to pull your weight around here. If you want back on this farm, then work on this farm. Jon does the milking twice a day, every day, and more besides.'

'You know I don't like cows. I'm a machinery man. I deal with all the tackle, always have done. That's fair, I say.'

'I'll be the judge of that,' said old man Wilson quietly. 'And I say, feed the livestock. You can do it with or without my boot up your backside. You're not so big or so clever that I can't give you a good hiding if need be.'

Mavis dropped the cups noisily into the kitchen sink. Debs disappeared inside the folds of the old knitted blanket on old man Wilson's favourite armchair. Jed strode across the kitchen. He walked at his father who was still sitting at the kitchen table next to the empty cake plate.

'Oh yeah? I'd like to see you try!' sneered Jed.

Old man Wilson stood up to his full height at a speed equal to or greater than Jed's strides. If Mavis' silver Christmas star had still been hanging above the kitchen table he'd have banged his head on the light of the world.

He was taller than his son, who was caught off guard by the sudden force of his straightening. Jed had to step onto his back foot to keep his balance.

'While you live under this roof, you will show respect to the ladies here present, respect to me, to your brother, to Carrie and to every creature and blade of grass on this farm. I've been watching you a long time, Jed Wilson. I don't like what I see. Buck your ideas up, or you're out of here. I'm not fooled by a few weekend's worth of you wanting to help out. I know what your game is.'

Still Jed pushed.

'And what's that, then?'

'There's ladies present, or I should tell you plain. Now, you will apologise to Mavis and Debs for your disrespectful words, and then you'll finish feeding the livestock.'

Old man Wilson spoke so quietly that Debs and Mavis could barely hear what he said to Jed as they faced each other down at the kitchen table; both were in no doubt as to the thunder and lightning that his words contained for Jed's face twisted through several different expressions before he finally spoke:

'I'm sorry, Mavis and Debs, if I've offended or upset you.'

'Oh Jed, you silly lad!' Mavis started to say, but Jed was already making for the door with his tail between his legs.

His father strode behind him and made sure that he left at speed with his magic hands that moved his son without touching him, and shut the door on him as he left the warmth of the kitchen. Jed muttered underneath his breath as he passed Debs:

'One day...he'll see...pay... 'J' too...'

Old man Wilson turned back to the warmth of the kitchen. He sighed. His shoulders dropped a little, and he rested one bony hand on the back of Debs' chair. She looked up at him. He looked so very sad; she tried to smile up some reassurance to him.

'I'm sorry about that, ladies,' he said. 'I'm not a violent man, but sometimes, it's the only way to deal with some folk. I've gone wrong somewhere with him and now I must try to put it right.'

Debs reached up to the cold, bony, hand that was resting above her head.

'Don't worry, Mr Wilson,' she said, 'it's not your fault. He's a grown up, but he just needs to grow up a bit more, and I'm sure he will do. You're not responsible for his choices, anyway. Look at Joe and me...'

Debs paused for a moment. It was the first time she'd spoken her husband's name since the night of the attack.

'I used to think it was all my fault...but it wasn't true...' Debs paused again; her tears were still mostly for Boxer.

Mavis helped her out:

'Ah, don't fret, Ezra, he'll be right!'

Old man Wilson looked through the kitchen window. It was a bitterly cold day. There was snow and ice and a razor sharp wind outside; the ground was frozen solid. He wondered how Carrie was getting on with Boxer the lamb; there was no way she'd actually be able to bury him in this weather; Jon would put her straight.

———————◆———————

Carrie didn't need Jon to tell her what to do. Boxer's little body had been lovingly laid to rest in the muck spreader. Carrie and Jon had grabbed a few minutes privacy in the calf shed, long enough to make it look like they'd had a hell of a job digging a hole. They'd been lying together on the corn sacks in the corner of the shed.

They sat up now. There was nothing to prove that they'd been there at all, except the still warm imprint that their bodies had left on the sacks and the considerably warmer memory inside both their heads of the moment they'd just grabbed. Carrie pulled her jumpers down and tucked herself back in. Jon's hands had been so cold she'd been pleased to be able to do for him what he'd done for her last weekend. He'd been alarmed at first.

She'd taken his hands and held them there. She'd held him there until the throbbing and pulsing in her breasts became so overpowering that he continued the rhythm himself. He had big hands. She wrapped her arms around his neck and breathed warm air into his ear. She could feel the softness of the fine layer of hairs on the back of his neck; her own were standing on end. Carrie stood herself up by reaching for his nearest shoulder. She turned to face him and he put his arms around her body and pulled her to him. Just like Boxer the lamb on Debs' lap, his chin found a cosy resting place in between her breasts.

'W..what?' he said.

'Nothing,' said Carrie. 'Thank you for warming me up!'

Jon straightened up to his full height, leaned forward, and kissed her on the lips.

'D..don't say that. Thank y..you!'

The shadow of a muttering man sloped past the fogged up window of the calf shed.

'...bastards...all of 'em...plague on his house...wretched farm...that bitch....once and for all...'

Carrie and Jon froze until the dark shadow had passed. She was heartbroken. She didn't want their moment to end, especially not with a dark reminder of Jed's presence.

'Did you hear that?' whispered Carrie. 'He frightens me sometimes.'

'He's all t..talk. The old man's probably making him d..do the livestock, that's all. He'll be b..better when he's b..been out t..tonight.'

'You don't know him like you think you do,' said Carrie.

Jon shrugged his shoulders and opened the shed door.

'C..come on. You think t..too much!'

The moment was complete and at an end; Jon was striding away. The joy was to be stored now and re-lived throughout the rest of the day.

'I must go back and tell Debs about Boxer.'

'I'll g..give Jed a hand.'

'O.K.'

Carrie walked back towards the farmhouse.

'No, it's not O.K. Don't give Jed a hand. He'd happily cut yours off and more besides, if he could. Why can't you see that? I've been wrong not to tell him the truth about Jed, and now I must try to put it right. I need to see Debs. I need to see Debs anyway. She'll probably tell me not to worry...'

It was a bitterly cold day. There was snow and ice and a razor sharp wind; the ground was frozen solid. She wondered how she was going to lie successfully to Debs and Mavis about Boxer the lamb.

'I probably don't need to worry. I probably don't need to say anything. Debs knows. Jon knows too...'

Monday 5th February

Carrie and her work colleagues heard shouting coming from Mr Pike's office. Dennis had moved in there last week. He'd inherited the job of proprietor and editor-in-chief, so it seemed quite normal to everyone that he should also inherit Mr Pike's large, mahogany wooden desk and all the trappings that came with the big fish's office now that he was, in effect, the new 'big fish'. Normal to everyone except 'Rosalind the Rottweiler'. She'd lost both her bark and her bite when she found out that Dennis was taking over. The handkerchief of grief that she'd been clutching to her face had temporarily disguised the real source of her distress; for some reason she really believed that she was going to inherit the earth.

She might not actually have managed to become Mrs Pike but, as far as she was concerned, that was just a formality. It was obvious common sense that she should take over after everything she'd done for him, wasn't it?

Obvious to no one except her own imagination. And now that imagination had had a whole weekend to stir and stew so that by Monday morning it was bubbling and boiling over the edges of reason. Dennis was a very laid back, bushy moustached Irishman, who never raised his voice unless it was to 'give three cheers' or 'tell a tale or two'. But he was raising it now, very loudly.

'Clear your desk immediately...Don't argue with me, Missy...He's dead and gone...Services no longer needed...Redundancy package...Newspaper of quality and integrity...No room for gold diggers here. Be gone with you...Call security? Sue me? Unfair dismissal? Go ahead! Written here in black and white...a message from the grave...wise to you...Good day to you, Mrs Greenacre.'

There was a loud bang. It wasn't a gunshot, but it was so sharp that it could have been. Carrie and her colleagues froze, suddenly anxious to hear some reassurance that it was indeed a door slamming and not a bullet being fired after all. They'd just lost one boss in unusual circumstances and they didn't want to lose another. It would look bad.

They didn't want the finger of suspicion pointing at themselves. They were all writers, they all had healthy imaginations. The police were already in the office probing and prying into every aspect of Mr Pike's life. They were all jumpy as it was, staring at each other and wondering how many skeletons were hiding in each other's cupboards; it had become a bit of a macabre game. What used to be a friendly jibe and a joke was turning into an inquisition. Nobody really knew and, of course, everybody likes to know, or think that they know.

'We are a newspaper of quality, integrity, and the backbone of our community...'

Mr Pike haunted them all as they worked. Their backbone was dislocated by current events and it was very painful. There was great relief, therefore, when the sound of fast moving, sharp heels ricocheted around the corner. 'Rosalind the Rottweiler' appeared at speed, clutching her handbag and coat; there was not a handkerchief in sight. Somebody somewhere started slowly clapping. Other hands joined together so that, by the time Rosalind had reached the stairwell, her heels were lost in a volley of machine gun hands.

She turned to see everybody on their feet, clapping and cheering her. It was tumultuous applause. 'Rosalind the Rottweiler' was overwhelmed. She'd always had the feeling that she was disliked by the staff; frankly, she didn't blame them. She'd been tough on their expenses claims, holiday requests, sick leave. She'd made their lives a misery, but she'd saved Mr Pike a lot of money. As it turned out, he hadn't appreciated it, or her, at all. So it was a great crumb of comfort that the staff clearly did so. All except Carrie Langford.

As Rosalind bared all her teeth to bask in the respect and affection of her now former work colleagues, she sent one last gnash of her smiling teeth in Carrie's direction. Carrie stood, silently, in the middle of the office floor, with her arms quietly folded.

'Bitch!' gnashed Rosalind.

Just then, Dennis appeared. Showing no signs of a gunshot wound, he smiled across the office at Carrie. Carrie smiled back. Then she turned her smile on 'Rosalind the Rottweiler.'

'You've been neutered!'

Rosalind froze. A dark shadow passed over her face as she realised that the tumultuous applause was not a fond farewell full of love and appreciation. She turned away and disappeared down the stairwell with her tail between her legs.

'Bet that handkerchief will be out by the time she reaches the bottom of the stairs,' said Carrie to Dennis, as the office settled down, calmed by his lovely lilting presence. 'You've made yourself an enemy there,' she continued. 'She'll bad mouth us for all she's worth.'

Dennis laughed out loud. He boomed, so that everyone could hear him:

'Don't ever forget, we're a newspaper of quality, integrity, and the backbone of our community!'

He winked at Carrie.

'Shall you just walk back with me to me office, Carrie. There's a young policeman needs to have a word with you.'

'What about?' asked Carrie, trying not to sound anxious or look guilty, sensing the relieved 'great, it's her not me,' faces around her.

'You knew Mr Pike a bit better than the rest of us, didn't you now?'

Somebody somewhere sniggered. Carrie wanted to shrivel up and die, but she managed a decent enough reply:

'Well yes, I suppose he came to my mother's social do's, and he encouraged me with my writing.'

Somebody somewhere choked on a guffaw; it turned into a snotty snort instead. Dennis swung his arm around Carrie's shoulders and steered her around the corner of the corridor and into his office. Dennis was a good sort. She felt so protected and safe she wanted to climb inside his sweaty armpit and stay there. Instead, Dennis released his arm, catapulting her into his office where Mr Pike's mahogany wooden desk and the clean cut, young police officer were both waiting for her.

'I'm glad that desk can't talk...'

The desk and the young officer were standing in the middle of the room, straight, square and neat. The desk looked the more comfortable of the two, being in the company of a pair of pin stripe suited legs, albeit much slimmer ones than it had formerly been used to accommodating.

'Miss Carrie Langford,' drawled Dennis, closing the door behind him.

'Please have a seat, Miss Langford, this won't take a minute,' said the young officer, sitting himself down in the more than ample imprint in the leather of Mr Pike's chair on the other side of the desk.

'I want to disappear and he looks like he really is disappearing.'

'My name is Detective Constable Steven Ranger...'

'I bet they call him the 'Lone Ranger' down at the station!' Carrie whispered to her side of the mahogany desk.

'...as part of our routine inquiries, to interview friends, acquaintances and beneficiaries of Mr Charles Pike. How long have you worked here at the paper, Miss Langford?'

'I came here straight from college, towards eighteen months ago now.'

'Not that long, then,' smiled the young officer.

Carrie smiled agreement and the 'Lone Ranger' wrote it down. He wrote everything down. He asked her all sorts of boring questions about her job at the paper, her hobbies and interests. It was more like a job interview than an interrogation. Carrie started to relax; she went into 'professional enthusiasm' mode.

'Ah! So you're the 'Twentieth Century Land Girl.' I've read some of your articles. They're very good, quite thought provoking at times.'

'Thank you,' said Carrie.

Will that do now? Don't you need to jump on 'Silver' and get back to Tonto at the station?'

'It's unusual to be given your own column like that after working as an office junior for such a relatively short time, isn't it?'

'Maybe,' answered Carrie, still enthusiastic. 'I had the idea originally and Mr Pike was very supportive and gave me the chance to try it. He was a great boss; he encouraged me with my writing. He knew how keen I was to get into journalism.'

'And how keen is that, Miss Langford?'

'Well, really keen. I love my job here.'

'Yes, I can see that. Did you ever meet Mr Pike socially outside of work?'

'Yes, Mr Pike was an acquaintance of my mother's; she always invited him to her social gatherings at home. She runs the 'Local Ladies Network'.

'Yes, so I've heard.'

Carrie stared across the mahogany wooden desk. Detective Constable Steven Ranger was suddenly looking bigger.

The 'Lone Ranger' wears a mask! What is this guy hiding? What is he getting at with all these questions?'

'Did you ever spend time with Mr Pike privately, apart from that?'

'No.'

'I understand you work late sometimes and are the last to go home.'

'Sometimes. That happens to all of us from time to time when there's deadlines to meet.'

'Did you ever meet with Mr Pike when you worked late?'

I feel sick. Very sick!'

'Occasionally.'

'He encouraged you, you say?'

'Yes he did. He was a very kind and generous man.'

'So I've heard. Did you encourage him back in any way, Miss Langford?'

Rosalind!'

'I beg your pardon, I don't know what you mean?' said Carrie.

'I mean,' he said, lowering his voice slightly as if he didn't want the desk to hear what he was about to say, 'that we've had reports from a fellow employee that Mr Pike treated you with favouritism above some other female members of staff and, since we're investigating the suspicious death of said Mr Pike, I need to clarify these matters. Where were you on New Year's Eve, Miss Langford?'

'Early on, I was at home with my mother. We had an intruder in the garden, and you should have a police report about that.'

'We have no record of you being there.'

'The police arrived after my mother had controlled the situation. I'd left by then to go to a party with my friends.'

'Who are your friends and where was the party?'

'Actually, it was going to be with the farmers where I do research for my articles, but they had an emergency, so we just spent the night at the farmhouse instead.'

'I'll need the name and address of the farm, please.'

'Is that really necessary? I have to keep my source material confidential you know.'

'Don't worry, it will stay confidential. It's just to confirm your whereabouts.'

'I find your line of questioning very offensive, Detective Constable Ranger.'

For the second time that morning, the staff heard shouting coming from Mr Pike's office. This time it was a woman's voice:

'The truth is, Mr Pike was a total sleaze bag! There's no point lying about it any more. Any woman who works in this office can tell you that! I've had to squeeze past him through this office doorway more times than I'd like to remember, and it was horrible! Disgusting! If I'd reported it to you, would you have done anything about it? Probably not. Would I have lost my job? Probably. Women's rights are still in the early stages of evolution, aren't they? Your ignorant line of questioning confirms that. The other truth that you need to know is that Mr Pike was a very sad and lonely man. He had an unlucky appearance. Something went wrong for him a very long time ago.

The only encouragement I gave him was to try to be kind to him and treat him with the respect that few other folk around here gave him. He warmed to me because of that. And I believe that he did genuinely want to help me, he wanted me to do well. I didn't realise until just before

Christmas just how lonely he was. Nobody cared and now it's too late. Even in death, folk still want to mock him and laugh at him. That's horrible! That's disgusting! Are you going to do anything about that? Probably not. You won't even interview them! All the ones who did nothing. You should be thanking me for trying to help him, not accusing me! Have you got any more questions, Detective Constable Ranger, because I'd like to get on with my work now, please.'

'No, thank you. That will be all for now. I'm sorry if I offended you, Miss Langford, but I have to do my job.'

'I know you do, I know you do,' Carrie told the mahogany wooden desk.

The mahogany wooden desk was the only thing standing straight, square and neat as Carrie closed the office door quietly behind her. Dennis grabbed her and hugged her and kissed her on the forehead with his big, bushy, Irish moustache.

'Don't you start!' said Carrie.

She no longer felt the need for protection from his armpits for some reason.

'I'm proud of you!' he smiled.

Somebody somewhere started slowly clapping. Other hands joined together so that, by the time Carrie reached the office floor, she was surprised to see everybody on their feet, clapping and cheering her. Carrie was overwhelmed. She sat down at her desk silently, and started work. Somebody brought her a cup of coffee, somebody bought her a tissue. Somebody patted her on the shoulder as they walked past her, and they did it more than once.

She was so keen on becoming a good journalist that she noted the exact time that the 'Lone Ranger' called out:

'Hi-Yo Silver! Away!'

He'd actually said:

'Goodbye, Miss Langford, thank you for your help with our inquiries. I look forward to reading your next article.'

Carrie was a going to be a good journalist; she had a good imagination. She worked for a newspaper of quality and integrity, and she'd just cracked its backbone back into place.

Friday 9th February

Joe had made a big mistake. He'd made several recently, so maybe tonight was not such a big deal after all. He'd just had a few too many down at the club. Pink ladies. They'd been the happy hour special. He hadn't had one for quite some time now, he was a beer man, but he was quite as capable as the next man to handle the sophistication of a lady. Besides, the cocktail glass looked pretty. Deep pink and frothy, his pork sausage fingers had difficulty grabbing its tiny waist at first. But he soon got the hang of it after a few tries. The reward for his effort was great. He drank the bitter sweetness from the ample bosom of the cocktail glass; it made him feel better much faster than beer did, and it had egg white in it so he wouldn't be hungry in the morning. It was an early breakfast. He felt great.

Friday night was music night; it was a 'Country and Western' singer tonight:

'Stand by your man....

Joe stared at his pink lady; her ample bosom beckoned to him:

'Bitch!'

The pink lady gave no reply, so he tried again.

'You didn't stand by your man, did you? Left me to cope on me own with this terrible injury. All this pain! Where've you gone? I was good to you, wasn't I? Always gave you a good time at the end of the day, didn't I? Even after you came in all mucked up from that precious garden of yours! I was going to buy you a new pink carpet with curtains to match....Bitch!'

Joe picked up his pink lady and squeezed her tight inside his sausage fingers. She couldn't take the pressure and broke in two in his hands; she ran away into the folds of the beer mat on top of the bar. Joe's hand was bleeding:

'Bitch!'

The barman gave him a final warning about his language. Friday night was music night and there were ladies present.

'I'm hurt!' cried Joe. 'She hurt me!'

'Well you've broken her and now you've lost your pink lady for good!' said the barman. 'I'm not giving you another one, you'll just go and break it again, and then you'll have to pay.'

Joe held up one sausage finger to the barman to show him his hurt; blood was pouring out of it. The barman didn't understand:

'You'll definitely have to pay now; I'll not have gestures like that in my bar. Now get out before I throw you out!'

The ladies present, and the men at the club, watched Joe get thrown out. He held up his bleeding finger to the last; he knew all about first aid since his recent experiences at hospital. They'd held his leg up when it was broken and now his finger might be broken too! The 'Country and Western' singer sang 'D.I.V.O.R.C.E.'

'Bitch!' he shouted as he disappeared through the door.

The perfect timing of his contribution to the song resulted in rapturous applause from the audience at the end it. The singer could not have produced better sound effects if she'd planned it. She was pleased; the club would probably book her again now.

It was a bitterly cold, February night. Very dark. The freezing night sky was a colour deeper than black. It didn't matter to Joe because he couldn't see where he was going anyway. He was on auto pilot, taking his usual 'short cut' route home through the park after a night out at the club. The park gates were always locked at night, but Joe had his own secret entrance through a gap in the wire mesh fence by the laurel bushes that he'd discovered quite by accident one time when he fell through it, quite by accident, on his way home after a night out at the club.

He liked his walk home through the park. It was always so quiet and peaceful after the noise and lights of the club which, much as he liked going there, always ended up giving him a headache. The people gave him a headache. The park never made a noise. He could throw up wherever he felt like it and it never said a thing about it. It was always dark so he was never dazzled by the stupid flowers that annoyed him so much in his own garden at home. She gave them more love and attention than she did to him and he hated them for it. Tonight, he wandered off the path more than once to trample a few, just because he felt like it. He never worried; his feet knew the way home.

He'd reached the high, metal, Japanese style bridge. This was the only tricky part of his journey. He had to think a little here, to steel himself and use his arms to cling to the widely spaced, metal railings at the side which always made him feel giddy. There was such a bitter wind in the air tonight that the bridge shook Joe so violently, that he had to stop, slap bang in the middle of it, to catch his breath. Joe stared down into the darkness of the river below. There was *so* much darkness. The bridge swayed to and fro with every gust of wind as if it was trying to throw him off it. Joe held on even tighter.

He felt dizzy and on edge. His feet were cold. Joe suddenly felt very alone. Surrounded by emptiness, it seemed like he'd been waiting forever.

There was a big, black, tree on the other side of the bridge; it looked like it was walking along the river bank straight towards him. Desperate for some company, he peered over the edge of the bridge to look for some fish. There were no fish. There was only darkness; just like the time he'd caught her on the bridge, waiting to meet that friend of hers.

'Bitch! It's all her fault. Her fault. She wouldn't do as she was told...she can't leave me...'

Joe trembled. The trees whispered in his ear. His face turned to ash. He thought he heard footsteps dancing along the bridge towards him. Joe clenched his sausage fingers and turned to face the intruder:

'It's that bloody tree...'

The bridge trembled violently; it was a bitterly cold, February night. Very dark. Joe's eyes, dark with understanding, let go. Head, hands, arms, face, hair. For a moment, his body trembled in the darkness:

'Debs! Debs! I'm so sorry!'

The fish lay still and quiet beneath the shadow that had joined their familiar darkness; they kept out of the way. The big, black, tree on the other side of the bridge stopped walking. It whispered in the darkness, long after the high, metal, Japanese style bridge with the widely spaced railings had stopped swaying:

'Sorry...so sorry...'

But the park was empty; the park gates were always locked at night. It seemed like it had been waiting forever; even the stupid flowers were asleep.

Saturday 10th February

The weather was a bit better; it was raining. There had been a thaw in temperature and temperament at the farmhouse. Old Ab had turned up for Saturday lunch; there was always a laugh and a joke and a good old fashioned story about the good old days when he was sat at the table. Even the rancid smoke from his battered old pipe didn't seem to offend anyone. In fact, it added a positive glow to the proceedings. Shrouded in smoke, old Ab sat at the far end of the table like a mysterious guru; the totally frail and helpless old man somehow managed to make everyone in the room feel protected and safe. It was the smell of old age.

It was the smell of peacefulness that the younger folk at the table could sense but never achieve for themselves; there was still too much life pumping through their veins. Even Jed sat quietly reading the paper.

'Hey up, Carrie! Did your old boss, Pike, give you anything besides encouragement?'

'*Oh no, not another 'Lone Ranger!'*'

'It's Mr Pike and no, he didn't.'

'Shame,' said Jed, 'thought he might have left you a bit of something in his Will. I can tell from reading this you'd got a soft spot for the old trout, I mean pike.'

'Show some respect for the dead, Jed Wilson,' said Mavis.

'Not everything is about money, you know, Jed,' said Carrie, quietly fuming that Jed had touched a slightly raw nerve.

'Of course it's not,' said Jed. 'It's about the 'spirit of opening' and 'moments of joy.' Have you had any of those recently, Carrie? Don't suppose you've had chance today, with Jon leaving for market so early.'

Jed flashed all his teeth in Carrie's direction.

'Jed!'

Mavis flicked Jed on the back of his head with her tea towel. Debs smiled across the table at Carrie:

'*Admit it; he gives you the 'hots'!*'

Carrie snatched Jed's paper out of his hands and batted him around the head with it.

'*No he doesn't!*'

Debs took the paper from Carrie's hands and started reading, still with a smile on her face.

'Well, I'm wearing my forwards looking face,' said Carrie, 'what have you got to look forward to, Jed?'

'A bit more of a battering from you, if I play my cards right!' laughed Jed, getting up from the table, stretching himself out to full height, before disappearing into the rain of the farmyard.

'You're right, yes he does, sometimes. He's just so like Jon.'

It wasn't long before they heard him returning. Jip was barking.

'Jed, why can't you leave that dog alone!' shouted Mavis.

She marched towards the kitchen door to give Jed a piece of her mind:

'Visitors!' said Jed, opening the kitchen door wide but not entering.

Jill and Bill entered instead. Carrie got up from the table, stretching herself out to full height:

'What the hell are you doing here?' she exploded.

Jill ignored her daughter. She ignored everyone:

'I'm Jill Langford, Carrie's mother, and this is my husband, Bill. I'm sorry to turn up at your door unannounced and uninvited like this, but I urgently need to speak to Deborah. Please can we come in?'

'Well you're already in and right welcome you are too. It's a pleasure to meet you. Carrie's a grand lady, just like her mum. I can see that,' said Mavis.

Jill ignored Mavis.

'Deborah dear, I need to speak to you in private. Is there somewhere?'

Jill kept her eyes fixed on Deborah. Deborah got up from the table, stretching herself to full height:

'What's the matter, Mrs Langford? Is there something wrong?'

'Carrie, take your Mum to me best room and I'll make a cup of tea.'

Carrie glared at her mother. If looks could kill she'd have dropped down dead on the spot. As it was, she followed Debs and a backwards looking Carrie to the doorway that led to the best room.

'Ah do!' said old Ab to Bill, from behind his smoke screen.

'Hello!' said Bill.

'Ah do!' said old man Wilson, who'd been pretending to sleep as Carrie had given Jed what for. Now, he got up from the table, stretching himself to full height to greet Bill.

'Sit ye down, sit ye down,' bustled Mavis.

Bill seemed relieved to join old Ab and old man Wilson inside the rancid smoke screen. He could see Carrie looking back at him, searching his face for answers that he couldn't bear to give her. Old man Wilson saw it too.

'What do you think you're playing at, turning up like this? What do you want with Debs that's so urgent?' she said to her mother.

'How dare you invade my private world!'

Jill closed the door on Carrie and her outrage. She glared at her daughter as she did so:

'Shut up or get lost!'

Carrie caught a glimpse of a worried looking Debs sitting herself down amongst a pile of cuddly toys on Mavis' best bench. Carrie chose the 'shut up' option and listened at the door.

For the second time that week she heard a sound that was so sharp that it could have been a gunshot coming from inside the room, except it wasn't a loud bang, or a noise, or a voice of any sort and yet, it was all three at once and the same time. Carrie quietly opened the door to the best room, afraid of what she was going to see.

Her mother was on her knees, holding onto a shaking Debs. Some of Mavis' knitted toys were fallen, lying scattered on the floor. Debs herself was bent double over her knees like a rag doll that had had the stuffing removed from its waistline and couldn't sit up straight unless propped up. Jill was trying to prop her up now. She was struggling to do it and so was the rag doll. There was very little stopping them both from joining the other toys that were scattered on the floor. At least they were quiet now.

'Oh heck,' said Mavis, instantly reversing away from the doorway with her tray of fine bone china tea cups.

'What's up?' she whispered to Carrie.

'I don't know,' said Carrie, hardly able to find her voice for some reason.

'But it's not good. She never hugs me like that...'

Carrie leant back on the doorframe to find her dad taking its place.

'It's Joe,' he whispered. 'Been found drowned in the river this morning. Looks like he had too much to drink at the club last night. Made quite a spectacle of himself, apparently, and somehow ended up in the park. The police think he fell off that high, Japanese style bridge. You know, the one that you and Debs were always so scared of crossing, with the widely spaced metal railings...'

'I feel giddy...'

'...might have banged his head as he fell...'

'Can you see any fish?'

'The cold would have got him...'

'Nah, they've gone to ground...they wait in the darkness...'

'...it was so dark, he wasn't found until late this morning...'

'*What if the light never comes back?*'
'*It always comes back...*'
'...a very sad end. Life has a funny way of working out...'
'*It has to...I just need a hug...*'
Old man Wilson was staring at Carrie.
'*Your eyes are the colour of pain. She loves you, too, you know...*'
'Let's have that tea, Mavis, before it gets cold. I'll put some extra sugar in for Debs,' said Carrie.
'Think she'll need a bit more than sugar in it,' said Mavis. 'I'll get me brandy.'
Everybody had tea with sugar and brandy. Old Ab's rancid smoke screen could no longer give protection or peace. It could not disguise the terror on the faces at the kitchen table, sipping tea, feeling the life pumping through their veins, remembering that it would not always be so. Peacefulness was not guaranteed. It was still raining outside when it was time for Jill and Bill to go.
Carrie followed them outside to their car. Jill ignored her daughter.
'See you later,' said Carrie, lamely.
'You can see me now and later darlin'!' called Jed across the yard.
Carrie glared at Jed:
'*Shut up and get lost, please...*'
'You haven't introduced me to your parents, Carrie.'
Jed swung his arm around Carrie's shoulders and pulled her close to him, ruffling her hair as he did so.
'You've got a great daughter here, Mr and Mrs Langford! She's a great worker; she really puts her back into everything I tell her to do. She's really eager to please, aren't you, Carrie, darlin'?'
Jill glared at Jed. She slammed the car door shut:
'*Shut up and get lost now...*'
She continued to ignore her daughter. Bill waved a good bye with his one good hand. The knuckles on his bad hand shone white on the gear stick as he watched Carrie wrestling with Jed through his wing mirror as he drove down the drive. He just missed the Land Rover that turned into the drive as he pulled out into the road. Jill glared at Bill:
'For goodness sake, be careful!' she snapped. 'I've had enough trauma for one day.'
'*Oh shut up, please...*'
Jon jumped out of the Land Rover. He'd had a good day at market and he was excited to see Carrie for the first time that day. She was in

451

the yard with Jed. She was talking to Jed. They were standing very close together. He was about to call out her name when she quickly turned and disappeared back into the farmhouse.

'What's g..goin' on? D..didn't she s..see me?'

'Sure she did. She saw you coming a long time ago, brother. I told you, you can't trust her. You don't know her like you think you do,' grinned Jed, striding away into the rain.

Jon watched his brother walk away, taking his moment of joy with him.

'C..come on. You think t..too much...'

He walked towards the farmhouse.

'I p..probably don't need to w..worry...do I?'

———◆———

Jill continued to ignore her daughter.

'For goodness sake, Mum, talk to me!' cried Carrie.

'I've got nothing to say to you, you're no daughter of mine!'

'What are you talking about? I thought we'd turned a corner! We've been getting on better, haven't we? Look at everything we've been through together with Debs!'

'So what? Deborah is an innocent, helpless, victim of a terrible crime. She didn't choose to marry cruel hands. She didn't deliberately choose to put herself in harm's way, unlike you!'

Jill was chopping vegetables and the wooden chopping board, faster than the speed of light. Carrie slammed her coffee down on the kitchen table.

'I knew you'd be like this! Just because it was raining and muddy at the farm. Just because they have dirty hands and dirty boots. Just because they're straightforward folk without any airs and graces. Just because old Ab smoked a pipe. Just because they got the fine bone china out for you. Just because you think they're not good enough. Good God, Mother, you're a total snob! Well, they're good enough for me! I'm ashamed of you! I've got nothing more to say to *you*. I'm glad I'm no daughter of yours because you're no mother of mine!'

'Agh!'

Jill rushed to the kitchen sink. Blood was pouring from her fingers. She bent double over the sink; she felt faint.

'What have you done?' said Carrie, wearily taking a tea towel to the kitchen sink to grudgingly offer first aid.

'It's what you've done that bothers me,' said Jill, very quietly.

It was a nasty cut. Deep, and at a funny angle.

'I think you'll need stitches,' said Carrie.

'I don't like hospitals. Fetch me the whisky,' said Jill.

'It's a funny time to start drinking,' muttered Carrie, in no rush to fetch the whisky bottle from the drinks cabinet in the lounge.

When she returned, Jill was sitting on a kitchen chair with her head between her knees, holding one finger up above her head.

'Up yours too!' thought Carrie.

How she longed to say it out loud.

'Pour it on my finger!' commanded Jill.

'But it'll hurt!' said Carrie.

'Life hurts, Carrie, haven't you learnt that yet?'

Jill made a sharp intake of breath as the whisky made contact with her wound.

'Agh! You stupid girl, this is your father's finest malt! Couldn't you have brought the cheap bottle that we keep for unwanted guests?'

'They all look the same to me,' said Carrie. 'A bit like people. I don't judge a book by its cover.'

'You're judging me,' said Jill, quietly.

'No I'm not!' said Carrie, loudly. 'The evidence speaks for itself. Just because I choose a different kind of life from you, a different kind of man from you, you don't just judge me, you want to execute me, and it's not fair!'

'Life's not fair, Carrie, haven't you learnt that, either?'

'Yes, I have learnt that. I'm here talking to you, aren't I? Has the bleeding stopped?'

'Not quite, it'll take a while longer; it's a very deep cut. Can you make me a cup of tea with some sugar in it?'

'Is that with whisky or brandy?'

'Don't joke about that, Carrie.'

'Why wouldn't you tell me about Joe? Why all that formal stuff at the farm about speaking to 'Deborah'?'

Jill cradled her bleeding finger in her arms as if it was a tiny baby.

'I didn't want you to have the pain of telling her. You needed to be clean of that. She's going to need you in the coming weeks and months.'

Carrie watched her mother rocking to and fro on her chair; her face looked deathly white. It was either shock, or loss of blood, or both.

'I think we should get that finger checked out.'

'No, I'll be alright. I'll just sit here awhile.'

Carrie sat down at the kitchen table, opposite her mother, who was becoming so pale by now that her cheekbones were starting to glow white beneath her skin. But Carrie couldn't help that; she was still feeling very angry.

'What did you mean about me putting myself in harm's way, anyway?'

'Exactly that. You're a fool, Carrie. I saw the way that young farmer treated you. No respect. Rough, cruel, hands. He might be exciting to start with, but he'll use you, Carrie, hurt you, and then leave you. A man like that will never love you, and he'll kill any love you have for him. He will destroy you. I don't know why it is that well brought up, educated young girls like you, always seem to want to go for the opposite in a man. If you've got any sense you'll stick to your own kind. It's the only way to stay safe. Your father should be telling you this, not me.'

Carrie started laughing. She couldn't help it. She laughed and laughed till her eyes filled with tears.

'What should I be telling you, Carrie? Have I missed a good joke?' smiled Bill, relieved to find a cheerful mother and daughter scene in the kitchen after what had happened at the farm earlier that day.

'How dare you!' cried Jill, with all the strength she could muster. 'Stop laughing! Stop it immediately. You must listen to me! Stop it! I'm trying to help you...'

It was no good, she couldn't help it. The tears that filled her eyes flowed and overflowed onto the tea towel that nursed her bleeding finger. Jill sobbed Carrie silent.

'What's going on here?' demanded Bill, suddenly realising that the joke was on him.

'Carrie!' he said sharply, 'It's not like you to upset your mother like this. Explain yourself.'

Bill glared at his daughter. Like her mother before her, now it was Carrie's turn to show the whiteness of her bones. It was the shock of hearing anger in her father's voice, and it was directed at her.

'It's not me. She's cut her finger badly and feels faint, *and* she seems to think I'm in love with Jed Wilson, which is why I couldn't help laughing.'

'And are you?'

Carrie glared at her dad. Why was he betraying her?

'Certainly not! You know that!'

'Well your Mother doesn't know it. All she knows is what she saw today. She saw Jed. And thank God she was too upset to look backwards as we left that farm today and see what I saw in my wing mirror. I'm not happy about it, Carrie, it's no laughing matter. Whatever your mother has said to you is probably right.'

'I'm not laughing about that! I can handle Jed Wilson. He might show off and mess around like he did today, but he'd never really hurt me. Jon wouldn't let him.'

'Who's Jon?' asked Jill, suddenly lifting her head.

Carrie lowered hers; she wanted to hide. Bill sighed and sat down at the head of the table. He paused before taking charge:

'You know, girls, all this trouble has come about because there's been a lack of truth in this family. I've been diplomat and counsellor by turns. I've put up and shut up more times than I can remember, just to keep the peace and have a quiet life. But it's not been quiet at all. It's been false, and I'm sick and tired of it. The truth must out and it's coming right now. So which of you wants to go first, or shall I do that for you as well?'

Both 'girls' looked up at the quiet man sitting at the end of the table; he looked different somehow. He'd just helped himself to a large glass of his best malt whisky that just happened to be out on the kitchen table; it always gave him a healthy glow. Tonight, he looked like he was on fire. He was; they could both feel the heat and it wasn't coming from the kitchen. There was no escape. Carrie went first:

'I'm sorry, Mum. I've been hiding the truth from you because I was frightened of you. Frightened of what you would say, what you would think of me, and I didn't want to hurt you. The thing is...'

Jill listened quietly. She listened so quietly that she could hear her tears, trickling down her face. She heard judgement, criticism, and condemnation, and it had all come from her. All these years, she'd been trying to destroy the thing she most loved, just to make herself feel better. It was Carrie.

'...and that's the truth. I would never be so stupid as to go for a man like Jed Wilson. I'd never get myself in trouble like you keep suggesting. You're right; I have been well brought up. I do have standards, just like you, Mum.'

Bill paused; he hadn't drunk any more whisky but he was looking hotter. He looked across at his wife:

'Jill,' he said softly, 'Jill, come on, love, it's time. It'll be alright.'

Jill started crying again.

'No, Bill, please! I can't do it, I just can't do it...' she sobbed.

'Whatever it is, can't it wait, Dad? She still doesn't look very well.'

Carrie was feeling better; full of forgiveness. Bill was right about truth. A great burden had lifted from her shoulders. It felt great. Carrie wanted to help her mother:

'Whatever it is, it can't be that bad, surely! Come on, Mum. Don't be afraid. I love you, you know.'

Jill was worn out. She could not lift her head, except to occasionally heave out a sob.

'No, no, I just can't do it. Please, Bill. Don't do it...'

Bill reached across the table with his one good hand and gently stroked his wife's golden hair. She was totally helpless; both her hands were wrapped up inside the bloody tea towel. He knew very well how that felt; at least he had one good hand that worked. He worked it now.

'It's alright, love. Let me do it for you.'

He got no reply, and took that as answer enough.

'We're sorry, Carrie. Your mother's been hiding the truth from you because she was frightened of you. Frightened of what you would say, what you would think of her, and she didn't want to hurt you. The thing is, she had a love. She was only sixteen, he was twenty five. He laughed when she got pregnant...'

Carrie listened quietly. She listened so quietly that she could hear her tears, trickling down her face. She heard judgement, criticism, and condemnation, and it was all directed at her mother. All these years, she'd been trying to forget. She had almost destroyed herself, just to make herself feel better.

'He laughed when she lost the baby, and so did everyone else. She'd been well brought up, you see, Carrie. She had standards, just like you. She haemorrhaged and nearly bled to death. She was so ill she never even got to hold her daughter...and still they laughed...and that's the truth. So never say never, Carrie. Look at Debs. It's easily done. What's happened to Debs has brought it all back for your mother and, in a strange way, I think it's helped her, hasn't it, love?'

He got no reply from either 'girl'.

'She's been determined to help Debs. Can you see that now?'

Carrie couldn't see anything but tears. She was worn out. Jill wasn't. She lifted her head:

'They took my baby away!'

'I know, love. I'm so sorry,' said Bill. 'But it's over now. You're going to be alright, now.'

456

And Carrie wanted to help her mother, so she cried for her mother.

'And afterwards,' Bill continued, 'her family fixed her up with me. She was damaged goods as far as they were concerned. Nobody would want her after what she'd done. And I was, likewise, already damaged by then.'

Bill held up his fingerless hand to prove it.

'Your mother never really trusted me because she thought I'd been pressurised into her. But I tell you, Carrie, your Mother was the best girl around. There was no one better than your Mother. She was the most beautiful woman I'd ever seen. And I loved her. But she's never been able to believe me, all these years. It was so hard for her, you know, the physical side of things. After everything she'd been through, after everything that was said to her. She saw it as a duty rather than a pleasure. We did manage to have you, but it was hard for her. Hard. So bloody hard. There was never any pressure from me because I loved her. And after you were born, it got a whole lot harder. But I've never stopped loving her, I never will. It's our journey and we're on it together.'

'I believe it now,' whispered Jill.

Bill was right about truth. A great burden had been lifted; it would probably feel great by morning, wouldn't it?

Wednesday 14th February

'Happy Valentine's Day ladies!'

'Give over, Jed, you great Lummox!'

'Where's the post, Mavis?'

'Where it always is, in the post box, now clear off from under me feet!'

'Your wish is my command, Fair Lady!'

Jed cleared off outside to check the post box.

'What a bastard!'

Carrie was sitting with Debs by the kitchen window. Debs was waiting for the funeral on Monday. Carrie was just waiting because she didn't know what else to do. The kitchen window looked out onto the front garden; it was dead at this time of year.

"Roses are red, violets are blue, Jed, be my Valentine, 'cos there's no one sweeter than you!' I know who that's from! Carrie, you shouldn't have. Or maybe this one's yours...'

Jed put on a squeaky falsetto voice:

'Jed, Jed, please visit my bed, and I'll be your Valentine!' No, I don't think so. I know who that's from. Sorry to disappoint, but it looks like I'll be out and about tonight, ladies. I've got some serious loving to do.'

'Come on, Debs, let's go for a walk outside,' said Carrie.

'But it's dark today.'

'It's February, it's always dark, but we can still see where we're going. Come on.'

Carrie's boots were heavy with mud as she pulled a reluctant Debs up the drive.

'Typical! Jed is the only one to get Valentine's cards and yet he's the least loving creature I've ever met!'

'You sound jealous,' said Debs.

'No I'm not. I'm not bothered about stupid Valentine's cards. I'm angry that he can be so thoughtless in front of you.'

Carrie realised what she'd just said:

'Just like me. I'm thoughtless too. I didn't mean it. I'm really not bothered about Valentine's Day. All I care about is you, right now.'

'I know you do,' said Debs. 'But Jon hasn't been in to see you this morning, and you haven't been to find him. You're bound to feel miserable. I would be hoping for a little romance today if I was you, it's normal.'

'There's no such thing as normal any more. You feel miserable. I feel miserable. We might as well make the best of it together. Let's have a walk in the orchard - that usually makes me feel better.'

'But it's dark in there.'

'But it'll be quiet. It's a very peaceful place somehow,' said Carrie.

'But all the trees are dead,' said Debs. 'They frighten me.'

'They're not dead. They're just asleep,' said Carrie.

'Like the fish at the bottom of the river.'

Debs started crying again. Carrie led Debs towards the stone bench at the foot of the sad looking tree; she hadn't visited it for a while, what with one thing and another. It still reached out to her in a gentle and pleading sort of way. She somehow felt comforted by it, today. She hoped that it would have the same soothing effect on Debs.

'What's up with that tree?' said Debs, suddenly grabbing hold of Carrie's arm.

'Nothing. Now that *is* a dead tree. Nothing grows on it, near it, or round it. It's quite harmless. Come and sit down,' said Carrie.

'I don't want to. It just moved!'

'Trees do move! They breathe the same air as we do.'

'You said it was dead. It reminds me of what you looked like, wearing that long black velvet dress in the farmhouse.'

Carrie shivered and sat down, pulling Debs with her. This little outing had been a mistake. All the trees looked like they were dressed in black today, the grass too. Carrie persevered:

'Are you saying that I look as dry, skinny, and withered, as a sad old tree?'

Debs managed a smile.

'Well yes! Frankly you do!'

'Oh...Well, a lot's been happening recently.'

'You know,' said Debs after a pause, 'we've all got to die. I've got to face my grief. Joe is gone now. His death has happened to me, really, not to him. It doesn't affect him in the slightest. It's up to me now to decide if I'm going to be happy or sad. What sort of memories I want to keep, if any.'

'You're totally amazing,' said Carrie.

A rustling, shuffling, sound came from behind the sad, old, tree trunk. Carrie and Debs jumped up off the stone bench as if they'd just been electrocuted. The sad looking tree *was* alive and moving. A very tall, dark shape appeared.

459

'What are you doing here?' said Carrie.

Old man Wilson looked from Carrie to Debs and back towards the sad looking tree.

'Facing my grief,' he said, simply. He walked away, dragging his memories behind him. Carrie and Debs watched him go.

'Everybody's miserable today,' sighed Debs, 'and it's all my fault.'

'No, it's not you, it's Valentine's Day.'

'It's this bloody tree...'

'I want to go back to the house, Carrie, it's dark here. I'm frightened.'

'So am I...'

Carrie's heavy boots didn't have to pull so hard on the return trip down the drive to the farmhouse.

'Look, there's Jon!' said Debs. 'Go to him, Carrie.'

'I can't be sure it's him without I see Jip first!'

Carrie's voice nearly broke at the sight of him. She so wanted it to be him.

'And here comes Jip! Go, you silly girl!'

Debs pushed Carrie down the slope of the drive that ran away with her feet. Jip ran forwards to meet her.

'Hello!' said Carrie, trying to sound cheerful and failing.

Only Jip wagged his tail. Jon looked terrible, like he hadn't slept.

'We all feel miserable today,' she continued.

He looked down into her face, reached out with one hand to touch her long, golden hair, and nodded.

'Are you alright?'

He let go of her hair.

'I've not been avoiding you, you know. It's just Debs. I need to be with her. It's the funeral...'

'It's other things too that I can't speak about just yet...'

'You do understand, don't you?'

He looked across at Debs and Jip, and nodded.

'Please talk to me!'

Jon looked down at the ground; something he'd not done in a long time in her company. Through the strands of his long hair that fell over his face Carrie could see his lips moving, but he was talking to himself. She put her hand on his arm.

'Jon, you're scaring me now. What's the matter?'

Jon sighed. He took in a deep breath, turned, and grabbed Carrie roughly by the elbows. He almost shook her. There were tears in his eyes:

'C...C...C...'

Carrie was good with tears. She'd seen and had so many of many of her own these last few days that she'd become quite expert at reading them. She put her arms around him. He stood still and let her do it; it seemed the right thing to do. She reached up and pushed his hair away from his face with her ice cold fingers. She pushed her face up as far as it would go, to get her eyes as close to his as possible. Then she cried him an answer:

'You're sad. You've lost your words because you feel for Debs. There's death in your home again. It's a reminder, and it hurts you. But it's different now, you've got me! Don't be afraid, your words will come back, I promise you they'll come back!'

She held him as tight as she could and he held her back. She closed her eyes. Jip's warm wag was tapping her on the leg. Another body pressed itself onto hers and Jon's, binding them tight together. It was Debs.

'Who needs words, anyway? There are no words for what this is...'

'Great! Is this a free love in? Can anybody join?'

Jed dug his chin into the back of Carrie's shoulder and leaned himself into Carrie and Debs from behind. Debs immediately buckled at the knees and sank into the mud on the drive:

'No, please, no!' she begged.

Jed immediately buckled at the knees and staggered backwards; Jip had bitten him on the side of the leg and was snarling towards him, threatening more. Jon had straightened out his arm and hit him hard in the middle of his chest, winding him. Carrie was on her knees in the mud, holding on to a shaking Debs.

'H..Happy Valentine's D..D..Day to you too!' mocked Jed, as soon as he could breathe again. 'Jon, I'm surprised at you! Such a display of violence in front of these ladies. Carrie won't like that, it's the wrong sort of violence, isn't it, Carrie?'

Carrie ignored Jed and concentrated as hard as she could on holding onto Debs. Jon stepped over the ladies, who were busy examining the mud on the drive and, like Jip, threatened more.

'Steady on, bro', can't you take a joke?' said Jed, backing away.

He rubbed at his chest:

'See, you've broken my heart, and I'm going to need it tonight. What am I going to do?'

'You've managed quite well without one up to now,' said Carrie, suddenly standing up, like Jon and Jip, threatening more.

'Jealousy's a terrible thing, Carrie, it'll eat you alive. Take care, Jon. I've warned you about this one. Anyway, better get on. Haven't you got work to do?'

Jed blew them all a kiss as he walked away, but nobody caught it, not even the black trees in the orchard. Carrie stood in the middle of the drive like a sad, withered, and black, old tree:

'There are no words for what this is...and it scares me. I'm in the middle...what will be the end?'

———◆———

She was in the orchard, surrounded by black trees. They were watching her. No, they were people, except that they had no words. It was raining. Hard. Everywhere. No, it was tears. But Carrie had none. She was lying down, all cosy and relaxed. She was well padded, tucked in on all sides, but she still felt very cold; she couldn't feel her toes.

'It's dark today, but I suppose it's always dark in February.'

It was getting darker and colder; still, it was very peaceful somehow. The black trees stood very still.

'They're not even breathing.'

She was surprised; even the sad looking tree had stopped reaching out to her. She couldn't see where she was going.

'What are you doing here?'

The Falcon hovered over her:

'Facing my grief.'

Jon was there too:

'Are you alright? You look terrible.'

He looked down at the ground. He stretched his arms out towards her in a gentle and pleading sort of way, but he couldn't reach her. There were tears in his eyes.

'C...C...C...'

'He can't talk to you!' laughed Jed. 'You do understand, don't you? You're dead! You're going down in the ground. You're going to be eaten. I warned you, Carrie, jealousy is a terrible thing. You've hurt him, Carrie. But it's different now, he's got me, and I'll see to it that his words will never come back. Who needs words anyway, when you've got a heart like mine?'

Jed blew a kiss to Carrie. She was falling, no, being slowly lowered, down and down and down.

'Here's your end, Carrie, that you were so bothered about. You wouldn't take mine,

and now you've missed out.'

Carrie lay all alone in the deep, dark, ground. She could hear Jed's voice in the distance:

'Hello, Debs, darlin', Happy Valentine's Day. Why don't you come in the mud with me and we'll mend our broken hearts together...'

'No, please, no!' begged Carrie.

She fought the darkness and the cosy padding with all her might until eventually, she fell free, onto the floor of her bedroom. She climbed back into her bed and held the covers tight.

'Think I'll stay in the middle for as long as I can...'

'Good idea,' said the Walnut, in her bedside table drawer.

Friday 23rd February

Dear Reader,

'Why, what's the matter, that you have such a 'February face', so full of frost, of storm and cloudiness?' [†]

Is that how you feel in the dark month of February, Reader? Was William Shakespeare right? The ancient festival of 'Candlemas Day' on February 2nd marks the midpoint of winter. Everything around us is dead.

The trees are black and frozen, and so is the grass. The ground is cold and hard and the snow, if we have any, is dirty. All in all, it seems like a suitable month for dying, wouldn't you say?

'Ah, it's a bad business,' says the old man who visits the farm to buy eggs every week; he says it about a lot of things and it certainly seems to suit this dark little month.

And of course, death is a part of life; we all have to do it, sooner or later. Down on the farm, some early lambs are being born. Some live, some die... 'Ah, it's a bad business...'

So what can be done to make us feel a little better about this darkness that surrounds us? What about St Valentine's Day? Traditionally a day for love and romance; but not everyone gets a card, do they?

Traditionally it's thought to be the day when birds choose their mates; they manage without cards. Does that make you feel a little better?

February comes from the word 'februa' which means 'cleansing' or 'purification.' The Romans undertook many such rituals at this time to prepare for the Spring. There's nothing like a spot of 'spring cleaning' to cheer things up, is there? Take stock of our homes, minds, and bodies. Prepare for a better time, for it will come for you. Spring always comes eventually.

And do you know the legend of the snowdrop? This tiny white flower, the first to appear in the depths of winter, is a symbol of hope. When Adam and Eve were thrown out of the Garden of Eden, Eve was ready to give up. She thought that the cold winters would never end. But an angel turned some of the winter snowflakes into snowdrops, proving to Eve that the Spring would eventually come again. My friend wears snowdrops on her coat and she grows them in her garden. Her husband bore them on his coffin. Feeling better yet?

'Ah, it's a bad business.'

But it's not all bad. Some live, some die. If we can keep our faith in beautiful things even when we can't see them, they will return, as sure as the Spring returns after Winter. Waiting for something makes it grow, whether it's a dream or a little seed planted in the ground. That's what February is for.

How's that 'February face' of yours now? Feeling any better? My friend wears snowdrops on her coat; she is feeling better.

Saturday 24th February

They held the meeting behind closed doors; Debs wanted it that way. She asked old man Wilson to stay with her. He was the closest thing to a father that she'd ever had; a good father, anyway. They stayed in the kitchen. It was the warmest place in the house. It was important to keep warm at this time of year. All three of them needed a bit of help from the kitchen fire to do so, they were all running a bit low on fuel themselves at the moment.

Drained of resources the trio sat huddled around the fire, drinking tea with a drop of something in it; old man Wilson had rum, Debs had brandy and Jill had whisky, finest malt from the little bottle that she carried in her handbag these days for first aid and medicinal emergencies. Bill wasn't happy about his wife's sudden interest in caring for the sick and injured. She was still ignoring the first rule of first aid. She was still not putting her own safety first. She was reaching for her little bottle in-between first aid and medical emergencies at an alarming rate. He'd decided to monitor the situation for the time being.

He hoped that 'Project Debs' would help her to see sense and keep safe. He took himself down to the tractor workshop at the end of the drive. He was very fond of Debs, but he also knew that she didn't need any more male energy in the room other than that from old man Wilson. He was a good man. She felt safe with him; that was all she needed right now. He didn't mind that she didn't choose him. He knew he was too close; he'd known her too long.

Mavis had retired to her best room. She'd made them tea and left them a plate of cakes and scones before she did so. She usually spent Saturday afternoons in her best room; it was her treat to sit with her knitting and listen to the radio. She liked a good story, a play, or sometimes there was even a documentary. It had always been her only chance to travel and see the world, to meet other people, to think other thoughts, and she loved it, once a week.

When Mavis returned from her travels, pleased that she'd finished her latest cuddly project, the meeting was over and 'Project Debs' was about to get under way. Jill was all buttoned up, coat on, standing by the fire.

'Are ya right?' said Mavis.

'Yes thank you, we are,' replied Jill. 'All done. Deborah has just gone to get her things. I'm taking her with me.'

'Ah, right you are,' said a disappointed Mavis.

'It's all been agreed. She's going to be alright,' said old man Wilson.

'Course she will! I shall miss her all the same.'

'Ah,' said old man Wilson, agreeing with Mavis and welcoming Debs back into the kitchen clutching her suitcase and little bag of personal stuff.

Debs smiled at the kitchen that had been her home all day, every day, for these last weeks. She'd never strayed far from old man Wilson's father bear chair by the fire with the old knitted blankets. She'd never drunk so much tea in her entire life. She'd never been so warm and cared for, never felt so protected and safe. Loved.

'Thank you!' she said, and promptly burst into tears.

'I'll just go and find Bill,' said Jill, knowing that 'project Debs' could not be rushed.

'Oh, Debs love, don't cry, don't cry.'

Mavis wrapped Debs up in her frilly apron and white whiskers. The two pink ladies hugged each other until their froth had settled.

'There now, that's better,' said Mavis. 'You shall come back and visit us with Carrie, shan't you?'

Debs smiled through her tears and hugged Mavis again. She was the closest thing she'd had to a mother; a good mother, anyway.

'You can come back here whenever you want. I'd be upset if you didn't,' said old man Wilson.

'I must see Carrie and Jon before I go,' said Debs.

'I'll find them,' he said, seeming glad to leave the heat of the kitchen.

Outside in the yard, he didn't need to look far. He hovered by the back door and watched as two worlds collided. Carrie and Jon were walking down the drive together towards the farmyard. Jill and Bill were waiting for Debs in their car, parked in the middle of the yard. He saw the look in Jill's eyes as she focussed in on her daughter. He saw the abyss open up in front of Carrie's feet; how was she going to cross it? She didn't have to, for Debs came out of the farmhouse with Mavis and sealed it up. Debs reached down into her little bag of personal stuff:

'Here, Mavis, I'd like you to have this. I won't be needing her any more.'

'But it's your little flower fairy!' said Mavis. 'She's special to you!'

'And so are you,' said Debs. 'Please keep her for me.'

'Only if you'll keep this for me!'

Mavis reached into her apron pocket and pulled out a tiny knitted lamb.

'Finished him this afternoon. Now don't you go crying again. Where's that lovely smile?'

'It's here,' said a soggy faced Debs.

Debs waved across the yard to Carrie and Jon and got into the backseat of the Bill's car. She'd got no words left. In fact, nobody seemed to have anything to say. Old man Wilson saw the look in Carrie's eyes as she focussed in on her mother. He saw the void in front of Jill's face; how was she going to get through it? Carrie tried:

'Mum, this is my friend Jon that I was telling you about.'

Jill sighed. She took in a deep breath, and promptly burst into tears. But Carrie was good with tears. She was an expert by now. She reached forwards towards the car door, but it reversed away from her. Bill was an expert with tears too.

'*Later!*' waved his hand; and then they were gone.

It was a bit of a shaky start, but 'Project Debs' had just got under way.

————◆————

Later came sooner than Carrie really wanted. It came the second she walked in through the kitchen door at home. Carrie had had very little contact or discussion with her mother since the night her truth was released into the ether; the atmosphere in the house had been a bit hazy since then. Like the uncertain February weather outside, the fog inside the house couldn't seem to decide whether it was going to lift or get thicker. Carrie braced herself because the climate looked like it was about to change. Carrie was ready.

'I saw what was waiting deep in his eyes,' started Jill.

'And what was that?'

'All his tomorrows.'

'Oh.'

'Deborah told me about it, and now I've seen it for myself.'

'Oh.'

'It's true for you. It wasn't for me.'

Carrie had to blink hard. The fog was lifting rapidly. She was suddenly being dazzled by a burst of very bright light; it made her eyes water. It caught her mother's eyes, too.

'I fell prey to a Jed. I was a fool. But you've got a Jon.'

'I know how to choose, Mum. I've had a great Dad.'

'I'm so sorry, Carrie.'

'It's alright Mum. We'll be alright now.'

'I just need a hug.'

The fog completely lifted. They had a hug. It was a bit of a shaky start, but 'Project Mum' had just got under way.

———◆———

'Bill?'

'Yes, love?'

'I've talked to Carrie.'

'Oh, good,' replied Bill.

It was dark in their bedroom and he couldn't see where she was going. She went in an unexpected direction; she climbed into his bed.

'Bill?'

'Yes, love?'

'I love you.'

'I know. I love you too.'

'Will you make love to me?'

'Of course I will.'

Bill turned towards his wife.

'I want to make love to you. I know how to choose, you know.'

'I know you do,' whispered Bill, starting to gently kiss her neck.

'I want to feel you inside me,' she said.

'Oh, Jill.'

'You've got all my tomorrows,' she whispered in his ear.

'Good. You've got something of mine as well.'

Jill giggled. One loving hand was better than two cruel ones. Jill reached down and pulled at Bill's fingerless hand. He knew it made her uncomfortable, so he always tried to keep it out of the way.

'No!' she said quite sharply. 'I want it. I want all of you.'

She made a fist with one of her own hands, tucked the fingers tight inside it, till her knuckles shone white in the darkness. She pressed her fingerless hand into his until their knuckles locked together.

'There, that's better.'

She took hold of his knuckles and kissed them gently, one by one.

'Oh!' said Bill.

'I'll be needing this, shortly, I'm going to need something hard to bear down on.'

'You're a very passionate woman. How have you managed all these years?'

'With difficulty. I'm so sorry, Bill.'

'It's alright. We'll be alright now.'

'I know. I've got a lot of catching up to do, starting right now!'

'Oh!'

'Ah! Look Carrie, there's a rabbit in the garden!'

'Don't talk to me about rabbits! Mum and Dad are at it 'like rabbits' night and day! They're driving me mad. All of a sudden, she can't keep her hands off him. It's embarrassing!'

'No, it's not. It's lovely!' said Debs. 'Your Mum's a teenager again. Sweet sixteen, before it all went wrong for her. After all those wasted years she deserves to be happy. Your wonderful, patient Dad, too.'

'Yes, you're right,' smiled Carrie. 'We all deserve to be happy, and that includes you!'

'I am. Well, I'm working on it.'

'You seem to be settling in here O.K. And there's not a spot of pink in sight! What's happened to you?'

'Yellow for the sunshine, white for a clean, fresh start and a bit of green and brown to remind me of the farm.'

'You should have been a poet.'

'Working with flowers all day does things to your mind! I love my new job at the garden centre. I shall never be able to thank your mum enough for what she's done for me. Never.'

'Even though she's fixed you up with a 'granny flat' to live in?' teased Carrie.

'I love it here! I'm surrounded by Mavises, who want to have a cup of tea and a chat. They're nothing like the real Mavis, of course, but it makes me feel right at home. It's only temporary, until the house is sold, but it's just the job for me right now.'

'How's about a cup of tea, then, or have you forgotten how to make one, since you've been waited on hand and foot all these weeks?'

'Carrie Langford, you cheeky young beggar! Me forget how to make a cup of tea? Pass me that there kettle, and I'll soon show ya!'

'Ah!'

The two Mavises made the tea together; one boiled the kettle and the other one produced a plate of cakes. They were from a packet, rather than the oven, but the end result was just about the same level of comfort. They collapsed into two faded, old, velour covered armchairs. No doubt like their previous owners, old age had sapped all their strength so that they gave comfort greater than the very finest new, soft, leather, sofa.

'Ouch!' squeaked Carrie, tucking her feet down the side of her chair.

A knitting needle dug into her ankle.

'Since when did you knit?'

'Since she showed me! You big nit, did you think I just sat in that chair by the fire all day, doing nothing?'

Debs disappeared into her bedroom. She returned with the beginnings of a new, old knitted, blanket. The multi - coloured squares were loosely tacked together. Carrie clapped her hands with delight.

'Wow! And still no pink!'

'I told you,' said Debs, quietly. 'It's time for a fresh start.'

'Start with a cream cake, then,' said Carrie, quickly holding up the plate to change the subject.

A few minutes of laughing and jokes about the shape of the cream cakes and they'd be sorted. It was just like old times. They watched a bit of telly. They relaxed. A new, old Debs was really, really back. Like the chair she was sitting in, life had frayed her around the edges, but her eternal smile, bubbly laugh and optimism, hadn't been blunted. So they had a laugh and a joke until it was time for Carrie to go home.

'Now go quietly when you get home,' warned Debs.

'Rabbits go to bed early you know. Make sure you don't disturb them!'

'They might go to bed early but they won't be sleeping, and neither will I, if the last few nights are anything to go by!'

Debs laughed:

'I promise to knit you some earplugs!'

'Give over, you silly old mare! See you tomorrow night!'

They had a hug and another laugh, before Carrie disappeared down the garden path.

'It's true. We all deserve to be happy...Well, I'm working on it...'

———◆———

'Where shall I put this?' asked Jill.

Bill laughed.

'You can put it on the workbench, but be careful, it's heavy and covered in oil, you'll get your lovely clothes dirty.'

'Dirty sounds good!' giggled Jill, pinching Bill's bottom as she walked past him to 'tidy up' the tool box he'd left open in the middle of the garage floor.

She made him jump; he banged his head on the car that he was working on. He stood up and watched her struggling with the heavy metal tool box:

'It's great you want to spend time here and help, but what about all your other work?'

'What other work? This is much more fun than housework. I don't know why I didn't realise it before. I can see why Carrie enjoys coming here so much.'

Jill had 'tidied' the tool box and now set about the workbench itself. The tools weren't so different from her cooking utensils at home. Bill just needed a system for them like hers, then his life would be much easier.

'I mean all your charity work. The 'Local Ladies Network.' They'd be lost without you.'

Jill picked up a mole wrench and started to open it wide. Her fingers were covered in oil.

'Bill Langford, are you trying to get rid of me?'

'No, of course not!'

Jill brandished the mole wrench. Laughing, she slowly walked towards him.

'Of course you are! I'd want to get rid of me if I was you. I know you've got your work to do. I've got some calls to make as well. I promise to leave you in peace for the rest of the day, but I'll just help you to adjust your nuts before I go!'

Jill pounced on Bill.

'You can't! Not here! A customer could walk in at any minute! That wouldn't do your reputation any good with the 'Local Ladies' would it?'

Bill removed the mole wrench and Jill's hands from the back of his neck. Jill smiled at him:

'There's always the store cupboard! I've never done it in a store cupboard. Have you?'

'Enough! We won't be able to afford a store cupboard if I don't get this car finished.'

'What about at the weekend, then?'

Bill smiled at his wife. It was an amazing feeling to see her looking so happy and feeling so full of life. They'd had an amazing few days, but he was getting really tired now. He did have to work as well.

'No, I've never done it in a store cupboard. So yes, *maybe*, at the weekend, but you'll have to leave me be for the rest of the week!'

Jill looked at her hands. They were black with oil and grease. They looked beautiful.

'If that's the case, I'd better go and get cleaned up, then.'

Bill put his arms around his wife and kissed her with all his might. 'Don't get too cleaned up,' he whispered in her ear. 'I like you like this...'

Saturday 10th March

'Please hurry up, Dad, or I'm going to be late!' pleaded Carrie.

'I'm going as fast as I can,' said Bill. 'I'm not a Formula One pit crew, you know. I can't change a tyre in ten seconds!'

'I know, but I mustn't be late today. I'm going to a farm sale with Jon. He wants to buy some cows, and he wants to go early so we can have a good look round before the sale starts.'

'Don't panic! I'm sure he'll wait for you if you're a few minutes late.'

'He won't, he can't. It's important,' wailed Carrie.

'You mean, it's important to you that you go with him!'

Carrie flicked her dad on the back of his head with her fingers:

'That as well. Now, is it done?'

'Done,' said Bill.

'Thanks.'

She'd kissed her Dad on the cheek, reversed the car and driven away, before he'd even had chance to get up from the ground.

'Take care today!' he called after her.

He knew she wouldn't listen. She was like him. Passionate. She drove her little red car like he used to race his vintage motorbikes. All out to cross that finishing line.

'*I wonder where she'll finish up today...*' he pondered, as he picked up his tool box.

He'd got back ache this morning. He smiled to himself as he stretched out:

'*The mind is still willing, but the body's a touch vintage. I could do with a gentle rub down instead of this all out racing...*'

He crunched the gravel a touch unevenly as he turned to walk back to the house.

'*Still, it's great to be loved and wanted. I'd better make sure I keep my spark plugs clean and firing on all cylinders, or she'll be replacing me with a younger model...*'

———————◆———————

His own younger model, daughter Carrie, pulled up in the farmyard with a squeal from her new car tyre. Jip was sitting in the flat, morning sunshine by the low, flat brick wall that edged the farmyard where there were no buildings. The cold March wind flapped his ears for him as he tilted his poorly chin up to such warmth from the sun that he could find; no doubt it soothed it for him. The down side was that he was blinded by the light from the sun, keeping his head at such an angle. He sat with eyes closed, squinting hard. Carrie noticed that he had something tied to his collar underneath his chin. Jip wagged his tail at Carrie as her approaching shadow soothed his eyes such that he could open them again. The folded piece of paper tucked into his collar said 'Carrie' on the outside:

'So sorry, I can't wait any longer. See you later, Jon X'

'Oh no, Jip! What are we going to do? Bloody tyre!'

A gust of cold March wind tried to rip Jon's words out of her hands. She held on tight to them. A shiver ran down her spine. It was an odd sensation to read his words; there was no stutter. She almost expected him to write like he spoke. In a way he had; there were very few words written here. She carefully folded up the paper and put it in her jeans pocket.

'At least he left me a kiss, Jip! Come on, let's find Mavis or the old man and see what needs doing. It'll be just you and me, today. We've done it before. We're alright, you and me; he'll be back before we know it.'

Jip wagged his tail; they set off across the yard together. There was no sound coming from behind the closed door of the farmhouse kitchen. There was no whistle of a boiling kettle, no clank of pots and pans, no music from the radio. Even the cold March wind could not touch her, standing in the shelter of the little porch area that was in front of the farmhouse kitchen door. It was eerily quiet. Ghostly. A shiver ran down her spine as she tried the door handle; it moved on its own.

'Hello, darlin',' said Jed.

'What are you doing here?' said an anxious Carrie.

'What does it look like?' said Jed.

Carrie chose not to answer Jed. She saw what it looked like. She took a step backwards. Jed was leaning against the farmhouse kitchen door dressed in nothing but a towel, wrapped around his waist. His upper body was wet, shining and steaming, as the cold March wind made contact with his skin. He looked incredible, like a living, breathing, God from all those tales of myths and legends. Carrie tried not to look at him. She tried not to think, 'that's what Jon would look like if he was standing here dressed only in a towel.' But it wasn't Jon, it was Jed. She tried to stop thinking, and failed. Jed smiled at her with all his beautiful white teeth. She knew he knew what she was thinking.

'I know I've missed Jon, but where is everybody else?'

She was determined to be brave.

'All gone! Jon left you to go in search of more four legged lady friends, old Mavis and the old man have gone to hospital with old Ab. He had a fall in the night. He might have broken his hip.'

'Oh no!' said Carrie.

'And I've just had a bath and got myself straightened up, just in case we decide to spend some quality time together while we're on our own.'

'We're not on our own. I'm with Jip, and Bob will be at the tractor workshop down the drive, so you keep right away from me today, Jed Wilson.'

'Or else what?' laughed Jed, tucking his thumbs inside the top of his towel.

'I'll leave you in peace to finish pampering yourself,' said Carrie. 'I'm going to get on with some jobs. Jon won't be late back, he left me a note.'

'He's so thoughtful, isn't he?' sniped Jed.

'Yes he is.'

Carrie backed away from the porch. The cold March wind pressed itself into her back. She was glad of it. She wanted to disappear into it, to be whisked away by it to safety. Jed grinned.

'Alright then, darlin', but give me a shout if you want anything.'

'Thanks, I'll be fine.'

Jed closed the door slowly, but not before he'd let his towel drop to the floor. Carrie pretended with all her might that she hadn't seen him do it; she hadn't seen anything at all. She walked away with Jip towards the cowsheds. She felt better and safer with every step. Jed was unlikely to follow them. It was Saturday; he didn't like work and he'd be no doubt getting ready to go out. He wouldn't want to get messed up again.

'What a complete idiot! Does he really think women are impressed by behaviour like that?'

Jip didn't reply. Neither did Carrie. She was suddenly thinking about her mother and another shiver ran down her spine. She walked, faster and faster, until she was up the drive and around the back of the farm buildings. She had a quick visit to the calf shed; it was full. Lots of cows were calving at this time of year. The shed next door was the maternity unit. Jon kept cows in here who were getting ready to calve. There was one in there this morning. It was his favourite; he called her J..Jenny.

J..Jenny groaned when Carrie opened the door.

'Oh my God! It looks like she's calving!'

Jip stood in the doorway and wagged his tail. J..Jenny had two little feet sticking out of her rear end. Another shiver ran down Carrie's spine:

'Don't worry, Jenny. I'll fetch Bob from the tractor workshop. I'm not telling Jed about this. I remember only too well what happened the last time he calved a cow. There's no way I'm letting him near you!'

J..Jenny groaned a thank you. Carrie closed the shed door and ran, faster and faster, down the drive to the tractor workshop. But there was no sound coming from behind its closed door. There were no men's singing voices, no clank of tools, no revving engines. It was eerily quiet. Ghostly. The door was locked. They were closed. There was no Bob the tractor mechanic today.

'Oh my God! What are we going to do, Jip?'

Jip wagged his tail.

'I'm *not* fetching Jed. I'll just have to do it myself.'

Carrie marched, faster and faster, to the outhouse to get the calving ropes; she knew where they were kept.

'Come on Jip, we're alright, you and me. We can do this!'

Jip wagged his tail. It soothed her hands a little as she nervously wrestled to loosen the loops on the calving rope. She suddenly felt very, very, alone. It seemed like a lifetime of longing and waiting had brought her to this moment. She still had a bit further to go, and she was going with J..Jenny. She had to help J..Jenny.

'All right, girl, it's alright.'

Carrie went into the shed and ran her hands along J..Jenny's back. She tried to do everything that she'd seen Jon do. She'd seen it many times by now, but it was the first time, with little Carrie, that she always came back to. And so Carrie became Jon. She became his hands, his eyes, his gentle voice; she knew them all off by heart. It was easy for her, but not for J..Jenny.

J..Jenny wouldn't stand still for the replacement Jon. The replacement Jon had kind hands but she was not as big or as strong as the real one. She had a real struggle to get the ropes onto the two little feet that were sticking out of J..Jenny's back end a little further by now. Round and round the shed they cart wheeled, until they both got tired and stopped for a rest in one corner.

'That's it, good girl.'

Carrie looked across to Jip for a bit of reassurance.

478

'That's it, good girl!' said Jed.

Jip didn't wag his tail. He was too busy laughing. His poorly chin was very poorly; bleeding and swaying from side to side in the cold March wind. J..Jenny pressed herself into the shed corner. Carrie pressed herself into J..Jenny. The cold March wind pressed Jed through the door and into the shed. The replacement Jon wished she was as big and strong as the real one. She stood her ground in front of the cow as best she could:

'I can handle this, Jed. I thought you were getting ready to go out. You go and enjoy your day.'

'Oh, I intend to, Darlin', but it looks like you need a hand first.'

'I know what I'm doing.'

J..Jenny looked round at Carrie as if to say *'are you sure?'* Carrie rubbed her ears as if to say *'look at the alternative!'*

'I'm sure you do,' said Jed, 'but Jon would be cross with me if I didn't come to the rescue of two of his most favourite ladies. He might thump me again and we can't have him getting upset like that again, can we? He might never speak to you ever again!'

'You really are a total bastard, aren't you?' spat Carrie. 'I've been right about you all along.'

Jed laughed. J..Jenny groaned.

'Well, if that's what you think I'd better see about proving it then, hadn't I?'

Carrie braced herself to defend J..Jenny, but Jed turned and walked out of the shed. Jip had stopped laughing by now and came back to the doorway with his ears hanging low, as if to say 'sorry Carrie.'

'It's alright, Jip. We'll be alright.'

Jip whined as if to say 'you're lying.'

Just then, the cold March wind pressed the sound of a tractor engine in their direction.

'We're saved! It'll be Bob at the tractor workshop.'

Carrie and Jip ran to the drive in search of Bob, but Jed blocked their path. He was reversing the tractor up the drive in their direction. And he kept going, so fast that they had to jump out of his way. Jed backed the tractor up to J..Jenny's shed door. Its enormous back wheels were so tightly pressed into the door that Carrie couldn't get past them. Jed climbed over the back of the tractor and disappeared into the shed to give Jenny a hand.

'I don't know what you're up to Jed Wilson, but you'd better leave that cow alone. We don't need your help!' shouted a frantic Carrie.

'Don't worry!' Jed called back, 'sometimes you have to be cruel to be kind. You don't want J..J..Jenny suffering in labour for hours if she doesn't have to, do you?'

Carrie remembered what happened the last time Jed had calved a cow. She remembered the pulley and the plank of wood. She remembered the cruel turning. She remembered suffering and death. Jed climbed back into the tractor seat, having wedged his cruel plank of wood across the doorway. He was going to use the tractor engine as a pulley!

'No Jed. Stop! I won't let you do it!' shrieked Carrie.

She launched herself at the tractor. With one swipe of his hand Jed batted Carrie off the tractor as if she was nothing more than a pesky fly. Like a pesky fly, Carrie flew through the air and landed flat and hard on her back in the mud. The fall winded her. The replacement Jon lost all her words.

'No!'

Her mouth moved but no sound came; it was terrifying. Jip was barking but no sound came; he was terrified. The only sound that came was the sound of the tractor engine revving; it was terrifying. Jed laughed; he hadn't finished proving himself yet.

Carrie sat up, in a daze. Inside the shed, she saw that J..Jenny had moved. She was standing in the doorway. She was probably groaning but she'd also lost her voice, just like Jip, beneath the deafening roar of the tractor engine. Carrie shook her head. She was seeing things. J..Jenny was still moving. There was a cracking sound like the firing of a gun as Jed's cruel plank of wood broke in two. Jed jerked the tractor forwards and pulled J..Jenny through the shed door.

Jed paused for a moment to make sure that J..Jenny was safely through the door. He shouted something at Carrie but no sound came; he was terrifying. With a wave of his hand, Jed slipped his foot from the clutch pedal and set off towards the drive on his beloved tractor. J..Jenny walked backwards as best she could. She looked at Carrie as she set off on her walk with the tractor as if to say *'Are you sure?'*

Carrie and Jip chased after her as if to say *'It's alright, we'll save you!'*

J..Jenny opened her mouth but no sound came.

'You're lying,' she mouthed.

Jed had reached the drive. J..Jenny wasn't moving fast enough for him. She was still suffering in labour. He changed up a gear and accelerated around the corner of the cow sheds. A short, sharp, run down the drive would probably do the trick. J..Jenny wasn't used to walking backwards, and certainly not at speed.

She couldn't keep up. Her legs gave up and she toppled onto her side. The two little feet that had been sticking out of her rear end were joined by two little legs. Cows can give birth lying down as well as standing up. It might speed things up for her now she was lying down. She wasn't going to suffer a long labour today; Jed was giving her a helping hand.

Carrie's hands reached out to J..Jenny, but they were only her hands. She wasn't a real Jon after all. She wasn't big and strong. She could do nothing with them but tear at her hair. She could do nothing with her mouth but make sounds that could not be heard above the revs of the tractor engine. She could do nothing with her legs but stand and watch as the tractor pulled J..Jenny round and round the farmyard. Round and round the yard they cart wheeled. J..Jenny looked tired, her tongue was hanging out; giving birth is thirsty work. Little Carrie's mother had drunk a whole bucket of water without stopping after she'd been born. But Jed wasn't tired, so there was no time to stop for a drink of water.

Besides, his method was working. Things were speeding up nicely. The two little feet and legs were joined by a nose and a head. J..Jenny wasn't going to suffer a long labour today. Jed paused from circling for a moment to check that J..Jenny was ready for one, final, push. He couldn't really see for sure from where he was sitting; J..Jenny wouldn't look at him. She held her head at a funny angle. She was being awkward, and he was trying to spare her suffering. She was Jon's favourite cow; she deserved that, didn't she?

Jed jerked J..Jenny and the tractor forwards again; their coupling broke in two. J..Jenny's calf lay stretched out on the ground as straight and lifeless as a plank of wood. Carrie stood still, in a daze. She shook her head. She was seeing things. The tractor had stopped, but J..Jenny was still moving. She was still alive. The deafening sound of the tractor had been replaced by the relentless sound of Jip barking. He'd got his voice back even if Carrie hadn't.

'Water! She needs a drink of water!'

It was all that Carrie could think to do. She grabbed a bucket that was conveniently already full of water from outside the nearest cowshed. She knelt down in the blood soaked mud of the farmyard to give such comfort as she could to J..Jenny. Carrie tried to pick up her head, but it was too heavy. J..Jenny wouldn't look at her any more than she'd look at Jed. Round and round, her eyes cart-wheeled in every direction.

In desperation, Carrie used her hands to spoon water onto her tongue, in the hope that it would soothe her. A shiver ran down Carrie's spine as Jed's shadow approached her from behind. Jed laughed. He *still* hadn't finished proving himself. He grabbed Carrie by the back of her hair and picked her up off the ground.

'Now it's your turn, darlin'. You've been asking for this for a long time, and now you're going to get it. It's just you and me.'

'*And me, don't forget me!*' growled Jip as he went for the back of Jed's legs.

Jip went mad. Jed went madder.

'Bloody dog!'

Jed turned and kicked Jip across the yard. He had to kick him more than once because Jip wasn't giving up any time soon.

'*Run, Carrie, run!*' he yelped as he flew through the air and landed flat and hard against the cowshed wall.

'No!'

Carrie's mouth moved; it was terrifying. Her legs moved; they started running. It was terrifying.

'*So sorry, Jip. I can't wait any longer.*'

Carrie ran.

'*Oh no, Jip! What are we going to do?*'

Jip lay still. He wasn't going to wag his tail any time soon. But he was still alive.

'*Run!*' he whispered.

Carrie wasn't moving fast enough. She changed up a gear and accelerated around the corner of the cowsheds. She could hear Jed's legs close behind her. He was catching her up. They'd reached the barn. There was no sound coming from his feet now that they were running on the soft bedding of loose hay. It was eerily quiet. Ghostly. A shiver ran down her spine as he grabbed her legs from behind. Carrie toppled onto her side. Her suffering was going to speed up now that she was lying down. Jed was going to give her a helping hand. He straddled Carrie and put his hand around her neck.

'Do you want me to tie you down?' he asked, reaching out for a stray piece of orange baler twine.

Carrie had no words for Jed. She lay very still. Jed stopped reaching for the string to check on her. She was still alive.

'Oh, come on Carrie! Don't be a spoil sport! You're not giving up already, are you? Where's the fun in that?'

Carrie lay stretched out on the ground as straight and lifeless as a plank of wood.

'Have it your way, darlin', it's all the same to me.'

Jed relaxed his hold on Carrie's neck. He used his hands to undo his trouser belt and buttons. Round and round, Carrie's eyes cart-wheeled in every direction. She wouldn't look at Jed. When he'd finished with his own trousers, he started on her jeans. His hands were big, her buttons were small. She was going to be awkward, just like Jon's cow.

Suddenly, in the triangular shaped gap that was still between their legs, Carrie's knees appeared from nowhere. With one enormous cart horse kick of both feet she batted Jed off her. He lost his balance and toppled over onto his side. Carrie was getting up and moving away, but Jed still had one helping hand free. He used it to grab hold of her ankle and bring her back down to his level. Jed laughed.

'That's more like it, darlin'! That's the Carrie I know and love!'

Carrie went mad. Jed went madder.

'Bloody Bitch!'

Jed slapped her across the face. He had to do it more than once because she wasn't giving up any time soon. Carrie stood her ground as best she could. It was difficult because she was lying down. She pressed herself deep into the layers of the soft hay bedding of the barn floor to get as far away from Jed as possible. Jed pressed his lips onto hers. The cold March wind pressed down on them both, coupling them together. Carrie suddenly felt very, very, alone. Had a lifetime of longing and waiting brought her to this moment? She still had a bit further to go, and it looked like she was going to go it with Jed.

She recognised his hands. They were big and strong, hard and rough. But they weren't Jon's. These hands were immovable. They had no gentleness. They went straight for the places she'd been keeping special.

Jed was pleased; his method was working. Things were speeding up nicely. The bare skin of her body was joined by that of her legs as Jed finally mastered her little buttons and ripped her jeans from her. All of a sudden, Carrie was back out in the fields, looking the cattle. The bull was there. He towered over her now; a King with beautiful white teeth and a glorious thick neck of long dark curls falling over her face. He made a funny snorting sound as something long, hard, and wet dropped out of his jeans. The King laughed. He rubbed himself up and down her belly. Carrie could smell him.

'Now then, Darlin', which way round do you want it? Are you wearing your forwards or your backwards looking face today?'

But Carrie was no lady in waiting. She reeled and shook, she kicked and punched. She was *not* going to let this King lay his immense weight on her. A shiver ran down her spine. She wasn't big and strong. She couldn't save J..Jenny. She knew couldn't save herself.

'I think forwards,' grinned Jed. 'I want you to see that I got you first.'

Jed paused for a moment to check that Carrie was ready for one, final, push. She wouldn't look at him. She held her head at a funny angle. She was being awkward and he was trying to show her how much he loved her.

'Cow!' he said.

She was Jon's favourite cow. He deserved her too, didn't he? Jed jerked forwards towards Carrie again, but their coupling broke in two. Carrie lay still, in a daze. She shook her head. She was seeing things. Jon had grabbed Jed by the back of his hair and pulled him off her.

'Now it's your t..turn, b..brother. You've been asking for this for a long t..time, and now you're going to get it. It's just you and m..me.'

Jed went mad. Jon went madder. It was time for him to prove himself. And he did. Their feet made no sound as they pressed each other, over and over again, deep into the layers of the soft hay bedding of the barn floor. Their hands, big and strong, hard and rough. There was no gentleness in them. They were immovable. They went straight for each other. Two Kings had to become one. It was eerily quiet. Ghostly.

'*Water!*'

Jip was licking her face. With his wet nose and bleeding chin, he lay down alongside Carrie on the soft hay bedding and gave such comfort as he could. Carrie's hands reached out to him. He let her hold him long after she stopped trembling.

Jed groaned. He was suffering. Jon hadn't finished proving himself yet. Round and round they cart wheeled around the barn and outside onto the drive. Jed looked tired, he had more than his tongue hanging out; he hadn't had time to do up his trousers properly. Both his tongue and his 'pith' drooped long, red raw, and slimy. Jon wasn't tired. Jed reeled and shook as his brother laid his full, immense weight upon him. Blow after blow pressed onto his lips, his head, his body. He tore at his hair. And still the cold March wind pressed him on.

Carrie, still shaking uncontrollably, somehow managed to get her legs back into her jeans and stand up.

'Oh my God, what are we going to do?'

Jip whined. Carrie and Jip chased after the storm that was bearing down on the orchard by now. The trees of the orchard were struggling to keep Jed and Jon apart. The sad looking tree in the corner looked straight at them. It reached out towards them in a gentle and pleading sort of way, but Jon and Jed were still too busy proving themselves to notice it. Just then, there was a loud cracking sound like the firing of a gun. Jip yelped. Carrie ducked down in panic. The sound came from the direction of the farmyard.

'We're saved! They're back!'

Carrie opened her mouth but no sound came:

'Help!'

She could still feel Jed's lips upon it, choking her. Jip must have felt it, too, because he'd lost his bark. But their legs still worked and so they ran towards the sound that still echoed around them in the cold March wind. Old man Wilson was standing in the yard, the shotgun in his hand hanging straight and lifeless as a plank of wood. Carrie grabbed his other arm:

'Help! Come quick, they're killing each other!'

Old man Wilson's long, silver grey hair batted at his face in the cold March wind. His palest of pale blue eyes stared down at J..Jenny. Carrie pulled at his arm again. He was immovable. He stood as straight and lifeless as J..Jenny who lay at his feet. He'd just given her a helping hand; her suffering was over.

'It's Jon and Jed! You must come now! Stop them!'

Old man Wilson's ears didn't seem to be working properly, nor his eyes for that matter. He only had eyes for Jenny and ears for the cold March wind. It was as if Carrie didn't exist. He didn't hear her calling him; he didn't feel her pulling his arm. He didn't see her red neck, her swollen, tear stained face, or the little buttons on her jeans that had been hastily fastened into the wrong holes. In desperation she tore at his hair. She grabbed hold of it and gave it an almighty pull. She jerked his head towards her. He stared down at her.

'No. It's time.'

'Where's Mavis?' No reply.

'Where's Mavis?' she shrieked in his ear.

'Stayed with Ab.'

'Think about Mavis, think about your wife! These are your sons and they're killing each other! Do something!'

'I am! Can't you see that?'

Old man Wilson shouted so loud that Carrie lost her balance. It was like being grabbed around the ankles and brought down by Jed all over again. She staggered backwards; he was terrifying.

'Run, Carrie, run!'

Carrie ran. Jip walked.

'Jon!'

It was eerily quiet in the orchard. Ghostly. No sound came except the cold March wind, pressing itself in and out of the trees. There was no movement except the cracking of their branches, a thousand broken planks of wood, giving way to Carrie and Jip. A shiver ran down her spine at the sight in front of her.

He was shaking uncontrollably. His brother sat, straddled above him, pressing him down into the cold, stone, bench. His hands were around his neck. Jed had no words for Jon. He stopped squeezing his neck.

'He's dead. I've killed him.'

He lay very still. He lay stretched out on the stone bench as straight and lifeless as a plank of wood. Jon stood up. His dark brown eyes stared down at his brother; he'd finally finished proving himself.

'No!' said Carrie.

Jed was still moving. He was still alive. Just. So was Jon. Carrie held him long after he'd stopped trembling. They had no words for each other.

Wearing her forwards looking face, Carrie looked up at Jon. He touched her tear stained face, he stroked her hair. He kissed her gently on the forehead. She recognised his hands. They were big and strong, hard and rough. They were covered with blood. They weren't Jed's. They were full of gentleness. His hair wrapped around her neck like a black necklace. She took hold of it. She kissed it. It was soft. Black velvet. His blood flowed for her like water over her hands and face; it soothed them. Mouths touching, they came together like branches of the same tree, sharing one root.

Long after Jon had finished kissing her, they stood together. A shiver ran down Carrie's spine. Had a lifetime of longing and waiting brought her to this moment? She still had a bit further to go, and it looked like she was going to go it with Jon after all. And Jip was there too, pleased to see that his master was still alive. They felt safe. They were far away in their own beautiful world, and nothing and nobody could take that away from them.

The Falcon saw the two trees standing together, growing together, in his orchard. He swooped down on them from out of nowhere. Old man Wilson grabbed Carrie and pulled her away from Jon.

'Go, Carrie! I'll deal with it. He's not dead.'

Carrie stood still in a daze. She shook her head. She was hearing things.

'Of course he's not dead. I'm holding him! He belongs to me!'

'Trust me. Do as I say and everything will be alright. Go! And stay away for a week or two.'

Carrie stared at old man Wilson. He was immovable. He stood straight and lifeless over Jed's barely breathing body.

'No!'

Old man Wilson's ears didn't seem to be working properly, nor his eyes for that matter. He only had eyes for Jed and ears for the cold March wind. It was as if Carrie didn't exist. In desperation she reached out towards Jon. He stood straight and lifeless, barely breathing. He'd finished proving himself and now he was finished. Old man Wilson pulled Carrie away from Jon once more. He had to do it more than once because she wasn't giving up any time soon.

Carrie wouldn't look at him. She held her head at a funny angle. She was being awkward and he was trying to show her how much he loved her. Jon saw:

'Go!' whispered Jon, finally breaking their coupling in two.

'Do as he says. It'll be alright. We'll be alright.'

'And get yourself cleaned up. I don't want you going home looking like that...'

———————◆———————

'Put your overalls straight into the washing machine, Carrie. I'll see to them in a minute!' called Jill from inside the kitchen.

'They're not dirty,' said Carrie, walking into the kitchen wearing her squeaky clean overalls by way of proof.

They were fastened all the way up to her neck.

'I didn't wear them today.'

'Oh,' said her mother, sounding disappointed. 'I was quite looking forward to doing a bit of scrubbing of some mucky overalls! Look at my hands, Carrie!'

Carrie looked.

'I've helped your Dad again today down at the garage, and I got covered in dirt! My clothes are ruined...'

'So are mine...'

'...my hands are stained...'

'So are mine...'

'...I've had such a great time...'
'....'
'...I could get clean by washing away your dirt!' laughed her mother.
I'll never be clean again...'
'I'll just go up and change,' said Carrie.
'O.K. Dinner won't be long. What have you done today?'
'Nothing much.'

Carrie took her usual route around the edge of the kitchen to keep away from her mother who was setting the kitchen table for dinner. She knew her mother couldn't bear farmyard smells. She couldn't bear them herself right now and they were very strong today. She felt sick. She couldn't cope with a bashing from her mother about it as well.

'Ah, come here! You look like you need a hug!' said a cheerful Jill.
'No, I'm alright,' said Carrie, continuing on her way.
'Well, I need one.'

Jill grabbed Carrie and pulled her towards her. She put her arms around her and held her tight. Her hair gently pressed against the side of Carrie's face. It was soft and sweet; it was almonds and coconut. It soothed her. Carrie stood still in a daze. She gave her mother such comfort as she could. She held her trembling deep inside.

'What's this?' asked Jill, suddenly breaking their coupling in two.
'What?' Carrie staggered backwards; her mother was terrifying.
'You've got blood on your face!'

Carrie stared at her mother. She opened her mouth but no sound came:

I have no words...'

'It's alright, Carrie. You don't have to protect me!' smiled her mother kindly. 'You've helped to calve a cow today! I bet you're covered in blood and slime underneath those overalls. I'm not daft, you know. I can smell it! And you didn't want me to see it, so you've covered up...'

'Yes.'

'Well you don't need to worry about that sort of thing any more. You must be exhausted. Get off upstairs and get changed. Drop all your dirty things down and I'll see to them. Was it a difficult calving?'

'Yes.'

'Ah, what a shame. I can't bear to see suffering. I hope that poor cow didn't suffer too long.'

'I'm going to have a bath now.'

Jill chased after Carrie as she was climbing the stairs. Carrie changed up a gear and accelerated into the bathroom.

'I've just had a great idea!' called her mother. 'Why don't we invite the Wilson's for Sunday lunch tomorrow?'

'No!' shouted the bathroom door, opening up very slightly.

'Why not? They're your friends aren't they? Why don't you ring them up and ask them? It wouldn't do any harm, would it?'

'No!' shouted the bathroom door.

Her mother's ears didn't seem to be working properly; she wasn't giving up any time soon. She pressed her head against the bathroom door. Carrie pressed her hands against it on the other side. The smell of coconuts and almonds was very strong. Carrie felt sick. She couldn't bear the sweet clean smell any longer. She locked the door and pressed herself deep into the bathroom, leaning against the sink, to get as far away as possible from her mother, the door, and the coconuts and almonds.

'They've got a lot on at the minute.'

'Oh, alright then. But I'm determined to get things right for you, Carrie. I didn't get the chance, but you're going to get it. I want you to enjoy your life and have all the things a young woman should be having at your age, if you know what I mean!'

Her mother was having a little giggle to herself on the other side of the door.

'Please! Not now Mum. I need a bath.'

'It's alright, Carrie. Trust me, everything will be alright. Everything's going to be different from now on!'

'Yes, it is.'

Jill cheerfully disappeared down the stairs, humming to herself, pleased that she'd done a good job of reassuring her daughter. Carrie disappeared into the toilet bowl, pleased that she was able to finally release the trembling that she'd been holding in her stomach.

'Do as he says. It'll be alright. We'll be alright.'

Carrie stood up, still in a daze. She got herself cleaned up.

'Yes, do as he says. It'll be alright. We'll be alright…We'll be alright! He's finally found his voice…'

'Good morning, boys. You won't mind if I just grab a coffee first, will you? I've got such a lot on this morning.'

Carrie breezed past the coffee machine queue and pushed in front of 'String.' She still hadn't found out what department this mouthy, spotty youth, was from, but she really didn't care. He immediately backed away at the sound of her approaching stilettos. She'd hurt his pride and his feet more than once. He wasn't taking any chances this morning, so he graciously made way for her to a chorus of moans and groans from the rest of the queue.

'Thank you boys. See you later.'

The 'boys' watched her steal her coffee and walk away, leaving them thirsty and still waiting in line. As soon as she'd gone, 'String' found his mouth worked again.

'Well, she might have got a lot on today, but it's definitely not clothes!'

The 'boys' laughed themselves through the coffee machine queue, but they still felt thirsty at the end of it. And it wasn't for coffee. It was going to be a long morning. Every time Carrie stood up from her chair, walked past them, leaned over her desk or, even worse, leaned over their desks, they suffered. The only solution was not to look at her. They had to hold their heads at a funny angle. It was very awkward and difficult to work like that. Carrie noticed it, too.

'What's the matter with you all today? Why are you all being so awkward? We've got deadlines to meet you know. You're just a bunch of jerks, the whole lot of you! Pathetic creatures...'

Carrie was determined to become a good journalist so she worked on her descriptive skills a little more, until Dennis stopped her:

'Carrie!' he called sharply. 'A word if you please!'

Carrie pressed herself into the office door with a waiting Dennis.

'Yes?'

'Have a seat, if you please.'

Carrie had a seat. Dennis escaped around the back of his big mahogany wooden desk. He only had to deal with half a Carrie sitting at his desk; her short skirt and matching long legs disappeared from his view.

'How are you doing today, Carrie?'

'Fine, thank you.'

'Good, good.'

'What do you want because I'm busy.'

'I can see that. You're giving everyone a run for their money at the minute, Carrie. Maybe you need to slow down a bit. Not everyone is as efficient as you, you know.'

'Are you complaining that I work too hard?'

'No! Not at all, at all,' soothed Dennis. 'I just want you to look after yourself, that's all. You're precious us to us, here at the paper.'

'Are you giving me a pay rise then, or do you want something else?' snapped Carrie, leaning forwards across the mahogany wooden desk.

'No, no!' smiled the bushy moustached Irishman, putting his hands up to be clear to himself and block Carrie's upper half from his view.

'I've got a bit of news for you that you might find upsetting, so I wanted to tell you in private.'

Carrie stared at Dennis; she'd got a lot on today.

'Well then,' Dennis continued, 'I've just had a telephone call from a Mr Wilson. I believe he's the farmer you go to for your 'Twentieth Century Land Girl' research.'

'Yes.'

'Well Carrie, love, he says he's very sorry but his circumstances are changed, and he can't have you at the farm any more.'

Carrie stared at Dennis.

'Is that it? I've got a lot on today.'

'Well not quite, Carrie. He said to tell you that his son has gone to Australia to work on a cattle ranch. He's been thinking about emigrating for some time now, as you may know. His other son has no interest in farming. He's a mechanic. Good with his hands but no interest in animals. You know the type. Now the old man's left running the farm on his own, he's got to wind it down. He's finished, basically, and he can't suffer the risk of having a volunteer on the farm any more. It's the insurance, you see. You're too much of a risk.'

'Obviously.'

'Well then, Carrie, does that put us in a bit of a fix for your 'Land Girl' articles? You've still got a few to run before your year is up.'

'Not at all! Why don't I do one last article and then call it a day? I'd just about had enough of it anyway. It was interesting while it lasted, but it's about time I moved on. You haven't got to be editor-in-chief without taking a risk or two in your career and it's about time I did the same. Do you still have any contacts in London?'

Carrie leaned forwards across the mahogany desk.

'I'm sure I could be useful to somebody.'

'I'm sure you could, Carrie, if that's what you really want.'

'I want.'

'Alright then. I'll give it some thought for you.'

'Thank you, Dennis. Can I go now?'

'Yes, thank you, Carrie.'

Carrie got up from her seat and turned to go, until Dennis stopped her.

'And Carrie!' he called sharply. 'One last thing!'

Carrie pressed herself into the office door once more and waited for Dennis. Dennis pressed his hands into her shoulders. He hadn't got to be editor-in-chief without taking a risk or two in his long career. He'd been around the block a few times. He'd seen and done it all before. But Carrie hadn't.

'It doesn't suit you, Carrie. This, (he lowered his eyes to her ankles and all the way back up to her face) doesn't suit you. You're so lovely as you are, I don't want to see you get hurt. Trust me, whatever it is, let it go!'

Dennis stared at Carrie, but her ears didn't seem to be working properly, nor her eyes for that matter. They were glazed over with a gelatine coating; tasty looking little tarts without any nutritional value in them. They were empty.

'Trust you, eh? Is that why you're pressing your hands into my shoulders?'

'Oh, I apologise, Carrie. I mean you no harm.'

Dennis backed away from Carrie; she was terrifying.

'Of course you don't. You're not the first boss who's said that to me, and look at what a sleaze bag he turned out to be! Trust! Men don't know the meaning of the word. Perhaps I should write an article about that! I could put you in it then, but I don't expect you'd like that, would you? Block it, wouldn't you? We're a newspaper of quality and integrity here, but only as long as it suits the men!'

'Carrie! It's me, Dennis!'

Dennis stared at Carrie; he was terrified.

'Are you going to let me go now?'

'Yes.'

'Thank you.'

Dennis let her go. He needed coffee. He was pleased there was no queue. The coffee didn't make him feel any better. It was going to be a long morning. He still had a few contacts in London if that's what Carrie really wanted. He'd be sorry to see her go. He'd been around the block a few times. He'd seen and done it all before. He'd a feeling that Carrie was setting herself up for a lifetime of suffering and there wasn't a single thing he could do about it.

Friday 23rd March

Dear Reader,

The month of March was named, by the Romans, after Mars, the God of war. Quite fitting, then, that he was also the guardian of agriculture. Mars was tall and handsome, mean, and self centred. He didn't care who won or lost the battle, he just liked to see bloodshed. Quite fitting then, for the guardian of agriculture, for down on the farm life is a constant battle. Farming is all about life and death; there is bloodshed a plenty on an almost daily basis.

You may have heard the phrase 'March comes in like a lion and goes out like a lamb.' The Anglo-Saxons called March 'the stormy month.' So, March is unpredictable. Down on the farm, the work at this time of year is very weather dependent. Take 'tractor' jobs, for example. There are a surprising number of uses for tractors beyond the usual one of driving around a field. I shan't list them all here; it would mean nothing to you, Reader. You'd have to see it to believe it. Trust me. Tractors speed things up nicely.

But March is not just weather dependent; it's 'whether' dependent, too. March is known as the month of expectation. We expect the Spring to spring. We expect things to get better. But expectation can be a dangerous thing. On the farm, chicks arrive. They are expected to grow up into hens and lay eggs. There's no guarantee they'll grow up or lay eggs if they do; just like people, really. Storms are unpredictable. You can never tell how or when they're going to end, or what damage will have been done. Charles Dickens describes it perfectly:

'It was one of those March days when the sun shines hot and the wind blows cold: when it is summer in the light and winter in the shade.' [†]

Unpredictable.

The March flower is the wild daffodil, called 'Narcissus' after the boy from a Greek myth. Narcissus was very proud and beautiful. He rejected everyone who loved him. Nemesis, the God of revenge, punished him. He lured him to a pool where Narcissus fell in love with his own, beautiful reflection. Eventually Narcissus realised that his reflection could never love him back. He died of grief. His body disappeared and a flower, the narcissus, our friendly yellow daffodil, grew in its place. Daffodils look very pretty at this time of year but their colours are short lived. They soon fade and die. Their story is a reminder of the dangers of loving someone who can't or won't love you back. Expectation causes suffering;

expectation is unpredictable.

It's 'Lady Day' on March 25th. In the religious calendar this is the 'Feast of Annunciation of the Blessed Virgin Mary.' Lady Day was traditionally a 'time of entry', a day when farmers 'entered' onto virgin soil, moved onto new farms and new fields. Sometimes they had to pack up their families and move far away to pastures new. And this is what I must do, Reader. This is my last 'entry' as your 'Twentieth Century Land Girl'. It is my 'time of exit' to pastures new. March has no room for ladies! The Gods want war! They will have their blood!

March came in like a lion this year. The cold March wind has been a wind of change for me. I hope, in the calm after the storm, it will go out like a lamb for you, Reader. I hope Spring will spring for you. I hope things will get better for you. I want to thank my farmers. I've been blown away by my experience 'down on the farm.'

It is an experience that will stay with me forever.

I hear the farmer say 'Ah, right you are, then.'

I say 'Ah, goodbye...'

———◆———

'Carrie!' called the Walnut sharply, from her dressing table drawer:

'A word if you please!'

'I have no words.'

'We all deserve to be happy, Carrie. It's true for me, but not for you.'

'No!'

'It's alright, Carrie. Trust me. Everything will be alright. You've been asking for this for a long time. I'll make you happy, darlin'!'

'No!'

'Do you want me to tie you down?'

'No!'

'That's it, good girl. Have you seen one of these before?'

'No!'

'Which way round do you want it?'

'No!'

'Give over, Jed, you great Lummox! I'll put the tractor on and make some tea. Let go of her neck, she's choking! She won't be able to drink me tea!'

'No!'

'It's alright, Carrie love, we'll save you!'

'You're lying!'

'Bloody bitch!'

'No!'

'That's it, good girl! One final push...'

'No!'

'See! I got you first...'

'No! Jon!'

'He's dead. I've killed him!'

'No!'

'Go, Carrie! I'll deal with it. He's not dead. He's gone to Australia.'

'No!'

'You're too much of a risk.'

'No!'

'Cow!'

'Ah, right you are, then.'

'No! No! No!'

'That's it, good girl,' whispered the Walnut in her dressing table drawer. 'There are no words for what this is...run, Carrie, run...'

Saturday 24th March

'Ah do!'

'Ah do Ab, how you getting on?'

'Not so bad, not so bad. I'm pleased to see ya! How are ya?'

'I've brought you the paper,' said Mavis, sitting down heavily in the blue, plastic covered, hospital chair next to old Ab's bed. Mavis sighed into the chair. It was actually a very comfortable chair. She allowed her letter 'R' shaped body to relax into a letter 'C'. She'd had a long bus journey to get to the hospital; she was exhausted.

'Ah, I've already seen it,' said old Ab. 'It's a bad business. Such a shame.'

'I've made you some little apple pies, your favourites,' said Mavis, rummaging around in her generous, frilly shopping bag.

'Well bless ya. Thank you. Just hide them in me cupboard, shall you?'

Mavis hid them.

'That's a right big bag you've got there. Have you been shopping?'

'No, I've just brought me knitting with me.'

'Ah, you like a bit of knitting on a Saturday afternoon.'

Mavis started knitting. She had a ball of white wool.

'What are you making?' asked old Ab.

'A little white dress for this here doll.'

Mavis pulled a small plastic doll from her frilly shopping bag. She held it up so that old Ab could see it.

'Ah, she's lovely,' he said, kindly.

The small plastic doll had long, golden hair. She was tall and slim. She was very pretty. She was smiling.

'Thought she'd make a good angel,' said Mavis.

'Ah, that she will, that she will.'

Old Ab tried, but could not keep the sound of sadness away from his voice. Mavis changed the subject.

'How are your bones?' she asked.

'Cracked but nowt broken!'

'We're all cracking up,' said Mavis. 'Cracked and broken, we are, and no trip to hospital can mend us.'

'Now, don't you fret, Mavis. Trust me. Everything will turn out right. Just you wait and see!'

Mavis measured her white knitted dress against the body of the pretty, plastic, doll with the long, golden, hair. It wasn't quite right just yet.

'No, it's not right.'

Mavis carried on knitting. Her eyes finally cracked open. Tears flowed, but she didn't need to see to carry on knitting.

'No, it won't be right! Our Jed's always been a bad lad, always been wrong in the head. Now he's really wrong in the head! Something's happened to him. He's lost his words, gone just like our Jon! He just sits staring out of the window all day! Alec the vet says he should get checked out at hospital but the old man's having none of it. Says we don't want folk round asking questions. And he's sent me lovely Jon away. And I'm never going to see him again, and not me lovely Carrie, either! How could she just up and leave us! Without any warning? Them two was made for one another, where's the kindness in that? It's just plain cruel if you ask me. I don't know what's been cracking off. Somat funny! She didn't even say goodbye! I just don't know where it'll all end...'

Mavis reached the end of her row of knitting and automatically started the next one. Old Ab reached out a long, cold, bony hand and stopped Mavis mid row.

'Ah, it's a bad business, but look here!' he said, giving the angel's white knitted dress a gentle squeeze, 'there are no ends, only beginnings!'

Old Ab pointed across at the newspaper lying open on his hospital bed trolley.

"Time for pastures new,' she said. We always knew she was going to go sometime. The lads have obviously had a falling out over it. Your old man's right, it probably is the kindest thing to let Jon go. He was sweet on her; it'll help him to forget. But remember what else she says here, 'it's an experience she'll never forget!' So don't fret, Mavis, she's sending you a message there. She loves you and she'll never forget you. She probably couldn't say it in person; it'd be too upsetting for her. She probably didn't have any choice in the matter. I reckon she'll be back to see you one day, when she's all big and successful, you mark my words. And Jon too. He'll not be gone long, just you wait and see.'

Mavis stared down at the pretty, plastic doll sitting in her lap. She shrugged old Ab's hands off her knitting, let out a big sigh, and took a big embroidered handkerchief out of her blouse sleeve and blew her nose.

'Ah, right you are, then. Now you'd best let me get on with this here dress. A naked angel don't seem right to me!'

'Ah.'

'It won't be the same without them, though. I shall miss them every minute of every day.'

'And I miss your cups of tea! Here comes the tea trolley. They don't make it like you, Mavis!'

'Well, let's have one anyway, and one of me little apple pies, before I've got to run for me bus.'

'Ah, right you are, then...'

Friday 30th March

'Ah, I'm glad you're both here. I've got some really good news!'

Carrie burst in loudly through the lounge door to find her parents looking and behaving like normal parents for a change. Bill was sitting in his own armchair, pretending to read while he watched the T.V. and Jill was sitting on the sofa with her embroidery. Carrie was shocked. She'd taken to making a dramatic entrance into the lounge to give her parents due notice to make themselves decent. They were usually draped all over each other on the sofa these days; it was tasteless and disgusting. It was the ultimate role reversal. And it was unfair.

'What's that, love?' asked Bill.

Carrie hesitated. She lost her words at the sight of the familiar, comfortable scene. It made her feel very uncomfortable all of a sudden.

'There's nothing like a bit of good news, especially if it's romantic!' smiled Jill, putting down her embroidery to concentrate on her daughter's face.

'Oh, no, nothing like that!' replied her disgusted daughter. 'I've got a new job!'

'Oh congratulations!' and 'Well done!' her parents called out at one and the same time.

'What is it?' asked Bill.

'Dennis has arranged it for me. I'm going to London to work on his old paper. It'll be the same sort of stuff that I've been doing here, but it'll be on a national paper. I've got to work three months' notice and then I'll be off!'

Jill and Bill stared at each other and then at Carrie. It was their turn to feel uncomfortable all of a sudden.

'Oh,' said Jill. 'I didn't see that coming. I thought you were leaning more towards farming than journalism these days.'

Carrie burst out, loudly:

'Good God, Mother, don't you know me at all? That farm thing was nothing! It was just a means to an end, and now I've reached it. I thought you'd be pleased for me!'

Bill hesitated. He was lost for words at the sight of his unfamiliar daughter. He was shocked. She was tasteless and disgusting.

'What about Jon?' he asked, quietly.

'What about him?' asked Carrie, loudly.

'Well, we thought you and him were, you know, going to get serious.'

'Yes,' said Jill. 'He's such a lovely, quiet, young man. I saw how he looked at you, Carrie. Are you sure you want to give that up for some career in London?'

'Get real, Mother. That's the trouble with women, they always think everything's about romance. But it's not. Men don't think like that at all, and unfortunately, we live in a man's world most of the time.'

'Not all men,' said Bill, quietly.

'Trust me, yes, most men,' snapped Carrie. 'Jon was fun, the farm was fun to begin with, but that's no life for me! I've got a lot more to give than that.'

'Well, they'll miss you at the farm, I'm sure. And Jon will be heartbroken,' suggested Jill.

'Sure, he's so heartbroken, Mum, he's gone to Australia to work on a cattle ranch. He's been planning to emigrate for some time now, and old man Wilson is winding the farm down to retire now he's gone. They want rid of me just as much as I want to be rid of them. Ask Dennis if you don't believe me!'

'It's alright, we believe you, Carrie. It's just a bit of a shock,' said Bill.

'Not at all! You know I've always wanted to be a journalist. And,' stressed Carrie, 'my other bit of good news is that we had a visit from a solicitor at the office today. Mr Pike has left me some money in his Will.'

'Oh, how lovely of him. Well, we always made him welcome here, despite what people used to say about him,' said Jill.

'At least Mr Pike believed in me. He knew how much I wanted to be a journalist!'

'Don't be silly, Carrie, we've always been on your side, and you know that,' said Bill.

Carrie ignored her dad.

'He's left me quite a lot of money, too. It'll be enough to set myself up with a place in London and to pay for any training I need.'

'Oh, well, congratulations love, if that's what you really want,' said Bill.

'Yes, I'll miss you every minute of every day,' said Jill. 'It won't be the same without you. But we want you to be happy, Carrie. Your Dad's right. We love you, so go to it, if it's what you really, really, want.'

'I want! I'm going to be a real journalist now. I've got what I've always wanted. I finally know who I am...'

Part Five

Spring Again –
'New Life…'

'Say something, then!'

'I can't, I'm lost for words,' stuttered Debs. 'This must be an April Fool!'

'It's too late in the day for that. You've moved on, why shouldn't I?' questioned Carrie, aggressively.

'Of course you should, you can, if you want,' soothed Debs. 'It's just such a massive, such a sudden, change of direction, that's all.'

'Well that's 'pot calling kettle black!' Look at you! You loved working at the garden centre and in a matter of weeks you've reduced your hours there to take on all these old biddies. Did you plan to become warden to these old folk here? Did you plan to do either of those things, in actual fact?'

'No, I didn't. You know that. But my situation was different. I had some bad luck, remember? Change was forced on me Carrie. I had to change or die. Thank God, I got the chance to change. I got the help I needed at the right time from you, your mum and dad, the Wilsons, and things are getting better for me. I'm one of the lucky ones. I wouldn't be a friend to you if I didn't question what you're doing, because it looks to me like you're choosing to die, and I don't know why. I can't see you being happy, living and working in London. That's not the Carrie I know; the Carrie that loves getting her hands dirty!'

'There'll be plenty of dirt in London to make me feel right at home. There'll be smog and pollution, litter on the streets, and I'll be working for a paper that specialises in dishing up dirt on a daily basis. If that's all you think I'm about then I'll fit in just fine, won't I?'

'That's not what I meant and you know it,' said Debs. 'Sarcasm doesn't suit you, Carrie. All this career stuff doesn't suit you. I just don't want to see you get hurt, that's all.'

'Deep down, you're just jealous I've got a career, aren't you? You always have been. It's not my fault that all you ever think about is men, and look where that got you! I'm not going to make the same mistakes as you. No man is ever going to be master of me!'

'Carrie! It's me, Debs! What on earth's the matter with you?'

Debs stared at Carrie; she was terrified.

'Talking of men, what about Jon? He's not a mistake, is he?' she tried.

'All men are a mistake! I'd have thought you, of all people, would agree with me on that!'

'Not all men. Not your Dad, not Mr Wilson. And definitely not Jon.'

'Yes, definitely Jon. He's gone to work on a cattle ranch in Australia. You've been away with the fairies, working amongst flowers and old folk, neither of which fight you back, for too long, Debs. I wanted to spare you the truth, but I think you'd better have it, after all.'

Carrie stared at Debs; she looked terrified.

'The truth is,' Carrie paused for a big breath, 'the truth is that the Wilsons don't want me on the farm. The old man sent me a message at the paper telling me I can't work there any more. It's the insurance; I'm too much of a risk. Jon's got this chance to go to Australia and so the old man's winding the farm down. He's finished with it all. Jon and me, it's finished. I'm finished.'

Carrie paused again, for dramatic effect. She was a journalist; she knew how to spin a tale or two.

'Going to London is a sudden change of direction, I know. Like you, this is a change that's forced on me. Of course I miss Jon like crazy. This new job, going away, will help me get over it. It's the help *I* need, come at the right time. Things are getting better for me, too. I'm lucky, too. It's a good thing, can't you see that?'

Debs paused.

'Yes, I can see.'

Carrie was pleased. She relaxed a little.

'I'll still come back at weekends. We'll still keep in touch just the same. I'm sorry I got angry with you before, I suppose I wanted to protect you. I didn't want to burst your bubble about the Wilsons. I thought if I just told you about the London thing I wouldn't need to hurt you with anything else.'

'You haven't hurt me,' said Debs quietly.

'I'm glad,' smiled Carrie.

'I just need a hug,' said Debs.

They had a hug. Debs held on tight to Carrie. Heads, hands, arms, faces, hair. Tighter and tighter. Carrie laughed.

'Are you going to let me go?'

'Oh, I'm sorry, Carrie. I mean you no harm,' said Debs, tightening her grip on Carrie's body still further.

Her ears didn't seem to be working properly, nor her eyes for that matter. She pressed Carrie deep into her closed kitchen door. Carrie held her head at a funny angle, she didn't want to look at Debs. Debs made her look. She grabbed hold of her hair and jerked her face towards her. Debs eyes were full of tears. They were full. She stared at Carrie.

'You're not going anywhere, Carrie. No, it's time. You're going to tell me the truth. Trust me, whatever it is, let it go...'

Debs held onto Carrie long after she'd stopped trembling.

'He hurt me...'

Debs gave Carrie such comfort as she could:

'Tea,' she whispered. 'I'll make the tea...'

'Drink your tea, love, it's getting cold.'

'Sorry, I was miles away,' said Jill.

'And I know just how far,' replied Bill. 'It's bothering me, too.'

Jill paused.

'I've got that awful 'déjà-vu' feeling about Carrie and I can't quite work out what it is.'

'I can,' said Bill. 'You're right; we've been here before, but not with Carrie...'

Bill reached his one good hand across the kitchen table and gave Jill's cold white hand a gentle squeeze. Her face turned as white as her cold hand as she joined eyes with Bill.

'No, no, no!' she cried out. 'Not my Carrie! No Bill, please! No! Tell me it's not true!'

Bill held on to Jill but she couldn't stop trembling. Bill cursed his own honesty. He gave Jill such comfort as he could:

'Hush now, darlin', I don't know the truth any more than you do but trust me, whatever it is, we're going to deal with it, I give you my word. I'm suspicious because...'

Jill finished what he'd started:

'...because she never once mentioned the other one! Jed! What about that bloody Jed? I told her Bill,' Jill's voice cracked open at the sound of her own memories, 'I told her, 'I got a Jed, but you got a Jon.'

Bill held Jill, tighter and tighter.

'What if Jed got to her first? Tricked her in some way?'

'We don't know for sure...'

'And that's why she's going away. That's what all this sudden journalist nonsense is all about...'

'She's always wanted to be a journalist...'

505

'She'll never get over it; it'll ruin her life...'

Bill held his head at a funny angle. He talked to the ceiling:

'You're not going anywhere with this!'

He pressed Jill deep into the kitchen table. His eyes were full of understanding, his voice full of memories. He wasn't just a man, he was Jill's husband - and he was Carrie's father. He wasn't cracking open any time soon:

'The truth is, we don't know the truth.'

'It'll ruin her life...'

'It hasn't ruined your life and it's not going to ruin hers. We won't let it, whatever it is. No, it's time. We're going to do what you do best, Jill.'

'And what's that?'

'Interfere!'

———◆———

'Bloody hell!' said Debs. 'I thought your last 'Land Girl' article was a bit weird, but it all makes sense now. Oh Carrie! I'm so sorry!'

Carrie sat, wrapped up tight in Debs' newly finished, knitted squares, blanket. She was newly finished also. She had no more tale to tell, yarn to spin. She sat completely helpless. Unravelled. Silent.

'You have to tell someone about this, it's very serious. You have to tell your parents, *and* the police! We can't let this go!'

Carrie went, at Debs.

'No police! No parents! No, no, no! That's what you said when it happened to you. I'm no different!'

Debs went back:

'Yes, you are. He raped you, Carrie! You were a virgin and he raped you!'

'But he didn't get very far. It was only for a second. Jon stopped him.'

'It's still rape!' shrieked Debs. 'And look at what he did to Jip and that poor cow! Carrie, it's alright! It's not your fault! Everybody will understand.'

'That's what Jon said, 'it'll be alright!' Well, it's not alright, is it?'

'You can't let him get away with this, Carrie, no matter how fond you are of the Wilsons.'

'He hasn't got away with it, any more than Joe did. Jon just about killed him!'

'But he's killed you and Jon!'

'That's just too bad,' snapped Carrie. 'I've got no choice. I have to protect Jon. Look, I'm alright! I'm dealing with it. I'm my mother's daughter, you know! This is nothing compared to what she had to go through, or you, for that matter. I can just turn the clock right back to the Carrie that I was before that fateful day I crashed into Jon's Land Rover. I never ever set foot on that farm. The farm wasn't real. Jed never existed. Jon was, Jon is, nothing but a dream. No harm done. Look at you, you've survived Joe.'

'I had a lot of help. I told!' cried Debs. 'And Jon wasn't a dream. He was and still is, very, very, real. You can't abandon him!'

'He's abandoned me! He's gone to the other side of the world. I'd never find him!'

'Maybe he thought he had no choice, the same as you. Maybe he thought that was the only way to save you pain. He looks exactly like his brother, doesn't he? How do you think he'd cope, every time he saw you, came near you? He'd never know if he was reminding you about what Jed did to you. He'll be hurting just as bad as you! Come on, Carrie, you reckon you're going to London to be a hot shot journalist and you can't even chase up an address in the outback. Tell your mum, she'll help you!'

'No! She must never know about any of this, it would kill her. She was right about Jed. And she's just starting to feel better about herself after all these years. I can't bring it all back to her door and make her live through that all over again. I just can't...'

Carrie cracked open once more. She buried her face into the nearest knitted square and sobbed herself dry. No stitches from the knitted blanket or hugs from Debs could hold her together. Carrie cried and cried. Debs could do nothing but wait.

'Listen to me,' said Debs, quietly. 'Listen!' she said again sharply, grabbing Carrie by the hair once more and holding her eyes in place as she did so:

'Remember what you said to me, not so long ago? You got cross with me like I'm getting cross with you, now. 'It's not your fault!' you said. 'You're as innocent as that flower fairy that you hold in your hands. She's been fixed and so will you be!' Remember?'

Carrie looked at Debs.

'Now I gave my flower fairy away to a friend of ours, but I hold an angel in my hands right now, and I'm not giving her away to anybody, and certainly not to that old, tight clothed, tight lipped, tight legged, uptight, Carrie, that lived in her head because she was afraid to be real! She's innocent and she will be fixed because I'm going to do the fixing. She's not got to deal with anything on her own because she's got me. She's longed to be real all her life. She's not going to give up and run away to London just because real life has turned out to be an uncomfortable ride. Get up, and ride that ride, Carrie! Look at your dad! How many times did he fall off his racing bikes? Look at all his accidents, losing his fingers! Falling down doesn't matter as long as you get back up again afterwards. So get up, Carrie! Trust me, everything will be alright. You're going to be alright. You can nod your head now.'

Debs forced Carrie's head up and down.

'Poor cow!'

'I know...' said Carrie, starting to cry again.

'No, you! You poor cow!'

It wasn't funny at all, but somehow Carrie managed a smile at Debs. Debs realised what she'd just said.

'Oh, I'm so sorry, Carrie. Words can be such terrible things. Are you sure you want to be a writer?'

'Tea, with sugar,' whispered Carrie.

Carrie and Debs did what they'd always done. They sat together and drank endless mugs of tea, and waited to feel better. They used to drink coffee but preferred tea these days, for some reason. They used to have a laugh and a joke but preferred peace and quiet these days. They waited and waited and waited but they just couldn't manage to feel better. It was just a matter of time before one of them cracked and gave up. Debs gave up first.

'You must go back!' said Debs.

'I can't. I just can't. I won't.'

'You must go back and find out!'

The blood drained from Carrie's tear stained face.

'You said that to me once before...'

'Well I'm saying it again. I was right before, and I'm right again now.'

Carrie stared at Debs; she was being strangled all over again:

'Cow!' she said.

'Thank you,' said Debs. 'I'll take that as a compliment.'

Debs had made it better. Debs was right. She had to go back.

'I haven't been able to stop thinking about you all day,' said Jill. 'How are you, Carrie?'

'Oh, I'm fine, thanks.'

'I've got some good news for you!'

'Oh?'

'Sit down, sit down,' said her mother excitedly, brandishing a mug of tea.

'Please, no more tea!'

'How about a sherry?' suggested Carrie.

'Good idea!'

'Old habits die hard...'

'Now then,' said Jill, quickly downing her sherry and starting the next one at the same time as her next word, 'your Dad and I have been out for a drive today, and guess where we ended up?'

'I don't need to guess given the look on your face...'

'We called in on the Wilsons at the farm!'

'Now there's a surprise...'

Carrie made to get up out of her chair; the sherry had suddenly made her feel light headed. Her mother's hands were pressing down hard on her shoulders.

'Now don't go running off. As I said, I've got some good news for you!'

'Surprise me, then...'

Carrie had no choice but to sit back down.

'Well, we saw old Mr Wilson himself. We'd only just turned into the drive and he appeared from nowhere. Striding down the drive he was, with those great long legs of his. We didn't even get chance to get out of the car, he moved so fast.'

'He must be nearly seven feet tall!' said Carrie.

'Yes, he must. He towered over us...'

'Look him in the eye! Even the smallest prey can still be brave!'

'I had to hold my head at a funny angle to look him in the eye, but he was pleased to see us. He asked how you were. Of course I told him about your fantastic new job in London and he was very pleased about that. He sends you his best wishes, they all do.'

'Did you see Mavis, then?'

'No, only him. I think it was a busy time of day, they were getting ready for milking, he said. I must say I was a bit disappointed he didn't offer us a cup of tea.'

'Oh, was that your news?'

'Oh no, I'm coming to that! Mavis sends you her love and this little parcel.'

Her mother pulled a paper bag out of her handbag and pushed it across the kitchen table. It was sealed with a piece of old, yellow sellotape.

'No prizes for guessing what that is, it must be one of her handmade cuddly toys!' continued her mother. 'And old Mr Wilson sends you this!'

Her mother shuffled around in the bottom of her handbag again and pulled out a piece of paper this time. She pushed it across the kitchen table. Carrie looked at the paper.

'What's this?'

Jill gave the piece of paper another little push.

'Have a look for yourself,' she said.

'I don't want to.'

'Oh, come on, Carrie! It's your good news, staring you in the face!'

'A grotty old piece of paper!'

Jill smiled and pressed the grotty old piece of paper against Carrie's closed hands.

'I bet she's been interfering again. She's pleased with herself about something...'

'It's Jon's address in Australia,' she said, gently. 'Old Mr Wilson says you can write to him if you want.'

Carrie's hands stayed closed; so did her mouth.

'He's only gone for a year,' encouraged her mother. 'You can keep in touch, and when you're back from London, and he's back from the outback, you can pick up where you left off, can't you?'

Carrie stayed closed; tight.

'Say something, Carrie! I thought you'd be pleased.'

'I'm not going to London now. Debs needs me.'

'Oh? But you can still write to Jon. He's such a lovely, quiet young man. His father says that he's sorry that Jon had to leave so suddenly, everything happened so quickly. The decision was forced upon them, especially with what has happened to his other son, that ghastly Jed.'

'Why? What's happened to Jed?'

'Apparently, he's had a nasty accident at work, got hit on the head by something. Been dangerously ill. He ended up in hospital for a while with fluid on his brain.'

'Oh.'

'Don't worry, he's home now. Mavis is looking after him as only Mavis can. But he's not the same. I can tell old Mr Wilson is cut up about it. Jed just sits, staring out of the window all day. He doesn't speak. He's turned into a complete simpleton.'

'*Oh.*'

'I reckon it's more as a result of his lifestyle than any accident at work if you ask me. He won't trouble you, or any other woman again, for that matter. I think Jed's the main reason Mr Wilson didn't invite us in for tea. I think he's embarrassed about his son and embarrassed about having to stop you going to the farm so suddenly. I saw the look in his eyes, Carrie. He looked so sad...'

'*He always looks like that.*'

'...especially when I told him how heartbroken you were about Jon going away.'

'You shouldn't have said that, Mum, that's not fair.'

'Well, it's not fair of him, sending Jon away without even giving you a chance to say goodbye. It won't do him any harm to suffer a bit for what he's done to you, and to his sons. I've seen how upset you've been, I can see it in your face!'

'*Thank God that's all you can see...*'

'Leave it be, Mum. We've all suffered enough. Let's just get up and get on with today,' said Carrie, finally finding her legs and standing up from her chair.

'Yes, you're quite right, Carrie. What a brave girl you are. Most girls your age would be in bits by now if they'd been through all this.'

Carrie moved her legs towards the kitchen door.

'Here, don't forget these!' called her mother, holding out the paper bag parcel and the grotty old piece of paper.

She forced them into her daughter's hands. Carrie closed her fingers around them and squeezed them tight.

'Oh, I forgot. One more thing,' called her mother as Carrie climbed the stairs up to her bedroom:

'Old Mr Wilson said to tell you one more thing.'

Carrie paused, mid creak on the middle of the stairs; their stair carpet reached all the way across; there were no shiny polished wooden edges here.

'He said, 'Tell Carrie to remember that he has a tree in his orchard.' Does that make any sense to you?'

Carrie shrugged a 'don't know' with her shoulders and disappeared into her bedroom. She didn't know everything. It was probably a good thing. She sat on her bed and stared at the parcel and the grotty, screwed up, piece of paper in her hand. She read the address, but she couldn't put pen to paper. She'd lost all her words. Debs was right, words are such terrible things; they hurt like hell. She wasn't sure she wanted to be a writer after all.

She opened the paper bag parcel. The sellotape was so old that it wouldn't budge; she ripped the paper around it instead. As expected, it was a knitted toy. Carrie put the grotty piece of paper in her bedside table drawer with her walnut. It rolled and banged loudly against the side of the drawer as she closed it. It made Carrie jump; it sounded just like a gunshot. She lay down on her bed as straight and lifeless as a plank of wood. She clutched Mavis' knitted toy to her chest.

'Help! Come quick! Do something!'

'I am! Can't you see that?' cried the Walnut in her bedside table drawer.

'He belongs to me!'

'Trust me. Do as I say and everything will be alright. I give you my word. I have a tree in my orchard. And get yourself cleaned up. I don't want you going down to dinner looking like that...'

Carrie got herself cleaned up. Before she went down to dinner she put Mavis' knitted toy in her bedside table drawer with her Walnut and piece of paper. The doll had long legs and would only just fit inside. He had long, dark, knitted hair that had been stuck to his head with yellow glue. He was dressed up in black tie; he was smiling. He was the third man.

'Are you alright, darlin'? You look like a little lost teddy bear! Do you want to come and have a cuddle with me?'

It was a good likeness, but Mavis hadn't got it quite right. The first time she'd met him he wasn't wearing a black jacket. He'd had rolled up, white shirt sleeves. He'd elbowed her in the face as little Carrie was born. But Mavis, like her mother, didn't know everything. It was probably a good thing.

'I'll look after him for you!' cackled the Walnut in her bedside table drawer, *'I've told you he belongs to me, all along...'*

Friday 6th April

Dear Reader,

This is not an April Fool! The 'Twentieth Century Land Girl' has not left for pastures new after all. I can't leave for pastures new, leaving my current field only half ploughed; that would be bad farming. I wouldn't be very productive and there would be no profit in it. As with all things, not just down on the farm or in our gardens, no matter how hard the work, the job has to be finished before we can move on. I'm not done just yet, Reader.

Perhaps that's what's behind the custom of April Fool's Day on the 1st April. This custom goes back hundreds of years, and no one really knows where it came from. The idea was, and still is, to persuade someone to do something silly before midday; it certainly provides a break from all that hard work for at least one morning every year, doesn't it?

No one knows the origin of the month of April's name, either. It may be from the Latin word 'aperire' which means 'to open.' Things are starting to grow again after the winter; the cuckoo arrives around about mid April as a sign that Spring is come. April 15th is 'Swallow Day', traditionally the date when swallows are seen again. Years ago, folk used to believe that they spent the winter months in the mud at the bottom of ponds, which just goes to show how easy it is for rumours to spread! We can't see everything, or know everything, so take care, and have a little faith. Be brave; wait patiently for the truth. Sometimes, we can only see what really matters by looking at other people's lives because we can't see it in our own. We're too close to ourselves and our eyes won't focus that close up.

April 23rd is St.George's Day. This patron Saint of England slew a dragon to protect a village. St. George was famous for his bravery, but he wasn't actually English at all. He was Turkish! He became a Roman soldier in the 3rd Century A.D. He complained about the Roman's cruelty towards the Christians. He was a Christian himself. The Romans tortured him horribly and finally beheaded him for his complaints. He was very brave, and is the patron saint of many other countries besides England. Truth often comes at a heavy price.

Down on the farm, life is opening up, being brave. It's time for Spring calving and lambing. Being born is one of the bravest things you and your mother will ever have to do! It's really hard work; it's a struggle. Taking that first breath. Life is a risky business. There are no guarantees.

'For everything there is a season, a time for every activity under heaven. A time to be born and a time to die. A time to plant and a time to harvest.' [†]

What happens in between, well, I'm not sure that too much planning is such a good idea. The 'Titanic' sank on the 15th April 1912. I repeat, maybe too much planning is not such a good idea, is it? Even the greatest plans can go awry. It's been almost a year to the day since I first started work down on the farm as a Twentieth Century Land Girl.

'For a healthy, happy job, join the Women's Land Army!'

What can I say about that, Reader? Well, I've got my hands dirty; I know what that feels like now. I've ended my year as I began - shovelling s***!

In 1945, after the end of the Second World War, womens' lives were never the same again. Many women felt unfairly treated. Even though they'd been successfully doing 'mens' jobs their contribution was dismissed by Government policy which encouraged them back into the home.

Lady Denman resigned over the Government's decision to exclude Land Girls from receiving financial benefits afforded to men. There was some increase in women's employment but they were very much seen as 'secondary' workers and their wages were lower than that of men.

Life is really hard work; it's a struggle. The Women's Land Army might have been disbanded but women must march on a while longer to achieve the longed for equality, value and respect that women since the dawn of time have been working for.

So we must be brave. We must open ourselves up, like all of nature, in the month of April. Whilst we may long for love, loyalty, beauty and salvation, we might never find them; the best thing we can do is do our best. We must be prepared to step into the darkness if we want to live in the light.

Life is a very precious thing that most folk and creatures will hold on to at any cost. The great Roman Emperor, Marcus Aurelius, said:

'When you arise in the morning, think of what a precious privilege it is to be alive - to breathe, to think, to enjoy, to love.' [‡]

He's right, isn't he?

Saturday 12th May

It was a bright yellow morning.

'Debs will be pleased.'

She's still in a yellow and white phase. She wasn't showing the slightest desire to return to being a pink lady. Carrie wasn't showing the slightest desire to pay attention to the contents of the meeting. She was on the editing team now. Denial had become her fuel. She had discovered that, with a combination of skilful day dreaming and mock enthusiasm, it was possible to live, no, to exist, very well indeed. Carrie had changed from being a 'go-er' to a 'going to.' Her polished, glazed, professional look was as hard as the lacquer on her beautifully French polished nails. She was stunning.

For weeks now, she'd managed to fool everybody, including Debs. In spite of all her talk she hadn't been back to the farm. She still hadn't put pen to paper, except when at work. Jon didn't exist. She still hadn't worked out how she'd worked it all out quite so successfully. She concluded that it was something to do with having intelligent hands.

When she switched her brain off her hands continued to function quite nicely. Nobody noticed she wasn't really there. Except Dennis, of course. She was free of the Falcon; old man Wilson would never stare at her again. Her dad was more relaxed these days and so generally less observant. But there was no escape from the all-seeing, all knowing, bushy moustached Irishman, whose lilting tones still pierced her tortured soul.

'News has just come in about a farm accident. Can you cover this one, Carrie? You're our resident farming expert. *Carrie,* are you with me?'

'Yes, of course.'

'If you hurry, Carrie, you might just catch the police officer in the foyer. He's just been in with the weekly updates. Get a copy of the police report from him and make sure you get your facts straight.'

Carrie nodded.

'Go now, Carrie! Give us a head start on this one!'

'Yes, I'll go now, then.'

Dennis watched Carrie open the door and click away down the corridor. He hadn't got to be editor-in-chief without taking a risk or two in his long career. He'd been around the block a few times. He'd seen and done it all before. He'd a feeling that it was time to shake things up a bit. He wanted to smile at his own, sordid, joke, about the 'head start', but thought it best not to. He'd a feeling that he was setting Carrie up for some suffering and there wasn't a single thing he could do about it now. He'd said it. He'd a feeling that he'd done the right thing.

———◆———

'Wait, officer! Please wait!'

'Ah, Miss Langford, how are you?'

'Very well, thank you, Detective Constable Ranger. My editor's just sent me down to catch you for a copy of the police report about the recent farm accident. Do you have one with you that I could take now?'

'I suppose, being the 'Twentieth Century Land Girl', this is right up your street,' said Detective Constable Steven Ranger, opening his efficient coloured, pale green police folder.

'Oh, I'm not doing that any more,' babbled Carrie. 'I stopped going to the farm ages ago.'

'Well, I'm sorry for your loss,' he said.

'Oh, it's no loss at all,' chirped Carrie. 'I'm on the editing team full time now. I was even thinking about moving to work on a national in London.'

'Why did you stop going to the farm, if you don't mind me asking?'

'I don't mind you asking,' continued Carrie. 'You're a detective. You're paid to be nosy, just like me!' she laughed.

'Well, why did you stop, then?'

'The farmer's son was emigrating to Australia and the old man had to wind the farm down because he couldn't cope on his own. I became an insurance risk. It's done me a favour, really. I was ready to move on, anyway.'

'Why did you so suddenly become a risk?'

'I don't know,' said Carrie. 'I was only a volunteer at the end of the day.

'And was your farmer prone to taking unnecessary risks? Cutting corners, that sort of thing?'

'Certainly not!'

Carrie was surprised by her own indignation. The Wilsons meant nothing to her any more but, nevertheless, the hairs on the back of her neck suddenly bristled at the questions from this Smart Alec police officer. He'd annoyed her once before. It was time to give him 'what for' once more:

'My farmers were wonderful farmers. Hard working and kind to their animals. Not all farmers are bad farmers, you know. You shouldn't believe everything you read in the papers!' she laughed.

'Well in that case, I'm doubly sorry for your loss. Given the circumstances, Miss Langford, if you could spare me a few minutes right now, I'd perhaps better take a statement from you. Can we go back up to your office for a few minutes?'

'Circumstances? What circumstances?'

Detective Constable Ranger held out the copy of his police report towards Carrie.

'The late Mr Pike would have been very proud of you, Miss Langford. His death turned out to be a tragic accident in the end. A bit like this one, by the look of things, but we still have to investigate it thoroughly, just to make sure there's no foul play or negligence involved.'

'What's it got to do with me?'

'As I say, Mr Pike would have been very proud of you. His faith in your talent for journalism was clearly well founded. There's not many folk who'd be willing to report this gruesome case when they'd had such personal contact with the victim.'

Carrie snatched the report out of Detective Constable Ranger's hand. Her intelligent hands were clever enough to keep still as she opened the paper, but her eyes trembled as she scanned it for key words. Detective Constable Steven Ranger was determined to be as helpful as possible to the aspiring young journalist:

'I'm sorry, Miss Langford, I assumed your editor had already told you that the accident was at your 'Twentieth Century Land Girl' farm. It must have been terrible for old Mr Wilson to find his son like that.'

'Run, Carrie, run!'

'Wait! Miss Langford, where are you going?'

Carrie ran. Back up the stairs to her office desk, kicking her padded, tweed covered, office chair out of the way to get to her car keys faster.

'Carrie, are you alright?' called Dennis in his lovely, soft, Irish lilt.

'Run, Carrie, run!'

'Where are you going, Carrie?' called Dennis.

'Home! I'm going home. I quit!' she shouted as she disappeared down the stairs.

She ran past Detective Constable Ranger, almost slashing his wrist open with her car keys as she forced his police report back into his unexpecting hands. He'd missed his chance to get a statement. There was a noise behind him as an out of breath, bushy moustached Irishman clattered down the stairs after her.

'Carrie!' called Dennis.

'She's gone!' reported Detective Constable Ranger with stunning accuracy.

Dennis bent down and picked up a stray piece of paper that she'd left lying on the floor in the doorway to the real world. He handed it back to the detective. It was the first page of the police report. He read the first sentence:

'Mr Jon Wilson, of Orchard Top Farm, has been found dead on the premises by his father, Mr Ezra Wilson. First indications are that the victim somehow became trapped in a heavy pulping machine and was unable to free himself...'

Dennis suddenly had an overwhelming urge to punch the Detective Constable in the face. He somehow managed not to. It was looking like he'd got a vacancy on his editing team all of a sudden, but he certainly wasn't going to offer this young man a job on his paper any time soon, despite the accuracy of his reporting skills.

Dennis allowed himself a twitch of his bushy moustache as he walked back up the stairs to his office. He'd shaken things up quite a lot. He'd done it, now. She was suffering. He'd a feeling that he'd done the right thing. He hadn't got to be editor-in-chief without taking a risk or two in his long career. He felt sure that Mr Pike would have approved. Now it was up to her.

——————◆——————

It was a lovely sunny day like it always used to be in the good old days when she first came to the farm. How can the days be old already? The bright yellow morning had matured into a golden day. The sun saw everything, touched everything. How could it be so cruel? How could it continue, warm and shining? Surely it must know that it wasn't wanted. Bright was brash and pointless. The sun was wasting its time, and hers. She would never feel its gentle touch; she would never feel warm again.

The wheels of her little red car skidded off the road and onto the incline of the farm's familiar drive; the clouds of white dust that they made as they ploughed recklessly through the white gravel minefield couldn't disguise the red brick of the farmhouse that loomed up at her, bigger and more derelict looking than ever before. Her little red car pulled into the perfectly square farmyard and parked itself in the middle of it.

Just like her first visit there were no signs of life anywhere. Just like her first visit her heart was thumping in her throat, choking her. Just like her first visit it hadn't actually taken her long to work out a reason to come back. Just like her first visit she was out of control.

Unlike her first visit, she knew why there were no signs of life; there was no life here. He was gone. She knew that she would not be able to speak; she had nothing to say. He was gone. She knew that she had no reason to come back; she was out of control. He was gone.

'Where's Jip?'

He might be gone too by now. Time to move. Carrie got out of her car. She couldn't feel her legs. She leaned against her little red car fearing she'd fall over if she let go of it. Her heels pressed into her stilettos, which in turn pressed into the dry, hard ground of the farmyard. It was rock hard, yet her feet seemed to be sinking without trace.

Why had she come back here? There was nothing here for her. Nothing. The wooden cowshed doors were either closed or dropping to bits and couldn't be closed. The entrance with no door at all led into total darkness. Why did she ever think that it was beautiful? It was empty.

A sudden loud sound startled her. Was it a gunshot? Carrie ducked. Actually, it was geese, flying over her head in loud formation. Everybody was leaving her. Even the gentle breeze died down. She looked around. She was in good company. She felt as wooden as the cowshed doors; empty, worn, warped and unhinged.

'Carrie!'

Yet another gunshot.

'Oh, Carrie, love, I knew you'd come!'

The voice hit her in the stomach. Carrie pressed her hands over the wound and leant on her little red car, to keep herself upright.

'Oh Carrie, I'm so pleased to see you!' cried Mavis.

She was standing in the farmhouse kitchen doorway. The sunshine lit up the red and black tiled floor behind her. No doubt it had been mopped, but it was dry now. It wasn't shining. Neither was Mavis. A very thin old woman was standing where the cheerful ghost in a frilly apron used to busily flicker to and fro. There was no warm, welcoming smell of baking. There was no cackle. There was only a very pale, very real, ghost. It must be so, for the ghost would not leave the shadows of the kitchen doorway, even though she called to Carrie over and over again. She couldn't walk upon the dry, hard, ground of the farmyard any more than Carrie could.

Perhaps it was because Mavis had no eyes. Her big, plastic glasses were completely fogged up.

'She's steamed up. She's been making tea.'

Carrie wanted to run to Mavis but her legs wouldn't let her. Mavis hadn't been making tea. She'd been crying. She was crying.

'Oh Carrie, it's been terrible. Terrible!'

'Why have I come here?'

Jed would be sitting, staring out of the window inside that red and black tiled farmhouse kitchen. That was terrible. She wouldn't, couldn't, set eyes on Jed. He was terrible. Carrie couldn't, wouldn't, budge from the single lump of rubble that her stilettos were balancing on in the middle of the farmyard. The rest of the ground had fallen away; Mavis might as well have been on the other side of the world.

'Why did he have to come back?'

'Oh, Carrie, it's been that terrible!' sobbed Mavis. 'It's driven him mad all over again! After what happened to her! He found him, you know. Go to him, *please,* Carrie love! Go to him! He's in the orchard. Help him. You can help him, Carrie.'

'Help him!'

Carrie hit Mavis right between the eyes. The old woman had to take off her big, plastic glasses to hold on to her hanging face; she was fast losing it. Carrie didn't care:

'Why didn't you tell me he was back? How could you do this to me! Why? Why didn't you tell me! Left me to find out through a police report! A cold piece of paper! Is that all I ever was to you? A would-be journalist, come to use you, like you used me?'

Mavis was sobbing something but Carrie couldn't make out what it was. Mavis was bent double by now; her letter 'R' body became an 'O.'

She didn't have a little red car to lean on. She had nothing. Carrie paused for breath. She shared the moment with Mavis; she had nothing, too. They were both at zero.

'...it all happened so fast...'

'Yes, it did...'

'We didn't get chance...'

'No, we didn't...'

'Our Jed's always been a bad lad...'

'Yes he has...'

'He blames himself...'

'He hurt me...'

'...he's killed us all...'

'Yes he has...'

'Why?' shouted Carrie, 'why did he have to come back?'

'He came back for Jed!' cried Mavis. 'He's always looked after his brother. Always.'

'He's killed him!'

Carrie's stilettos fell off their piece of rubble. Her ankles fell, to their surprise, onto solid ground. She could feel her legs; they were angry.

'He didn't! It were an accident! A terrible, terrible, accident. Go to him, please, Carrie love! He's in the orchard.'

'Don't you dare offer to make tea...'

Just then the red and black tiles of the farmhouse kitchen changed colour as the bright morning sunshine walked across its threshold. Now they were black and white at Mavis' feet.

'Now look who's here, Jip! It's our Carrie,' stroked Mavis, gently.

Jip looked. He looked just as empty, worn, warped and unhinged as Carrie. He held his head on one side; his chin was laughing. He looked as though he was tired of laughing. The extra weight of his sense of humour was being carried by only one front leg; he kept the other one raised as far as he could. But he used it now to hobble towards Carrie. He was a brave dog. He did what Carrie and Mavis could not; he walked across the dry, hard ground of the farmyard. He was not giving up any time soon. Carrie felt ashamed. She dropped to her knees and held out her arms to Jip. Mavis found her face and put her glasses back on.

'Oh Jip! Jip! I'm so sorry,' whispered Carrie. 'Come here, boy! How are you?'

Full nerved and still warm, Carrie held Jip's fur. Big hands, strong and gentle, once touched this fur, once touched her. She would never again feel her blood pulsing beneath his hands; neither would Jip. But now she had something. They had something. They had each other. They were real. This was real. What did he always say?

'B..Better get on,' said Carrie.

There was work to be done. Carrie stood up. She walked across the yard towards Mavis. She put her arms around her.

'We need a hug,' she said.

Carrie closed her eyes. She didn't want to see the inside of the farmhouse kitchen. If Jed was in there, he was a ghost of his former self, for it was eerily quiet. There was no breath, not even from the steaming kettle. Wearing her forwards looking face, she'd face him later. Wearing her forwards looking face, she opened her eyes and let go of Mavis. The smell of wet old lady was overpowering; it was the perfume of great courage and perseverance; it was intoxicating.

'Now I'm going to the orchard. We'll all have a cup of tea and a piece of cake a bit later. Shall you get it ready, Mavis?'

Mavis had no words but she managed a nod. She was a brave Mavis. Carrie turned and walked back to Jip. She picked him up.

'I carried you once before. Now we'll carry each other.'

She could feel his heart thumping in her hands, keeping her alive. It was a long walk to the orchard carrying a big, heavy dog. There was time to cry on the way. The last time he'd spoken to her he'd found his voice:

It'll be alright. We'll be alright...'

No stammer. No stutter. If he could do it, so could she. She had to speak. She had to say something. For him.

'Look him in the eye! Even the smallest prey can still be brave!'

But what eyes! Was he really mad or did he just look mad? Old man Wilson was sitting on the stone bench in the orchard.

'It'll be alright, Jip. We'll be alright.'

She was a brave Carrie.

———————◆———————

The two stone gate pillars without gate let them pass. The orchard was still amazing. Wild and beautiful with neglect. There was no breath. No sound. The sunlight hardened in front of her eyes, and grew cold. The shadows beneath the trees did their best to soften its glare. The pink and white blossom on the trees and the carpet of yellow buttercups on the ground tried their best to distract her. Carrie and Jip listened to their own breathing as they made their way through the silent grass. There was a slight rise in the ground in front of the stone bench. Carrie carried Jip until she could carry him no more.

She laid him down like a sacrificial offering at the feet of the man who was himself, laid out upon the stone bench. He sat, no, hung; a man in the last stages of crucifixion. He had no visible wounds. The branches of the sad looking tree behind him held him up, and nailed him down. Carrie remembered her first visit to the orchard. The sad looking tree was reaching out to her in a gentle and pleading sort of way. But it was punishing old man Wilson.

'Your orchard is very, very, beautiful, Mr Wilson. Thank you for showing it to me. (Well, he hadn't actually shown it to her, or had he?) 'I bet Mrs Wilson likes coming here, to pick the fruit.'

'My wife died.'

The sad looking tree was weeping. Sap poured from eye shaped markings on its trunk; eyebrow shapes frowned above them. Above old man Wilson's head a face with two weeping eyes, a runny nose and an open mouth, screamed at Carrie and Jip. Tear shaped marks in the tree bark cried all the way down to the ground. Carrie had never noticed the face before, but she noticed it now. Nothing would grow near this tree.

There was no green grass here. Black and white, Jip lay upon the black ground at old man Wilson's feet. Jip was her strength and protection, but she had to look away from him. It was old blood that made no grass here. It was nothing to do with this stupid, crying, tree. The sunlight could not move old man Wilson; he would not look away. Dazzled by the sun, he stared in front of him with white hot eyes.

Carrie stood over him as he had once stood over her.

'Ah do,' she said.

The white eyes flickered and writhed in his face at the sound of her voice. He bowed his head. His fine head of long, silver grey hair would have been dark once upon a time.

His hair wrapped around my neck like a black necklace...It was soft. Black velvet.'

Carrie was no priestess. She wasn't there to anoint him. She could not ease his pain, nor he hers. She could not bear to sit down on that bench. But hands suddenly grabbed hers and pulled her down.

'Do you want me to tie you down?'

'No!' cried Carrie.

She landed on the stone bench. It was cold and very hard. Silence.

'It's al..r..right.'

'You've left me alone here all day, picking plums on my own, and now a wasp has stung me on my face! You've left me all alone!'

Carrie touched her face. All of a sudden, it felt red and swollen. It was stinging. But Jip was leaning against her legs.

'Why don't you cut this tree down?'

'My wife died.'

'He's died!'

'It bears no fruit, and nothing will grow near it.'

'It was her tree. Our tree. Our walnut tree.'

'*Yes, it was.*'

'Maybe it's bad luck.'

'She was so lovely.'

'*So was he.*'

'She's not here any more. She's gone. Just like Jon. Gone forever.'

'No!'

'Yes!'

Old man Wilson tore at her hair. He grabbed hold of her head and jerked it towards him. She recognised his hands. They were big and strong, hard and rough. These hands were immovable. She recognised the violence. He stared into her. She saw utter despair; utter desolation. His lips pressed towards hers:

'You look like her! You walk like her! You breathe like her! You smell like her!'

'I know! I've always known it. The way you look at me. The way you don't look at me! But I'm not her! You have to let her go. She's a ghost. She's not real! Mavis is real. You're real. I'm real.'

Carrie reeled and shook. She was not going to let this King lay his immense burden on her. She was big and strong. She had to save them both.

'Now let me go, you're hurting me!'

Old man Wilson's lips whispered against hers but landed softly with a kiss on her forehead. He loosened his grip on her but he didn't let her go.

'I would never hurt you. You're so very precious.'

'Jed hurt me.'

'I know.'

He waited for her to know that he knew.

'I should have ended it a long time ago. He was a bad 'un through and through. Sometimes you get the odd one. Cattle are just the same, you know.'

Carrie took hold of his hands and pulled them away from her face. But she didn't let him go. She recognised his hands. They were big and strong, hard and rough. They were full of gentleness.

'I had no choice, Carrie. I've blamed myself all these years, but he might have been the same even if she hadn't died.'

'He had Mavis. He had choice...and so have you.'

Old man Wilson lowered his voice and his eyes to Jip, who gave such comfort as he could to the bloodless, pale, hand that sought sanctuary in his warm fur.

'I had no choice, Carrie.'

'Forget about Jed. It's not your fault.'

Old man Wilson's ears were not working properly. He wasn't listening:

'No matter what I did, I couldn't do any good with him. He had an aggressive streak in him that would *not* be tamed. When you came to us,' old man Wilson gasped for breath, 'I didn't think it would end like this. It's all my fault.'

Carrie touched his face; it was dissolving in her hands.

'I had no choice,' he whispered.

Carrie stared at old man Wilson. The heat was gone from his eyes leaving only grey, haunted, orbits. Dark eyes didn't look natural on him. She remembered the first time she'd seen Jon's eyes; little Carrie had just been born. They were dark:

'C..Carrie it is, then.'

'What have you always said to me?'

She waited for him to remember.

"Trust me. Do as I say and everything will be alright."

'And they were the last words that Jon ever said to me. 'It'll be alright. We'll be alright.'

She paused, before continuing:

'It's my fault. If I'd never come here in the first place, none of this would have happened. And now he's dead. Jon's dead. *I've* killed him.'

'No! It's not true!'

'Yes, it is!'

Jip's warm body was pressing down on her feet. She could feel his rib cage rising and falling underneath his fur. He wasn't giving up any time soon. Neither must she.

'Why? Why did he come back?'

'Loyalty. Love. Thank you for being so loyal, Carrie. I shouldn't have sent him away. I was wrong. He loves you. I'm so sorry.'

'It's all my fault.'

'No, Carrie! Don't say that. You've helped him so much. Through you he's found his voice again.'

'And now it's gone forever. This is real. Jon is gone!'

'No, Carrie, you're not listening. He came back. He's here!'

'No, you're not listening! How can you be so cruel?' she exploded.

'Stop it! I know everything! I've seen the police report. 'Mr Jon Wilson, of Orchard Top Farm, has been found dead on the premises by his father, Mr Ezra Wilson. First indications are that the victim somehow became trapped in a heavy pulping machine, and was unable to free himself..."

'No, Carrie! You're wrong!'

'I've seen it! Written in black and white! As white as Jip's chest lies here on this black, blood soaked ground. Blood he shed for me, after his brother....Right here...It's all I have left of him...'

Jip was struggling to his feet. Perhaps he'd heard mention of his master's name. Carrie didn't see him get up, she couldn't see a thing. She had no choice. She had to let go. Her eyes let go first. Jip rested his chin in her lap and whined up at her. She reached down for his ears with her hands.

'It's alright. We'll be alright,' she whispered.

Two big, strong arms wrapped around her. They held her long after she stopped trembling. Jip licked her hands. She closed her eyes. There was no more dark. She was back in the calf shed. He lifted her tear drained face and gently kissed her on the forehead.

'Oh I'm so sorry, so sorry,' she sobbed into the warm, big, strong hand that was holding her face.

'It was Jed. Jed's dead,' he whispered.

He kissed her again. And again. On the mouth. He couldn't help it. He really knew how to do it. So did she. He pressed his whole body into hers. She just sat still and let him do it. It seemed the right thing to do. Light broke through the branches of the sad looking tree. Jip panted in the heat. It lasted for an eternity. Carrie opened her eyes. She could see. Everything.

The sunlight swung itself in and out of the trees. The girl, the man and the dog sat together. The stone bench was cold and very hard. They shared the warmth from the sunshine. They held on to each other. They were not giving up any time soon.

'Jon's back. Jed's dead. Trust me, Carrie. Do as I say and everything will be alright.'

Old man Wilson was staring at her. Was he mad or did he just look mad? He had the palest pale blue eyes that she'd ever seen; almost ice white. Almost.

'It's over. Go to him, Carrie! He's not dead. He's in the top field.'

Carrie stared at old man Wilson. She could see. She saw. Jed. Jon. Everything. A shiver ran down her spine.

'I belong to him.'

'I know. I've always known it. He belongs to you. Run, Carrie. Run!'

———◆———

Carrie ran.

'Run up the field and undo the wire.'

How many times had she done that? There was no Jip to run with her today and no electric wire fence to sting her.

'Agh!'

She hurting just the same. She was live. She ran as fast as she could to the gateway at the top of the field. The gate was closed. A gust of wind hit her body as she stepped into the top field. How many times had it done that? She wasn't giving her body up to the ravages of the wind today; it belonged to someone else. She made ready to let go her feet from the ground; it was time to fly.

Across the sloping field, at the top of the next hill, the tall tree stood alone. It watched the Falcon. Seemingly far away, yet so close that it could see every detail of its outstretched wings. It held its breath and waited. Suddenly, in less than the blink of an eye, the Falcon swooped. Flying in a straight line, across the rippling hill of the top field. Flying in a straight line, the ground rose and fell in ridges. Flying in a straight line, it pushed through the vortex of swirling grass and cows, towards its sanctuary. On this day, sanctuary was given.

It wasn't a very elegant landing. The Falcon crashed into the outstretched branches of the tall tree. Talons extended, wings thrashing, but she was held fast. She was powerless. He would not let her fly. He wasn't going to lose her again. He weighed her down with his hands, his arms, his eyes, his lips, his hair. She just stood still and let him do it. It seemed the right thing to do. She wrapped her fingers around his hair and held him tight.

'I love your hair.'

'It's grass day,' he said.

'What's that?'

'Twelfth of May. Traditonally when the cows are let out to grass for the first time in the year. It means f..freedom.'

Carrie looked up into Jon's eyes; they were dark.

'Freedom it is, then,' she said. 'Do it!'

527

'Do what?'

'It's Grass Day! Give me my freedom, Jon. Cancel out my pain. Cancel out our pain. I want to feel you inside me. Now! Do it like he did it, like Jed did it. It's the only way.'

'I don't want to hurt you.'

'You have to, to take my pain away. I trust you completely.'

Jon looked down at the ground. It was green. He saw. Everything.

'It's alright. We'll be alright,' she said, gently.

Less gently, she ripped at the metal buckle of his trouser belt. Her hands were small; his belt was stiff and tight. She hadn't got very far with it when Jon suddenly grabbed her by the back of the hair.

'Grass day it is, then, Darlin'. You're coming on the grass. It's just you, and m..me.'

Jon dragged Carrie onto the soft rye grass beneath the trees. It was eerily quiet. Ghostly. A shiver ran down her spine. Her feet were very cold and wet. She'd kicked her stilettos off in the orchard; she didn't need them any more. Her white blouse and black, tightly fitting office skirt, her old life; she didn't need them any more. Suddenly, Jon pushed out a hand to Carrie's shoulder and knocked her to the ground. She pressed herself deep into the soft green grass where she fell.

Jon pressed his lips onto hers. Light broke through the branches of the trees above them. Its warmth pressed down on them both, coupling them together. A lifetime of waiting and longing had brought her to this moment. She recognised his hands. They were big and strong, hard and rough. But they were not Jed's. Carrie opened her eyes.

She could see. Everything. She wanted to. The bare skin of her body was joined by that of her legs as Jon finally mastered her little buttons and ripped her black, tightly fitting office skirt from her. Black and white her clothes lay at her side.

'Jip!'

But there was no Jip. There was nothing to guard against here. Carrie panted in the heat. Her hands reached out to Jon. It was time for him to prove himself. And he did.

———————◆———————

The clock was ticking. The mantelpiece above the Rayburn cooker flinched as the farmhouse kitchen door burst open, but the clock was unaffected. It carried on ticking just like it had always done. It had no choice. It was the farmhouse kitchen clock. It belonged to Mavis; it just kept going whatever burst in through the door. The flames of the little cooker fire shivered in the draught created by old man Wilson laying Jip down on the floor in front of it. A wave of bright orange heat pressed Jip deep into the soft rag rug. He panted in the heat.

A door banged upstairs. It sounded like a gunshot. He'd heard it many times before but never so loud. He knew which door it was. The hairs stood up on the back of his neck. He stood over Jip, stooped and helpless as a tall and sad looking old tree. He watched Jip. He was still alive. He reached down to him. He stroked his black and white fur. He held his breath and waited. Mavis came in from the pantry.

'Are ya right, Ezra?'

'No, I'm not.'

Old man Wilson straightened himself up. He let go of Jip. He had no choice. It was time to let go. He turned to face Mavis:

'I've been a bad man, Mavis. It's time. I want to put things right.'

'No, Ezra. Please, no! Don't tell me, I don't want to know.'

'It's alright.'

Old man Wilson gently took hold of Mavis' hands and pulled her down onto a kitchen chair; she landed hard. He knelt down at her feet. He didn't let her go.

Silence.

He waited for her to know that he was a bad man.

'You've been an angel to me all these years, Mavis. I've disrespected you. I've taken you for granted. I've hurt you. All these years I've been chasing after a ghost from my past that wasn't real.'

Old man Wilson touched her face; it was red and swollen from days of crying.

'You're a real woman. You're good and kind, loyal, and a real grafter. You're beautiful inside and out. You matter. You're the most precious thing I've had in my life. It's been right here in front of me all these years and I couldn't see it.'

'More inside than out, I should say,' interrupted the beautiful, white-whiskered woman.

'I see it now. Everything. Please forgive me.'

'It's alright, Ezra,' said Mavis, quietly. 'You haven't hurt me. I've been happy with my lot here. You know I've loved the lads as if they were me own. You gave me that chance and I thank you for it.'

Old man Wilson bowed his head. His fine head of long, silver grey hair fell on to her pale white hands.

'I know I don't deserve you, but please, Mavis! If you'll have me! It's your turn to be dressed in white. Mavis, let me put it right. Will you have me?'

Mavis touched his face; it was dissolving in her hands. He recognised them. They were big and strong, hard and rough. They were full of gentleness. They were the hands of an angel. Mavis lowered her voice and her eyes to the sad looking, pale man who sought sanctuary in her lap. On this day, sanctuary was given. The angel took his pain away.

'Get up, you great daft Lummox!' cackled Mavis. 'My mop'll always be at your door! Of course I'll have you! I never expected, never needed, flowers and a white dress from you. Still, I'd be a fool not to take it, since you're offering! And right chuffed I am too!'

Two big, strong arms wrapped around him. They lifted him up.

'I'm so sorry, Mavis.'

'Now give over,' said Mavis. 'I've always belonged to you, and you to me, and that's all there is to it!'

Ezra struggled to his feet. He was nearly seven feet tall.

'Where's Carrie?' asked Mavis.

'With Jon, in the top field.'

'They'll be a while, then,' cackled Mavis, standing up and stretching into a well-rounded, capital letter 'R' shape.

'Ah.'

Jip whined. Perhaps he heard mention of his master's name. He was struggling to his feet, but he couldn't do it.

'What's up, Jip, lad?' asked Mavis, hobbling across the kitchen.

She'd been sitting down for too long. Jip's warm body pressed down on her feet. She could feel his rib cage rising and falling underneath his fur. He wasn't giving up any time soon. He had no visible wounds.

'I don't think he's going to do any good. We'd better call Alec,' said Ezra.

'No!' said Mavis. 'He's waiting for Jon. He'll hang on for Jon.'

She knelt down at his black and white side. She gave him such comfort as she could.

'Ah Jip, lad. Don't fret. It's alright. Jon's coming. He's coming...'

———◆———

Jon groaned. Loudly. Carrie answered him with a low sound which grew in her belly. It grew and grew. She'd finally found her voice. It startled her. She didn't know where it came from. It broke the silence as he broke her. Those big hands moved very slowly and gently. She pressed herself deep into him; she just couldn't get close enough to him. She loved his hair. It was around her neck and on her breasts. She stroked it. She wrapped her fingers around it; it was hers. They were joined forever by the same hair.

Mouths touching, she wrapped her body around his; he was hers. And gradually, their limbs fused together and they became each other, like branches sharing the root of the same tree.

The high branches above them cast a warm, half light. They shared their deep silence with the blurred shapes of the trees. They half closed their eyes. A soft, rocking breeze rippled the waves of green grass around them. He watered her face with his tears. He felt her growing beneath him.

'I love you!' he cried.

They cried together. Carrie reached up and put a finger on his lips.

'You talk too much!'

She smiled up at him. Jon lowered his eyes and shivered. He kissed her tear stained face. He stroked her hair. Her blood flowed for him like water over their green grass, turning it into a bed of soft, black, velvet. Without thinking, without hesitating, he grabbed a handful of fresh grass and began to wipe it away. All of a sudden, Carrie was cold. She was back in that little shed on the night of the party, on a bed of fresh straw. Little Carrie's mother was licking her body dry. No, it was the third man. She let out a big shiver. It didn't seem an odd thing to happen at all. She just lay back and let him do it. He breathed life into her.

'What's your name?' she cried out.

'Jon,' he whispered. My name's Jon. He reached out to her again, and went inside. Carrie followed him. He pulled her hair. Hard. In the high branches above their heads, a bird sang to its mate. The voice of their despair, it drifted solemnly down from the trees. It anointed them. It took away their pain.

'We don't need words,' she sang. 'There are no words for what this is...'

———◆———

A thudding, thumping, sound vibrated underneath his feet. It got stronger and louder and louder and stronger as Jon walked down the hill towards the orchard, cradling Carrie in his arms. Her feet were red, swollen, and bleeding, from running up the drive to him in the first place. He wasn't going to let her get hurt ever again. He didn't need to any more. It was done. Finished. He carried her into the orchard. The odd leaf detached itself now and then from the trees and fell on them, soft as confetti.

In the far corner of the orchard, old man Wilson was chopping down the sad looking tree with an axe. Carrie shivered. The sad looking tree held its branches out towards her in a gentle and pleading sort of way before finally letting go and falling to the ground. There was one final, cracking, sound as old man Wilson gave the sad looking tree a helping hand. It lay at his feet, straight and lifeless. He let the axe fall to the ground. His suffering was over.

'It's time,' he said. 'It's brought us nothing but bad luck all these years. Sometimes you have to cut back in order for things to grow again. All things must die to grow again. It's done. Finished.'

Old man Wilson turned to Carrie and Jon.

'See, Carrie? I've trusted you. 'Do as I say and everything will be alright.' Right?'

Carrie smiled at him as Jon lowered her gently to the floor. He didn't let her go. He wasn't going to let her go ever again. She balanced her feet on his boots; he had big feet. She wrapped herself around his trunk like ivy. She was never ever going to stop growing on him. Old man Wilson walked across to them.

'I knew you'd bring us good luck the first time I set eyes on you. I gave you a walnut from this tree. It was her tree. Our tree.'

He reached with a finger and thumb into his tweed waistcoat pocket, and pulled out a little tin.

'Hold out your hand,' he said.

'You said that to me the first time I met you! I'm not sure I'm going to do it again,' teased Carrie.

'Hold out your hand!' he commanded.

Carrie held out her hand but she didn't close her eyes this time.

'You must always wear this. Never take it off.'

Old man Wilson placed the small, plain gold ring on her right hand ring finger.

'This was hers. You will always be safe if you wear this. I think she'd want you to have it.'

'Thank you, I promise I'll never let it go.'

'I know,' he said. 'You will bear great fruit.'

'Dad! She's not a tree, or a cow,' said Jon.

'I know,' he said. 'But she's pedigree all the same!'

Carrie laughed.

'Carrie!' called Mavis from the orchard gateway. 'Do you want your shoes? I've dried them out for you. You'll catch your death wandering about half dressed,' she cackled.

Carrie hobbled across the orchard grass to Mavis; her feet were sore.

'Thanks, Mavis.'

'You're right welcome, Carrie, love. And talking about dresses, do you fancy being me bridesmaid?'

Mavis' pale blue eyes swelled beyond the usual magnification of her big, plastic rimmed spectacles. She waved across the orchard at 'the lads.' Carrie hugged Mavis.

'Oh, Mavis, I'd love to, but I might have to be your maid of honour instead, depending on which one of us gets down the aisle first!'

'Tell them to come on, I've got the kettle on,' said Mavis, giving Carrie her stilettos.

'I'll tell them.'

Mavis bustled back to the farmhouse. The orchard was very beautiful with pink and white blossom at this time of year, but she never walked through it. Some things might belong to her, but the orchard wasn't one of them.

Old man Wilson, Carrie and Jon followed Mavis across the farmyard. They saw her disappear into the red and black farmhouse kitchen floor tiles, only to come straight back out again.

'Jon!' she shouted, 'Jon, come quick! It's Jip!'

'Oh Jip! Run Jon, run!'

Old man Wilson ran after Jon. Carrie couldn't follow. He was Jon's dog. She stood in the middle of the yard and looked up at the red brick farmhouse; it wasn't derelict and empty any more.

She remembered the first time her eyes had scanned the Georgian windows, looking for any signs of life. She had the uneasy feeling that she was being watched all over again. She was drawn to the black window at the far end of the house. She knew which room that was. It was a lovely sunny day. The sun always shone on her farm days. Was the light chasing the shadows, or the shadows chasing the light? For a fraction of a second, she saw her reflection in the black window. She was smiling.

'So Debs did see me on New Year's Eve! Debs was right. I had to come back. To stay.'

'Carrie!' called Mavis. 'Come quick, we need you!'

Carrie followed the stripes of light and dark flickering across the windows. The black window was empty; it was soft black. Velvet.

'Trust me. It'll be alright. We'll be alright...'

Epilogue

Saturday 14th May 1983

'Tell me the story about the roses, Grandad!'

'Now these roses are very special. Your daddy planted them for his dog, Jip. Jip was a very brave dog, and a very good friend to your Mummy and your Daddy.'

'Like my Jip?'

'Yes, just like your Jip. Now one time, poor Jip got badly kicked. He died from his injuries. He was so very brave. Your daddy buried him here, in the orchard, because he loved it here. He loved to come and play in the orchard. He liked to run through the trees with your Mummy, and he liked to sit with your Mummy and Daddy by this old stone bench.'

'Just like my Jip?'

'Just like your Jip. Go on then - run!'

She ran. Jip ran too.

'Grandad, come and see what we've found!'

'What's that?'

'It's a baby tree!'

He stared at the tree.

'Well I never, so it is! This old tree died a long time ago. I cut it down.'

'Well, it's my baby tree now. What sort is it?'

'It's a walnut tree.'

'It's growing like the baby in Mummy's tummy!'

'Yes, it is.'

'Hello!' called a familiar voice.

'Aunty Debs, come and see what we've found!'

'Can we see too?'

Nanna Jill and Grandad Bill appeared at the orchard gateway, closely followed by Grandma Mavis, pushing old Uncle Ab in his wheelchair, and Mummy and Daddy.

'I've got a baby, just like Mummy!'

'Oh my goodness!' said Aunty Debs. 'All these babies! How shall we manage?'

'It's alright,' she said. 'Mine's a baby tree, it won't cry. It's a Walnut tree.'

'Come here!' called her mummy.

She reached her arms out to her daughter in a gentle and pleading sort of way. Her little girl ran. Jip ran too. She picked her up.

'I'm glad your baby tree won't cry, because my babies will. We've just found out that I've got two babies growing in my tummy!'

'Oh!' chorused the trees of the orchard.

'Grandad, why are you crying?'

'I'm crying because the tree can't.'

'Why?'

'Because the tree is happy - and I'm happy.'

'Oh.'

Daddy put his arms around Mummy and kissed her gently on the forehead.

'I'm going up to the top field to look the cattle. Do you want to come with me?'

'Yes, I do!'

'And we'd better find some water for this baby tree. Come on Jip, come on Grandad!' said Aunty Debs.

'And I'll put the kettle on,' said Grandma Mavis.

'They'll be a while,' said Grandad Wilson.

'Ah,' cackled Grandma Mavis.

They watched them walk all the way up to the top of the top field. They stood together by the gate, like two tall trees, growing together, their fruit ripening, before disappearing over the horizon.

'Ah.'

He looked up at the sky. It was clear and blue. The palest pale blue, almost ice white. Almost. And high in the sky, a Falcon hovered over them all.

Sources

The author gratefully acknowledges the use of quotations from the following poems and texts:

Page

324 † : From *For the Fallen*, Laurence Binyon, 1914

337 † : From *Venus and Adonis, poem 1593*, William Shakespeare

337 ‡ : From *Sonnet 86*, William Shakespeare

337 ᐃ : From *Othello, Act V, Scene II*, William Shakespeare

338 † : From *Romeo and Juliet, Act II, Scene II*, William Shakespeare

362 † : From *O Little Town of Bethlehem*, Rector Phillips Brooks, 1868

363 † : From *In The Bleak Midwinter*, Christina Rosetti, 1872

373 † : From *Away in a Manger*, author unknown, first published 19th Century

432 † : From *Letter To His Mother*, Flight Sergeant Clifton Wedd, 1942, by kind permission of Marcia Gifford

464 † : From *Much Ado About Nothing, Act V, Scene IV*, William Shakespeare

494 † : From *Great Expectations*, Charles Dickens, 1861

514 † : From *Ecclesiastes 3*, scripture quotation is taken from Holy Bible, New Living Translation, copyright © 1996, 2004, 2007, 2013 by Tyndale House Publishers Inc. Carol Stream. Illinois 60188. All rights reserved.

514 ‡ : From *Meditations*, Marcus Aurelius

Journey to the End of the Night

Dear Reader,

Find out more about Jon and Carrie in *Journey to the End of the Night*, the sequel to *The Walnut Tree*, available in 2016. Their story continues from the very moment we have left them in the top field at the end of The Walnut Tree...

'I don't want to hurt you.'

'You said that to me once before,' laughed Carrie, 'and look where that got me!'

'I know,' he smiled. 'You make me feel creative.'

Carrie gave Jon an almighty shove and knocked him to the ground.

'Here,' she whispered, lowering herself down onto him, 'feel the fruits of your creation!'

'Our creation,' he pushed back at her.

'We should celebrate while we can,' gasped Carrie. 'I don't think we'll have time for a lot of loving a few months down the line.'

'Yes we will,' Jon pressed on. 'It will be a different sort of loving. Trust me, we'll be alright, it'll be alright...'

Will it be alright?

What is true love?

When is bad blood real?

How do you forgive the unforgiveable...and survive?

'If you're not afraid to die, you can live...'

About Caroline Wedd

Caroline Wedd was born in 1963 at Burton on Trent, Staffordshire, and grew up on a small dairy farm. She was educated at Hatton School in Derbyshire, and went on to graduate from Southampton University with an honours degree in music and a post graduate certificate in education from London University Institute of Education. She has spent most of her working life teaching music to school children of all ages but has also worked as a stewardess in a hotel, as a country and western singer and as an animal portrait artist.

In addition to her novels, she also enjoys writing music and songs for children and choirs. She lives with her family in the Midlands.